THE WAR LESS CIVIL

An American Saga
1864–1991

Joseph Lewis Heil

Lake Lore Press LLC

Published by
Lake Lore Press LLC

Copyright © 2012 by Joseph Lewis Heil.

The cover photograph is of the author's maternal grandparents taken on their wedding day in 1901.

First softcover, paper edition: December 2017, published by Lake Lore Press, LLC.

ISBN-13: 978-0-69291-829-6
ISBN-10: 0-69291-829-9

The HELDEN FAMILY TREE appears after the Acknowledgments page.

Cover and interior by Gary A. Rosenberg • www.garyarosenberg.com

Contents

PART 3 ~ 1957 TO 1976

PART 4 ~ 1980 TO 1991

A.M.D.G.

&

To those I love.

Acknowledgments

In 1990, my friend Andrew Clarke (www.andrewclarkestories.com) inexplicably suggested I write a novel. I thought about it for several years before I began to conceive the nature of the novel that I wished to write. Finally, in December 1996, I began.

After several chapters were written, I asked family and friends to read them. My wife, Ursula, accepted the invitation and proved to be an outstanding in-home editor. She was the first to read and edit the book in its entirety, for which I am deeply grateful. Without her encouragement and constant, unfailing support throughout many years, *The War Less Civil* would not have been written.

My brother, John, himself a published author, also expressed great enthusiasm for my writing, as did my sons, Joseph Jr. and Jeffrey.

I mailed chapter copies to many friends and, for the most part, received favorable comments and feedback. I also received valuable constructive criticism, all of which contributed to a betterment of the novel.

In 2012, I submitted a draft copy to the Faulkner-Wisdom Novel Competition, at https://wordsandmusic.org/william-faulkner-wisdom-competition, in New Orleans where the book was named a finalist. I thank Rosemary James for her wonderful support, not only of me, but all aspiring writers.

I thank Mr. John Wallbank in Los Angeles for his superb professional editing of the entire novel. Without his involvement, instruction, and insights *The War Less Civil* would be a far lesser work.

Lastly, I thank my parents, John and Anita Heil, whose lives and stories, whose joys and sorrows, so enriched this book.

Joseph Lewis Heil

The Helden Family Tree

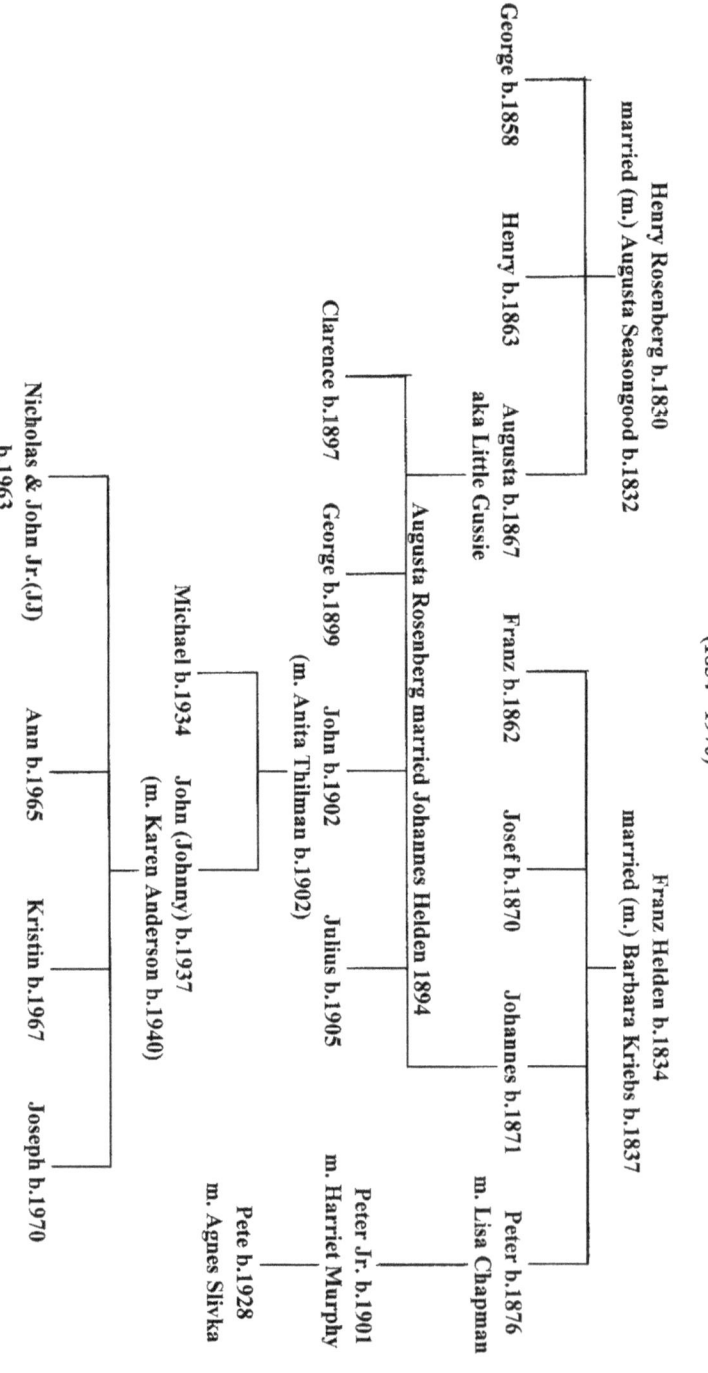

The Helden Family Tree
(1834 - 1970)

Franz Helden b.1834
married (m.) Barbara Kriebs b.1837

Henry Rosenberg b.1830
married (m.) Augusta Seasongood b.1832

George b.1858

Henry b.1863

Augusta b.1867
aka Little Gussie

Clarence b.1897

George b.1899

Augusta Rosenberg married Johannes Helden 1894

Michael b.1934
(m. Anita Thilman b.1902)

John b.1902

John (Johnny) b.1937
(m. Karen Anderson b.1940)

Nicholas & John Jr.(JJ)
b.1963

Ann b.1965

Kristin b.1967

Joseph b.1970

Franz b.1862

Josef b.1870

Julius b.1905

Johannes b.1871

Peter b.1876
m. Lisa Chapman

Peter Jr. b.1901
m. Harriet Murphy

Pete b.1928
m. Agnes Slivka

PART I ~ 1864 to 1932

Chapter 1 ~ 1864

L incoln. The name caused within the mind and heart of Augusta Rosenberg revulsion for the president who bore it. *A grotesque, wicked man . . . .* "That deceiver, murderer, a tyrant," she told her husband.

Augusta could not understand how Congress allowed Lincoln to wage war against the southern States into a fourth year. "He's incompetent, as are all his generals. The war should have been over in six months. Nay, it never should have been fought at all."

Augusta's loathing of President Lincoln so alarmed Henry Rosenberg that it confirmed in his mind the wisdom of the States not to have bestowed the voting privilege on their women citizens. Henry voted for Lincoln in 1860 and had every intention of voting for him again in 1864, even though Henry was a Democrat.

"War is difficult, my dear. The Confederacy is a determined and treacherous foe. They are traitors and will not easily lay down their arms."

"There is too much bloodshed, Henry. That is the greater evil, not that the South seceded. The death of thousands of young Americans at the whim of Mr. Lincoln is the real evil. And it's all so senseless. Tell me, for what are they dying?"

"For heaven's sake, Augusta, how many times must it be said? To preserve the Union and rid it of slavery . . . those *are* reasons to die for."

"I do not mean to defend slavery," she replied, "but I must condemn war. It seems to me a war that slaughters thousands is

1

much worse than a benign slavery in which only wicked slaves are punished. Indeed, most live happy lives under the protection of a compassionate master."

"Nonsense, Augusta. Would you want us to be slaves of a compassionate master?"

"They're darkies, Henry. It's all they know."

"They are *Men!* Men and women enslaved by greedy Southerners who prosper off the hard labor of those Negroes and barter their children for horses and land. It's evil, Augusta – evil."

"Is it not evil that thousands die on the battlefields? More soldiers die in a month of Mr. Lincoln's war, I dare say, than do slaves in ten years on the plantations. Indeed, yes, slavery is evil, but war is the greater evil."

At least, Augusta reflected, *the fighting is far away, and my husband is here.* At thirty-four, Henry had not been called to serve, and every day Augusta prayed he would be spared conscription into the Union army. Augusta was thirty-two, their son, George, six; little Henry had just passed his first birthday. They lived peaceably except for an occasional disagreement about Mr. Lincoln's war. They got along well with their neighbors and the friendly Potawatomi who roamed Muskego Township, fishing its lakes and hunting small game with bow and arrow. Left behind in fields and hardwoods were the stone arrowheads that Henry and Augusta's grandsons would find fifty years hence. Augusta was reasonably content, but Henry wasn't content at all. He longed to join the *Cause*; he longed to go to war.

+ + +

Augusta Saisongut's parents came to America from the German kingdom of Saxony in 1831, a year before her birth. Henry Rosenberg's parents had arrived ten years earlier in one of the first waves of German immigration. Both couples settled in Manhattan where they learned *some* English though markedly accented by their native tongue. Their children, however, educated in the public schools, spoke and read the language well. At a young age, Henry learned the machinist's trade. Then in 1853 he met and, as winter came, married Miss Augusta Seasongood.

Henry and Augusta's first, halcyon summer was marred by an outbreak of cholera in Brooklyn that took many lives. It terrified them. After ten hard years Henry had wearied of factory work, while Augusta, overwhelmed by the swarms of Europeans that kept coming to New York, wearied of living in the restless, teeming city.

In the 1850s, New York's population swelled from five hundred thousand to over eight hundred thousand. It often seemed to Augusta that most of the immigrants moved into their building or onto their street. She could hardly walk to the markets for the constantly surging milieu, and then by the summer of 1857 she realized she was pregnant.

That November there was widespread labor unrest; fifteen thousand unemployed men marched down Wall Street, as Henry and Augusta watched in wonderment and worry. After much discussion they decided to move upstate where Henry hoped to find work, and their baby would be born far from Manhattan's unyielding intensity of crowds and commerce.

In Albany, he found employment as a brass finisher. Their sparsely populated block with its passable sidewalks, trees, and fresh air made Augusta's life much more tolerable, but even then a new idea took root in Henry's mind. When he told Augusta, she, too, was intrigued: acres of affordable farmland in the distant western states were available to anyone who wanted them. Their innate frugality let Henry dream of owning land to work in the open air with boots against the soil, his gaze upon the sky. He intended to become a farmer. By reading books – they both read newspapers and the Bible daily – Henry learned about wheat farming, Augusta learned about vegetable gardening, and both learned about faraway Wisconsin. Granted statehood in 1848, newspaper articles described it as splendid country with fertile land and hardwood forests rich with game and fowl.

Indiana newspaperman John B. L. Soule advised and Horace Greeley, editor of the *New York Tribune*, echoed, "Go west, young man, and grow up with the country." So Henry and Augusta did.

Several months after the birth of their son, George, they made the long train trip to Chicago and then north to Wisconsin. Henry bought forty acres in a valley near the little town of Tess Corners about twelve miles southwest of Milwaukee. He hired two carpenters to help build a cabin of logs: three rooms, a fieldstone fireplace at the center of the plan, a front porch, and a roof covered with lapped cedar shingles. He hired a well digger, but dug the latrine himself, building its outhouse one hundred paces from the well out front.

They moved into their new home in September, 1860. Earlier that summer they bought chickens and planted a large garden knowing the first winter would be difficult. In spring, Henry planted wheat and harvested a good crop that assured their survival for the second winter. The year 1862 yielded another good crop. By that fall, Augusta was pregnant again. They never regretted leaving New York though it was difficult to part from parents and siblings. Nor did they regret coming to this beautiful land. The only overshadowing darkness was their beloved country now at war, tragically, with its divided self. That division even seeped into homes far from the anguished battlefields.

+ + +

One afternoon in the late summer of 1864, Augusta, with baby Henry in her arms, stepped onto the front porch and saw her husband striding along the rising road that led to the Watry farm, their neighbors a half-mile north. She watched as he reached the crest of the hill and then disappeared behind it. *He went yesterday, that he told me; but why today,* she wondered. *Twice this week to visit Mr. Watry; now why would he do that? And why would he walk and not hitch the wagon or ride the horse?*

When he returned, Augusta asked, "Were you visiting Mr. Watry then?"

"Yes, yes, I was. We had business to discuss."

It puzzled her. "May I ask what sort?"

Henry sighed and, if there was meaning there, Augusta didn't sense it. "Could we talk later? I've things to tend."

After the evening meal, Henry read the newspaper Franklyn Watry had given him. The days were growing shorter; Augusta lit the oil lamps and candles a little earlier each evening. She drew a chair and sat close to his rocker with the baby on her lap. Outside, Georgie, as they called their firstborn, played in the fading light.

"Can we talk now," Augusta asked.

"Can we wait 'til the boys sleep?"

"Of course."

"There's a chill in the air; I'll build a fire."

Augusta called Georgie in and began to ready the children for bed. Occasionally she glanced at Henry, absorbed in the newspaper. "Is there any progress?"

"General Sherman is approaching Atlanta; there's speculation the city might fall. That would be a great loss for the Confederacy."

"But will it hasten the end?"

"Yes, I think so; it would be as though Chicago fell. Atlanta is important. It's a rail center, you see."

After the children were tucked in, Henry went to kiss them goodnight. When he returned, Augusta said, "I do not mean to pry, and I know you always share any matter concerning the children and me, but you spoke of some business with Mr. Watry. I'm wondering if this is something you wish to tell?"

Henry gazed at her fine face reflecting the swaying shadows of the fire's flames. He felt reluctance, knowing that what he was about to say would sadden her. "Augusta, dear," he drew her hands into his, "I have decided to join the Union army."

Horrified, Augusta's hands recoiled from his grasp, as though they found thorns. She stood and began to pace. "No, no, no, you shall not go to war."

"Augusta, I have given this much thought."

"You are not going to war . . . you promised me solemnly you wouldn't go. You must not break that promise. You cannot do that to the children and me."

"Augusta, please, you must listen to what I have to say."

"No, I will not . . . I've heard enough," and then, "I'm going to bed."

She disappeared into the darkness of their room. Henry sat bewildered. *She must listen,* he thought. *She is my wife.*

He went to the log pile to replenish the fire. The night was cool; the sky moonless and white with stars. In bed, Augusta lay still as stone, facing the wall. Usually Henry heard her light breathing, while she slept. Now he heard nothing.

"Gussie?" There was no response. "Goodnight, Gussie," he whispered, knowing she heard.

When he woke in the early morning, Augusta was gone. He went to the boys and found them sleeping soundly. From the front porch he scanned the long road and the garden at the side of the little house. He went to the back, looking out over the bright fields of ripening wheat, but she was nowhere to be seen. *Stubborn woman,* he thought.

He built a fresh fire in the fireplace, then the stove to boil water for the morning tea. *Went to confer with Mrs. Watry, I suppose.* He sat in his rocker with a cup of hot tea in his hard hands wondering how he might overcome Augusta's powerful opposition. After a while, he went to the porch and glancing northward saw his wife coming down the road.

The sun was already high. Augusta, not even acknowledging Henry, walked straight past to the garden where she paced up and down the neat rows, as was her manner. There she liked to be alone with her thoughts. Now, as Henry watched, he noticed she didn't even bend down to pull a weed or two. He realized she was upset, but he felt much better having her near.

When she entered the house she said, "Henry, I made my opinion very clear last night, but I realize I must at least listen to yours. Understand, though, nothing you say will alter my mind about such a foolish decision. I am appalled that you would be so inconsiderate of your family; nevertheless, I will listen. I have that obligation as your wife, and I shall honor it."

"Oh, good, good . . . thank you, Gussie." Then in good humor, "I was beginning to fear you might never speak to me again."

Georgie tugged at his mother's skirt. The baby fussed. Augusta went to change his diaper. She handed him to Henry, while she made the morning meal. They did not resume their disagreement until the children took their nap.

"You must always understand, Henry," Augusta began, "that your repute in my heart is ensured only by your faithful duty to our children and to me."

"I do understand . . . my duty is sacred. Never would I forsake it."

"Good – can I take that to mean then that you have abandoned your silly notion to go to war?"

Henry looked at her, amazed how she turned his words to her advantage. "Augusta, for me to be dutiful to my country in time of war does not mean I forsake my family."

"Yes it does, for only I have the right to make that judgment."

"But if I fail in my duty to my country, I fail also in the duty to my family, for my family is part of my country."

"Nonsense – it is the other way around. If you fail your family, you fail your country."

Henry sensed the superiority of her argument.

"We've a bountiful crop this year, Henry. You've a harvest and horse to tend, house and barn to maintain, firewood to gather and split, another winter to help your family endure. Your two little sons need you to teach and guide them. And your wife needs you. These are duties your country expects you to honor."

"The war, Augusta, has lasted this long because the army has difficulty getting men. I feel the call to join where others do not. It is rooted in my conscience. For me to ignore that call would be despicable. I'm a patriot. I can't let others fight and die when I believe, as strongly as they, in the righteousness of the *Cause*. I must join them. Were I not to, I could not live my life, for I'd have no honor at all."

"But, Henry, honor isn't only found amid the bloodshed of war. To farm your land and protect your family is just as honorable."

"It is too tranquil, Gussie. I'm impelled to join the fight by everything I know and believe. That is where my honor lies. The Union army desperately needs men. Unless she gets them the war will never end. Surely you don't want that."

"I want you alive, here, with us."

They fell silent until Henry said, "It is my opinion, Gussie, that it would be a far worse fate for me to live my life without honor than it would be for you to live your life without me."

Augusta looked at him in disbelief. Angered by his selfishness and horrified at such recklessness, she wouldn't allow herself to speak until she had controlled her emotions and composed her thoughts, for she wanted her reply to be exactly to the point. After a long pause she said, "You are presumptuous to think you could ever imagine the boundaries of my sorrowful heart. Were you to die in this terrible war, they would extend to my grave. Throughout this life my sorrow would be shrouded in a bitterness caused by your indifference to my feelings and your carelessness for your little boys' needs for a father's love and guidance."

"Augusta--"

"Don't interrupt. I am perplexed by your willingness to forsake the solemn promise you made when the war began. How peculiar it appears to me that as a younger man, before your second son was even born, you vowed not to go to war, and now you decide to renounce that wise vow in order to place yourself and your wife and children at such great risk."

"Please, Augusta-"

"Let me finish. That you would break that sacred promise and dishonor yourself in *my* eyes so that you *might* find honor in your own, strikes me as selfish and foolish. Would not your honor be forever tarnished by the betrayal of your wife and sons? And yet, you tell me you cannot live without honor here, for there, beyond that terrible betrayal, is where you imagine your honor lies. Indeed, sir, we have very different understandings of the nature of honor."

Henry never imagined that would be the basis for his wife's strong objections. He made the pledge years ago when everyone believed the war would end shortly after it began.

"Augusta, dear, I can hardly remember that. Things have changed over the years. You can't expect me not to change my thinking given the danger the nation faces. The Union army needs men now. It didn't think, nobody thought, it needed men then."

"We need you much more because now we are three."

"If I must ignore my youthful promise, I do so because I sincerely believe I can perfect my character in this war. The preservation of the Union and eliminating slavery are worth fighting and, yes, even dying for. Thousands of men have already given testament to that. Though I, perhaps, disappoint you for a short while, my dishonor in your eyes pales beside the dishonor I would bear for the rest of my life if I fail to serve my country."

"Is it honor you seek or dishonor you wish to avoid?"

"Both, of course. One begets the other."

They heard Georgie get up and the baby fuss. Augusta shooed George outside, ignoring little Henry who whimpered back to sleep. She said, "Is there no dishonor for you at all, sir, in breaking a solemn vow not to abandon your wife and sons? We need you more than the army needs you. It cares nothing if I am left husbandless and your sons fatherless. Do you think the army does not know that men your age are needed to work the farms? Has it not occurred to you that the government wishes you to remain a farmer? That is your sacred duty and the reason you have not been called. You are needed here, not just by me, but by the very army you wish to serve."

While she spoke, Henry fetched a cup of water. Sitting down again, he said, "The farm will be worked by Franklyn Watry. That is the business I resolved with him. He will harvest and share the profits equally with you. In spring, if I have not returned, he will do our planting. He'll also tend the horse."

"My God, Henry, you are so terribly stubborn. You should honor my arguments, but you do not."

"Yes, indeed, I am stubborn, Augusta, but I must go in spite of your arguments because in my deepest soul I am called to join."

"And if I tell you it will harm us – that it will harm our love – would you still go? I fear something will be forever lost in me."

"And if I stay, something will be lost in me. Is that what you want for your husband? Am I to live the remainder of my life without honor?"

"Is it right for your wife to live without her husband because he sought a false honor in needlessly sacrificing his life? What good is such honor to you or to us if you are dead?"

"My joining the *Cause* does not ensure my death."

"Nor does it ensure your honor. Indeed, ignoring my deepest wishes destroys it. Does that not matter?" Her eyes searched his.

"Oh, yes, Augusta, yes . . . that matters more than anything, but I beg you not to dishonor me simply because I choose what my conscience tells me is right. Do not present me such a choice. Accept my decision, please. I go to war not to forsake you, but to serve my country. Try to understand that."

For a moment Augusta fell silent, her face deformed by sadness. "I have invited the Watrys for tea Sunday afternoon." It was pointless, she knew, to continue arguing because Henry yielded not at all.

"You've invited the Watrys to dissuade me . . . ."

"Yes, I have."

They shall not, Henry thought, but his silence gave Augusta hope.

+ + +

In 1862, frequent Union military defeats and waves of arbitrary arrests had turned many Northerners against Lincoln's conduct of the war. War weariness proved fertile ground for a peace campaign; many prominent Wisconsin Democrats took up the cause of compromise and an end to the hostilities. They argued that restoring the Union as it *was* would be sufficiently honorable and certainly preferable to Lincoln's disastrous war, but they had no specific strategy to bring it about. They dreamed peace and reunion might somehow come to the war-ravaged country while choosing to ignore the Confederacy's determination – because it was winning – to carry the fight to the death.

In early 1862, Henry and Augusta read an editorial in the *La Crosse Democrat* by Mr. Marcus Pomeroy who wrote:

> *The people do not want this war. Taxpayers do not wish it. Widows, orphans, and over-taxed workingmen do not ask or need this waste of men, blood and treasure. There is no glory to be won in a civil war, no more than in a family quarrel. If politicians would let this matter come before the people, there would be an honorable peace within sixty days. But so long as blind leaders govern and fanaticism rules the day, so long will there be wars, tears and desolation.*

They had agreed with Mr. Pomeroy, but with the passing of time their opinions began to diverge.

+ + +

Franklyn and Veronica Watry were the Rosenberg's nearest neighbors, having built their house in 1856. They had three children: Virginia was twelve; Jack, ten; and Rudy, seven. The families got along well: both were Lutheran, all were Democrats. After several years, Franklyn and Henry became friends though both remained solitary men. Georgie liked playing with the Watry boys, while Ginny, as Virginia was called, had reached the age in her young life when she enjoyed her mother and Augusta's company far more than her brothers'. She regarded Rudy and Georgie as little more than irksome children, though baby Henry enchanted her.

Founded in 1857, St. Paul's Lutheran congregation in Tess Corners built their small frame church a year later. Sunday services were held twice a month plus the holy days of Christmas and Easter. To augment this formal worship, the Watrys and Rosenbergs, in their homes, occasionally conducted makeshift services comprised of readings from the Old and New Testaments. The children were expected to sit quietly and listen to the readings, but afterwards could go outside and play, while their parents visited.

"Why don't you begin now, Mrs. Watry," Augusta said, after the boys were seated, but still struggling to control their outward signs of pleasure at being together again. The baby was on Augusta's lap. Ginny studied him with great interest.

"I would like to read," Veronica began, "from the Epistle of Paul to the Colossians, Chapter Three, Verses 12 to 15." She turned toward her boys, looking right at Jack who struggled not to grin. She said, "Children, you behave and listen well . . . this is church for today, and this is St. Paul:

> *Put on therefore, as God's chosen ones, a heart of mercy, kindness, humility, meekness and patience. Bear with one another and forgive one another, if anyone has a grievance against any other, even as the Lord has forgiven you, so also do you forgive. But above all these things have charity, which is the bond of perfection. And may the peace of Christ reign in your hearts . . . . Amen."*

"Amen," all responded, even the children.

Augusta glanced at Henry who sat motionless staring at his clasped hands. He was contemplating the word *grievance*.

"That was a fine reading, Fronnie," Augusta said. "Mr. Watry would you give the next, please?"

Mr. Watry cleared his throat. "This is from Matthew, Chapter 18: 15 to 17. Our Lord is speaking to his disciples." He cleared his throat again; Jack did the same at the exact same moment, which made his sister and brother gag with suppressed laughter.

> *"But if thy brother sin against thee, go and show him his fault, between thee and him alone. If he listen to thee, thou hast won thy brother. But if he does not listen to thee, take with thee one or two more so that on the word of two or three witnesses every word may be confirmed. And if he refuse to hear them, appeal to the Church, but if he refuse to hear even the Church, let him be to thee as the heathen and the publican."*

When Mr. Watry finished, all the grown-ups seemed in deep reflection. Henry realized the Watrys chose their texts to rebuke his decision. He wasn't looking forward to Augusta's reading though now he had to ask, "Augusta, would you like to read next?"

"Why thank you, Henry." She handed the baby to Fronnie. "I have chosen from Psalm 139." She was thrilled to have found something so befitting Mr. Lincoln. She read:

> *"Deliver me, O Lord, from the evil man: rescue me from the unjust man. Who have devised iniquities in their hearts: all the day long they designed battles. They have sharpened their tongues like a serpent: the venom of asps is under their lips. Keep me, O Lord, from the hand of the wicked: and from unjust men deliver me. Give me not up, O Lord, from my desire to the wicked: they have plotted against me. Do not thou forsake me, lest they should triumph . . . ."*

She closed the Bible without finishing the psalm and declared, "Amen."

Everyone except Henry and the baby echoed the word. With a faint smile, Augusta slid the bible towards her husband, confident the three readings had disarmed his foolish resolve.

They all looked at Henry; he had not the slightest inclination to look at any of them, especially, Augusta. The previous readings made him uncomfortable just as Augusta hoped, but he had anticipated his wife's strategy. He positioned the Bible in front of himself having placed his marker at Chapter Ten of Matthew's Gospel. Then he began, "This is our Lord giving instruction to the Twelve.

> *Do not think that I have come to send peace upon the earth; I have come to bring a sword, not peace. I have come to set a man at variance with his father, and a daughter with her mother, and a daughter-in-law with her mother-in-law; and a man's enemies will be those of his own household. He who loves father or mother more than me is not worthy of me; and he who loves son or daughter more than me is not worthy of me. And he who does not take up his cross and follow me, is not worthy of me. He who finds his life will lose it, and he who loses his life for my sake, will find it. Amen."*

"Amen," the others repeated, with little enthusiasm.

"Children, you may go outside now," Fronnie said. After a nod from Augusta, Georgie followed.

"Tell me, Henry," Mr. Watry began, "do you believe that passage can be used to justify war?"

"I believe the passage clearly indicates that our Lord anticipates enmity between believers and heathens. I think the struggle between good and evil oftentimes results in war, such as our struggle with the Confederacy."

"But our Confederate brothers are Christians just like ourselves," Franklyn said.

"They espouse a great evil. Collectively, they are guilty of a great sin."

"And I suppose then, it's Mr. Lincoln's role to judge and punish them – is that right?"

Henry resented the interrogation, but his good manners and Fronnie's presence let him suffer it. He clasped his hands behind his head, leaning back in his chair. Augusta didn't like when he sat that way. He answered, "The south seceded because their wealth is built upon slavery, which they intend to maintain. But secession is contrary to the spirit of unity within the Constitution, a document those States willingly bound themselves to. Lincoln's role is to preserve that union and, as has become necessary, to abolish the evils of slavery that mock the Declaration of Independence."

"The only reason, Henry, the southern States originally agreed to join the Union was because the slavery issue was left alone. You know that. It was left for the states to decide . . . they had that right. Perhaps now they see themselves betrayed."

"And how sensible is it," Augusta said, "to wage *civil* war, which I think is the most heinous of wars? To me it's senseless. Just think, Americans killing Americans."

"Yes, it's a senseless war to my way of thinking, as well," Franklyn Watry said.

Henry leaned forward. His chair thumped. "Preserving the Union is not senseless nor is ridding the country of slavery. The Founders erred. I, too, regret the bloodshed, but those two causes are worth fighting for."

"The problem, as I see it," Augusta said, "is that Mr. Lincoln, in addition to being wicked, is also incompetent. The war never should have lasted this long. A general as president would have concluded the matter in swifter fashion than a country lawyer with no military understanding."

"Yes, General McClellan is the better choice now, no question at all," Mr. Watry said.

Henry squirmed in his seat. "McClellan would end the war without resolution. If he's elected there will be two Americas, and slavery will exist in one of them. Then all who have died will have died in vain. No, no, not McClellan; I could not in good conscience vote for him, though I am a Democrat."

"If women could vote, General McClellan would be elected," Veronica Watry said.

"Absolutely," Augusta said. "Mothers would not vote for Lincoln. They want their sons home where they belong."

"That is precisely why women are not allowed the vote," Henry said. "Women use their hearts to make decisions rather than their minds. Any thinking man who understands the Constitutional unity pledged in blood by the revolutionaries – as well as the evils of slavery – is compelled to vote for Lincoln."

Franklyn looked askance at Henry. "Well now, I like to think of myself as a thinking man, but, by God, I am not compelled to vote for Lincoln. I've had enough of this damn war. It obviously can't be ended by Lincoln and his generals so let McClellan end it."

"Hear, hear," Augusta said.

"The papers are saying it will be close," Mr. Watry said, "even without the women's vote."

At that, Augusta recalled a point. "And, Henry dear, I must remind you: the heart is a far more sensitive and accurate arbiter of human affairs than is the head. If I must choose between the conclusions of my reason and the urgings of my heart – were they in opposition, which they seldom are – I shall always choose my heart to guide me."

Henry struggled to stay calm. "McClellan's skill was training an army, not fighting with one. That's why Lincoln discharged him. *He* was incompetent, not Lincoln. He was a terrible field general . . . he'd be a terrible commander-in-chief."

Franklyn Watry stood, gazing down at Henry. "We don't want

him as commander-in-chief. We want a statesman who'll sue for peace."

Fronnie and Augusta clapped their hands.

Henry stood, facing Franklyn. "How could there be a just peace if half the nation remains chained to slavery? So many have already died that it would be unthinkable to sue for peace when nothing has been resolved. Will McClellan sue for a peace in which the continent is divided and slavery triumphs over the blood of so many dedicated men? That is unthinkable. No, no, a just peace would be impossible under McClellan."

Eye to eye with Henry, Franklyn said, "Aah, yes, a military man knows well the horrors of war and, therefore, is reluctant to wage it. But a country lawyer knows nothing of war and, like a fool, rushes into it. I'll tell you this, Henry: McClellan will certainly end it more justly than Lincoln has fought it, if only the voters possess the wisdom to send Lincoln back to Illinois where he can engage in less deathly mischief."

"Dear Henry," Augusta said, "you worry too much about union and slavery. I read an editorialist who wrote unity would be restored *with* time, while slavery would be abolished *by* time. Do you agree, Mr. Watry?"

"Indeed I do, Mrs. Rosenberg. I've never been to the South and have no desire to wage war against the Americans living down there. I've never seen a plantation, never talked to a slaveholder though I've read the writings of Washington and Jefferson, both slaveholders and both, I dare say, civilized and intelligent men. Henry, let me ask you this." At that, both men sat down again. "How can slavery in which so few Negroes are maliciously killed be worse than a civil war that slaughters thousands of America's sons on both sides of the line?"

For months, Henry had struggled with that question. "Simply because slavery has existed for thousands of years does not bestow upon it the legitimacy of a virtuous institution, even if not a single Negro is killed or mistreated. It is inherently evil; it always was and always will be. Did we not learn this in *Exodus?* For one group of men, simply because of power and might, to enslave another group and then portray it, with the passage of time, as a benevolent economic institution, is an affront to God who created all men equally free."

"Henry, you evade my question. We all concede that both slavery and war are evil, do we not?" He glanced at the women who nodded in concurrence. "Which is the greater evil? Answer that question. Is the slaughter of thousands in a never-ending war less or more evil than a benign slavery where few are ever killed? And, as Augusta said, the passage of time itself will end slavery, and probably without bloodshed."

Tired of arguing, Henry said, "They fired the first shot. They seceded from the Union."

"So what?" Augusta fidgeted with the cuffs of her sleeves. "Had Lincoln simply let them go and not behaved like a tyrant, eventually they would have been drawn back to unity when wiser men – on both sides – had come to governance."

Fronnie said, softly, "Our Lord taught, *He who lives by the sword shall perish by the sword.*"

"Oh, my," Henry said, "What's the use of arguing? You will never concede my point, and I will never concede yours. Why should we even talk at all?"

"Because, my dear Henry," Franklyn answered, "it is from such debate that the truth can be distilled."

"Can it? Believe me, if Lee and his Army of Virginia were marching towards Wisconsin, you'd all whistle a different tune."

"If a *foreign* power invaded us or attacked our ships, I'd be the first to join in defense of my country," Franklyn said, ignoring the dilemma posed by Henry's comment. "I would defend this country with my life, as I know you would. But this is *civil* war. And that raises completely different moral issues."

"Franklyn," Veronica said, "I think we had better be going."

Augusta, sensing Henry wanted them to leave, said, "Well, thank you so much for coming. It was very pleasant visiting again."

Henry and Augusta, the baby in her arms, followed onto the porch, as the Watrys gathered their children, boarded the wagon, and prepared to leave. Georgie pretended he'd climb aboard too.

"Georgie, stop that," Augusta scolded.

"Thank you for coming, Fronnie," Henry said.

"We'll see you again soon, I trust," Augusta added.

They watched, as the wagon turned towards the road. All the Rosenbergs waved, and all the Watrys waved back. Augusta and little Henry went into the house expecting Henry to follow, but instead he grabbed Georgie's hand and walked around back to gaze at his land. He needed to recompose himself.

"See how beautiful the fields look, Georgie? See how thick the grain has grown? See the color? That's fine wheat. We had just the right amount of rain."

"I sure do like Rudy and Jack," Georgie replied.

When they entered the house, Augusta was mending; the baby played at her feet. A pot of stew simmered on the stove. Augusta greeted them with silence. Henry replied in kind. Georgie drank a cup of water then went outside again to play.

"Gussie, it was wrong of you to conspire against me in my own home."

"I will do whatever I can to dissuade you."

"I can assure you, those readings did nothing to change my mind. On the contrary, because they angered me, I am more determined to join than ever."

"It's a foolish man who lets the *Good Book* anger him."

"It wasn't the Good Book . . . it was your foolishness to contrive with the Watrys. I would respond more favorably to your pleadings than to any such conspiracy with those *Copperheads*."

Augusta never thought of herself as anything but a true American though she was as much a *Copperhead* as the Watrys. In her mind, Lincoln was the venomous snake.

"Henry, what are you saying?" She rested the mending on her lap and looked at him sadly. "You always were a good Democrat until Mr. Lincoln poisoned your mind. You told me your father wept when Jefferson died. How can you possibly support Lincoln?"

"Because Lincoln is right. I agree the Union must be preserved. I'm sure, if Jefferson were alive, he'd agree too, just as I'm sure he'd agree slavery must be abolished."

"Aah, but as Mr. Watry pointed out, Jefferson was a slaveholder."

"That was forty years ago. He would have changed. He would have confessed the evil and rejected it."

"Surely, though, you must confess the war is a terrible evil because of the bloodshed," Augusta implored.

"Yes, I do Gussie; perhaps you are right. Perhaps, the war is a huge mistake, never should have been fought; but now that opinion doesn't matter because it's being fought to the death. If the army doesn't get more men, I fear the war will last for years with even more bloodshed – just what you don't want. Don't you see, Gussie, the country needs me . . . I must go."

"No, I don't see. Your presence won't hasten the end one bit."

"But, if there are ten thousand others . . . ."

"There aren't a hundred who would leave wife and children to join a bloodbath."

"You underestimate how patriots feel. They want slavery abolished, once and for all."

"No, I do not, sir. I believe they want the war to end. This is why General McClellan will be elected. The killing must stop."

"Evil is always veiled in benign trappings," Henry said. "The veils are usually placed by those who most profit from the evil doing. It is the slaveholders who spread lies about life on the plantations."

"It is the armament manufacturers who profit from the killing."

"But no one attempts to disguise the war as anything other than the awful reality that it is. That's the difference. No one can mask the evils of this war, yet the slaveholders always portray life on the plantations as happy and peaceful. In fact, it is slave labor that builds the mansions, dresses the women in French gowns, and provides the men with stables of fine horses." Henry's voice grew louder, frightening Augusta. "Give me fifty slaves and I'd be a wealthy man too," he shouted. "I'm one man . . . I can barely work forty acres. With slaves I could work hundreds. We'd have hundreds of acres of wheat, Augusta. We'd be rich just like those g--damn Southerners."

Henry's curse shocked Augusta. *And on Sunday . . . what a disgrace.*

"You'd live in a fine house," Henry ranted on. "You'd have a cook, a laundress, and pretty, little nigger girls to sweep the floors and make the beds. It'd be so comfortable for us, but it's wrong, Augusta – wrong! What will it take for you to understand that? I'm going to join. There's nothing you can say to stop me."

Augusta, too, felt anger. And scorn. "The government you wish to serve doesn't want you; you're too old. Old men should remain at work so society can function though war is waged. Young men can join more carefree than a tradesman with wife and children. If they are killed, no one is left behind to mourn. The government's conscription practices are wise. If all the old farmers go off to war, who will feed the army?"

"You've said all of this before. I don't want to hear it again."

"Well, you will hear it . . . , if you can speak your mind, I can speak mine."

Henry fell silent. He was tired of arguing, tired of his wife's insolence. He had resolved that nothing would dissuade him.

She sensed his weariness. "Don't you see, Henry, you behave dishonorably by breaking your old vow, and then you join the army in hopes that you serve honorably. It's a contradiction; it doesn't make sense. Truly honorable men are consistently honorable."

"Why do you ascribe such maliciousness to my decision? Is not my sense of my own mature purpose more valid than your opinion of a rash promise I made as a young man?"

"Then you deliberately misled me. You bore false witness. You violated God's Commandment. It is a sin just like using God's name in vain. Tell me, would you rather die in sin for your country than live in virtue with your family?"

"No, of course not."

"Well, if you're not prepared to die for your country, how can you possibly serve as a soldier?"

"Not every army man gets killed," he shouted. "I do not intend to get killed."

"My heavens, what a silly thing to say; tell me, Mr. Rosenberg, do you know the mind of God?"

"To the extent that I recognize evil, yes. Slavery is a great evil – at least I understand that." He paused, but then added, "I'm a free man. My country needs me. There's nothing you can say. I'm going."

Georgie came into the house and stared at his parents in bewilderment. Never before had he heard their loud voices.

Augusta looked at Henry in anger and amazement. "I am your wife; these are your sons. *We* are your country!"

She scooped little Henry off the floor, ordered Georgie to come along, and went to the wash basin. Henry stepped outside. He walked to the road and back. Augusta lit the lamps and fed the boys their supper. Henry went 'round, stared at the dark fields then strolled to the road again. When he finally came in, having calmed his anger, he sat at his writing desk watching the lamp shadows tremble upon the wall. He heard Augusta saying bedtime prayers with Georgie.

From the moment he made the decision to join the Union army he knew Augusta would be displeased, but never did he anticipate such unrelenting opposition. In his mind, she was not being reasonable at all nor considerate of his deepest convictions as a patriot and free man. In her mind, Henry was completely unreasonable and totally inconsiderate of her and their children. This, for her, was nothing less than treason.

When Augusta came into the room, Henry heard, "Night, Pa."

"Goodnight, Georgie," he called, as he watched Augusta move to the dining table to seat herself as far from him as she could. He rose and sat across from her.

"Gussie, I intend to leave in the morning."

She looked at him, but did not speak. His supper waited on the stove.

"I'd like to leave with your blessing and the knowledge I'll be in your prayers."

"I suppose I have no choice though my heart is angry at you for abandoning us. It will be difficult to overcome my bitterness. You are going to war against my deepest wishes. Quite frankly, I'm not sure my prayers will be sufficiently pure to secure your safe return."

"Without them I fear this service, but with them I know I shall return."

"You know nothing of the sort. Don't be presumptuous. You know very well the war is claiming many. What are my ambivalent prayers for an errant husband beside the sacred pleadings of so many mothers for their innocent sons? No, Henry, I'm not sure, once you leave, we shall ever meet again."

"Then, dearest Gussie, let us sleep together this last night."

Her eyes flashed with anger. "No – you have no right to ask that."

"Gussie, you are my wife."

"You make me feel more like your widow. I fear that is what I shall become. Were I to conceive, the child might be born fatherless. That is wrong, and I shall not allow it."

"Oh, my dear Gussie, I'll be safe; I'll return to you. Please let us sleep together that I might carry that sweet memory with me."

"Henry, I beg of you. If you but renounce your intention to go to war, I shall welcome you into my bed as though it were our wedding night."

"No, I cannot. I've made up my mind. I leave in the morning."

"Then you are not welcome in my bed."

"It is *our* bed, Gussie." His voice edged with anger.

"Then you may sleep in it, and I shall gladly sleep on the floor."

Henry grabbed both her hands across the table. "I beg of you, Gussie, let us sleep together. Please, please . . . ."

She yanked her hands away. "No, Henry, it is all I have."

+ + +

It was the fifth night since he told Augusta of his decision to join the Union Army. Because of it, neither of them slept peacefully. Henry woke often, unable to control thoughts running wildly through his mind. Augusta woke at the smallest hours unable to control her feelings, sobbing until her heartache pressed her to sleep again. They both woke just after first light. Augusta would lay still and silent, waiting for her husband to begin to move about, pull his boots on, and go to the privy. She'd get out of bed, dress, and wait for him to return. When he did, she'd slip past on her way to the privy.

But this morning she stayed in bed. When he came back she heard him dress, gather his things to pack his valise, and then, with her eyes closed and feigning sleep, she lay motionless, as he stood in the passageway hoping for some sign she might be stirring.

"Gussie, are you awake?"

He approached the bed. She turned to face the wall.

"Gussie, I must leave now . . . bid me God's blessings."

She began to turn towards him, but turned away again, as he sat beside her. "You should not go . . . it is so wrong of you."

He placed his hand on the hill of her hip. "I love you Gussie. I love our sons. I'll return to you, but, please, pray for me. Look at me now, please. Let me see your sweet face once more before I go."

She turned towards him. In the sunless, early light her face appeared pallid and swollen. Tears from her shadowy eyes ran down her colorless cheeks. Her blue-gray lips were thin and inward drawn; her hair disheveled. "You should not go."

"I must. God bless you Gussie, and the boys. Keep me in your prayers."

He leaned towards her. She allowed him to kiss only her cheek. "Farewell," he said.

Tears welled in his eyes; he turned from her before they ran. In the room where his sons were sleeping, he kissed Georgie without waking him, then bent way down to kiss little Henry in his crib. As he passed the doorway to Augusta's room, he heard her exclaim, between her pitiful sobs, "I shall, I shall . . . ."

She barely heard the door close, as he left. She lay there almost as though paralyzed, half expecting any moment to hear Henry come right back in again. But, as the moments passed, only the fervent chirping of the birds and the occasional sad coo of a mourning dove graced her consciousness. Suddenly, regret and sorrow flared into panic. She flung herself out of bed and raced to the door.

From the porch she could see Henry, almost two hundred yards distant, trudging along nearly all the way up the long slope of road leading to the Watry farm. *Maybe there's news,* she hoped. *Maybe the war's . . . . Maybe Franklyn can dissuade. Yes, yes, he must. Oh, God, please, please.* She stood at the corner of the porch hoping Henry would turn that he might see her. He kept walking until he reached the crest of the hill, then stopped to gaze back upon his little farm in the wide valley below.

Augusta saw him clearly because the risen sun shone upon him. She waved wildly and shouted his name, but he could neither see nor hear her. The low sunlight pierced his eyes; the breeze diffused the patterns of his name, and the side of the porch where Augusta stood, waving and weeping, was hidden in shadow. He turned and was gone.

Chapter 2 ~ 1864 (Continued)

Days passed before Augusta could think of Henry without tears, but when those sad feelings abated they were replaced by anger. Never would she concede what Henry did was anything less than a betrayal of his sacred familial duty. Her conviction that he'd be killed in the war strengthened that feeling. *He'll sacrifice his life for a foolish cause,* she thought; a sacrifice that would make no difference in the war's outcome, but one that would force her to endure life without the husband who, on their wedding day, had vowed his eternal fidelity.

When she pondered her future, she saw a lonely widow whose sons were forced by their own poverty and lack of education to work at hard labor in a bleak, distant city and who had little time or money for their pitiful mother. Augusta's thoughts were anything but rational. She finally realized it one morning when she woke and felt neither sadness nor anger. She had slept particularly well. After the morning meal of biscuits, honey, tea, and baked apples, she stepped outside with the baby in her arms to enjoy the warm sunlight of the cool September morning. Then she saw a wagon trailing a dusty cloud; it was Veronica Watry come to visit.

"Oh my dear Fronnie, I'm so happy to see you. Oh my God, I've been having an awful time."

The women embraced.

"I've brought a pot of blackbird stew, fresh bread, apples, and some newspapers. Franklyn and I have been wondering how you're getting along. How are the children?"

"We are reasonably well, thank you. I've been out of sorts, but I woke this morning feeling almost like my old self again. For the first time since Henry left I don't feel quite so sad."

"Let's put the food inside then we'll talk. Georgie, you may tend the wagon if you'd like."

He bounded to the high bench and, grinning, took the reins. Veronica had tied the bridle to the porch rail and set the hand lever brake so there was no danger of Georgie going anywhere except for the happy journey he'd take in his mind. Augusta, smiling, carried baby Henry into the house, put him on the floor, then placed the gifts of food in the cupboard.

"Would you like a cup of tea," she asked.

"Nothing, Augusta; just come, sit . . . tell me about yourself."

"Oh, Fronnie, I haven't done so well since Mr. Rosenberg left. I'm frightened. I just don't know what to expect."

"What do you mean?"

"I fear Henry will never return. I fear what might happen to us. I'm so frightened because I . . . ," she paused to compose herself. "I believe Henry will be killed. I've convinced myself of that."

"The newspapers say things are going better now. Perhaps, it won't go on much longer."

"For years Henry told me the war would be over next week or next month, but it never is. And now that foolish man is in it. Oh my God, Fronnie, how could he have done such a thing?"

"Franklyn admires Mr. Rosenberg's courage. He said only a true patriot would make such a decision, given his age and all."

"But it wasn't honorable to break his vow to me. I know he's a good man, a dear man, just stubborn as a mule. I couldn't dissuade him no matter what I said. Tell me though, did Mr. Watry take him to Tess Corners or did he walk?"

"Franklyn took him."

"That was kind . . . thank him for me. Henry took the coach to Hales Corners then?"

"Yes, Franklyn said Henry would enlist in Milwaukee and then go to Camp Randall in Madison to learn to be a soldier."

"Oh, dear God, my Henry a soldier!" Augusta slapped her hands to her cheeks. "I cannot approve such foolishness. What am I to do, Fronnie?"

"Well . . . ," but she had no answer.

By mid-September, the harvesting was underway. Veronica told Augusta she had never seen the wheat fields look so beautiful. Franklyn Watry hired men by placing notices in the General Store and Post Office in Tess Corners; he even recruited some hands by going early to the tavern. Those he hired, including several

Indians, were older; most worked from farm to farm throughout the township.

The first week of October, Augusta marked Henry's absence at one month. She hadn't received a letter, but didn't expect it so soon. *After all*, she realized, *he has to learn to be a soldier* – she didn't have the faintest idea how long that might take – *and then he has to go off to fight his first battle*.

"I doubt," she told Georgie, "your father has time to write letters."

Georgie didn't understand; his father taught him how to write letters.

Dear God, she prayed, *I beseech Thee: let Mr. Rosenberg become a cautious soldier*.

She hoped to receive a letter by the first of November, but that, she knew, depended on Henry's attitude. Was he still angry with her? Had he forgiven her for refusing him? Would he ever return? All terrible questions that stabbed her heart.

In one of Fronnie's now weekly visits, she suggested Augusta give serious consideration to moving in with them for the winter rather than being isolated in her little cabin during that long, difficult season. Augusta didn't have to give the invitation much thought because she knew how vulnerable they'd be once the deep snows and bitter cold came. The Watry's generosity touched her heart, and even though their house was larger, Augusta knew it would be an imposition whether they admitted it or not. "Certainly, no later than the middle of November," Fronnie advised.

"I'll help with everything: cleaning, baking, cooking . . . ."

"You and little Henry can sleep in Virginia's room. She's so fond of you and the baby. She'll be thrilled you're coming."

"And Georgie?"

"He can sleep in the attic with Jack and Rudy. Oh my, what fun that will be, but, I dare say, we'll hear giggles all night long."

As they all agreed, on the morning of the national elections, Franklyn fetched Augusta, her sons, and her trunk packed with clothes and blankets. Henry's tethered horse trailed behind. After the Rosenbergs were moved and the horse quartered, they all rode to the schoolhouse in Tess Corners to accompany Franklyn who proudly cast his vote for General George B. McClellan, the Democratic nominee for the Presidency of the United States.

After Henry went to war, Franklyn picked up Augusta's mail. Now, leaving the children with Veronica at the schoolhouse, Augusta walked alone to the Post Office. But still no letter, two months after Henry left. Sadness overwhelmed her: sadness that Henry was somewhere far away, that he hadn't written, and that she had refused him the last night, knowing full well her wifely duty. She rejoined the others, struggling to hide her sorrow. Mr. Watry suggested they go to Schaumberg's Tavern for supper.

"He has an excellent chance of beating Lincoln," Franklyn said, as they sat down. Both women were confident he was right.

In the noisy, smoky tavern the baby fussed. Augusta and Veronica overheard all the talk about re-electing Lincoln, abolition, and winning the war. Lincoln posters bedecked the walls, but not a single one for McClellan.

"In Milwaukee," Franklyn said, "I've heard all the posters are for McClellan."

"Good," both women said. Never had they felt as certain of the righteousness of McClellan's candidacy.

+ + +

During the fall campaign, copies of partisan newspapers spread across the state. Their vigorous life lasted only until a disgusted partisan with the opposite viewpoint either pitched them into the fire or relegated them to privy duty. Enough, however, survived to reach the general store in Tess Corners where Franklyn Watry picked up papers partisan to Democrats. He shared them with his wife who shared them with her friend, Augusta Rosenberg.

Months earlier, Veronica gave Augusta a tattered issue of the La Crosse *Democrat*. In it she had the pleasure of reading the aggressive Mr. Pomeroy for the second time:

> *Abraham Lincoln is a traitor. It is he who has warred against the Constitution. We have not. It is his policy, his Administration, which has prolonged the war. We have not. It is his proclamations, not our editorials, which have disgusted the country. Abraham Lincoln was elected President by the people; he has been President but for the Republican Party.*

After Henry read it, he crumbled it into the fire.

Another editorial that strengthened Veronica and Augusta's attitudes against Lincoln was written by Stephen Carpenter, editor of the Madison *Patriot:*

> *The re-election of Lincoln would produce nothing but evil, for such has been the bitter fruit of his administration. The people must know the truth of what we say. They must know that Lincoln is an unfit man for the high station he occupies. His inconsistencies and his faults have been so glaring that they must be apparent to every disinterested mind. In view of these things, the incompetence, the blunders, violations of law, and fearful corruptions which have characterized his administration, and the dire consequences which are sure to follow his re-election, we cannot see how such a calamity can happen by the free choice of the people.*

Mr. Carpenter's words seemed restrained and reasonable when compared to Mr. Pomeroy who, when he learned Lincoln sought a second term, wrote:

> *May God Almighty forbid that we are to have two terms of the rottenest, most stinking, ruin-working smallpox ever conceived by fiends or mortals in the shape of two terms of Abe Lincoln.*

In the August 23, 1864, issue of the La Crosse *Democrat* that Augusta read with feelings of both anger and horror, Pomeroy placed a picture of Lincoln on the front page. Over it he boldly wrote, *The Widow Maker of the 19th Century and Republican Candidate for the Presidency.*

After reading that day's editorial, Franklyn Watry expressed alarm to Veronica that an editor would so abuse the liberty of a free press. Pomeroy wrote:

> *The man who votes for Lincoln now is a traitor and murderer. He who pretending to war for, wars against the Constitution of our country is a traitor, and Lincoln is one of these men. And if he is elected to misgovern for another four years, we trust some bold hand will pierce his heart with dagger point for the public good.*

"No Christian man, no patriot regardless of party could subscribe to such a violent suggestion," he told Veronica. "Pomeroy hurts the Democrats with such viciousness. The man has no restraint; he's every bit as ruthless as Lincoln."

"Rage has overtaken his reason," she replied, "but I think it's important to ask why so many are enraged."

As the fall of 1864 approached, the tide of war turned in the Union's favor. Sherman moved against Atlanta, while Grant gained ground near Richmond. The sea blockade drained the life out of the Confederacy, while prosperity in the North, brought on by the war, strengthened Lincoln's campaign for re-election. Demand for wheat was strong; the army bought the surpluses that assured high prices for a bushel of Wisconsin's golden grain. Such prosperity helped heal some of the wounds of war and bolstered Lincoln's chances, while McClellan's declined. And yet, McClellan ran much stronger in Wisconsin than even his most ardent supporters had expected. Milwaukee, a bastion of Democrat Party politics, gave McClellan 6,875 votes to only 3,175 for Lincoln. Statewide, *Little Mac* received forty-seven percent of the home votes, losing by only 6,000. However, when the soldiers' votes were counted, Lincoln's plurality swelled to over 15,000. One of those was cast by Corporal Henry Rosenberg.

Nationally, Lincoln won the electoral vote in a landslide, 212 to 21, but the popular vote narrowed with McClellan drawing 45 percent. It proved small comfort to Augusta who was devastated by his defeat. She really believed McClellan would win. She simply could not understand why so many men decided to vote for the hated Mr. Lincoln.

"If only women could vote," she told Veronica, "such tyrants would never be elected."

"Oh, Augusta dear, once the war is over we won't find Mr. Lincoln quite so loathsome."

"The problem I see," Mr. Watry said, "is that Lincoln has garnered massive power for the government. Jefferson would be horrified. Oh, the war will end, Augusta, but I'm not sure the power of the federal government will ever be limited again. Where that will lead us, God only knows."

"Well," Augusta said, "with Lincoln re-elected, I simply shan't read the newspapers. I'm sick to death of him and all he has wrought."

Franklyn and Veronica laughed. They knew how much Augusta enjoyed reading newspapers, especially those friendly to the Democrats. In a matter of days, they suspected, she'd enjoy them again.

But that night Augusta fell asleep disheartened by three awful realizations: Lincoln had been re-elected, the war still raged, and Henry hadn't written. Even when little Henry began to walk, Augusta's sadness overshadowed any brief feelings of happiness caused by something so dear to her heart. As the year wore down into December and still no letter from Henry, Augusta's spirits, day after day, sagged noticeably. Ginny told her mother she had heard, on several occasions, Augusta's soft weeping during the night.

One evening with a bright moon rising, Franklyn saddled his horse and rode to Tess Corners to hear a speech by a colonel on leave from a Wisconsin regiment. It gave the women an opportunity to talk privately. After the children were in bed, Veronica and Augusta sat by the fire, as was their habit. Veronica said, "I can't help but notice your sadness, dear. Would you like to confide in me?"

Augusta stared at the flames. She didn't answer.

"I know how difficult it must be not knowing where your Henry is and why he hasn't written. I understand your sadness and find it to be the most normal of states."

Augusta sighed. "I know why."

It puzzled Veronica but she was reluctant to pry.

"I just hope he's safe wherever he is," Augusta said.

"Well, remember what Mr. Watry said about the government being efficient at, if nothing else, notifying next of kin. I think it's safe to say he is not dead. If he were ill or wounded, I think he would have written from his hospital bed. I suspect, Gussie, Mr. Rosenberg is in good health and off somewhere very busy with his soldierly duties."

"Oh, I do hope so."

Suddenly, from her bedroom, Ginny called, "What are you whispering about?"

"Nothing dear," Veronica said. "We don't want to wake the baby."

"You're talking about something you don't want me to hear."

"It's nothing at all," her mother replied. "Just go to sleep now, Ginny. We're waiting for your father."

The women sat in silence a little while until Veronica called to her inquisitive daughter who failed to reply. "She's asleep now," she said, and then waited for Augusta to speak.

"You know I didn't want Henry to go."

"None of us did."

"We had saved the three hundred dollars to keep him out if he was drafted. All these years we've had that money, and then that foolish man enlists. He promised me several years ago he wouldn't go. I took that as a solemn vow, but he betrayed me, Fronnie. He betrayed us by putting himself in a situation where he might be killed. Do you know how difficult my life will be if Henry dies? Never will I understand why he did this. He's relatively old. Let the younger men go, I say. I cannot, try as I might, understand how a man would make such a terrible decision having a wife and two little ones. His going will not affect the war one tiny bit, but do you have any idea how it will affect my life if he doesn't return?"

"Well, yes, I think I do. It would be terrible."

"I was angry at him, angrier than I have ever been in my whole life. Sometimes now I get feelings of longing, but the next moment I'm loathing him again. How could he have done such a thing? He knew how I felt about the war. So, what does he do? He goes to war. Oh, my God, Fronnie, never did I think he would so betray me. That's why I . . . ."

Veronica waited before asking, "What were you going to say?"

"I rejected him. I hardly talked to him. I wouldn't let him sleep with me. I didn't even say good-bye the morning he left."

"Augusta, I'm surprised. That's not like you."

"I felt such coldness in my heart; a coldness and hardness I never felt towards any other living soul. I could barely stand to look at him. I rejected him and that is why he hasn't written. I doubt he ever will. I don't believe he'll return even if he isn't killed. Quite frankly, Fronnie, I don't ever expect to see Henry again."

Shocked, Fronnie said, "That is not like your Mr. Rosenberg. He's a loyal husband and father. He'll return to you, God willing."

"Oh, I pray he will, but I'm not so sure. Not after what I did."

"And what was that?"

Augusta wondered, *should I tell?* And then, *yes, better if she knows.* "The night before he left, he begged me to sleep with him. He begged me to give him that sweet joy, but I refused. I refused him, Fronnie. I expelled him not only from my bed, but, more terribly, from my heart."

Augusta sobbed into her hands. Veronica went for a clean handkerchief, which Augusta took without words. She wept for a long while. In her bed, Ginny heard the familiar sobbing and finally fell asleep.

"Did I ever really love him at all," Augusta asked Veronica. "Have I lost him forever?"

Again Veronica could offer no answers.

In the morning, Franklyn told Veronica and Augusta about the speech given by Colonel Ambrose Payne, a Milwaukee man who indicated with great confidence that the war would not go on much longer because of the overwhelming strength of the Union forces and their ability to press forward on every front. "Six months at the most," the distinguished colonel had said. "Maybe less if the weather proves favorable."

"Foolishness – I've heard it all before for years," Augusta cried. "Back in '61, Henry said the war would be over in three months. No, I don't believe a word of it. The war will last forever."

"No, Augusta, I think the colonel is right. The Union is winning now, and it will end, maybe not in six months, but certainly within the New Year."

"Let's not talk about the war, please," Veronica implored. "Christmas is coming."

The first week of December marked the third month since Henry's departure, and Augusta still hadn't received a letter. Not only did she feel acute sadness about that grim fact, but she also felt profound shame. *What must the Watrys truly think,* she asked herself. *How strange it must seem that my own husband hasn't written in all that time.*

Sympathetic as he tried to be, Franklyn didn't concern himself with Henry's failure to write. *No sense in wondering about that,* he realized, nor the wellbeing or whereabouts of his neighbor. *What good does it do?* Besides, what could he do about any of it? Franklyn was more concerned about Henry's horse. *Him I can take care of.*

Henry had asked Franklyn to work his horse, for it did the animal no good to be lazy. The thought of a two horse team pulling his wagon intrigued Franklyn. The cost of the rigging, however, gave him pause. Nevertheless, he declined to discuss the purchase with Veronica; she'd consult with Augusta, and their mutual opinion, he suspected, might be complete opposition. The harvest, though, had been profitable, and Franklyn had money to spend.

So without any marital discussion, he hitched the wagon to Henry's horse and drove to the livery in Muskego where he bought the gear. When he returned, he unhitched the wagon and led the animal to pasture.

In the house he greeted Veronica, Augusta, and the children, then went back to the barn to re-rig the wagon. He had purchased a fine, two-horse harness with leather breast straps and breeching made specifically for farm wagons. The breeching enabled the horses to back up the wagon as well. He also purchased an evener or doubletree as some called it, a movable front crossbar that attached to the pole of the running gear with a hitch pin. Franklyn aligned and marked the pin location several times before he augured it, as he couldn't afford to ruin the pole. At both ends of the evener, singletrees hung to attach to the harness pole chains. After several hours work, Franklyn had the wagon outfitted, but decided not to tell anyone until Christmas day when he'd surprise them. He left the new harness and breeching in the wagon, then pushed it into the back darkness of the barn.

When Veronica asked, he said, "Just some minor repairs . . . ."

By mid-December, heavy snow still hadn't fallen. An inch of dry, dusty snow fell a week before Christmas. The sun came out for a day, but then more clouds moved in. Every day Franklyn studied the sky. "Let's hope it doesn't snow. If the weather holds," he announced, one evening at dinner, "we'll go to church."

By Christmas morning it still hadn't snowed so they could reach Tess Corners on open roads. After breakfast, Franklyn enlisted the boys to help rig and hitch the wagon to what the women presumed to be just one horse. When Virginia saw the two-horse team she squealed with delight. *Even the horses look proud,* she thought. In the wagon, the boys shouted and waved as though it was the Fourth of July.

Franklyn bounded from the high bench and offered Augusta his hand. "May I help you board, Ma'am? We've fresh hay and clean blankets for your comfort."

"Why, thank you sir."

Franklyn offered his hand to his wife who glanced at him with bemused skepticism. Veronica's expression appeared far too stern for a Christmas morning, revealing her disapproval of the expenditure.

With everyone seated, Franklyn lightly snapped the reins; the horses walked out the rutted lane. Reaching the road, he cracked the reins; the horses surged in a fast trot.

"Oh, my, Mr. Watry," Augusta said.

"We're going fast, Papa," Virginia shouted.

The boys cheered.

"Faster, Papa," Jack said.

Veronica tightened her bonnet. "No, no, it's fast enough. At that, I'm quite amazed at our swiftness. We'll be on time for church today, no question."

Grinning, Franklyn replied, "No question at all."

"And how much did this fancy rigging cost us," Veronica asked.

"It's Christmas," Franklyn said. "I'll not discuss the devil's dung on this holy day."

Franklyn and the women rode in silence, enjoying the quick pace and brisk air. Behind them the children chatted happily.

Finally, Franklyn said, "You know, Mrs. Rosenberg, Henry asked me to work your horse. That's why I bought the two-horse rig. That and the speed . . . amazing the difference a second horse makes, eh?"

"Yes," Augusta answered.

Veronica, between them, stared straight ahead.

"We want to keep your horse lean and strong. They get slow and fat if only put to pasture."

"Indeed they do."

At the little junction of Tess Corners, the chilly air compelled both families into the church with its pot-belly stove. Discreetly, the women looked around for familiar faces, as others entered. They also admonished the boys not to look around so much. As more families filed in, the church grew warmer.

The Watrys and Rosenbergs were fond of Pastor Hubert Berner. They knew him to be intelligent and kind; a man who had mastered the principles of Christian living and exemplified them by generosity to those in temporal or spiritual need. Stories were freely shared about such matters throughout the township; news of his good deeds traveled almost as fast as news of another's scandal. In this way, he became a beloved minister to his mostly farming flock.

Pastor Berner stood six feet tall with a powerful frame, the result of hard labor in his youth when he helped his father farm eighty acres. But his mother had, in the end, more influence. Her love for the Lutheran faith inspired the boy to holiness and to choose divinity school as a young man. His father had mixed feelings: on one hand he was proud of his minister son; on the other, he wanted him to work their farm once he passed on. When the young minister married a city girl after his ordination, there'd be no further discussion of farming. His assignment to a country town's church and the help he gave his wife tilling their vegetable garden was as close as he'd ever get to the soil again.

On this Christmas morning he bore a grave countenance. He climbed the steps to the canopied pulpit, opened the large Bible, and began to read:

> *"And seeing the crowds, he went up the mountain. And when he was seated, his disciples came to him. And opening his mouth he taught them, saying, blessed are the poor in spirit, for theirs is the kingdom of heaven. Blessed are the meek, for they shall possess the earth. Blessed are they who mourn, for they shall be comforted. Blessed are they who hunger and thirst for justice, for they shall be satisfied."*

He paused, raised his eyes heavenward, then glanced about the room. "Matthew, Chapter Five, verses one to six. Good morning, my brothers and sisters."

"Good morning Pastor," the congregation replied.

Then in a loud voice, "Blessed are they who mourn, for they shall be comforted."

Pastor Berner scanned the faithful, his expressive eyes moving from family to family, person to person, pleased to see the little church filled, but not so pleased with the sermon he was about to give. Twice he looked directly into Augusta's eyes.

"We all mourn this Christmas day," he began, "for our divided nation, but when shall we be comforted? Our Savior promised that we would, and we must never doubt His promises. Sadly, this is the fourth wartime Christmas, and I again must offer words that provide some meager comfort against the harsh fact that the nation still groans under the weight of a terrible civil war. Though I welcome you this Christmas morning – what should be a morning of great joy for all of us – I do not welcome this opportunity to address you, but address you I must.

"It is difficult to be merry while the nation remains at war though merriment is not a necessary attribute for the celebration of our Savior's birth. Joy definitely is, however, and we must distinguish between the true joy of the spirit's deep realization of the coming of our Savior those many centuries ago and the silly merriment so many people seem to think is proper disposition for the celebration of this holy day. But few today feel such merriment. Most struggle earnestly to find a bit of joy in their hearts knowing that loved ones are still away at the dreadful conflict."

The Pastor's opening remarks touched Augusta's heart.

"Many of you have sons, husbands, and brothers in the war. We pray to Almighty God that they return safely. And yet, we know that not all will and, therefore, it is difficult for any of us – because we are brothers and sisters in Christ – to be joyful on this sacred day. I know, too, that many of you have strong anti-war convictions." He paused then added, "I share those noble sentiments."

Hearing their pastor express his opinion pleased Augusta and Veronica. They smiled at each other. A rush of admiration for his courage stirred Augusta's heart. This was, after all, Lincoln country.

He continued. "Nevertheless, I have studied the issues and prayed for enlightenment and have concluded, as terrible as the war is, it must be fought and won to finally rid our nation of the evils of slavery."

Augusta's mood slumped.

"We cannot be, before God, a nation of slaveholders, slaves, and those politicians and editorialists who tolerate such evil. We must not imitate the ancient Egyptians who enslaved the Israelites simply because they had the power to do so. Our nation's birth was too rich with idealism and promise to allow this evil institution to continue any longer within our borders. Therefore, I urge all of you in solitude to beseech Almighty God to guide the President, the Government, and the Generals to lead the country to a just and swift end to the conflict.

Augusta did not appreciate her minister expressing his altered political opinion, for she realized he, too, had succumbed to Lincoln's rhetoric. *In the early years, he felt differently.*

"I believe the prayers of millions are absolutely necessary to persuade our heavenly Father that the nation has suffered enough. Pray not for your temporal needs, for they will be enhanced once the war is over. Pray instead for forgiveness of any word or deed that might have caused a war between you and a loved one or a friend. Pray in adoration of a heavenly Father who sent his only Son into the world for the forgiveness of sins that you might have the opportunity for eternal life. Thank God for all the blessings he has given you, and pray with all your heart for the swift conclusion of the war and the safe return of your loved ones."

Pastor Berner paused for a moment and, as he did, became aware of the sadness on every face in the little church. He sensed the congregation felt his sermon a bit long. He shuffled through the pages to the conclusion.

"Remember always that Christ disdained worldly things, but did not disdain the world. He taught us to love the beauty of the flowered fields and to be compassionate to strangers because to do both is to be like Him. Oftentimes we are not content with what we have in this life. Then we must remember the Son of God did not even have a place to lay His head. Not until he reclined on the wood of the cross did he have a moment of repose, and then it was only an instant before the first nail pierced forever the palm of his sacred hand. Thus, we must not complain about our lot in life, knowing well that God's only begotten Son suffered so terribly at the hands of evil men. By this divine example, I urge you all to bear your sufferings with great dignity.

"Those of you who have already lost, or who will yet lose a husband, a son, or brother, must remember that God Himself lost His Son to a cruel but noble death – a death that earned for us the gift of eternal life. Remember your loved ones who fall in battle not only with sorrow, but also with great joy, for they shall be with God."

The thought of Henry's death crushed Augusta's heart. Tears welled in her eyes.

"It is the deaths of good men in a just war, a war with a true, moral purpose that will enable our nation to undergo a transformation where none brandish the whip of the slaveholder, and no Negro cowers beneath such vicious cruelty. Yes, many have died, but ultimately there will be a renewal born of this sacred blood. When slavery is forever eradicated from America's soil, we shall experience a resurrection into the light of true justice, liberty, and peace.

"It is my prayer for all of you that this holy celebration of Christ's birth will sustain you to the feast of Easter, our Lord's resurrection, when, hopefully, our terrible national conflict will be over. God bless you in the days and months ahead. As always, Mrs. Berner joins me in wishing a joyful Christmas to you all."

The solemn congregation then partook of the Lord's Supper. The service concluded with a rousing singing of the old Latin hymn, *Adestes Fidelis*, with Mrs. Berner working the organ. Augusta rose, but could hardly sing a word. Outside, the winter air revived her. After they all greeted the pastor and his wife, and chatted with acquaintances, Franklyn was ready to leave.

Tis a sullen Christmas day, Augusta realized, as the horses trotted towards the Watry farm. She sat on the front bench with Veronica in the middle again and the children in the rear with little Henry quite content on Virginia's lap. *So colorless*, her thought went on, *so lacking warmth and pleasantness. How I long for blue sky and spring.* Henry flitted about her mind.

She whispered to Veronica, "I could not bring myself to pray for Mr. Lincoln though I pray earnestly for a swift end to the war and Henry's safe return."

"I understand, Gussie. I, too, pray for conclusion and your Henry. I'm not so sure, however, that it is our Christian duty to pray directly for Mr. Lincoln."

Veronica and Augusta planned a grand dinner around the large, wild turkey Mr. Watry had shot a week before Christmas. They stuffed it with a bread and onion dressing with the giblets boiled tender, finely diced and thoroughly mixed in so the children wouldn't detect, though they occasionally discovered a lead shot in the great bird's meat. The women, with Ginny's help, boiled potatoes, caramelized carrots, sugared sweet potatoes, sweet-soured the green beans, and baked bread and apple pies enough to last all January. Candles and mistletoe were placed all about the house. Franklyn built a fire and kept it roaring all evening with some of his best split hardwood.

"Mr. Watry always reads St. Luke before our Christmas dinner," Veronica said.

"Oh how nice," Augusta replied.

Everyone gathered at the table. Franklyn stood at the head with the Bible in his hands. He cleared his throat. Rudy and Jack giggled; Georgie did too.

"Boys, hush," Veronica said.

"Now it came to pass in those days that a decree went forth from Caesar Augustus that a census of the whole world should be taken," Franklyn began.

The children paid rapt attention to the ancient tale. Augusta stared at Franklyn though in her mind she saw Henry. Occasionally, Veronica glanced at Augusta and found a distinct sadness traced on her pretty profile.

". . . there was with the angel a multitude of the heavenly host praising God and saying, 'Glory to God in the highest, and on earth peace among men of good will.'" Franklyn closed the book and returned it to the high mantel above the fireplace.

"Please, everyone, remain seated," Veronica began. "Before we serve dinner we have a little present for" – she paused to build suspense – "our dear friend, Augusta Rosenberg."

Virginia clapped, and the boys joined in.

Veronica turned towards Augusta and smiled. "Do please come here, Augusta."

She stood little Henry at Virginia's chair, then rose from her place, moving gracefully to stand in front of Veronica. "What are you up to, you sly thing," she asked.

Veronica held her hands behind her back. Franklyn stood beside her, smiling at Augusta. "Well," Veronica said, her eyes bright with pleasure, "we have a little present for you, but it's not really from us."

From behind her, where Franklyn had placed it in her hands, she withdrew a faintly tinted article tied with fresh ribbons and graced with dried wildflowers that Veronica had lovingly attached to this most slender and delicate of gifts.

"Oh, my God . . . ," Augusta gasped. "A letter from Henry."

Chapter 3 ~ 1907

In 1881, ten year old Johannes Helden came to America from the little town of Duesmond, Germany, with his parents and brothers: Josef, fourteen, and Peter, five. The oldest brother, Franz, had been conscripted into the Prussian Army, but, true to his parent's abhorrence of all things military, at his first opportunity went absent without leave. Fleeing to Hamburg, he booked Atlantic passage *ein weg* to New York and from there, by letters, urged his parents to follow him to the New World. His father, also a Franz, set about to persuade his fearful wife to leave her beloved Germany forever. He insisted Europe was a hotbed for war. He wanted no part of it for themselves and no part, especially, for their budding sons.

After nine difficult months the family reunited in New York City where young Franz had made inquiries. He recommended they settle in southeastern Wisconsin, a distant western state where the sparse immigrant population was mostly German and acres of serene, wooded hills, and wide, fertile valleys were available for homesteading.

Franz Helden acquired forty acres at Prospect Hill in Muskego Township. After he built a house, little money remained, but now the family possessed shelter and fine farmland. As the years passed they prospered; the youngest of the sons, unsuspected by all, would prosper beyond any of their imaginings. Peter's wealth, though, wouldn't come from the grains of this gentle land, but from steel milled from the ore of iron-rich earth scraped and scarred in northern Minnesota.

Within several years the boys had new names: Franz became Frank, Josef became Joe, and Johannes, John; even little Peter's name was pronounced with the long *e*. They became young men in America, but the three oldest never forgot their boyhoods in Germany. Only Peter, as he grew, remembered less of the old life and, of all the boys, mastered the English language most easily and spoke it without the slightest accent while retaining his ability to speak perfect German. Indeed, the family had become bilingual. At home the language at first was German, but then, because of the boys' schooling, it became part English. After a decade, more often than not, they all spoke English.

In September, 1892, at the Muskego Township Fair, John Helden met a pretty, young woman, Augusta Rosenberg. He was twenty-one; she was twenty-four though in John's eyes no age difference was evident. As they began courting, she proved herself as sweet and gentle as John's own mother.

Augusta's father, Mr. Henry Rosenberg, was a distinguished veteran of the Civil War. After he had been appointed Postmaster in Tess Corners, he sold his farm to his neighbor, Franklyn Watry. For many years now, Henry lived in Tess Corners with his wife, Augusta, and their daughter, also named Augusta, whom he affectionately called "Little Gussie" right from her birth on the last day of 1867.

Two years after they met, John and Little Gussie married in St. Paul's Lutheran Church in Tess Corners with Augusta's minister presiding. The Heldens were Catholic and expected Augusta to convert. However, when John announced he would marry Augusta in her church, his parents were shocked.

The young couple moved to Milwaukee where John and Peter Helden turned their attention to learning the new technology of electric arc and gas welding. By 1901, John and Peter had started their own company to weld streetcar tracks for the burgeoning lines that kept extending farther into the outlying areas of Milwaukee and the growing suburbs of West Allis, Shorewood, and Wauwatosa. But that wasn't enough for Peter. Older brother Joe, a skilled draftsman, also became a partner in the young firm. Peter described his ideas for Joe to turn into engineering drawings. From these Peter and John fabricated welded steel storage tanks and bins of varying capacities, and welded steel truck bodies that could be pulled either by horses or the new, gasoline powered trucks that were becoming, year after year, more common.

By 1907, Peter envisioned automobiles and trucks becoming so widespread that gasoline would have to be stored at fueling stations in large, underground, welded steel tanks. He convinced his brothers to build a prototype with a gravity inlet valve, air vents, a pump outlet valve, and a long, oak, measuring rod. Peter's ability to look ahead, to anticipate a need that had not yet become evident and determine how to fill that need, made his brothers marvel at his intelligence, foresight, and decisiveness. Eventually, those qualities would make Peter a rich man.

+ + +

In 1897, Augusta Helden gave birth to her first son, Clarence, and, at her husband's urgings, converted to the Catholic faith. Two years later, George was born, named after Little Gussie's older brother who lived in Chicago. That same year, Augusta Rosenberg died at age sixty-seven. Henry, her husband of forty-six years, sold the house in Tess Corners and came to live with Little Gussie and John Helden in their new bungalow in Milwaukee. In 1902, Augusta gave birth to John Junior, and three years later to her last son, Julius, who everyone called Juley.

On the first warm, spring Sunday of 1900, Henry Rosenberg did something he hadn't done in thirty-five years: for the first time since his return from the Civil War in June of 1865, he put on his old, blue uniform. It still fit, though his body, especially his upper torso, had shrunk with age. That he donned the uniform only months after his wife's passing was no mere coincidence. Henry knew full well he couldn't wear the uniform while Augusta was alive lest it brought back those awful memories when Henry went to war in spite of Augusta's mighty objections. He considered himself fortunate she didn't burn it, so strongly did she hate the memories of that horrible war. Augusta didn't need any reminder from him or anyone else to occasionally turn sullen and withdraw. Henry rightly suspected she was recalling how terrible he was for going to war, leaving her and the children to fend for themselves that long winter, even though they lived in the comfort of the Watry's pleasant house.

But now, the more Henry wore the old uniform the more he enjoyed it, though he only wore it on Sundays and then only when the weather was clement. That he was given to reminisce about those events so many years ago was, he thought, perfectly normal for a man of seventy. All the old veterans he knew did the same, and they all talked about their war-time experiences, especially among themselves. Henry looked back on it with a strange fondness in spite of the horribleness of so much of it. He was young then and desired adventure even though the great event proved a tragedy of epic proportions. He had been changed by the war; as the years passed, he believed it had made him a better man.

Henry's regiment had fought its way eastward at Gravel Run, at Five Forks, and in fights along the Weldon Railroad. Henry had been with Grant and Sheridan at Appomattox and had even seen the great, gray general, Robert E. Lee, serious in expression and straight in the saddle at war's formal end. Only the old veterans knew these things, and they couldn't really explain what it meant to anyone who hadn't been there. As the decades rolled relentlessly along, fewer and fewer people, especially the young, had any interest in it at all. By 1900 even the assassination of President Lincoln was, for most people who were alive when it happened, just a dim, distant memory, an old, isolated event because now the nation was vigorous with life and growth and looked forward to the coming of the twentieth century.

+ + +

"Boys, get ready . . . we're going to church. Where's your father?" Augusta, with baby Julius in her arms and three sons clustering about, moved as one grand being through the front door.

"I'm a-coming, Gussie," John called.

"Grandpa," Clarence asked, "how come you never go to church?"

"What do you mean?" Henry gently glided on the two-seat swing suspended by chains from the porch rafters.

"How come you don't have to go to church?"

"Because your mother isn't my mother."

"Who is she?" little Johnny asked.

Henry laughed. "She's my daughter."

Augusta pinned her hat. "Pa, why don't you come? That'd be nice."

"I'm not Catholic. I'm Lutheran like you used to be."

"It doesn't matter. We all pray to the same heavenly Father."

"Let me tell you something, Gussie. When I put this old uniform on, I feel just as though I'm slipping into church."

"How's that, Pa?"

The boys milled about their grandfather. "Because I did more praying in this here uniform than all the churches I was ever in, in all my life. If that doesn't make it a church nothing does. Church doesn't have to be timber and stone, you know; fine wool cloth is just as honorable as the harder, more earthly materials."

"Grandpa," Clarence said, "Can I wear your coat and stay here in your church?"

George snapped to attention. "Grandpa, can I wear your pants?"

"Boys, stop your foolishness." Through the screen door Gussie called, "John, are you coming?"

A moment later her husband strode out barking, "Boys, to church! See you later Henry."

The old Civil War veteran watched as they headed towards Lincoln Avenue. He waved though no one turned to see it. In the rear of the formation, Augusta held little Johnny's hand. Her husband walked ahead carrying two-year-old Julius. In between, Clarence and George stumbled along, side by side, on the narrow sidewalk.

Nice family, Henry thought. *John's a good provider, that's for sure.*

In the warm, morning sunlight, Henry appreciated an hour alone. He needed that, living in a house filled with exuberant boys. Sometimes they interfered with his inner life; as boys they weren't aware of anything like that yet. Henry wanted quiet time with his thoughts, and to remember those wonderful days, those terrible, wonderful days so long ago when, as a young man, he had gone to war.

+ + +

Winter, 1865. In dangerous territory Henry's scouting company marched eastward through open fields alongside a badly damaged plank road. Intersecting another road, the company halted; the officers considered where they might encounter Rebels. The road led southeast; after half a mile it bent eastward against the long north edge of a wood. The lieutenants and sergeants suspected they'd most likely discover the enemy hiding in those woods, just hoping for a column of Union Blue to come marching serenely by.

Anticipating a skirmish, the officers figured they'd be shot at by Confederate ambushers long before they'd reach the east end of the wood two miles distant. They gave the order to spread the column in a quick march with several yards between pairs of soldiers with loaded *Springfields*. In the event of an attack, gaps in the column would be safer against Rebel sharpshooters; a compact march couldn't be missed. A long battle line would be formed directly against the heaviest fire. The response would be a concentrated volley at the hidden enemy by half the Company's rifles followed by a second volley, while the first shooters reloaded. The officers hoped there'd be fewer Rebels and the heavy Union fire would kill or injure enough to rout the survivors. Then the Second Lieutenant, Mr. Curran, would lead a party to hunt down the Reb's camp. That was the plan.

"Would you like to wager we pass the wood unshot upon," Corporal Hayes asked.

"I'll take the bet only if you give me the ambush," Henry said.

"No, no, I get the ambush. You bet the peace and quiet. That's what you're praying for."

Henry laughed. "I never bet my prayers. Methinks there's a limit what the good Lord can do once the Rebs decide to fight."

The long column of Company D, Sixth Wisconsin Volunteers, Infantry, approached the wood. The lieutenants on horseback trotted ahead of the flag bearer. All three knew if sharpshooters with *Enfields* were waiting and sighting, they'd be fired upon first. Their lives, in only moments now, would be in imminent danger.

"Watch for a puff or two of smoke, Mr. Curran," the First Lieutenant said. "Look sharply."

"Yes Sir."

The column advanced another two hundred yards at a quick pace before they spotted the first telltale puffs of rifled, musket smoke billowing from a small area of the gray wood. A tremendous clamor rose among the men, as the shots rang out. The Company formed their battle line. Three Union soldiers had been hit, emitting loud screams. One was killed.

"This is it," the officers shouted. Both heard *Minie* balls hiss by. Yanking their horses left, they trotted behind the men who had dropped to their knees, firing a tremendous first volley from a line that stretched a hundred yards behind the officers. All that fire converged at the small area where the musket smoke rose. Lieutenant Curran galloped well past the center of the line exhorting the men to reload. He realized the right flank was exposed, but saw no Confederate troops anywhere.

A second volley from the ambushers rang out; Curran counted less than ten puffs. Two privates screamed when hit. Almost immediately the second volley of Union fire rang out in return. Then the Company's third volley roared against the wall of trees and reverberated back across the line. At that point, no more musket smoke was sighted. The lieutenants shouted, "Hold your fire," as they rode back and forth behind the men, realizing the skirmish ended as suddenly as it began.

The men sat down with their rifles across their laps, aware of little more than the sound of the horse's hoofs, which ceased when Lieutenant Curran reached his commanding officer. Many of the privates lay down in spite of the cold ground, propped their heads on their packs, and stared at the bleak sky, happy to be alive. Most concerned themselves not at all with the several wounded and the one dead. Nothing was seen or heard from the spot where the Rebels had ambushed. Minutes after the skirmish, it seemed to most of the men nothing more than a brief, disagreeable dream.

Corporal Hayes was ordered to tend the wounded. For the time being, he ignored the dead soldier. The First Lieutenant ordered Sergeant Mechler to take five men and search for Rebels, dead or alive. Then he ordered the Second Lieutenant to have the men encamp.

"Rosenberg, get four men," Mechler barked.

Henry went down the line glancing at those still standing. He pointed at one, then another, then a third, and, lastly, a young boy about eighteen. He presented the privates to the sergeant who ordered them to prepare their rifles. Mechler examined his pistol, while ordering Henry to procure one for himself. He sensed the sergeant hoped for a close fight. Henry hoped they'd encounter no one.

After the six were ready, they marched towards the wood where the Rebels had ambushed. As they neared it, Mechler addressed the small group. "You do two things: first, listen for groans; second, look for blood."

"What if we're fired at," the youngest private asked.

Mechler barked, "You fire back, you dumb shit. What the hell do you think you're supposed to do?"

"Look at this, Sergeant," Henry said, deflecting Mechler's attention.

A wide band on the trees had been mutilated by the Company's fire. At waist height and above, the trunks, dozens of them to the left and right were ripped and shredded.

"Man, glad I weren't no Reb in there," Mechler said. "They like hiding behind trees, but these are too damn skinny. Maybe we got lucky and killed some of the sons-of-bitches."

"It's all Confederate gray," Henry said. "We could have been looking right at them and not even known it, let alone know if we hit 'em."

Mechler ignored the comment. "Everybody shut up, spread out, keep your eyes and ears open. When I say 'halt' you just stop and listen for moaning and groaning. Let's go."

They entered the wood searching for a splatter or rivulet of fresh blood on the brown, leafy ground. They strained to hear something other than the soft crunch of their own boots. Glancing upward, Henry noticed taller trees barely swaying in the light breeze, not strong enough to make itself heard through the leafless hardwoods. *A stronger wind*, he knew, *would set off a howling*.

Mechler said, "If they're groaning, they're groaning mighty quiet. Man, you'd think we woulda hit some of 'em." They walked a dozen more yards. Suddenly, Mechler shouted, "Halt."

They stopped, straining to hear.

"Water . . . ," someone said.

"Yeah," Mechler agreed. "We'll need it."

They turned towards the stream. After fifty yards Mechler again halted the men. Now there arose something not at all like the brook's sweet tumbling. From the east came a strange sound unlike anything they had ever heard.

"What the hell is that," Mechler asked.

Above the sound of the gently flowing creek, a forced, guttural, freakish uttering of a groan cut through from their left, some distance away.

"Sounds like an animal," Henry said.

At that moment, one of the privates, way left of Henry, shouted, "Sergeant, I've found blood."

They rushed to see it, discovering enough to create an

intermittent trail. Mechler disregarded it. "We don't need to follow. He'll come to us."

Again they headed towards the stream. Every few minutes they heard the grotesque groan drawing nearer.

Mechler shouted, "Hello, Johnny Reb – come to me, boy. Meet us in the creek." Then to Henry, "It's easier to navigate if he's hurt bad." He paused then added, cheerfully, "I think we got ourselves a prisoner of war, Corporal."

A bank covered with tangled brush and closely spaced trees dropped to the stream. As they struggled through the rugged thicket there sounded, ever closer, the recurrent groan of the wounded Confederate, as though he was calling them. Reaching the creek, all six Union soldiers stood on the loose gravel in the shallow rapids. They gazed upstream, but there was no sight of the Reb, only the low, guttural groan that now and again lumbered through the woods, gray and bleak as the February sky.

The young private stood next to Henry, as far from Mechler as he could get. When Henry turned towards him, the boy was trembling. "It's alright," Henry whispered. "Stick with me."

The boy's voice quivered. "Thank you Sir."

In minutes, the young Confederate rounded the nearest bend fifty yards from where they stood. The sight stunned the men.

"Holy shit," Mechler muttered.

"Oh, my God," Henry said.

All six gasped, as the young Rebel, the right side of his face white with shock and blood loss, staggered towards them. The left side of his face drooped red with bloody flesh.

"Holy shit," Mechler said again.

At twenty yards the rebel stopped. A Union bullet had slashed beneath his left eye, destroying his cheekbone and nose. His eye sagged into the grotesque cavity of the wound. A remnant flap of flesh hung limply exposing the profile of his blood-outlined teeth and lower jaw.

Blood oozed down his face and neck onto a tattered uniform towards a long, deep wound in his gut that he pressed against with his right forearm. Another bullet had sliced across his abdomen; dark blood soaked the front of his pants.

He had stumbled and fallen into the stream several times before reaching his enemies in Blue. He could not speak. His jaw had locked; unable to use his tongue or lips he groaned a deep, fearsome sound, "hooee, hooee . . . ."

"What the hell's he trying to say," Mechler asked.

"Hooee . . . ."

"Shoot me," one of the privates guessed. The rebel nodded.

"Oh, he wants us to shoot him, eh," Mechler said, in mock surprise. He looked into the rebel's one good eye. "You want us to put you out of your misery, eh? Do I got that right, boy?"

"Aaah, aaah . . . ."

"For God's sake, Sergeant, the man is suffering," Henry said.

"Oh really Corporal," Mechler sneered. "Thanks for informing me. You musta figured I'm just too g--damn stupid to know what the hell his problem is, eh?"

A private snickered. The rebel soldier struggled within himself, praying to God he'd find the strength to keep standing. Behind Henry the young private trembled. Henry sensed it and reached with his left hand to grasp the boy's forearm to calm him. He didn't see Mechler withdraw his pistol.

"Corporal, I want you to put this fine Southern boy out of his – what was it you called it – oh, yeah, *suffering,* that's it. I'm gonna let you take away this good old rebel boy's suffering. Course, I would've preferred a trip to the surgeon, but . . . ." His voice trailed off, suggesting a skilled physician might save the Reb. He offered Henry the handgun. "That's an order, Corporal. Kill the son-of-a-bitch!"

Henry reached for the weapon, but balked. His mind had locked on one thought: *I cannot shoot a helpless man at point blank range in cold blood.*

"What's wrong, Corporal? I gave you an order – take my pistol."

"I can't do it."

"Well you will do it, you son-of-a-bitch," Mechler screamed. "I'm ordering you to do it. You don't do it I'll shoot you for insubordination right here. I'll kill you before I kill him."

His heart racing, Henry grasped the pistol. He searched the Rebel's one good eye, certain the boy was bleeding to death. He raised the handgun and, as he did, the others saw the violent trembling of his arm.

"Stop shaking," Mechler ordered.

"I can't."

"I'm commanding you – stop it! Kill him, damn it – kill him now!" Mechler grabbed one of the private's rifles. He stepped back, raised the rifle, aiming at Henry's head. "Corporal, you've got to the count of five: one, two . . . ,"

Henry tightened every muscle in his shoulder, bicep, forearm, and wrist, but still could not control his trembling hand.

"three,"

Senseless that we both die. I'm sorry Son . . . .

"four,"

Forgive me . . . .

"five."

Between the steep banks two shots cracked sharp and deafening. The privates, hands over their ringing ears, recoiled in horror. By chance the bullet from Henry's pistol entered the Rebel's chest in line with his heart, killing him instantly. Not by chance, the bullet from Mechler's rifle passed half a foot above Henry's head.

The Reb's body fell backwards with both legs stiff until one buckled, downing him in an ugly, contorted twisting. The blood from his face, abdomen, chest, and back stained the stream.

"Get him outta there, for chrissake," Mechler ordered.

Two of the privates grabbed the Rebel by his coat shoulders, dragging him from the shallows.

"He stinks like shit," one said.

"He crapped in his pants," Mechler said. "Let's get the hell outta here."

Three of the privates, but not the youngest, fell in behind Mechler, as he scrambled up the high bank. He stopped and stared back at Henry who stood motionless in the stream. "Corporal, if you ever disobey me again, I'll kill you. Get that through your g--damn thick skull – I will kill you."

For Henry Rosenberg the instant he shot the boy the war ended. He might be commanded to continue fighting, but his spiritual and emotional commitment to this or any other war ceased when he pulled the trigger, killing the forsaken Reb. No longer trembling, he had absolutely no fear of Mechler or anyone else, indeed, not of death itself. If he was killed in this war, so be it. He had joined the *Cause* against his wife's better judgment, and now he would accept the consequences with dignity and resignation, but also with profound regret. "Sergeant," he called, completely indifferent to Mechler's threat, "We must bury the man. We can't let him rot in the stream."

"You're in command now, Corporal. Do with him what you will."

The sergeant, grabbing one tree after another, struggled up the bank in silence. When he was gone the youngest boy sat on his haunches and cried.

Henry put his hand on the boy's shoulder. "Get hold of yourself, Son."

One of the other privates asked, "What are we going to do with the Reb, Corporal?"

"You three go back. Get spades, a litter, and some coils of the smaller rope. And for God's sake hurry – double-quick! We don't have time for this, but we must . . . ."

After they left, Henry looked in the boy's eyes. "Son, come with me. We have to find a place to bury him."

They headed downstream. The boy strained to compose himself. He wiped his wet, whiskerless cheeks with the back of his hand, glad the others were gone.

"What's your name?"

"Andrew Schmedler, Sir."

"Where're you from?"

"Sheboygan Township, Sir."

"When'd you get here?"

"Two weeks ago."

They came to a bend in the stream where the south bank, to their left, was a shelf of broad, smooth clay that sloped upwards to what appeared to be a clearing.

"Climb up and take a look," Henry ordered.

But the moist, clay slope was slippery as pond ice; the boy couldn't reach the top. He struggled to no avail until Henry told him to quit. Henry looked farther downstream, but saw no suitable site.

They headed back towards the dead Rebel. "Tell me Andrew: how old are you?"

"Eighteen."

Henry searched the boy's eyes. "Truly?"

"Seventeen, Sir; I lied to get in. But, please, don't-"

"I won't . . . ." *My God, half my age,* Henry realized. *He's too young to be in it, and I'm too old.* "Why'd you lie?"

"I had friends who were going. I didn't want to be left behind. Besides, I believe in the *Cause.*"

"Couldn't you have waited a few months . . . till your birthday?"

"No. My pa didn't want me joining so I ran away. He was gonna buy my way out just like he did my brothers. I got six brothers. Not a one of 'em is gonna serve because my pa paid the three hundred dollars. I didn't want him buying my way out. I wanted to serve my country. To my way of thinkin' my brothers are cowards. At least they're cowards to let their pa tell 'em what to do at a time like this."

"What's your pa do?"

"He's got two hundred, forty prime wheat . . . claims he needs my brothers to work it. To my way of thinkin', he could get by with three. He certainly doesn't need me."

"It's your mother – she doesn't want to lose her youngest boy. Are you the youngest?"

"No, Sir, I got a kid sister – an older sister, too – there's nine of us. I guess it won't matter much if they lose me."

"Stay away from Sergeant Mechler. Stay awake, no daydreaming . . . ."

"He scares the heck out of me. I didn't think the war would be this bad." Andrew's voice broke. "I couldn't believe what happened to that poor Reb . . . ."

"Just think, only two bullets . . . ."

"You okay with what you did?"

"No."

When they got back to the dead soldier they heard the other privates coming through the woods. Henry ordered the four to lift the body onto the litter and tie the ankles to the handles. He passed a rope over the dead rebel's chest, tying it under the litter. The sour stench from the Reb's soiled pants forced the men to step away to refresh their nostrils. After Henry secured the body, he tied on the spades and ordered the men to carry the litter downstream towards the broad bank he and Andrew had found. There they set the litter down on the clay slope with the rebel's head pointing towards the top of the bank.

"How are we going to get him up," Andrew asked.

"We'll pull him, which means we've got to get to the top first," Henry said.

With spades, Henry and Andrew cut steps into the steep bank. One of the privates tied rope to the stretcher's handles. After the men reached the top, Henry ordered the privates to pull. The litter slid up easily.

A broad, fallow field spread away from the narrow band of brush that bordered the stream. In the distance, farther south, a house and barn appeared abandoned, for no smoke rose from the chimneys though the day was cold.

Henry ordered the men to pick up the litter and follow him to the open field. To his left, he spotted an old oak whose branches overhung the brush line.

"There," he said, pointing at the tree. "We'll bury him there."

The soldiers set the litter down beside where Henry stood to mark the gravesite. They turned away from the reeking body and breathed deeply. Henry, holding his breath, searched the soldier's pockets for papers, but found nothing. Then all five began to dig. They worked in shifts until the hole reached four feet.

"Good enough," Henry said.

Using the ropes tied to the litter's handles they lowered the body into the grave.

"Now, before we cover him, we have to say a prayer to honor his passing," Henry said. "Would any of you like to lead?" He knew full well what their answers would be. "If not, I trust you have no objections to my presiding."

"No Sir," they said.

Henry bowed his head, thought for a moment then prayed aloud. "Dear God, we humbly ask Thee to look kindly on this honorable soldier whom we lay to rest today and be merciful to his soul because we think he suffered sufficiently in his final hours to gain forgiveness for just about any man's sins.

"We ask Thee to comfort him on his journey to your heavenly kingdom, and we pray Thou might also comfort his loved ones, left behind, who will forever wonder what happened to him. To my way of thinking, Lord, and I do not mean to be presumptuous, I, we – I mean all of us – just powerfully believe this poor boy deserves to be with you this day in Paradise."

He paused to control his emotions then said, "Amen."

Andrew and another private were crying at the appalling sight of the Reb's mutilated face and lifeless body. All responded, "Amen."

"If any of you would like to add a prayerful thought . . . ," Henry said.

The four stood beside the open grave shuffling their muddy boots, horrified at all they had witnessed, and praying without words that what had happened to the poor Reb would never happen to them. One began to pray, "The Lord is my Shepherd, I shall not want; he maketh me to lie down in green pastures . . . ."

"Good, good," Henry said when the private paused. "Go on."

"That's all I know." The young soldier stared into the grave. "I shoulda learned more. My ma wanted me to . . . ."

"We all should have," Henry said. "But now we've got to finish and get back."

Henry removed his coat and blouse. He felt a hard chill when his soaked underwear met the cold air. Right away he put the coat back on. Then he knelt at the side of the grave, draping his blouse over the destroyed face of the young Southerner.

"Why are you doing that," Andrew asked.

"I don't want any earth falling on his head."

"What difference does it make," a private asked.

"He died honorably and bravely. Such a man should not have soil fall directly upon his face. He deserves a fine, pine box, but we can't give him that so we bury him as best we can."

They worked fast filling the grave. When they finished, Henry marked it with a cross fashioned from two thick branches that he tied with a short length of rope. He wanted to carve at least *Johnny Reb* and *Feb '65* on the cross arm, but didn't have time. As they made their way back, Henry realized the simple grave would be forever lost as soon as a few strong winds pushed the cross to the ground, and the mounded earth, rained upon for a while, resettled level. But it would not be forgotten. Not until the five of them were dead and gone, and their children, to whom they'd tell this, were dead and gone, would the poor, nameless Confederate soldier, his death, and burial be forgotten.

+ + +

As the five hiked back through the woods, someone shouted, "Wake up old soldier." Henry Rosenberg opened his eyes out of the memory to encounter John Helden marching up the porch steps, leading his family home from church.

Little Gussie passed by. "Pa, I'll start dinner now."

At half past noon they sat down to fried pork chops, boiled potatoes, sauerkraut, and freshly baked rye bread from the bakery on Lincoln Avenue.

"Honestly, Gussie," Henry said, "you'd think Clarence and George had never eaten before in all their lives, the way they shovel it in. They eat like men, but they're skinny as girls."

"They're growing, Pa."

"All they do is run around all day," John Helden said. "They've got an awful lot of energy for running. I'm not so sure there's much left for growing. But I'll tell you this, one of these days I'm gonna put Clarence's energy to good use."

"How's that Pa," Clarence asked.

"The day you turn twelve, you're coming to work . . . ."

". . . at the shop?"

"At the shop . . . ."

"What'll I do?"

"You'll learn what it means to work hard, and we'll pay you a quarter a day for it."

"But what will I do?"

"Well," John Helden enthused, "you'll sort nuts and bolts, pick up steel drop-offs we sell to the scrap iron man, sweep floors . . . things like that. Your uncle and I run a clean shop."

Augusta frowned.

"When George turns twelve, he'll work too. That's how old I was when I started real work, and that's how old my sons will be."

Wanting to change the subject, Augusta asked, "Pa would you like some tea?" Her father enjoyed tea after a meal. John Helden retreated into silence. He didn't drink tea.

"Why, yes, I would. Thank you, Gussie."

Clarence and George shot out the back door before anyone could ask them anything. They raced to Lincoln Avenue to meet their pals. Augusta put Johnny and Julius down to nap. Then she cleared the table and tidied the kitchen.

On the porch, Henry rested on the swing again, while John, cross-armed, leaned against the railing. They said little to each other. When John spotted his neighbor, Mr. Plewa, he went over to chat with him.

Through the screen door Augusta said, "Pa, I'm going to lie down."

"All right, Gussie." Henry felt in a dozing mood too. Most days now he felt sleepy after the noon meal. *Never felt that when I was young,* he realized. He glanced at his son-in-law still chatting with the neighbor then closed his eyes. *I'll just snooze for a moment.* Warm in his uniform and comfortable on the gentle swing, a train whistle wailed in the distance way to the south, coaxing Henry to recall other trains and other days, as he nodded off.

+ + +

The train lurched. Turning to Andrew Schmedler, Henry said, "We must be nearing Chicago."

Andrew laughed. "Didn't you hear the conductor? He said 'about thirty minutes' . . . that was at least fifteen minutes ago. You dozed off."

"My goodness, I believe I did. You know, Andy, if we're lucky, we'll be in Milwaukee today."

"I hope so. I'm mighty anxious to get home. Boy, will my family be surprised."

Merchants, veterans, couples, parents with children, and an assortment of stragglers filled every seat on the train to Milwaukee. Henry and Andrew were lucky to sit together. Both of them realized they'd finally part ways in Milwaukee because Sheboygan was north from there and Tess Corners southwest. They became friends the day they buried the Confederate soldier and stuck together as their regiment, part of Sheridan's army, moved eastward. Both men wondered if they'd ever meet again.

"I suspect your mother will be overjoyed. Your pa might feign a little displeasure left over from you running away, but he'll get over it. And I suspect you're going to enjoy your ma's cooking like never before in your whole life."

Andrew laughed. "Yeah, and I'm also looking forward to my own bed."

"As am I . . . ." Henry often wondered about Augusta's reaction to his presence in her bed again. *How will she be, and how in heaven's name will she treat me? At least I'm alive to find out. Course, she could be angry for me surviving.* He chuckled to himself. *She can't possibly be as angry as when I left . . . .*

Arriving at the Everett Street Station, Andrew asked about the train to Sheboygan.

"Not here," an attendant said. "Spring Street station at the lake."

"Where's that?"

"Two blocks north . . . then east . . . can't miss it."

"Coach Yards?" Henry asked.

"South of where he's going – follow your nose."

"Thanks," they said, struggling through the crowded waiting room.

Outside, Andrew looked around. "Wanna get somethin' to eat?"

"Sure, but first maybe we should check your train."

The next train to Green Bay with a stop in Sheboygan wouldn't leave until nine in the morning. Henry's coach to Hales Corners would leave an hour earlier. After supper and two glasses of beer at a restaurant near the station, they stepped outside into the mild June evening.

"Where we gonna sleep?" Andrew asked.

Henry turned around and, gracious as a doorman, opened the same door through which they just passed. "This is a hotel my fine fellow. We'll sleep here."

They crossed the crowded dining room to an arched passage that opened into a small lobby. The hotel was full; the desk clerk said they'd probably not find a room in the entire city unless they were willing to sleep in a sporting house where they'd pay dearly. "No thanks," Henry said.

Outside, the lamplighter went about his quiet task. Henry and Andrew strolled along Spring Street, as it curved north in front of the train station. Lake Michigan, to their right, was black save for a long, thin wedge of moonlight that reflected straight at these two, homesick veterans. Ahead, at the end of Mason Street on a grassy bluff, several campfires already burned, built by men who intended to sleep there. At the base of the bluff ran the railroad track heading north to Green Bay. Across the tracks the great lake lapped against the rugged shore.

"Have you ever slept beneath the stars before?"

"This is the last time," Andrew vowed.

As had become common, Henry slept with strange, disjointed dreams. The dawn woke him, but he waited till six to rouse Andrew. They were among the first in the hotel's dining room. After breakfast they hiked to the coach yards where Henry bought his ticket to Hales Corners. Coachmen, horses, liverymen, stable boys, ticket agents, and passengers filled the yards beneath a blue, cloudless sky.

"It's a splendid morning, Andrew." Then Henry realized, *my God, today I'll be with Augusta.*

"I'm mighty grateful this day has finally come."

Henry chuckled. "Me too . . . except I hate to say goodbye."

"Yeah, me too . . . mighty glad I met you, though."

"Just to see how foolish it was for an old geezer to go to war, eh?"

Andrew smiled, aware of his own foolishness at joining. The coach to Hales Corners was ready to board. "Thank you Sir, for everything, for all your help, I mean. I'm not sure I could've got through it so good without you."

"You did fine Son, just fine. Honorable discharge – don't forget that."

"You too . . . ."

"I won't," Henry said.

They peered into each other's eyes while shaking hands. Henry boarded, as a livery boy tossed his valise onto the roof rack. Through the rear window, Henry spotted Andrew waving. He waved back until Andrew was lost in the milling crowd, and Andrew waved until Henry's coach rolled out of sight.

Oblivious to other passengers, Henry reached inside his coat's breast pocket and pulled out his *Honorable Discharge,* folded sharply in thirds. Dated June 8, 1865, and signed at Lincoln General Hospital, Washington, D.C., by an Army Surgeon whose signature Henry could not discern, this was his first chance to study it. He had been pronounced in good health, free of lice, tuberculosis, and venereal disease. After shaking hands with the examining doctor, Henry Rosenberg was also free of army life – forever.

Chapter 4 ~ 1907 (Continued)

On May 24, 1865, Andrew Schmedler and Henry Rosenberg marched in the grand parade of the Union western armies down Pennsylvania Avenue past the White House where President Andrew Johnson, Lincoln's fated successor, and General Ulysses S. Grant reviewed the troops for two full days. After that, Andrew and Henry waited two weeks for their medical examinations and formal discharge papers before they could return home. They did not, as many veterans did, remain in Washington to sample its illicit offerings. At war's end, more than fifty thousand prostitutes prowled the streets of the nation's capital.

In his last letter to Augusta, Henry wrote he hoped to be home by the first of July. Now in mid-June, he was on a coach headed towards Hales Corners.

A patrician-looking gentleman, about sixty and seated directly across, noticed the double chevron on Henry's sleeve. "On your way home, Corporal?"

"Yes, at long last." Henry smiled at the bespectacled man with a high forehead and thinning white hair.

"Was it difficult?"

"Yes, it was. If we weren't scared to death, we were bored to death. But it's over; that's all that matters."

The gentleman nodded and fell silent.

To Henry's right, a rough-looking chap, unkempt, and nearly fifty years old, muttered, "All a big waste to my way of thinkin'."

Henry turned to the man. "Not a waste, my friend . . . necessary to rid our country of slavery."

"So now they ain't slaves no more, eh? What are they?"

"They're free men, just like us."

The patrician cut in. "But what do they do now, now that they are free?"

Henry had often wondered about that, especially after Lincoln signed the *Emancipation Proclamation* in 1863.

"I'll tell ya what they do," the rough fellow said. "Since they can't do nothin' but pick cotton, they go back to their masters and beg for their old cotton pickin' jobs back. They gets paid ten cents a day, and the master charges ten cents to feed and lodge 'em. So what's the difference? What's been changed by all that killin'?"

Pleased with himself, the ruffian fell silent. Henry suspected that might be the kind of argument Augusta would raise once they began to discuss the war's aftermath.

The patrician shifted his weight, re-crossing his legs. "To the extent that we educate the Negro, both morally and academically, well or ill, to that extent will we justify or not the blood spilt in this war. Failure to educate the Negro will condemn him to a fate nearly as wretched as slavery itself. With education he can be assimilated into the economic and political life of the nation. Without it, he will never be woven into its social and cultural fabric."

"What are you saying . . . we gotta school 'em?" the rough fellow jeered.

"Precisely, but not just them, all our young citizens, at least eight grades, preferably twelve."

The ruffian didn't reply. His own schooling ended after the fifth grade, embittering his heart.

"Corporal, there are four million Negroes in the United States. What do you expect them to do, now that they are free?"

"Well, they know agriculture . . . farming, I suppose. I'm sure some have learned mechanical trades. I've heard there are many fine Negro cabinet makers in Charleston."

"Yes, but the question is what do you think they might be doing as free men in ten, fifty, or one hundred years?"

"Oh, shit, who gives a damn," the ruffian said. "As far as I'm concerned they can all stay on the plantations for the next hundred years. I sure as hell don't wanna see 'em up north."

"In one hundred years my good man, there will be twenty million Negroes in the United States. They will be in every county, city, town and hamlet. We all have to give a damn, so to speak."

Henry took off his cap, rubbed his forehead and stroked his hair. "Yes, I see. Without education they'd have all the problems begotten of ignorance. Freedom without education wouldn't be worth much to any of them or to us, for that matter."

"Exactly," the patrician said. "Freedom without education, especially moral education, begets a personal anarchy."

The ruffian didn't know what *anarchy* meant. He kept quiet, unwilling to disclose that.

After a pause, the gentleman said, "So, perhaps, it really isn't over."

"What isn't?" Henry had forgotten his initial assertion.

"The war or at least its ramifications . . . ."

"Oh for chrissake, it's over," the ruffian said, intending to have the last word. Uncomfortable with the patrician's opinions, he began pounding the ceiling to signal he wanted to get off. The coach neared a junction; when it stopped, the rough fellow bolted out the door. He had no valise.

The patrician said, "Good day," but the man never looked back. Then to Henry, "Allow me to introduce myself. I'm Willard Tillema."

Henry extended his hand. "How do you do?"

They had an amicable conversation all the way to Hales Corners. After exiting the coach, they shook hands and said goodbye. A distinguished gentleman in a fine surrey was waiting for Mr. Tillema. After he climbed aboard, the horse trotted off in an easterly direction. Had they been going west, Henry would have enjoyed riding along. Mr. Tillema gave Henry not the slightest indication of his profession though Henry disclosed he was a wheat farmer with a wife and two children. He suspected, *perhaps a teacher.*

Henry grabbed his valise and crossed to the tavern on the corner of the Janesville road. He asked the bartender if and when a coach would be heading west. "You missed it. He had early fares so he left. I'd say he's back here in an hour, hour and a half. Can I pour you a shot? First drink for an army man is always on the house."

But Henry had no interest in whisky or waiting for the coach. At a good pace he could be in Tess Corners, three miles distant, in less than an hour: not much of a march for a sole-calloused veteran of the United States Infantry. *And if I'm lucky,* he thought, *some friendly wagon might give me a lift.* That didn't happen. Nevertheless, when Henry finally reached the last crest overlooking his small, sunlit town, his heart filled with joy.

At the Tess Corners junction he greeted several boys who

wondered at his blue cap and uniform. Their dogs barked after him, as he headed south the half-mile to his lane. He quickened his pace when he spotted Watry's house in the distance.

"Oh my God," Veronica said, opening the door. "I don't believe my eyes. Oh my God, let me look at you. Oh, thank God you're home, Henry Rosenberg."

She rushed to the rear door, flung it open, calling to her husband. Then she rushed back. "Henry, are you well? All in one piece, I trust? Let me look at you."

"Yes, I'm fine, all my limbs intact, thank God. And you, my dear Fronnie, you are a most pleasant sight for this weary, old man."

They embraced just as Franklyn came in with the children behind. "Henry Rosenberg, welcome back my friend." They shook hands vigorously while Veronica, Virginia, Jack and Rudy circled round. "So, you finally made it home, eh? Well, we're mighty glad, Henry. Praise God for it. Have you seen Augusta?"

"Not yet . . . you're my first stop."

"Well, we're mighty honored to have a veteran of the Union Army cross our threshold, that's for sure," Franklyn said. Everyone agreed.

Henry requested a cup of water that Virginia fetched. After drinking, he expressed his wish to be on his way. The Watrys' minds had filled with questions. They were reluctant to let him go.

"We'll visit soon; I'll tell you all about it," Henry promised.

Franklyn walked him to the road.

"You didn't tell Augusta I asked you to take her in?"

"No, Henry, of course not. She thought it Fronnie's natural idea and was most grateful. Actually, it was quite pleasant. The children certainly enjoyed it."

Now nothing remained save for the familiar rising road that led to Henry's farm. When he reached the final crest and beheld the wide, bright valley with his little house, the planted fields, and the hardwoods on the far ridges that wore the green of early summer, he paused just as he had the September morning he left for the war. *I'm home*, he thought. *At last, I'm home.*

He was halfway there before Augusta, as she often did, glanced out the open door and noticed the man in blue coming down the road. It puzzled her, for she had never before seen a uniformed stranger hike their lane. On the porch she watched him draw nearer. Then, seeing the slender form, the well-remembered stride, and the green valise, she recognized her husband. Without a thought, she flew off the porch, running towards him, as Henry ran towards her.

"Henry, Henry . . . ."

She ran into his open arms. He swung her in an arc, her skirt sweeping the air like a scythe through the waiting wheat. Whether she wanted him to kiss her or not was immaterial, for he kissed her passionately.

"Oh, Henry, you came home to us, my God, you really came home. I didn't think . . . I didn't know . . . I wondered if I should believe you."

"Of course I came home. You're my wife, my family. Where in this whole world should I go if not here?"

"Are you alright?" She pushed back to inspect.

"I am whole and in one piece. Everything works just fine."

He took her in his arms again, bending to kiss her, but she turned away.

"No, Henry, don't force me, please." Her tone was tense. "Let me go."

In spite of it, he held her close. She began to pound her little fists on his chest that was as hard as the clay road they stood upon. "Please, Henry, let me go."

Her violence amused him, so gentle was it compared to what he had seen in the war. *My God, she's nearly as angry as the day I left.*

His gratitude even relished Augusta's fury. As she beat his chest and shoulders, he was completely confident she would be his wife again. After she exhausted herself, she collapsed in his arms weeping. Henry, inhaling deeply her wonderful scent, cupped her bundled hair in his left hand, while his strong, right arm pressed her soft body against the hardness of his own. For him it was an extraordinary joy. His deepest desire, held in struggled check for almost a year, yearned to be free. *She will be my wife this night,* he vowed.

"I'm mighty grateful to be home, Gussie."

She pushed him away. "You should not have left us. How could you do such a thing? How *could* you?"

"Gussie, you must forgive . . . ."

She hurried back to the house. Their shy sons stood in the doorway.

When Henry saw his little boys he cried out their names, ran to them, and swept them into his arms, kissing their sweet faces. Tears flowed from his eyes, as though he was the child. He put them down, but Georgie clung to his right leg, while little Henry baby-stepped to his mother.

"You know, he wasn't walking when I left," Henry said, laughing through his tears.

"I know . . . he started right before Christmas."

+ + +

Little Gussie touched his shoulder, causing the swing to sway. "Pa, are you awake?"

"Oh, Gussie, yes I am. I was just thinking of the old days."

"Pleasant thoughts, I trust."

"Well, yes, for the most part. Maybe I dozed off for a little while. I get tired during the day now. Never used to . . . ."

"Should you see Dr. Schwartz?"

"Good heaven, no . . . if my tiredness can't be cured by sleep, it certainly can't be cured by that quack. I fear it's begotten by old age. I doubt there's a cure save the sleep of death."

"Oh, Pa, don't talk foolish. You're still hale and hearty. Would you like some lemonade?"

"Yes, that'd be nice."

+ + +

She was my wife that night, he remembered. And then afterwards he slept on and on, hours past the bird songs at daybreak. It was his longest and best night's sleep since last August before he told Augusta he decided to join the army. When he woke, sunlight filled the little room.

In the front room, he smiled at Augusta. "It's wonderful to be home . . . ."

She smiled back. "You slept well."

"I did indeed, but I believe I failed to thank you for that wonderful meal last evening. Best meal this year by far."

"You are welcome sir." Henry loved the music in her voice.

He excused himself to use the privy, kissing his sons on the way. When he returned, Augusta was on the front porch watching the boys play. Henry approached from behind, putting his arms around her.

She turned in his embrace. "Henry, I think it important that you understand what happened last night did not entirely meet with my approval."

"Gussie, you're my wife."

"Yes, but you've been gone a long time. I still feel somewhat distant. I think we should not be intimate again until those feelings have left me."

"But Augusta, last night was heavenly. It's my God-given right."

"I've thought of that, but, quite honestly, I didn't want it to happen. I didn't expect you home until July, like your letter said, so I had not, perhaps, properly prepared myself. Indeed, you caught me off my guard."

"What guard do you need against a loving husband who's missed you so and longs to hold you?"

"I admit that last night our passion overcame my resolve to avoid passion, but that shall not happen again, Henry. Not until the last and faintest feeling of estrangement has, like a butterfly, flown from my heart."

Henry gazed beyond her, towards the greening hills. "And how long might that be?"

"That depends on how well you woo me, and if you should win me." She glanced at his eyes, smiled, and slipped through his arms into the house. Her answer seared his memory.

+ + +

"Here's your lemonade, Pa." Little Gussie handed him the glass. "Mind if I sit?"

"No, no . . . please do."

"Juley's still sleeping," she said.

"And Johnny?"

"Out back with Cousin Peter; they play together all the time now. They're real pals."

Henry took a hearty swallow. "I was thinking of your mother."

"Well that's nice. Do you often?"

"Off and on, to be sure; she was my wife for over forty-five years, you know. When I got back from the war she was strict with me; told me I had to woo her again. Can you believe that; a wife telling her husband something like that?"

"Oh, for heaven's sake, why?"

"Because she didn't want me going to war; that was the point. I don't believe she ever really completely forgave me for it. After I got back she said it would take a while to get used to me again before she-" His discretion made him pause. "Well, I had to win her hand again, a second courtship, so to speak. She was still angry. In a sense, I couldn't blame her. I admitted I was wrong. She was right; I conceded that. What else could I do? I felt like a damn fool. I was too old. I had two little sons. I could have been killed. I was foolish, damn foolish."

"You must have been successful in your wooing though. You must have won her again because I came along. Am I not proof that Mama loved you?"

"Indeed you are, Gussie. She was ecstatic when you were born. Oh my, how she longed for a little girl. We prayed for that, you know."

"It was always my impression, Pa, that you two got along just fine."

"Well, we did, but it was – oh, I don't know – it just was different after the war. There was a joy in our life before, when we were young. I didn't think anything could ever change that, but my going off affected your mother in ways I didn't anticipate. It was almost as though she could never quite allow herself to be so care-free again, so trusting. And it wasn't just that I went to war, Gussie. I had promised her when the war began I wouldn't go. Breaking my promise hurt her, and I lived to regret it, but never did I intend to hurt her. I thought my youthful promise far less important than the call to serve. I was idealistic. I believed my duty was to serve my country, and her wifely duty was to accept it. Of course, she didn't see it that way. In her mind the war was a waste, never even should have been fought. In her mind, my true duty was strictly to her and our children, and you know what, Gussie? She was right. I was thirty-four when I joined, way too old."

"Why was she so against that war?"

"Because of the killing; over six hundred thousand died, I've read. Just think of that. She thought it horrible, which it was."

"But, Pa, we couldn't live in a country that tolerates slavery, could we? How would that be now if there still were slaves? What kind of Christians would we be?"

"Maybe slavery would have died a natural death. Many people believed that, but I don't know. In any event, the war was fought, and your mother blamed Lincoln for every horrible minute of it."

"Did she really hate Lincoln so?"

"Well, she didn't like him, that's for sure. I prefer not to call it hate, but it certainly was a damn, strong, negative disposition," Henry said.

In fact, Augusta did hate Abraham Lincoln. She knew it was wrong to hate another human being, and she prayed to overcome it. Nevertheless, her feelings were passionate because, as so many editorialists pointed out, Lincoln squandered lives and resources and trampled on the Constitution. She believed in Constitutional limits on the federal government and the strict separation of powers. She was a Jeffersonian Democrat, through and through, a believer in States' rights. When Lincoln got the country into civil war over secession, it seemed foolish and unnecessary to many Northerners. Augusta even believed that individual States had the right to secede, for she wondered, *why a State should be bound to something its people no longer wish to be bound to. What kind of liberty is that?*

In Lincoln's conduct of the war, Augusta loathed the waste and graft, as corrupt suppliers and industrialists cheated the government out of millions. She hated that the war dragged on, year after year, with all the senseless killing and dying. She believed in Jefferson's ideal of people well educated in moral and democratic virtues so they'd govern themselves without the need for endless laws, without the burden of federal taxes, and certainly without a civil war. Lincoln and his radical Republicans created a powerful central government, something Augusta's favorite editorialists believed akin to tyranny. Lincoln even threw Northerners into jail without a trial if a government spy accused them of being sympathetic to the South. All of it appalled Augusta. In her mind, without the slightest doubt, Lincoln was a despicable tyrant.

"What did she say when Lincoln was assassinated," Little Gussie asked.

"I don't know; I was still in Virginia. Everyone in the army was horrified."

"Did her opinion of Lincoln change after the war?"

Henry shook his head. "No. Several months after the war I asked how she felt when she learned Lincoln was assassinated. She told me she thought it fitting that someone who sacrificed so many innocent lives should himself be sacrificed. I was surprised by such a distorted idea because most of the nation mourned Lincoln's murder, not in the South, but certainly the rest of the country. He was regarded as a great and good man."

"Well, she certainly had strong opinions . . . ."

"Yes, but then your mother said something I've never forgotten. She said, in that sense, the sense that Lincoln was sacrificed for the deaths of so many innocents, John Wilkes Booth wasn't an assassin at all – he was a priest."

"Oh my God!"

"From that point on, I never discussed Lincoln or the war with your mother again. That was it for me. Booth was a cold-blooded murderer. He shot Lincoln in the back of the head at point blank range. Think of that. Lincoln was completely defenseless. I thought your mother's opinions simply weren't worth getting upset about because there wasn't a force in heaven let alone earth that could change her mind about any of them."

"I suppose that's true, but she did enjoy politics, didn't she?"

"Yes, to a point. She liked Andrew Johnson after Lincoln because he was a Democrat, but after that the Republicans kept winning. I voted for Grant in '68 but never told your mother. She wasn't happy until Cleveland, another Democrat, won in '84. She was furious in '88 when he lost to Harrison because Cleveland won the popular vote. But when Cleveland won again in '92 she was happy. Her emotions went back and forth just like this swing. William Jennings Bryan came along in '96. She loved him, but was bitterly disappointed when he lost to McKinley. You must remember some of this, Gussie. You grew up through all those elections."

"At the time I didn't pay much attention because I couldn't vote. She told me several times, though, she was angry with you for voting for Lincoln and going to war. I also remember she talked about women eventually getting the vote. She even said I'd live to see it."

Henry chuckled. "Don't bet on it."

"Tell me, Pa, do you think women should have the vote? I suppose I'd have more interest if I did."

"Of course they should. They birth the boys who fight the wars and bury them if they're killed. Seems to me that's plenty more than sufficient to have earned the right to vote."

"I think so too, though Mama only would have voted for pacifists. She hated war so."

Henry laughed. "She only would have voted for Democrats."

"Well, they are the pacifists."

He finished his lemonade. "I never told your mother what happened to me in the war. She didn't want to hear about it. She made that very clear."

"You mean you never told her about the Confederate soldier?" Gussie knew the story.

"Never – she would have been horrified that I killed a man, especially, as I did. So I said nothing. Your mother made it difficult for me when I left. I didn't write for several months, but then I told her very forthrightly that it was proper for me to join and that she, as my wife, had better learn to accept that. Of course, that was before I was shot at. Once we came under fire and I saw men suffer and die, I realized I was a damn fool to have joined, but I never could really bring myself to admit that to your mother. I realized I might get killed. All I wanted was to go home. But there I was, trapped in the army like a damn fool. I ignored my wife's good counsel and went off to have my head shot off. My God, how I suffered with that realization.

"After I got back it was never quite the same with your mother. Oh, I used to tell myself we were just growing older, but, in fact, I hurt your mother too deeply. It changed her and changed us, and I never imagined anything like that would ever happen. I've often wondered, had I known that, if I still would have gone. When she died, I realized she had slowly withdrawn over the years, and it became impossible for me to ever truly win her back, and, yet, I still believe – if I'm honest about it – that I would have joined."

"Maybe, Pa, you should have told her what you experienced . . . told about that poor Confederate. It might have helped her understand what you had to endure."

"You know, I've often wondered about him, Gussie. Who he was, where he came from, who was left behind to mourn his going to war, and then mourn forever that he never returned. I wondered what it was like for him when he joined his Cause: his enthusiasm, his idealism, and the belief in the righteousness of his State's secession. Of course, they couldn't defend slavery, but they could defend States' rights. They certainly believed they had to defend the South against tyranny and the evil Mr. Lincoln, a tyrant every bit as bad, in their minds, as any English king."

"Only God knows, I suppose."

"Was he just a lad when he left? Did he leave a sweetheart or wife with little children, like I did? Did his loved ones tremble at his decision, yet stand in silent praise of his courage and nobility of heart? I don't think so. I suspect he was an orphan boy caught up in a patriotic fervor he didn't understand and couldn't control. He was doomed to go to war and was probably thrilled about it, but believe me, from what I saw of him, there was no one – no mother, no sweetheart, no innocent children – nobody was saying any prayers for that boy.

"Did he imagine his Rebel lads could win the war and preserve the old South forever? It's one thing, Gussie, to march through a friendly town under a clear blue sky, the drum and fife stirring your heart with the most noble sentiments, and quite another to have half your face shot apart and be abandoned by your comrades. He staggered towards us, trying to give us – just think of it – a command.

"What swirled wildly in his brain then? Did his drooping eye see the stream bed jiggling at his boots, while his good eye fixed on six Union soldiers with their jaws dropped? Were those images commixed somehow in his brain? Tell me, Gussie: where were his idealism and noble sentiments then, eh? Did he still believe in the South's damn *Cause*? Did he still want to defend States' Rights? If he had a father, did he still think it was his right to own slaves? Did he think someday he'd possess slaves to do the work God intended him to do? No, no, I assure you, nothing like that.

"All that poor fellow wanted was to be put out of his wretched misery because his life, his hopes, dreams, everything was over, gone forever. And he was so young. He had only one life, just like any of us, and now it was over, and he damn well knew it. All was lost, everything except his pride."

"My goodness, Father . . . ." Gussie held her hands as in prayer, pressing them against her lips.

"I'll tell you this, though: he was one proud soldier to the end. He struggled mightily just to stay on his feet, just to reach us still standing. He surrendered everything, even his life, and he did it, by God, with more dignity and courage than anyone I'd ever seen. All he wanted was to be shot like some foaming-mouthed dog, and he had to beg, he had to plead with these strangers in Blue to do it. 'Could you please spare one bullet, Sir? I mean please, Sir, to put me out of my misery?' That's what he said to me; at least that's what I saw in his one good eye. That's why I shot him, Gussie. He was going to die anyway. I did it to end his suffering. I meant not to slay him cruelly. I meant only to ease his dying."

Augusta saw the moist glistening in her father's eyes. She placed her hand on his. "It was good you took pity on him, Pa. No one should suffer so. Strange to say about the act of killing, but it was, to my way of thinking, the Christian thing to do."

"That night I couldn't sleep. Another corporal, my friend Johnny Hayes, shared my tent and was snoring away, but I couldn't get that poor Reb outta my mind, or the awful fact that I killed him. I killed a man, Gussie. Some would say in cold blood even though I believe with all my heart it was an act of mercy. To my knowledge he was the only man I ever killed in the war, and I pray God that's true. After that, I lost all interest in battles and fighting. I wanted nothing to do with any of it. Army life was mostly just marching and setting up and tearing down camp, an awful lot of moving about, then just waiting around. It was terrible wondering about the next fight, and I was miserable for it. And it was my own damn fault for joining because I didn't have to. My presence in that war didn't make a damn bit of difference just like your ma said it wouldn't.

"I crawled outside my tent. The sky was filled with stars, perfectly tranquil, not a trace of wind, not the blemish of a cloud. It was almost as though – to God's way of thinking – nothing disturbing at all was happening down here on Earth, and I thought to myself,

I finally realized, I had become what your dear mother always was – a pacifist. I hated the war, hated the thought I might kill another man, hated myself for leaving my family and might never return. Believe me, Gussie, I could have been killed any number of times. More than once I heard a Minie ball zip closely by."

"Oh, Pa, I in particular am very glad you lived," Augusta said.

"Oh my God, Gussie, just think, had I been killed, you wouldn't have been born. Nor your sons . . . ."

"Well, we mustn't have such morbid thoughts. The good Lord blessed you, and I'm grateful for it, and I love having you as my papa. That's a fact."

Smiling slightly, Henry nodded.

"And I really believe you did make a difference in the war regardless of what Ma said. You told that sergeant he couldn't just leave that poor Southern boy dead in the stream. You were there to show him true mercy, which he begged for because he knew he was dying. You buried him properly and prayed for his immortal soul at a time when he was most needful of prayers. And also, Pa, all of it most certainly set a good Christian example for those young soldiers. They would have just blindly followed that sergeant and left the poor boy's corpse to rot. His blood and bile would have spoiled the stream – that's for sure; might even had made someone downstream who drank of it mortally sick. No, Pa, it's good you went to war if only to ease that poor boy's dying."

Johnny crept onto the porch. He stood at his mother's knee with his hands on the armrest of the barely moving swing. He was studying his grandfather's old face.

"What do you want, Johnny?" Augusta Helden asked.

"I was thinking about something."

"What?"

He turned towards his grandfather. "Grandpa, next time I'm supposed to go to church, can I wear your soldier cap and pray with you?"

Chapter 5 ~ 1910

Aristotle, that old Greek cogitator, opined that comets were earthly things comprised of water and air, moving in the sub-lunar realm well beneath the dome of the fixed stars. His opinion endured for about two thousand years until 1577 when Tycho Brahe, the clever Danish astronomer, determined without a telescope that a visible comet did not display parallax, an observable attribute if it did in fact exist beneath the orbit of the moon.

Aristotle also believed comets to be omens. That opinion survived much longer. For most people a comet's physical composition, size, orbit, and period were far less important than its significance of foretelling some earthly calamity. Among intelligent Europeans that opinion persisted until Halley's predicted reappearance of the comet of 1682, which was confirmed seventy-six years later on Christmas Day, 1758, sixteen years after the great astronomer's death. So thrilled and relieved were people with this celestial return that they named the beautiful, infrequent, and now benign comet in Mr. Halley's honor.

If a comet is not a portent then the questions of a comet's composition and behavior again become topics of scientific investigation: what is it made of? How close to us does it come? How close to the sun does it pass, and how far out into space is it flung?

Nevertheless, the old tales among more simple folk still lingered. When a great comet – not Halley's – was observed in the United States in 1861, it was regarded retrospectively as a warning from God of the horrible carnage of the Civil War.

Halley's Comet was due again in 1910. Its reappearance was even more intriguing because planet Earth would pass through the comet's tail. That fact caused a great deal of apprehension. If people had known, through reading and study, what Mr. Halley had discovered and published so many years earlier, their fears would have been eased by insight. In the 1680s Halley, in his late twenties, calculated the orbit and period of the comet using Newton's recently published equations of motion, as well as his own and prior observations. He determined that the comet at its closest point was only fifty-five million miles from our Sun. At its apogee, well past the outer planets of Uranus and Neptune, it reached three and a quarter billion miles from our star. The orbit was an elongated ellipse at a steeply inclined angle to the orbit of the Earth. Its mass was at least ten billion tons. As it accelerated around the Sun it reached the incredible speed of one hundred and twenty-two thousand miles per hour.

Still there were many people, perhaps most, trapped in the escapable cage of ignorance who didn't know what to think about comets at all: not their orbits, their frequency, composition, and certainly not their tails.

For the boys and girls who hung out around 31st and Lincoln, nothing thrilled them more than the comet's coming. And there was absolutely no doubt, at least in the boys' minds, its coming would be spectacular. Many newspaper articles said so, as did many fathers. The girls in the neighborhood, however, reflected some of their mothers' feminine skepticism, though they always took a keen interest in the antics of the boys.

"Think of it as a Chinese rocket roaming freely amongst the stars," Mr. Zimmermann, the builder, once told a gullible group of kids. "Perhaps even ridden by the creatures of a strange, faraway world . . . ."

That profound misstatement most impressed Paul Jablowski who was, owing to his pinkish-white complexion, well known in the neighborhood as *Pinkey*.

"Ain't nothing gonna stop Pinkey from doing exactly what he says. He says he's gonna do it, he'll do it. You just wait and see," George Helden, eleven, told his younger brother, Johnny, and their cousin Peter.

Johnny didn't know what to say about Pinkey's powerful resolve nor did little Peter. Finally, Johnny said, "I just can't figure out how it's gonna fly down Lincoln Avenue."

"It ain't flying down Lincoln Avenue . . . just its tail."

Just as confused, little Peter Helden asked, "How's its tail gonna?"

"The whole world's gonna pass through that tail. Lincoln

Avenue's part of the world, ain't it? So the tail's gotta come here too. And when it passes by, Pinkey's just gonna reach up and grab it. I'm thinkin' maybe I'll grab it too."

"No, don't Georgie," Johnny said. "I don't want you going. Let Pinkey go himself."

At the dinner table it didn't take long for George to bring up Pinkey's daring adventure. Oldest brother Clarence, thirteen, greeted it with sneers of ridicule.

"That boy's a bit of a boaster, I suppose," Augusta said. "I'm not so sure the comet's tail can be grabbed. I've read nothing of the sort."

Sitting across from George, Grandpa Rosenberg said, "You've read nothing because no one knows, not even the scientists."

"Oh, foolishness," John Helden said.

"Maybe, maybe not . . . ." Henry winked at George.

"How could anyone grab a comet's tail," Clarence said. "It ain't like some big old slow fat horse."

"Clarence, mind your manner of speaking," Augusta said.

"Sorry Ma."

"If anybody can do it, Pinkey can," George said. "I know Pinkey. I've seen him do lots of stuff nobody else ever woulda done."

Clarence jeered, "Ya, cause nobody's that stupid."

"No need to speak unkindly," Augusta said. "The boy does have a certain flair."

"He's a big talker, but he don't do nothin. When he gets around older kids he shuts up fast. He's got you hoodwinked, George."

"Please Clarence, your language . . . ." Augusta feigned exasperation.

"Sorry Ma."

"So, George," Henry said, "your friend is planning to fly off to space on the comet's tail. Is that the idea?"

"Sure is," George said, glad that at least his grandfather showed some interest.

"And how might I observe this great event?"

"Pinkey's selling tickets for chairs set up in front of church for a real good view of the exact instant when he's gonna grab that tail. We're gonna watch him fly into space, right Johnny? Pinkey's gonna write the newspapers and get reporters and maybe even a photographer."

At that, everyone laughed out loud except Augusta who kept the hum of her laughter to herself. Her father remained composed and unsmiling.

John Helden said, "The only space that boy will ever encounter is the big, empty one between his ears."

Everyone laughed again except George and his grandfather who searched George's sad eyes.

"Pa," George said, "Pinkey's my friend."

John caught his wife's disapproving glance. "Sorry, George . . . ."

The next day Pinkey, walking along Lincoln Avenue on his way home, noticed the old man on the bench in front of the tailor's shop, but showed no interest until he heard, "Hello there, Pinkey."

He knew George's grandfather. "Oh, hello, Mr. Rosenberg."

He would have continued on his way, but Henry said, "I'd like to buy a ticket."

Pinkey reached into his pocket for one of the worn, cut in half playing cards that he always carried about. He offered it, saying, "ten cents please."

"I thought they were a nickel."

"That's kids. Grownups is ten cents."

Henry handed him a dime. Pinkey thanked the old man, but before he could escape Henry said, "I've something to tell you, if you can sit a minute."

"I guess I can." He agreed only because it was George's grandfather.

"I want to tell you something I've never told anyone. But before I do, I'm wondering how well you keep a secret."

What's he talking about, Pinkey wondered.

"Can you?" Henry asked.

"Huh?"

"Can you keep a secret?"

"I guess . . . ."

"Guessing isn't good enough. You're friends with George aren't you?"

"Yup."

"Then you have to promise that what I'm going to tell, you will never in your whole life tell George or your mother, father or anybody else. I mean it to be confidential, just between you and me. Can you promise that?"

Pinkey wasn't sure, but his interest had been roused. "Ya, I can promise."

"Good, now remember, I've never told this to anyone since the day it happened because it is rather unbelievable." Henry smiled imperceptibly. "After you hear it you mustn't tell anyone because it really only involves you and me; besides, I don't think anyone would believe us. However, if you tell someone and were they to ask me about it, I'll deny the whole thing. I'll deny I ever told you anything of the sort, understand?"

"Ya, I guess so." Pinkey hesitated because he wasn't sure he did understand.

"Last night at the supper table George was talking about you planning to grab the tail of Mr. Halley's comet and flying off to space."

"Ya, so what? You got your ticket."

"Well, let me tell you, all of us were greatly impressed with your courage and derring-do. Even Mr. Helden and you know what a skeptic he is."

Pinkey nodded though he didn't really know what a skeptic was.

"When I heard about your daring plan, I realized I had to tell you what happened to me during the war, the Civil War. You've heard of that great event, I trust?"

"Ya."

"We were in a terrible fight at a place called Five Forks. Lots of shooting and hollering and some of our fellows were killed. A young soldier I knew was awfully upset because one of his pals was killed. He hated the war, hated the killing, the fighting, the food, hated being tired, dirty, and smelly all the time, so he decided, after his friend died, that he wanted to get out any way he could. But he couldn't desert because he knew the army'd hunt him down like an old 'coon and hang him from the gallows. So he felt trapped – which he was – and he was miserable for it. And, Pinkey, he was scared. Scared of dying 'cause he was so young."

The thought of death terrified Pinkey.

"Now, here's where the story takes a turn. Several nights before that fight, we had seen a comet coming." Henry, for his own curious purpose, moved the famous comet of 1861 forward a few years. "Our captain got a telegraph from Washington warning that the earth was going to pass right through the tail, and all us men should remain calm, just let it pass by and be on its way. They didn't think it would hurt us, but they didn't know for sure what exactly its true nature was. Well, after the fight, my young friend came to me, his name was Andy, Andy Schmedler, and told me he was planning to grab the tail of that comet – just like you're planning – and use it to escape. Well I was amazed at his daring just like I'm amazed at yours. But you have to remember, he wanted to get out of the army real bad. He was just desperate to get away from all that bloodshed. Can you understand that?"

Pinkey nodded.

"A couple days later we saw the comet's tail a-coming."

"What'd it look like?"

"It was unlike anything I'd ever seen; strange looking, hard to describe, definitely something from far out in the heavens." He paused.

"What'd it look like?" Curiosity hushed Pinkey's voice.

"It was luminous, filled with bright sunlight. That's how we could see it coming, but we could barely feel it. Why, Pinkey, it passed right through us gentle as a breeze. It was like thousands of brilliantly shining strands that seemed to me like ropes of golden glass, yet they were just as soft as cotton, but much stronger, stronger even than rope or chain, and just the right size to make it easy to grab hold, and all them shining things hanging down, swinging from the sky, high as the eye could see, and all just waiting to be grabbed."

Pinkey's eyes swelled.

"Definitely something from another world. It's a miracle my whole company didn't grab hold and fly off to space. I almost grabbed it myself. It was like a temptation, you see, like the Siren's song. In fact, I did grab one for just a second. Lifted me about ten feet before I let go, but my young friend, Andy, oh my, he didn't let go."

Breathless, Pinkey asked, "What happened to him?"

"Well, we watched him rise higher and higher. It was unbelievable because he was higher than a mountain, though I've never
seen a real western mountain. When he was up maybe a hundred
feet he was smiling and waving like the happiest man in the world.
I couldn't believe my eyes, but I figured he was okay because he
was grinning and smiling and looking happier than I'd ever seen.
But remember, Pinkey, he was escaping the war. That's why he was
so happy. Then we all let out a big cheer. He waved again, and we
waved, and next thing I knew he was out of sight. And, would you
believe, I haven't seen that boy since that very day."

"Where'd he go?"

"Told me he planned to get off at the moon. I asked him how he
was going to get back, but he said he just didn't care to worry about
that. Said he'd figure it out once he got up there. All he cared about
was getting away from that awful war."

"Wow!" Pinkey screamed.

"Now, Pinkey, here's what I want to propose to you. Unfortunately, my friend never did figure out how to get back 'cause he
promised he'd visit me, but he never has in all those years. Not
many people in this world know that poor old Andy Schmedler is
still up there. But now, the way I figure, you have a chance to not
only be the first boy in space, but also to be a true hero if you can
bring Andy home."

Pinkey jumped up. "Me a hero?"

"Yes, a great hero." Henry searched Pinkey's yearning eyes. "A
truly great hero . . . someone even the newspapers will write about.
But, first things first: what are you planning to do once you grab
that comet's tail?"

"I guess I was gonna get off at the moon, like your friend." He
sat down.

"Good, good, but how are you planning to get back?"

"Well, that's the only thing I ain't got quite figured out yet,"
Pinkey said with fearless puzzlement. "Mrs. Helden said I could
catch a moonbeam, but I ain't so sure . . . moonbeams sure don't
feel like streetcars."

"You've got a fine scientific mind, Pinkey. Moonbeams sound
neither reliable nor sufficiently substantial to me." Henry paused.

"You do know that comet is gonna whiz 'round the sun and come right back this way again? Couldn't you . . . ?"

"Ya," Pinkey said, catching Henry's thought. "I'll just wait 'till I see it comin' back. Then I'll grab it and jump off at Lincoln Avenue right where I started."

"Good thinking, Pinkey. That's exactly what I'd do. But don't forget, when you get to the moon you'll meet my friend Andy. Tell him I say *hello,* and that I'm looking forward to seeing him just as soon as that old comet brings you both home."

"You can count on me, Mr. Rosenberg."

"You're going to see wonderful things, things we ordinary folk never could dream. I can't wait for you to get back and tell me all about it. Course, you'll be a hero, while I'm just looking forward to seeing my old friend, Andy Schmedler. Can you remember that name?"

Pinkey nodded; he'd remember. He repeated it several times in his head. Then he jumped up, thanking Mr. Rosenberg. He felt much better, much more confident now that his problem of how to get back from the moon had been solved, and that he'd return a great hero simply by bringing along old Andy Schmedler. That night Pinkey fell asleep happy for the talk with Mr. Rosenberg. Henry fell asleep amused, but also a little ashamed for having planted such outlandish ideas into Pinkey's fertile mind.

For a week after their conversation, Pinkey felt tremendous confidence. Even his father confirmed that the comet would round the sun and head back just like old Mr. Rosenberg said. Only when his teacher mentioned something about "millions of miles" did Pinkey's confidence waver. The newspapers were filled with stories about the approaching comet, some of which were scientific. Those Pinkey ignored. The few he did read always seemed to speculate pessimistically about the earth's impending intersection with the comet's tail, but Pinkey simply recalled that old Mr. Rosenberg himself had seen and touched such a tail, and it was nothing to worry about at all. "Perfectly rideable," Pinkey often told himself based on Mr. Rosenberg's testimony. For if there was one thing Pinkey could count on, it was that George's grandpa would bear no false witness.

And yet, the day before his daring adventure, a sense of grave foreboding seized Pinkey's soul. With George Helden's cheerful help, they set up forty chairs on the sidewalk in front of Holy Ghost Church for his ticket buyers on a first-come basis. George couldn't say enough about Pinkey's courage and daring, nor could he be more enthusiastic about Pinkey's upcoming journey to outer space. Nevertheless, in spite of George's encouraging chatter, it was terror that had effortlessly slipped into Pinkey's heart, and, even more effortlessly, courage that had slipped out. His mother and father noticed his sullen mood, as he picked at his supper.

"Where's your appetite," his mother asked. "You didn't fill up on candy?"

"No, Ma . . . ."

"Then what's the matter? Eat your supper."

"I ain't feeling so good."

He fought not to cry. The thought of flying off into space on the tail of that fast approaching comet the very next day was proving far too difficult for his emotional capabilities even though he knew long ago young Andy Schmedler did it with a cheerful wave and a happy smile. He didn't have the heart to tell his parents he had promised the whole neighborhood he'd do it "no matter what." How could they know about the light-filled rope smooth as glass, soft like cotton, and strong as chain? How could they understand that he had to rescue Mr. Rosenberg's old friend who was still living on the moon so many years after he deserted the army? How could they possibly understand that Pinkey would return a true hero? As far as Pinkey could tell, his parents were the only ones in the neighborhood who didn't know he was flying into space, and he resented it. Thus, he was all the more surprised by his father's first question.

"You worried about riding the tail of that comet?"

"How'd you know about that?"

"Mrs. Helden told your mother. I understand everybody's talking about it. I heard you even sold tickets."

"You had better take your winter coat, dear," Mrs. Jablowski said. "I read those scientist fellows think it's real cold in space. Take your cap and mittens too."

Pinkey's chin dropped onto his rising fork. "Oow!"

"You eat well tonight, Paul. I don't have the faintest idea what you're planning to eat out there in space. Maybe your mother should pack some food"

"How can he carry food, dear, if he's going to grab the tail of a comet? Surely he'll need both hands for that."

Pinkey never felt so wretched in all his life. What had been a triumph just three weeks earlier when he announced to all the kids who hung out around 31st and Lincoln that he decided to be the first boy in space, and the constant adulation he had received in the passing days from nearly all of them with, perhaps, the exception of a few older, more skeptical boys, had since degraded into the most frightening anticipation imaginable. Even Mr. Rosenberg's promise of heroism failed to comfort. His head ached; his bowels rebelled several times during the day; he couldn't eat, not even candy, and he didn't want water for feelings of throwing up. He had no hope for sleep and doubted he'd ever make it back to Lincoln Avenue again. If he did, he doubted he'd be alive even if he brought old Mr. Schmedler back with him.

I need a miracle to get out of this one, Pinkey lamented, as he crawled into bed. He was too tired to kneel, but on his back under covers, staring into the blackness, he prayed with such intensity and perfect desperation that the good Lord took pity on him. During the night a cloud mass slid over southeastern Wisconsin covering Muskego, Tess Corners, Hales Corners, and finally Milwaukee. By morning it was completely overcast for thousands of square miles. Pinkey's miracle came disguised as a cold, steady rain. His prayer had been answered by a shrewd God who wanted to ensure Pinkey would remain a grateful believer the rest of his life. A nearby low-pressure system made it all the easier to spin off the miracle.

In the morning when Pinkey woke, he heard rain. Its significance wasn't appreciated until he had fully awakened. Or was it, perhaps, a subconscious realization of the importance of rain that did fully waken him to the happy prospect that he wouldn't be leaving Earth this day or any day in his immediate future? He peered out the small, back window at a thick, gray sky and bleak rain, falling into long puddles in the rutted alley. *There ain't gonna be no sun-filled rope this day,* he realized. *I'm saved.* He was joyful. *Saved!* To his credit, not forgetting the source of his salvation, he said out loud, "Thank you God, thank you. I'll be good, I promise. I'll be good in everything . . . you'll see."

It rained all day. Pinkey wondered about the chairs and if Father

Grobschmidt had the custodian bring them in. After school he met George in front of church. The chairs were gone.

"Doesn't look like you can grab a comet's tail today," George said. The rain had stopped but the overcast lingered.

"Can't see the comet a-coming . . . that's the problem I got. Have to have light . . . can't see the tail without light. Boy, I'm mad at this stupid weather. Just when I was all set to go . . . ."

"I want my nickel back."

"What'd ya mean?" Pinkey forgot about the money in the glass jar under his bed.

"I mean I want my money back. Everybody's gonna want their money back. You ain't going to the moon."

"Nobody's gettin' a cent," Pinkey jeered. He turned and ran home.

Pinkey went to public school; the Helden boys to Holy Ghost parish school. Next day after classes, he thought it better not to meet George, as they always did, so instead he cut between the back of the church and the rectory. He spied George waiting for him at the front. When George strolled west, Pinkey ran across 31st Street and made it home without being spotted.

The following day he tried the same maneuver, but Father Grobschmidt was waiting. "Pinkey, I want to talk to you."

The priest led him into the Rectory. In his office he sat at his desk with Pinkey in a chair across. He reached for something on the floor, placed it on the desk, and looked with amusement at Pinkey's astonishment. "This jar of coinage, Pinkey, appeared on my front doorstep this morning. The doorbell rang, but when my housekeeper answered no one was there . . . only this jar. Do you recognize it?"

"That's my money, Father."

"I assume your mother or father brought it here. Now why would they do that?"

"Impossible. They didn't know where I hid it."

"Where did you?"

"Under some old stuff under my bed. My ma never looks there."

"How do you suppose it got here then?"

"I don't know. It just wasn't my ma or pa."

"Of course it was."

Pinkey shook his head. "Coulda been my angel."

The sarcasm annoyed the priest, but he didn't show it. *If the nuns had him,* he thought, *he'd not be such an insolent boy.*

"Paul, your guardian angel is there to light, guard, rule, and guide you, not to convey your ill-begotten coinage by some meta-physical sleight of hand. I am absolutely certain he's in agreement with your parents and me that you should turn this money over to the Church. If not the Church, then return it to the people who bought your worthless tickets. I'm sure your angel advised you not to promote your ridiculous adventure, but you ignored his good counsel. He gets in your head, Paul, and when he's in there you have to listen to him. That's how angels work."

The priest paused, but the boy said nothing.

"You sold tickets to an event you knew very well could never happen. You tricked your friends, little children, and even my custodian into paying good money to watch you stand like a big dummy in the middle of Lincoln Avenue grasping at the undetectable tail of a comet so far away and moving so fast that astronomers can hardly keep track of it. You are guilty of committing fraud, Paul, guilty of the sin of bearing false witness."

"No, Father. I was gonna do it. I really was. You ask Mr. Rosenberg. He'll tell ya."

"Mr. Rosenberg? What's he got to do with it?"

"He told me his friend, Andy Schmedler – during the war he was in – did the exact same thing I was gonna do. He told me all about it, how his friend grabbed the tail of a comet and flew to the moon. It's true, Father. He saw it. You gotta believe me. I was even gonna bring him back."

"Mr. Rosenberg told you a tall tale, Paul. He should know better than tell such a story to a boy with a lively imagination. You listen to me now: no such thing ever happened. I studied astronomy and physics. I know these things. If he projected that tale as the truth then he, too, is guilty of bearing false witness."

"He saw it, Father; I'm telling you, he saw it. He described it perfectly, just like it was. He saw his friend disappear in the sky hanging on a comet's tail. You gotta ask him. He'll tell ya."

"Indeed I shall."

Then Pinkey recalled Mr. Rosenberg's pledge to deny to

everyone the incredible story of Andy Schmedler's long ago journey to the moon.

"Aaw, he'll just deny it. He won't tell nobody."

"No, Paul, you're wrong. He'll tell me. Mr. Rosenberg is an honest man."

At that, Pinkey felt saved. "You're right, Father. Holy cow, don't you see? There ain't no way he'd ever lie to me 'cause I'm George's friend. He did see Mr. Schmedler grab the tail of a comet. Father, I'm sure of it; you gotta believe me now!"

"Pinkey," the priest struggled for patience, "the issue at hand is what we, or rather what you, are going to do about all this money? There's almost three dollars here."

Pinkey lunged for the treasure; Father Grobschmidt pulled it back.

"It's my money, Father. I earned it fair and square."

"Under false pretenses, my boy. It was not an honest endeavor."

"It was honest, Father. I woulda gone to the moon except for the rain."

"You would have done no such thing, Paul. Even if the comet's tail could be grabbed, which it could not, you would have perished in space."

"Andy Schmedler didn't."

The priest slammed his palm on the desk. "No more talk, boy! You have two choices: return the money or give it to the Church." Gary, I don't know why this happened.

"Oh, no, Father . . . ." Pinkey buried his face in his arm on the edge of the desk. He groaned, "You gotta gimme my money."

"I'll make the choice easy for you. If you give the money to the Church, I'll give you twenty-five cents."

Pinkey, guided by his invisible angel, knew it was the best deal he'd get.

"You can buy a lot of candy with a quarter, my boy."

Next day after school, Pinkey met his best friend at their usual spot and knowing his preference said, "Come on, George, I'm gonna buy you some licorice."

After that, there was no more mention of Pinkey's ill-fated trip to the moon. The only humiliation he continued to suffer was at the merciless tongue of George's brother, Clarence. For weeks he shouted after Pinkey, "Hey, space-boy," or "Hey, there's moon-boy," or "Hey, it's the comet tail kid." If nothing else, Pinkey became masterful at avoiding the hated Clarence Helden.

That evening, Augusta detected licorice on George's breath. He didn't eat as much supper as usual, but she ignored it. Something else concerned her.

Chapter 6 ~ 1910 (Continued)

After Augusta Helden tidied the kitchen, she sat with her husband in the parlor. "I received a letter from my brother. Henry said we can bring the boys out the first Sunday of June or the second."

"Good," John said. "I want Juley to go this summer."

Augusta's head jerked. "What?"

"I want Juley to stay at Henry's this summer. He's old enough now."

"Oh my God, John, no; he's only six. He's too young . . . I want him here."

"No, Gussie, he's old enough. Now's as good a time as any for Juley to learn to be away from his mama."

"John, he's only six. Johnny was seven when he first went, and then it was only a month. I need Juley here with me."

"No, Gussie, he's going to Henry's. Johnny needs a companion."

"What are you talking about? Johnny has a companion. George is going."

"No he isn't."

On the edge of anger, Augusta said, "And may I ask why not?"

"You know the reason, Gussie."

"No, I don't know the reason."

John wondered how she could be so unaware of his thinking. He had mentioned it several times. "George isn't going because he starts work in June. We talked about that . . . we went through this with Clarence. I don't want to go through it again."

"John, you said the boys didn't have to work until they're twelve. George is only eleven. That's not fair."

"He turns twelve in a month. He's going to work just like Clarence did, and just like I told you he would."

"John, dear, he's too young. Let him have this one last summer to play with his brother and be with his uncle. Please John, don't make him work. He's so looked forward to going out to Henry's. Let him go, please."

"I told you when Clarence went to work that George would follow when he turned twelve. You didn't object then, don't object now. Besides, how fair is that to Clarence?"

"Clarence was twelve and a half. He was bigger and stronger . . . smarter. He could handle it, but George is still – oh, in so many ways – just a little boy. He has a more sensitive nature. You can't expect him to go into that dirty shop with all those rough men. He's too young."

"No, he isn't. I was twelve when I went to work. I had a sensitive nature if one believed the silly stories my mother told. It didn't hurt me, didn't hurt Clarence, and it won't hurt George."

The prospect of her two younger sons sent away for the summer to her brother's little cabin on Basses Bay, and two older sons forced to work in the harsh confines of their father's metal working shop, deeply troubled Augusta. She feared for little Juley's health and George's safety. She dreaded being alone with her failing father, feared what might befall him, and how she'd handle it. And then there was the growing resentment she felt towards her husband's stubbornness. After he decided something, he'd not consider any contrary arguments though Augusta always made them for the wellbeing of their sons.

"Well, he's not twelve yet," Augusta said, "not for four more weeks. I will not allow him to work until then."

"I'm not asking that, Gussie. But the day after his twelfth birthday he's going to work. And when Johnny turns twelve he'll start work the next day too."

She hated hearing it. She undid her hair, letting it drop onto her shoulders. "We'll let George go to Henry's even if it is only three or four weeks. And don't forget, John, Clarence was in school two months after he turned twelve. You didn't object to that."

"No, we won't."

"But why, John? Why deny George those few weeks with his uncle?"

"Because in that time you'll find some damn reason for me not to go out there to bring him back. George isn't going, Augusta – that's final. No more talk. I have no interest in arguing about matters where you have nothing to say. It's how I intend to raise my sons. Good heaven, they could turn out like your brother and never work at all."

"You leave Henry out of this; you know very well he's a worker. You work all the time. He views life differently. He works sensible hours. Perhaps money isn't so important to him."

"He doesn't have a wife and four hungry sons. If he did, he'd work like me, or he'd beg on the street. I suspect the latter, so I'll make damn sure my sons aren't raised like that."

"Mind your language," August said. "Henry is a reader, a thinker. He writes poetry, and he's a fine carpenter. He emulates Thoreau, a man you would do well to read."

"I have no time for foolishness. Peter and I are building a business that's provided you with plenty of money, which you don't seem to mind one damn bit. Were you married to someone like your brother you'd think different. Believe me, you'd notice the difference laziness and poverty make. Thoreau, whoever the hell he is, would lose his appeal mighty quick."

Desperation flashed across Augusta's mind. "John, don't you remember Henry told us at the end of last summer that George hadn't mastered swimming? I think it best if our sons become good swimmers. If you allow George just one more summer at Henry's, he'll become a strong swimmer. I'm sure of it."

"Tell me, Gussie, how many summers has George spent with your brother?"

The question sparked suspicion. "He started when he was eight: so eight, nine, ten, and eleven . . . four."

"If he can't learn in four summers I doubt he ever will. Besides, George will work his entire life on dry land. So what if he can't swim? I can't either, but I made it across the Atlantic Ocean when I was a boy. I couldn't swim ten feet, but I know how to put bread on your table. My duty is to make sure that someday George can put bread on his wife's table."

"But John, I fear for Juley. He told me he's afraid of the water."

"Don't baby him, Augusta. Henry will watch Juley. Your brother's conscientious. For all his aversion to real work he'd never be careless with our boys. That I know. If he were, I'd never let any of them go out there."

Augusta knelt on one knee beside his chair. She grasped the armrest with both hands. "Please, John, for my sake, don't make George work this summer. He's not ready. And please let Juley stay with me. I need him to help with my father. He has so many aches and pains . . . he talks of nothing else. Juley's sweet company distracts him. Pa's face lights up when Juley enters the room, Johnny too. Oh, John, I beg of you, let Juley stay with me, please, please . . . ."

John put his hand on Augusta's shoulder. He didn't want to be angry with her, but refused to be moved by her humbling entreaties. "My dear Gussie, please understand this one thing: if I fail to teach my sons to work while they still are boys, how will they ever learn to work when they become men?"

"One last summer for George, John, that's all I ask." On both knees she pleaded, "One last summer for little Juley with me here . . . please, please, I beg you."

"No," her husband said, reaching for the newspaper. "I've made up my mind. It's not something for you to object to. You must accept my decisions in matters like this without argument. You're my wife – you are to obey. We'll drive out to see them often enough. I promise you that."

He stood and left the room. Still kneeling, Augusta bowed her head as though in prayer, but it hung in disappointment and sadness. In the faint light she looked older than her age. Small, fine wrinkles had engraved themselves about her darkening eyes and extended halfway to her temples. Her once pink cheeks had faded, and the corners of her mouth bent, ever so slightly, downward.

Before she went to bed she made sure Juley and Johnny's hands and faces were washed, and teeth brushed. She tucked them in then tended to her father. All the while her heart wept.

John knew she was upset, but he was too tired after an eleven hour day to even think about a matter on which he had so firmly resolved not to yield. He fell asleep quickly. Augusta, unable to stem the flow of sad thoughts, fell asleep much later. John didn't wake her to make breakfast, as she always did before he and Clarence went to work. They left by six-thirty without eating anything. Augusta and the younger boys never heard them.

The next evening, her voice quivering, Augusta announced she wanted a piano. It didn't surprise John; years ago he had promised it. "I'll buy you a piano, Gussie." He hoped it would ease her ill-temper.

Augusta said little that evening though John tried engaging her. She had conceived a plan: she would instill in her two younger sons' a love for music that would enable her to protect them from starting work at the age of twelve. If she could delay that merely one year she would consider her plan a success. She knew music; she knew how to play the piano though woefully out of practice. She'd begin teaching Johnny and Juley at the end of summer and continue through their twelfth and, hopefully, thirteenth years. Even her husband would be forced to concede that their sons' mastery of the piano was far more important than sorting nuts and bolts, and sweeping concrete floors. In Augusta's heart dwelt the dream that, perhaps, one of her dear, younger sons would display real talent for the piano, real virtuoso gifts: the gift of the artist.

+ + +

Augusta's farewell to her two little boys swirled with hugs, kisses, and a flow of maternal tears. Seeing his uncle again thrilled Johnny Helden. Henry was so delighted to see the boys after almost a year, so enthused about their staying for the summer that even Juley was seized by excitement. Any apprehension he felt on the long drive out was dispelled by the joyous arrival. Johnny and he beamed with happiness on a June afternoon when Basses Bay gleamed as blue and radiant as the sky and sun above. As the pleasant moments embraced them all, even Augusta's copious tears dried in the glorious light.

"Stay for supper," Henry urged his brother-in-law. "No need to leave so soon. I'm roasting a big chicken."

"Alright," John agreed. It surprised Augusta. She imagined he couldn't wait to leave.

As Henry and his appeased sister went about preparing the meal, John Helden took his sons by the hand and strolled to the shore to get a better view of the little lake.

"You behave for your uncle," he said. "Help with chores. No foolishness when you swim. Let Henry teach you . . . maybe you'll learn it."

They gazed over the water. John studied their faces. "Juley, are you all right?"

"Yes, Pa."

After dinner, Henry lit his pipe, Augusta cleared the table, and John pronounced, "It's time to go." Augusta knelt beside the open door of the automobile, embracing her sons, one in each arm. She trusted her brother; she knew they'd be safe. It was her concern about being separated from Juley that saddened her. She struggled to suppress her tears, for she knew it better if the boys didn't see her cry again.

The evening light lingered as, in June, is its habit. After John and Augusta left, Henry, a nephew on each side, sat at the end of the wooden pier. Six bare feet dangled above the silver-gray water, as the first faint stars appeared high above the eastern shore. Henry whispered about the wonderful summer to come. Eight year old Johnny Helden had never felt so happy in all his life.

Later, when the boys finally climbed the ladder into the dark attic, little Juley was overcome with longing for his mother. They crawled under the blankets that Henry had placed over two mattresses, no more than five feet below the ridge beam. Juley whimpered not wanting Uncle Henry to hear, but not caring if Johnny did.

"What's the matter," Johnny said.

Juley sobbed. "I miss Ma."

"Come here."

"Where?"

". . . in my bed."

Juley crawled into the safe bend of his brother's slender arm, his head resting on Johnny's chest.

"It's okay, Juley; you can cry."

"How come you ain't crying?"

"Cause I like it here. We're gonna have so much fun you won't believe it. In a few days you won't be thinking about Ma or Pa."

"I like Uncle Henry."

"I love Uncle Henry. George and me always had fun. You just wait and see, Juley. You're gonna have more fun than you ever had in your whole, entire life, and you're gonna see how nice Uncle Henry really is."

After a while Juley fell asleep. Henry heard neither words nor whimpers. The second night Juley cried again, and again Johnny held him and told about all the fun they'd have. Juley admitted that very day he had fun, but he still missed his mother. The third night, Juley didn't cry, but now he liked falling asleep in the crook of his brother's arm. He asked Johnny if he could, and Johnny said, "Sure . . ." because he didn't mind his little brother at all.

The fourth night Juley was just plain worn out and fell asleep almost instantly in his own bed. He had gone fishing with Uncle Henry in the warm morning. After lunch he played with his brother in the shallow water for hours. Henry promised he'd teach Juley to swim "real good," and in a few summers he'd be a sidestroker just like Johnny was learning to be.

The boys loved to fish off Uncle Henry's pier. Using cane poles and black line with red worms on small hooks, they'd catch perch and bluegills, throwing most back, only occasionally keeping a bigger fish that Johnny put in Henry's live box. They could sit there for hours, never tiring of it. Henry made them quit only to eat their meals.

Henry never regarded fishing a sport. It was a quest for food, no different than when he hunted blackbirds with his shotgun. As delicious as his blackbird stew tasted, his pan-fried fillets of bluegill, potatoes fried in butter and onions, and green beans soured with vinegar and sweetened with a little sugar, was a meal the two boys relished as much as any gourmet who ever dined at the table of the Prince of Wales. If Henry went so far as to bake a wild blackberry pie, Johnny and Juley considered themselves the best fed boys in the whole world.

Henry fished alone or with Juley. He couldn't take both boys because the skiff was too small; he never left Juley by himself. At Henry's favorite spot, he'd drop a couple lines with a barbed hook shrouded with worm to entice the pretty pan fish with dark blue coins on their golden gills. A fish as big or nearly as big as his hand, he'd keep. Anything smaller went back into Basses Bay to grow another inch or two and gain a few more ounces.

For the boys, though, fishing was great sport. While catching a bucket full of plump fish it became pure joy.

When Johnny first asked Henry if Juley and he could go fishing by themselves, Henry said no. But as the weeks passed, and Johnny showed that he had mastered handling the skiff, Henry began to think it might be okay.

"Course, you have to be mighty careful. The skiff is awfully tippy if you stand up. If you stay seated she's safe. But once you stand up, because she's a flat bottom, she becomes tippy."

"We'll stay seated. Juley never stands up when he goes with you, does he?"

"Never, he always sits nice and still, right Juley?" He smiled at his youngest nephew.

Juley's suntanned face glowed. His eyes twinkled with pleasure. His homesickness had evaporated; now he was as content and happy as his brother.

The early August evening turned cool. After supper, Henry built a fire. They sat in front of the fieldstone hearth on the pine plank floor with blankets around their shoulders talking about fishing. Johnny stayed wide awake, while Juley grew sleepy.

Johnny enjoyed Henry's tales of big pike he had caught over the years, and now Johnny wanted to fish for pike. He dreamed of catching a big fish. Last summer he went twice with Henry; he remembered how his uncle rowed slowly across the small lake and back again making sure the deep bait was always moving. But no fish struck.

"This is my special pole." Henry held up a fine cane pole, longer and stouter than the ones used for pan fishing. "In the morning I'll string it with good line and a wire leader. Pike have mighty sharp teeth; teeth that can cut right through the line. Then we put on a silver spoon with a big hook and a strip of pork rind." He reached into his tackle box, withdrawing the lure for the boys to marvel at. "Then a big bobber tied about six feet from the hook." Henry had fashioned it out of cork and white paint. "And Juley," the boy was falling asleep, "when a pike strikes, you'll see that big bobber go way under. Then you know you've got one."

Johnny said, "But I'll fight it, right Uncle Henry?"

"Sure, Johnny, but first you gotta row. You gotta keep the bait moving so Juley can hold the pole until you get a strike. Then he'll hand it to you, but no standing up. You have to remember that."

Something startled Juley. "What?"

"Do you want to sleep now?" Henry asked.

"Okay." He curled between his uncle and brother, pulling the blanket around his shoulders. Fire shadows played on his sandy hair.

"We'll let him sleep . . . you tired or wanna keep talking?"

"Keep talkin'," Johnny said.

"When you get a strike, take the pole from Juley, but don't stand up. If you stay calm and think about what I'm telling you, you'll have a good chance to land the fish. First thing you gotta do when you have the pole in your hands is set the hook. But, remember, no standing up; you gotta stay seated. Now watch me, here's how it's done."

Henry sat in a straight-back wooden chair with the pole in his hands. "You hold it at an angle like this . . . grasp it with both hands. When you see the bobber moving around below the surface, raise the pole straight up real hard, like this" – Henry demonstrated – "with your hands and arms . . . see?" He did it again. "Not with your body because watch what happens."

Henry leaned forward holding his arms tight against his sides. He pretended to set the imaginary hook by throwing his body backwards. As he did, the chair tipped back, crashing onto the floor. Johnny howled with laughter, but Juley barely stirred.

On his knees, Henry righted the chair and sat down again. "Had I been in the skiff, Johnny, I do believe I now would be in the lake."

Johnny controlled his urge to laugh again.

"That was an important lesson on how not to set the hook. You have to use your wrists and arms, not your body. Understand? I don't want you falling in."

"I understand, and I promise, Uncle Henry, I will not stand up."

The morning broke sunny and windless; as it aged, a light breeze blew from the southeast. The surface rippled, but not nearly enough to keep the boys off the water. By the time Henry had everything all set it was mid-morning. High cirrus clouds had moved in from the west halfway across the sky, but the sun still shone brilliantly.

Henry shoved them off and Johnny got right into the rhythm of rowing. A hundred feet off shore, he tossed the baited spoon into the water. Juley, on the stern bench, held the pole. Johnny rowed hard to get the big, white bobber out behind the skiff. It floated high on the water, easily seen, while six feet down the bait trailed along.

Johnny, looking back, could easily track the bobber. Juley, facing the bow, stared at his brother.

"Juley, keep the pole up."

When Juley raised it to the correct angle, Johnny said, "Good, keep it there."

Slowly, Juley let the pole drop until it neared the horizontal. "Get the pole up, Juley."

Up it went until it began again its slow descent, causing Johnny to repeat the command. At no time did the bobber disappear.

They were half way across Basses Bay when Juley asked, "Do you think we'll get one?"

"Hope so," Johnny replied.

"What'll we do?"

"What do you mean?"

"If we get one . . . ."

"Land it."

"How," Juley asked.

"I'll pull it in. We'll bring it in the skiff."

"We can't stand up."

"I know," Johnny said.

Johnny rowed towards the opposite shore. In cattails he turned the skiff around in a tight circle to point back towards Uncle Henry's. He aligned the bow with Henry's pier, then rowed steadily and evenly. Finally, he searched for the bobber, but didn't see it.

"Juley, where's the bobber?"

All they saw was the black line cutting through the water, as though the line itself, twenty feet behind them, was alive.

"Here," Juley said, handing the pole to Johnny.

Johnny set the hook with a hard jerk. He felt the heavy fish, deep in dark water.

"Juley, we got one, we really got one."

The hook was set just fine. After several minutes the pike swam close, causing Johnny to raise the end of the pole as high as he could. Both boys saw the fish.

"Wow, it's big," Johnny said.

Impressed, but puzzled, Juley asked, "What should we do?"

Johnny handed him the pole, telling him to keep it high though it bent in a bow. When the fish came closer, Johnny grabbed the line.

Hand over hand he brought it in until the fish neared the surface. Then the pike dove burning the line across Johnny's left hand, right in the crease where fingers join the palm. Screaming, he released the line and plunged his hand into the lake.

Frightened, Juley said, "What happened?"

Johnny sobbed. "The line burned my hand."

"Should we let it go?"

"No – never!" The tiring fish fought against the flexing of Henry's stout pole. Johnny pulled off his shirt and wrapped a sleeve three times around his left hand. Again he grabbed the line. Hand over hand, he slowly brought the pike back to the skiff. Exhausted, it did not fight. Johnny started to lift, but felt the little boat heel.

"Sit back." Instinctively, Juley moved to counterbalance the overturning.

With the skiff flat, Johnny brought the big pike into the boat.

"Wow," Juley said.

"What a fish . . . Uncle Henry ain't gonna believe it."

Johnny laid the fish on the floor between Juley and himself, placing his bare left foot on its flank. The hook had pierced the tough side skin of the fish's mouth, but Johnny worked it out while pressing on the fish's head with his stinging left hand.

"Wow," Juley said again.

"Put your feet on it," Johnny ordered. Juley didn't like feeling the slick slime on his tough little feet, but knew he had to do it.

The skiff had drifted towards the northwest. Johnny rinsed his hands, rubbing them on his pants while scanning the west shore for Henry's pier. Then he began rowing towards it. He grinned at his little brother.

"It's big," Juley said.

". . . really big." Johnny admired the splendid Northern pike under Juley's feet.

Johnny decided they might as well troll, as he rowed home. The pike had swallowed the rind, but Uncle Henry sent along a small jar with more. Johnny hooked a strip onto the spoon then flipped the bait back into the water. Juley held the pole, but couldn't look back to watch the bobber without lifting one or the other foot off the fish. Occasionally, he felt the pike flex its muscled body; he pressed down harder to keep it still. Uncle Henry warned them, "Never let a big pike flop around in a boat . . . that's very dangerous."

Johnny kept his eyes on the bobber. Ripples played with it. Johnny thought several times it went under, but it was only a small wave washing over. As they neared Henry's shore, Juley spotted his uncle.

"We got one," Juley hollered, but Henry couldn't hear the high, shrill voice.

Nearing Henry's pier Johnny saw the bobber go under. He took the pole from Juley and set the hook hard. "We got another one," he shouted.

He gave the pole back to Juley. Its bent tip almost touched the water. Juley tried to raise it, but Johnny said, "It's okay. Just let it fight against the pole."

"It's heavy."

Johnny rowed towards Henry who stood watching and waiting. "You got a fish on?"

"Yeah," both boys screamed.

As the skiff came closer, Henry yanked off his boots, rolled up his pant legs, and waded in. Johnny swung the oars onto the stern bumping Juley twice. Henry grabbed the truncated bow; he edged alongside the gunwale until he reached Juley. Henry's eyes followed the movement of the line in the water never spotting the pike on the floor of the skiff beneath four little feet. Juley handed him the pole.

"Feels like a big one." Henry gave the pole back to Johnny without looking into the skiff. "I'll bring him in. We'll beach him."

Instead of keeping the pole and dragging the fish onto the narrow, sandy shore, Henry grabbed the line. Then the fish did something unexpected: it swam right towards Henry. They all saw it. It was larger than the first pike.

"Holy cow," Henry shouted, as the fish swirled then swam right between his legs. In a stride towards shore, Henry's weight swung off balance just when the fish decided to head back to deep water. The length of line around Henry's left leg restrained the fish's thrust causing Henry to totter and lean. He went over like a toppled tree, shouting "holy shit" and making a terrific splash that showered the boys. At the sight of their uncle's disastrous predicament they laughed uncontrollably.

The first echo the boys ever heard was that vulgarity, as it bounced off the dense woods on the eastern shore. They laughed even harder as Uncle Henry struggled to get up. The pike swam in short, angry figure eights about ten feet away with the line still wrapped around Henry's left leg. He assessed the situation then calmly limped towards shore dragging his leg. The pike, as it felt the shallows, began to thrash wildly.

The boys watched in wonder, but wisely stopped laughing.

Henry hauled the fish into the long grass beyond the narrow strip of beach while pulling out his pocketknife to free himself. "Boys, that's the first time I ever landed a fish with my leg."

They all laughed. Henry told them to wait a minute. Johnny and Juley held the skiff to the pier. They could see the big fish flopping in the grass. Henry came back with a long, tough, cord stringer with a metal point at one end and metal ring at the other. He pierced the stringer through the lips of the panting pike. Holding the stringer in his right hand and the fish's tail in his left, he raised it high for the boys to admire. It was over three feet long.

"That's a fine fish, boys. I'm mighty proud of you."

They said nothing. On the pier, Henry put the fish in the live box then tied the stringer to a top slat.

Johnny said, "Uncle Henry, look here . . . ."

Henry spotted the pike under the boys' bare feet and muttered "holy shit" again. "I'll change clothes and hitch the wagon. We'll go to Tess Corners and show off these lunkers. We'll leave 'em at the icehouse. Then I'm gonna treat you fishers to a meal fit for princes."

As they headed towards Woods Road, Henry noticed dark clouds sliding in from the west. He had put each fish in a burlap sack; now and then the larger one flopped at the back of the wagon. The first pike had died. "Won't rain for a while," Henry said.

+ + +

That same early afternoon in Milwaukee, Augusta noticed her father's ashen face and glassy eyes. He refused to eat or drink. "Pa what's wrong? What hurts?"

"I can't breathe right, not deep. I'm wet . . . feel me."

She palmed his forehead, feeling the cold sweat on the burning brow. She touched his nightshirt, wet as wash.

"Pa, I'll fetch Dr. Schwartz." She ran next door to Mrs. Plewa and asked if she'd get the doctor, a block away on Lincoln Avenue. Then she ran back to her father. She thought he was sleeping, but he heard her and tried to open his eyes.

He groaned. "Gussie, hard to breathe . . . ."

"Mrs. Plewa is getting the doctor, Pa. He'll be here soon." She prayed, *dear God, let him be there.*

With a towel she began drying her father's face, neck, and forearms though he was too weak to let Augusta remove the nightshirt. He groaned again, as she dabbed his face. His open-mouth breathing was short and rapid. Paste-like saliva congealed on his lips. She touched his forehead again with its terrible fever. *What is wrong,* she wondered. *You weren't this sick yesterday.*

Mrs. Plewa came in through the back door. "Dr. Schwartz will be here in a few minutes. He has his automobile."

The doctor placed the stethoscope on Henry's chest and, with Augusta's help, rolled Henry on his side to listen to his back. It didn't take long to reach a diagnosis.

". . . pneumonia in both lungs; they're filling up." Palming Henry's forehead, he turned towards Augusta. "I don't think he'll recover from this. I'm very sorry."

Horrified, Augusta asked, "Is he dying?"

"I'm afraid so. How long he'll linger I don't know. I don't think long."

"Oh my God," Augusta gasped.

Henry raised his arm. Augusta bent down to hear him whisper, "Get George and Henry."

Augusta turned to the doctor. "I have to let my husband know. Can you stay till I get back?"

"How quickly," Dr. Schwartz asked.

Mrs. Plewa motioned to Augusta. She had been listening just outside the room. "In half an hour. We can take our tandem."

The doctor glanced at his watch. "I'll stay."

The women knotted their skirts above their ankles to keep from catching the bicycle's chains. They pedaled at what Augusta thought was *surely a dangerous speed.* At Layton Boulevard they headed south towards the Helden plant, but not as fast because the burst of exertion tired them.

Clarence and George Helden stood open-mouthed and speech-less, as their mother flew into the shop. She burst into John Helden's office. Startled and baffled at the sight of his flush-faced wife, he asked, "Augusta, what the hell are you doing here?"

Words shot from her mouth. "My father's dying – you have to get Henry and the boys. He's asked for George too. Send him a tele-gram, but you've got to get Henry and the boys – now!"

"For God's sake, Augusta, calm down . . . I have work."

"No, please, John, you have to leave immediately. My father's asked for Henry. Please – he's dying. It's his last wish. Please, John, don't argue . . . just do as I ask, please."

"Can't it wait 'til evening?"

"No, it cannot. Take Clarence and George, and get Henry and the boys. You have to leave now – please."

John Helden gave orders. He took them from his baby brother, Peter, but not from his wife. His voice was hard. "Augusta, I told you, calm down. How are you so sure your father's dying?"

"Dr. Schwartz said so. He's with my father. Please, John, do as I ask . . . please."

John shuffled papers on his desk without looking at his wife. "Well, it seems to me your father isn't going to die quite that fast. He wasn't deathly ill last evening. So, it's gonna have to wait until I'm done here. Now go home!"

Enraged, Augusta stared at him with disgust, realizing she could be quite content never to look at him again, never to speak with him again, so sharp was the pain of his unwillingness to honor her. A frantic rancor emanated from her deepest being. Leaning towards him, she planted her palms on his desk. Her eyes fiery, her voice passionate, she said, "So help me God, John Helden, if you do not do as I ask and do it immediately, I swear by God in heaven, you shall never enter my bed again." She spun out of his office in a fury. "Never again," she screamed. Every worker's head turned. "Never again," she screamed, over and over, but no one suspected what she was forever excluding.

As she rushed from the shop, Clarence and George looked even more dumbfounded than when she had rushed in. She shouted, "Go by your father!"

John Helden, fearing Augusta's vow, left the shop in a foul

mood with his two older sons. All the long drive to Tess Corners, the boys knew to keep their mouths shut. Reaching Basses Bay in the late afternoon, John brought Henry, Johnny, and Juley back to Milwaukee. He maintained his foul mood because he detected liquor on Henry's breath. He showed no interest in the story Johnny and Juley tried so hard to tell. Henry said the boys had caught two big pike that morning. John wasn't interested. Henry added nothing more. His thoughts were of his father. For most of the ride home, the inside of the crowded automobile remained silent as a tomb.

When they arrived at the Helden home, they all clamored up the porch steps and into the front room. Augusta stood there weeping with Mrs. Plewa beside her. Henry Rosenberg had died minutes before.

Henry embraced his sister. They clung to each other for some time, while the others waited in silence. Finally, they all went in to view the body. The four Helden boys had never seen a dead person. It took only moments until George began to cry at the sight of his gray grandfather; when he did, his brothers joined the weeping.

John Helden edged to Augusta's side. He whispered, "I'm sorry, Gussie." She looked at him with eyes of ice and turned away.

For Augusta everything seemed unreal. Thinking about it later, she could scarcely remember how or when her father's body was taken away, how she cleaned his room, how she prepared the meals, how they all ate, where her brother slept, how or if she herself had even slept at all that long, sad, terrible night. By the evening of her father's wake, however, she had regained her composure and was beginning to feel like herself again. *After all,* she realized, *my father lived a long, good life.*

Augusta first noticed the stranger standing at the rear of the funeral home's parlor. As people mingled near the coffin, he wondered whom he should approach, for he knew no one in the room. Finally, he stepped forward. As he neared the open casket, Augusta moved to greet him. They met a short distance from where Mr. and Mrs. Jablowski and their notorious son, Pinkey, were talking with other neighbors.

"Hello, I'm Augusta Helden, Henry's daughter."

"How do you do, Mrs. Helden. I'm Andrew Schmedler. I was with your father in the Civil War."

Pinkey Jablowski heard the name clear as a bugle call. He stared at the man in stupefied amazement.

"Oh, Mr. Schmedler, yes, I remember my father mentioning your name. I remember very well. He spoke fondly of you."

"Well, I just wanted to pay my final respects. You know, I haven't seen your father for forty-five years, not since the war. That's an awful long time."

Pinkey's eyes bulged to twice their normal size. His mouth went dry. He couldn't whisper a word had he wanted to, nor could he move. His heart pounded in a body nearly as rigid as old Mr. Rosenberg's.

"Come with me." Augusta took Andrew's hand and led him to the coffin. Pinkey, transfixed, stood open-mouthed.

Andrew gazed in disbelief at the shrunken, wrinkled, ghostly, old man in an oversized Civil War uniform. He groaned and pressed his fist hard against his taut lips. "Oh, my God, was it really that long ago?"

"He was eighty," Augusta said. "You're quite a bit younger."

"I'm sixty-three. I was eighteen when we were discharged, so your father was seventeen years older, thirty-five when we got out. My God, in my memory I see him as such a fine-looking young man. I was just a boy."

"I wasn't born until two years after my father got home from the war."

"He told me about his sons, that I remember. I know one was named Henry; I think the other, George. And, of course, he talked about his wife."

"Well, he couldn't talk about me. I wasn't even a twinkle in his eye."

Andrew chuckled. Henry's amiable daughter delighted him.

"I want you to meet my brothers." Augusta led him towards George.

When George saw his sister approach, he excused himself from a small group. He turned towards Augusta with the stranger in tow.

"George, I'd like you to meet Mr. Andrew Schmedler."

"Oh my God," George said, as they shook hands. "You're the fellow who was with our father when he shot that Confederate soldier."

"Yes."

"Let me get my brother. He'll want to hear what you have to say."

As Henry and Andrew shook hands, Andrew remarked how much the son resembled the father. Then George asked Andrew to tell them what their father was like in the war.

"Your father, thank God, took me under his wing. I was there only a few weeks when he picked me for an assignment that turned out to be the unfortunate incident with the Reb. From that day on, we became friends. I was scared. He knew it, so he told me to stick by him. I was mighty foolish to have joined. He'd always tell me my foolishness was wisdom beside his stupidity for having joined because he had a wife and children. He told me, 'You expect boys to be foolish but not old men.'

"I was underage and could've gotten myself killed, but your pa was like an older brother. When I was scared he'd offer some lesson in courage. When I was homesick he'd tell me the war'd be over soon. I believed everything he ever said . . . gave me hope, you see. When we came under fire, he'd be at my side telling me to keep my head down just when I was craving to see what the hell was going on. We saw plenty new recruits get shot right between the eyes because they didn't believe the skill of a rebel sharpshooter. When the war was over we went through the discharge together, but he wouldn't let me so much as look at one of them street-walking ladies in Washington. 'You're a Christian boy,' he'd say. 'Remember that.'" Andrew paused. "Your pa was a good man. I doubt I would've made it through without him."

"He acted bravely, I trust," George asked.

"As brave as any other. Course so many were just plain scared, those with a little bravery stood out. When there was a skirmish – we weren't in any major battles that late in the war – everybody found the courage to do what was expected. Every man I ever saw die, especially that young Reb, died bravely. Yes, your father was brave; most were brave . . . ."

"There's something that's always bothered me," George said. "I know it haunted my father, and I think it bothers Henry and Augusta too; that is, whether that Reb could have somehow lived?"

"Impossible . . . he would not have lived another hour. He was bleeding to death before our eyes. No, your father did what he was commanded to do, and he did it courageously. I don't think I could've done it."

"I find it hard to believe, Mr. Schmedler, that you were actually there," Augusta said. "My father told me that story several times. He always mentioned your name, and now here you are with us. I find it quite remarkable. Just think, you were witness to the most tragic event in our dear father's life, years before I was even conceived."

"Well, your father was good to me. I just wanted to pay my respects."

He shook hands with George and Henry who thanked him for coming, and then Augusta offered her hand. They said goodbye, but he wanted to revisit the coffin. Looking down at his comrade in arms, he promised, *we'll meet again, my friend; we'll meet again.*

In the vestibule, as he was leaving, Andrew's eyes met the gaze of a ghastly looking boy who wondered for a week how that old man-on-the-moon finally got back to Mother Earth. For Pinkey's peace of mind, Augusta Helden finally put the matter to rest. Yet, in a curious way, Pinkey didn't appreciate the truth nearly as much as Mr. Rosenberg's wonderful tale, and, especially, how Pinkey would have returned a great hero. The Heldens never met Andrew again. In 1923, by chance, Augusta read his small obituary in the evening newspaper.

When Augusta finally got to bed, completely exhausted, her mind could not stop reliving the evening, could not stop greeting people, could not stop the repetitious conversations, and most of all could not stop thinking of her dear father finally gone to his eternal reward. *All that remains,* she realized, *is to bury him.*

John's snoring annoyed her. *How can he sleep,* she wondered, *on such a night.* It wasn't until she let her grief overcome all, sobbing softly so the house wouldn't hear, that she finally drifted off in the small hours. In the morning she felt just as exhausted. *Help me through this day,* she prayed.

When Father Grobschmidt learned of Henry Rosenberg's death, he realized he had never asked Henry about the tall tale he told Pinkey Jablowski. The priest agreed to bury Augusta's father; however, since Henry was not Catholic there would be no Requiem Mass. In a simple service he said what priests and ministers say on those occasions. As he prayed aloud, he sprinkled the casket with holy water. There was no doubt in Augusta's mind that her father was in the company of the angels, the saints, and his wife.

Peter Helden watched the carriages and a few automobiles gather behind the horse drawn hearse. He'd speak with Mr. Bruskiewitz again in a few days about mounting the hearse on a small, flatbed trailer powered by a Ford truck and get rid of, once and for all, "those damn indiscreet horses." To the undertaker's chagrin they always seemed to evacuate themselves at the most inappropriate and solemn moment, usually when a refined woman, like Mrs. Helden, was standing nearby and couldn't help notice.

John Helden approached his brother. "Thanks Peter for letting me use your automobile. I'll be back as soon as I can." John's family and Augusta's brothers were already loaded into Peter's larger car.

"Take your time . . . ." Peter watched the meager cortege slowly wind westward on Lincoln Avenue. He spotted several old men in blue uniforms trudging along in a slow march behind the last carriage. *Theirs was a different world,* he thought. Then he uttered, though no one heard it, "Such old-fashioned fellows . . . ."

Before the funeral procession reached the corner, Peter Helden had turned and was striding towards Layton Boulevard. *Smells like rain,* he realized. He put Henry Rosenberg's death and funeral out of his mind. Peter Helden was not a man of the past, but of the present and, most of all, a man of the future.

At thirty-four years of age, in robust good health with boundless energy and enormous passion for the business he had created, Peter Helden walked resolutely but without pride, just the self-realization that things had gone pretty well by his own cleverness and hard work and, if he had anything to say about it, they'd go even better in the years ahead.

Peter was a thinker, and everyone in the family knew it. Now, with the opportunity to walk alone back to his office, he did what came naturally.

Sales, he thought, *that's the key. What the hell good is it if we build the best weldments in the country, but don't have salesmen? John and Joe don't get it . . . engineering and shop methods, that's all they talk. Production follows sales, boys . . . without sales they'd sit on their ass and twiddle their thumbs. It's more than shearing, bending, and welding . . .*

someone has to make the sale. Hell, it's the salesman with a train ticket and suitcase that builds a business. I need more men selling . . . that's the key. I need men willing to live in trains and hotels . . . salesmen willing to leave their families for months at a time . . . like I did in South America. I build damn good products . . . I can out weld every shop in this town, this state, maybe even the whole West. I can build a weldment as good as anyone, but what the hell good is it if I don't have a customer to build it for. Joe's more interested in pretty drawings . . . just put down the right dimensions, Joe. Show 'em where to cut and bend. Don't spend so much time making the damn drawings look pretty . . . just tell the shop what they gotta do. And John, forget about sweeping floors and organizing those damn bins. I'll get you so damn many orders you won't have time to pick your nose let alone clean the shop. I wanna see that shop run sixteen hours a day. You're tired . . . so what? You both make damn good money . . . .

For a moment his thoughts became ineffable, but prescient, certain, and inevitable. He had a visceral sense of his destiny: that the perfection of his life would come in the fulfillment of his youthful dreams, dreams of producing great works and great wealth.

Nothing like what I'm gonna make though. They just don't understand the potential . . . they think nickels and dimes. I want a million and, by God, I'm gonna get it. Sales are the key . . . sell out East, down South . . . the country's building, changing. It needs what I build. I gotta get men riding the rails, get men selling everywhere. I should have at least fifty, no, a hundred. Production . . . John and Joe don't have the faintest idea what real production is. I'll get so damn many orders they'll never go home . . . mass production off an assembly line like Mr. Ford preaches. Maybe I'll get 'em beds in their offices . . . .

He chuckled to himself. Passing the butcher's shop, he nodded at Mr. Pacyna. Peter felt raindrops while glancing at the darkening sky. In minutes he'd be at his office.

They gotta learn to work like me . . . stop running home to their wives . . . stop looking at the damn clock. Those dummkopfs in the shop, that's all they do . . . such collective ignorance. If only they realized the power of work. I learned it well, Pa . . . it's the key, the one, true key. Work twelve hours a day, six days a week, then you get somewhere . . . .

With hurried steps, two women approached. Peter smiled while tipping his bowler.

If Lisa ever complained, I'd kick her fine fanny. Of course, if I sat in a tavern like the shop men, she'd kick mine. One day I'll be free, truly free . . . financially free. Maybe Lisa understands that . . . that's what real freedom means, and maybe she knows it. Enough damn money to tell anyone to go to hell . . . never have to work again. Sit under the shade of the old apple tree . . . or work . . . that's my play. Never have I enjoyed anything as much as my work.

He strode past the nondescript buildings where several cross-armed shopkeepers in center doorways waited for customers and the rain. They all said hello to this prosperous and good-looking young man. Many knew of Peter Helden, knew that he was a comer, a man on the rise, as they say. The shopkeepers, for the most part, lived with their wives and children in apartments above, but Peter's interest wasn't in shopkeepers. Looking up the street he saw more horse drawn carriages and wagons than automobiles and trucks.

That's going to change . . . in a few years there'll be more. That'll happen sure as winter. The world's changing, he knew. *Nothing's going to stay the same. It needs heavy equipment, and I build heavy equipment. If you wanna move the earth you need dump trucks . . . if you wanna store gasoline you need underground tanks. If you wanna haul water or gasoline you need tank trailers. I build 'em all . . . ya, a million bucks easily . . . that's the goal. Easily done . . . a hundred men selling . . . simple multiplication. If I make twenty grand on a hundred thousand in sales, I can make two hundred on a million. I just need more men willing to ride the rails. Give me time . . . ten, fifteen more years . . . when I'm fifty . . . two million. By God, I'll do it.*

He enjoyed the fresh, rain-washed air. *Good to walk,* he realized. He didn't care to look at the collective ordinariness of his provincial town. He raised his eyes above the low-level building tops and ragged trees to the broad, gray sky. He envisioned great cities with great buildings and bridges. He would meet great men with big dreams who had the brains and strength to make those dreams real, for he knew that he, too, was such a man.

Above and beyond the dull profile of this humble street, he saw a vigorous, changing world. In that world he saw markets for what he could build, and in those varied, heavy weldments he saw his fortune. *I need men,* he thought, as he entered his office. *Salesmen . . . that's the key!*

Chapter 7 ~ 1918

In the presidential election of 1916, the incumbent, Woodrow Wilson, pledged to continue his policy of *waging neutrality* to keep America out of the war that had raged across the European Continent since August, 1914. His campaign slogan, *He kept us out of war*, was naively extrapolated by millions of German-Americans to mean *he'll keep us out of war*, especially if it meant joining the fray on the side of the English and French. But Wilson was too honest to offer the slogan in the future tense, for by the fall of 1916 he wasn't sure he could keep America neutral and unarmed. Wilson realized the only sensible way to keep the United States out of war was to end it. As head of the last great world power still at peace, he felt it his grave responsibility to literally drag the warring nations to the peace table.

After his astounding re-election in which Democrat Wilson lost the three most populous states of New York, Pennsylvania, and Illinois to the Republican challenger, Charles E. Hughes, he asked the European combatants to state their terms. Regrettably, both sides responded with demands that their enemies would never accept unless they were totally defeated. Wilson, reflecting on the foolish intransigence of the European leaders, argued before the Senate for "peace without victory." A victor's peace, he prophesied, "would leave a sting, resentment, a bitter memory upon which terms of peace would rest only as upon quicksand. Only a peace between equals can last."

Such profound insight and vision was lost on the European leaders. As curators of empires, they could not subdue their appetites for power, dominance and wealth. Compromise with hated rivals was unthinkable. Tragically, for the world's future, their pride and greed far exceeded their foresight and common sense. They were arrogant men, falsely educated, and worse, they lacked compassion: the suffering and deaths of others, even of their own people, meant little to them.

By early 1917, Britain was winning the propaganda battle. America leaned ever more precariously towards joining the British and French in fighting the barbaric *Huns* even though millions of German-Americans and Irish-Americans, who had suffered under the cruelty of their British rulers, still hoped and prayed the United States would ally itself with Germany. After all, Britain first violated international law by imposing a blockade on German and neutral ports. Britain planted mines in the North Sea, unlawfully boarded and inspected American ships, restricted trade with European neutral States, opened American mail, and even put food on the list of contraband materials not to be exported to Germany. The British had every intention of starving the German people into complete submission.

Desperate to retaliate against this stranglehold, the German government announced on the last day of January, 1917, the resumption of unrestricted submarine warfare. Ships in waters near the British Isles, France, and Italy, regardless of flag or purpose, risked attack without warning. Germany would starve England into submission. Once Germany made that fateful decision, albeit a decision to relieve the hungry plight of her people, as well as to gain strategic advantage, America was compelled to follow a course that inevitably led to war.

In early February, President Wilson, son of an English mother, broke diplomatic relations with Germany. On April 2nd, he asked Congress for a declaration of war. In June, 1917 ten million young American men, including Clarence and George Helden, and Paul – Pinkey – Jablowski, registered for the draft. By the early summer of 1918, one million American soldiers reached France ready to fight.

During the summer and fall of 1917, the nation's factories, foundries, mills, and machine shops began to retool for the production of the materiel of war. Bernard Baruch, a Wall Street speculator who headed the *War Industries Board,* made countless offers throughout the industrial heartland to let military contracts. In Milwaukee, where over sixty percent of the four hundred thousand residents were of German descent, three brothers, all born in Germany and owners of a thriving, metal fabricating business, wondered where all of this was going to lead. The youngest brother, Peter Helden, had a pretty good notion.

"I won't be here tomorrow," Peter said. "I'm going to Chicago."

John squinted with curiosity.

Peter, not one to procrastinate, realized he'd have to explain sooner or later. "I'm meeting with an army procurement officer. I'm curious what's available in government work. This war is going to keep metal fabricators busy. We can make money if we get some contracts."

"Armaments?" John asked.

"Well, I suppose." Peter grinned at his brother's naiveté. "It is war, after all. I'll see what's needed and what fits our capabilities."

"We've never done government work."

"That doesn't matter. Look, John, I can either get a half-million dollar contract from the army, or I can chase down a thousand contracts pounding on doors. You tell me how you think I should spend my time and energy."

"We should not build armaments for war against our homeland, Peter. Have you lost your mind?"

Peter stared at him coldly. "America is my homeland. The Kaiser and his henchmen are barbarians. They don't represent my homeland. I certainly hope they don't represent yours."

"Their soldiers are our cousins, relatives, sons of old friends. Germany is our heritage. My God, Peter, you don't wage war against your own sacred heritage."

Peter didn't reply. At the window he glanced at the dreary afternoon, his arms folded across his broad chest. John sat rubbing the back of his neck, waiting for his brother to speak.

"Did you read Wilson's address to Congress," Peter asked.

"That traitor . . . ." John voted twice for Wilson; Peter had not.

"That traitor is our President. Did you read the speech?"

"No."

"Well you should. Wilson made it clear our quarrel isn't with the German people; it's with the Imperial Government. You don't read enough, John. As my Works Manager, I want you better informed."

The singular possessive angered John. "I'm as much an owner of this company as you."

"Yes, you are." Peter's voice dropped with regret. "I don't want to talk anymore. Read that speech; then we'll talk."

Unappeased, John rose at the command of his younger brother.

He felt anger that America was going to war and sorrow that persons he loved supported it. In his mind, his brother was as much a traitor to Germany as Wilson was to his pledge to keep America neutral. As he left Peter's office, he asked, "Did he really say our quarrel isn't with the German people?"

"Yes, he did, John. He's a wise man. He knows the regime is no good, but that doesn't make the people bad. Our quarrel isn't with the German people – remember that."

John crossed the street to his shop office and tidied up his desk. He checked the doors, locking the last one behind him. He hadn't decided if he'd read Wilson's speech regardless of his younger brother's insistence. This late, he certainly had no intention of driving by a closed library. *It's enough I know that son-of-a-bitch asked for war.*

It was almost unbearable to him: America at war with his beloved homeland. His parents left Germany to escape Europe's wars, and now America and Germany were enemy combatants simply because, in John's mind, of the treachery and lies of the scheming British. "Those bastards," he muttered out loud, in the solitude of his automobile. "Those devils . . . what a disaster." *Peter doesn't understand Germany,* he thought. *He remembers nothing of it, nothing of her beauty, the good life . . . , wonderful people.*

John often pondered his childhood there, a time drawn sweeter and more idyllic with the passing of every hard year and the soft amendments of memory. He could still see his father, the wagon reins comfortable in his hands, and hear his pleasant humming, as they traveled along the Mosel River road. The vineyards rose on the hills above them, stretching eastward all the way to the Rhine where the town of Koblenz nestled in the river valley beneath bluffs and fields adorned with wild flowers. His uncle Ludwig's house sat on a narrow shelf above the Rhine; little Johannes could see, almost directly across, an ancient castle loom high above the mythical river. He'd watch the rising moon emerge above it, enormous and glowing, to light in paleness and shadow the sloping rooftops and high steeples of the ancient town. They ate at cafes where musicians played lovely melodies that were forever lost to him, and where happy, contented people often sang, in spontaneous chorus, songs he never heard again. He slept in a cozy bed in a large room with his two older cousins, cousins who were kind to him, cousins still in Germany to whom he always wrote at Christmas, and now, sadly, cousins with their own sons in the Kaiser's army.

"What a disaster," he muttered again, as he parked his automobile on the quiet street in front of his bungalow.

Wilson's election in 1912 thrilled John and Augusta Helden. Wilson defeated, as Little Gussie derided, "both the arrogant Teddy Roosevelt and that good-for-nothing Taft," the incumbent. Roosevelt, candidate of the new Progressive Party, split the Republicans enabling Wilson to win with only forty-two percent of the popular vote. Wilson, a true intellectual, a civilized man eloquent in speech and manner, a man with liberal ideals, loathed war and understood its futility. While he wasn't a true pacifist, he was close enough to satisfy both John and Augusta who loved Wilson. He was, she told her husband fervently, "the perfect Democrat."

Oh my, she often reflected, *how Mother would have loved him.*

"Peter's going to Chicago tomorrow," John began. "He's going to get army contracts to build armament. When he told me, I couldn't believe it."

Augusta heard the disgust in his tired voice. "I suppose that's the kind of thing salesmen must do when circumstances are such."

"Nonsense, the company doesn't have to build armament to kill Germans. There's plenty of other work . . . civilian work."

Augusta leaned against the sink. "So that's what's bothering you?"

"Ya, Gussie, very much . . . ." So sad was his voice, Augusta thought he might weep. But then his anger impelled him to shout, "I didn't come to America" – he pounded his fist on the kitchen table and dishes jumped – "we didn't come to America" – he pounded again – "to build armaments to kill Germans."

She stared at him. "I would hope you didn't come to America to build armaments to kill anyone."

"Of course we didn't; my parents hated war. Frank deserted the Prussian Army. Had he been caught he would have been hanged. And now Peter wants to build armament to fight against our homeland. I can't believe it, Gussie. I can't understand how Peter can be so greedy, so completely ruthless."

"It isn't necessarily your homeland that America is fighting, John. The Kaiser's regime is barbaric. The same Prussian army that would have hanged your brother is part of that. Such a regime must be opposed."

"It's the French, Gussie, and the English and Russians. They hate Germany, especially the French. In the last war the Prussians beat the French." He paused. "Just think, that was 1870, before I was even born. That should have been the end of it, but, no, now the damn French want their revenge. They've all ganged up against Germany even though it was a crazy Serb who assassinated the Archduke. If a crazy German had killed the Prince of Wales, I could understand it."

"But to sink unarmed ships, and the rape of Belgium? John, those acts are outrageous. Surely you can admit that."

"And the British blockade? Not a ship can reach a German port, Gussie. Germans are starving. Are they to do nothing? Just take whatever the damn British shove down their throats?"

Little Gussie didn't reply. She turned to the waiting dishpan, but then back to the table to retrieve the last of the dirty dishes. Finally, she faced her husband in gloomy silence.

"You're for this war, aren't you, Gussie?" John studied his wife's face. "Your parents were pacifists, but now you're for this war. Well let me tell you; they would be shocked."

Augusta did not want to argue. She didn't want to incite him or bear his anger.

John went on. "It's Wilson . . . a Democrat. To you that's all that matters. Whatever Wilson says or does, you accept. Were he a Republican you'd be as opposed to this war as I am. You choose to abandon the great principle of pacifism in favor of the blindness of partisanship. Your parents would be shocked."

"John, I'm going to bed. I'm too tired to talk. Good night."

As she rose, he asked, "Did you read Wilson's speech, the declaration of war speech?"

"Of course," she replied, with a tone suggesting: *hadn't everyone?* She left John alone to brood in the shadowy parlor.

In the morning, he went over the day's work with the foremen. Then he went to Joe's office to tell him he was leaving.

"You're not supposed to leave when Peter's gone." Joe swiveled on his stool away from the drafting board. "He always wants two of us here, you know that."

"He told me to do something; I'm going to do it. I've gone over everything with the foremen. There won't be any problem. If there is, you handle it. I'll be back in a couple hours."

"Peter won't like it."

"I don't give a damn. I'm doing something he wants me to do. Besides, he needn't know . . . don't tell him."

"He'll find out. He finds everything out."

"Do you know what he's doing?"

Joe didn't answer.

"He didn't tell you, did he? He's in Chicago trying to get army contracts."

Joe grunted a short, derisive laugh. "That's foolishness. I'm not capable of designing armaments, and this shop isn't capable of building them."

"Bull shit. Peter'll figure it out."

At the Layton Boulevard library, John inquired about newspaper back issues. "How far back," the librarian asked.

"April, Wilson's speech, the declaration of war speech."

The librarian, a nice looking woman in her forties, smiled. "Oh, that's a special project of mine. I save all his speeches. I'll get them for you."

She returned with a leather bound scrapbook, placing it on the smooth, oak counter. "Isn't he wonderful?" She expected confirmation.

"I don't share your opinion, but I have to read that speech."

At that, the librarian decided she disliked John's German accent. She wasn't sure she should trust him with Wilson's collected speeches.

John sensed her reserve. "I won't harm your book. I just want to read that one speech."

"All right," she agreed.

With a persistent bias, John Helden scanned the speech, not agreeing with any of it. He read it a second time, noting Wilson's major points. After a third reading he understood the most important arguments, and now, in his leisure, he'd think how to rebut. At best, John found Wilson's speech mediocre and filled with faulty logic. At its worst, he thought it criminal for the President to mislead the nation into joining the bitter French and malevolent British against the better nation, Germany.

Next morning, Peter scheduled an after-hours meeting in his office with John and Joe. John looked forward to it.

"I need your help," Peter began. "We've an opportunity to build something for the army that's right up our alley."

"Anything for the army we construe as armament," John responded. "You know we oppose that."

"Joe, do you feel that way?"

"We're not qualified to build armament, Peter. You know that."

"Yes, I do," Peter said. "But what about building transport tanks to take water to the troops in the field? Could you be comfortable with that?"

Surprised, John said, "That's what the army wants?" They had been building welded, steel tanks for several years. They knew how to do it well.

"*Needs*, John . . . what the army needs."

John expected something far more draconian. It was humane to transport potable water to the weary troops. Peter knew it would be difficult for John and Joe not to agree.

"We have to submit a proposal for a prototype and, on the presumption the prototype is accepted, a bid for one hundred units," Peter said. "Five hundred gallon capacity, rugged conditions, truck mounted or horse drawn, has to be interchangeable. I've got the specifications. Joe, I want you to make some sketches so John and I can price it out. John, you have to figure the best and cheapest way to build 'em."

Peter paused and studied their faces. Now he sensed he'd be able to persuade them regardless of their opposition to the war. "What do you say, boys? Can I count on you?" As always, his enthusiasm was palpable. "We've got to have the bid in by next Friday, twelve noon in Chicago. I'll deliver it myself. What do you say?"

Joe glanced through the specification booklet. "I don't see a problem with this." He handed it to John.

"I'd see no problem if we could sell the same equipment to Germany; otherwise I'm against it. If we do it, it strengthens Wilson's war effort. I can't be party to that, not against my homeland."

"Then you're party to treason," Peter replied. "We're Americans now."

John didn't have the courage to say what his heart exhorted: *you're the traitor; you betray our homeland. It is you who drives the dagger into Germany's heart and for what . . . money, profits?*

"Remember, John, our quarrel isn't with the German people. It's with the Imperial Government. Wilson separates the two; that's an important distinction."

Since reading Wilson's speech, John pondered that point often. "Tell me, Peter, exactly how are the people separate from their government?"

John's question caused Joe to search his brother's sad eyes. He wondered why John was so obstinate. In his mind, there'd be nothing wrong with building this equipment. Somebody had to do it.

The question surprised Peter. "The Kaiser's regime does whatever it wants without consulting the people. It isn't a democracy. He's a tyrant. We live in a democracy."

"Did Wilson consult the people before going to war?"

"Of course he did. He asked Congress for a declaration and got one. That's asking the people."

"That's asking a bunch of politicians in a closed room."

"Don't talk foolish . . . that's the way our government works. The people elect Congress. It's perfectly legitimate, and you know it."

"It's no more or less legitimate than Germany going to war for its reasons."

Leaning forward, Peter rested his right elbow on the front edge of his desk, his right hand at his face. His index finger moved lightly over his lips. Perplexed, he stared at his older brother wondering what the hell the point of all this was. To the side, Joe sat there like an audience.

John continued. "It seems to me, regardless of the form of government, you can't separate the people from that government. Any regime, good or bad, tyranny, monarchy, or democracy, is joined to the people by the army itself. The army, while a tool of government, is also the dwelling place of the fathers, sons, brothers, and uncles of the people. Every man in that army, in any army, has parents, brothers, sisters, uncles, aunts, nephews, and nieces. The older men, the officers, have wives and children. It's the army, Peter, that binds the government to the people tight as brothers."

Peter leaned back in his chair. He never thought of an army that way, but now he conceded, at least to himself, that John's point was insightful. Joe thought John's comment self-evident.

"The army of any nation is an extension of the people," John continued. "A nation mobilizes in support of its soldiers and sailors to train, equip, feed, and clothe them. It is the procreator of the army just as the army is its progeny. Wilson is foolish to suggest we have no quarrel with the German people while waging war against the German government. If we kill German soldiers and sailors we are killing the German people themselves. It is ridiculous to suggest our fight is only against the German government. That regime is little more than a protected cadre of cowardly loyalists huddled around the Kaiser far from the front lines and subject, at some point in time, to change. But the people, the citizens of a nation, never change."

"Well, he was speaking more to somewhat placate, I suppose, the people of German descent in this country," Peter admitted.

"Ya, to placate us," John agreed. "But that's a major point in his speech and, in my opinion, a false one."

"But what about the sinking of unarmed ships, sinking of hospital and supply ships to Belgium; is that a false point?" Peter asked.

"It's a state of war . . . what the hell do you expect? My God, Peter, the British and French are every bit as ruthless as the Germans. American newspapers don't publish that. They're too damn biased. I despise it on both sides. I condemn all parties. But people are stupid if they think Germany is the only vicious dog in the fight."

"They never should have gone into Belgium. That was a violation of a neutral country. That was Germany's fatal mistake. That got the French in, then England, now us."

"Some people see it that way, I suppose. But is that really sufficient reason to go to war on the side of the British? Germany, after all, never directly violated our neutrality, as Britain did. If violating a nation's neutrality is such a grievous offense, why didn't Wilson advocate that the United States go to war against the British when they violated ours?"

Peter did not respond.

Joe nodded. "Wilson should have stayed neutral . . . ."

"Well, we're not anymore," Peter replied. "We're in it."

"You know Wilson's mother is English," John said.

"So what?" Peter asked.

"If she had been German I think Wilson would have joined the Kaiser."

"Ach, don't talk foolish."

"People are loyal to their heritage. Wilson is loyal to his English mother. I respect that. Blood makes a powerful argument."

"And you think I'm not loyal to my heritage, eh?"

"That's right, Peter; you are not." For once, John sensed he had gotten the better of his brother. "If you build armament now it's an absolute betrayal of your German heritage . . . something Wilson would never do to his mother's England."

"Water transport tanks are not armament. This is different. You can't accuse me of betrayal. The army has to deliver fresh water to the troops whether in exercise or battle. Even if we weren't at war, it still needs that equipment."

That ended the discussion. The gray afternoon became a cheerless evening. The three brothers sat in silence, anxious, but late for their suppers.

"Well, think about it," Peter said, his voice drained of enthusiasm. "This is something I intend to do. Give me your decisions in the morning."

Augusta, along with a single plate, waited for John at the kitchen table. Johnny and Julius were upstairs doing schoolwork; in the parlor, Clarence and George were reading the newspaper.

"Peter wants to build water transport tanks for the army," John said, after washing up. "He doesn't think that's armament, but it's for the war so I think it is."

"It's not like guns, though," Augusta replied.

"No, I suppose not." His wife's response aroused John's suspicion. He finished his meal in silence.

After Augusta poured his coffee, John began again. "I'm five years older than Peter, but in every other way he's the older brother. You wouldn't believe how he's the boss now, Gussie. Even though we invested the same amount, Joe and I jump at every command."

"Is it things he shouldn't boss you about? Is he unreasonable?"

"No, not at all . . . he's just very smart. He's rarely in the shop anymore, but he understands fabrication better than men who've worked at it for years. Almost better than me, Gussie, and I'm Works Manager. No, Peter is just brilliant. What a difference between him and his three brothers. In comparison we're a bunch of dummkopfs. He's the baby, but he's the boss. Frank is lucky not to work for him."

"Would you ever consider leaving?" Augusta feared that, because John made good money.

"I've thought of it, Gussie, especially with this damn war. Here I am, at my age, forced to build equipment for war against my homeland."

"You remember the old country. Peter is more American. He's not emotional about Germany, not like you."

"I know; I know . . . ."

"But, John, it's to your credit that you don't agree with everything he thinks. You're respectful of your heritage, and that's good even though-" She stopped herself.

"Even though you think it's right that America opposes Germany, eh, Gussie? That's what you were going to say, wasn't it?"

"I can't think like you in everything, John. I believe Wilson is right to oppose the Kaiser's regime because that regime is evil."

"You agree with Wilson because he's a Democrat. A Republican you'd oppose to the death."

Augusta felt the stab of scorn, but defended herself. "That's not true."

"Your parents were against war as a matter of principle. They'd oppose Wilson even though they were Democrats."

"Must I remind you that my father fought in the Civil War under a Republican president?"

"Ya, and must I remind you that the Civil War made your father a pacifist? He learned it's easy to espouse war if others have to fight it. If Clarence and George have to fight, you'll change your mind real quick."

Augusta regarded President Wilson a principled man. She believed he was absolutely correct in going to war against Germany, but she also knew her own heart. John was right about their sons: if Clarence and George were called, she'd feel differently, perhaps unbearably so. She wondered about her parents. Her mother was a true partisan, through and through, so she might support Wilson even though she was a pacifist. Her father wasn't as passionate about politics, but he had become a pacifist because he experienced war first hand. Would they support Wilson's going to war? In all honesty, Augusta didn't know.

In the morning, John still hadn't decided what he'd tell Peter. He saw Joe first who told him he decided to go along with Peter. John resented being pressured to make a decision that went against everything he believed to be right and just. The equipment itself, however, mollified his attitude. The troops on both sides of the line, he realized, needed fresh water. That was legitimate. But if he agreed with Peter, he'd be helping the American war effort against his beloved homeland. That was almost impossible for him to accept.

"John, we're Americans now," Peter began. "Your boys are Americans by birth. Your wife was born in this country."

"I think of myself as much a citizen of Germany as America, maybe more so. What you're asking strikes against the loyalty I owe my heritage. How can I do that?"

Peter spoke calmly. "Someone will get this contract. That equipment will be built, with or without us, by somebody," he argued. "Why not let it be us, John? It'll help our families and the men in the shop and their families. We still have to put bread on people's tables."

"We could get other work. We always have."

"No, you're wrong. It's a war economy now. Every shop will build for the war. Our salesmen are telling me civilian work is drying up fast."

Like so many other arguments with Peter, John eventually reached a point of discouragement. Even if he'd counter again he knew his brother would argue against it. But now John's silence drew something out of Peter's mind, something he saved for the last, something he was sure would bring John around.

"You know, John, with army work come certain privileges . . . ."

John didn't know what Peter meant.

"We can name Clarence, George, and, when they come of age, Peter Junior, and your Johnny, as critical personnel, critical to the manufacture of those tanks. Draft board won't touch 'em."

John Helden responded, "Are you trying to bribe me? Has it come to that? Are you that desperate to get your hands on government money . . . blood money?"

"Listen, dummkopf, that's not bribery. That's the way the government does business. I'll save my son's rear end, but if you're not willing to save your boys then maybe I should have a little chat with your wife. She'll tell you what to do, and, by God, you'll do it."

It's always his way, John realized. *Right from the start, he's always gotten his way.* John grew bitter years ago: bitterness accompanied by the weary realization that Peter's intellect and willfulness would always prevail. John and Joe, the older brothers, had been relegated to subservience.

+ + +

Throughout 1916 America remained in a state of nervous peace. Newspapers brought the distant war home, while certain editors speculated whether America would be *dragged into it*. Augusta's brother, Henry Rosenberg, kept the conflict far away from his little house on Basses Bay. He didn't like reading about the war; it upset him too much, for he saw it all as madness. Yet, he did read about it, and the more he read the more he embraced not only neutrality but pacifism. And then, too, summers for Henry weren't what they used to be, now that Johnny and little Juley were too grown up to spend those happy months with him. He missed his nephews. To relieve his loneliness, he spent many evenings at Sobek's tavern out on Woods Road, but left when men started discussing the war. They knew Henry opposed it, and most of them resented that.

In May, Johnny Helden turned fourteen. In June, he went to work in the Helden Company's shop sweeping floors, picking up scrap metal, and sorting nuts and bolts, just as his two older brothers had done before him. Juley didn't want to stay at Uncle Henry's by himself, nor did Augusta want him there because she knew her own precious summers with her youngest son were slipping away. She, too, hated reading about the war and didn't care about the minutiae of tactics and battles; nor could she bear the horrible suffering and death. *It was enough,* she decided, *to know that across that big ocean a terrible war rages.* She was more interested in political news: what Wilson was saying in his campaign and if he would, in fact, be able to keep America neutral. But whoever picked up a newspaper that long year and scanned the front page couldn't help notice that a certain battle near the French town of Verdun was constantly in the headlines.

Augusta and John often wondered why Europe descended into this catastrophic war. John blamed the French for scheming revenge, while Augusta judged the Kaiser and his henchmen the aggressors. Popular opinion blamed an assassination that triggered alliances that demanded to be honored. All of it was true, but the roots of the causes extended far back into the nineteenth century.

Four *isms* infected the combatant European states to varying degrees: *imperialism* expressed a nation's greed; *nationalism* expressed a nation's pride; *militarism* expressed a nation's anger, and the fourth, *secularism,* expressed a nation's public rejection of God. No nation was more perniciously infected with all four *isms* than France, the second largest imperial power after England. France seethed with a vengeful anger at her loss to Prussia in the War of 1870, and her pitiless secularism was nothing short of pure fanaticism. Between 1880 and 1900, France expelled one hundred thousand Catholic nuns and eight thousand priests. She expelled the Jesuits and illegally seized their property, as she did convents and schools. French primary and grammar schools removed all religious instruction. Universities suppressed the faculties of Catholic theology. Army chaplaincies were abolished, and nuns were forbidden to serve as nurses in the hospitals. A spy system established in the army harassed and drove out officers known to be practicing Catholics. Into this dark, spiritual void something terrible came to France: it came in 1916; it was brought by war, and it settled in the hills and fields surrounding a place called Verdun. What came was *Hell.*

The Germans began the battle of Verdun on February 21, 1916, with an intense artillery bombardment of the forts surrounding the town. To relieve the desperate French, the British on July 1 attacked the German positions along the Somme River near Bapaume. On that fair, summer day, twenty thousand young British soldiers died; forty thousand were wounded. By November, after enormous loss of life on both sides, the British acknowledged their failure to break the German line at the Somme just as the Germans, by December, conceded failure to break the French line at Verdun. No strategic advantage, absolutely none, had been gained by either side. When the battle finally ended on December 19, there were seven hundred thousand French and German casualties including a quarter million men dead.

The American Civil War began as a war of movement, but ended statically in trenches. Nine months of trench warfare ensued when Lee's forces dug in to resist Grant's army outside Richmond. It was that long, final siege that foretold the western front of the Great European War half a century later.

In the trenches of 1916, the dead piled up amid the barely living. Excrement and urine mixed with the virulent oozing and bursting of the gaseous, rotting corpses. The stench was the stench of hell. Surely, somewhere along that battle line there must have been at least one exhausted, broken soldier, his face black with filth and fear – British, French or German, it didn't matter – who rose above the putrid, death-filled trenches and, on behalf of all, screamed at his Ministers, Princes and Generals, "What good are your philosophies, your music, your art, the sweet poems, and brave novels of your literature if, after all of it, you still hate your neighbor? Look amidst what I stand. If, after all this, you still believe war to be a reasonable expenditure of human life and treasure, then you have learned nothing from any of it. Better that all your philosophies, music, art, your literature, and all the culture had never been created, but you had learned instead the one, simple, profound truth that war is the business of madmen and fools."

Clearly, the western front became a hopeless stalemate. Germany didn't attack again until March, 1918, when the British bore the brunt near St. Quentin. In May, another German attack was launched against the French who were pushed back to Chateau-Thierry. But by early summer, the American army had reached France in force. With these fresh troops the decision was made to counterattack at Chateau-Thierry. On August 2, the town of Soissons was taken. Suddenly, the Germans were in broad retreat, unable to resist the overwhelming superiority now possessed by the Allies. By the end of the summer of 1918, the Crown Prince would telegraph the Kaiser, "All is lost . . . ."

Chapter 8 ~ 1918 (Continued)

John Helden idly rolled a coffee cup between his palms when he noticed someone at the rear door. *Who the hell is that,* he wondered. He was in no mood for company.

Augusta, already thinking of tomorrow's supper, heard the soft knocking. She opened the door to Mira Jablowski who entered the kitchen pale as paper. She stood before them, but said nothing.

"Mira, what is it," Augusta asked.

She did not answer; she just stood there straight as a sword, her face kneaded by sorrow.

"Mira, tell us."

She spoke so quietly, John and Augusta barely heard. "Pinkey is dead. He was killed in France."

For a moment, silence captured the kitchen.

But then John, looking right at his wife, exploded. His fists slammed the table. "See!"

"Oh, my God," Augusta groaned. "No, no . . . ."

She moved towards Mira, embracing her.

"My son," Mira said, staring like a blind woman. "My only child . . . ."

John shouted, "So, Augusta, now do you see what Wilson has wrought?" He pushed back from the table. "That g--damn son-of-a-British bitch." He kicked the chair aside. "Now do you see his treachery? Wilson's a devil. What do you think of his g--damn war now?"

Augusta and Mira huddled together, terrified at John's outburst, though Augusta felt far more shame than fear.

"You think war is some kind of game, eh? Well, people get killed, or didn't you know that? What the hell were you thinking, woman? You've been for this g--damn war right from the start, and now Pinkey is dead."

"John, please, control yourself, please," Augusta begged.

"You're a stupid woman, Gussie, and Peter is a greedy

son-of-a-bitch." Facing the grieving mother, John Helden said, "And for it, Mira, your son is dead. As far as I'm concerned, Pinkey's blood is on the hands of my wife and my brother."

"John, please, calm down." Augusta didn't care what John said about her, but was horrified that he spoke so viciously of his brother.

John ignored her. "The only reason Peter got that government contract is money. He doesn't give a damn how many boys die – American or German. Money is all he thinks about. He's made money his god, and, by God, he'll rot in hell for it."

"John, don't say such terrible things . . . please."

Anger, frustration, and bitterness consumed John's energy. He reached for the chair, set it right then collapsed on it. With both forearms on the table, his breathing came short and rapid. Perspiration stood on his face and neck and slid from his armpits down the sides of his chest. He felt the first swipe of shame for losing his temper in front of his wife's friend, but not once did it occur to him to express sorrow to the dead soldier's mother.

Mira observed him with disgust. "You should remember, Mr. Helden, my husband and I support this war. Pinkey supported this war. Do not forget we are Poles. Our relatives in Poland support this war. For years Germany has treated the Polish people with disdain. We are not even allowed to be our own country. Germany forces Polish men to fight her wars. It is Germany that refuses to live in peace with her neighbors. How can there be anything *but* war?"

"I am German, Mira. I was taught to love my neighbor. Germans are God-fearing, Christian people just like you Poles."

"Nonsense, I don't believe that for a minute. If they were, their bishops would have far more influence with the generals in Berlin."

John stared at her in disbelief. The animosity in her face appalled him. *What have I done*, he wondered. He didn't want killing. He didn't want Pinkey dead. *What the hell is wrong with these women?* He struggled to stand then stumbled out the rear door, slamming it in disgust.

"Oh, Mira," Augusta said, "I'm so sorry . . . please forgive him. He's blinded by his love for Germany. He still has the same childish ideas of Germany, as when he left there as a boy. But, truly, he wants no war, no killing."

Mira's eyes pierced Augusta's. "My son is dead. Your husband's opinions mean nothing to me."

She began to weep. Augusta led her to the parlor. On the sofa, Augusta slowly rocked Mira in her arms and, every so often, whispered, "I'm sorry, I'm so sorry." There was nothing else she could say.

John Helden headed towards Lincoln Avenue. Feelings of self-righteousness and self-pity fed his anger. "Stupid women," he muttered. *How can they be in favor of this damn war? Pinkey's killed, and they're still in favor of it.*

He paused at the corner tavern, thought of entering, but then crossed Lincoln Avenue to Father Charles Grobschmidt's rectory. The housekeeper greeted him by name. John was well known in the parish; he served on the building maintenance committee after construction of the new church. She asked John to wait a moment, while she fetched Father Grobschmidt.

"Have you heard about Paul Jablowski," the priest asked right away.

"Ya, Father, Mira told us."

"Very sad . . . ."

The men faced each other across the same desk where, eight years earlier, Pinkey disputed how his pastor came into possession of a certain jar of coins. John blurted, "I blame Wilson for Pinkey's death . . . and all who support him."

"And your wife?"

"Ya, she's for the war. Her parents were pacifists, but she's a big Democrat . . . loves Wilson. Makes me sick."

"Did you get angry at Augusta?"

John lowered his head. "Ya, Father, very angry . . . in front of Mira, too. She's all for this damn war. Poles hate Germany."

"John, I'm of German descent. From what I've read, the Kaiser and his henchmen are the reason the war doesn't end. If they had any sense they'd end it by negotiating. To my mind, it's pointless to continue, but the Kaiser just fights on and on. Don't forget, his troops are in France. He's the invader. He should call his army home. But he's stubborn as a Prussian peasant, so now America will have to end it. Wilson had to get us involved; he really had no choice. Millions have died. It's gone on long enough. One way or the other, it has to end."

"It would end without our involvement from sheer exhaustion," John said.

"Perhaps, but now America is involved. You and I can't change that. We can pray for a speedy end, but that's about all."

"Ya, tell that to my wife, Father. Whatever Wilson does, she supports. If he fights ten more years, she'll support it. She'll pray for him before she prays for peace. Right from the start, I opposed the war, but she's a partisan. I'm a pacifist."

"John, you're from Germany. Augusta was born here. She doesn't think the same way. There are issues involving justice. The Kaiser and his warmongers have violated the rights of innocent, peace-loving people. You have to let your wife form her own opinions."

"Even when they're wrong, eh?"

The priest shrugged. "Who's to say? This isn't a simple matter. Great injustices have been done on both sides. But now the war has to end. There's been enough killing. Germany should go home lest the American army chase her home with more dead on both sides."

"That's no solution, Father. Germany will fight."

"Well, there is a solution, John, but, unfortunately, it's one that all parties are far too proud to initiate."

John didn't ask to hear it. He was exhausted, despondent, and thirsty. He slouched in his chair.

"Let me tell you a story about my father," the priest continued. "He was the only man I ever knew who really understood how to properly end a fight."

John asked for water. The housekeeper brought them each a glass.

When he finished drinking, he said, "Okay . . . tell me."

"Five years after the Civil War," the priest began, "my family moved to the far west side of Chicago. I say 'far west side' . . . now it's the middle of the city. I was twelve when my parents bought a nice house from a Mr. and Mrs. Dorfman, a Jewish couple. We settled in, got to know our neighbors and joined the nearby parish where I was enrolled in school. My father was an insurance man who traveled throughout Illinois and Indiana. One of the problems we, or I should say, I had was at school. There was a boy in my class whom I disliked. His name was Anthony – his mother was Italian – so everyone called him Tony. I didn't like the way he looked, how he dressed, how he talked, the way he blew his snot-filled nose, even the way he sat at his desk. I just decided I wasn't going to like this boy. However, and this is important, there was nothing wrong with him. I had no valid reason to dislike him, absolutely none. I created that prejudice because his mother and father were, for some completely unknown reason, the only people in the neighborhood who weren't welcoming to my mother and father."

John shifted his weight in the uncomfortable chair.

"My parents were genuinely nice people. They tried to be pleasant to all our neighbors, but these folks – their name was Hoch – just weren't friendly to us at all. On several occasions Mr. Hoch rebuffed my father's overtures of neighborliness, and Mrs. Hoch cold-shouldered my mother even though she was the sweetest, friendliest lady you would ever hope to meet." The priest glanced heavenward. "God rest her soul." He cleared his throat.

"Well, my parents didn't understand it. So, what I did, in foolish retaliation, was to dislike the Hoch boy. Not a Christian response, to be sure, but I was a rather stupid lad back then. For no fault of his own, I taunted him. I mocked him in front of other boys, and I did it with impunity because I was bigger and stronger. I became a bully for no good reason other than my anger towards his parents for their unfriendliness towards my parents. Had they been friendly, I would not have behaved that way. Tony and I might even have become friends. In fact, had he been bigger and stronger, I would have left him alone. In my heart I was still very much a cowardly fellow.

"A house was being built on the lot next to the Hoch's. They lived a half block north. I was there once with a gang of kids. For no reason I picked a fight with Tony. After some harmless punches and just scuffling around, I threw him to the ground and pinned him. He didn't put up much of a fight or, maybe, he was just too weak to fight. I held his wrists to the ground and felt how thin they were. I put my knees, my weight, on his upper arms and pinned him hard. He could barely move. He squirmed and kicked, but couldn't break away.

"It was then I did something I'll regret to my dying day. It was cruel and degrading and something that weak little fella didn't deserve. Mind you, I wasn't physically trying to hurt him. It was enough I had him pinned and had complete control over him. For poor Tony it was humiliating. All the other kids, mostly boys but some girls, gathered 'round, kind of screaming stupid things. One boy urged me to smash his face, but I couldn't do that. Tony was too helpless and I, for all my stupidity, wasn't that cruel. Other kids, mostly girls, were telling me to let him go. At this point I didn't want to hurt him, but some of the tougher boys were egging me on to do something. So I leaned over him, my face directly over his, and I dropped a big glob of spit on the bridge of his nose right between his eyes. Those boys laughed hard when they saw it, and it must have been their laughter that prevented me from hearing someone coming towards us who called out my name, '*Grobschmidt!*'

"I glanced down at Tony. He was crying. He hadn't cried before I spit on him, but that made him cry – not hard, mind you, not out loud. No kid wants to cry in front of other kids. Well, I saw my spittle flow into both his eyes, mingling with his tears. He couldn't even wipe away my spit because I still had him pinned. It disgusted me, or, rather, what I had done disgusted me. I actually felt shame. I was ready to let him go when an unbelievably powerful hand gripped my shoulder. That physical pain far exceeded any I had inflicted on poor Tony. I was pulled straight up by a force far greater than anything I ever experienced. Behind me stood Tony's father; he spun me around and glared at me. He wasn't tall, but very broad, very powerfully built. He was a stonemason by trade, a bricklayer.

"'Why don't you pick on someone your own size,' he screamed; his face flushed with anger.

"Of course, I was a wise guy and said with a smirk, 'He is my own size,' but it wasn't true.

"Well, with that, Mr. Hoch slapped my face harder than I had ever been hit anywhere on my whole body. I had never been struck in the face before – or since, for that matter. Oh, let me tell you, John, it was an enlightening experience. The blow knocked me to the ground, and yet I had the feeling, had he wanted, Mr. Hoch could have hit me much harder. But then I roused my little boy temper. The side of my face burned. I stood up, dusted myself off and said, my shrill voice ringing with hatred, 'Why don't you pick on someone your own size, you big, fat, ugly slob?' He lunged at me, but I was too quick. I turned and ran all the way home.

"I told my mother I got into a fight with Tony and what his father did. She was horrified. 'Oh, what a terrible man,' she said. 'Don't you worry; your father will know how to deal with him. We could have him arrested for striking a child.'

"Oh my, she was angry. Of course, I was too afraid to tell her my own bad behavior, so I said nothing. We waited for my father to come home. After my mother explained to him what happened, my father looked at me and asked a simple question: 'Who started it?'

"Meek as a lamb, I replied, 'I did.'

"At that my mother gasped. 'Why?' my father asked.

"'I don't know,' I said.

"'What do you mean you don't know? Tony Hoch isn't your size and strength. He's not a boy for you to fight. You know how unfriendly his parents are . . . .'

"I had no answer. How could I possibly convince them I did it precisely because Tony's parents were so unfriendly to them? And I was terrified my father would ask for more particulars. Then I'd have to reveal that I spit into Tony's face when I had him pinned, and *that* I did not want to tell.

"My mother asked my father, 'What are you going to do?' He didn't answer, but then said, 'Charlie, come along. We're going to visit Tony and Mr. Hoch. We're going to put an end to this before it gets any worse. I want to know why he struck you and why they're so unfriendly towards us.'

"Let me tell you, John, my father was a very smart man. He knew the value of controlling his temper. By the time we got to the Hoch's, he was calm enough to ring their bell rather than pound the door. Needless to say, Mr. Hoch was not happy to see us. He growled, 'What the hell do you want?'

"My father, in an even voice, said he did not believe Mr. Hoch was the kind of man who struck other people's children. 'You've shown your dislike for my family, but I don't understand it,' he went on. 'Now you strike my son, and even though he fought your boy, I can't believe you would strike him unless you were taking out your anger against me. I suspect you have a quarrel with me. I wish, by heaven, you'd come out with it.'

"'Your boy spit in my son's face when he had him pinned; my boy was helpless,' Mr. Hoch said, to my great shame. He glared at me. 'I'd strike him again for that.'

"My father turned and looked at me with an expression that broke my heart . . . an expression of such profound disappointment that I would have done anything to atone to him and to God for my terrible sin.

"'As bad as that is,' my father said, struggling to recompose himself, 'I do not believe that is why you struck my son. For God's sake, tell me. Let's resolve it, once and for all.'

"'I have nothing to say to you,' Mr. Hoch shouted. 'Get the hell off my porch. Go home! You're not welcome here.'

"At that I detected my father's frustration. He had offered to resolve whatever it was between them, but Mr. Hoch refused. Also, my father's discovery of my terrible behavior made the situation much more difficult. Then, to my great surprise and horror, my father said, 'Mr. Hoch, I want you to step outside and strike me, as you struck my son.'

"'You're crazy . . . go home,' Mr. Hoch shouted.

"I could see Tony and his mother huddled in the shadows behind Mr. Hoch.

"'If you're a man, come out and strike me, as you struck my son,' my father demanded in a loud voice.

"I was horrified. I didn't know what to think. I didn't know what my father was getting at. He wasn't a fighting man; he was a Christian gentleman. He wouldn't fight except to protect his family or himself. He certainly wouldn't start a fight. Needless to say, I was very confused."

"Did you say anything?" John asked.

"I was too afraid, too filled with shame. After the way my father looked at me, I wanted to run away and hide."

The priest paused to sip some water. John saw the sadness in his eyes.

Father Grobschmidt went on. "Well, finally, Mr. Hoch did step out, probably because of my father's reference to his manhood. Without saying anything they descended the steps to the front yard. My father spoke very calmly: 'I would prefer that you not strike me with your fist. You hit Charlie with an open hand; I ask that you strike me the same.'

"Standing in their doorway, I saw Tony and his mother with her arm around him, motionless and silent and probably, like me, very frightened.

"Mr. Hoch just glared at my father, his face red with anger. There was hatred in his eyes, but I knew no reason why he should so hate my father. Me, yes, because I spit in Tony's face, but not my father. I didn't learn until later his hatred was indeed meant for me. In truth, Mr. and Mrs. Hoch didn't hate my parents. They were hurt by them although my parents, at that point, didn't even realize it."

'No, no," John interjected. "How could that be? Nothing ever happened between them."

The priest smiled. "Let me continue. Mr. Hoch spit into his big, rough hands, rubbing them together while eyeing my father." The priest paused at the memory. "My dear father, his arms hanging limply at his sides, just waited. They looked intently at each other for what seemed an eternity. Then, suddenly, Mr. Hoch reared back with his right arm and shoulder" – the priest's voice faltered – "and slapped my father incredibly hard across his face, much harder than he had hit me. I heard Mrs. Hoch's muffled shriek. My father swayed then spread out his right leg so as not to fall. At the sight of it, I began to cry, but I couldn't move except for my trembling. I couldn't speak except for my sobbing. I felt terrified and helpless at what I was witnessing, for I knew, in my heart, my father was taking the punishment I so rightly deserved.

"Well . . . after striking my father, Mr. Hoch did something I hadn't expected, something almost comical. He jumped into the classic stance of the prizefighter, left leg and foot out in front, his fists up and at the ready, as though expecting my father to attack. But my father, after steadying himself, just rubbed the left side of his face. Then he put both arms at his sides and said, just as calmly as before, 'Now, Mr. Hoch, I want you to strike the other side of my face.'

"'You're crazy,' Mr. Hoch shouted. In my mind I had to agree. I really thought my father had gone mad. Still shouting, Mr. Hoch said, 'Go home! I want nothing more to do with either one of you. You've done enough harm already. Leave us alone!'

"But he didn't turn away. He just stood there waiting for us to leave. My father, however, gave no indication he was ready to go. Instead he said, very calmly and evenly, 'Mr. Hoch, our Lord taught that I must offer you the other cheek as well.'

"Well, at that, Mr. Hoch realized what my father was trying to accomplish, for he, too, was a Christian man and knew the Lord's teaching. He threw up his hands and without shouting asked us to please just leave, go away and leave them alone. He climbed the steps, slumping under the weight of the encounter, and went in through the door held open by his trembling wife.

"My father and I walked home in silence. He uttered not a single word, but at home told my mother what I had done. She groaned in disappointment then sent me to my room where I gladly went. Her gaze was even more condemning than my father's. On my bed I wept until I slept. When I woke early in the morning I wept some more."

"But how did your parents hurt them," John asked. "I don't understand."

The priest chuckled. "Let me finish the story. That early morning after I dried my tears, I got dressed and snuck out of the house before my parents awoke. I went to Tony's house. I sat on the bottom step at their front porch and waited, praying for God's forgiveness and that He'd give me the strength to do what I knew I had to do."

"Which was?"

"To apologize to both Tony and Mr. Hoch and beg their forgiveness."

John nodded. "Ya, ya . . . and did you?"

"Yes, repeatedly, with tears flowing down my sad face. Both Mr. Hoch and Tony came outside. Mr. Hoch held me gently, by my shoulders, and said, 'and you please forgive me for striking you and your father.'

"'Yes, Mr. Hoch, I do, I do,' I said, still unable to control my tears. I wept like a baby beside a very calm and serious Tony Hoch who, at that moment and to this very day, remains my moral superior."

"But what possible harm could your parents have caused them," John asked.

The priest sipped a little more water. "Well, that's the sixty-four dollar question, isn't it? My mother remembered when we bought our house that Mr. Dorfman mentioned he had another offer, but the people needed more time to save for the down payment plus they had to sell their house. Dorfman told them if he got better terms he'd have to accept. Since my parents had sold their previous house, and had money in hand, it was a quicker deal.

"My father decided to write Mr. Dorfman who replied that, 'yes, those people were indeed the Hochs.' Even so, my parents still couldn't understand why they would be angry with us, precisely because Mr. Dorfman had disclosed his intention.

"'There must be something else,' my father said, but we were stumped. So a week later he took me by the hand, and we paid another visit to Mr. Hoch. He was surprised to see us, but not unfriendly.

"'Mr. Hoch,' my father began, 'I learned from Mr. Dorfman that you had made an offer to buy his house prior to ours, and I'm wondering if that caused you to have resentment towards us. If that's the case, my wife and I are sincerely sorry, as we were completely unaware of the situation and that it offended you and Mrs. Hoch so deeply.'

"'Ya, that's it,' Mr. Hoch replied, with a hopeless shrug.

"'But your house is every bit as nice,' my father said.

"At that moment, Tony came out. Without giving it a thought, I extended my hand and said, cheerfully, 'Hello Tony.' We shook hands in the most normal, natural way. He said 'Hi Charlie.' Then we both shut up and waited for our fathers to resume their conversation. Well, that made a great impression on Mr. Hoch. He smiled at my father and extended his hand, which my father gladly shook. It was the first time, but it would not be the last.

"'I'm sorry, Mr. Grobschmidt,' he said. 'I behaved badly, but I . . . .' He glanced at me. I knew it was my cruelty that sparked his anger and, perhaps, even increased his disappointment at losing Dorfman's house.

"'Please, let's forget that,' my father replied, knowing the shame I still felt. 'We've no quarrel with you.'

"Emitting a great sigh, Mr. Hoch said, 'Ya, I suppose our house is as nice . . . .'

"My father and I started to leave, but Mr. Hoch and Tony offered to walk us to the corner. At Franklyn Street, my father extended his hand to Mr. Hoch. We all said, 'good night.' We were set to cross the street when Mr. Hoch, out of the blue, said, 'Ya, our house is as nice, but yours has the treasure.'

"Well, treasure is a powerful word; it stopped us in our tracks.

"'Treasure?' my father asked.

"'Right in front of our eyes,' Mr. Hoch replied.

"'I'm afraid I don't see any treasure. Do you Charlie?'

"'No, Pa,' I answered.

"Mr. Hoch said 'You see treasure, Tony?' And Tony answered, 'Sure do, Pa.'

"All my father and I saw was our house with the barest, flattest, nearly treeless, five-acre rear lot one could ever imagine. In the distance, beyond our property, was a line of scrub oak and an old barn. We were at the very western edge of Chicago. At the horizon, the sky was graced with a band of fading evening light under thinning, pink clouds; beneath that glorious sky, my father and I saw not a hint of worldly treasure."

"What did they see?" John Helden asked. "Was there oil on your land?"

The priest laughed. "No, nothing that precious. Mr. Hoch explained it by saying, 'See how your house sits in the corner to the left and see how Franklyn Street lines up with the center of your property. I wanted to buy Dorfman's place, not because of the house, we like our house well enough, but because of the land. I wanted to extend Franklyn Street all the way to the west property line and then subdivide on both sides of the street. I figured I could sell twenty-nine lots. I've never had a chance to make any money except what I've made in the masonry trade, and that's a damn hard way to make a living. That was my one great opportunity, but you stole it from me.'

"'We had no idea,' my father replied. 'I didn't know the offer was yours.'

"'Doesn't matter . . . fact is you stole my dream,' Mr. Hoch said, bitterly. 'You knew Dorfman had a prior offer. Had you any decency you would have let his property pass. There were other houses you could have bought.'

"Well, John, my poor father was utterly dismayed. He was not a man to frustrate someone else's dream, nor did he lack decency.

He looked at me sadly. I could see he was struggling to make some kind of sense of it, for he didn't think Mr. Hoch was being reasonable at all. Dorfman never mentioned the Hochs by name. He willingly sold my parents his house. He had that right, and they had the right to buy it. If anything, Mr. Hoch should have been angry with Mr. Dorfman, not my parents. But even that would have been unreasonable.

"We went home, and my father told my mother the whole story. She asked what we could do. He answered that he didn't know, but, as I said before, my father was a very smart man. A week later, on a Sunday afternoon, we again paid a visit to Mr. Hoch.

"When we arrived, Mrs. Hoch invited us in. Tony was there. He and I had grown more friendly, as often happens after a fight, and all my stupid prejudices were gone. My father and Mr. Hoch greeted each other courteously; then Mrs. Hoch asked us to sit. Well, what my father had to say then really put an end to the war. There's no doubt in my mind that the war ended when my father turned the other cheek, but maybe the peace couldn't begin because there still was that lingering disappointment in Mr. Hoch's heart.

"'Mr. Hoch,' my father began.

"'Call me Anton,' he interrupted.

"'Anton, I'd like to make a proposal, a business proposal.' Believe me, John, that got his attention. 'I will deed my land, except the land that our house sits upon, to a partnership if you would be willing to provide your expertise to subdivide the land just as you envision.'

"Well, you should have seen the look on Mr. Hoch's face. He was totally dumbfounded, utterly flabbergasted.

"My father continued. 'If you hire the surveyor to plat the land and get all the necessary permits for streets, sewers and water, I will pay the bills for those services, provided you allow me to recover those costs once we begin to sell the lots. Any profits we make over our costs, we split fifty-fifty. What do you say?'

"Well, Mr. Hoch didn't know what to say . . . didn't know if he should laugh, cry, sit, stand or shout. Finally, he grabbed his slender wife, and they began to dance the *Schottische* in a tight, little circle in the middle of the parlor, while he shouted out a wordless tune. Well, the *Schottische,* danced by a portly man and a petite woman with such dubious musical accompaniment in a tiny space with heavy feet stomping dangerously close to dainty ones, looked awfully silly. We all began to laugh and no one harder than Tony. My father stood. Mr. Hoch embraced him. It was then, at that precise moment of their embrace, that I realized my father truly knew how to end a war and build the peace. They worked out the deal without a lawyer. Nothing was written down. They spoke clearly. They trusted each other, and their handshakes were sacrosanct. My mother invited the Hochs for coffee and kuchen the next Sunday. She and Mrs. Hoch became best friends, as did my father and Mr. Hoch. He got the land surveyed, got the permits to extend the street and sewer, hired the road contractors, and even painted the big sign advertising lots for sale that Tony and I helped plant right across from our house. And, wonderfully, old Mr. Hoch realized his dream. He and my father both made money. Every single lot sold for a profit."

"There was a man by the name of Hoch involved in the building of our church," John said.

"Yes," the priest answered. "That was my dear friend, Tony Hoch. He went to the University of Illinois and became an architect. I went to the seminary and became a priest. We've remained friends ever since our boyhood. I asked him to design our wonderful church."

"Well, well, quite a story . . . ."

"The church's stone exterior is in honor of Tony's father: a simple, honest, kindhearted, hardworking stonemason . . . a bricklayer."

"Very nice, very good indeed . . . ."

"Now, John, do you see what is needed to end the war," the priest asked.

"Ya . . . France and England must turn the other cheek."

"What about Germany?"

John didn't answer.

"We've always agreed Germany is the better nation. If that's true then she must turn the other cheek. She must lay down her arms. She must withdraw from the fields of France."

"The French and British would chase her to the Rhine."

"Let them. Then they certainly show the world they are the lesser nations."

"They'd occupy the Rhineland."

"They'd tire of it soon enough," the priest said. "Wives, mothers, and sweethearts want their men home. The occupation wouldn't last long."

The priest escorted John to the front door. They stepped onto the concrete stoop. It was a black night, save for the spherical halos glowing around the street lamps, and very late.

"Goodnight, Father."

"Goodnight, John; get a good night's sleep. Things won't seem so bleak in the morning."

"Oh, I'm not so sure about that. Pinkey will still be dead, and my wife will still support this damn war."

Before closing the door, the priest said, "If you truly are a pacifist, John Helden, make no war with your wife."

+ + +

When George Helden learned of Pinkey's death he went "all to pieces," as his mother later told Mira Jablowski. He refused to eat his supper, which was not in keeping with his nature at all. He wept on his pillow, wept wandering about the house, and wept in his mother's arms. His mutterings began with either "how" or "why," but he never allowed his parents to offer an explanation. All evening his soft crying or loud wailing continued until it finally drove Augusta, Johnny, and Julius upstairs to bed. Clarence was lucky; he wasn't home.

George's behavior disgusted John Helden. He realized he had to do something for his second son, so he made George sit at the dining room table. John removed Augusta's centerpiece and, in its place, set a bottle of whisky and two shot glasses.

Still sobbing, George buried his face in his arms.

"George, you've got to get hold of yourself now. Pinkey's gone, and you crying like a baby isn't going to bring him back. I want you to stop crying . . . look at me."

George didn't move.

"Look at me George," John demanded.

George raised his head. His red eyes streamed tears onto his cheeks and chin. John handed him his handkerchief. George blew his nose. "I can't believe he was killed, Pa. I just can't believe it. I've lost my best friend forever." He began to cry again.

"I know, George, but you've gotta get over it."

"I'll never get over it."

"Well, in a way you're probably right. You'll miss Pinkey, that's for sure, but now you've got to get over this damn crying. You gotta work in the morning. You can't bawl like a baby in front of the men."

That made sense to George. John, his arm rigid as a beam, grasped the whisky bottle and raised it towards his son. He held the open end at an angle waiting for George's approval to pour the fiery liquid into the shot glass.

"It's medicine, George. It'll do you good. You need a good night's sleep."

"But Pa, Ma said we should never drink whisky. She calls it the devil's brew."

"I know, but this is different. You're taking it for medicinal purposes."

"Pa, I don't know . . . ."

"Have some George; it won't hurt you. You'll sleep better."

"Maybe I should ask Ma . . . ."

"Damn it, George, your mother's asleep. I don't want you asking her anything. I'm your father, and I'm telling you – you won't get Pinkey outta your head until you have a little medicine to help ease your mind towards rest."

"I don't want to disappoint Ma."

"Damn it, George, don't disappoint me." John hated George's crying and felt disgust at such obvious weakness in his second son. Besides, John wanted to go to bed. "Come on now; let me pour you a little."

"Okay," George agreed.

He wiped his eyes with the backs of his hands, leaving the soiled handkerchief on the table edge. He watched his father's hand rotate, lowering the neck of the bottle until the amber liquid flowed like quicksilver into George's shot glass. John poured it two-thirds full, then his own. In his nineteen years, George had never tasted whisky. He raised the glass to his mouth, sipped a little and grimaced.

"No, no, George. This isn't sipping whisky. Watch me."

John Helden put the shot glass to his mouth, tilted his head backwards, then with one, sudden, swift arm movement swallowed it all.

"Now, you do it, George, the same way . . . then we go to bed."

In spite of his father's example, George drank the whisky like milk. Grabbing his throat, he bolted to the kitchen sink, turned on the spigot and, ducking his head under the spout, gulped to ease the burning. He coughed hard then gulped more. Finally, his father put his arm around his waist and helped him climb the stairs.

George woke wondering if he had slept at all. He stared at a ceiling he could not see. He had no lingering feelings of sleepiness, no idea how long he had been in bed, and when he thought of Pinkey, felt no sadness, realizing, perhaps, he was at last getting over the horror of his friend's death.

He heard Clarence's steady breathing, but nothing else. *When did he get home?* George scarcely remembered going to bed; still in his clothes, he couldn't remember crawling under the covers.

He thought of his father and drinking the whisky; "the medicinal," as he called it. *It burned bad . . . Pa must have helped me to bed.* George lay still, staring blindly into the darkness. *I needed water.* He felt thirsty now. After several moments, he got up and descended the stairs in shadowy silence. Putting his mouth under the spout of the kitchen sink he drank. When he finished, standing there wide-awake, he told himself, *I'll never get back to sleep.*

From that point, it took little to conclude that he probably needed just a tad more of his pa's powerful medicine. He turned on a light and leaned against the door jamb between the kitchen and dining room. *Ma doesn't want us drinking whisky, but Pa drinks it and calls it medicine. In the tavern it's poison, but not at home . . . I don't understand the difference, but I sure need a good night's sleep.* Then, his arm trembling slightly, he reached to the top shelf of the cupboard where his father – George recalled ever since he was a little boy – always kept an open bottle of whisky.

An innocent remedy to ease the sorrow of a son launched a dark, inexorable passage through a wasteland of pain, disillusionment, and sadness. Augusta Helden, helpless and hopeless, witnessed her second son's dissolute wanderings; at their end, her heart was broken. By his twenty-first birthday, the witch of whiskey had enslaved George Helden.

Chapter 9 ~ 1930

Of all human conditions, situations, and states, none holds more potential for true happiness or genuine misery than the ancient and illustrious institution of marriage. A young man and woman, upon meeting and perceiving one another, correctly or incorrectly, as mates, move inevitably toward the act of becoming a *couple*. One day they discover within themselves an unlimited source of faith and hope regarding the blissful possibility of finding everlasting happiness with each other as husband and wife. Nothing seems beyond attainment with this uniquely special person. The trust each places in the realization of being in love becomes a self-fulfilling triumph, immune to any attack of reason. Thus, joy and optimism in the mere feelings of love replace such unexciting considerations as the study of another's character, analysis of personality, a penetrating insight into family background, and an objective comparison of goals, values, preferences, interests, similarities, dissimilarities, likes and dislikes, especially as they all pertain to child rearing, in-laws, social relationships, religion, politics, housekeeping, and the handling of money. Beauty and charm conspire with faith and hope to beget sublime feelings such that when the exalted transcendental emotional level is finally attained, nothing on earth could dissuade the lovers from marching down the aisle, radiant and beaming, arms and hearts locked like links of chain, toward the secret, veiled, and mysterious future of their married life that stretches before them like a bright, limitless fog.

Luella Schmidt and her fiancé hosted an elegant dinner party where John Helden Jr., a handsome chap of twenty-seven from Milwaukee's south side, met Anita Thilman, a doctor's daughter of alluring beauty from the north side. Her loveliness and quiet grace prompted an immediate interest on his part. If Anita, however, had a similar reaction it wasn't obvious. During the course of the evening John became quite charmed by this lovely young woman, while she demurely retained a dignified detachment. Luella later noted that John became the "life of the party," not because he wished to impress Anita, but rather because of his great pleasure at being part of such a splendid soiree in the presence of an unattached beauty. He proved in an easy, natural, and even humble manner to be the best conversationalist at the dinner table. His style of speaking was so engaging that others who didn't know him were truly impressed. For her part, Miss Thilman enjoyed John's presence far more than she was willing to reveal.

Luella knew John in high school as a young man of good character and considerable promise. She had every intention, when she decided to throw this party, of introducing him to Miss Thilman whom she had befriended at Marquette University several years before. She suspected John and Anita just might get along. Nevertheless, by the end of the evening only Anita knew that this tall, charming, dark-haired man did indeed interest her.

Several days later John called Luella.

"No, I haven't spoken with Anita since the party," she lied. "Yes, I think she might have an interest in going out with you. Actually, I thought she responded to you quite favorably. No, no, John . . . you made a good impression. You certainly were talkative. Yes, as a matter of fact, I do have her phone number. Would you like me to call for you? No, of course I don't have to . . . I just thought . . . well, I know you're perfectly capable. My goodness, a talker like you could charm Mrs. Hoover. All right then . . . let me know what happens and don't forget little Luella if you two become lovebirds. Bye-bye."

He called Anita the second Monday evening after Luella's party. He didn't want to seem too eager. From the hallway telephone at his father's house where he and his younger brother, Julius, lived, his opening remarks went better than expected. The lilt in her voice, when she agreed to a date the following Saturday evening, delighted John.

Dr. and Mrs. Dominic P. Thilman had built their fine home on the northwest corner of North Avenue and Grant Boulevard in 1921. Twenty years prior, with a five thousand dollar wedding gift from his bride's wealthy parents, Dr. Thilman bought a large, two story framed building on North Avenue between Tenth and Eleventh Streets. He remodeled the upstairs into a residence; downstairs he built the *Thilman Sanatorium* where he administered the famous

European water remedy, the *Kneipp Cure*. Many patients came from the Midwest and East including, in 1911, Mr. Connie Mack, owner of the Philadelphia Athletics baseball team.

For twenty years the apartment above the Sanatorium remained the Thilman's home, as they raised three children: Anita, Lewis, and Dominic. But the doctor's wife, Mary Louise, grew to hate the place. It was cold, drafty, and difficult to heat in the winter, insufferably hot in the summer and, in all seasons, the wood walls quivered like sounding boards. The family, patients, and staff heard street noise almost as though there were no walls at all. The architect for their new home specified clay tile block behind the exterior brick veneer knowing it was important to the Doctor and his very particular wife to have the noise on North Avenue muffled. All three knew, in the years ahead, the street would get even busier, as the city continued its relentless growth westward.

Dr. Thilman's new office, with its entrance on North Avenue, occupied the wing off the southwest corner of the house. The home's formal entrance faced east on Grant Boulevard where two flights of concrete steps led from the sidewalk to the entry sun porch. Above was the window dormer of Anita's small front bedroom. Now she stood discreetly out of sight behind a lace curtain in the dimly lit room and watched, as the handsome, young man ascended the steps to the front door where Anita's mother waited impassively to greet him.

"Mr. Helden, how do you do? Please, come in." Mary Louise Thilman was fifty-two. The moment John met her, he knew the source of Anita's great beauty.

He stepped into the foyer. To the right a staircase with carved newel posts, well-proportioned balusters, and a dark-stained, polished banister rose to the second floor. Carved, wood panels adorned the staircase wall and below the balustrade. Above the wainscot, several oil paintings ascended the stair wall. To the left, a wide, cased archway framed the view into the spacious parlor where John spotted an ebony grand piano. A large fireplace faced with green and black Italian marble dominated the far wall. John realized, in comparison, the ordinariness of his father's house.

"May I take your coat?"

"Yes, thank you."

"Sit down, please." She gestured towards the sofa. "The Doctor will be here in a moment . . . I'm sure Anita is almost ready." Mary Louise noticed what John was admiring. "Do you play?"

"A little." He hadn't expected a Steinway grand. He learned to play on a fine, old Steinway upright that his father bought for his mother when John was eight. She gave him his first lessons and recognized his talent. Even as a boy he had a beautiful touch. "It's a true gift," his mother often told her husband and boasted to friends. "The gift of an artist . . . ."

A large, imposing man entered the room. His face intimated a life of unrelenting work, sacrifice, and dedication. John rose in awe of Anita's father. *My God,* John thought, *he looks like he carries the weight of the world.*

"Mr. Helden, I'd like you to meet Dr. Thilman."

John extended his hand. "Dr. Thilman, how do you do, sir?"

"Fine, fine . . . sit down, please. I understand you're a member of the Helden manufacturing family."

"Yes I am. Presently, I'm a sales engineer."

"Tell me, John, are you a graduate engineer?"

The question stung like a slap in the face. "No sir. I had two years of mechanical engineering, but then went to work full time in the engineering department at the Company."

It took only that single question and its honest answer to deflate John's confidence and restore his humility. He regretted he hadn't obtained his degree, for he had the opportunity. His parents urged him to.

"Mr. Helden plays the piano." Mrs. Thilman wished to defer her husband's inquiries to a later time if, indeed, there would be a later time.

Anita had descended the stairs and now entered the room. Standing beside her dignified parents, John found her even lovelier than at Luella's. She smiled so sweetly at him that, when he thought about it later, he decided at that moment she was the girl he wished to marry.

He rose. "Good evening Anita."

"John, how nice to see you again."

The four chatted until Anita asked, "Would you play? I know my parents would enjoy it."

Had John the choice, he would have preferred Dr. Thilman's

interrogation. He was uncomfortable playing for people he didn't know well, let alone people he didn't know at all. His nervous self-consciousness changed playing the piano into work. Rather than letting his natural gifts of touch and technique express themselves, as they did in the privacy of practice, he concentrated too hard on his effort, which diminished it. Nevertheless, the beautiful tone and perfect action of the Steinway so thrilled him that he played Poldini's *Marche Mignonne* well enough to make a good impression. His fingers stumbled a few times at the more intricate passages, but no one in the tiny audience seemed to mind.

"Well, nicely done my boy," Dr. Thilman said. "You play very beautifully."

Anita smiled at John, silently clapping while raising the point of her hands to her lips. That John's playing delighted her parents pleased her though John knew he could have done better. Anita's parents realized John's playing indicated intelligence, discipline, and hard work; necessary virtues if they were to consider a young man suitable for their daughter's hand. John, in spite of his academic shortcomings, had gotten off on the right foot, as people used to say.

As the weeks passed, there were more dates for John and Anita. After two months they were seeing each other every Saturday evening and, occasionally, on Sunday afternoons. He called several times during the week; they'd have long, pleasant conversations about their everyday lives. Anita worked as a secretary in a downtown law firm. John, by far the most ambitious, hardworking, and enthusiastic young sales engineer for the Helden Company, was perceived by all who knew him – including Anita – as a young man with a future. Inevitably, they became a couple, not only in their own hearts and minds, but also in the minds of their families. Soon, John and Anita's Saturday and Sunday dates became as regular as a metronome.

Dr. and Mrs. Thilman grew comfortable with the realization that their daughter might very likely marry this agreeable fellow. It pleased them when John and Anita started attending Sunday Mass together. After all, Mary Louise Thilman had three brothers who were priests; one of them, her beloved brother Johnny, had been Secretary to Archbishop Messmer in the early years of the century.

The family convinced itself that one day Father Johnny, too, would wear the bishop's miter.

But tragedy struck. In 1912 Father Johnny at the age of forty died of peritonitis on a trip to Europe with the Archbishop. He had suffered a burst appendix several years earlier; surgery saved him then, but couldn't save him twice. The family stumbled into a state of shocked disbelief and most of all Mary Louise who wept for days.

Father Johnny's coffin, at his elderly father's directive, was prepared for transatlantic passage to New York and then by train to Milwaukee. It arrived at Dr. Thilman's Sanatorium in early 1913 where the entire family, including five brothers and two sisters, gathered to grieve. Eleven children had been born into the family although they were never all alive at the same time. In 1872, when their mother was pregnant with Johnny, a smallpox epidemic claimed, in a period of only two weeks, the lives of three of her children: a girl fifteen, a boy eleven, and another girl nine. Father Johnny was born shortly after she buried those three, dear children. Six years later, in 1878, Mary Louise was born, the last of the offspring. She became the favorite, little darling of her brother Johnny.

Silent and sorrowful, Mary Louise gazed upon Father Johnny's coffin encased in zinc. She watched with trepidation, as her brothers prepared to cut it open to expose the well-constructed wooden box within. There was concern if they should open the nailed lid because they wondered about the possibility of decay. Nevertheless, the desire to see in death this wonderfully accomplished brother, a Doctor of Divinity, overcame their apprehensions. To everyone's amazement there was no odor save the sweet fragrance of the chamomile blossoms that surrounded the body like garland. Father Johnny, in the white vestments of his pure priesthood, wore a finely trimmed beard. When the family escorted their mother to view the body, she who gave birth to him forty years earlier shrieked a mournful scream that Anita, then only ten, never forgot. Years later she could still hear it in her mind's ear: a perpetual remembrance of the immense loss and sorrow of her grandmother's life. But now, Anita had met John Helden Jr., and it was he who began dominating her thoughts.

Lew and Dom enjoyed teasing their big sister about her beau. They had their opinions. "He's pleasant enough, but not a college grad. You should think about that. A man's education means so much nowadays," Dom said.

"His job's at the same level as other men who are graduate engineers," Anita replied.

"Nepotism," Dom, the little brother in age and stature, shot back. "He's a nephew of the owner . . . nepotism, plain and simple." Dom always enjoyed offering a quick contrary opinion.

"You're a fine one to talk about nepotism. You've never had a job in your life. If it weren't for Dad, where would you be? He pays everything."

Lew sensed the need to defend the largesse both brothers received from their successful, physician father. "Dom's preparing for a distinguished legal career."

"You think law school's easy?"

"No, I just don't think you should criticize John. He's at the same salary level and has as much, or even more, responsibility than other young engineers. And he makes enough to support a wife and family."

"Ooooh," Dom sang. "And who might the little wife be?"

Anita blushed. "I just mean he's doing well financially, that's all; better than either of you."

"Yeah, you just wait till I'm outta law school. I'll make a hellava lot more dough than some half-educated engineer."

Lew knew better; times were tough for new lawyers. He had a chance to join a downtown law firm after graduating from Northwestern, but decided to go into private practice instead. After a few months, it proved a mistake. Now he wasn't at all sure he wanted to make law his career, but he wasn't ready to reveal that to Dom. Increasingly, financial investments and politics attracted Lew's attention. Stocks were cheap; he bought, for himself and his parents, good companies at low prices, well off their 1929 highs. He predicted, "Someday these companies will come back. We'll all make money. This damn depression can't last forever."

Lew, however, let his younger brother stick to the idea that *Thilman & Thilman, Attorneys at Law,* would "set the town on fire," as Dom liked to say. "Within a year after I graduate, folks will be talking about a fantastic new lawyer, namely me, D.J. Thilman. They'll beat a path to our door Lew . . . you'll see. I've got big ideas."

"Good, Dom. I like your enthusiasm."

Anita listened placidly to the banter of her brothers, something she had done a great deal in her life. Everyone in the extended family knew that Lew and Dom were indulged by their generous parents. *They seem almost like spoiled children,* Anita thought. She preferred John Helden's more mature companionship. He had worked ever since he was a boy. Her father was like that, but *not my brothers,* she realized. *They even complain when Mother asks them to shovel the walk.*

"Yeah, Anita," Dom said. "You say I never had a job, but what about my music? Playing in an orchestra is honest work. It makes people happy and pays well . . . more than you think."

"Playing the clarinet on a Saturday night isn't my idea of a career," Anita said. "You sleep most of the week . . . when you're awake you talk like a big shot."

"Sis, I'm still in law school. I need summers to rest my brilliant but somewhat overworked brain. And, hey, I play more gigs than you'll ever know. I just don't talk about it. You'd be surprised how I get around this town, the people I meet, places I go, what I see." He winked at Lew. The previous Saturday night he played at a party where, after a few drinks, a remarkably compliant young woman took off her clothes and danced nude.

"Hey Dom," Lew said, "when we have a trial, bring your clarinet. During lulls you could play a little *Blue Skies* . . . I'm sure the judge would get a kick out of that."

"I'll serenade the jury, while you hand out our business cards. On the back we'll print, *Acquit Thilman's client and earn one free clarinet lesson.*"

"That's a terrific idea, especially if you wanna get us disbarred."

The brothers laughed. Anita rolled her eyes and left the room. John Helden Jr. was coming; she had to get ready.

Since their first date, John visited Anita's family on many occasions. He got to know her parents, brothers, and even her uncles, Father Jean Pierre and Father Joe. Mary Louise's priest brothers had parishes in small towns an hour's drive from Milwaukee. John and Anita often went there on Sunday afternoons. He met other uncles and aunts and many of Anita's fifty-six first cousins. All her relatives, including the priests, thought John a fine fellow.

During that congenial period, however, Anita didn't have occasions to meet John's family. The first several months it wasn't a concern because they were still new to each other, and it was his responsibility to come calling. Living with her parents there were more opportunities to involve him with her family. After another month, though, Anita decided it was time to meet his father and three brothers. John's mother, Augusta, had died suddenly in 1927, when John was twenty-five.

"My mother and I were very close. Her death was completely unexpected."

Anita asked, "How old was she?"

"Fifty-nine . . . died in her sleep of heart failure. It was very sad; she was the loving heart of our family."

"I'm sorry, John. My mother and I are close, too."

"We did a lot together . . . things my father just wouldn't do."

"Like what?"

"Concerts, plays . . . my father has little interest in the finer things. When I was eighteen, my mother and I heard the great Russian pianist, Josef Lhevinne, play at the Pabst. That made an unforgettable impression on both of us . . . he played so beautifully. I try to imitate him."

"You play very well."

John grinned in appreciation. "I remember that spring day vividly. On the way to the theater we passed a pet shop. There was a little English bulldog in the window. He got very excited when my mother tapped the glass. He was a cute little fella. She found joy in simple things, but she loved the finer things, too."

"Including puppies . . . ."

"Oh, sure . . . ."

"Didn't you once tell me she was a convert?"

"Yes. My parents were married at St. Paul's Lutheran Church in Tess Corners in 1894. When they moved to Milwaukee they attended a Catholic Church – my father was Catholic – and, after a while, my mother expressed an interest in converting. Several months later she was pregnant, but the baby – a little girl – was stillborn. My mother told me it broke her heart, but she offered her sorrow to the Lord and, like so many converts, became a devout Catholic.

"Two years later she was pregnant again. My brother Clarence

– thank God – was born alive and healthy. George came next, then me, and Julius – Juley, as he's called – is the baby."

"And now the baby is a young doctor," Anita said.

John chuckled.

"Your family, especially your father, must be very proud."

"We are, but my father just doesn't enjoy life the way he used to."

"Since your mother died?"

John nodded. "Anita, I haven't told you much about my father, but he made a terrible mistake in his life."

"Is it something you'd rather I didn't know?"

"No, you should know. He's Works Manager at Helden; ever since my mother died all he does is work. I think he's still trying to get over her death."

"That's not a mistake . . . seems like a normal reaction."

"That's not what I'm referring to. He was a co-founder of the company, but in 1920 sold his stock to his brother – my uncle, Peter – for fifteen hundred dollars. There was a slowdown in metal fabricating after the Great War. My father tired of working in a business that didn't seem to be going anywhere, so he decided to buy a shoe store. He wanted to be his own boss. The store didn't do well, so after several years he sold it and went to his brother and asked to buy his old stock back. He wanted to work at the company again. Uncle Peter said, 'Sure but now the stock's worth three thousand.' Well, my pa didn't have that kind of money, so my uncle hired him for his old job as Work's Manager. Then the company really began to grow. My father realized had he not gone into the shoe business, but kept his stock, he'd be much better off. The whole family knows he made a tremendous mistake. He calls it the biggest mistake of his life. It's true because now he'd have almost the same wealth as Uncle Peter. My pa can't get it out of his mind; he's haunted by it. I think that's why he works so much. He's from the old country, Anita. He was only a boy when he came . . . spoke no English, worked on the farm, never finished high school. Now he leaves early and gets home late, day after day. All he's ever known his entire life is hard work. He'll never have enough money to buy back his old stock and probably not even to retire, not until he's in his seventies. He's not up-to-date like your father."

"Who cooks his dinner?"

"One night he goes to Clarence's, then George's, then Aunt Lizzie's. There's no shortage of cooks in the family. I suppose he'd prefer his dinner at home, but he's helpless in the kitchen. He never cooked a meal in his life. I'm afraid he might do something foolish because of it, like remarry."

Anita grimaced. "John, why say that's foolish? It'd be good for him. He should have a companion . . . someone at the end of the day to cook a good meal. Maybe he'd work less."

"My mother always said he was hard to live with. He's stubborn, has a temper. I suspect a new wife would find him just as hard to live with."

"Is he difficult for you?"

John laughed. "No . . . we get along fine."

Eventually, Anita came to know John's three brothers. Clarence lacked his mother's refinement, but it didn't matter; he was smart, aggressive, and tight-fisted. For it, Uncle Peter made him the company's Purchasing Agent. Clarence had a dog's nose for a bargain and was a tough negotiator. He made, in spite of not having a college education, an excellent buyer. He knew little of literature, history, and philosophy and didn't possess the musical talent of his brothers. Only occasionally would one hear him humming an off-pitch tune.

He became absorbed in the success of his uncle's growing company and devoted his life to it. With a tough sell reputation many suppliers lavished him with Christmas gifts of fine cheese, sausage, fruit baskets, candies, nuts, cigars, and bottles of good Canadian and Scotch whisky, and English gin, especially, during Prohibition. He was treated to dinner by steel salesmen, machinery and equipment salesmen, and parts vendors who hoped to become suppliers to the company. That's the way business was done in the twenties. Clarence reveled in it. He loved his work, relegating his home life to a secondary position. He abandoned his family so many evenings that his wife became a treacherous nag. The more he went out with salesmen and stayed late drinking and playing bar dice, the more his wife nagged. The more she nagged, the more he went out eating and drinking.

Clarence relished the city's German restaurants. Over the years, he gained excess weight; indeed, he looked bloated or, as Julius once remarked to John, "He looks like he might burst." Clarence enjoyed cigars, inhaling them as casually as he smoked cigarettes, which was a decades' long habit.

Initially, prohibition was nothing short of a personal disaster for Clarence, but he compensated just fine. He knew every high-class speakeasy in town and every good restaurant that served liquor on the sly. All this rich living took a toll on his health and cut short the life he devoted to his uncle's thriving company. He suffered gout his last five years, and, finally, in a sense, he did burst, or at least one, tiny, blood vessel in his brain did. That was all it took. After forty-one years of loyal servitude, he died at fifty-three, outlived by his wealthy uncle, seventeen years his senior, and outlived thirty years by his bitter, unforgiving wife.

George Helden also worked for the company since the age of twelve and would work in the shop until he retired at sixty-seven: fifty-five years of hard, physical labor. He began by sorting nuts and bolts in the machine shop, but showed no interest in learning the machinist's trade though his father urged him to. George wasn't strong in mathematics, a requisite for a boy to become a skilled tool and die maker. Instead, he learned to operate the heavy brakes and shears that bent and cut steel sheet and plate. He mastered gas and electric arc welding and gave excellent instruction to other men who wanted to learn the welder's trade. He became a skilled overhead crane operator, picking a ten-ton load and placing it as delicately as his mother set china on her dining room table.

Best of all, though, George played ragtime piano. He never had any lessons; unlike his two younger brothers, his mother gave him no instruction. He never learned to read music, but his hands and heart could imitate the syncopating rhythms he heard at the taverns and pool halls along Lincoln Avenue. George sat for hours at the Steinway upright, entertaining the family who never tired of his improvising. John studied serious music with good teachers and played with the artist's touch. But he could no more sit down and play ragtime than George could play Chopin. The sharp contrast of their respective talents amazed Augusta, though she never fully appreciated George's. Sadly, he knew how his mother felt, and, as the years passed, he played less and less.

At age twenty, when he was coming into his own as a skilled mechanic in the great metal working shop of his uncle's rapidly growing company, George discovered the simple pleasure of stopping after work on a Friday for a shot and a beer. After his initiation at the time of Pinkey Jablowski's death, he discovered he had a real fondness for whisky, a genuine appreciation of it. Unfortunately, what he had was what the family called, "the weakness." By the time Prohibition began, he was on a path to alcoholism. Every Friday night he got rip-roaring drunk to the profound sadness of his forgiving young wife. Irene bore George a fine son and daughter whom George loved more than he ever could express. Finally, at age thirty-one, he quit drinking because of Irene's incessant threat that she and the children would leave him if he didn't.

Once in his late twenties and still drinking heavily, George mistakenly went to his father's home late on a Friday night, though he had his own little house to go to with Irene there waiting. When he staggered in, reeking of booze and cigarettes, his brother, John, became furious. Of the brothers, George's weakness most troubled John. That night his patience ended. He beat up his defenseless brother with his fists. Of course, George was in such a hopeless state that he could barely stand anyway, and John's first, glancing blow knocked George down with such a terrific crash that it woke up their father and brother, Julius, who came running to the front hall. George had passed out, though John boasted afterwards that he knocked him out. Once down, George never got up till morning when he remembered nothing. The first question he muttered was his wife's name, as though she might help him understand why in the world he was waking up on his father's floor. After John threw the first harmless punch he began to weep. The last thing he wanted was to hurt his pitiful, alcoholic brother. He wanted to help, but only Irene could, and eventually she did. George, to his great credit, finally quit drinking and, in the forty-one years until his death, never touched another drop.

Julius, the youngest brother, was the star of the family. Eventually, John knew he had to introduce Anita to all his brothers and, in Clarence and George's cases, to their wives and, of course, their father. But John thought it wise to first introduce Anita to Julius, the brother of whom all were most proud. John knew Julius would make a good impression because he always did. When Anita learned Julius was a doctor, she took note. She knew what a special man her father was. For years she observed how hard he worked caring for thousands of patients. Because of him, Anita respected the medical profession greatly.

They were driving to County General Hospital on the far west side to visit Julius who interned there. Anita said, "Tell me more about him."

"From early on, Juley wanted to be a doctor. When company came and Juley got talking, sooner or later he'd tell them when he grew up that's what he was going to be. I remember one night at the dinner table – maybe Juley was in third grade – he asked our pa what he had to do to become a doctor. My father thought about it and told him, 'Juley, you start tonight by doing your homework, and you do it better than ever before. If you don't understand something, ask your mother. Then read ahead in your Reader, at least one story. Tomorrow do your homework better than tonight, and when you finish, practice your sums. You have to study every day all through high school, always learning what you're supposed to, and always doing more than what's expected. If you master science and mathematics, then when you get to college you'll be ready to study to become a doctor.'"

". . . excellent advice."

"Yes, and Juley took it. Every evening he studied after supper; not once did he have to be told. In high school he took four years of science and mathematics and graduated near the top of his class. There were some smart kids at South Division, but I don't think anyone was smarter in science."

"John, at Holy Angels I had three years of math and one of biology, half of what your brother had."

"Well, you never intended to be a doctor."

Anita laughed out loud. "No . . . I didn't graduate near the top either."

"Juley did well in pre-med, but had to work hard to get his M.D. He was above average, no question, but med school was tough, even for him. Now he's interning and waiting for the results of his State board exam."

"My father told us if he had to take the examinations now, he'd probably fail. He said it's difficult to keep up with all the changes and reading. We went to California in 1911 to see my uncle, my dad's brother, and we liked California. I really think my mother would have loved to live there. My uncle wanted us to move west, but my dad said "no" because he was afraid he'd fail the California examinations."

"I'm glad your folks stayed in Milwaukee."

"Are you? And why is that?"

"Well, I'm glad we met." Right away, John regretted he said it so matter-of-factly. He realized his tone didn't convey the force of his feelings.

In the darkness of the Ford's interior, intermittently lit by the headlights of an oncoming car, Anita stared at him in disappointment.

They were quiet for a while until John, his voice low, passionate, and resolute, said, "Anita, I'm very glad we met, very glad."

She was overjoyed to hear it.

At the hospital, the receptionist paged Dr. Helden. John and Anita waited in the lobby. When Julius arrived, his short stature surprised Anita. He was only a little taller than her brother, Dom. Nevertheless, Julius was nice looking, and Anita certainly could tell he was John's brother.

Julius smiled. "So, finally I get to meet the lovely Miss Thilman. Johnny said you're the prettiest girl in Milwaukee. I think he might be right. I'm delighted to meet you."

Anita extended her hand. He had charmed her just as John had hoped, for Julius stood as the most inviting portal to the rest of the family. He had a pleasant demeanor, but Anita sensed his seriousness. As they walked towards the elevator, Julius, talkative and light-hearted, expressed pleasure that John brought Anita to visit. They took the elevator to the fourth floor.

"This is my domain," Julius said. "There's a senior doctor-in-charge and another intern. For the most part, barring the need for a specialist, the three of us look after all the patients here."

Anita glanced about. "What medical conditions?"

"General practice . . . pretty much everything: appendicitis, heart trouble, broken bones, and anything else that's not highly contagious. We see all kinds of stuff. I like that. Remember, Johnny, what I used to tell you? I don't want to specialize."

A slender, young man approached, not as tall as John, but taller than Julius. From two steps away he said, "Dr. Helden, introduce me to your guests."

If Julius experienced any kind of emotional reaction to the command, which indeed he did, it wasn't apparent to John or Anita. "Dr. Messert, I'd like you to meet my brother, John, and his sweetheart, Anita Thilman."

"Well, well, well . . . how do you do, Miss Thilman?" Messert, his black hair combed straight back, grinned at Anita, as he eyed her beauty from face to feet. He completely ignored John.

Anita tentatively extended her hand that Dr. Messert prepared to shake just as tentatively, mocking her initial reaction. "I had no idea the Helden men had such fine taste in women." He leaned towards John. "How the hell are you?"

Before John could answer, Messert addressed Anita. "Why is the name *Thilman* familiar to me?"

Julius answered. "Anita's father is Dr. Dominic Thilman. You might have heard of him."

"Oh yes, he was a top baby doctor, right? I guess I did read something about that."

"Yes," Anita said. "For seven straight years he delivered more babies than any other doctor in Milwaukee. We're very proud of him."

"You should be . . . methinks that makes him a damn good midwife." Dr. Messert laughed, though Anita and Julius didn't find the remark funny. John chuckled; Anita noticed it. For the first time since they met, she was displeased.

"Anton and I were in med school," Julius said, "now we intern together."

John cut in. "Is this the fellow you used to study with?"

"Occasionally."

"Listen folks, I helped your little brother get through med school. Don't let him tell you otherwise. Now I've got to run. Miss Thilman, it was a distinct pleasure." Then a perfunctory, "So long John." He left without shaking John's hand.

When Messert was far enough down the corridor, John said, "Well, he seems like a nice enough chap . . . ."

"I didn't like him at all," Anita whispered. "He seems arrogant . . . used vulgar language. And, John, he ignored you. Plus, it was uncalled for to joke about my father. Julius, what's he really like?"

"Arrogant, vulgar . . . ."

"Well," John said, "I didn't want to say anything bad about someone I just met."

"If it's true, why not?" Anita asked.

"Johnny, you've got yourself a no-nonsense young lady here."

For the first time since he met Anita, John's confidence plunged. He knew he shouldn't have laughed at Messert's disparaging remark about her father. He regretted it, but could say nothing to mitigate the damage he imagined he had done.

Julius headed towards the elevator. "We're going down to the third floor. I want to show you one of the more unusual cases I've dealt with."

He unlocked the door to the lab and turned on the light. Personnel were gone for the night. With a small key he opened a white, metal cabinet, took out a glass specimen jar and set it on the counter. John and Anita stared at its contents, while Julius raised it towards the light.

"What is it?" John asked.

"A human embryo, in formaldehyde, about six weeks old. It's only two inches long, but if you look under the microscope, you see remarkable detail"

"Did the woman miscarry?" Anita asked.

"No." Julius paused. "She aborted it herself."

"Oh my God," Anita exclaimed. "How desperate she must have been."

"Yes, a young woman, only twenty. Alone here in Milwaukee . . . afraid what her parents would think if they found out she was pregnant. Not in love with the boy, at least not enough to marry him."

John stared at the tiny creature. "What did you have to do, Juley?"

"In trying to abort, she induced bleeding. It was very fortunate she didn't harm her uterus, but she did damage the placenta. She came to Emergency bleeding heavily. I was on duty. The only thing we can do in such a case is what we call a dilation and curettage, a D and C, where we actually scrape the uterus to clean it out completely . . . placenta and embryo. The baby simply can't be saved. Without that, we never could have stopped the bleeding. She would have died."

"Who was she," John asked.

Julius looked askance at his brother. "Don't ever ask that, Johnny . . . you should know better. Never ask a doctor the name of his patient – never!"

"I know, I know." Now John regretted two things.

"It's terribly sad," Anita said. "I imagine she was desperate beyond belief. What a shame she couldn't trust her parents or someone. Was she taken advantage of?"

"She told me she was as much to blame as the boy, maybe more so."

"Of course, but it's the woman who gets pregnant," Anita said. "The man, if he isn't honorable, just runs away."

"Actually, she said the boy wanted to marry her. Now she regrets everything. She's really suffering with it. I'm having a tough time just getting her to stop crying. She's sad and weepy one minute; the next she's relieved she's not pregnant. It's perplexing."

"Can we go?" Anita asked.

"Yes, of course. Let me turn off the lights. I'll walk you to the elevator. I'm going to let you show yourselves out. I have to get back to work."

At the elevator, Julius again told Anita how pleased he was to meet her. "I hope we can get together real soon. I'd like you to meet my girl." He shook his brother's hand vigorously while thanking them for coming.

John and Anita smiled and waved, as the operator closed the heavy door.

Chapter 10 ~ 1930 (Continued)

Julius climbed the stairs to the fourth floor. At the nurses' station they told him, "It's been quiet . . . nap if you'd like."

When Dr. Messert was scheduled, Julius went home to his father's. After an exhausting twelve hour shift, he fell right to sleep in his own bed. At the hospital, however, napping on a narrow cot proved difficult. He always imagined some calamity would arise after he dozed off. Generally, nurses were indifferent to his need for sleep. When roused, he'd get up, slip on his shoes, white coat, grab his stethoscope, and rush to the distressed patient. But this night, without a crisis, Julius slept until five-thirty.

He met Dr. Messert in the cafeteria for breakfast. After they settled down with eggs, toast, juice, and coffee, Anton said, "Your brother's girlfriend is quite a looker."

Julius had no intention of discussing Anita Thilman. Messert, however, had been charmed by her beauty and, like most men, felt a vain curiosity in knowing something about such a lovely young woman even if she were unattainable.

"What the hell does she see in your brother?"

"A gentleman," Julius said, "unlike what I'm looking at."

"Yeah, yeah, but what does he do? What does he know? He didn't seem too bright to me."

"He's a sales engineer and very smart."

"Oh, no, not an engineer," Messert laughed. "Why the hell would a sweet little honey lamb like that, a doctor's daughter no less, get involved with an engineer?"

"You can be such a horse's ass, Tony. Not every woman wants to marry a doctor and certainly not an arrogant son-of-a-bitch like you."

"Please Julius, save the flattery. As a matter of principle, she shouldn't marry a dumb engineer, for all engineers, in my opinion, are dumb. She could marry this brilliant, young doctor I know. Do me a favor. Call your brother, tell him to go to hell, and then get Miss Thilman's telephone number. I'll take care of the rest."

"Oh, sure, but can I finish eating first?"

"Seriously, Julius, a doctor's daughter of such extraordinary sensual appeal should not be wasted on an engineer, surely you understand that. Only a doctor with my unique and somewhat perverse insights into female sexuality knows how to treat such a woman. An engineer, impossible; your brother? Never."

"Johnny has two things you totally lack: class and character. How do I know? Because I just had this conversation with you; I intern with you; I went to med school with you. Of course I know. I'm a national authority on the deficiencies in your character. For crying out loud, stop talking about my future sister-in-law."

"Julius, you don't understand . . . I intend to marry that girl."

"Shut up, Tony."

Messert raised his hands at the harsh command. "Just one more thing then I'm done. You probably won't agree, but I think your future sister-in-law – oh, pardon me, I mean my bride-to-be – is even sexier than 407." He grinned at Julius knowing it was a sensitive subject.

Julius was mildly annoyed by Messert's teasing about John's girlfriend. He expected that from Tony, but reference to the patient in Room 407 angered Julius. "She has some real problems. Can't you respect that? Can't you maintain some degree of professionalism?"

Messert stood while saying, "You worry about your own g--damn professionalism." He walked away.

It was apparent to Anton Messert that Dr. Helden had become protective of the young woman in 407. Julius did the initial exam, performed the D & C under Dr. Ragen's supervision, did the follow-ups, and made her the first stop on his rounds. If both young doctors were on duty, Julius made sure he'd see 407 before Dr. Messert and then insist there was no need for Anton to check on her. He even went so far as to tell Messert that he should treat her as Julius' patient exclusively. At first, the request bemused Messert, but he came to realize that Helden wished, for indiscernible reasons, to insulate the patient from him. He complained to Julius, even calling him unprofessional. Finally, he decided to take the matter to Dr.

Ragen. In a spirit of fair play, he invited Julius to defend his obviously inappropriate behavior.

In medical school there had been a developing friendship between the two, but as they progressed into their internships, Dr. Helden backed away from Dr. Messert. Tony resented it. He didn't understand Julius's withdrawal because he thought it natural for them to be friends as well as colleagues. As he observed Julius becoming more distant and even at times aloof, he suspected Dr. Helden of arrogance, which he thought laughable. Julius was, after all, just a kid from the south side who really had to work hard to get through medical school, whereas Anton, an *Eastsider* from a well-to-do family, scored consistently higher grades. More than once he had patiently tutored the struggling Julius. After breakfast, Messert went to Dr. Ragen's office and requested a meeting later that morning.

They sat in straight-backed, leather armchairs facing their mentor. Though the young doctors regarded relationships with patients important, and though Anton was angered by Julius's protectiveness of 407, both men approached the meeting with levity, realizing it wasn't a serious issue as it related to the doctor-in-charge. They both, in their own way, were committed to the wellbeing of the young woman and did not want to appear excessively upset with each other. Both thought Dr. Ragen would see it just as they did and would rule in their respective favor to the chagrin of the other.

Dr. Ragen began. "What's bothering you boys that you need to involve me like this? Can't it wait till our regular meeting?"

"Actually, it's a question of territory," Dr. Messert said. "Julius doesn't want me checking the young woman in 407, claims she's his patient, and I should leave her alone."

When Anton put it that way, Julius's attitude did, indeed, sound unprofessional, not only to Dr. Ragen, but to Julius as well.

Ragen asked, "Julius is that true?"

"He makes me sound possessive, but that's not the case at all. I'm trying to be medically protective of her emotions. It's been tough for her."

"Protected from what," Dr. Ragen asked.

"Protected from whom should be the question," Dr. Messert said.

"My interest is simply in protecting her emotions. On one hand she feels a lot of guilt; on the other, she's relieved she's not pregnant. She's confused, so I try to help as best I can. She asked for my help."

"I understand, but why don't you want Anton involved?"

"Well, with all due respect, Tony just doesn't take it seriously. He minimizes the whole thing and tries to minimize it in her mind and her conscience. She's got to let her own true feelings come out without any interference from him. He'll just confuse her."

Messert clasped his hands behind his head. "Yeah, Julius, but it's okay for you to confuse her, right?"

"Confuse her about what," Dr. Ragen asked. "Come on, what are you boys really talking about?"

"Tony thinks the only mistake she made was not going to him . . . to have him do the abortion."

"Oh, bullshit . . . I'm not in private practice."

Now Ragen understood the contention. "For a woman to abort herself is a serious matter, but for a doctor to do it, that's against the laws of this State. Anton, you don't believe in performing abortions, I hope."

Messert seized the opportunity. "So it's all right for a woman to do the aborting and potentially mutilate herself, maybe even kill herself, and then come here to be treated. But if she goes to a doctor who can safely end the pregnancy, that's against the law, and the doctor goes to jail. That makes no sense to me whatsoever. None at all."

"No, no, no, you have to understand women shouldn't be aborting themselves," Dr. Ragen said. "A desperate woman might attempt it, as this young woman did, because she doesn't want to be pregnant. I understand that. But women know the consequence of sexual intercourse; if they let themselves get into such a situation then they run that risk. But aborting their pregnancy? No, totally unacceptable. The State is absolutely correct in prohibiting abortions. If it didn't, men and women would behave even more irresponsibly. There'd be an outbreak of illegitimate pregnancies because they'd think, well, if I do get pregnant I can always get an abortion. It would be an utter disaster for women, believe me."

Julius nodded. "Invading the womb to destroy new life is morally and medically wrong."

Messert responded, "Must you always cite your dull morality?" They had argued the issue before.

Dr. Ragen cut in. "But it is a moral issue, definitely, except in the case of an ectopic pregnancy. There a woman has the right to protect herself. She has a right to a therapeutic abortion; otherwise she'd die. Tell me, Julius, is the young woman religious?"

"She's Lutheran."

"Has she talked with her minister?"

"No. She said she has to work this out with God in her own way. She knows it was wrong, but she's confused because, while the guilt is really haunting her, at the same time she's relieved she isn't pregnant. She's torn between two conflicting emotions."

"Yeah, and I wonder which one you dwell on," Dr. Messert asked. "I'm sure sin and guilt are the big winners in your psychotherapy. I've never seen her cry. I'd tell her she should be damn glad she's not pregnant and damn lucky she didn't kill herself."

"Dr. Messert, please, not so harsh," Dr. Ragen said. "Of course she suffers guilt. What God-fearing woman wouldn't? Whether you believe or not, you must respect the faith of your patients."

"Tony's a good agnostic," Julius said.

"I beg your pardon," Messert said, his voice rich with sarcasm. "I am neither good nor agnostic. I am an atheist. I can assure you, it has nothing to do with goodness."

"Keep that to yourself around your patients, Anton," Dr. Ragen advised. "If you doubt the efficacy of faith then you are naive at best. There are going to be times in both your careers when prayer will be the only medicine you've got.

"Let me tell you what happened this past January. I had a patient, a man forty-one years old, who was seriously ill with lobar pneumonia. I examined him at his home. He was so critical I called the ambulance immediately.

"Over the next several days his condition worsened. His temperature rose above one-o-four, blood pressure dropped, lungs filling up, erratic heart rate, plus great difficulty breathing. The man was clearly dying, and there wasn't a thing I could do about it. Of course, I had him in oxygen and on sulfa, but his condition just kept getting worse. Day after day I had no good news for his wife, and, finally, I just told her, 'the only thing that's going to save your husband is a miracle. I suggest you and your family pray morning, noon and night; otherwise I don't think your husband will make it.'

"Well, several days later his fever broke. Now, I say this with absolute certitude: that man was dying. The only reason he lived was because of the prayers of his wife and family. She told me she promised God she'd pray a rosary every day for the rest of her life if God would spare him. They had two little girls; she didn't want them growing up without their father. So, don't ever doubt the power of prayer in healing. Sometimes it's all we've got."

"I'm a man of science," Dr. Messert said.

"So am I," Dr. Ragen replied. "I like to think of science as theology in the lab. All scientists really do is study the world as God created it, whether they acknowledge it or not. That's what theology is all about, isn't it? We study God through His created works and revelation? Science, in my view, is simply the branch of theology that looks at God's creation under the microscope and through the telescope."

"Well, I think we're getting away from the point," Dr. Messert said. "Let's discuss the issue of that girl trying to end her own pregnancy. That's profoundly real. No woman should ever have to resort to that."

"I agree," Dr. Ragen said, "but don't ever advocate that a physician provide an abortion. A woman can be helped in other ways. Most doctors in this town would be happy to deliver her baby free of charge, plus many families are eager to adopt. Or there's the orphanage.

"Look, as physicians we've taken the Hippocratic Oath; we pledged to protect and preserve life, not destroy it. Illegitimate pregnancies, in an ideal world, shouldn't occur, but, regrettably, in this world they do. It's a consequence of bad behavior, but not necessarily the woman's. Mostly the man's, I suspect. Sometimes in a marriage, it's lack of consideration or restraint on a husband's part. Unfortunately, such behavior can have serious, negative ramifications. That's how women learn that men of low character must be avoided. For some, that's the only way they ever learn. If there weren't negative consequences no one would ever learn to behave responsibly."

"Human nature isn't always rational or responsible," Dr.

Messert replied. "People like to copulate, married or not. You can't change that. It's a powerful urge."

"Nonsense, human nature also includes free will, forethought, and self-control. If men and women don't utilize those attributes then they should suffer the consequences. And when they do, hopefully, they'll learn to behave properly."

Dr. Helden sensed Dr. Ragen had grown irritated with both Messert and the course of the argument. "So what about 407? Can I continue to protect her from this free-thinker?"

"No, you may not," Dr. Ragen answered. "I'm mentor to you both. Both of you are to care for all the patients on this floor and learn, from all of them, the art as well as the science of medicine. For heaven's sake, I don't want a rivalry between you two. We're all colleagues here.

"407 is, obviously, in a delicate emotional state. Don't release her until she has better control of her emotions. Dr. Messert, you are not to express any of the views you expressed to me. Dr. Helden, if you feel you can help her regain some emotional stability, then continue to do so, but if you don't succeed in a few more days then I suggest we consult either the Lutheran chaplain or a psychiatrist or maybe both. How long has she been here?"

"This is day five," Julius said.

"Five days after a D & C she should be strong enough to leave," Dr. Ragen said.

"She claims she feels very weak," Julius said. "Picks at her food. Her vitals are normal, have been right from the start. There's never been any infection."

"Well, give her a few more days. Keep after her to talk to the chaplain. Make her walk the halls."

"Frankly," Dr. Messert interjected, "I suspect she pities herself. With all due respect Julius, I think you're perpetuating that. I think we should tell her she's being discharged tomorrow, and she should get back to whatever the hell she does with her life, get her mind off the whole, stupid affair."

"We'll let Dr. Helden be the judge of that," Dr. Ragen said. "Quite frankly, Julius, I think she's been here long enough. Don't let her sink into depression. I think there's some truth in Tony's opinion. Go tell her right now you're going to discharge her in two days. See how she reacts."

"Fair enough," Julius replied. He thanked Dr. Ragen, nodded at Anton Messert, and left the office.

He went directly to 407. The young woman stared out the window at the willows weeping beside the lagoon that filled the long swale between the hospital and the road. Her mind was far away. She turned to face him. "Hello Doctor."

"Hello, how are you today?" Julius asked.

"So-so, still weak . . . sad."

"You do understand there's nothing wrong with you physically? No fever, no infection."

She shuffled back to bed.

"I met with Dr. Ragen and Dr. Messert. We all agree that you should be discharged day after tomorrow. I want you to walk the halls today, regain your strength. It's not good for you to stay in bed all day."

"I still feel so sad. How am I ever going to get over that?"

"Would you please see the chaplain now? He'll help you more than I can."

"I suppose . . . ."

"Dr. Messert will check you this afternoon, but I'll see you again tomorrow and the next morning when you're discharged. I'd like to see a smile on your face tomorrow, okay?"

"I'll try . . . ."

"And walk . . . you'll feel better getting some exercise. When your lunch comes, eat. You need nourishment."

"I don't have an appetite."

"That's because you aren't doing anything. Look, these are doctor's orders, okay? I'm going to have the nurses make sure you walk and eat. And smile for heaven's sake. That's also a doctor's order. You have a very pretty smile. The sooner you start using it again, the better."

She smiled faintly while gazing into his eyes. She always found kindness and gentleness there. In only five days she had grown fond of the young doctor. *Not romantically fond,* she argued with herself, *just respectfully fond,* the fondness one feels for another human being who has been patient and kind throughout their acquaintance, however brief.

In the early afternoon, Julius met Dr. Messert at the nurse's station. Anton asked, "Did you tell her she'll be discharged day after tomorrow?"

"Yes, and I told her to walk. Make sure she does."

"She'll be okay, Julius. Women are tougher than they look."

"Physically, perhaps, but her emotions are delicate. Respect that. She agreed to talk to the chaplain."

"Oh, boy, you and your silly religion. I don't know about you, Julius. Maybe you should've been a priest." He laughed. "The seminary would've been a lot easier, that's for sure."

He started to walk away, but Julius grabbed his arm. "You know I've finally figured out how we're different – I mean in medicine, as doctors."

Anton's expression questioned Julius.

"You look at a patient; all you see is a body. You don't give a damn about their soul, their faith, family, work, sorrows, their joys, nothing; just a body for you to work on, to analyze, diagnose. It's no different than when you were cutting up cadavers. It makes no difference if a patient is dead or alive."

"Bullshit!" Messert turned and walked away.

Julius shouted, "Be kind . . . ."

Dr. Messert ignored him.

The morning she was to be discharged, the young woman in 407 waited for Dr. Helden. He glanced at her chart: temperature, pulse, and blood pressure all normal. The youthful sweetness of her appearance touched Julius: her black hair full and frizzy, lips slightly reddened with lipstick, which he hadn't seen before, her nose small and perfect. It was her eyes, though, that always drew his attention. There was an ever so slight hint of the Oriental in her deep, dark eyes. *Unusual, but most attractive,* he realized. Her navy blue dress, straight and loose, completely hid the beauty of her curvaceous figure. Over her left arm she carried a grey, cloth coat, and, in her right hand, a small, black purse.

"So you're all set . . . I trust you're up to it?"

"I think so. I know I can't stay here forever. The chaplain was very nice. He talked some sense into me. It's hard to explain, but I finally feel like I want to put this all behind me. Plus, I have to find a job."

"That's very good. You know you have to settle with the cashier . . . ."

"I've done that. I really was just waiting for you."

"Would you like me to walk you to the lobby?"

Surprised, she asked, "What about your patients?"

"I can push them back a few minutes."

They took the elevator to the ground floor, walking in silence to the east entrance where a city bus waited under the porte cochere. Julius helped with her coat. Stepping outside, she checked the bus's destination. The coolness of the moist air felt wonderfully refreshing after a week indoors.

Through the open door the driver said, "I leave in a couple minutes."

Walking back to Julius, she said, "That's my bus."

They looked at each other knowing they were about to part after a brief, seven-day encounter in which so little happened between them. They both felt an unspoken fondness, an attraction, and yet both knew they very likely would not meet again.

"Take good care of yourself . . . use good judgment."

"I will. I don't ever want to go through that again. Thank you for helping me. I truly appreciate all you've done."

"Glad I could help. I'll miss your pretty smile."

His admission thrilled her. "Goodbye . . . ."

She extended her hand, but then Julius did something to her no man had ever done. He bowed and kissed her hand; an act that shocked him almost as much as it surprised her. She said nothing, smiled slightly, turned, and boarded the bus. Through the rear window their eyes met one last time, as the bus rumbled away. Julius waved then entered the hospital. Walking to the elevators he looked back, but the bus was out of sight. She was gone. Neither of them could have imagined in the moments after their parting that they wouldn't see each other, would not meet again, for over forty years.

Julius took the elevator to the fourth floor. Dr. Ragan left a message at the nurses' station asking Dr. Helden to see him in his office.

He knocked on the half open door. "Come in Julius; have a seat." Dr. Ragan put aside a medical journal. "I've some unexpected news." He straightened the few items on his desk. "Dr. Messert is leaving us."

The news stunned Julius.

"He's transferring to Columbia Hospital . . . has an opportunity there. He wants to specialize now."

"He's leaving County for Columbia? I don't believe it. He's been talking general practice a long time. This is a wonderful place for that."

"That might be, but his father is friends with a Dr. Roger Chambers, a gynecologist on the east side. I've met him several times. He's got a good practice, right in the heart of the north shore: Milwaukee, Shorewood, and Whitefish Bay. Apparently, he's always wanted Tony to climb on board, and now he's made him an attractive offer. Dr. Chambers is on staff at Columbia. They had an opening for an ob-gyn intern, called Anton, and he decided to take it. I was just as surprised as you."

"He's specializing in obstetrics and gynecology?" Julius asked. "He used to talk orthopedics, but then we agreed general practice offered the broadest experience. Neither of us wanted to specialize because of the repetition. I'm surprised, really, especially ob-gyn."

"He told me the patient in 407 interested him; said he always had a latent interest in gynecology. The more he thought about Dr. Chamber's offer the more he realized that's what he wants to do."

"Baloney – he had no latent interest in gynecology. I knew him so well in med school. He never once expressed an interest in gynecology and certainly not obstetrics. The only thing he said about 407 was she should've had a doctor do the abortion."

"Well, he did mention that Dr. Chamber's practice is lucrative. I suspect Anton is interested in the financial potential of being a gynecologist in the right neighborhood. I know Dr. Chambers has done very well, plus Anton's father is wealthy. People from that background get used to having money. Making money is important to them. I don't think he's a lawbreaker. Women talk. That would get around; I mean if he were to do abortions. This town's too small; the DA would find out. I doubt Anton wants to go to jail."

"When's he leaving?"

"Friday's his last day. This is going to be somewhat of a burden for you, Julius, but I'll call the Dean. He'll put up a notice down there. I'll have a new doctor lined up real quick; we'll bring him in after graduation. In the meantime, you'll have to make part of Anton's rounds every day. I'll cover as much as my schedule allows and bring in another staff doctor to help. We'll have to see about an occasional day off for you."

"You do know I'm engaged? I'd like to spend a little time with my fiancée. Quite frankly, I need that now."

"Of course, Julius; when are you getting married?"

"We haven't set the date. We need to save a little more."

"What does she do?"

"She's an RN at Children's."

"Good for her," Dr. Ragen said.

+ + +

Dr. Helden did not speak with Dr. Messert until his last morning at County General. Julius didn't just want to say goodbye; he wanted to gain insight into Anton's thinking. Dr. Messert and Julius hadn't conversed nearly as much the past three months as when they began their internship. Julius, for his own reasons, decided to distance himself from Messert, socially and professionally, and now he realized that would be easily accomplished by Anton's move.

"I was surprised when Dr. Ragen told me you're leaving," Julius began. "But more surprised when he told me what you intend to specialize in."

"Why?"

"I thought you wanted to be a GP."

"Your little heartthrob got me thinking about gynecology again."

"What the hell are you talking about? You never thought about gynecology here or in med school."

"Don't expect me to believe you've forgotten 407 so quickly. Really, Julius, you shouldn't become emotionally involved with a patient, certainly not such a sexy, little kitten. I'm surprised, especially you being engaged. My, my Julius, what were you thinking?"

"I was not emotionally involved. I had an interest in her spiritual and physical wellbeing – strictly professional. For you to suggest otherwise shows how stupidly you think."

"Come on, she's a hot, little number, and you know it. I know you, Julius; had you met her under different circumstances you would have been severely tempted."

"I resent that. Who the hell are you to judge me or her? Who are you to suggest she isn't a decent girl? For a doctor that's truly unprofessional."

Messert laughed. "I'm only judging you and your opinions, which have grown very tedious. You're the main reason I'm getting out of this public hellhole. It used to be the niggers and white trash, but now it's just you: Julius Helden, all-American, all-around asshole. I thought we were friends, but you treat me like monkey shit. What the hell did I ever do to you?"

"Why are you going into gynecology?"

"What the hell business is that of yours?"

"I don't trust you with women. Why would I trust you as a gynecologist?"

"You arrogant son-of-a-bitch . . . stay the hell out of my life, out of my practice. Who the hell do you think you are?"

"I've got to be your conscience because you don't have one."

"I'm telling you, Julius, mind your own g--damn business. Don't ever stick your nose in my affairs, understand?" The blood of anger reddened his face.

"And I'm telling you, Messert, if I ever hear you're doing abortions, I'll go to the DA. You'll never practice medicine again."

"Are you threatening me? You lousy son-of-a-bitch – don't you ever threaten me."

"I'm not threatening, just stating a fact. If I ever hear you did one, single abortion, I'll call the DA. It's not a threat, just a statement of intention."

Dr. Messert struggled to control himself. Never had he felt such anger. He wanted to strike Julius, but knew better. Helden's arrogance and self-righteousness destroyed any lingering interest Anton might have held, just days earlier, for an ongoing friendship. Messert saw no point in continuing the ugly confrontation with his old, medical school chum. He looked intently into Julius's eyes, spewed, "Go to hell," and walked away.

Julius watched him momentarily then headed back to his office. Their last encounter unfolded just as he had imagined.

Chapter 11 ~ 1932

John Helden and his sweetheart, Anita Thilman, married in the early spring of 1932 on a dismal, wet Wednesday poorly suited for silk top hats, white gloves, and black and white film. John's younger brother, Dr. Julius, was best man. Anita's lovely country cousin, Susie, was matron of honor, and Luella Schmidt, the triumphant matchmaker of Layton Boulevard, was one of three, slender bridesmaids all of whom were striking in their Celeste blue chiffon, empire style gowns. However, on this day, Anita, in a princess gown of white chiffon with long, draped sleeves, proved most resplendent. Her skirt trailed a circular train over which swept a tulle veil that fell from a cap caught with orange blossoms. In her arms she carried a bouquet of Lilies of the Valley – May bells. As she approached the altar at her father's side, John thought her the most beautiful girl he had ever beheld.

Anita's brother, Lew, looked dashing in his groomsman's morning coat, the sight of which caused more than one of Anita's girlfriends to feel fluttery. Dom Thilman ushered and attended, especially to the pretty, young lady guests of both families, joking with every single one, as he escorted them to the proper pew. Anita's dear uncle, Father Joe Pierron, offered the solemn, nuptial Mass though Mary Louise would have preferred her favorite brother. As she awaited Anita's entrance through the ornately carved, double doors of St. Ann's, she could scarcely believe twenty years had passed since Father Johnny's tragic death.

To everyone's way of thinking, particularly Mary Louise's because she and Anita planned it, the wedding was a wonderful affair. The Thilman's, however, were puzzled that John's rich Uncle Peter came without his wife. Even more surprising, John's cousin, Peter Jr., and his wife, Harriet, didn't come at all. Anita couldn't understand it because John told her that he and Peter Jr. were pals from early childhood.

"Then why wouldn't he come?" she asked.

Without a credible answer, she concluded they were snobs, which John vehemently denied. They did possess, however, enough etiquette to send a place setting of Anita's chosen Spode ware. As for the elder Mrs. Peter Helden, she was "a bit under the weather," according to her wealthy husband. In fact, she was home dead drunk.

Most interesting though to John and Anita was how well Dr. Thilman and John's Uncle Peter got along. Peter Helden, a millionaire-industrialist, appreciated Dominic Thilman for what he was: a dedicated and successful professional man without pretense or guile who spoke good German, the well-remembered language of Mr. Helden's childhood. Peter Helden respected the medical profession greatly and took pride in his youngest nephew, Julius, who became a Doctor of Medicine. He wasn't nearly as proud of his only son, Peter Jr., who had a degree in Business Administration, something his father thought any man with half a brain could obtain on the job if he just kept his eyes and ears open. Peter Helden had no university degree, but administered his business brilliantly and spoke "the King's English," as John liked to say. Anita read some of the letters Uncle Peter wrote as a young man when he sold mining equipment in South America. Their precise expression and descriptive beauty impressed her because, when he came to the United States, he was just an impoverished, uneducated boy. Nothing stopped him, however, from mastering *English* because he knew, from early on, to succeed in America he had to speak, read, and write the predominant language well.

To his credit, Dr. Thilman easily held his own with this successful, rich, bilingual manufacturer, and hemispheric traveler. The doctor was smart, accomplished, and trilingual – he also spoke Luxembourg – and, like all truly great men, possessed humility.

On the other hand, John's father was not the poised and polished, self-educated man his younger brother, Peter, had become and, as a result, spent little time at the reception conversing with either Dr. Thilman or his own remarkable brother. He was, after all, just a shop man who owned no stock in the company and, thus, knew his place. Nevertheless, with considerable help, he might have written a text on manufacturing processes and techniques based on excellent principles he had discovered and devised, literally hands on, all for the purpose of ultimately making his younger brother a very wealthy man. At his third son's lovely wedding he appeared to be quite the ordinary fellow, content to visit quietly with his two older sons, Clarence and George, and their shy wives.

Mary Louise Thilman, however, got along splendidly with her new son-in-law's rich uncle. At fifty-four, she was such a charming woman, so quick to make just the right remark with the most delightful Luxembourg accent – she rolled her 'r's with great style – that Peter Helden was quite taken with her. Before the evening ended, he invited Dr. and Mrs. Thilman to visit "Mama" and him at their mansion on Lake Drive, which, with John and Anita in tow, they did only once in the year after the wedding.

"All in all," Mary Louise told her tired husband, "the wedding and reception were very successful indeed."

The newlyweds spent their wedding night at the Drake Hotel in Chicago. They had a leisurely breakfast. Afterwards, in their room, the groom hung the *Do Not Disturb* sign on the doorknob. They checked out at the last minute, not leaving Chicago until after lunch.

Their honeymoon trip, at the directive of Peter Helden, would include fact-finding visits to several of the company's distributors in the eastern part of the country. For it, John would be paid his full salary for the six-week excursion, while the worsening depression continued to devastate more and more workers across the country. To Anita, her new husband's job and paycheck seemed wonderfully secure.

Before they went to Indianapolis to meet with the Helden distributor, John drove to South Bend to see Notre Dame University. He followed their football team and liked Knute Rockne, the great coach who died in a plane crash in 1931. Hand in hand, John and Anita roamed the spacious, pastoral campus, admired the great Golden Dome with the statue of Our Lady – *Notre Dame* – high on top, and made visits at the church and the Lourdes Grotto.

Gazing towards St. Mary's Lake, Anita remarked, "This is a beautiful place."

John wondered out loud if they might have a son go there one day. Anita only smiled.

The drive south to Indianapolis on the Dixie Highway crossed the flat, rural country that covers so much of Indiana's midsection.

They arrived at the hotel late. The following morning they met with the Helden distributor who wasn't able to spend much time with them even though he knew John was coming. He mentioned some problems mounting Helden's equipment and let it go at that. Afterwards, the Heldens strolled the Monument Circle area downtown. They found a nice restaurant, had a pleasant dinner, and stayed at the hotel a second night.

Next morning they headed south to Louisville. The weather grew warmer, as they neared the Ohio River valley. Wooded ravines alive with blossoming Magnolias, lilacs, flowering crabs, Dogwoods, and an occasional Carolina Silverbell delighted them.

Friday night they slept in Louisville. By Saturday noon they reached Frankfort, Kentucky. The Helden distributor's office was closed, and John got no answer when he called him at home. After covering hundreds of miles, John learned absolutely nothing from the two distributors he was obligated to call upon. Uncle Peter would not be pleased.

From Frankfort they drove north to Cincinnati. The next day, leaving early, they headed east across southern Ohio all the way to Belpre where they crossed the Ohio River into West Virginia. They had gone through towns with funny names like Hoagland, Bainbridge, Chillicothe, Hebbardsville, and Little Hocking, all of which amused them. It was good they did because much of what they saw in and between those towns disturbed them.

"It's the depression," John said. "People are hurting."

"They should do something . . . ."

"There's no work. Farmers can't make a profit. What do you expect men to do?"

"Clean their yards, paint their houses, the barn . . . anything to keep busy."

"They don't have money for paint," John replied.

"They do for cigarettes."

At Parkersburg, arriving late, they slept well. In West Virginia the rural poverty seemed even worse. "This is depressing," Anita complained. "Can't we take a different route?"

"No, this is the shortest to Philadelphia."

Just east of Aurora, West Virginia, a chunk of Maryland comes down like an Indian arrowhead splitting West Virginia from itself.

After crossing the narrow width of the arrow near its tip, they were back in West Virginia again, which puzzled Anita until John showed her the map. They crossed the northeast neck of West Virginia, finally entering Virginia. Several miles east, they picked up US Highway 11 out of the town of Winchester, and before they knew it, they were back in West Virginia, confusing Anita even more.

"What is going on here?" She laughed at the apparent silliness of the border makers. "Are we going in circles?"

"Look at the map," John said.

West Virginia, shaped like a bloated sea creature with a small head and straight jaw at the upper northeast corner on top of a thick neck, separates the small western triangle of Maryland from the State of Virginia. Oftentimes rivers are more important than surveyors in establishing borders, but to get into Pennsylvania, John and Anita had to cross America's most famous survey line, the Mason-Dixon Line that demarcates Pennsylvania and Maryland. At Chambersburg, they picked up US 30 pointing towards Philadelphia. The road passed through Gettysburg. It was there John wanted to stop ever since he first planned his route.

He turned right, heading south past the Military Cemetery on the Baltimore Pike. Without another car in sight, he parked on the crest of a ridge. The young couple gazed across the broad sweep of grassy fields where General Lee and the Army of Northern Virginia encountered the Union Army of General George Meade those fateful, first three days of July, 1863.

"Your grandfather was in the Civil War," Anita said. "Was he here?"

"No, but he ended up at Appomattox where Lee surrendered to Grant."

"When did he join?"

"September, 1864, over a year after Gettysburg."

"Why did he go?" Anita realized that was the better question.

"My mother said he was an idealist, very much opposed to slavery. He didn't have to join; he was relatively old. My uncles were little boys. My mother wasn't even born."

"You're a lucky man."

"Yes, I suppose he could have been killed."

"How many died here?"

"I don't know . . . too many."

"Well, I'm certainly glad your grandfather wasn't here." She tugged his arm.

"Me, too."

"It's so tranquil now." Anita gazed at the rolling fields of greening land. "War is stupid. The Great War was stupid just like the Civil War."

"Perhaps, but at least the Great War was the war to end all wars, so maybe that wasn't so stupid."

"We'll see," Anita replied.

They got into the car and headed back towards Gettysburg.

"So why was there a Civil War?" Anita asked.

"To save the Union and free the slaves. You know that."

He turned east onto Highway 30. They passed a road sign: *Philadelphia 100 miles.*

Anita still wondered about John's grandfather. "So why did he join?"

"I told you: he opposed slavery. He wanted to do something about it."

"I can't imagine this country ever having slavery, although my father claims Negroes still aren't free."

"What do you mean? Of course they're free."

"Slavery and not being free are not the same thing. Negroes are poor and uneducated. My father has seen how they live, how they suffer. That isn't freedom."

"How does your father know?"

"Remember those years – well, actually, it was before we met – when he delivered the most babies?"

"Yes, that was impressive."

"It was because he delivered so many Negro babies."

"Oh, interesting."

"Yes, and he did it under very difficult circumstances."

"Like what?"

"Well, at the time, we still lived in the Sanitarium on 10th and North. Negroes were moving into the neighborhood south of us along Walnut Street. Oftentimes, a Negro would ring our bell at two or three in the morning; he'd plead for help for his wife. And, John, my father never refused. That happened once or twice a month for years until my father just couldn't do it anymore. It wore him out. Then we moved to Grant Boulevard, farther from where the Negroes lived."

She paused to recall the stories her father told her. "Once he went to a Negro's home where the wife was in hard labor. Her water had broke so my father began to prepare her, but he sensed another presence. There was only a single lamp next to the bed and some candles, so he moved the lamp closer. When his eyes adjusted to the dim light, he turned and saw children, curious as cats, just standing there. He hadn't noticed them when he entered the room. They wanted to watch their mother give birth. Can you believe that?"

"How old were they?"

"Young – four, five, six; I don't know. He shooed them out."

John laughed. "I should hope so."

"My father washed and wrapped the newborn, and placed it in the woman's arms so she was comfortable with the baby at her breast. Then he dealt with the afterbirth and cleaned her up. When he finished, he asked the husband for payment. The Negro showed him his purse. It contained some coins, a five dollar bill and a one dollar bill. The man offered it all, but it was still less than the ten dollar fee. My father asked if that was all his money, which it was, so my father took only the dollar because he had to leave the man money to feed his family. Can you believe that? My father, almost fifty years old then, went out in the middle of the night to deliver a Negro baby and received only a dollar."

"My goodness . . . ."

"My father never complained though. He said he had to do that whether he was paid or not."

"Doctors are great men."

"Some . . . my father, certainly, but not every doctor."

"I suppose not."

The road sign read: *Philadelphia 55 miles.*

"Once my father treated a man who complained of constantly feeling ill. Other doctors found nothing wrong, and my father didn't either except for a slight fever. At first he didn't know what to do, but then he told me he had an inspiration. Because of the fever he suspected an infection somewhere, but there were no visible signs so he pressed all over the man's body with three fingers – like this."

Anita pressed firmly against the top of John's leg with her middle fingers.

"Why?"

"Well, I'll tell you." She smiled at her husband. "He pressed everywhere on that man's body until he found what he was looking for."

"Which was?"

"A deep abscess on the inside of his upper leg. Once he found it, he extracted the pus with a syringe, and the man was cured."

"Wonderful – I bet he thought your father a great doctor."

"Absolutely!"

John pointed at the sign: *Philadelphia 25 miles.*

"I'll tell you another," Anita began. "When my father told me this, I realized that he truly is a great doctor because-"

John interrupted. "I have to stop for gas."

Anita strolled about in the mild weather, while the attendant filled the tank, checked under the hood, and washed the windshield. John complimented him on the cleanliness of the station. The man, the owner, told John his wife cleaned every night after they closed. John wanted to ask if the gasoline was delivered in Helden tankers, but decided not to, as he realized the man probably never noticed the nameplate.

Driving northeast again, Anita said, "I started to tell you about a woman who came to my father; she, too, complained about always feeling ill. She hadn't had her regular monthly flow for some time, but then it started again so she knew she wasn't pregnant."

"How old a woman?"

"Early forties, I think. My father examined her and found nothing wrong: normal temperature, no infection, plus he confirmed she wasn't pregnant. However, he did tell me she was overweight, which hindered his diagnosis."

"How?"

"I'll tell you . . . don't always interrupt."

"Sorry."

"He felt over her entire body, just like with that man, looking for an abscess again, but found nothing. Then he told me he had a suspicion. He examined her abdomen very carefully, but her innards were under" – Anita giggled – "a considerable layer of fat, and it was difficult for him to feel what he needed to feel. He searched only with his touch, but finally, pressing down very hard, he found something. At first he thought it was a tumor, but the more he felt it, the more his fingers were able to sketch in his mind what he had discovered."

Anita paused. Now she waited for John's curiosity to interrupt. "Which was," he asked.

"My father told the woman she needed surgery."

"For what?"

"I'll tell you – don't be so impatient."

"We're getting close now." John referred to Philadelphia.

"Well, my father performed the surgery. In fact, it probably was best described as a cesarean."

"You said she wasn't pregnant."

"She was, and she wasn't," Anita said, coyly.

"I don't understand," John said, somewhat annoyed.

"My father made an incision through all that fat and the abdominal wall and into her womb and found exactly what he suspected."

"Which was?"

In triumph, Anita answered, "A calcified fetus!"

"No, really?" Astonished, John had never heard of that.

"Oh, yes, but it is most unusual, most rare. My father removed it, and the woman was restored to perfect health."

"Wow – quite remarkable." Then John recalled the aborted fetus Julius had shown them, but decided not to mention it. Anita seemed too content, too happy, reflecting on her father's wonderful career, as they entered the city of *Brotherly Love*.

Bill and Naomi Gunther were delighted to meet the Heldens. Bill's distributorship, one of the largest in the country, included Pennsylvania, New Jersey and Maryland. Every year, even during the depression, John sold hundreds of thousands of dollars of equipment to Bill who resold it all. Now, in return, the Gunthers looked forward to showing the Heldens historic Philadelphia.

John and Anita checked in at the Benjamin Franklin Hotel downtown on Chestnut Street. "As grand," they agreed, "as Chicago's Drake." That first evening they were guests of the Gunthers in the main dining room where they enjoyed an elegant dinner. An orchestra played dance music, and, after dessert and coffee, the four of them fox-trotted and waltzed with great pleasure. Anita commented that Bill was a good, strong lead; she enjoyed dancing with him. Naomi, however, couldn't say the same about John who had a tendency to keep the beat by *pump handling* with his left arm. In spite of it, she found him charming and liked his good looks.

The following morning after breakfast, the Gunthers picked them up and drove to Bill's office. Naomi snatched the car keys announcing that she and Anita had some important shopping to do. John kissed Anita goodbye prompting Naomi to comment, "Oh, how sweet."

Bill had been married long enough to know a goodbye kiss wasn't necessary on a workday morning. He wanted to show John his business. In the shop, men were mounting a newly arrived Helden tank on a truck chassis. "See our problem?" Bill held up a Helden U-bolt with legs too short and the gage too narrow. "Every damn one . . . ."

"Oh, no," John groaned.

"And look at this. The only way we can get the tank to completely drain is to put tapered shims under both sides. We end up having to fabricate shims and new U-bolts. Quite frankly, John, that shouldn't be our responsibility. It cuts into our profit. Helden should anticipate these problems. The manufacturer is supposed to do the engineering."

Bill's disclosures diminished John's enjoyment of Philadelphia, if not the whole trip, and yet they were exactly the kinds of things Uncle Peter wanted him to discover. John knew it was a costly mistake because if they had a problem in Philadelphia they had it at every other distributorship throughout the country. They spent two more days with the Gunthers visiting historical sites, but John seemed distracted. Finally, Anita asked about it.

"They're installation problems," John said. "It's serious because Helden didn't anticipate them, and it costs Gunther money."

Now John wanted to get to New York. He crossed the Delaware River at Trenton, New Jersey, and continued to Newark and then Jersey City where he found the entrance to the Holland Tunnel.

"We're under the Hudson River," he told Anita.

"Under?"

"Yeah . . . what did you think?"

"I thought they put a tube on the bottom of the river."

John laughed. "No, they bore through bedrock."

In Manhattan they had a reservation at the Roosevelt Hotel on Madison Avenue, but John turned north at Sixth Avenue. He had spotted a high beacon on top of a tall building. "That must be the Empire State."

"My goodness," Anita said. "I didn't think it was that tall."

At a stoplight a scruffy fellow hopped on the running board on Anita's side, wiping the windshield with a dirty rag. Then he hustled around the front and wiped John's windshield before the light changed. It happened so fast that John and Anita said nothing. When he finished, he stared with dark and sunken eyes through the side window that John instinctively rolled down.

"Gov'ner, can you spare a quarter?"

John reached into his pocket, but before he found the coin, Anita shouted, "We didn't ask you to wipe our windshield. We certainly won't pay you. Now go away . . . get off our car!"

"Gov'ner . . . a dime?" the man implored.

Horns honked from behind.

"Go away," Anita said, again. "Get off our car – it's private property."

The man slid off the running board and disappeared amid cars and cabs. John let out the clutch; his car slowly accelerated through the intersection.

"Anita, the man has no job."

"He had no right to do that. He wouldn't do it if a policeman were around."

"He might have a wife and children . . . ."

"Nonsense – he's a bum. Bums have no respect for other people's property."

"But you said men should work."

"Not if they trespass."

John conceded the last word. After they checked into the hotel they spoke little, except to comment on the loveliness of the room. They both needed sleep. John believed Anita's outburst stemmed from tiredness, so he forgot about it.

The next morning, rested and relaxed after a good breakfast,

John called George Pohlman, the largest Helden distributor in the country.

"We'll take the train in and meet you for lunch," he told John. "We'll meet you in the lobby – the Roosevelt, right?"

"Yes," John answered.

George Pohlman, twenty years John's senior, was a powerful, gregarious, outgoing man, a true salesman type. *A little taller than John,* Anita noticed, *but not nearly as handsome.* His wife Linda's cheerful, eager personality readily bowed before her husband's dominance. She was a pretty woman who obviously dyed her hair, but Anita found her pleasant company.

After a delicious meal in the hotel's dining room, George put his arm around John and handed him an envelope. "Read this," he began. "We've got problems mounting your equipment, but rather than dragging you out to my shop, I summarized the main issues. You're an engineer, right? You comprehend written English, right? If not, we'll talk about it some other time. For the next few days, Linda and I are going to show you a good time in New York. It's your honeymoon, right?"

"Yes, it is," Anita answered. "John tends to forget that. He worries too much about engineering problems."

"George replied, "Lady, he's got problems he should worry about."

"I'll read it this afternoon," John promised.

"Right . . . let's meet here this evening at seven. We're busy this afternoon. Can't have dinner with you, but we've got tickets for a Broadway show. It's a big hit. You'll enjoy it."

"Oh, yes," Linda chirped. "*Of Thee I Sing* . . . we've heard it's great fun."

Four seats together, Row J, Center, Music Box Theater, West 45th Street, half a block from Times Square. Shortly after they were seated, a young man with sleek, dark hair, and dark eyes appeared in the orchestra pit to great applause. When the house settled down, he raised his baton.

Leaning in front of his wife so George and Linda would hear, John asked, "Who's that?"

"Gershwin," George replied. "He and his brother wrote the songs."

The Overture began. John settled back for an evening of pure enjoyment. He took Anita's hand. The show delighted everyone in the sold-out theater. Throughout the play John and George laughed heartily, while Anita and Linda displayed more restraint.

They walked east on 45th Street back to the hotel: two long blocks from Seventh to Fifth Avenue then the short block to Madison.

"What a show," John said, over and over.

"Winterbottom for President," George shouted. Everyone laughed, even passersby.

"Love is sweeping the country. Waves are hugging the shore," John sang.

"A show about love . . . oh, how thrilling," Linda said.

"It wasn't about love," Anita chipped in. "It was about sex."

"Anita!" Linda feigned shock.

George sang, "Sex is sweeping the country. Waves are banging the shore."

They all laughed, but Anita missed the crudity of George's second musical phrase. After that exuberance, they walked quietly, hand in hand, with John and Anita trailing George and Linda.

When they reached the hotel, George said, "Too bad we can't get a drink here."

"We don't drink," Anita said.

"We do." George wanted one. "Tomorrow night we're taking you to a real New York club where we can drink liquor. We'll pick you up at eight."

Anita noticed a change in George. He was anxious to leave. Had they been able to relax with highballs in the hotel's lounge with a pianist playing, he would have been happy to stay another hour; without that he wanted to get home, pour himself a drink, and go to bed.

"And then on the fourteenth," Linda added, "we've a special treat. We love opera so we're taking you to the Metropolitan. They're doing Puccini's *Madama Butterfly*."

"Bring a pillow, John," George said. "We'll catch up on our sleep."

In fact, the invitation thrilled John. George had no idea how deeply John loved serious music.

All agreed the food at the nightclub was only fair. Anita drank iced tea; Linda had a glass of Chablis. George started with *bourbon, rocks,* continued with *bourbon, rocks,* and would end with *bourbon, rocks.* John ordered a highball after which Anita whispered, "Only one . . . ."

"This place is popular with the administration," George said, "even top cops."

"Aren't the laws enforced?" Anita referred to Prohibition.

"Only for those who don't play ball," George answered. "You need connections, and it costs. You don't pay, you can't serve liquor. If you serve it, they'll shut you down."

"That seems rather hypocritical," Anita said.

"Hey, it's New York City," George said. "This town wants to drink."

After tables were cleared and fresh drinks ordered, the floor-show began. When the girl dancers appeared wearing only tiny panties with their breasts completely exposed except for pasties over the nipples, Anita was speechless. *They might as well be naked,* she realized. She felt George's leg graze her own when he kicked John under the table. She noticed how they looked at each other. *Lechers,* she thought. George was on his way to having too much liquor, while John, forced by the look in Anita's eyes, nursed his second. Anita appeared anxious to get out of there. Linda recognized the unpleasantness and finally suggested they leave. George balked, but Linda prevailed. The cab ride back to the hotel even lacked small talk. George slurred some ignored comments, while John thought it better to say nothing. Anita and Linda gazed indifferently out the side windows.

"We'll pick you up Thursday at seven," Linda said, as John and Anita got out of the taxi. "The opera starts at eight. I promise you a far more pleasant evening."

John leaned into the cab. "Goodnight George."

Anita, in no mood for any physical attention from her husband, feigned sleep. John's tired breathing in the other twin annoyed her. She was glad he didn't try to be romantic. She wouldn't have allowed it after that terrible nightclub. *To think that men have the gall, with their wives sitting right beside them, to lust after half-naked show-girls . . . disgusting . . . thank God it wasn't John's idea.*

Actually, the nightclub surprised John just as much as it did

Anita. She noticed, though, how slyly her husband eyed the dancers. She understood his pleasure at seeing their lithe, curvy bodies
because John was a normal man. That George, however, dragged
them to such an awful place to put temptation before her husband
angered her. She regretted it because now, perhaps, she would have
liked John to be romantic, but certainly not after seeing those shame-
less women. She would not allow herself to be used to gratify the
passion of her husband when that passion was enflamed by tawdry,
exhibitionistic showgirls. She knew her worth. She knew she was
every bit as beautiful. She knew her husband needed no such visual
stimulation except what she herself was willing to reveal.

At first, Anita thought George quite nice; now she saw him as
a voyeur. Plus he drank heavily. She had no use for a man of such
low character, a man who might even be unfaithful to his wife,
something Anita would never tolerate. He might be successful in
business, but Anita wasn't impressed by that. She didn't care at all
that he was the largest distributor for the Helden Company. *What
are his morals,* she asked herself. *I know only too well.* In the morning
she'd tell John her assessment of George Pohlman. She'd point out
his many and obvious faults, and she'd tell John of her anxiousness
to leave New York. *This is a wicked city,* she concluded. *Wicked . . .
wicked . . . wicked . . . .* Finally, she fell asleep having forgotten to say
her prayers.

Thursday, April 14, 1932, turned out to be one of those blissful days that honeymooners deserve. At breakfast, Anita expressed
her low opinion of George; John generally agreed. Nevertheless, he
pointed out he had to deal with him. Anita certainly understood.

"It's not a problem," she said. "He lives in New York, and we
don't. I just feel sorry for his poor wife."

After breakfast they strolled to St. Patrick's Cathedral. Side
by side they knelt in prayer and, as they left the church, dipped
their fingers in the holy water fount and blessed themselves. They
walked, that lovely spring morning, all the way to Central Park,
crossed Fifth Avenue to the plaza in front of the large hotel there,
then headed back on the west side of the street. They enjoyed a
delicious lunch in the hotel's dining room before returning to their
room. Both felt romantic.

The Metropolitan Opera House on West 39th and Broadway

comprised a beautiful, high-ceilinged auditorium. John and Anita were thrilled to see it. Linda, elegantly dressed, beamed as she entered the vast hall. Anita had dressed more plainly. George appeared remarkably well groomed, friendly, and polite. *So much so,* Anita thought to herself, *that Linda obviously gave him a good talking to.* They certainly seemed happier than in the cab after the nightclub.

"We heard this several seasons ago," Linda began. "It's a gorgeous opera; the music is out of this world. You'll love it." She spoke charmingly. "Elizabeth Rethberg is wonderful. She's German, but tonight she sings the role of a young Japanese girl, *Cho-Cho-San.* The Italian tenor, Merli, is singing the American, *Lieutenant Pinkerton.* An Italian wrote the opera, but it's based on an English play. It takes place in Japan, and we're seeing it in New York City. That's what I love about opera. It's so international . . . a veritable League of Nations."

John and Anita laughed, as did Linda. George smiled contentedly, gazing about the large hall with its five, rising horseshoe tiers. He and Linda seemed completely comfortable with each other, a difference from the previous evening that amazed Anita. *It was that terrible nightclub,* she realized. *It brought out the worst in George. Good for Linda for straightening him out.* In fact, unlike John and Anita, they shared a nightcap when they got home and then the same bed before they slept.

"Did you bring your pillow, George," John asked.

George smiled. "Actually, I like this opera very much. It's very beautiful. I'll stay awake."

The house lights began to dim.

"What is *Madama Butterfly* about," Anita whispered to John.

"I don't know," he whispered back.

+ + +

In 1894, Great Britain consented to a treaty with Japan that abolished *extraterritoriality.* Shortly after, the Emperor of Japan issued an edict declaring it was his desire to remove all legal distinctions between natives and foreigners.

Extraterritoriality exempted foreigners from the jurisdiction of Japanese courts of law; foreigners could only be charged with and tried for a crime by their own consular courts. With travel and time, however, the Japanese government became aware that other nations regarded them as a people who could not be trusted to administer justice to foreigners. This insulted their national pride. By 1899, at Japan's insistence, all the major world powers had concluded treaties with Japan rendering extraterritoriality an historical artifact.

Giacomo Puccini saw David Belasco's one act play, *Madam Butterfly*, in London in the summer of 1900. Belasco based his play on the novelette of the same name by Philadelphia lawyer, John Luther Long, first published in early 1898. Long claimed his story was based on a true incident related by his sister, the wife of a Christian missionary stationed in Nagasaki. That incident, therefore, would have occurred before the abolition of extraterritoriality and necessarily after Commodore Perry's expedition in 1854 when Japan finally opened herself to the world.

In Act I of the opera, B.F. Pinkerton, the American naval lieutenant, and Goro, the Japanese marriage-broker, admire the house Pinkerton has leased on a hill overlooking the Bay of Nagasaki. Soon they are joined by Sharpless, the American Consul, as they await Pinkerton's Japanese bride-to-be, the fifteen-year-old Cho-Cho-San, *Madama Butterfly*. Sharpless is horrified at her tender age and that his friend intends to take her as his wife. Pinkerton responds, *everywhere the roving Yankee takes his pleasure . . . . He drops his anchor at random . . . . He's not satisfied with life unless he makes his own the flowers of every shore . . . .* Sharpless, older and wiser, replies, *an easygoing creed that makes life delightful, but saddens the heart.*

When Butterfly arrives she freely reveals she has already worked as a geisha to support herself. She sings, *I don't hide it; neither do I feel hard done by. Why do you laugh? It's the way of the world.*

Sharpless knows, however, the truth of her heart. He tells Pinkerton, *She came to visit the Consulate. I didn't see her myself, but I heard her speak. The mystery of her voice touched me to the heart. True love surely speaks like that. It would be a great sin to strip off those delicate wings and plunge a trusting heart into despair. That heavenly, meek, pretty, little voice shouldn't utter a note of sadness.* Moments later Sharpless proposes a toast to Pinkerton's family back home, and Pinkerton callously adds his own ultimate desire: *. . . to the day when I shall get married in earnest to a real American bride.*

Pinkerton marries *Butterfly* solely to satisfy his immediate craving for carnal pleasure, safe in the knowledge that he need fear neither moral and social reprimand nor legal reprisal for his egregious self-indulgence. He marries with absolutely no intention of honoring his vow, for he values Cho-Cho-San not as an authentic bride, but as an available and willing courtesan. She is a mere trinket for his amusement and the gratification of his lust. If he did commit a crime against the marriage laws of Japan, which he did not, only his own Consul, Sharpless, could charge and try him, but it is clear that Sharpless is more avuncular than harsh. Were Pinkerton guilty of a crime in Japan, he would not merely be protected by extraterritoriality and a sympathetic Consul. He was also psychologically protected by his own indifference to the moral law having any relevance to a sham marriage on this remote, Oriental island. Before the ceremony, he even scorns and mocks Butterfly's relatives. When Sharpless finally takes his leave of Pinkerton and Cho-Cho-San on their wedding night, he can only naively hope that Pinkerton won't betray her, but betray her he will.

Lieutenant B. F. Pinkerton is an arrogant and promiscuous man, indifferent to the universality of moral law. He rebels against the divine admonition, *thou shall not commit adultery,* the day he weds Kate, his American bride, for it is with her on their wedding night that he betrays his Japanese wife. Indeed, he gains no understanding, no insight into the wretchedness of his behavior until the very end of the opera when Cho-Cho-San, profoundly loyal in her long wait for Pinkerton's return, is implored by both Sharpless and Kate to give her beloved son to his American father. Finally, Cho-Cho-San realizes she can no longer *live with honor,* for honor, indeed life itself, is taken from her when her son is snatched away. By the traditions of her ancestors she must end her own life, which she does with her deceased father's dagger at the very moment Pinkerton comes to claim their little child. Witnessing the young mother's suicide, Pinkerton, in horror, can only thrice cry out her name. What the audience witnesses is the profound failing of his young manhood, just like so many others who refuse to recognize their own reprehensible behavior until tragedy has occurred.

+ + +

"He reminds me of you," Anita whispered, comparing Merli's dark hair and good looks to John's. It pleased him.

John Helden heard music with his ears, mind, and heart. He had the ability to detect the beauty of an unfamiliar score faster than most: those who might need to hear a work several times before discovering its great beauties. From the beginning of the first act, John grasped the gloriousness of Puccini's music, which captivated him and kept his attention focused and rapt. Though he could roughly follow the dramatic action, he wanted to know the meaning of every word. In the great love duet a solo violin sang sweetly above the hushed sighs of the orchestra. When Cho-Cho-San uttered with impassioned tenderness,

> "Vogliatemi bene, un bene piccolino,
> Un bene da bambino
> Quale a me si conviene.
> Noi siamo gente avvezza . . . ,"

John longed to know exactly what she sang, for he sensed its deep and profound intimacy.

Now he felt a pure, lust-free passion that desired not the gratification of flesh, but the ineffable comprehension of that which was beautiful. He longed to possess beauty just as he longed for beauty to possess him, whether it was this new, wondrous music, the glories of nature, or the loveliness in the face and form of his young wife. He loved all that he found to be beautiful with a sense of joyousness. It exists, he knew, to nourish and refresh his soul. Fleshly desires were mere appetites incapable of nothing more than an ephemeral satisfaction. But it was beauty that had charmed and delighted him since his boyhood and beauty that would come closest to satisfying his deepest longings until his death. And now, at this wonderful moment in his young manhood with his beautiful bride beside him at what was, he was certain, the grandest opera house in the world, the music of Puccini filled his heart and soul with intense, pure, and perfect joy, a transcendent joy that most people never experience. He sensed he could never be happier, and he was right.

After the opera they took a cab back to the hotel. George told the cab driver to wait, while Linda and he got out of the cab to say goodbye to their guests.

"Well, we hope you enjoyed New York."

"It was wonderful," John and Anita agreed.

The evening at the Met changed Anita's opinion again. Now she thought George a gentleman and forgave him for taking them to the nightclub. She told Linda, "I like your spunk."

"Come back sometime, and we'll do it again, except for that horrid club." Linda's glance scolded her husband.

"We will," Anita promised.

George and John shook hands, while Linda and Anita embraced. Linda climbed into the cab; George followed, but quickly backed out again. "John, you make sure your uncle understands our problems – right?

"Right."

George got into the cab, and they drove off.

John and Anita spent nine honeymoon days in New York City with the last proving the best. And this final night, in the hotel room they had grown so accustomed to, they slept well. But before John fell asleep, he resolved when home to read the libretto of *Madama Butterfly*. In his memory, he burned two words: *piccolino* and *bambino*. They were the clue.

In the morning, the Heldens drove north along the Hudson River before heading west. The next distributor was in Buffalo. They stopped at West Point to visit the great Military Academy and gaze at the magnificent vistas of the Hudson River to the north and south.

"It's a beautiful spot . . . ."

"Yes, but I'd prefer our sons at Notre Dame."

"Right," John said.

That night they slept in Elmira. The following afternoon they arrived in Buffalo at the east end of Lake Erie. From there, the Niagara River flows north into Lake Ontario. Several months later, John would write in his report, *Mr. and Mrs. Jack Davis showed us around Niagara Falls and Canada for three days. They certainly did everything to show us a good time.*

After Manhattan, though, nothing seemed quite as exciting except for the beauty and power of the famous falls. At Jack's shop, he pointed out the same problems Bill Gunther identified in Philadelphia and George Pohlman wrote about in New York. More and more now, John and Anita were anxious to get home. They had been gone over four weeks.

The last scheduled stop was in Detroit. The distributor, Fred Ehler, repeated the difficulties trying to mount Helden tanks with improper U-bolts. John was sick of hearing it. "We'll fix that," he promised.

Fred knew Henry Ford's personal pilot. After lunch he drove his guests to Willow Run, surprising them with an airplane ride in Mr. Ford's private Tri-Motor. Neither of them had flown before. Anita was eager; John was not. After thirty minutes aloft, the plane landed. Anita enjoyed the wonderful views, but her husband suffered profound discomfort that bordered on deathly fear. The plane vibrated so incessantly that John felt it would shake itself apart. Back on solid ground he vowed never to fly again.

Chapter 12 ~ 1932 (Continued)

W hen they finally returned to Milwaukee, John Helden drove straight to Anita's parents. The Thilmans, including Anita's brothers, were delighted to see them after the long, five-week honeymoon. After John called his father to let him know they arrived safely, Mary Louise invited them to dinner.

A sense of lightheartedness hovered about the dinner table. John told of their trip in detail, and everyone found his accounts entertaining, especially Anita. He raved about *Madama Butterfly* though now there were only a few melodies and two Italian words he could recall. Dr. Thilman mentioned he had read of the opera's great beauty. In contrast, Anita ranted about the "poverty born of idleness" she observed from Kentucky nearly all the way to Philadelphia. She even grumbled about that "terrible looking bum" in New York City who expected a handout for wiping their windshield.

Nevertheless, by the time Mary Louise served the chocolate cake, John's enjoyment of the evening was complete. Anita's too. She liked how well her new husband spoke, making it so interesting that even Dom held his capricious comments in check. Anita was proud John could command the respect and attention of her family. Overjoyed to be home again, she hid her enthusiasm much better than her husband. Whereas John was eager to get back to work, Anita looked forward to spending time with her mother.

From the Thilman's, it was a short drive to the lower flat on Sherman Boulevard. John hauled in the suitcases, while Anita turned down the twin beds. She and her mother had set up the apartment before the wedding. Now Anita quickly undressed, slipped into her robe, and told John she would bathe. He was hopeful. He desired his beautiful wife in his own new bed, in his own new home.

Next morning at seven thirty, John burst into the Helden office. Secretaries and sales engineers were delighted to see him. They pounded him with questions, while he fingered through the stack of papers on his desk before retreating to Uncle Joe's office. Joe welcomed him warmly. After a short visit, John headed across the street to the plant. Inside he waved to some of the shop men though he didn't spot his brother, George. He went into Clarence's office where they greeted each other with pleasure.

"Great to see you, Johnny, glad you're back."

"Me too . . . we had a wonderful time."

"Good, glad to hear it. Have you seen Pa?"

"I'm going now."

"Don't let him upset you."

John couldn't imagine why Clarence said that. His father's greeting was restrained, but John made nothing of it because, in the telephone conversation last evening, his father claimed he was "mighty glad" to have him home.

"Now it's time to get back to work."

"Yes, Pa, I'm anxious to."

"Have you seen Uncle Peter?"

"He's not in."

"You do understand your uncle has been very generous to you?"

"Yes, Pa, I know. I'm very grateful, as is Anita."

"A six-week honeymoon with full pay at the height of a depression . . . not many men get that. If the men in the shop knew, it wouldn't be good. Did you tell George?"

"Uncle Peter told me not to."

"Don't tell him or Clarence."

"I won't," John said, "but I did work, Pa."

"I certainly hope so, and that's another thing . . . Uncle Peter wants a typewritten report on all your meetings with the distributors. For your sake, I hope you discussed more than the weather."

"I discovered some serious problems . . . ."

"Put it in your report."

"I think we should talk-"

"I said, put it in your report. I don't have time now."

John left his father's office and went looking for George. After almost six weeks away from the plant, the aroma of metal grindings and burning welding rods in the hazy, morning air delighted John. He spotted George in the cab of the overhead crane. He grinned and waved, but continued picking and placing, so John went back to his office. Crossing the street he noticed Peter Helden's Cadillac. John intended to greet his uncle, but he was in a meeting with the door closed.

The papers on John's desk contained numerous requests for quotes. He knew the importance of getting them out as quickly as possible. That's what Uncle Peter expected. Writing the report would have to wait.

In no time, John felt back in the swing of things, as people liked to say. He spoke only briefly with Uncle Peter who acted as though his nephew had never left. Uncle Peter told him to write the report at home on his own time because he didn't want it interfering with John's sales work.

What John found most unusual, though, was that his cousin didn't approach him for several days. When they bumped into each other, Peter Jr. asked, "I trust you had a pleasant trip?"

"Yes, it was wonderful . . . ."

"Save it, John. We'll talk some other time." Peter Jr. scrambled upstairs to his office leaving his cousin alone in the lobby.

For a while, John looked forward to telling Peter Jr. about the trip, but as the weeks passed that became increasingly unlikely. He sensed Peter distancing himself. He showed little interest in talking business and showed no interest in non-business matters. He made no attempt to be friendly, as John always did. It made him wonder again about Peter and Harriet not coming to the wedding. Like Anita, John believed his cousin had become snobbish, but John couldn't fathom why.

It became clear that the Heldens weren't nearly as interested in John's travels as Anita's family had been. Of course, his brothers were happy to see him, but no one, including his father, expressed any strong desire to hear about their sightseeing and adventures, simple as they were. It seemed to John that his family was too engrossed in work. His uncle and cousin showed the least interest.

John told Anita, "I actually think they resent my being away that long."

The Depression decreased the Helden Company's sales, but segments of their product line withstood the economic downturn. Heating oil and gasoline underground storage tanks were still being sold, and petroleum and milk transport tanks were still being delivered. America's rolling equipment fleets were aging; tankers took tremendous abuse on the rugged roads. Nevertheless, the company's sales and production dropped almost twenty-five percent. To compensate, shop and office payroll had been slashed. If one, large, metal fabricator in Milwaukee would come through the Depression reasonably well, it was the Helden Company. Because of it, John Helden Jr., his two brothers, and their father never knew the deprivation and hardship that many of the unemployed workers in Milwaukee and across the nation suffered.

Even with reduced sales, Uncle Peter's wealth increased dramatically. Company ownership became Peter's exclusively when his brother, Joe, sold his stock to Peter in 1924 for four thousand dollars. By 1932 that same stock was worth forty thousand dollars; by the end of the Second World War it would be worth four hundred thousand with more appreciation to come. Of the three founding brothers, only Peter owned stock, and now he owned it all.

On the Fourth of July, John Helden Jr. began his report. He sketched a chronological outline with Anita's help, as she easily recalled all the dates, all the people, and every place. John filled in critical, technical details, as he reflected on what he had seen and discussed with the distributors. He worked on the report several evenings a week, finishing in early August. His secretary typed a draft for his review. In mid-August he submitted a revised, final copy to Uncle Peter, Uncle Joe, and his cousin Peter Jr.

With dignified formality, John presented the report to his father, who tossed it, haphazardly, on his desk. "Thanks," he said, and then, "You have to visit Uncle Henry."

It surprised John. "Don't you want to discuss this?"

"Not till I've read it. When did you last see your uncle?"

"Which one?"

"Henry," his father answered.

John thought for a moment. "Ma's funeral in '27." He detected a deep sadness in his father's eyes.

"Ya, she's gone five years already, five years . . . . Well, it's time you pay her brother a visit."

"What have you heard?"

"Henry's getting old. George and Irene went out there. George said he asked for you . . . wants to meet your bride."

"We'll go," John promised.

The next Sunday, a beautiful, late summer day, John and Anita drove to Henry's cabin on faraway Basses' Bay. It was nostalgic for John; he hadn't been there for years. On straight roads, he held Anita's hand.

As John drove into the yard, his uncle approached. When the car stopped, he was right there to open Anita's door.

"Thank you," she said, "and hello."

John rushed around to introduce them properly.

"Nice to see you, Johnny."

They shook hands.

"Nice to see you too, Uncle Henry."

The dreary interior of the little cabin shocked Anita. It shocked John, too, for when he was a boy, Henry kept everything clean, well-organized, and cheerful.

"My God, how do you live?" Anita asked.

"Quite well," Henry answered. "I've got happy chickens and a bountiful garden."

Anita turned away. That wasn't what she meant.

"Can I show Anita where we slept?" The ladder to the attic was gone.

"I haven't been up there in years, Johnny. I filled it with hay . . . keeps me a little warmer in winter and a little cooler in summer."

"We were right under the rafters . . . thunder reverberated on the roof like a drum. Scared the heck out of Juley and me."

"Those were nice years," Henry said. "Now they're lousy."

"Why do you say that?" Anita asked.

"Men have no work. Banks can't be trusted. Farmers can't make any money. We need a change . . . ."

"You mean political change?" Anita asked.

"Of course, a man can't even buy a cold bottle of beer. What kind of a country is that?"

"I believe in Prohibition," Anita said.

"Let's not talk about-"

Henry cut John off. "I don't. What the hell ever happened to government for the people? What kind of liberty is it if a man can't enjoy a glass of beer?"

"Drinking caused more problems to more men than it ever gave benefit," Anita said.

"Nonsense," Henry replied.

"Well, President Hoover doesn't agree with you."

"Anita-" John tried to interrupt, but Uncle Henry, a staunch Democrat, cut him off again.

"And for it, he'll be out a job come November and damn good riddance, too."

Anita gasped.

John cut in, "Now's not the time to talk politics."

"Don't be silly, Johnny. I talk politics anytime," Henry said, cheerfully. He grinned at Anita. "Nothing personal, of course."

Anita forced a smile. She thought Hoover a fine president.

Sensing his wife's discomfort, John suggested he show her the lake. Henry held the door for his guests. In silence, the three strolled towards the pier. Its dilapidated condition surprised John because Henry always maintained the pier, even taking it out every winter to protect it from surging ice. Now, leaning posts and loose or missing deck boards prevented walking on it. John gazed sadly at the far end of the pier, recalling how he had fished there so many happy summer hours so many long years ago. In the tall grass behind the narrow beach he saw the old skiff overturned and weather beaten. Henry hadn't launched it in years.

"Pier needs work," Henry grumbled.

He'll never do it, Anita thought.

"The lake looks smaller," John said.

"Same size," Henry replied, "you just got bigger."

"Water seems high, though." John wanted to stretch the conversation.

"We had plenty rain . . . too much, actually. Carp swim up from the marsh. Every now and then I shoot a big, fat one."

It surprised Anita. ". . . with a gun?"

Henry laughed. "With my pistol . . . carp make good fertilizer, especially for tomatoes."

"Oh, my," Anita said.

John never knew Uncle Henry kept a pistol. They walked back to the cabin, but Anita was reluctant to go in again.

When they reached the steps leading to the lakeside door, Henry said, "I'm sorry I can't feed you a little supper."

"That's all right, Uncle Henry," John said, tenderly.

"I picked you a bag of tomatoes, though."

"Oh, how nice," Anita said. And then, "We really can't stay . . . ."

"Suit yourself," Henry muttered.

George was right. Henry looked and talked like an old man. It saddened John. "We don't want to put you through any trouble," he said. "We're having dinner with Anita's folks . . . ."

". . . so thanks for coming. Nice to meet you, Anita."

"Yes, nice to meet you, too, Uncle Henry." The sweetness in her voice pleased John.

They drove out Henry's bumpy lane to Wood's Road; John headed east towards Tess Corners. On both sides of the gravelly road, breezes blew across the flower heads of wheat and through the tall corn tassels. The fields surged and swayed almost as though they possessed a kind of life, like a swelling sea. In less than a month farmers would begin harvesting, not knowing if they'd earn a penny profit. John's Model-A rumbled along, its top barely higher than the corn. Inside, conversation was sparse.

"He seems old," Anita commented.

"He was born in '63 during the Civil War; he's almost seventy."

"Seems older than that . . . his place is a mess."

"He kept it very nice when I was a boy."

"I'm sure he did," Anita said, coldly.

+ + +

By the summer of 1920, thirty-six States had ratified the Nineteenth Amendment to the Constitution thus granting American women the right to vote in the November national elections. Wisconsin's ratification, along with two other States in June, 1919, thrilled John's mother, Augusta Helden.

The Republicans nominated for the presidency a senator from Ohio, Warren G. Harding. Though not a national figure, women suffragettes regarded him highly for his outspoken support for a woman's right to vote. That would not be sufficient, however, to gain Augusta's vote; she remained a *Wilsonian* Democrat.

The great State of Ohio emerged extremely important that

election year, as the Democrats nominated her governor, James Cox, for president. Most of the country had turned against President Wilson's plan to participate in the League of Nations, fearing a loss of sovereignty. The issue hurt Cox. Harding wisely emphasized the need to return to a more normal economy with less government involvement, a lingering holdover from Wilson's wartime regime. That, however, would not be sufficient to gain Augusta's husband's vote. John Helden, Sr. remained a *pacifist* Democrat in spite of policies that ultimately dampened the metal fabricating business.

As Cox's running mate, the Democrats nominated a relatively unknown thirty-eight year old assistant secretary of the Navy who had served throughout Wilson's two terms. This brilliant man earned his bachelor's degree in history from Harvard in 1903. He married a niece of then Republican President, Theodore Roosevelt; she bore him six children. He had first been elected to the New York State Senate in 1910 at the age of twenty-eight and re-elected two years later. He then served in Wilson's administration with great distinction and, for it, received the nomination for Vice President in 1920.

Harding's landslide victory disappointed Augusta Helden, her uncomplicated husband, and fledgling sons. The extraordinary vice presidential candidate for the Democrats, to whom the Helden's paid little attention, contracted polio in 1921, never fully regaining use of his legs. However, with the encouragement of his wife and children, he returned to politics and, at the 1924 Democratic National Convention, nominated New York's governor, Al Smith, for president. Smith lost the nomination to West Virginian John W. Davis who got trounced in the Electoral College by a tight-lipped Calvin Coolidge who became president at Harding's death in 1923.

In 1927, Augusta Helden died. The following year, Al Smith, a Catholic, won the Democratic nomination for president. That gave John Helden, Sr. and his four sons two reasons to vote for him. Smith relinquished his job as governor of New York and nominated the partially paralyzed, former Navy secretary to replace him as governor of the nation's most populous state. Even though Herbert Hoover beat Smith in another landslide, greatly disappointing all the Helden men, the people of New York elected Smith's young protégé, Franklyn Delano Roosevelt.

In late 1932, after FDR served two successful two-year terms as Governor of New York, and after the calamity of the economic crash, John Helden, his four sons, and their wives were poised to vote for Governor Roosevelt for the presidency of the United States. Only Anita Helden, nee Thilman, had reservations, and that was because her parents remained loyal Republicans.

+ + +

At the dinner table, Anita mentioned that John's Uncle Henry favored repeal of Prohibition. She expected everyone to be as horrified as she was.

"He'd just like to enjoy an occasional glass of beer," John said.

"So would I," Dr. Thilman agreed.

"Father!" Anita exclaimed.

"Prohibition is stupid," Dom cut in. "Everybody drinks bootleg, criminals get rich, the cops are corrupt . . . it's a disaster. I'm in favor of repeal."

"So am I," Lew added. "What about you John?"

That put John on the spot. He respected his wife's opinion, but believed Prohibition was, at best, a well-intentioned mistake. Long before passage of the Eighteenth Amendment, his beloved mother favored Prohibition because she saw in her own brother a weakness for alcohol and feared it might corrupt her sons. Sadly, Prohibition never did stop George Helden from becoming an alcoholic. Augusta's other three sons, however, did not succumb to that insatiable craving for liquor. John knew he'd enjoy an occasional glass of beer just as he enjoyed a highball now and then. He never frequented speakeasies and thought the nightclub in New York City immoral. He had no desire, however, to disappoint Anita. He had to answer Lew's question carefully. "I'm not sure . . . I see pros and cons on both sides."

Anita accepted John's safe and easy answer because she was more interested in her father's opinion. "What about you, Dad?"

In his long medical career, Dr. Thilman had seen the ruinous consequences of alcoholism. He treated men with the profound weakness, noting how it destroyed their lives. He knew men who, in drunken rages, beat their wives and terrified their children. He had treated those poor women and because of it, back in 1919, favored

Prohibition. Nevertheless, he answered, "Jesus changed water into wine at Cana. That's hardly the work of a Prohibitionist."

"Brilliant," Dom said. "The Pope couldn't argue that."

"Hoover could," John said, hoping the family would find it funny, though no one did.

"Roosevelt will be elected," Lew predicted, "and Prohibition is going to be repealed. The country will be better off getting rid of Prohibition, but I'm not so sure about gaining Roosevelt."

"Dom's point is well made," Dr. Thilman said. "People drink bootleg, the criminals get rich, and the police are corrupt. In my view, prohibition is worse than legal alcohol even with all its dangers."

"We saw that in New York," John said.

Mary Louise folded her napkin and placed it aside. "The problem with Prohibition is that it merely bans alcohol. Make something illegal and people want it. Children have to be taught the dangers of drinking. My father told me years ago that the whisky makers had a convention in Chicago; one of the speakers urged the salesmen to peddle whisky to young boys. He said something to the effect that if you get them early, you'll have them for life. Can you imagine deliberately corrupting young boys that way, ruining their lives? Think of the harm. That's why Prohibition came to be. Many saw the whisky purveyors as truly evil."

"If the States repeal Prohibition, which I think they will," Dr. Thilman said, "then laws have to be passed prohibiting alcohol to youngsters."

Mary Louise excused herself and went to the kitchen. She returned carrying a silver tray bearing a lovely cut-glass decanter and six fine, sherry glasses. The decanter contained a dark, red liquid, raising Dr. Thilman's suspicion.

"What have you there, Mary?"

"I am guilty of breaking that terrible law. I have become a vintner. Tonight I'm serving my finest raspberry dessert wine."

Everyone clapped except Anita.

"So, what exactly is in there?" Dr. Thilman asked.

"Partially fermented red grapes, a sufficient quantity of medical alcohol stolen from your office, and a strained puree of my homegrown raspberries. I do hope you all like it, and none of you, especially you Anita, will report me to the Feds, as I've heard them called."

They all laughed hard.

After Mary Louise poured the dark, viscous wine, Dr. Thilman, a Republican ever since he first voted for McKinley in 1896, proposed a toast. He looked at Mary Louise who held his gaze with bright, contented eyes. "To my dear wife . . . may she never stop delighting me. And to the end of Prohibition and this damn Depression."

"Hear, hear," everyone shouted.

On the drive home, Anita said, "John, if Prohibition is repealed, promise me you won't drink."

"I can't promise that."

"No, I mean to excess."

"George told me that once he took that first shot he couldn't quit till he passed out. I never craved liquor like that. I've never been drunk in my life. I doubt I ever will."

"That would frighten me . . . ."

"Of course, I'll drink your mother's wonderful wine."

Anita laughed. "Well, even I'll do that."

+ + +

That same evening across town, Peter Helden, Sr. sat in a comfortable, leather chair in the library of his spacious Lake Drive home with the door closed, the blunt sign he gave his wife to leave him alone. A neatly typed document lay on his lap. The cover page read: *Report on Eastern Trip by John Helden Jr., Spring, 1932.* Peter expected an arduous, prosaic read, but as he got into it, the report commanded his interest. His nephew's writing pleased Peter, but what John wrote angered him:

I noticed at all our distributors that they have hundreds of sets of U-bolts on hand, which could not be used on the tanks for which they were intended. The U-bolts as they come from our factory were either not long enough or the gage was not right and in many cases the thread lengths were too short. The result is that our distributors must go out and pay a high price for bar stock, make up new U-bolts to fit, and use those to mount the tank we furnish. It was necessary for our Detroit distributor to have two men spend the greater part of the day making up new U-bolts for the two 3000 gallon tanks they were mounting when I was there.

Peter couldn't believe it. Hundreds of sets of U-bolts furnished to all the eastern distributors proved worthless. Obviously, they represented a good deal of money, but, far more importantly, they represented the incompetence of the Helden Company itself. *How did this happen*, he asked himself. How could his brothers, Joe in engineering and John in manufacturing, have allowed this to happen? And why, he was confounded, didn't the distributors let him know? It cost them money so why the hell wouldn't they have said something, if not to him, at least to the sales engineers? He read on:

Many of the compartment tanks when mounted do not drain properly. When I was in Philadelphia a 1000 gallon tank was being mounted and in order to make the compartments drain, it was necessary to place a sleeper tapering from seven inches to two inches underneath the sills of the tank. Obviously, with a condition of this kind it is necessary to make up new U-bolts also.

Peter dropped the report to his lap. *Why didn't Joe, John, and I think of that? It's a disgrace. They must think we're all a bunch of dummkopfs.* He read more:

Another thing that causes trouble is the interference of the compartment outlet or piping over the rear axle under maximum load or maximum spring deflection. This is also true of raised truck cross members. Of course, many times units are mounted on old trucks for which we have little or no engineering data. I told all the distributors that in such cases they must take time to make a sketch of the chassis and send it to us before manufacturing begins.

Peter finished the report. While reading it again, he noted the significant points. His nephew, to his credit, had discovered issues vitally important to the Helden Co.'s reputation. It angered Peter; anger he directed at his brothers and the entire sales engineering department, even John Helden Jr. *Why hadn't someone discovered these problems sooner,* he wondered. Peter Helden didn't give a damn what people thought of him personally, but he did care what his distributors and customers thought about his company. From the very beginning, over thirty years ago, he was determined to do things better than any other manufacturer. Every product he made would be of incomparable quality, but now, he realized, the company must appear grossly incompetent in the eyes of its distributors. *Thank heaven,* he thought, *that my distributors are more resourceful than my*

brothers. Hopefully, they never disclosed any of this to their customers.
Peter shook his head in disgust. His two older brothers would bear
his wrath.

The next morning he called Peter Jr. into his office. "Did you
read John's report?"

"Yes."

"What'd you think?"

"It was alright . . . ."

"Just alright?"

"Yeah, he seemed to get along well enough with the distributors, if we can believe him."

"What the hell are you suggesting . . . that John's a liar?" Peter
Helden turned in his swivel chair. He gazed out the window, deep
in thought. "You were against my paying John for the six weeks."

"You only paid me for four," Peter Jr. replied. "I'm your
son . . . ."

"You went to Florida and sat on your ass. Do you have any idea
what was significant in John's report?"

"You know I don't like technical stuff. I didn't pay much attention to that, but I'm sure that's what you're thinking."

"That technical stuff cost our distributors thousands of dollars.
What John learned, because he's a pretty damn good engineer, is
worth about a hundred times what I paid for his trip, maybe more.
He pointed out we're a bunch of knuckleheads."

"That wasn't in his report," Peter Jr. scoffed. "He'd never write
something like that. You'd fire him."

"You're right," Peter replied, surprised that his son missed the
point. "He didn't have to. All he had to do was tell me, in a few
well-written paragraphs, that we failed to ship our equipment with
the proper mounting hardware. That doesn't sound like much to
you, does it? But I'll tell you something Peter, had John not discovered what was really going on, this company – which provides you
and me a damn comfortable living – would have been seriously
harmed. Thanks to your cousin we can correct those problems.
Uncorrected they'd jeopardize our relationship with every distributor, not just the eastern ones, all of them, all over the country. You
think they wouldn't tell our competitors of our incompetence and
offer to represent them and tell us to go to hell? I'm telling you, they

certainly would. I'll solve these problems. I'll visit every one of our distributors and apologize for being so incompetent, and I'll pledge it will never happen again. And all of this because your cousin, who you think is so beneath you, was smart enough to recognize serious problems when he saw them, and you don't even make the g--damn effort to understand his report."

"I'm not a technical man."

"No you're not, but this company is a technical enterprise. Too bad for its future you didn't study engineering."

"What do you mean by that?"

"I mean you can consider yourself damn lucky I bought out your uncles. Had I not, your cousin would succeed me – not you."

His father's admission stunned Peter Jr. "John doesn't understand that this company needs to run on modern business principles. Engineers like him are a dime a dozen. I'll hire and fire those guys like clay pigeons."

"I've built this business on common sense and hard work. You think that crap they feed you in college makes you worthy to run my business? Don't make me laugh. You should have studied engineering. You'll never really understand this business because of it. You'll never have the insights you need for our products to change, to improve, and compete. Your cousin has shown me he has those insights. If you were smart, you'd go back and get an engineering degree."

"Never," Peter Jr. sneered.

"Get the hell out of here," his father snarled.

Peter Jr. went to his office and in that brief moment, walking those few steps across the hall, the seed of hatred in his heart that he had already planted for his cousin grew wildly. His own father had marked the enemy. Now the son recognized, among all the men in the company, that his cousin was his one, true, and dangerous rival. There was always the possibility that something might arise to alter the clear, smooth path Peter Jr. envisioned for his ascension to the head of the company after his father retired or died. There was the very real possibility, at least in Peter Jr.'s mind, that his first cousin, John Helden Jr., might be named president by acclamation of the board of directors at the posthumous directive of Peter Helden Sr. simply because John was perceived as the more talented potential successor. In fact, John had a better intellect and a more outgoing personality than Peter Jr., and most employees in the company knew it. So whatever that something was, Peter would seek it out, find it, and destroy it. He would even destroy John if he had to. Nothing was going to deny him his rightful place at the top after his father was gone. Nothing was going to deny him the great wealth that the company afforded the sole owner, now and in the future. He would inherit ownership of this prosperous, growing company, and he would inherit the extravagant salary that the head so properly deserved. He was the only son, the only child, and he would rightly inherit his father's entire fortune and legacy. He would do anything and everything to prevent his cousin from becoming the president of the Helden Company, for he had already decided, in his darkest and most secret thoughts, that the company was destined to be his and his alone, and his father – dead or alive – his uncles, his cousins, and the entire board of directors be damned.

+ + +

Some instant known only to God in the third week of October, 1932, Henry Rosenberg died alone in his bed at the little cottage on Basses' Bay. In a simple, hand-written will he named his four nephews sole heirs. Three of them elected John Helden, Jr. executor of the meager estate. The question that dominated the brothers' discussions was whether they should retain or sell the property on the west shore of the little lake in faraway Muskego. It appraised at eight hundred dollars, enough to make all four realize they'd prefer two hundred dollars in hard cash rather than owning a shack on a parcel of mosquito breeding lowland. After they decided to sell the property, the wonder became who would buy it, and how long would it take? A local realtor agreed to list and show the property for fifty dollars, and then, in those incredibly difficult economic times, a buyer came along almost miraculously and paid the full asking price.

John and George assumed the job of cleaning the property, keeping the few items of some value – they found Henry's holstered pistol under his bed – and burning the rest. The fire pile welcomed most everything including the old, dry-rotted skiff. When John and George drove away from Basses' Bay for the last time, they took only a small chest of drawers that just fit into John's trunk. The drawers were filled with Uncle Henry's papers, his Bible, and a few books including Thoreau's *Walden*. John put the pistol under his car seat. Some usable furniture and all the fishing gear were left for the new owner.

With his four sons and daughters-in-law, John Helden Sr. attended Henry's funeral at St. Paul's in Tess Corners. After burial in the church graveyard, they drove in procession back to Milwaukee where John Sr. treated everyone to a roast duck dinner at Kegel's Inn. Throughout the day, John Jr.'s feelings were ambivalent. He had so much good in his life now with his beautiful young wife and her congenial family that the happy memories of his boyhood summer days with Uncle Henry didn't seem nearly as precious and important as they used to. How he'd come to think of those long ago days in another fifteen or twenty years he could not imagine.

+ + +

On Tuesday, November 8, 1932, America elected Franklyn Delano Roosevelt its thirty-second president. Right after John Helden Jr. came home from work, he and Anita went to vote. In the school's crowded cafeteria polling place not a single Hoover button was seen. After dinner, Anita quickly tidied the kitchen, brushed her hair, and put on fresh lipstick. Their friends, Rudy and Ella Laab, invited them to an election night party at their home in Shorewood. In the mild evening, the Heldens wore light coats and high spirits. John, born and raised a Democrat, would always look upon this night as the triumph of his parents' and grandparents' fondest political hopes. Democrats would be swept into Congress and the White House, and the incumbent Republicans banished to the impotent fate they so richly deserved.

When John and Anita arrived, people were already boisterous and loud. Anita attributed it to election expectations, but John knew it was bootleg, especially among the men.

"John plays," Rudy shouted. He thrust sheet music in front of him, but Anita grabbed it knowing John wasn't comfortable playing for a crowd. She glanced at it, noted the key of *G* and announced, "I can play this."

Ella approached. "Not yet Anita, I want to show you my new mixer."

"Tonight's the night," Rudy shouted above the din. "Tonight's the night the people take back their country."

Everyone cheered, while John smiled with absolute certainty Roosevelt would win in a landslide.

Rudy put his arm around John's shoulders. "What can I get you Johnny?"

"Highball . . . not too strong."

"Anita?"

"Same, but no whisky."

Laughing, Rudy went downstairs where the hooch was hid. After a few minutes he returned with their drinks. Anita and John gazed into each other's eyes, clinking their tumblers happily. John took a sip and detected the bourbon; he found the drink delicious. Anita tasted her ginger ale. She wasn't suspicious at all.

As the evening wore on and the radio's early returns showed a growing Roosevelt lead, Anita sat down at the piano and began stumbling through *Happy Days Are Here Again*. Everyone joined in at the top of their voices. Anita's miscues were hardly noticed. She had to play it again and again. Cake and coffee were served after the radio predicted a decisive win for the Democrats. As the party finally began to break up, John and Anita said their goodbyes and left.

While everyone at the party sang that optimistic tune of instantly returning prosperity, a cold front pushed across southeastern Wisconsin. Fog formed in the mild, moist November air immersing Milwaukee within a thick, white cloud that slowed the drive home. On the way, John talked cheerfully about the good times coming: about laborers and shop men going back to work for a decent wage, small businessmen reopening their doors, dairy farmers earning a fair price for milk, increasing sales at the Company, and even about the end of Prohibition. Tired and sleepy, Anita chose to believe it all.

As she fell silent, John began to dream of his future. He was convinced, as the economy strengthened, that he would eventually be named Vice President of Sales, the position his cousin held, and the position John believed destiny meant him to have. He anticipated Uncle Peter, in ten years or even less, would retire, and Peter

Jr. would rightfully become president of the Company. John would become the most important, trusted, and loyal man in top management, serving Peter Jr. well, especially, helping him understand engineering issues. For it, Peter Jr. would be forever grateful. He and John would be friends again, as they had been when they were boys. They would run the company in tandem just as their fathers had. John would make more money than he ever imagined; he and Anita would have a wonderful marriage, and, hopefully, they would be blessed with children.

He envisioned his happiness extending his entire life, the same visceral happiness he felt in New York at the Metropolitan Opera, and the same happiness he felt this incredible, victorious, political night. John believed in the inevitability of all his hopes and dreams, believed in it with all his heart. The entire drive home the fog never lifted.

PART 2 ~ 1935 to 1948

Chapter 13 ~ 1935

In the spring and languid summer of 1935, Hildegard E. Neubauer pondered her life and future. She had lived in Milwaukee five years and worked as a waitress five to six days virtually every week, all that time. In early 1934, the *John Ernst Café,* one of the city's fine German restaurants, hired her; there she became acquainted with many distinguished customers. By this casual association and observation, Hildy, as she was called, resolved to improve herself. She knew it was solely up to her if people were ever to find *her* distinguished.

Mr. and Mrs. Ernst treated their staff well. Hildy earned a decent wage: forty cents an hour plus tips. She enjoyed serving in the three spacious dining rooms with their wood paneled walls and high, beamed ceilings. A magnificent stone fireplace, roaring with burning hardwood most fall and winter nights, delighted her. Nevertheless, on mild April days, walking to the Cafe from her little apartment on the east side, she realized she did not want to work as a waitress for the rest of her life. Now, she felt, was the time to make a change.

At twenty-five, Hildy craved more education. Her high school history teacher, when once questioned by a brash student about the value of book learning, calmly replied, "It is wiser and easier to work with your brain than your back," saying nothing more to the blank-faced boy. The admonition stuck in Hildy's mind, though for years she bore the weight of laden trays. A waitress, however, also had to use her mind. After diners finished, Hildy carefully and quickly added the charges, priding herself that no customer ever found an error in her addition. She knew her service and personality were pleasing because she often received compliments and generous tips. Yet, many nights after work, as she walked alone to her apartment, her back ached. *At my age, that shouldn't be,* she thought. The older waitresses constantly complained about their tired backs and sore feet; the waiters too, at the end of a busy night, looked tired and old. Hildy knew, unless she made a change, their fates would be her future. Slowly, over a period of weeks, she made a decision: she would go back to school, find a job in a business office and resign permanently from the tough ranks of waitressing.

Hildy often passed the *Stratton Business College for Women* on Van Buren, kitty-corner from the Cafe. Recently, she overheard a lunch customer mention that he hired a Stratton graduate and was "very pleased with her." Shortly thereafter, Hildy went to the admissions office and inquired about classes and registration. That night she read the bulletin for courses she'd take the first year.

The idea of going back to school thrilled Hildy. Her determination to succeed was as solidly rooted in her heart, as in her brain and back. *Someday,* she anticipated, *I'll prove myself useful to a real business.* Curiously, she never regarded her job at the Cafe as real business.

After she registered and paid a small down payment on an installment tuition plan, she wrote her parents:

August 16, 1935
Dear Papa and Mama,
  I am so excited to be writing you because I've made a most important decision. This morning I registered at the Stratton Business College for Women and I begin classes the first week of September. At the end of the school year, I'll receive my One-Year Certificate and, if I want, I can go a second year with more advanced courses and earn a Two-Year Certificate. Girls who attend Stratton get good jobs and I decided I just don't want to work as a waitress the rest of my life. Also, I hope to meet some nice girls my age. I can still work evenings at the Cafe and there'll be time in the afternoons for study. I am so happy to be doing this.
  I hope you both are well. I'm already looking forward to my

Christmas visit. I know I always say this but I do hope someday you'll come visit me.

How is your garden? I think of you often. Presently, I'm not dating anyone so you don't need to ask if I have a new beau. I don't and right now I'm glad because I want to work hard in school. No distractions, if you please.

Mama, write me soon. I always look forward to your letters.

Love, Hildy

Once classes started, Hildy felt boundless enthusiasm. She enjoyed her courses, teachers, classmates – all young women – and learned the material fairly easily. She liked bookkeeping because, since childhood, she enjoyed numbers. It was, she realized, little more than keeping track of money received and spent. "For every debit there has to be a credit," old Mr. Schmitz often said. He expected his students to clearly understand the differences between income and asset accounts and between expense and liability accounts.

Learning typing also thrilled Hildy. "It's such a modern thing," she told her co-workers at the Cafe. The goal was fifty words a minute by the end of the school year. When Hildy first struck the stiff keys on the big, black *Underwood,* she doubted her fingers could ever attain such blazing speed. But she was determined. She came to class a few minutes early and stayed after as long as possible, practicing whenever the room was available. She would have loved a typewriter in her apartment, but laughed at herself when she realized how unrealistic that was.

She even felt renewed enthusiasm for her job at the Cafe. The day's classes stimulated her mind; she welcomed the change waitressing afforded in the evening. She was in excellent health and her active life, with all the lifting and carrying of trays, and walking to and from school and work, kept her strong and slim. She enjoyed exchanging simple greetings and making small talk with her customers more than ever. She felt wonderful about her life because now she had a goal. It gave Hildy hope; when she felt hope she gained confidence. Importantly too, she thought of her affair with Arthur only rarely and, when she did, put him out of her mind without getting nearly as upset as she used to. If Arthur sneaked into her consciousness she'd expel the intruder with happier dreams of days to come. She attained control of her emotions, and only infrequently did she lapse into bitter memories of those past months, nearly a year ago, when she had kept company with Arthur.

At Christmas, the restaurant's busiest time, Hildy arranged to take several days to visit her parents. The other waitresses appreciated her absence, just to gain extra time and tips for themselves. They all needed money. The day before Christmas Eve she rose early and packed. From the payphone in her building she called a taxi to take her to the Everett Street station.

Hildy waited in a long line at the ticket window and struggled to board and find a seat. In Madison, she walked several blocks to the bus depot where she took the Greyhound headed to Dubuque. It stopped at every little town along the way. In Mineral Point, her father met her and they drove the eight miles to Albertsville exchanging pleasantries amid the simple joy of being together again. He was delighted to see his daughter, his only child, but his appearance surprised her. He looked older, heavier, and his breathing seemed more shallow and rapid. At home, Hildy embraced her mother, but she, too, appeared older and remarkably plain in ways Hildy never noticed before.

At the kitchen table, Hildy and her mother chatted, while her father read the newspaper, eavesdropped, and occasionally commented.

"Tell us about school," her mother said.

"Well, I really like it. I want to learn about business because I'll be able to get a better job, earn more, and save more. I mean if I can find a good position after I get my certificate."

"The country's still in this damn depression," her father said. "Be grateful you've got a job."

"Oh, I am, Papa, but there are so many businesses in Milwaukee. The breweries are working again, thanks to Mr. Roosevelt."

"That's a strange way to get the country out of a depression. He's been in almost three years, and the economy still stinks. Catering to the weakness of workingmen for a cold glass of beer hardly seems sound economic policy. Helps those fellows forget the misery they're in, I suppose."

"Hildy, I saw Eddie Cassidy the other day," her mother said.

"He's married, married a girl from Willow Grove. Her father has a farm near there."

"Oh my, I haven't seen him in years." Her mind flashed with gratitude for *not* being married to Eddie.

"He came here a few years ago, just dropped in after you moved to Milwaukee. He said he liked you very much, but couldn't understand why you left so suddenly. He said you were his one, true, high school sweetheart."

Hildy laughed out loud. "Oh, Mother, I was so young then. I never was serious about Eddie. I mean I couldn't see myself married to him. He was nice, but I never loved him or anything like that. I want someone who interests me and likes the things I like. All Eddie and I ever did was school dances and football games."

"You dated him after high school," her father reminded. "He drove his father's car and picked you up here."

"Maybe a little that summer, but never after that," Hildy protested.

"And what about the other fellow, what was his name . . . Arthur? You dated him quite recently," her mother said.

Discussion of past romances annoyed Hildy. She didn't want to think about those times much less talk about them. "I dated him for a while and realized he wasn't my type so I stopped seeing him."

Sensing her discomfort, her father said, "Your mother and I want you to use good judgment, Hildy. I'm glad you told us he wasn't your type. Good you knew that before getting involved. A man can make demands on a woman, especially, if she's easily available. If someone isn't your type, don't waste your time. You're better off with a good book."

Hildy placed her hand on his. "Papa, I completely agree."

Her mother cut three Macintosh apples into wedges: apples from the benevolent, old tree in their backyard. They snacked and talked about less consequential things. Every night her father enjoyed a cup of coffee with sugar and cream along with a piece of pie or cake, and a final cigarette before retiring. He was one of those lucky persons never kept awake by the coffee or the sugar. He claimed they eased him to sleep. If for some strange reason he couldn't sleep, which was rare, he'd blame the cream. Tonight if necessary, he'd blame the apples.

"You know, Papa," Hildy said, "you and Mama should visit me in Milwaukee. In all these years you never have, and I've asked you so often. If you don't want to drive take the train; it's only an hour and a half."

"Your mother and I don't like big cities."

How can he say such a thing, Hildy wondered. She couldn't recall her parents ever visiting any city other than Madison or Dubuque. "Milwaukee isn't real big . . . it's nice."

"Cities like that have swindlers and panhandlers, bums who'd just as soon pick your pocket as look at you. It's a wonder you haven't been robbed."

"Mama, you'd like to visit me, wouldn't you? Milwaukee isn't a criminal town. I've never had a problem."

"Yes, I would dear; perhaps we will one day." She glanced at her husband who said nothing, sipped his coffee, lit another cigarette, and retreated behind the newspaper. She didn't think *she* disliked big cities. She had been in Chicago years ago and really didn't know what to think.

"Lake Michigan is beautiful; it looks like an ocean. Come to the restaurant; I'll serve you. Oh Papa, please come. I would be so proud to serve you and Mama."

"Hildy, calm down; I don't want to talk about it. I'm tired." He looked at her sweet, round face, her thick, curly, black hair, and the dark, blue-black eyes. It was a daughter he loved dearly yet to whom he could scarcely utter a word of affection. "I'm glad you're home, but now I want to go to bed. You know I don't like contentious discussions before we sleep."

"I'm sorry Papa." She kissed his forehead and whispered, "Goodnight."

Hildy climbed the narrow, winding stairs to the small bedroom of her childhood. Every Christmas since she left Albertsville she returned to this house, this room, and her old bed. She realized in the almost six years since she moved away, her parents' home had become like a rarely opened drawer of old letters, photographs, and costume jewelry that evoked, if not unwanted memories, then at least unnecessary ones. Her true home couldn't be this house. She had grown completely away from it and the country town in which it was rooted. Her home wasn't even the little apartment in

Milwaukee. As she thought about it, she realized home was much more about the attitudes of her heart towards school, the Cafe, the streets she walked every day, her new friends, especially Anna, her sister waitresses, Mr. and Mrs. Ernst, Glorioso's Market where she shopped: the entire, simple fabric of her life in Milwaukee and the happy feelings it enlivened had all melded to become home. She had dreams now. She wanted a good life, and she wanted it in a city her father was afraid to visit. *I could never live here again,* she told the darkness. And then in a startlingly simple insight she envisioned the life she desired. *I want to marry a smart, good man and have babies, and I want to become a businesswoman.* It made her laugh out loud. *Oh, Hildy, you a businesswoman? You are such a silly girl.*

She gazed down at the lonely street lit only by a solitary lamp. Behind clouds of wispy gauze, the dim moon cast faint tree shadows on the hard, winter ground. She thought of how, in front of this house, she had sat with Eddie in his father's car with the windows rolled down on warm, summer nights. They talked, as long as she could, knowing her father's impatience was growing. She paused for a moment to watch Eddie turn the car around and then wave as he drove away. She might dawdle a moment before she went inside just to inhale the wonderful breezes sweet with the aroma of field crops that encircled the town like an enormous wreath.

At the side window she glanced at the snow-streaked fields sloping to the crest of the frozen horizon. She drew the shade, closed the curtains and, in the cold darkness, felt her way into the bed of her childhood. In a while, she grew comfortable and warm.

She thought of Eddie again and how stupid they had been, how stupid *she* had been. He was always sweet to her. She never meant to hurt him. She knew he hated to see her leave. But she just couldn't bring herself to tell him she was pregnant; he would have wanted to marry her. *Now he's married to some little schaumtorte,* she thought. *Just as well; better I never see him again.* And then, *oh, God, were he to know what I did.* She shuddered at the thought and if her parents were to ever know.

Horrid memories of Arthur intruded. A loathing seeped into her mind and heart. She had taken her revenge, a revenge that hurt her, she knew, far more than Arthur, for she never even told him. *I mustn't have these thoughts, not at Christmas,* she warned herself. *God bless Mama and Papa,* she prayed. *Dear God, help me to forget, please . . . forgive me . . . forgive all.* In minutes she fell asleep.

Christmas morning, Hildy and her parents drove to the Lutheran Church in Mineral Point. The choir sang *Oh Holy Night,* which she loved. She enjoyed the service realizing, as she sat between her parents, that she hadn't been to church since last Christmas. She knew better than to disclose that.

At home, Hildy helped prepare the Wienerschnitzel, boiled potatoes, and red cabbage. Her mother had baked an apple pie, garnishing each piece with a chunk of fine, room-temperature cheddar.

After they finished the wonderful meal and final cups of coffee, they exchanged gifts. Hildy gave her mother a bottle of cologne and a beautiful, lace-trimmed handkerchief. She gave her father a book titled, *The New Germany.* Her parents gave Hildy a special, bank envelope with an oval opening that revealed Alexander Hamilton's serene countenance. They all thanked and hugged each other and wished each other "Merry Christmas" over and over.

Her father paged through his present. "A *new* Germany, eh? Well, this Hitler fellow is not a good man. He's ended their depression and war reparations and, for that, Germans like him, but I tell you, he is not a good man. He talks of *Lebensraum.* Hildy, do you know what that means?"

"Living space, Papa . . . I did have two years of German in high school, if you recall."

"Ya, he talks *Lebensraum,* but I hear *Krieg* – war. He's a rabble-rouser and hates the Jews. In my opinion he's a dangerous man."

"I've heard people at the Cafe talk about him. They say he's been good for Germany. People seem to admire him."

"Because he helped the German economy, I understand that. But he is not a man Europe can trust. Believe me when I tell you this."

"The Olympic Games are going to be in Berlin next year," Hildy said.

"Your father knows that. He knows all about Germany. The Madison and Dubuque papers are filled with European news."

"I appreciate the book, Hildy, and I'll read it . . . *Dankeschoen.* It looks like propaganda, but that's all right so long as one knows one is reading propaganda. I want to learn about this so-called new Germany. After all, I came from old Germany when I was only five."

"Oh, Papa, I know nothing about politics," Hildy laughed. "I hear things at work, that's all. I overheard someone mention the Olympics. If you tell me Hitler isn't a good man, I certainly believe you more than anyone else."

"Why of all people, must we talk about him?" her mother asked. "Germany might as well be on the moon, for all I care."

Hildy laughed again, while her father shrugged. "Well, I'm just saying: he is not a good man."

At the end of the evening, Hildy hugged and kissed them. She washed her face, brushed her teeth, then went up to her room. Just as the night before, she looked out at the quiet street that ended right there at the end of their yard and the yard of the house across the way. The sidewalks ended there, the street lamps, the naked American elms; the little town itself ended right there at the south survey line of their lot. A wood plank barricade painted with black and white angled stripes stood firmly fixed at the end of the street so no tipsy motorist would drive into the broad field that bordered the short, south edge of town. Gazing out the window, Hildy thought, *I was raised on a dead-end street in a dead-end town. I'm so different now. Oh, I'll be glad to get back to Milwaukee.*

That Christmas night, Hildy slept well, but not in the bed of her childhood though it was the same comfortable bed against the same flowered wallpaper in the same cold, dark room. Her innocent childhood was over long ago, and the bed, in spite of itself, had become the bed of a woman. She realized she was merely a guest now, and that was all she ever could be. *I'm not their doting daughter anymore,* she knew. *I have my own life . . . I don't belong here.* As sleep enfolded her, she wondered, *where do I belong?*

Chapter 14 ~ 1936 [Part 1]

J ust days after starting school in the fall of 1935, Hildy Neubauer
met Anna Eastwood. They found each other amusing, interesting, smart, and within a month became good friends. They attended
the same classes, ate lunch together and, occasionally, on weekends
went to a movie or strolled the bluff in Juneau Park overlooking
Lake Michigan. Anna, a west side girl, lived with her parents in
the uptown area along North Avenue. Evenings, she worked as a
waitress at the Boulevard Inn, a restaurant as fine as the Ernst Cafe.
Soon enough, the young women were exchanging stories of their
favorite and not-so-favorite customers.

Anna, straight and slender, had long, reddish-brown hair, light
brown eyes set widely apart, and a perfect nose. When she dressed
for Sunday Mass, congregants, especially men, noticed her regal
bearing. While Hildy had an interesting and appealing face, Anna's
beauty stunned at first glance. Pretty as she was, though, she wasn't
conceited. Like her new friend she was considerate, friendly, and
pleasant.

Near the end of the school year, Anna and Hildy began searching for jobs. They read every *Help Wanted: Female* ad in the newspapers and discussed what they felt might hold promise. They wished
for jobs as secretaries, but Hildy also considered bookkeeping. Anna
liked the west side, while Hildy preferred downtown. She hoped
for a job near her apartment so she could walk to and from. "Plus,"
she told Anna, "I'll save bus money."

"But Hildy, you'll wear out your shoes."

Hildy figured thirty fares for a pair of pumps and decided she'd
take the bus.

In early May, 1936, Hildy invited her parents to the *Awarding
of Certificates Ceremony,* the first Saturday in June. She practically
begged, pleading it was the perfect occasion to come to Milwaukee.
She also mentioned her wish to serve them at the Cafe and to meet
her friend, Anna.

The young women even talked about their parents spending a little time together, though Hildy expressed a concern. "Anna, my father's not from America. He came from Germany and still speaks with an accent."

Anna laughed. "Hildy, my father came from Germany when he was seven."

"Oh, I'm glad. Everything German interests my father, even that awful man Hitler."

"My father doesn't like him at all."

"That's good . . . we wouldn't want an argument. But tell me, Anna, how come you have an English name, I mean, if your father is German?"

"He changed our name. It used to be *Ostwald* with the *v* sound, but he wanted to change it to *Oswald* with the *w* sound because it sounds less German, but my mother wouldn't agree. So he changed it to *Eastwood*. That's the English translation, you know, and that my mother likes."

"I do too. It sounds so refined. *Oswald* sounds like something in the funnies."

Anna giggled. "You're something in the funnies . . . ."

A few days later, Hildy received a letter from her mother. *It wasn't easy*, she wrote, *convincing your father that this was something he had to do*. She warned him, "If you won't go, I'll go alone." At that, he relented.

Anna and Mrs. Eastwood began planning a dinner party for the evening after the young women received their certificates. Anna's success in finding a new job would also be celebrated. The vice president at the Plank Road Brewery thought her an excellent choice not only for her high grades, but also her graceful beauty. A proud parent of three, he was a resolutely married man, old enough to be Anna's father. Nevertheless, he decided to wait awhile before introducing his wife to his striking new secretary.

"Now we have to find you a job," Anna told Hildy.

But as graduation neared, Hildy had no luck. She consoled herself that she could keep her job at the Cafe until she found a suitable position. Like so many other things in life, she realized, *it's just a matter of time*.

Her parents planned to arrive Friday and stay until Monday.

Anna and Hildy arranged to meet before the ceremony to introduce everyone. Later, at the Eastwood's, they'd become acquainted. They presumed their parents would get along just fine, as their fathers thought similarly about German politics, and they simply weren't concerned about their mothers. "Women are so much more adaptable," they agreed.

That Friday, Hildy slept late, ate breakfast, bathed leisurely, and washed her hair. Her frizzy curls she'd let dry in the mild breezes. She wore a newer dress, one her parents hadn't seen. Hildy and Anna planned to meet at two o'clock, have a bite to eat, then walk to the station. After so many years, her parents' coming thrilled Hildy. She gazed out her open window at the blue, sunny sky. Small, silver-gray clouds floated eastward, their edges radiant with sunlight.

The intercom buzzer startled her. She pressed the speaker button. "Yes, who is it?"

"Western Union for a Miss H. Neubauer."

Her dread was instantaneous. Rushing to the lobby she suspected her father changed his mind. In her room she read: *Dear Hildy* Stop *Papa ill* Stop *can't come* Stop *so sorry* Stop *Love Mama* Stop.

She sat on the bed and sobbed, her heart numb with disbelief. "Oh Papa, no, not now, not today . . . ."

For five years, Hildy longed for her parents' visit. Now a sudden, bitter resentment tainted her mind and heart. She paced the room in anger and helplessness. She couldn't call home because her parents didn't have a telephone. It was pointless to call her father's store, and she didn't know the doctor's number. Finally, she freshened her eyes and lipstick, grabbed her purse, and left. She'd walk to the telephone company's office on Broadway, call the doctor from there, then meet Anna as planned.

Mr. Neubauer had suffered a gall bladder attack. Confined to bed for three days, he had to abstain from food, but could sip warm water. After that, the doctor prescribed hot tea, broth, toast, and baby food. If the patient endured that lean regimen for a week and his condition improved, a heartier diet would be allowed. Without improvement he'd require surgery in Madison to remove the gall bladder and its mahogany-like stones that the doctor suspected Neubauer had in abundance.

Anna recognized the disappointment in Hildy's voice and eyes, as she explained her father's condition. After an hour, though, Hildy's inherent resilience began to assert itself.

"Well, there's absolutely nothing I can do . . . except pray. I certainly intend to get my certificate tomorrow. I don't know what you and your mother will do about our dinner party."

"Hildy, for heaven's sake, we'll have the party just as we planned. Your parents would want us to."

"Oh, Anna, I'd like that."

In the school auditorium, eighty-seven young women received their one-year certificates with both Anna and Hildy earning top honors. Hildy was the only graduate without a blood relative in attendance. Then fifty-two candidates received their two-year certificates. Hildy thought, *maybe I'll go the second year*. More than likely, she wouldn't find a new job so she concluded, *I might as well stay in school*.

Anna's parents expressed their regrets and, without thinking, told of a friend of theirs who died from a gall bladder attack. Shocked, Hildy declared her hope that one day they would meet her very much alive father and mother.

Mr. Eastwood invited her to sit in the front seat of his automobile – she rarely rode in such a fine car – and when they arrived at the Eastwood's home, its loveliness surprised Hildy. A floral centerpiece and crystal candleholders adorned the dining room table. Bone white china shimmered above a golden tablecloth. Hildy had never seen such an elegant setting. Her parent's house in Albertsville didn't even have a dining room. The Cafe's tables, in comparison, seemed terribly plain.

"Mrs. Eastwood, everything looks so beautiful," Hildy said. "I just love the flowers. They bring so much joy to a room."

"Thank you – yes, they do."

"Let me show you our new piano," Anna said. "Perhaps my father will play."

"Do you play?"

"I took lessons, but I have no talent."

Overhearing, her father said, "Nonsense, you have talent; you just don't have the desire. You didn't work."

Hildy feigned surprise. "Anna Eastwood didn't work? Let me check that certificate. Is that really your name there?"

Mrs. Eastwood offered Hildy lemonade. "We're having a Mosel wine with dinner, but this will quench your thirst."

Hildy sipped the pale, sweet-sour juice. "I've served Mosel wines at the Café, but I don't know exactly where that region is."

"The Mosel River," Mr. Eastwood began, "flows into the Rhine at the city of Koblenz. The vineyards extend far to the west along the river valley. I saw those beautiful vineyards once when I was a boy."

"I understand you were quite young when you came."

"Ya, just a little shaver . . . ." Mr. Eastwood's words fell like a sad tune. "I regret your parents couldn't come. I was looking forward to meeting them. Anna told me your father is also interested in Germany."

"Yes, very much so. He's concerned Hitler wants to expand Germany and fears that might lead to war."

"Your father is insightful. If there is another war in Europe it will be Hitler's doing, and America, whether it wants it or not, will be dragged in, just like 1917."

Mrs. Eastwood didn't want to hear such talk. "Tell me Hildy, what are your plans?"

"Well, until I find an acceptable position, I'll work at the Cafe."

Without being coaxed, Mr. Eastwood sat at the piano and played a waltz by Brahms, its lilting melody unrecognized by Hildy. When he finished, she said, "That was lovely; it made me feel like dancing."

Anna announced, "Dinner is about to be served . . . won't you please come?"

Mr. Eastwood offered Hildy his arm. She felt remarkably content given the circumstances of her father's illness and her parent's absence. In the dining room the table candles diffused a glowing charm. Mrs. Eastwood served fresh Lake Superior trout steaming with a tomato and bread stuffing, and garnished by spears of asparagus. She set the silver platter in front of her husband, as he poured the chilled *Mosel* into Hildy's glass.

Standing at the head of the table and forgetting he was the only man, he said, "Ladies and gentlemen, I would like to propose a toast to our dear graduates. May they have successful careers in the world of business, and may the goodness in their hearts always guide them in their dealings. To Hildy and Anna – congratulations!"

All clinked their glasses before sipping the dry, fruity wine. Hildy was touched by his words, doubting her father could offer such a perfect toast.

As they began to dine, Hildy asked, "Tell me Mr. Eastwood, Anna said you were involved in exporting and importing. What exactly do you export and import?"

"Actually, we only import musical instruments: brass and woodwinds from Europe. We sell American instruments, too, but I prefer the European. Mostly we sell to schools. They have excellent band and orchestra programs . . . our business has been very good these past several years. We sell sheet music and employ several part-time teachers. Some parents want their children to have more than just the school instruction, so they take private lessons with us. I love music . . . it's a wonderful business for me."

"I certainly can understand that," Hildy said. "Someday I intend to be in business for myself, something I really love."

Anna's eyes quizzed Hildy.

"No, seriously, I just don't know what kind of business."

"Basically, all business is the same," Anna's father said. "You buy or make something and sell it for more than it cost. Whatever you sell has to pay for the cost of the goods, all your other expenses, salaries, rent, and so forth. Hopefully, there'll be a little profit left for you.

"All you have to worry about is that your customers don't stop buying whatever you're selling or that the country gets stuck in a depression. I'm fortunate now because people are buying wind instruments. They're more affordable than pianos. Years ago all the children took piano lessons. Now the parents buy a clarinet or trumpet. It's made our business very good, but the piano business is down. In fact, that's why I bought a new piano. I got a very friendly price."

Anna's mother interjected, "Hildy, Mr. Eastwood fears war for his business's sake. If war comes, then it will be more difficult, if not impossible, to import from Europe."

"While that is true, Clara, I fear war primarily because of the suffering it will cause. We must never forget the Great War . . . millions died. The thought of turning instrument factories into armament works, here or in Europe, is abhorrent to me. Ya, I have a business interest in not having war, but I would gladly forsake extravagant prosperity to avoid such a conflict – that I can assure you."

"Yes, of course, dear. I just want Hildy to understand your business is dependent upon peace in Europe. If war comes, many people will be affected including us. Tell me, Hildy, what does your father do?"

"He runs the General Store in Albertsville."

"So he also is a businessman," Mr. Eastwood said.

"Funny," Hildy replied, "I've never really thought of him that way." Relaxed and calm, she vaguely realized the wine had something to do with it. The concern for her father retreated to the edge of her awareness. She had two choices: she could worry about him or enjoy herself. She chose the latter.

Mrs. Eastwood went into the kitchen, as Anna cleared the table. Hildy rose to help, but Mr. Eastwood restrained her. "No, no, Hildy, you keep me company. You are our guest."

"I enjoyed your playing," she said. "Do you also play a wind instrument?"

He laughed. "No, I have enough trouble playing the piano."

"You play very well."

"Thank you, but tell me, have you ever heard a concert pianist?"

"No, I have not," Hildy answered.

"Well, someday you will. Then you'll recognize the difference."

Anna and her mother served hot fudge sundaes in pretty glass dishes.

"Oh, my goodness," Hildy said." I'm not so sure I can do this justice."

"We'll walk to wear it off," Anna said. "Hildy, why don't you spend the night? Mother, could Hildy stay?"

"If she'd like. Hildy, you're certainly welcome."

"I have to work at one . . . ."

"The bus will get you there. Oh Hildy, please stay," Anna said.

The invitation delighted her. The young women helped clean the kitchen, while Mr. Eastwood read the newspaper. When Anna and Hildy stepped outside, a reddish glow lingered in the western sky. Lilac blossoms scented the air.

"They remind me of Albertsville."

"Do you miss your home?"

"No. I miss my parents, but I'd like them here. They would have enjoyed today, especially meeting your parents."

"Yes, it's a shame. I know my father looked forward to talking with your father. Do you think they're right? Do you think there will be war?"

Hildy laughed. "Anna, how in heaven's name should I know? I hope there isn't. Just because our fathers think so, doesn't mean it will happen."

"Oh, I don't know. My father reads about Europe. He said Germany is rearming."

Hildy didn't care to speculate. "It was a good year for us, wasn't it?"

"Yes, a wonderful year, just perfect . . . , but what will you do now?"

"Maybe I'll go the second year; I mean if I can't find a job. But I'll miss you."

"I don't want you going to school without me."

Hildy laughed again. "Well, quit your job then."

They walked in silence until Anna said, "I start a week from Monday."

As they approached a hedgerow of mock orange bushes, Hildy asked, "What's that wonderful scent?" She spotted the small, white flowers. "Oh, so lovely – Anna, smell them."

"I know. I like them too."

"Were I ever to have a home of my own, I'd have mock orange bushes and lilacs and all kinds of flowers," Hildy said.

"Do you think you will?"

"Have a home someday?"

"Yes, I mean, do you think you'll ever get married?"

"If I meet a nice fella, someone I could trust . . . , but who knows? Maybe I will; maybe I won't. I certainly won't marry just for the sake of being married. I'd rather be an old maid than marry some young jerk."

Anna laughed. "Me too; God knows I've known my share."

"So have I." Hildy thought of Arthur.

"The stars are out. I love that."

Hildy laughed. "My dear, you should visit Albertsville. On a moonless night, the sky is white with stars. It's breathtaking. This is nothing." She dismissively waved at the sky. "I don't miss much about Albertsville, but I miss that."

"Seeing the stars makes me think of God," Anna said. "Do you ever think of God?"

Hildy laughed out loud. "My father used to say that God means for us to see the stars every night before we sleep, just so we think of Him."

"Oh, that's a beautiful thought. Your father sounds very wise."

"I suppose so," Hildy said, without much conviction.

"And Sundays, God means for us to go to church. In the morning, come to Mass with us. I know you're Lutheran, but it won't hurt."

"Oh, that's fine." Hildy studied Anna's beautiful face in the street lamp's soft light. She thought her *a very good girl*. And then, *I'm good now, too.*

When they got home, Anna showed Hildy the guest room. Her parents had gone to bed.

"This is very nice and Anna, thank you for making everything so special today. Your parents are wonderful. It was a wonderful evening."

"They like you too. I'll see you about seven, okay?"

"Okay," Hildy whispered. "Goodnight."

Early sunlight in the unfamiliar room woke Hildy. She yawned, stretched, and recalled the pleasant evening and then her sick father. Anna rapped and greeted her cheerfully. After Hildy showered, Anna offered some dresses and hats for Hildy to choose. She decided to wear her own dress, but did borrow a cute little hat.

The Eastwoods belonged to St. Sebastian's Parish, St. Seb's, as it was called. The church and bell tower loomed high above Washington Boulevard. As they climbed the steps, Hildy's eyes caught the cornerstone: *Anno Domini, 1929. I was nineteen . . with Eddie . . . .*

Mr. Eastwood marched halfway down the center aisle. Hildy sat, while the Eastwoods knelt. Bells signaled the start of Mass. The church had filled, and now everyone stood, Hildy too. Anna opened her missal and whispered, "I'll point out what the priest is praying so you can follow." There were two columns of text: the left in Latin, the right, English.

The priest began, "In nomine Patris, et Filii, et Spiritus sancti, Amen. Introibo ad altare Dei . . . ."

In the name of the Father, and of the Son and of the Holy Spirit, Amen. I will go unto the altar of God . . . . The trailing phrase surprised Hildy: *the God who gives joy to my youth.* She had never thought of God that way.

Rapidly, the four altar boys recited, "Confiteor Deo omnipotenti, beatae Mariae semper Virgini . . . ," as Hildy read, *I confess to Almighty God, to blessed Mary ever Virgin, to blessed Michael the Archangel, to blessed John the Baptist, to the holy Apostles Peter and Paul, and to all the Saints, and to you, Father, that I have sinned exceedingly in thought, word and deed, through my fault, through my fault, through my most grievous fault . . . .*

That prayer of profound contrition made a tremendous impact on Hildegard Neubauer, inducing deep regret. Her eyes drifted from Anna's missal, but her mind's voice repeated, *through my fault, through my fault, through my most grievous fault.* And then: *yes, it was wrong of me, terribly wrong, horribly wrong even though he . . . .*

Nearly half the congregation received Holy Communion, the Body and Blood of Christ. The priest placed the sacred host directly on their tongues. Hildy studied Anna's face as she returned from the Communion rail. *How virtuous she looks . . . how sweet . . . I wonder if she . . . what her life has been . . . if she knows . . . .*

Walking to the car, she asked Anna, "Do you really have to go every Sunday?"

"No, we're not forced to, but it's our religion. I go because I'm a believer; it's good for my soul."

"I don't go very often . . . I mean, to the Lutheran church."

"We have to make some effort, Hildy. Christ died for us. You have to show a little gratitude."

"Well, I know that." Then in the car, "So why is the Mass in Latin? Wouldn't it be better in English?"

"You certainly are full of questions," Anna said.

Mr. Eastwood answered, "The Catholic Church is the universal Church. All over the world the Mass is offered in Latin. It's symbolic of the unity of the Church."

"But wouldn't it be better in English? I would have understood."

"You have to follow the missal," Anna said.

"But Anna, how is Latin better? Not everyone had a missal. Wouldn't it be better if everybody could understand the priest?"

"No, Hildy, our faith is an ancient one," Mr. Eastwood said. "It can be traced back to the Apostles, back to Christ himself. They all spoke Latin."

"What?" Mrs. Eastwood screamed. "Herman, the Apostles were Jews . . . they spoke Hebrew or Aramaic. Only the Romans spoke Latin."

Anna and Hildy laughed out loud.

"Ach, ya, point well made."

Hildy persisted. "So why then isn't the Mass in Aramaic?"

At that, Anna said, "This is ridiculous. Obviously, it was an arbitrary decision. I think Hildy's right . . . it should be in English."

"It's been Latin for a thousand years," Mr. Eastwood said. "I dare say, a thousand years from now it will still be Latin."

Anna doubted it so she said, "I'm hungry."

Mrs. Eastwood prepared breakfast, while Anna set the table with everyday dishes. The candles were gone, but the centerpiece remained. In the bright daylight, the room lost its elegance, but remained cheerful and comfortable. They ate and talked about the ceremony, Anna's new job, the lovely weather, what annuals would be planted in the backyard gardens, and other pleasant topics. Hildy felt in no mood to leave.

Anticipating Hildy's inevitable question, though, Anna said, "The buses run every fifteen minutes. I'll walk with you."

"Ya, Hildy," Mr. Eastwood said, "It was very nice having you as our guest. You come again. And I hope your father will be well soon. Tell him and your mother to come too."

"Thank you Mr. Eastwood, for everything. And thank you Mrs. Eastwood . . . dinner was perfect, and breakfast hit the spot. I was hungry. I'm not used to fasting like you Catholics."

As the bus approached, Anna said, "Call me when you know about your father."

"I will." They hugged goodbye, and Hildy boarded.

Seated at a window near the back, she reflected on all that happened since her mother's telegram. Thinking about what the

Eastwoods told her, she realized her father could die. At sixty, he wasn't young anymore, nor, at fifty-seven, was her mother. Her father's heaviness and shortness of breath had alarmed Hildy at Christmas, though she made no comment. They were symptoms, she sadly suspected, of his failing health.

Stop after stop, the bus filled with quiet or murmuring passengers. In their midst, Hildy felt entirely alone. She had no relatives in Milwaukee, her parents lived far away, and she had no siblings. Anna was her only close friend. Since leaving Albertsville, life forced her to learn to be alone without suffering loneliness. Small talk with customers was an ephemeral pleasure. Acquaintances came and went, especially, when she changed jobs. Friends weren't easily made, and possibilities often fizzled if a girl Hildy liked met a fella.

Not until Hildy fell for Arthur did her heart discover the joy of love. Those first thrilling months sketched an outline of happiness she could scarcely believe. And yet when she thought of how terribly their romance died, she concluded it would have been far better never to have met Arthur. Still, she longed for something beyond what her parents, Anna, or anyone else could offer, and she wondered if she'd ever find it. Like most women, she sensed marriage presented the best hope for happiness. That, however, depended so greatly on the character of the man. After Arthur, she questioned if she'd ever meet a decent man and even wondered if there was such a creature. Only her memory, or was it a dream, of a young doctor who once was kind to her, sustained her yearnings for an enduring love.

At Holton she transferred. After the short trolley ride to Ogden Avenue, she walked to her building, wondering if a second telegram awaited her. It did not. She washed her hands, put on a clean uniform, redid her lipstick, brushed her hair, and left the apartment.

At the Cafe, she told Mrs. Ernst about her father. "Oh I'm so sorry," she replied. "I was looking forward to meeting your parents."

The busy dining room allowed Hildy no time to worry. After closing, she set tables for Monday's lunch then ate supper with the staff. They understood her silence. She finished before the others, excused herself, and left.

At her apartment she made a list: *laundry, write Mama, call Anna, card for Papa, pick up school bulletin.* She opened the window. The temperature had dropped; a cool breeze whispered in off the lake. She spread a second blanket and turned off the lamp. Within minutes she was asleep.

Her mother's letter came Tuesday. Yes, Hildy's father was very ill, but her mother offered no prognosis – good or bad. Most of the letter expressed disappointment that *she* was denied the trip to Milwaukee. Hildy realized her mother's self-pity exceeded the concern for her husband. Nevertheless, she was there with him and could observe, so Hildy concluded her mother sensed he was going to be all right.

She needs to get away from that God-forsaken town, Hildy realized. When her father insisted they didn't like big cities, Hildy suspected he wasn't speaking for his wife. Her mother failed or refused to express her true feelings and probably hadn't for many years. It angered Hildy.

In her reply, Hildy asked if she should visit her father. She added a postscript: *Mama, we'll get you to Milwaukee yet, don't worry. We'll have a good time, you'll see.*

Chapter 15 ~ 1936 [Part 2]

arly summer crept into July, as Hildy's life settled into a pattern of repetitious toil at the Cafe. She worked every day except Tuesdays and every other Sunday when she'd try to get together with Anna. At the restaurant, several male customers approached, but she wasn't interested. The lingering bitterness she felt towards Arthur transferred itself to most other men.

Constantly aware that she wanted more satisfying work, she longed to find a job in a respectable business. Tuesday mornings she answered help wanted ads in the newspaper and then wrote her parents; afternoons, if nice weather, she'd walk to the Main Post Office and then window shop westward all the way to the library at Eighth Street where she read magazines. Late in the afternoon she'd take the bus back to her apartment. Occasionally, in her mailbox she'd find a polite reply informing a sought position had been filled. After her solitary supper, she'd call Anna from the lobby pay phone to make plans for the Sunday afternoon when Hildy was free.

At the Cafe another pattern emerged. A young man had come to the Cafe several Wednesdays in a row. He sat at one of Hildy's tables in the center room and chatted pleasantly with her, as much as he could throughout his dinner. Hildy found him "kinda nice." She asked another waitress, "Have you noticed that guy?"

"Yeah, he's become a real regular," Doris answered. "I suspect you know why."

"What do you mean?"

"Could be your pretty face and cute figure . . . ."

"Oh good heaven, I hope not."

Doris laughed. "Happened to me when I was younger. Actually, he's quite nice looking."

"Hmm, I suppose so, but we're not to fraternize, you know that," Hildy said.

Good looking or not, once she realized why he was coming, she felt the same caution she seemed to feel towards all men. Next

Wednesday he returned and quipped with Hildy, while he ordered a cocktail. He sensed her new reserve, but wisely didn't change his soft approach. He'd proceed carefully, patiently; he'd bide his time because he had confidence, *she'll come 'round.*

Hildy's mother wrote that her husband finally showed some improvement though he despised the bland diet. The doctor ordered Mr. Neubauer to "lose at least fifty pounds." No longer confined to bed, he wasn't to resume work for at least another week or two. The doctor ordered him to walk daily to gain strength and lose weight. Neubauer so feared the return of the terrible abdominal pain and the thought of surgery that he meekly accepted the doctor's directives. At home, though, his unceasing complaining ruffled his wife's nerves. She saw no point in Hildy visiting because her father couldn't pick her up in Mineral Point, plus Hildy's mother didn't drive. *Come at Christmas unless this year,* Hildy's mother wrote wistfully, *we come to Milwaukee.* Hildy doubted that would ever happen.

As time passed, the midweek encounter with the young man became an inescapable part of Hildy's job. In spite of his friendliness and generous tips, she knew what he wanted; she felt she dare not drop her guard. He didn't seem threatening, but she sensed she could not trust him, or perhaps, could not trust herself. He made no advance, and if he were to ask her out the Cafe's policy provided an easy excuse. *So why am I so uncomfortable,* she wondered? *He's polite and well mannered. Sometimes he tries a little too hard to be funny, but I guess that's all right. What is it about him,* she asked herself, pretending not to know.

The following Wednesday she caught him staring. When their eyes met he didn't avert his gaze, but grinned a thin smile where the upturned corners of his mouth hid behind his droopy mustache. Hildy found his expression more a smirk: an arrogant, intrusive, offensive leer. She turned away, as though she hadn't noticed, but still had to do her job. At his table she poured him coffee.

"So Hildy, all these weeks I've been a pretty good customer, wouldn't you say? We've known each other long enough for you to call me 'Bob' . . . don't you think?"

She considered them reasonable questions, but an unwanted advance. "I didn't know your name," she said, off the mark then headed right back to the kitchen.

Mrs. Ernst noticed Hildy's odd expression. "What's the matter?"

"I don't know . . . nothing. Do you know the young man at C-3?"

Ernst peeked through the small pane in the kitchen door. "That's young Mr. Schmitt. He used to come with his parents. He hasn't been here for a number of years, though I've noticed him these past several weeks. Why do you ask?"

"He comes every Wednesday, sits at the same table, and always wants to chat . . . seems a little too friendly, I guess."

"Does he flirt?"

"Not really," Hildy lied.

"Then don't worry; do your job. You are not to fraternize with customers – you know that. If he asks, tell him."

"Yes, I will . . . thank you."

She slapped his bill on the table and uttered a perfunctory, "Thank you sir, good night." She made no eye contact and retreated quickly.

For a moment, Schmitt just sat there. Hildy rebuffed him, and he hated it. For all the Wednesdays he dined at the Cafe, he had gained nothing. He glanced at the bill and thought, *this is the last time, you little bitch.* He threw money on the table and left.

Walking home she wondered why Schmitt made her so uncomfortable. *What is it about him? For all I know, he might be a really nice guy. Maybe he's lonely. If I were to go out with him, so what? Mrs. Ernst wouldn't have to know. It's really none of her business.* And then, from the deepest, darkest corner of her soul, the unspoken question emerged: *And if I were to go, what would I . . . ?*

The following Wednesday broke the pattern. Young Mr. Schmitt wasn't there at seven-thirty and still not there at nine. Hildy wondered, *why didn't he come tonight? Did I hurt his pride? I know what he wants, but how would I . . . ? No, no, no, it'd be Arthur all over again.*

Both men had the same cocky self-assurance and raw aggressiveness expressed so boldly around women. Some women are drawn to it, others repulsed, and yet some have both feelings, irrational as that may seem. Hildy felt her emotions straddling the pivot of a teeter-totter. Engrossed, she was unaware of the slow moving automobile about a half-block behind her and barely aware of its passing, as she entered her building.

Sunday, Hildy told Anna that Schmitt hadn't come. She

expressed her dislike of him while at the same time feeling she might be judging unfairly. She couldn't quite put her finger on it, but when she caught him staring at her it was as though, "He was looking at me with evil intentions. Perhaps," she added, "with lust."

Anna laughed. "Hildy, men enjoy looking at attractive women. That's not a crime. You're very attractive. When I worked at the restaurant I noticed men looking at me all the time. I ignored it."

"But did you ever have a man come in week after week and just stare at you?"

"No, that's a little too obvious."

"Honestly, he frightens me."

"So what are you going to do about it?"

"I don't know. I tried changing my day off to Wednesday, but it doesn't work with the other girls. I could ask Mrs. Ernst to move me to the east room, but Schmitt can just as easily sit there. I don't want to give in to my fears; maybe I'm just imagining the worst. Maybe he's a decent guy. I just don't know."

"Hopefully, he'll stay away now. That's what you want, isn't it?"

"Of course, I've no interest in him at all," Hildy insisted, almost as much to convince herself as Anna. What she had interest in, though, she was reluctant to say: *I'd like a fella now. Maybe Schmitt would be someone I could get to know.*

He didn't return to the Cafe until the last Wednesday in July, three weeks after he asked Hildy to call him by name. She had wondered if she'd ever see him again, but there he sat, staring at her with a little smile, most of which was hidden by his mustache. He had missed two Wednesdays through which Hildy allowed herself the hope he'd never return. Now she had no choice but to smile back, for she had to be, as Mrs. Ernst instructed, friendly and cheerful to every customer.

Hildy hid her emotional confusion because she knew exactly what he wanted, but she wasn't at all entirely sure what she wanted. She had to serve him and maybe just as well, she thought. *Hopefully, I can resolve this now, one way or the other.*

For his part, Schmitt returned to find out, once and for all, if he would ever possess what he wildly desired. In a pleasant voice he said, "Hello, Hildy. Did you miss me?"

The question infuriated her; she knew the answer – or thought she did – but couldn't say it. She simply could not answer honestly. She was amazed he could be so completely wrong about her perception of him and just as amazed at her reluctance to offend. She felt it rude to utter "no," but far more dangerous to whisper "yes."

In lieu of an answer she said, "Good evening."

"I'm Bob, remember? Bob – a damn easy name not to forget. Now say it," – his voice was harsh – "say it like a good girl."

"Yes, Bob," she obeyed, struggling to control herself in the face of such crass intimidation. She hated the way he made her feel. Or was it disappointment? Nevertheless, she was not defenseless. Her shifting eyes revealed a guarded indifference. With a frozen voice she asked, "May I get your usual drink, sir . . . Bob?" She fought to keep a calm exterior if not an interior one.

"Ya," he said, indifferently, as he scanned the menu.

When she set the cocktail in front of him, she asked, "Will it be the usual," referring to his favorite steak, baked potato, and salad. No longer, though, was it the sweet, cheerful voice Schmitt had grown fond of in the early weeks.

He despised her distance, hated her detachment. *Why*, he wondered. Why hadn't he been successful in gaining a little foothold at least on her plane of interest if not her plane of trust? Never before had he worked this hard to convince a pretty waitress to go out with him. He had money, came from a respectable family, had a university degree, dressed well, and was reasonably good looking. He could make a girl feel special even if only for a few months before tiring of her. But the signals Hildy sent convinced him he'd have no success with her. It wasn't a matter of time anymore. His efforts had come to nothing. He felt a sharp, bitter, vengeful anger spawned by what he regarded as a severe and stupid rejection.

"Ya, rare . . . ." He raised the cocktail to his mouth, gulping it like water.

The confrontation was subtle in its unexpressed hostility. Hildy realized she was abrupt and unfriendly. He was a customer, after all, and had a right to the pleasant service the Ernsts expected of their waitresses. She served him a basket of rolls, rye bread, and butter, but said nothing.

I was fine when he came in, she thought. *So why did I react so badly?*

Oh yeah, he asked if I missed him. I should have told him I was overjoyed not to . . . .

Schmitt motioned to her. "Yes, sir, what can I get . . . ?" She refused to speak his name.

He raised the empty tumbler. "Make it a double."

Oh, great, she thought, *now he'll get drunk.*

She brought his salad. Minutes later when she passed close by, he barked, "This salad's awful. Where's my drink?"

"That's your usual," she said. He never complained about the salad before.

"Get me my drink . . . then we'll talk about my *usual.*"

At the bar station, Doris had been eyeing the situation. "Not so nice, eh?"

"Oh my God, he's awful." She called to the bartender, "Double whisky *Old Fashion* with sweet."

As she brought his drink, Schmitt watched with passive, expressionless eyes, but hatred hid there. "I didn't order this hot bacon crap . . . ."

"Oh my goodness, did I serve the wrong dressing?"

His voice reeked ridicule. "Yes you did . . . you know I always order French Roquefort. Is that too much for you to remember?"

"I'm so sorry."

"You should be . . . I think I deserve a little of your precious attention." Then, for no reason, he raised his glass and, looking right at her, toasted, "Heil, Hitler!"

She turned and walked away. *Oh my God, he's a Nazi.* Oddly, Schmitt's toast relaxed her. It confirmed what she sensed. From the start something would not let her trust him. All those weeks his sweet talk never swayed her. She knew what he wanted. She wasn't naïve. She knew the dark desires of men. After the affair with Arthur she raised her guard. That caution had served her well. Schmitt wasn't so charming that she couldn't resist, and now she had every reason to believe he admired the German leader her father warned against.

She brought him a second salad without incident, then his dinner. She served him quickly and carefully, without any of the small talk she so easily made with others.

Moments later, he ordered a stein of beer. He ate slowly,

leisurely. When Hildy glanced his way, she caught him staring, but he averted his gaze. Hildy sensed something in Schmitt had changed. She was right, for now he knew she would never succumb.

After Schmitt finished dining, she cleared the table, served coffee, then retreated to the kitchen to total his bill. When she presented it, though, he ordered Cognac.

My goodness, he certainly drinks a lot, she thought. *Yeah, I'd really like to get involved with a lush who's fond of Hitler. He'd be a big hit with my father.*

After serving the Cognac, Hildy reached for the bill. "Leave it," he said. "I might want another."

Schmitt had sat there over two hours, one of the few, remaining customers in the Cafe. Hildy realized he could dawdle until closing. But Schmitt didn't order another drink, and when she approached his table he handed her the bill. Like a reflex, she said, "Thank you, sir." In the kitchen she added the Cognac and recalled she hadn't deducted the cost of the offensive salad. If a customer didn't like something, they didn't have to pay for it even if a satisfactory substitution was made. Looking at the bill she realized, *not the tidiest . . . .*

She placed it in front of him. "I'll be back in a moment."

Doris passed close by and whispered, "Bet you'll be glad when this night is over."

"Oh, it was terrible. He was awful. I was awful. Would you believe he said 'Heil Hitler'?"

Doris laughed. "These days I believe anything." She entered the kitchen, as Hildy headed back towards Schmitt.

"I'm not sure I understand this," he said, while pointing at the bill and holding it flat on the table with his left hand. "I think you made a mistake."

Hildy reached for the little slip, but he wouldn't let go. "What did you scratch out? I can't read it."

"I deducted for the salad . . . let me see."

He slid the bill to the table edge, but wouldn't release it, forcing her to move closer so she could find the reputed error. She moved beside him, leaning over to examine the bill, which he held and stabbed at with his index finger, saying, "Here . . . look . . . here . . . ."

It was difficult for Hildy to decipher her scribbled changes. Her angle of sight was poor; the lighting wasn't as bright as in the kitchen. She strained to add the numbers in her head, searching for an error she couldn't find.

Unaware that he had drawn his right hand off the table onto his lap, Hildy didn't sense as he guided it lightly above her backside at her waist, so delicately that his fingertips barely touched the fabric of her uniform.

He let his palm follow the dramatic break of her hip. He had often studied her figure and was excited by the narrowness of her waist, the sudden flaring of her curvaceous hips, and the beautiful taper in her upper legs.

In an instant, he shifted his right hand until it was directly behind her buttock, while Hildy hunted for the elusive error.

Then he struck.

He grabbed the full cheek of her bottom, lightened his grip and fondled the soft, firm flesh, even pushing the length of his thumb against the deep, anal crevice. It lasted barely a second.

Instantaneously and violently, she spun her body so rapidly and stepped sideways so quickly that her weight shifted faster than her feet. She stumbled, taking three, quick little hops to keep from falling.

Schmitt laughed.

When she regained her balance, she bore into his eyes, saying with muffled rage, "How dare you . . . how dare you?"

He sat upright in the chair, his hands folded on the table, as though nothing had happened. He grinned like a schoolboy sitting at his desk. "What," he said, with mock innocence and feigned surprise, the sound of the word curling downward.

"How dare you," she said again, with a vicious loathing. She snatched the disputed bill and rushed to the kitchen.

In his mind, Schmitt taunted, *how'd you like that, you little bitch?*

In the kitchen she called, "Mrs. Ernst, Mrs. Ernst, where are you?" She said it so passionately that Mrs. Ernst dropped what she was doing and rushed towards Hildy. "We have to speak privately," Hildy said.

Mrs. Ernst pulled her into the pantry and closed the door. "What is it?"

"He touched me. He touched my bottom . . . ."

"Who touched you?" Mrs. Ernst noticed the clutched bill in Hildy's hand.

"He did – Bob Schmitt – that son-of-a-bitch."

Mrs. Ernst decided her husband should hear what Hildy had to say. She led her by the hand and, passing through the kitchen, shouted, "Cover for Hildy, cover for Hildy, coffee to C-3. Don't let him leave . . . he hasn't paid . . . . "

A waiter brought Schmitt fresh coffee. The waiter didn't know, no one knew, what had happened. "Thanks," Schmitt said, cheerfully. For all of Hildy's cold indifference, he had settled the score. He knew she wouldn't go out with him, as he had hoped all those weeks, all those evenings he had been so nice to her, always leaving a generous tip. It had come to nothing, he realized, so he had every right to extract a small measure of revenge.

Hildy explained as calmly as she could. When she finished, Mr. Ernst asked, "Are you absolutely sure he touched you there?"

"Ach, Johannes, don't be a dummkopf. A lady knows when she is improperly touched, for heaven's sake."

"Yes," Hildy answered, "it was deliberate."

"Johann, add the bill; see if Hildy made a mistake."

He checked it several times, found no error, then rose from his chair. "I'll handle this. You both wait here."

Schmitt wasn't surprised to see Ernst approaching. Ernst began, "I haven't seen you since the days you came with your father. Tell me, how many years since he passed?"

"Three," Schmitt answered.

"Hmm, that long already . . . . Your father was a decent man," he paused, peering into Schmitt's eyes, "or so I thought."

The inference angered Schmitt. "Of course he was."

"My waitress said you found an error in the bill. I checked, but can't find it. Perhaps you can show me." He placed the crumpled slip in front of Schmitt.

"Let me see." For a moment, Schmitt feigned studying it. "Looks like I was wrong. Sorry – she must've fixed it." Grinning, he handed the bill back to Ernst.

"She didn't have to fix anything. It was a ruse. You wanted to take her out, but she wouldn't go. She knows a pig when she sees one. Why did you touch her?"

"Bullshit, I didn't touch anyone, certainly not that lying bitch." Schmitt's face reddened.

"Her service is a disgrace. This place is a disgrace. You should fire her, the way she treated me. My parents gave you a lot of business in the old days."

"Then why did you come here all these weeks? You didn't complain about her service then. You wanted to pick her up."

"Bullshit . . . I've no interest in sluts."

The slur enraged Ernst. Thirty years older than Schmitt, had he struck him he would have done great harm to Schmitt's delicate face. As a youth in Germany, Ernst mastered the butcher's trade, which made him strong. "Get out of here, you worthless piece of shit." He said it with such passion that Schmitt had every reason to fear the large, hard fist bobbing in front of him.

He edged past Ernst towards the door. "I haven't paid my bill."

"The last meal a man eats at my restaurant is on the house. You show your ugly face in here again, I'll throw you in the gutter where you belong."

He followed Schmitt into the small vestibule. Schmitt opened the door. As he stepped outside, he turned towards Ernst, sneering, "Fuck you, old man."

Infuriated, he lunged at the nimble Schmitt who easily jumped aside. He ran across the street so fast that Ernst could only marvel at how he vanished into the shadowy darkness. He went back into the Cafe muttering, "Worthless piece of shit . . . ."

"He won't be back," he told Hildy and his wife. "If he comes, I'll throw him out again."

"Did he admit what Hildy claimed?"

"Every word admitted it. Hildy, I'm sorry. His parents were customers for many years. They seemed decent enough, but judging by this son who knows."

Hildy had been crying. Mr. Ernst knelt beside her in a gesture of such spontaneous and simple kindness that it even surprised his wife. Taking Hildy's hands into his own, he said, "I know you've been frightened, but he's a worthless fellow. He won't be back. I can assure you of that."

"Thank you . . . I'm sorry to have caused so much trouble."

"Nonsense," Mrs. Ernst said. "You didn't cause anything. Now, will you stay for supper? You don't have to setup tonight."

"I'm not hungry, thank you. I just want to go home."

She thanked them again and left the office. Doris approached, but Hildy said, "I'll explain tomorrow." She got her purse and left the restaurant.

A warm, humid, summer night's moon hung low in the southwest. The soft glow of streetlamps shone against the windless elms that lined so many of the streets of old Milwaukee. Exhausted, Hildy headed towards her apartment. She never imagined Schmitt would behave so terribly. It was beyond belief that he touched her that way. She felt relief and gratitude that Mr. Ernst banned Schmitt from the Café. *Perhaps,* she thought, *it was necessary to get rid of him once and for all. I never want to see him again. I never want to feel that way again. I never want to be touched like that again.* And then, *Oh, God, how I wish I could find a decent job.*

At Van Buren Street she waited for the traffic light to change. She paid little attention to the headlights of the oncoming cars and barely noticed the Buick roadster, as it drew alongside her. Then, from the black interior, a familiar voice shouted, "You fucking slut!"

It so startled her that she looked around to find the object of the attack. There was no one. She realized, *my God, he's in that car.* It turned the corner and roared away, but she feared he'd round the block and come after her again. Terrified, she turned back towards the Cafe. When she reached Van Buren, an automobile approached from the east. *Oh no, no, it's him.* She crossed the street dodging the honking traffic and ran all the way to the locked front entrance at the Cafe. She ran to the side, staff entrance, but that was locked. The only other door led to the Ernst's second floor apartment above. Hildy rang the bell repeatedly. "Please answer, please . . . please . . . ."

Mr. Ernst hurried down the stairs. "Hildy, what's the matter?"

She panted, "He was in a car. He screamed at me. I'm afraid. I ran here. I'm sorry . . . I don't want to cause trouble."

"Come up . . . ."

Standing in the doorway at the top, Mrs. Ernst, in a green, silk peignoir, heard Hildy's fear. "Come, Hildy, sit by me. Johann, call a taxi. Bring Hildy a hot chocolate." She took Hildy's hand. "We'll have a little *klatsch*."

Mrs. Ernst's lovely appearance with long, gray hair falling to her waist surprised Hildy. She always thought her a rather plain woman.

Mr. Ernst made the call then served Hildy. A marshmallow floated on the steaming liquid, and a fine, silver spoon nestled on the saucer.

"Thank you," Hildy said. Now she felt embarrassed, suspecting the Ernsts might find her frightened reaction to Schmitt's verbal attack extreme.

"The cab will be here shortly. Then we know you get home safe and sound. Schmitt won't be back . . . ."

"You didn't think he'd be back after he left the Cafe," Mrs. Ernst reminded. "He is not only dishonorable, he is unpredictable. Hildy, be on guard, watch what's happening all the time until you're absolutely sure he's not around."

"I will." She sipped the chocolate.

"I'm surprised he behaved so terribly. We knew his parents. They seemed decent enough. Strange the son would act so brazenly knowing we know who he is. We could call the police, if you wish."

Hildy looked at Mr. Ernst. "He'd deny it . . . your word against his."

The bell rang. Mr. Ernst went downstairs and brought the cab driver into the small entry. Hildy hugged Mrs. Ernst goodbye. "I'm so grateful to you both."

"That's quite all right, Hildy. Get a good night's sleep now."

Mr. Ernst overpaid the driver, instructing him to wait until Hildy was safely inside her building. She thanked Mr. Ernst and offered her hand. She wanted to hug him, but decided not to because she felt he might think her silly. In fact, he would have liked it.

At her apartment, Hildy thanked the cab driver, got out, and hurried to the entrance. She turned to wave just as Schmitt's Buick emerged from the shadows. She heard him scream, "You fucking whore!"

She was stunned. She couldn't believe he came back again. She wondered, *my God, will this never end?*

The driver jumped out, shouting after the Buick, as it sped away. He ran to Hildy. "Who was that? Are you all right?"

"I'm all right . . . please. I must go in. Thank you for helping me."

Hildy left the puzzled cab driver standing on the stoop. She climbed the stairs to her apartment. Once inside, she locked the door and set the chain bolt. In the dark stuffiness, she crept to the window and raised the sash. Through the gap framed by the corner's edge of the building next door, she watched and waited, certain that at any moment Schmitt's car would rumble by. She leaned tiredly against the window casing and wondered, *what did I ever do to deserve this?*

Perspiration ran down the sides of her body. Exhausted, she couldn't believe Schmitt shouted a filthy obscenity in front of the taxi driver and the many tenants who must have heard because they all had their windows open this warm, summer night. She could not repeat the ugly words in her mind; they were too terrible. *What would my parents think,* she wondered. *They'd be horrified. My father couldn't imagine anything so awful. He'd want me back in Albertsville for sure.*

For ten minutes she stood watching; not a single car passed. In the darkness she took off her uniform and slip. At the bathroom sink, she washed her hands and face, rinsed her face and wrists with cold water then sponged her sweaty body with a washcloth.

Again at the window, no traffic; only several cars parked at the curb.

In bed she felt the weight of exhaustion press against her whole body. Her anxious mind prayed, *Oh God, what did I do wrong? I know what he wanted . . . I had to be that way. Forgive me . . . I don't know why he was so cruel. Protect me . . . help it so he stays away. I don't ever want to see him again . . . please . . . please . . . .*

She wept, but still she prayed. *Dear God, help me find another job. I don't want to work like this the rest of my life.* She sobbed face down in her pillow, her shoulders rising and falling in unison with her sobs. Then she thought of her father. *Bless him,* she prayed simply, *and Mama.*

Whispering, she faltered through the Lord's Prayer. She wiped her eyes on the hem of the sheet before turning on her side. Barely aware of her body, tiredness overwhelmed all her senses. She felt herself nearing the edge of consciousness. As she slid towards sleep, her last terrifying vision was of her leering enemy – his cruel face and sour breath pitilessly close – attempting an act of unspeakable violence.

Chapter 16 ~ 1936 [Part 3]

Hildy didn't see Anna again until the second Sunday of August when they met at their favorite cafeteria for coffee and, if the visit lasted long enough, dinner and a piece of strawberry pie mounded high with whipped cream. Once the initial pleasantries were aside, Hildy told Anna about her last encounter with Schmitt, even whispering, word for word, the filthy obscenities shouted at her.

"What kind of man would do that? How could he be so cruel to a waitress, of all people? You ought to have him arrested. Really, it's that terrible."

"If he bothers me again, Mr. Ernst said he'd call the police. He knows the name of his company."

"I should hope so. Sex fiends and Nazis belong in jail."

"Well, I'm not sure he's a Nazi. Mr. Ernst told me that during the Great War, Schmitt's company did army work. That's how his father became rich. If there is another war, Mr. Ernst thinks Schmitt would do the same."

Anna extended her hands and held Hildy's. "What will you do now?"

"I pray a lot . . . that he leaves me alone, I mean."

Anna frowned. "Oh Hildy, I'm not so sure God answers prayers like that. Schmitt is free; he can do whatever he wants. If he wants to scream obscenities at you, he knows where you live, where you work. You have to make sure it won't ever happen again."

"I take a taxi every night now . . . what else can I do?"

"You should move."

Hildy shook her head. "I don't want to move. I like my apartment."

"Yes, but he knows where you are, and, therefore, you're vulnerable. He could come after you any night of the week. Is that how you want to live? If it were me, I'd move."

Hildy had expected some soothing words, not such bossy advice. She withdrew her hands while gazing at the passers-by.

"Hildy, look at me. You have to think seriously about this. He knows where you work and where you live. He touched you. Who knows what he might try next. You don't want to be a sitting duck, do you?"

"No, of course not."

"As long as you work at the Cafe – even if you do move – he can always find you. You have to vanish completely . . . from him, I mean. You have to change everything, and you should do it now because you just don't know what he might be plotting."

"Anna, you make it sound so terrible."

"It is terrible. What if he kidnaps you . . . rapes you?"

Hildy gasped.

"Who knows what he might try? Did you ever think he'd touch your bottom?"

"Never!"

"Then protect yourself while you can."

The young women quietly watched the avenue traffic. Finally, Anna said, "Hildy, move to the west side. We'll see each other more, and you'll be safe. He'll never find you there."

"And my job . . . you want me to quit that too?"

"You can waitress at the *Boulevard Inn*. I know the owner. I'll give you an excellent recommendation. He'll hire you on the spot. I'm sure of it."

Hildy gazed out the window.

Anna sensed her sadness, but didn't share her bleak outlook. "Are you more afraid of Schmitt or making a change? You haven't found a job downtown, and now a terrible man is after you. Don't fear moving or changing jobs – fear Schmitt. You've got to protect yourself. Moving to the west side is the solution. The area north of Washington Park is very nice. At least come look at it."

"And I suppose I shouldn't complain about the bus to school and the fare, and what if the restaurant doesn't hire me, and what if I can't find a decent place to live?"

"I took the bus," Anna said. "I studied or read magazines. Let me call the restaurant tomorrow. I'll bet you a dollar they hire you. Look in the classifieds; you'll find lots of nice places to live. Hildy,

I'm trying to give you good advice. I don't want to upset you. You're my dear friend."

Hildy smiled.

"And think about that awful man. He certainly doesn't want you to move, does he?"

For Hildy that question posed a powerful argument.

"Every now and then, when he gets the urge to scream obscenities, he knows where to find you. Why make yourself so accessible?"

The questions pulled Hildy closer to Anna's attitude. She didn't like answering them, not because Anna's suggestions were bad, but because Hildy thought it terribly unjust that she should have to make drastic changes to protect herself from someone so despicable. To her way of thinking, Schmitt should be punished for being the attacker rather than Hildy being inconvenienced for being attacked. But Anna was right: Hildy had to make sure he would never find her. A move and job change were prudent. *I certainly don't want to move back to Albertsville,* she realized, knowing that's what her father would demand.

"Will you at least consider moving?" Anna asked.

"Yes, I shall. I know there's truth in what you say. Call the restaurant. See if they need a really excellent waitress to replace that silly girl who went to work for a brewery."

Anna laughed out loud. She sensed once Hildy became familiar with the west side she'd love it.

"You know, Hildy," Anna said, "what he shouted at you was exactly what he wanted you – for him – to become."

"What are you saying?"

"He wanted you to be," Anna looked around then whispered, "his *fucking whore.*"

Hildy gasped again. "Anna, that's a terrible thing to say."

"Well it's true. He would have used you for a month or two then thrown you away like a piece of trash, for that is what you would have become."

"Anna!"

"That kind of man uses foolish girls to gratify his lust, but then, when it comes to marriage, he'll take some sweet, little, virgin home to Mommy."

"Anna, you sound so bitter."

"No, not really, but it does happen to the stupid ones. I certainly don't want it happening to you."

"It won't. I know what he wanted." She inferred Schmitt, but remembered Arthur.

By the time they said goodbye, Hildy had resolved to escape her enemy. The Ernsts would want her to stay, but she knew they'd understand. She didn't like the thought of taking the bus to school, but Anna had and so could she. She was always on her guard now, always aware of the goings-on around her. Every night after work, stepping out of a cab, she searched the street. If headlights approached she'd slide back in and wait for the suspect car to pass. Her sense of awareness had been greatly enhanced but at a grave price: she never felt safe anymore, nor did she feel free. *Next weekend,* she vowed, *I'll visit the west side.*

Hot, humid, August air settled over the city, even along the lakefront. Hildy perspired under a light, print dress and wide brimmed hat. On the bus, women fanned themselves; men shed their coats, loosened ties, and rolled up their white shirtsleeves. Open windows occasionally blew oppressive air into Hildy's face; futilely, she fanned herself with her flimsy hat.

Getting off at Sherman Boulevard she spotted the *Boulevard Inn* beyond a large, cast bronze horse and rider in the little square where the thoroughfare ends at Lloyd Street. She presumed it must be General Sherman gazing southward over the great expanse of Washington Park. To the north, fine large homes lined both sides of the wide street.

Walking east she passed a drugstore; above, through open second-story windows, curtains fluttered outward. Then a car horn, loud and close, frightened her. She turned towards the street, quickening her pace. She knew the shape and dark color of Schmitt's Buick, searching for it, she walked right past a small, non-descript shop.

In the Sunday *Classifieds* Hildy found a room for rent – *Ladies only* – on LaPointe Avenue, a narrow street enfolded by tall, arching elms. People lounged on the front porches of closely spaced, well-kept houses. Children played on the sidewalks. A triangular, grassy area bordered the first house on the west side of the street, the address she sought. Though larger, the white, clapboard siding, steeply pitched roof, and front porch suggested her parents' house in Albertsville. She climbed the steps and rang the bell.

The door opened a crack. In her print dress, sun hat, and purse held at a belted waist, Hildy appeared a very proper, young lady.

"Yes?"

"I'm inquiring about the room."

"Oh, good . . . come in." The woman seemed about Hildy's mother's age.

Inside, the air felt cooler. "It's very nice here," Hildy said.

"I keep everything closed. We don't open windows until evening. It's one of my rules. I have many." The woman waited for Hildy to speak.

"My name is Hildegard Neubauer."

"How do you do, Miss Neubauer – I'm Mrs. Margaret Walker. Let me show you the room."

The second floor rental had two windows; out the side, a corner of the park was just visible. The front window overlooked the street and houses across the way. After Hildy glanced out, Mrs. Walker lowered the shades and closed the curtains. "Helps keep the room cooler, you see."

A bed, dresser, mirror, small clothes closet, reading chair between the windows, and floor lamp comprised the room. Hildy thought it just fine.

"The bathroom is down the hall. You'd share it with two ladies. Come, I'll show you."

It appeared adequate, though Hildy had grown accustomed to her own tub and toilet.

"Regarding the kitchen, we all share the ice box and pantry. That arrangement works well only if everyone respects the others' food. I have no tolerance for anyone who doesn't respect other people's property. Do you understand?"

"Yes, of course."

In the front parlor, Mrs. Walker motioned for Hildy to sit.

"The rent is five dollars a week due on Saturdays. I'm very strict about that. I have rules that you will be expected to obey. If you do not, then I'll ask you to leave. Is that clear?"

"Perfectly."

"You may not, under any circumstances, have a young man in

your room. You may, however, entertain in this parlor on Saturdays and Sundays. Your young man or friends must leave by ten o'clock. The other girls might be doing the same; then you can all get to know each other, which is a good thing. I, too, am always free to join in. Understand?"

"Yes."

"Well, you seem to be a very nice young lady. Tell me about yourself."

"I'm originally from Albertsville, southwest of Madison. I came to Milwaukee six years ago and, presently, work at the *John Ernst Cafe*. I don't have a young man in my life and have no prospects, so I wouldn't be entertaining for quite a while. Eventually, I hope to find employment on the west side, but, until I do, I'll work downtown. I'm twenty-six; I have my one-year certificate from Stratton, and I intend to go to school again this fall for my two-year certificate."

"Why did you leave Albertsville?" Mrs. Walker asked.

"There's no work."

"What did you say you do?"

"I'm a waitress, but I hope to find a responsible position in a business enterprise."

"Where did you say you work?"

"Downtown at the *John Ernst Cafe* . . . mostly evenings."

"How late?"

"The restaurant closes at ten; I'm usually out by 10:45."

"Then you'd have to take the bus, which means you probably wouldn't be here until about 11:30, would you say?"

"Yes, I suppose."

Mrs. Walker stood. "I'm very sorry. I couldn't sleep peaceably with roomers coming in that late. I'm sorry because you seem like a nice girl, but, really, I couldn't sleep knowing you weren't home by eleven. Sunday to Thursday the curfew is eleven; Friday and Saturday it's midnight."

"I'm going to apply at the *Boulevard Inn*," Hildy said. "I'm sure I'd be home by eleven."

"If you find employment close by, if you can keep my curfew, and if the room is still available, then I'll be happy to have you."

Mrs. Walker escorted Hildy out of her home. "Thank you for coming . . . goodbye." She went right back in and closed the door.

Surprised how quickly the interview ended, Hildy realized, *this would have been perfect.*

On her way to the restaurant, Hildy passed a flower shop that she didn't recall seeing. She wondered, *how did I miss this?* Then she recalled the startling horn, searching for Schmitt's Buick, and rushing right past the little shop.

Potted asters, carnations, daisies, gardenias, zinnias, and colorful ceramic vases of all sizes and shapes clustered in the windows. Small terra-cotta pots of African violets, just like the ones her mother tended in the parlor in Albertsville, bordered the display along the front windows and at the entry recess.

Painted on the glass entry door were *Carolyn's Flower Shop* and its hours of business. Two hand-lettered signs were taped to the angled window of the recess. Hildy could scarcely believe her eyes: *Help Wanted – Clerk* and *Help Wanted – Bookkeeper.* She stared at the word *Bookkeeper* almost in disbelief. "Oh my God," she said out loud.

I'll apply first thing in the morning, she decided, *and, if I'm hired, I'll visit Mrs. Walker to rent the room.* If Hildy wasn't hired, she'd inquire at the restaurant. She crossed Lisbon Avenue to the bus stop all the while thinking how wonderful it would be to work as a bookkeeper, live on the west side, spend more time with Anna, and, most importantly, be lost to the loathsome Bob Schmitt.

In the morning, minutes after nine, Hildy entered *Carolyn's.* A little bell above the door jingled her arrival. "Good morning," a voice sang. A smiling woman, tying an apron behind her, appeared from the rear of the shop. "May I help you?"

"Good morning . . . yes . . . ." Hildy recognized the woman's *Irishness*: sparkling blue eyes, perky nose, flowing reddish-brown hair, and freckled cheeks. "I'd like to apply for the bookkeeper's job if it's still available."

"Oh how silly of me . . . I thought you were a customer."

"I saw your sign yesterday. I decided to come early."

"Do you have experience? Oh, I'm sorry, forgive me. I'm Carolyn Rabach. My husband and I are the owners. And you are?"

"Hildegard Neubauer."

"How do you do, Miss Neubauer? My, what a pretty name."

"Thank you. Yes, I have my certificate from Stratton Business

College. I had two semesters of bookkeeping and earned two *A's*, so I do have a good understanding of the subject."

"Unfortunately, my husband isn't here. He'll interview you. He's our salesman. That's what he loves, and, just between you and me, he sells a lot better than he keeps the books. Could you come back at eleven? He should be here by then."

"Well, yes, of course," Hildy said.

She crossed Lisbon Avenue, walking in the shade of the elms that lined the sidewalk bordering the park. She strolled all the way to the *Boulevard Inn* and stared, as though she were studying its prosaic architecture. In fact, she did not want to work as a waitress there, at the Café, or anywhere else. Six years was enough. *I wonder what Mrs. Ernst will say,* she thought. *Well, I can't worry about that. Of course, maybe I won't get it. Don't count your chickens, Hildy.*

She followed a looping path into the park, thinking of her father who, two months after taking ill, wasn't doing as well as the doctor had hoped. Hildy wanted to visit him, but her father just didn't want her to come now. *If I get this job,* she speculated, *I certainly won't be going to Albertsville until Christmas – if even then.*

Hildy had tremendous ambition. She knew she was smart and sensed she could do significant work if given the opportunity. Now, in less than an hour, she'd discuss the possibility of working as bookkeeper for a little flower shop. She wondered, *how much business can they possibly have? Will I be locked in some back room?* And then, *where will it lead?* She re-entered the shop a few minutes before eleven.

Carolyn called, "Charles . . . ."

In a moment he appeared. His manners, movements, and smile disclosed a man who engaged life with tremendous enthusiasm. Thinning hair on top, solidly built, neither tall nor short, he looked right at Hildy and said, "Hello there, Miss Neubauer," in such a sincere and robust manner that it completely calmed her. "I'm Chuck Rabach . . . I understand you know my wife."

The comment was so unexpected and disarming that both women laughed out loud. "We just met. I'm glad she remembered my name."

"*Hildegard Neubauer* isn't easy to forget," Carolyn said. "You know there's a local chanteuse by that name, at least the first name, but I think she's moved to Paris."

"You can't move to Paris until I've had a chance to talk to you," Charles said. "Come on in. Carolyn, are you coming?"

"Leave the door open . . . I'll hear."

"When you see my office you might decide *you* want to move to Paris," Charles said.

Unlike the tidy shop, the disheveled room shocked Hildy. Newspapers, files, and magazines were piled everywhere. The desktop, strewn with clutter, wasn't even visible. She waited for him to speak.

"You're wondering how it got to be such a mess, huh?"

"Well, I . . . ." Hildy's head shook in disbelief.

"Well, it's not going to be my mess much longer. If we hire you, it's all yours." He laughed.

Her mind turned anxious at how quickly he inferred she might get the job, but her heart was thrilled.

"We need someone who can manage our money. I'm no good at it. I'm a salesman. I enjoy people. Actually, selling is all I really want to do. I can't do the books – I've tried. Look at this mess. If you ask how much money we're owed, I don't have the faintest idea. Bills to be paid . . . I wait for my suppliers to call. I don't even know where their bills are . . . somewhere in here, I imagine. They know I'm good for it though. I've never not paid a bill . . . I'm just not real prompt. See this stack of envelopes . . . know what they are?" He didn't wait for Hildy's answer. "Checking account statements . . . I haven't reconciled our account in over a year. How much money do we have in the bank? I don't know exactly, but I make sure I don't bounce checks, which means I call my banker a lot. Carolyn is the best flower arranger on the west side, but she wants nothing to do with the books, and neither do I. So tell me, what should we do?"

"How do you track your receivables?" Hildy asked with such authority that it surprised him.

"We don't. My accountant wants me to, but I keep forgetting."

"You have to know who owes you money."

"I'd have to go through all our customer files and add it up."

"Haven't you created a *Receivables Account* in your ledger book?"

"No, in fact, I rarely open that book. That's why we need

a bookkeeper. That's why you and I are having this friendly conversation."

"Well, that's the first thing I'd do," Hildy said.

"Good. Now let me tell you a little about our business. Carolyn creates centerpieces for banquets and dinners at all the big hotels. We even sell to banks; they put arrangements in the lobby to make people feel better about not having any money." He laughed again. "Of course, we have weddings, funerals, and our walk-ins; considering the times, our business is pretty good, but I don't quite know where we stand financially. Understand?"

"Yes, perfectly."

"Have you ever worked as a bookkeeper before?"

"I worked as a clerk in my father's store, summers when I was a girl." She shifted in her chair, realizing she failed to answer the question. A stream of sunlight, alive with dust particles, distracted her. Suddenly, she remembered her father's store, and how she liked waving her hand through those same dusty beams, sweeping them into chaos.

"Miss Neubauer, I asked, have you ever worked as a bookkeeper?"

"Excuse me?"

"Did you ever work as a bookkeeper before?"

"No, I did not, but I assure you, I can put your books in perfect order. Once I do, you will never not know your financial situation again."

The assertion impressed Charles and surprised Hildy.

"Do you live nearby?" he asked.

"No, but I intend to . . . ."

"Carolyn, can you come in?"

Carolyn smiled at Hildy. She had heard the entire interview.

"Do you have any questions?"

"Yes, just one: tell me, Miss Neubauer, do you like flowers?"

Hildy's smile and bright eyes answered unmistakably, and, at that moment, the Rabachs sensed they had found their new bookkeeper.

The job was only four hours a day, but Hildy had an idea. "May I apply for the clerk position as well?" she asked.

Carolyn looked at her husband. "Charles, why not?

The joy Hildy felt at her double hiring was sweeter than

anything she had ever known. She wanted to hug and kiss her new employers and shout the news to strangers on the street. She could hardly hold her happiness till she reached Mrs. Walker's house.

On hearing the news, Mrs. Walker said, "I trust then you'll be home by eleven."

"Yes, of course, and I promise I'll be a good renter. I hope you'll come to the shop, if not to buy flowers then at least to say 'hello' and see my office. It's quite a mess right now, but I'll clean it up just fine. I'll introduce you to Mr. and Mrs. Rabach. They're very nice. You'll enjoy meeting them. It's small, but a lovely shop, really."

"Miss Neubauer, calm down, please. I'm not used to such excitement. Yes, I know the Rabachs. I've bought flowers there."

Hildy's good fortune at being hired at *Carolyn's* surprised her friend, Anna Eastwood, who presumed Hildy would work at the *Boulevard Inn*. Hildy attributed her good luck to Anna's wise counsel, but Anna could only say, "Why, I never would have imagined . . . ."

Hildy wrote her parents including the telephone number at the shop and Mrs. Walker's address. She regretted she couldn't come home until Christmas and closed by writing, *I miss you both*. Feeling a little successful, she wanted them, more than ever, to visit her in Milwaukee.

But Hildy also suffered doubt. Was she really capable of organizing the bookkeeping, as she claimed? Would the Rabachs be pleased with her? Would the tedious work bore her? Would she miss living downtown? Would she miss the casual sociability at the Cafe?

Once she started, Charles and Carolyn accepted her without question. She was free to do whatever she wished, and the Rabachs, from the first day, treated her office no longer as their own. Indeed, that first day the mess overwhelmed Hildy. *Good heaven, I have to clean this place before I can even think of keeping the books.*

By the end of the first week she had thrown out most of the old magazines except a small stack Charles took home. Newspapers ended up in the back room where Carolyn had use for them. By the start of the second week, Hildy attacked the clutter on her desk. More pleasantly, she also received her first telephone call.

"Oh, Anna, how nice to hear your voice. I'm fine, happy to be here."

"I'm so glad. When did you move?"

"A week ago Thursday . . . a cabbie helped me. Friday I organized my room, so I'm all set."

"How's your landlady and the other roomers?"

"She's strict, but pleasant. The two women keep to themselves. I guess I do too . . . they're older. But Anna, I'm so happy to be a *Westsider*. I feel safe again.

By the end of the second week, Hildy had organized all the papers on Charles's desk into piles on the floor beneath the window that angled the morning sunlight into her office. She cleared enough of her desk to do some real work including preparing her first paycheck, which thrilled her even though Charles had to sign it. The checkbook, however, lacked a running balance, which concerned her, along with blank check stubs and missing deposits, even though Charles went to the bank twice a week. She had to analyze the bank statements, over a year's worth, bring the checkbook up to date, and reconcile every month. She resolved to know exactly how much money the shop had, not because of an intrusive curiosity, but rather to show Charles and Carolyn that she was capable of determining their financial situation. *How can I pay bills,* she wondered, *if I don't know how much money they have?*

Anna called again the second Wednesday. "I forgot to ask: how did Mrs. Ernst react when you told her you were leaving?"

"Oh, she was good about it . . . said they'd miss me, but people come all the time looking for work. She didn't think it would take long to find a replacement."

"Would you like to get together Sunday?" Anna asked. "If you want, come to church and have breakfast with us. Then I'd love to see your room."

"Sounds wonderful," Hildy said.

+ + +

By October, Hildy had the office well organized to both Charles and Carolyn's amazement. In five weeks she had scarcely clerked though she greatly preferred bookkeeping: work that demanded thinking, analyzing, and executing.

Besides, Carolyn was competent, quick, and graceful whether wrapping cut flowers, potting plants, or arranging centerpieces.

She engaged customers in pleasant small talk that Hildy enjoyed overhearing. Only when Carolyn worked in the rear room, and a customer came, did Hildy clerk.

"Ladies always appreciate roses; your wife will enjoy these," Carolyn remarked to a man Hildy couldn't see from her desk. "Is it a special occasion?"

"No, just a little surprise. She's expecting in January."

"Well, these will please her, Mr. Helden. Every woman loves to receive roses." Carolyn handed him the wrapped flowers.

"Thank you," he said.

Neither Carolyn nor the customer noticed the quiet figure behind the office door. When Hildy heard the name *Helden* she stood and peaked at the tall, handsome man. After he left, Hildy asked, "Did you say his name is *Helden?*"

"Yes . . . why?"

"I knew a Dr. Helden several years ago."

"They could be related, I suppose," Carolyn said. "Next time he comes, ask him."

Hildy's organization of the office was, in Charles' most enthusiastic voice, "nothing short of a miracle." One day late in the afternoon, she called Charles and Carolyn into her office. Not only had she paid all current bills and reconciled the checkbook, but she also had created an Accounts Receivable Ledger. The checkbook balanced at three thousand, nine hundred and twenty-seven dollars, and sixty-two cents. In addition, there were over four hundred dollars in current receivables. Charles and Carolyn looked at each other in disbelief.

"You mean to say, there's over four thousand dollars here," Charles asked, "after all our salaries."

"Yes, you have a very profitable business."

"My goodness, Charles, I had no idea," Carolyn said.

Walking to her room that amber October evening, Hildy treasured the Rabachs' reaction. On the strength of her intellect and industry, she had made herself an important employee. Bookkeeping demanded, at least in the Rabachs' case, solving some difficult problems. She enjoyed waitressing, but it could never satisfy her lively mind. Organizing both the office and the checking account required total commitment. Neither Charles nor Carolyn had that resolve. Hildy did, however, and she was proud of herself. That night she wrote her parents telling them how pleased the Rabachs were with her.

During the week, Anna called Hildy at least once. Sometimes Hildy described her work, though Anna showed little interest in bookkeeping. She had far more interest in her much simpler job at the thriving brewery in the Menomonee River valley. She took dictation, typed a few letters, answered the phone, and occasionally chatted with the charming thirty-year old grandson of the original founder. He had an interest in Anna and she in him.

Saturdays, Hildy worked half a day and oftentimes all day, so Sundays were better to get together with Anna. For all the times she had gone to Mass with the Eastwoods, Hildy almost felt Catholic. Breakfast afterwards with Herman and Clara was always pleasant. Often, the young women took the bus to Washington Park to stroll amid the golden elms and fiery maples. If it rained, they'd visit the caged animals indoors at the odorous zoo or catch a movie at the *Uptown*.

"I don't believe it; when did all this happen?" Hildy asked, after Anna told how she and young Mr. Pfaltz had been dating nearly a month.

William Pfaltz had his eye on Anna since her first day on the job. Because of his friendliness and her demure openness, they began exchanging morning greetings. Now and then, he'd stop at her desk just to make some perfectly harmless comment about nothing really important. If he was near her at the end of the day, which he usually was, he'd make it a point to say "goodnight" or "see you tomorrow."

"He's always been really nice," Anna said. "My folks think he's a perfect gentleman."

"You're a lucky girl, if he proves as good as he seems."

"I know. I learned a long time ago to be extra careful when some guy starts talking like a Romeo. But sometimes I just pray it works out. He's been so nice, right from the start."

At the shop, Carolyn usually answered the telephone. When the call was for Hildy, she got into the habit of saying "hi" instead of the more conventional "hello" because it always was Anna. She said "hi" now.

"Hildy is that you?"

"Yes, Mother? Can you hear me?"

Without a reply, but not silence either, Hildy strained to make sense of the sounds in the receiver. Long distance calls always crackled, but there was something else now. Hildy heard her mother weeping.

"Mother, what is it?"

"Oh Hildy, your father died this morning."

+ + +

The family was small. Hildy's aunt, her mother's older sister, lived in Indiana. They hadn't seen her for six years. Her father's two younger brothers lived in Los Angeles, and they hadn't seen either of them for ten years. Two of Hildy's first cousins lived in Indianapolis and five in California. By the time Hildy's mother wrote them all and they received the letters, Mr. Neubauer would be long buried.

He had been well liked by townspeople and farm people too, from miles around. Many of them came to his funeral. For a while, the line went out the door into the cold November morning. They paid their final respects to the weeping widow and the mature daughter from Milwaukee whose faces revealed intense sorrow. Not another blood relative shared the women's grief for the loss of the only man intimately in their lives.

Albertsville was a churchless town, so Mr. Neubauer was laid out in the General Store with the approval of Mr. Harvey, the store's owner and Mr. Neubauer's employer for the past twenty years. He drove from Madison for the funeral and other sudden and necessary business. He moved display counters, rolled barrels into the back room, covered the colorful candy jars with blankets, and cleared an area for the pine box coffin in front of the cash register where Mr. Neubauer stood sentinel for two decades. The Lutheran minister came from Mineral Point to conduct the service. Afterwards, they buried Hildy's father in the hardening ground of the small cemetery northeast of the little town.

+ + +

"Of course, you can take off," Carolyn said. "Just let us know how long you'll be gone. The bookkeeping can wait."

"I've worked less than three months, and now I have to leave. I'm terribly sorry."

"You don't have to apologize. Your mother needs you."

The train ride was as bleak as the weather. November takes Wisconsin from the soft, Indian summer to freezing, hard winter in a matter of days. By Thanksgiving snow is on the ground nearly everywhere; many years there can be as much as a foot of snow somewhere.

The train wasn't crowded. Hildy sat by herself because she was in no mood to chat with a stranger. She cried occasionally, but was careful not to let others notice, although the conductor suspected something when he took her ticket from a hand holding a balled handkerchief.

She remembered, as a girl, how she loved when her father took her to his store. On summer days, cooling breezes funneled through the open doors, front and rear. On a rolling ladder, she stocked shelves with blankets, sheets, towels, work shirts, coveralls, and long johns that the farm women bought for their husbands, plus canning jars, pots and pans, wooden spoons, and bolts of colored fabric and dress patterns they bought for themselves. She helped her father keep the barrels filled with nails and spikes, electrical wire, outlets and switches, and black-iron plumbing elbows and fittings. She wasn't allowed, however, to open the dark-stained oak and glass cases filled with knives, hunting rifles, and shotguns under lock and key. She loved the candy jars that stored her colorful wages and the fun she had picking three hard pieces. Hearing her father greet customers by name and listening to them talk gave her great pleasure; sometimes it was just chitchat, but oftentimes serious things. That was why, Hildy realized, her father didn't converse so much at home.

And now, after seven long years, she had to deal with Eddie again. Her mother arranged for him to pick Hildy up in Mineral Point just as her father used to. Hildy felt it was all too much yet when she thought of her father, her apprehension about seeing Eddie evaporated.

"Hildy," his unmistakable voice called.

Crossing the road, she stared at the wet pavement rather than confronting Eddie's gaze. He bounded from the pickup, took her small suitcase, and placed it in the back, covering it with canvas. He walked 'round and opened the passenger door for her.

Putting the truck in gear, Eddie said, "I'm sure sorry about your pa. He was a good man, always nice to me, that's for sure."

"Thank you, Eddie."

She didn't know what to say. She didn't want to talk, not just to Eddie, not to anyone except her mother. *Oh dear God,* she prayed, *how I wish I could talk to my father.*

For several miles they rode in silence. Grateful for it, Hildy finally said, "I understand you're married and have children."

"Yup . . . I've got a little girl and boy, three and one. Cutest little shavers you ever saw. Our little guy just started walking."

"That's nice, Eddie, really nice. Good for you."

To Eddie's credit and Hildy's relief, he didn't bring up their past. Years ago he thought about it more, but his marriage proved happy. With the birth of two children and the many, good qualities he discovered in his wife, he let his passion for Hildy die. When he was eighteen and nineteen, though, he loved Hildy so much he thought he'd die without her. Now, he found his own wife prettier.

He parked in front of Hildy's old home. Both of them recalled the times they often sat in Eddie's father's car at this same spot, talking and holding hands on those lovely summer nights when they were so young back in 1929. Now neither said a word. She glanced at him and felt nothing, not a speck of emotion. He helped her from the truck and carried her suitcase up the porch steps. Her sight settled on the front door behind which she imagined her father pacing, just as he had while she dallied after a date with Eddie. Mrs. Neubauer opened the door. Hildy thanked Eddie, grabbed her bag and scurried inside. The two women fell into each other's arms and wept.

Chapter 17 ~ 1937

Carolyn noticed Hildy's sadness after she returned from her father's funeral, and as it lingered into December. After Hildy's Christmas visit to her widowed mother, and well into January, Carolyn noticed Hildy still wasn't getting over her father's death. Carolyn didn't think it normal for a young woman at all. "She's just not herself, Charles. She works hard, but she's not happy. It's not right; she's too young."

"Carol that happens; a parent's death isn't easy; I don't care how old you are. She's sensitive. It'll take a while."

"Well, I really think we should introduce Hildy to Paul."

Charles grunted.

Carolyn knew what it meant. "No, no . . . before you reject the idea, you have to listen."

"Your solution to all your girlfriends' problems for the past fifteen years has been to fix them up with a man, as though that's some kind of magic cure-all. She just needs a little time to put her father's death behind her. Time, Carol, that's all . . . she doesn't need a matchmaker or a man."

Carolyn didn't mention it again until several evenings later, then a couple evenings after that and, finally, she brought it up nearly every evening, but always in a brief and clever way. Eventually, Charles embraced the idea because Carolyn so skillfully convinced him of its merits, not only for Hildy's sake, but Paul's as well. Charles even agreed to present the idea to his younger friend.

Nevertheless, Carolyn decided not to rush Hildy into meeting Paul until she sensed Hildy felt a little happier. When that didn't happen she mentioned it anyway. With no apparent enthusiasm, Hildy replied, "Let me think about it."

By mid-January the city, burdened with two months of snow and cold, yearned for a thaw. Near the end of the day, Hildy and Carolyn chatted at the counter when they noticed a customer approaching. Carolyn recognized the man and asked Hildy to wait on him. It was John Helden.

Hildy felt a wisp of anxiety before saying, "Good evening sir."

She wore a white apron over a red woolen dress that revealed her shapeliness. Her eyes sparkled in anticipation. John smiled at her.

"May I help you?" she asked.

"Yes, I'd like a dozen roses. My wife gave birth to our second son today."

"Oh, how wonderful . . . congratulations!"

"Thanks."

"Would you like long stem or regular?"

"Long stem . . . don't you think," John said.

"For a birth, yes, definitely."

Hildy chose twelve from the cooler, all with closed, tight buds.

"They're very beautiful," John said.

She wrapped them and offered a small, greeting card.

"No thanks; I bought one earlier." He put three dollars on the counter; Hildy gave him change. "Thank you very much. Give my regards to Carolyn."

"I shall, Mr. Helden."

He started to leave, but turned wondering how she knew his name. Hildy caught his curiosity. "Last time you were here, Carolyn mentioned your name. It interested me because I knew a Helden once, a Dr. Julius Helden."

"Julius is my younger brother. How did you happen to know him?"

"I was a patient of his at County General . . . years ago."

"Oh, yes, I remember when he interned there."

"Is he . . . ?" Hildy sustained the pronoun hoping John would reveal something about the young doctor she had been so fond of those many years ago.

"He's in private practice on the south side and doing well. He and his wife have a little girl and they're expecting again."

"Oh, how nice . . . he was a very good doctor and very kind to me."

"May I tell Julius I spoke with you?"

"Of course . . . I'm Hildegard Neubauer, but everyone calls

me Hildy. Perhaps he'll remember. He helped me very much. I've never forgotten him so please say *hello* for me."

After John left, Hildy put on her boots, coat, hat and mittens, and said goodnight to Carolyn. "So he is the brother of the doctor you knew."

"Yes, small world isn't it?"

"Big world, Hildy," Carolyn replied, "just a small town. Goodnight."

Walking to her room through the cold, dreary evening, she recalled her brief encounter with Dr. Helden. *My God, almost seven years,* she realized. *He was so sweet. His brother seems very nice. How lucky their wives are to be married to such fine men. They must be very special women.*

And then Hildy confronted a deeply buried truth, one hidden in her heart that gave both exquisite joy and enormous pain. *I could have loved you, Julius Helden, dear, sweet doctor, my beautiful young man. I could have so easily loved you.*

At the side window in her darkened room, she stared at the desolate park across Lisbon Avenue. Several cars and a bus crawled slowly by. Snowflakes shimmered in the soft light of the street lamps. Usually, Hildy found winter scenes lovely, but this night appeared bleak and barren. In her flannel nightgown a chill overcame her. *I would have loved you so well, dear Julius.* Tears poised in her eyes, then ran down her cheeks and fell to the hardwood. *Julius, my love . . . Julius, never shall it be.* Under the weight of a great sadness, a bitter realization of an untold, inevitable, and irreplaceable loss, she fell asleep. It was the first night since her father died that she didn't think of him in the final, conscious moment.

Several days later, Carolyn sensed a change in Hildy. *Perhaps,* she speculated, *it's the weather.* The sky became brilliant, a cloudless blue, but still no thaw. From the little shop filled with flowers and sunlight, they could see Washington Park laden with the white weight of winter. The temperature barely reached twenty degrees at noon; at night it fell below zero, but Hildy was beginning to smile again, and her voice regained its lilt. Within days, Hildy agreed to meet Paul; she didn't say when, but once ready she'd let Carolyn know.

Anna and Hildy hadn't seen each other for several Sundays

because Anna was spending more time with Bill Pfaltz. Hildy understood how enjoyable that was for them and even admitted to a little envy. The second weekend in February she went to Albertsville.

"Mother, what will you do now," Hildy asked.

"I don't know."

"Will you stay here?"

"I haven't thought about it," she lied. "I really don't know."

"Move to Milwaukee. You don't have to live in this tiny town anymore. We can rent a two-bedroom or an upper flat."

Hildy's suggestion came not as a surprise. Her mother had the same idea, but felt reluctant to mention it fearing Hildy might find her presumptuous. Once Hildy offered it, though, her mother was delighted. In her mind it was the only logical thing for them to do. She chose, however, not to disclose her elation.

"I'll have to sell the house; it could take a while."

"It doesn't matter. At least we'll be able to look forward to being together."

"You're a good daughter, Hildy. We should be together. We're all we've got now. I didn't think," she dabbed her eyes, "your poor father would pass so soon."

In February, Carolyn, for the first time, invited Hildy to church and then afterwards breakfast at their home. The Rabachs belonged to St. Anne's, the wedding church of John and Anita Helden back in 1932. Hildy felt more *Catholic* with every Sunday Mass; between the Eastwoods and Rabachs the Catholic influence on her grew steadily. Hildy grew so accustomed to the Catholic service that on Sundays when she didn't go, she missed it or, perhaps, just missed the congeniality of being with friends for breakfast and coffee. Over time, though, she gained a deeper sense of worship. She understood both the blessings of life and its sorrows come from God; they were hers to cherish or regret, deal with, learn from, and finally to accept – good and bad. All the beauty she discovered in the world, and in those she loved, came, she now recognized, as divine gifts. Her prayers beseeched God's blessings on her loved ones, thanked Him for everything, and begged forgiveness for her unthinkable sins.

Charles explained that every Mass offers instruction from the Old Testament and the Gospels. Within its structure resides the opportunity for contrition, forgiveness of lesser sins, thanksgiving, and professing one's faith in the universal *Nicene Creed*. At its most essential, elemental core, however, a remembrance of the passion and death of our Lord is offered in the transubstantiation of bread and wine into the Body and Blood of Christ. St. John's profound and beautiful *Last Gospel* filled Hildy with the wonder and mystery of Creation and the Incarnation. The missal's English translations were like poetry to her. After several months, both Charles and Carolyn sensed she would eventually convert.

But Hildy had questions. "Why so many rules: not missing Sunday Mass, not eating meat on Fridays, Church on Holydays, fasting during Lent? Don't you sometimes feel like you're in the army?"

Charles loved it. He considered himself both an evangelist and an apologist. "Let me ask you this: how often did you go to church before you met the Eastwoods and us?"

"Not very often, once or twice a year, Christmas and Easter with my folks, but, you have to understand, I was not a very good Lutheran."

Charles laughed. "Not eating meat teaches people to make little sacrifices. The Church tries to teach people the wisdom of denying physical desires. There's value in fasting and abstaining because it teaches us to control our appetites. If a person learns to deny himself something that is not, in itself, morally wrong – like eating meat – then it stands to reason that that person is better prepared to resist the temptation of serious sin."

"You would have made an excellent priest, Charles. Of course then you couldn't be married to Carolyn, which brings up another point: why can't priests marry?"

"Oh, I agree with that," Carolyn said. "I mean, I agree priests shouldn't marry. Think of the distractions . . . ."

"Like what?"

"Well, there's the matter of children, in-laws, bills to be paid; maybe his wife wants to go dancing on Saturday night when he has to hear Confessions."

"What's Confession like? Do you really tell everything?"

"Sure," Charles answered. "What good is it if you hide a sin from the priest? God knows. He reads our hearts. After Confession I feel incredible peace because all the guilt is gone. If I die, I know I'm going straight to Heaven."

"Maybe a little stop in Purgatory, Charlie," Carolyn said, "especially for the state of your office when Hildy first came. That was a sin if ever I saw one. I hope you confessed it."

"Oh, boy," Charles said, drawing the women's laughter.

+ + +

Several days later Hildy told Carolyn, "I'd like to meet your friend sometime . . . ."

Carolyn smiled. "Oh, good, good, I'll take care of it."

Paul called Hildy at work and suggested a Sunday afternoon walk in Juneau Park and afterwards a bite to eat. She gave him her telephone number at Mrs. Walker's, asking that he call her several days in advance to confirm the time.

Carolyn warned Hildy that "Paul's a pretty serious guy. Once you get to know him, though, you'll discover a pretty neat sense of humor. We always have fun with Paul. Really Hildy, he's very nice. Give him a chance, okay?"

"Oh, I will . . . tell me about him."

"Well, let me see: he's a mechanical engineer, Marquette grad; Charlie says he makes a good salary, given the times and all. He's thirty-three. His older brother, Phil, was one of Charlie's best friends, but he was killed in the Great War. I never knew Phil. Paul also has two real nice sisters. The family grew up on the south side. After Phil was killed, Charlie kept in touch; he and Paul became close. I've fixed him up a few times, but no one as special as you."

Hildy smiled.

"Oh, and Paul's Catholic," she added.

"Gee whiz, I wonder why *that* doesn't surprise me."

Six women had an interest in Hildy meeting Paul. Carolyn, because she thought they might find happiness with each other and also to vindicate her role as matchmaker. Anna, because Hildy was a dear friend for whom she wished happiness, but also Anna fancied the fun of double dating. Hildy's mother wondered if it would lead to marriage, but in any event, she'd move to Milwaukee to live either with Hildy or by herself, and that was that. Mrs. Walker, because Hildy had proved an excellent roomer; she didn't want to lose her. Paul's mother had great interest because he was too old to be living at home and should have a wife. And lastly,

Hildy herself, because she was feeling the desire to love and be loved. So much good had happened the past year in spite of her father's death and the horrible encounters with Bob Schmitt that she wondered if this first date would lead to anything at all.

Carolyn couldn't wait to get to the shop the Monday after Paul and Hildy's first date. Hildy sat demurely at her desk, as Carolyn rushed through the front door. She asked, "How was it? Did you like him? Was he nice? Will you see him again?"

Hildy smiled, but said nothing.

"Hildy, don't toy with me. I could hardly sleep wondering about you two. Tell me . . . ."

"Well, Paul is very nice, but you're right . . . he's a serious guy."

"Does that mean you won't see him again?"

Hildy laughed. "I don't know. It's really not up to me, is it? If he asks, then I'll decide."

"Don't tease me Hildegard Neubauer. Be honest – did you like him?"

"Yes, I liked him. He was very sweet. I did see glimmers of a sense of humor under all those layers of seriousness; but don't ask silly questions, Carol. It was only one date. I don't know if he'll even ask me out again."

"He'll ask . . . I guarantee it," Carolyn said, with the authority of a born matchmaker.

"Carol," Charles's voice boomed from the back, "don't be a butt-inski."

"I'm not. We're just talking for heaven's sake. My goodness, he's my friend, too, you know." Charles's command flustered Carolyn. "He can be so bossy," Carolyn whispered. She winked at Hildy and left the office.

A moment later, Charles stood at her door. "Good morning Miss Neubauer. How are you this fine Monday?"

"Oh, good morning; I'm fine, thank you." Then she added, "Charles, may I speak with you a moment?"

He sat in the same chair Hildy sat in when she interviewed last August, but now she oversaw a desk cleared of clutter and arranged according to her wishes. Charles's expression, as always, was open and friendly. She found him, right from the start, to be remarkably pleasant, so much so that she asked Carolyn if he was like that in the privacy of their home. She answered, "I hate to admit such near perfection in a man, but for the most part, yes, he is." Pattern resumed.

Hildy asked, "Tell me Charles, what one must do if they wish to become a Catholic?"

Chapter 18 ~ 1937 (Continued)

Hildy could have asked Anna or Carolyn the same question, as she did consider it before settling on Charles. She felt he'd sense her seriousness, not wasting her time or his for that matter. All he had to do was send her to the right priest who, like a skilled bricklayer, would set her decision in the mortar of sound theology to bind her to the sacramental life of the Church.

"You have to take instructions, usually in a small group."

"Can you give me the name of a priest, someone you think I'd be comfortable with?"

"I've got just the man for you, I mean, just the priest for you," Charles laughed. "Maybe Paul's the man for you."

Hildy didn't react. She wouldn't allow his remark to lead to any conversation about Paul, not after only one date. Besides, Paul wasn't the reason she asked the question.

Father Jim Fahey taught chemistry at Marquette University. Charles took the course his sophomore year and proved, to both teacher and student, that he shouldn't consider chemicals for a career. His junior year he had Father Jim for moral theology; in that class Charles proved himself both a lover and defender of the Faith. Students found Father Fahey an excellent teacher and a kindly, spiritual man, esteemed and beloved by young men and women alike.

After Charles graduated, he and Father Jim remained friends. The priest loved classical music and literature, whereas Charles's interests focused on business and sports. The Christian Faith, however, held their mutual interest. Charles kept in touch by referring several people for instructions. Father Jim baptized them all.

Forty-eight years old when Hildy met him, Father Jim respected what a potential convert brought to the Church. He knew their minds and hearts were filled with anger, pain, doubt, guilt, confusion, as well as a longing for knowledge, forgiveness, peace, and the truth they all so desperately hoped would set them free. He possessed a deep insight into human psychology and forged his own obstinate and somewhat self-righteous nature to be compassionate and forgiving of all human weaknesses. He heard the first confession of so many adult converts and so many confessions of practicing Catholics as well, that the constancy and universality of the frailties of human beings ceased to amaze him. He recognized all too well that many of those same weaknesses lurked in the deep, dormant crevices of his own soul.

The great, Gothic church at Marquette University, *Gesu,* sat prominently on Wisconsin Avenue at the southern terminus of North 12th Street. Well-staffed by the school's Jesuits, it also served as parish for Catholics in the neighborhood west of downtown. Twin spires flanked its large rose window and were visible miles to the north. Above the steeply pitched cruciform roof at the intersection of transept and nave, a shorter steeple was visible from east and west. Two bus lines and a streetcar line converged at this junction making it a transfer point for many riders. A block north, the Wells streetcar brought students from the old village of Wauwatosa, six miles west. Buildings surrounding Gesu included stores and shops with apartments above, an insurance company, and movie theater. On the south side of the avenue the main buildings of Marquette's lower campus, old Johnston Hall and the Science Building, flanked the great church. The sidewalks on both sides of the street teemed with people.

Built with cut, grey stone, the magnificent upper church hovered above a catacomb-like lower church that abounded with student and neighborhood worshippers coming and going at all hours of the day. It was a popular place for the sacrament of Confession, available six afternoons of the week, every week of the year except Holy Week. Spending several hours in the dimly lit lower church offered an opportunity to view a cross-section of the city's sinners and saints, all with their own secret vices and virtues, all with their own unique and evolving relationships with a necessarily merciful God. Father Fahey, knowing well the passive intensity of this restless milieu, thought it better if Hildy came to the quiet rectory on Michigan Street to make her first Confession. He knew she'd find it less intimidating.

She arrived at ten o'clock the Saturday morning following her Baptism. Anna Eastwood was her Godmother and Charles Rabach her Godfather. Even though Father Fahey explained that Baptism washed away all the sins of her past life, she insisted on making her first Confession with him as soon as possible.

The housekeeper led the young woman to the parlor. Father Fahey would be down shortly. Now Hildy felt an overwhelming apprehension. As an adult making her first Confession, she couldn't possibly acquire the easy acceptance of the Sacrament that a well-instructed child would. Anna and Carolyn assured her it was nothing to fear. She hoped with all her heart Confession would provide the peace she so desperately craved. She vowed to disclose everything. She reminded herself of Father Fahey's oft-stated instruction that God was a God of infinite mercy. She wanted, with all her heart, to believe that yet wondered what the limits of Father Fahey's mercy might be. He worried her more than God did. Throughout the weeks of her instruction, however, he had been so patient, so kind, and encouraging that she could hardly imagine he would change in the secrecy of the confessional. He greeted her, cheerfully, "Good morning Hildy."

She smiled and extended her hand. "Good morning, Father." Her voice veiled her anxiety.

"We'll go in my office; it's quiet and secluded."

"Next time I'd like to go to Confession in church like regular Catholics."

Father Fahey chuckled. "You are a regular Catholic, Hildy. In the church confessional there's a kneeler that faces a curtained opening where the priest sits; you whisper your sins to him. You receive some spiritual guidance, your penance, absolution, a blessing, and you're on your way. You'll do that often enough in your life, I suspect. Today it might be more comfortable in my office, as long as you don't mind looking at my old Irish mug."

She laughed. "I don't mind Father."

He closed the door then went right out again to tell the housekeeper they were not to be disturbed. He was back in a moment, seated at his desk facing her. "Hildy, do you remember how to begin?"

"Yes."

"Okay, then. May the Holy Ghost enlighten your mind and heart to know your sins and confess them completely in the Name of the Father, and of the Son, and of the Holy Ghost, Amen." As he spoke, he made the Sign of the Cross at her, as she made it upon herself. Then he turned away so their eyes wouldn't meet, while she confessed.

"Bless me Father for I have sinned. As you know, this is my first Confession, and these are the sins of my life." Hildy had prepared for this moment a long time. "Father, not being Catholic I missed Mass every Sunday before I met the Eastwoods and Rabachs. I didn't go to my Lutheran service very often except when I was little with my parents.

"I've eaten meat on most Fridays my entire life, but it wasn't forbidden like for Catholics, although now I enjoy fish-fries so I won't eat meat on Fridays anymore. I do not use God's name in vain. I have always prayed, but sometimes they were angry prayers although now, since I've been taking instructions with you, I don't have such angry prayers anymore."

Father Fahey interrupted. "And you want to develop the habit of saying both morning and evening prayers."

"Yes Father." Hildy paused. "I've always honored my mother and father."

Now a feeling of terror overcame her. Regardless of how painful it might be, though, she knew she had to reveal the darkest sins of her life. With all her being, she hoped confessing would provide the peace of mind and heart she so ardently desired.

"Father, when I was nineteen I had sexual intercourse with a boy my age. We did it only once, but I got pregnant. I was scared; I told no one, not even the boy. I couldn't possibly tell my parents. I didn't know what to do so I came to Milwaukee and took a room at the YWCA. I had told my parents I wanted to get a job and live here, which really was true. I thought about it after I got out of high school because there wasn't any work in our little town, so when I told them I was leaving, they weren't completely surprised. At first, my mother didn't like it, but in the end she didn't object because my father insisted I was grown up and had to find my own way in the world. When I got to Milwaukee I was frightened. I had no one to talk to. I was alone and felt desperate, plus I had very little money." She paused, fighting for courage. "Father, I tried to abort myself. It was terrible, but I just couldn't let myself be pregnant."

Nearly speechless, Father Fahey uttered, "How?"

"With a coat hanger. I flattened it out as best I could, I mean, I squeezed it together into a loop so it would fit. I bought a jar of Vaseline and put some in me and on the wires so it would enter more easily. I didn't want to hurt myself. I was afraid of that, but I didn't want to be pregnant either. I just couldn't bear that."

Hildy broke down weeping uncontrollably. Father Fahey had not expected such a secret sin. He gave her his handkerchief and let her cry for several minutes. Then, in a firm voice he said, "Hildy, tell me everything now. Don't be afraid, you'll feel better for it."

Sobbing, she said, "I turned it in me. I worked it around in a circle and tried to-" – her voice faltered – "I don't know what I tried to do. I didn't know what I was doing, but I wanted something to happen. When I took the hanger out, I was bleeding." Her voice trembled. "It wasn't heavy, but it didn't stop even after several hours. It frightened me. I put a pad on, got dressed, and took a bus to County General. I was scared, but in a strange way relieved because I thought maybe I had gotten rid of it. At the emergency room I told a nurse what I had done. She was very kind. She got a doctor to see me right away. He was kind too but, after examining me, said I'd have to have an operation. I had to have my womb scrapped, and the fetus – he called it that – would be lost. When he told me, I was terrified at what I had done. I knew I had killed my baby."

Again Hildy broke down. The priest struggled to control his own emotions.

She blew her nose then said, "After a while, I felt relieved I wasn't pregnant anymore. I was in the hospital a week. I had no money so I wrote my parents and told them I had gotten very sick and had to go to the hospital. My father sent the money. In addition to aborting my child, Father, I lied to my parents."

He nodded.

"When I was in the hospital it was strange because I was glad I wasn't pregnant, but then I'd think about the baby, and I'd feel horrible. I realized I had killed this tiny, little person. I couldn't stop crying because I remembered when I was a little girl how good my mother was to me. I thought of my baby that never would be born, and I felt very bad for what I had done, and yet at the same time I was relieved. I was confused, Father, and I couldn't stop crying. I cried for days until the doctors told me I had to leave. They said I couldn't stay because there wasn't anything wrong with me. Finally, I realized, even though I did this terrible thing, I had to live my life."

Hildy paused. Father Fahey presumed she had finished. He was silent while she blew her nose again. Then he began, "Hildy, I taught you that God is a God of infinite mercy-"

"Father, I have more . . . ."

"All right, go on."

"When I left the hospital, I vowed not to have intercourse again until I got married. I knew that was the right way. I was very good until I met a man who I thought wanted to marry me. He was very charming, but ten years older . . . I was twenty-four at the time. He was so attentive and considerate, but he kept pressuring me, in very sweet, nice ways, to make love, but I told him, 'No, not unless we get married.'

"One night he took me to a high-class restaurant in a downtown hotel. They had a dance orchestra. I never even knew a restaurant would have such a big orchestra, that's how dumb I was. Well, the music was very nice; people were dancing, having a good time. We drank a few highballs. I was happy . . . he seemed happy and hinted that he intended to ask me something very important very soon. I really believed, Father, he was going to ask me to marry him even though we only knew each other about four months.

"Well, maybe we both had a little too much to drink. When he took me home he made very strong advances. At first I resisted, but then realized I didn't want to . . . resist I mean. We had intercourse and then began to do it regularly, and I was surprised how much I enjoyed it because I really believed he'd be my husband. He always seemed so nice, but he never asked me to marry him, and I kept thinking he would any day. After a few months I got pregnant. At first I was happy about it and expected he'd be happy, too, but I didn't tell him right away – I don't know why. Finally, one evening we went out for supper. I told him I was pregnant and very happy to be carrying his child. At first his reaction wasn't so good, but then I said, 'Arthur, we'll get married now. That's what we must do, and everything will be fine.' Then he said, 'Sure, no problem, you're right. I'll be your dutiful little husband, and we'll live happily ever after.'

"I was relieved to hear him say that, but when we got back to my apartment he got very aggressive. He wanted to make love. I think that was okay with me, but his advances were so strong, so rough. I told him not to be like that. He ripped my blouse open, and a button came off. He touched my breasts so rough like he had never done before. He made love to me, but he didn't spend time with me, if you know what I mean, Father. It was not so nice for me; I almost felt like I was being raped. I was angry at him because I told him I was going to have his baby, and he should treat me nice. He left, and I didn't hear from him for days. I called, but he never answered. I'm sure he knew it was me. Two weeks later I received a letter. I have it with me. I've kept it these past three years, but after you read it, I want to burn it. Would you read it Father, please?"

"If you wish . . . ."

She handed him the sharply creased letter. He read silently:

Hildy,

I'm so mad at you I'll never talk to you again. To think you'd try that old pregnancy trick on me is beyond belief. You think I'd let some country hick lead me to the altar with a empty shotgun? Maybe once I was thinking about marrying you but I'm glad I didn't cause I learned what a liar you are. I don't want to marry someone who tried to trap me. I don't want to marry a girl of easy virtue not fit to kiss my Mother's shoes. Forget me cause I've forgotten you. Don't write back and don't ever call me again.

Arthur

Father Jim was stunned. Holding the letter up, he peered into Hildy's eyes. "This is terribly cruel . . . I trust you did not reply in kind."

"No I did not, Father. I never saw him again, much less respond to such an ugly letter. But I was angry, Father, angry beyond words. I know in my heart I wanted to kill him. I swear to God I would have, if I had the chance."

"What did you do?"

She stiffened in her chair, shifting her eyes from his. "I killed his child. When I was at County General, I met another intern who's a gynecologist now. He told me if I ever got in trouble again he could help me safely, provided I came early enough. I looked him up in the phone book after I received that horrible letter. Oh, Father, I was so angry . . . I wanted to kill him, but instead I killed his child. I swore to God I would never make that mistake again, but I did. I went to Dr. Messert. He did the abortion. I've suffered with all of this for years, Father. Can God forgive me? Please tell me God will forgive me. I'm sorry . . . ; I'm so sorry . . . ." She wept, bitterly.

Fr. Fahey watched her whole body tremble. "Yes Hildy, God can forgive you. The question is, can you forgive yourself?"

He let her weep. She wiped her eyes, blew her nose, but refused to look at him. In his years as a priest, Father Jim heard many diffi-cult confessions. This one surprised him only because he regarded Hildy as a rather innocent young woman, never suspecting she had had two abortions. Finally, after she regained a semblance of com-posure, he spoke.

"Something people don't realize, Hildy, is how God limits Him-self. God will not create human life without the participation of a man and woman. He has made them equal partners in the creative act. Of course, He made it extremely desirable for human beings to want to participate in creation, that is, by having sexual inter-course. Nevertheless, without that act, God simply doesn't create new human life. So, in that sense, He limits His divine power and is dependent upon a man and woman joining together in the act of love. If and when conception occurs, God infuses a soul that gives the fertilized egg – what is called the zygote – its life. The soul comes from God – God is the origin of all life. In a sense, the soul ignites life. It is what the theologians call the *Principle of Life*. The egg and sperm, the physical matter for the new human person, come from the woman and man, but the soul comes from God, and this newly created life is precious beyond all human understanding."

He glanced at her sad, downcast expression then continued. "For example: who wonders what really happened when Shake-speare and Beethoven were conceived? Who imagines such enor-mous genius contained and hidden in the tiny embryo and soul? But it was all there, or, I should say, its potential was there, right from the beginning. Who'd ever think of Shakespeare's parents hav-ing intercourse, and then, with God's divine love, Shakespeare's genius was created. People don't think those kinds of things, only an old Jesuit like me, but they're absolutely true. Shakespeare and his genius were created at the instant of his conception, for if it wasn't Shakespeare, who was it? Of course, he had to learn and experience life to write his plays, but he was who he was from his conception. His genius was present in the fullness of its potential right from the start.

"What you did, Hildy, is seriously sinful in that you deliberately destroyed the new life within you, created with God's love, and bestowed as a gift even though you and the young men weren't married. Who knows what those two, tiny, human beings might have become? Do you see why marriage is so important if people wish to have sexual relations? Indeed, as a follower of Christ, you must understand the only proper context for sexual intercourse is the married state. Do you understand that, Hildy?"

"Yes, I do, Father."

"Going forward now you must be careful when evaluating a young man. You have to learn his character, and that takes time: months, perhaps even years in some cases. I would suggest you get to know a young man for at least a year. After that, if he's interested in marrying you and if he's truly honorable, he will ask for your hand. If you find him of decent character and he has other traits and virtues that are important and pleasing to you, you'll say 'yes.' But then, Hildy, don't marry for at least another three to six months. He might put pressure on you to have intercourse. However, if he truly is a Christian gentleman, indeed any kind of gentleman, he will respect your wish to delay intercourse until you're married. I don't mean to say that you have to wait a year to get married, perhaps six months is sufficient. The point is, the more time you take to evaluate a young man and his family – and don't forget he's also evaluating you – the more likely you are to have a happy marriage.

"And shouldn't you want with all your heart, and more than anything else, to have a happy marriage? People must know each other extremely well before they marry, plus it helps greatly if they have the same religious faith. The more a couple has in common, the more likely they are to agree about the important things in their lives. Someone said that opposites attract, but the Roman poet, Ovid, said, 'If you would marry suitably, marry your equal.' Do you understand, Hildy?"

"Yes, Father."

"You've been hurt by a dishonorable man – this Arthur fellow – and his sins are great, very great indeed. But God does not want you to ever sin that way again, and I'm sure you yourself don't want to commit those sins again."

"No, Father, I do not."

"I'm also sure you hope to find your earthly happiness in the married state, and I think you definitely should. For you to have sexual desire for a man is perfectly normal. You must, however, express that desire in marriage with a man who will cherish you, a man who will provide for you and your children, a man who will help you attain your heavenly reward, as you will help him."

"Yes."

"You know, Hildy, the surest way to get someone thinking about God is their impending death. You're a young woman; I'm sure you don't think about that, but eventually it comes to all of us. Always remember, when we die and stand before our Creator, we don't want to be ashamed of our lives. Henceforth, you must avoid serious sin. In marriage, a husband and wife help each other reject the temptations of this world and yet fully enjoy the sexual gifts that God bestows upon them. Then, if they are blessed, they'll delight in the children God sends. What I'm telling you, Hildy, will make you a happy woman, but only if you marry the right kind of man, otherwise you will never find happiness. Don't be influenced by how much or how little money he has or how good looking he is. Examine his character because everything else is superficial. You have been hurt twice, don't let it happen again. There are evil men who will take advantage of you if you let them. But there are also good men. Maybe you have to look a little harder to find them, but there are men of good character who also might be nice looking and have a good job. Do you understand?"

"Yes, Father, perfectly." She thought of Paul.

"The danger for you now . . . now that you've experienced the pleasures of the flesh, is that you could yield more easily to future temptations. Beware Hildy, be on vigilant guard. Do not allow yourself to be enslaved on the bed of fornication. It could cost you your immortal soul, a soul like every other that Satan covets to possess for all eternity."

The priest paused and rested his chin on the prayer point of his hands. His thoughts were inexpressible. He did not look at her.

Horrified, Hildy sat motionless, her hands wringing the soiled handkerchief. Never in her life did she think there was a possibility she could be eternally damned.

"Now is there anything else you wish to confess?"

"Yes Father . . . remember that passage in the Gospel, something about a man committing adultery in his heart? You mentioned it once. I've heard the passage in church, but I don't know what it's from."

Father Fahey reached for his Bible, his "office copy," as he called it. He well knew the passage in *Matthew*, Chapter Five. "Let me read it . . . our Lord says, 'You have heard that it was said to the ancients, Thou shalt not commit adultery. But I say to you that anyone who so much as looks with lust at a woman has already committed adultery with her in his heart.'"

"Yes, that's it."

He detected fear in her eyes. "What is it, Hildy?"

"Does that passage refer to other sins or just adultery? What if I thought about stealing a necklace? Would I be guilty of sin simply because I thought . . . ?"

"Yes, I think you would. To covet another's possessions is condemned by the Tenth Commandment."

"Then, I must tell you Father," her voice trembled, "I am a murderess. In my heart I've killed Arthur a thousand times. I loathed him, despised, and hated him so much that I swear to you, if I had a pistol and saw him on the street, I would have killed him. I would have shot him a hundred times." She began to sob again. "Oh, God, what have I become?"

"My child," the priest stammered.

"I'm not a child, Father." Her voice was hoarse; teeth clenched. "I'm a murderess, three times. Do you understand that? Do you understand what I've done? Does God have mercy on a murderess of two, little, innocent ones, and a dirty, lying son-of-a-bitch?"

Hildy's face filled with terror. Tears streamed down her cheeks. Her lipstick and rouge, so fresh in the morning on her washed face, were gone, transformed into smudges and smears on the priest's fine, white handkerchief.

Finally, Father Fahey screamed in a whisper, "You are not a murderess. Do you hear me? You are not a murderess."

She looked at him, her eyes demanding. "What am I then?"

"A murderess would have procured the pistol . . . would have sought him out and killed in cold blood. That's what a real murderess would have done."

"Then what am I," she demanded again.

"You're a wretched, miserable sinner, just like everyone else on the face of this planet."

Hildy shuddered in relief, sensing a great weight lifted from the shoulders of her soul. She had told everything; every offense had been revealed. She withheld nothing from Father Jim or from God. Now another human being knew the horror of her sins, which gave her enormous comfort.

After several minutes, the priest asked, "Is there anything else you wish to confess?"

Hildy shook her head. "No, Father, nothing."

She waited for the priest to speak, but he remained silent, struggling with his thoughts, struggling to collect his scattered emotions, struggling to respond as Christ wanted him to respond. He didn't know what to say so he decided to tell an old story, a story and a truth he had never found necessary to share inside the confessional before.

"I knew a family – really the history of a family – that came to this country from Luxembourg in the 1840s. They settled north of here in one of the early farming communities in Ozaukee County. When they arrived, three sons were already born. Four daughters were born here. In the old days, farmers had big families because they needed workers, especially as the parents grew older. Well, in time, this father of seven became a successful businessman who, in addition to his large farm, was a grain trader, invested in real estate, and founded, with some other men, a bank. Eventually, he grew quite wealthy. The oldest son, from an early age, was groomed as heir to the father's business interests. The second son was less worldly and became a Catholic priest. The youngest son, for lack of any other interests, joined his father and brother in the managing of their many ventures.

"The children grew up, married, and had families of their own.

The youngest son and his wife had three children. His mother knew a German immigrant girl in her early twenties who needed work, so she arranged for this girl to help the youngest son's wife with the housekeeping. In those days they were called chambermaids.

"As time passed, this younger son who, I was told, was a very charming, vigorous fellow, befriended this girl. She spoke German, of course, which is similar to Luxembourg, so they could communicate. Unfortunately, they did more than talk. To the family's horror, he impregnated her. It proved an absolute catastrophe for everyone involved. The betrayed wife took her children, left her husband, and demanded a divorce, which, in those days, was unheard of for a Catholic couple. Plus, she demanded a large, financial settlement. Obviously, the father and two older sons were furious with the youngest brother's terrible behavior. They decided to banish him not only from the affairs of the family, but also from the community where he was raised and lived. They ordered him to take his pregnant chambermaid, leave Wisconsin, and never return.

"And that's exactly what he did. The father bought two one-way tickets to Cincinnati. How they decided on Cincinnati I don't know, maybe because of its large German population. Anyway, they gave him some money to make a start, but his father cut him completely out of his will. When he died that son got nothing, not a plug nickel. Well, in Cincinnati, he and his chambermaid became parents of a son born out of wedlock. After his divorce, he married her, but not in the Church; they couldn't because the Church doesn't recognize divorce. They had two more children, a son and then a daughter. Well, as you can imagine, this transgressor had to work very hard to reestablish himself, which he eventually did. He never grew rich by any standard, but to his credit both sons became medical doctors. That was a wonderful achievement, quite remarkable, actually."

"When was that?" Hildy wondered.

"Early 1890s . . . the scandal occurred in the mid-1860s, so they went to Cincinnati sometime after the Civil War. They had a third child, a girl born in 1870. This little girl – oh wait, I want to tell you something else first. The youngest son's first wife died sometime in the late 1870s, and then he married his second wife, I mean remarried her in the Church. Both he and the chambermaid were born and raised Catholic. Once the first wife was dead, they could remarry in the Church, that is, they could receive the *Sacrament* of marriage.

"Well their daughter, the youngest child, was a quiet, serious girl who married a young teacher in Cincinnati, a scholar in English Literature. He taught at different colleges, working his way westward through Indiana, Illinois, Iowa until, eventually, he became a professor at a college in Nebraska where he and his wife finally settled down for good. They had three children, two beautiful daughters and a son." He looked at her intently. "Hildy, I am that son."

She stared at him in disbelief.

"I was born because my grandfather committed the sin of adultery. Had he not, I wouldn't be here. Certainly, one can argue that actual sin is worse than sin harbored in the heart, notwithstanding our Lord's instruction. This is true regarding your desire to kill Arthur. Yes, it's a serious sin of evil intent, but the point is, because God created us with free wills, we can begin to make good decisions even after we've committed serious sins earlier in our lives. If we change, God's blessings will flow to us. We can choose to obey God's Commandments and the teachings of Christ at any time regardless of how old and sinful we might be.

"My poor grandfather didn't just lust in his heart for the chambermaid; he actually committed adultery with her. By doing so, he destroyed his marriage, profoundly hurt his first wife, was forced to abandon his three little children whom, to my knowledge, he never saw again, and was banished from his own family forever. Think about that. I could argue all of it was a tragedy, but then, and I truly believe this, my grandparents tried to make good decisions consistent with God's will, as they struggled to understand it. Once they did that, good things began to happen. They raised their children in the Faith, two sons became doctors, and one of their little grandsons – me – became a Catholic priest. And today, you could say because of my grandfather's mortal sin, I am alive and here to receive your confession. Life is strange Hildy, very strange, very difficult to understand sometimes." His voice trailed away.

Enthralled by the story's irony, Hildy said nothing.

The priest began again. "Every person who has ever lived has the potential to do the greatest good or commit the most terrible of human sins. Each of us can be sinner or saint. It depends entirely on our free will choosing to align itself with the will of God as disclosed in the Commandments and the teachings of Christ. Or we can reject those teachings and live a life of selfishness, lust, greed or whatever. Do you understand?"

"Yes, Father."

"You are not a murderess, but you are a sinner, just like everyone else, just like my poor grandparents. But, I must warn you: do not commit those sins again, I mean the sins of abortion and the murderous thoughts. Those sins are too grievous, too terrible. They risk the loss of your immortal soul. I know you are flesh and blood, and you'll have temptations regarding sexual matters. That's a normal part of life; it happens to all of us, even priests. But those other sins, Hildy, never commit them again, never for the sake of the salvation of your immortal soul."

"I understand."

"You also must understand that unless you are truly sorry, indeed, perfectly sorry for your sins, God will not forgive you. You must not harbor hatred for Arthur. You must forgive him, difficult as that might be. You must change your heart and attitude so you can experience God's forgiveness completely. Can you do that?"

"Yes, I believe I can. Hating Arthur just hurts me."

"That's right. Now, Hildy, is there anything else you wish to confess?"

"Sometimes I fear God will punish me . . . I mean for what I've done."

"God doesn't operate that way. He forgives and forgets, and you must too. If God is willing to forgive you, then you must forgive yourself. God is slow to anger, but quick to forgive. He never marks any sinner in this life for punishment. However, when we finally stand before Him, as each of us certainly shall, His justice will be swift and absolute.

"In this life, Hildy, God wants all of us to repent and gives us, as He's given you, the time and opportunity for it. We have sorrow and joy in our lives because that is the nature of the human condition. Now that you have confessed, God will forgive you. All He expects is a perfect expression of sorrow from the sinner. That is why Christ came into the world: to redeem us and forgive our sins that we might have eternal life. Now is there anything else you wish to confess or ask me?"

"Father, I've met someone who, I think, is very good; someone, perhaps, after I spend more time getting to know, I could marry. Must I tell him my past?"

"Absolutely not! Why would you mention any of this to anyone ever again? You must believe God forgives your sins completely. Forgive yourself now, forget the past, and begin your life anew. If you were to tell a young man, it might drive him away. What good is that? No, Hildy, don't tell him or anyone else. There are sins in his life he's ashamed of; would you want to know them? Of course not. The past is over, gone forever, for all of us."

Father Fahey reached for his Bible and quickly found the passage he always referred penitents to when this issue arose. "This is *Luke*, Chapter 9. Jesus said, 'No one, having put his hand to the plow and looking back, is fit for the kingdom of God.'" Hildy looked at him quizzically. He still detected sadness in her eyes.

"What the passage means, Hildy, is that once a person takes up the Lord's work, that is, once you put your hand to the plow, you must never look back. You have to forget the sins of your past. If you fail to do that, you are not worthy of God's kingdom. Understand?"

"Yes, Father."

"And Hildy, you mustn't be sad now. You have to get over that. I'll give you absolution and then your sins are truly forgiven, not by me but by God. We Christians are not to be sad."

The priest stood beside her. He placed his hands above her head while saying the words of absolution. "Almighty God, the Father of mercies, through the death and resurrection of His Son, Jesus Christ, has reconciled the world to Himself and sent the Holy Ghost among us for the forgiveness of sins. Through the ministry of the Church, may God give you pardon and peace, and I absolve you from all of your sins in the name of the Father, and of the Son, and of the Holy Ghost. Amen."

Normally, he would have given absolution in Latin, but he wanted Hildy to understand. "For your penance pray the Rosary at your earliest convenience, dwelling on the Joyful Mysteries. You are to go in perfect peace now. Know that God loves you and has forgiven all your sins. Never doubt that. Now, do you remember the Act of Contrition?"

"Yes, I've memorized it, Father. I say it every night."

"Good. Pray it now."

"Oh my God, I am heartily sorry for ever having offended Thee. I detest all of my sins because I dread the loss of Heaven and the pains of Hell, but most of all because they offend Thee, my God, who art all good and deserving of all my love. I firmly resolve, with the help of your grace, to confess my sins, to do penance, and to amend my life, Amen."

It was over. *Not as bad as I feared,* she realized. Fr. Fahey did not frighten her into deceit, omission, or silence. She confessed her secret sins and finally felt unburdened of their enormous weight and the guilt she suffered for nearly eight years. The haunting and persistent sadness was finally and forever flushed from the caverns of her heart. The priest had been compassionate at the moment of her greatest fear and need, and had, for her, truly been *Christ.*

"Thank you Father. Thank you for everything."

"Thank you Hildy, for making such a good confession, I mean. You see and hear me, but always remember it is our Lord who hears you, who understands, and forgives you. I'm just His poor intermediary."

"You're very kind, Father. I carried those things in my heart a long time."

"Forget them . . . you've chosen the plow, remember that. Don't look back. Leave your guilt here, don't take a penny's worth with you."

Finally, she smiled. "I'll leave it, Father. Shoo it out the window for me."

"Hildy, there's one more thing I must tell you." He peered into her eyes. "At the very least, receive our Lord every Sunday. You will find great strength and comfort there. The Eucharist will strengthen you in ways the world cannot comprehend."

He opened the office door. Hildy walked to the vestibule and waited for him to open the entry door. She stepped onto the front porch. "Goodbye, Father. I hope to see you soon. Oh, I almost forgot . . . I'll wash your handkerchief and return it."

"Anytime you'd like . . . just give me a call."

She descended the steps but turned back. "Father, what of God's work am I to do? I mean, now that I've put my hand to the plow."

"It's all around you; keep your eyes and ears open, you'll know. Read the Beatitudes. Someday our Lord might call you for something special. If and when He does, you'll know."

The early spring sunlight warmed the quiet street lined with shrinking piles of dirty snow. Father Fahey watched the slender, comely, young woman walk away until she turned the corner and passed out of sight. He was emotionally exhausted.

God have mercy on me, he prayed, aware that he could have done better. He went into his office, found Arthur's letter and slipped it into his pocket. He'd burn it later.

His lunch waited in the dining room; the other priests had finished. He nodded in appreciation to the housekeeper, but when he contemplated the sandwich he had no appetite. "I'm sorry, Mrs. Winter; I'm just not hungry. Can you save it?"

In the living room, several priests were listening to the Metropolitan Opera radio broadcast from New York City. He asked no one in particular, "What's playing?"

His friend, Father Jerry Boyle, glanced up at him. "Verdi's *La Traviata*."

"Oh, yes," he said. "Yes . . . ."

Chapter 19 ~ 1942

The Seventy-fifth Congress of the United States sat from 1937 to 1939. Comprised of three hundred and thirty-three Democrats, only eighty-nine Republicans, and thirteen members of minor parties, it was the largest plurality in the history of the Republic. With Franklyn Delano Roosevelt in the White House it was, for all intents and purposes, one-party rule. And yet, for all that political power, the Democrats simply could not lift the country out of the worst economic depression in its history. Regrettably, they were more interested in creating a welfare state than a prosperous one. Their policies were *liberal,* which meant not the enhancement of individual liberty, but rather more federal control over the lives of ordinary citizens by creating a political and bureaucratic leviathan. The federal welfare state and its bureaucracy were born between 1932 and 1939. Ostensibly, the objective was to help the poor, the downtrodden, and those devastated by the Great Depression. Nevertheless, lurking in the back of the Roosevelt Administration's collective mind was the realization that citizens would be forever beholden to the political party that so generously offered them easy access to the federal treasury. Thus, political power could be sustained for years by doling out benefits to all classes of citizens save the rich. In due time, however, the rich, too, would come to benefit greatly from this strange, new liberalism. Thomas Jefferson must have rolled over in his grave several hundred times throughout those fateful six years.

+ + +

In early 1938, thirty-four year old Lew Thilman sensed an opportunity and decided to take advantage of it. The nation's economy, for all the Democrats' toying and tinkering, had not improved. Lew reasoned, because Congress was so overwhelmingly Democrat, the voters would be in a changing mood for the midterm national elections. Though he had never run for public office, he entered the Republican primary for Congress. His family name was well known. Lew's physician father was widely respected in the district he had tirelessly served for over three decades. The day of the election, Dr. Thilman told his son he believed he'd win. Lew, trailing late in the evening, went to bed believing he lost, but woke to the morning *Sentinel* that proclaimed, to the family's delight, *Thilman Wins!*

Prior to the general election in November, Dr. Dominic Thilman suffered a heart attack after driving an appendicitis patient to St. Joseph's Hospital. As the doctor rushed up the entrance steps, powerful chest pains overwhelmed him. He collapsed and tumbled down the concrete stairs badly abrading and bruising his face, head, and body. He died the following day with his wife Mary Louise, sons Lewis and Dominic, daughter Anita and her husband, John Helden, at his bedside. He whispered farewell to all. He told Anita he regretted he wouldn't see her two little boys grow up. He predicted Lew would win the election in November and begged Dom to give up his career as a jazz musician and return to the practice of law. At sixty-eight, after spending forty-one years as a dedicated physician, Dr. Thilman proved to be Lew's single, most effective campaigner. When it came time to elect a new congressman, people who knew him voted for the son of this beloved physician. Even the young chap who was being taken by Dr. Thilman to have his appendix removed, proudly voted for Lew because it was Lew's father who brought him into the world two decades earlier.

Thilman received over forty-seven thousand votes, the Democrat, thirty-one thousand, and the Progressive candidate about twenty-nine thousand. Lew did the math; though he won the three-man race he received only slightly more than forty-three percent of the total votes cast. He was a minority congressman, and it worried him from the start.

In the election of 1938, the Republicans gained an historic eighty seats in the House to hold one hundred, sixty-nine seats to the Democrats two hundred, sixty-two. The balance of power, however, had shifted to the conservatives. Now the large block of southern Democrats, in coalition with northern Republicans, could impede any further extension of Roosevelt's New Deal. The President, in his annual message to Congress in January 1939, announced that he would introduce no new programs of liberal reform to an appreciative

Senate and House. Roosevelt increasingly turned his attention to the ominous European situation. He realized America faced, day after day, the increasing threat of another world war.

Lew Thilman based his winning campaign on the failures of the Democrats to solve the nation's economic problems and on a strong isolationist position to avoid entanglement in any future European conflict. On the first day of September, 1939, Germany waged sudden and violent war against Poland. Four days later, the United States government again declared its neutrality in this new war that involved, by treaty, the British and French. American public opinion remained solidly isolationist. Lew, though deeply troubled by Germany's attack, was convinced, as were many House members of both parties, that American troops shouldn't get involved. So prevalent and widespread was that opinion that even President Roosevelt, as late as the summer of 1940 during his third campaign for the Presidency, pledged in a speech in Boston, "I have said before, but I shall say it again and again and again. Your boys are not going to be sent into any foreign wars."

Germany's Hitler and the Soviet dictator, Josef Stalin, signed a nonaggression pact in August, 1939, that was quickly overshadowed by the outbreak of war. Its significance, however, was not lost on the young congressman from Milwaukee. Lew Thilman observed with trepidation Stalin's invasion of eastern Poland in late September and his forceful intimidation and occupation of the countries of Lithuania, Latvia and Estonia that buttressed the eastern shore of the Baltic Sea. But Finland to the north, presented with the same Soviet demands as the three, smaller, Baltic States, refused to capitulate. On November 30, 1939, Stalin ordered five Soviet divisions to attack Finland. The following March, after facing an army with fifty times as many troops, Finland surrendered. Lew now knew, without the slightest doubt, that the communist Stalin was as ruthless and evil as the socialist Hitler. Neither respected the rights of the individual nor the sovereignty of nations, and neither feared God. All these events caused a powerful idea to take shape in Lew's mind.

By the summer of 1940, the issues of intervention and isolation cut across political party lines. Many Democrats who supported Roosevelt's liberal domestic policies were hard isolationists, while many conservative Republicans who abhorred the New Deal favored massive aid to Britain. As the national elections approached, the battle between interventionists and isolationists was fought in both parties. However, after the Republicans nominated Wendell Willkie as their standard bearer in June, and the Democrats re-nominated FDR for an unprecedented and controversial third term, it represented defeat for the isolationists, effectively removing the issue from the fall campaign. Roosevelt and Willkie were both *financial aid* interventionists.

Lew Thilman campaigned as a reluctant interventionist who believed the administration should do everything in its power to keep American boys out of the European conflict. It was exactly the right message, as almost seventy-four thousand of his constituents voted to return him to the House. He could hardly believe he received twenty-seven thousand more votes than in 1938, but again he was a minority congressman with just over forty-four percent of the total. With more than ninety-two thousand voting for the two liberal candidates, Lew's seat wasn't safe, and he knew it.

Near the end of 1940, President Roosevelt proposed that America become the *Arsenal of Democracy*. The President settled in for a third term, while pondering the Nazi conquests of central and western Europe, a seriously weakened British ally, an imperial, military regime in Japan that waged war throughout Asia and, at home, continuing problems in the economy. He believed, but was reluctant to say it to anyone outside his closest advisers, that eventually, if Europe was to be liberated and Britain made secure, the United States would have to participate with its armed forces. Roosevelt saw more clearly than anyone that American military involvement to liberate the world from the scourge of expansionist tyranny was inevitable. When he spoke of America as an arsenal the industrialists knew what he meant, the labor union leaders knew what he meant, and his military chiefs knew. Roosevelt had linked the two great problems that vexed him and saw with chilling clarity the answer to America's chronic, economic crisis. The way to full employment was a simple, three letter word: *WAR!*

+ + +

John and Anita Helden spent Christmas with their sons, Michael, six, Johnny, three, Anita's mother, and Dom and his new wife, Dorothy. Shortly after Dr. Thilman's burial, John, Anita, and the boys moved into the Thilman's gracious home on Grant Boulevard.

After Christmas, the Heldens, leaving their sons with Mary Louise, drove their new *Nash* sedan to Washington to visit their congressman. They stayed at the Mayflower Hotel where Mary Louise had stayed when she visited Lew in the spring of 1940.

On January 6, 1941, in the House Chamber, the Heldens heard President Roosevelt deliver to a joint session his brilliant *Four Freedoms* speech in which he enunciated the four, essential freedoms for all mankind: freedom of speech, freedom of religion, freedom from want, and freedom from fear. As a memento, Lew autographed his official White House copy of the speech and gave it to John and Anita. Anita carefully packed it with her things.

"It was a great speech," John Helden said, in the Mayflower's dining room that hummed with relaxed excitement.

"The more I listen to Roosevelt, the more I appreciate his brilliance to communicate difficult concepts," Lew said. "Short, simple sentences, but powerful and to the point. I wish I had that ability."

Seeing and hearing the President thrilled Anita. "His age and countenance give him such an aura of authority. I felt in awe and find that a little hard to admit about a Democrat we didn't even vote for. I don't think I'd feel in awe of Willkie."

"You might, had he been elected, and you saw him in the same setting," Lew replied.

A trio began to play; John turned its way. He was delighted to be having dinner with his beautiful wife of eight years and his brother-in-law whom he respected for being remarkably successful at age thirty-seven. He recognized the music, but couldn't name it. Anita guessed, ". . . a Strauss waltz?"

"I'll ask the waiter," John said.

Lew wanted to talk issues. "The big question now for Congress is: Do we aid Britain?"

A tall, slender, Negro waiter, perhaps fifty years old, dressed in a starched, white jacket with banded collar and black, sharply creased trousers, took their drink orders. John asked if he knew what the trio was playing. The waiter replied he'd return in a moment with their drinks and to take their dinner orders.

Lew answered his own question. "Britain will get aid. Roosevelt will get his way on that, but he'll have to pledge to keep our boys home."

"Would you support that?" John asked.

"Sure, if he promises to keep us out of it."

"Oh, God, I pray we aren't dragged into another war," Anita said.

The waiter brought their drinks, leaned towards John saying, *"The Emperor Waltz, sir."* Lew and Anita heard too.

John smiled at his wife. "You were right . . . so let's toast the emperor."

"Would you like to order now, sir," the waiter asked, looking at John without knowing Lew was the member of Congress.

"Give us a moment . . . we haven't quite decided."

The waiter bowed and withdrew.

"Are you going to toast the tune, or did you have someone in mind?" Lew asked.

"FDR . . . who else?"

Anita giggled. "Yes, FDR is most certainly an emperor, or as Mother likes to say, 'Any president who seeks a third term is a tyrant.' Mother's exact words, honestly."

"Unfortunately, most Americans didn't see it that way."

"Well then," John said, "to our esteemed emperor, tyrant, president, or whatever else you'd like to call him – to FDR." He raised his glass, grinning at his lovely wife and brother-in-law. Lew did not grin back. John added, "Let's hope he keeps us out of war."

"Oh, yes," Anita chimed. "I'll drink to that."

"If he wants to," Lew added, sarcastically.

It surprised Anita. "You don't think he wants to keep us out of war?"

"I don't know . . . maybe I'm getting cynical in my old age." He glanced around and lowered his voice. "Several weeks ago, after a subcommittee hearing, an admiral told me privately that the Navy received secret orders from the White House to fire on German ships to provoke an incident. So, what would you think?"

"My God, that's hard to believe," John said.

Anita looked at her younger brother. "Lew, vote your principles. That's why the people elected you."

Lew chose not to remind her that a decided majority had voted against him.

In March, 1941, after two months of raucous debate, Congress passed the *Lend Lease Act* providing seven billion dollars in military credits for Britain. Thilman voted with the majority, but in the fall, when *Lend Lease* was proposed for the Soviet Union after Hitler's invasion in June, Thilman took a principled stand. He was one of the most vocal opponents on the House floor arguing that Stalin and the Soviets were just as treacherous and untrustworthy as the Nazis. Lew even cited Roosevelt's *Four Freedoms* speech in asking the House, "Why should we aid a regime that denies its own people freedom of speech and freedom of religion?"

But an answer could be given to Thilman's question, and many people thought it an excellent answer. A two front war with a powerfully-armed ally on Hitler's eastern front would drain Germany economically and militarily, thus hastening the end of the war. Nevertheless, Lew argued even more forcefully before the House. "A well-equipped Soviet army would march all the way to Germany, and we'd never get them out of eastern and central Europe. Better not to make them strong. Their country is big enough that even without our aid they'll wear down the Germans."

A majority of the House rejected his argument. In November, 1941, *Lend Lease* for the Soviet Union was approved by Congress. Lew flew back to Milwaukee convinced Congress had made a tremendous mistake. In spite of that, he looked forward to spending Christmas and New Year's quietly and happily with his family. He was physically and emotionally drained. It took several nights before he slept well again.

December 7, 1941, was a quiet, dreary Sunday in Milwaukee. At ten, the entire Thilman household went to Mass at St. Ann's. Mary Louise planned an early dinner for everyone including Dom and Dorothy. Michael and Johnny ran around the house, happy their Uncle Lew was home, and Uncle Dom was coming. John Helden played the piano, while Mary Louise, Anita, and Lewis read the newspaper. After John finished, Lew turned on the radio. When the startling news came, Lew knew exactly what he must do. He called the airline, asked his brother-in-law to drive him to the airport, then went upstairs to pack.

"Lew, what does it mean?" Anita asked. "Where's Pearl Harbor? Why would Japan attack us? I thought Hitler was the problem."

"We're at war now . . . I have to get back to Washington."

John, with Anita and the boys, drove Lew to General Mitchell Field on the far south side. The airport was named for Billy Mitchell, a local boy who graduated from West Point in 1901 and, as an Army colonel in the early 1920s, argued that strategic bombing from aircraft would become a vital military tactic in future wars. He maintained, contentiously, that the Air Corps should be entirely separate from the Army, and this separate *Air Force* should be equal in stature and importance with the Army and Navy. He demonstrated that air power could sink the largest battleships with skillful and accurate bombing. Mitchell argued his ideas with officers of higher rank; to him it was always a matter of principle, of vision, of the future of warfare, and how best to protect the United States. Never did he make it an issue of personalities. Finally, in 1925, his persistence in championing his outrageous ideas earned him a court-martial. He died in 1936 at age fifty-seven, spared the tragedy of Pearl Harbor and the realization that the Japanese warlords had so perfectly adopted and executed his visionary and terrifying recommendations. Nineteen ships were sunk or damaged, and two thousand, four hundred Americans died in the smoking, fiery Hawaiian harbor, including a twenty-four year old Navy lieutenant who was supposed to have had his appendix removed by Dr. Dominic Thilman back in 1938.

John Helden, his wife, and sons stood at the fence bordering the tarmac, as Lew boarded the big DC-4. When he reached the top of the steps he turned, waved, then disappeared inside the cabin. Michael and Johnny watched the large, silver aircraft's four propellers sputter and spin, their engines belching ugly puffs of black smoke. They held their ears against the roaring, as the aircraft taxied toward a runway that pointed to the east-southeast, almost directly in line with Washington, D.C., a thousand miles distant. They watched the plane poised for flight and then slowly roll, gain speed, and become airborne.

On Monday, December 8, 1941, Lewis Thilman voted with Congress to declare war on Japan. On Thursday, December 11, he voted to declare war on Germany and Italy after both had declared war against the United States. That night, in his small apartment near DuPont Circle, unable to sleep, he wondered, *where it will all lead?*

Buried in the muck at the bottom of Pearl Harbor were the issues of isolationism and interventionism. All that mattered now was the nation totally at war on two broad fronts. It would fight under its aging Commander-in-Chief with the full power of its industrial might and an armed force that would eventually enlist more than sixteen million men and women. The proud and lowly people of Japan and Germany – for the hell that was about to be unleashed upon them, for the hell their insane leaders unleashed upon an innocent and peaceful world – were to be pitied.

In May, 1942, the American people had their first chance to cheer a naval victory over the Japanese fleet in the Coral Sea off the east coast of Australia. It was described in the Government's release as a *narrow victory,* but welcomed news nevertheless. In June, an immense flotilla of the Japanese navy turned back after heavy losses in a three-day battle near Midway Island, west of Hawaii. Those two engagements of American forces with the Japanese Imperial Navy were historic because for the first time in modern naval warfare, surface gunships did not exchange a single shot. Planes and submarines, on both sides, inflicted all the damage.

Had he lived, Billy Mitchell would not have been surprised. However, Lew Thilman was both surprised and gratified. He reasoned if the United States could win a major naval battle after being in the war only seven months then, as new ships, tanks, and planes were produced in American factories, and young men were trained as sailors, soldiers and airmen, the war on both fronts would be inevitably won.

As early as May, 1940, President Roosevelt publicly discussed American manufacturers producing 50,000 warplanes a year. Many skeptics in government and the press thought him crazy. Yet, by 1942, American manufacturers produced over 90,000 military aircraft, while the Army Air Corps taught the nation's young men to fly them exceedingly well. By 1944, military plane production rose to 120,000 in factories far beyond the range of Jap and Nazi bombers. When Roosevelt referred to America as the great *Arsenal of Democracy,* he knew what he was talking about.

After the attack on Pearl Harbor and the formalities of declaring war against the Axis powers, the issue of foreign policy was suspended from American political debate. There could be only one foreign policy: to wage all-out war against our barbaric enemies. It didn't matter to the American people what effort was required regardless of the enormous sacrifices they would be called upon to make. The whole nation geared for the war effort. Our enemies were clearly defined and recognized in the collective mind of the people. We had been cruelly and wrongly attacked by Japan just as our European allies had been by Hitler. After Japan launched a violent attack against us, Germany declared war upon us. We had to fight to protect our nation, our homes, our women and children, and our lives. We fought with the only perfect justification for a nation going to war: *self-defense.*

Lew Thilman belonged to a group of anti-communist House members who privately, after-hours over drinks, discussed the inappropriateness of Stalin and the Soviets being our ally. Britain's Prime Minister, Winston Churchill, had effectively silenced public debate on the issue. When Hitler invaded the Soviet Union in June, 1941, Churchill declared, "I have only one purpose, the destruction of Hitler. If Hitler invaded Hell, I would make at least a favorable reference to the Devil in the House of Commons."

By early summer, 1942, Lew began to think about his second re-election campaign. He was confident he would win, indeed, more confident than in 1940. Powerful members of the House minority leadership offered him an opportunity to address the American people in a nationally broadcast radio speech. In it, he could make the case to change the attitude of the American people regarding the administration's policy of aiding the Soviet Union. He went right to work writing the speech.

Lew returned to Milwaukee over the July Fourth recess and told his enthusiastic family that he would deliver a national radio address prior to the November elections. Dom reacted cautiously. "Lew, if you want to be re-elected, don't talk about cutting aid to the Soviets."

Lew thought, *he's always so damn contrary . . . .*

After Mary Louise's picnic supper, the entire family settled on the front porch to enjoy the summer evening. John Helden said,

"It's quite an honor to give a national address. You can be proud of that, Lew."

Dom said, "Of course it's an honor, but, realistically, Russia is our ally, and Hitler's the enemy. Don't buck conventional thinking, Lew. You'll just give your enemies the ammo to beat you."

"I'm giving a philosophical policy speech. Someone's got to raise the issue of what happens after we defeat Hitler. If the Soviet Army reaches Germany – and the only way it could, would be because of our aid – then we'll have to contend with Stalin. He'll subjugate eastern and central Europe and annex them to the USSR, just as he did the Baltic States. Then what do we do? What's our policy then? Believe me, it's a hell of a lot smarter to keep Stalin weak."

"Well," Dom stretched the word, "that's the future; people don't care to think that far ahead. We have to concentrate on the task at hand – defeating Hitler. Once that's done then deal with Stalin. In any event, they're being ravaged by the Germans. Hitler might conquer Russia; then what do we do?"

John Helden leaned towards Dom's opinion, as did Anita and Dorothy. Mary Louise had read enough to know Stalin was ruthlessly evil. She knew of the killing purges in the 1930s and loathed communism for its suppression of religion and individual liberty. Now, siding with her congressman son, she asked, "How long do you think the war might last?"

It was a tough question. "Five, ten years . . . if only Germany, maybe less. But we've got Japan too."

"If that's the case, doesn't it make sense to aid the Soviets to get the war over as fast as possible?" Anita asked.

"Sure, unless after we get Hitler out of the countries he's not supposed to be in, we have to get Stalin out of all the countries *he's* not supposed to be in. We trade one huge problem for another. I'd like to see Hitler and Stalin fight to the death in the east; then we come in from the west and set up free democracies from one end of Europe to the other."

"You're a dreamer, Lew. No one's gonna buy that," Dom said. "If we stop helping Russia, they'll sue Hitler for peace. Then he puts all his forces back in the west to fight us. Lew, I'm telling you, don't give that speech. Give an old-fashioned, patriotic, support our boys in uniform speech."

"No, I will not cheerlead for the troops. This is a national audience. I'm raising an issue that has to be debated in a national forum. Helping Stalin is a mistake; I can articulate the reasons why. The American people need to hear this; they need to know. What comes out of this is going to be a major foreign policy debate in Congress. Someone has to raise the issue."

Dom shook his head and waved his hands. "No, no, Lew, you raise that issue you'll be buried by it. It might be a national forum, but the voters in this district will listen too, and they want Russia as our ally. Everybody understands if we aid Russia that makes our job on the western front much easier. This is the way people perceive this now. Do you want to be reelected and do some good in Congress, or do you want to sit around here twiddling your thumbs?"

Anita asked, "Dom, what do you hear at work?"

"Everybody's for Roosevelt. Everybody's for beating Hitler and the Japs, as fast as we can."

Dom worked in a plant on the east side where, under tight security, bombsights were manufactured. He never talked about his job, remarking once to John that he and his coworkers were warned by their supervisors never to discuss their jobs with anyone, even family members.

"So am I," Lew said, in his defense. "But someone has to raise the issue of what happens in Europe after Hitler. Who draws the new borders? Who governs whom? Does Communism become the new Nazism? Does Stalin become the new Hitler?"

"Lew, don't do it. The district's changed since Dad died . . . more working people, more union people. Negroes have moved in. They're big Roosevelt supporters, as are Jews. They all support Roosevelt. Everybody wants to aid Russia and beat Hitler. Hitler and the Japs are the enemy. Trust me, Lew; it's a mistake to give that speech. Your enemies will kill you with it."

Lew turned to his brother-in-law. "John, what do you think?"

"I think Dom's right. Of course, it's a terrific opportunity. How many ever get such a chance? If you think the issue should be raised, then raise it, but if you lose then what? How much influence will you have then? We want you in Congress where you can do the most good."

"Anita?"

"If you really believe it's that important then raise it, but how will you feel if you're not re-elected? Personally, I don't think you'll lose because of one speech, but if you're not sure then don't give it."

Lew turned towards his sister-in-law. "Dorothy?"

"I think Dom's right."

Lew fidgeted. After a moment, he said, "My re-election isn't going to hinge on a single speech. I got seventy-four thousand votes in '40; I'll get more this time. A national speech will enhance my reputation. Voters know that only well respected congressmen are asked to give a national address. John's right; this is an honor. The longer I'm in the House, the more influential I become. Voters understand that."

Dom had enough. He looked at John and asked, "Where's your brother, Julius, now? Have you heard from him?"

"East India. I don't know exactly; he can't put that in his letters. The last one was postmarked London. It took a month to get here and a month to get from India to London. His patients are mostly American and British airmen. He said their biggest problem is hemorrhoids."

Finally, everyone had reason to laugh.

"How are Helen and the girls?"

"They're fine. Helen and I talk every week. She's holding up pretty well."

"Dorothy, it's time we go." Dom stood and stretched. "Lew, think about what I said. Goodnight Mother." He kissed her forehead. "Goodnight everyone . . . ."

After they left, no one had much more to say. John and Anita checked their sleeping sons. Mary Louise retired to Anita's old room at the front of the house above the sun porch. She had given the master bedroom to John and Anita when they moved in after Dr. Thilman's death.

In bed only a few minutes, Anita began to whimper. John sat by her, placing his hand on her shoulder. "What is it darling?"

"If the war lasts ten years, Michael will probably have to go. Oh, God, John, how I hate that thought. Think of the parents who will never see their sons again. That would break my heart. I'd never get over it."

"Ten years is a long time. It might end sooner. We were in the last war only two years. We're stronger now. Lew doesn't know for sure. Even if it is ten years, Michael will only be seventeen. Best if you put it out of your mind now."

He longed for his wife to turn on her back and place her lovely, slender arms around his neck, as she did when she wanted to make love. It wouldn't happen. In the dark, Anita whispered, "John, do you pray the war ends soon?"

"Yes, of course . . . ."

"I do too, all the time."

In his bed, hearing Anita's slow, faint breathing, John thought of the first evening he had come to this house back in 1930. *Life was so simple. Dr. Thilman was still alive. My father was alive. Julius was at County General; now he's in India. Lew was in town. Dom was still in law school. Anita and I didn't have a worry in the world.*

But John had reason to worry now. Before the start of the war, he and Anita hired an architect to design and build a house far out in Wauwatosa. The architect was having difficulty getting building materials; he couldn't even estimate when they'd be able to move in. If John had known war would come so soon, he'd have put off building indefinitely. It was pleasant living with Anita's mother. He had the Steinway to play to his heart's content. His wife and mother-in-law were good cooks, plus the boys were beginning to appreciate their father's musical gift, especially Johnny who was five.

Several days later, John received a letter from his Draft Board.

Chapter 20 ~ 1942 (Continued)

For some newspaper editorialists, freedom of the press means, as it relates to politics, that they are free to write false, bad things about good men and false, good things about bad men. What matters to these editorialists is not which candidate is, in fact, in their personal behavior moral or immoral, but rather whose political philosophy more closely agrees with their own. They will affix virtue or vice to a man's character, as it suits their purpose to praise or smear.

Nevertheless, in fairness to all editorialists, it *is* philosophy of government and not a candidate's character that ultimately determines how people decide to vote. If one believes in socialism, he or she will not vote for a conservative of high moral character just as a conservative wouldn't vote for a saintly socialist.

Had Al Capone been alive to run as a liberal Democrat against Lew Thilman in 1942, the city's leading newspaper would have enthusiastically supported the former Public Enemy Number One. They would have written sappy, silly, illogical editorials to rationalize their endorsement, dwelling more on the character deficiencies of a man who once was an isolationist rather than a man prone to such minor imperfections as murder and bootlegging, so long as he favored America going to war.

Lew Thilman, however, made it very clear he was not an isolationist in 1941 and 1942. World events compelled him to change his views. His votes in Congress in those years were entirely supportive of President Roosevelt's requests to build up the armed forces and to support Britain with military aid. Lew didn't mind that the dominant, daily press opposed his re-election bid in 1942. He expected it; he was, after all, a Republican. But he did mind that the newspaper deliberately bore false witness to his constituents on where he now stood on the all-pervasive issue of America's total involvement in the World War. Allied nations brutally overrun, Pearl Harbor savagely attacked, America's east coast threatened by Nazi Germany, and its west coast by Imperial Japan: no American patriot could remain an isolationist. Lew Thilman was, above all, a patriot.

+ + +

Dom remembered only one line from Lew's national radio address the first week in October, 1942, just a month before the mid-term elections. When he heard it, he thought, *that's it . . . Lew's finished*. The line was spoken passionately and bumped around Dom's brain for days. Lew said, "President Roosevelt made a mistake pushing Lend Lease for the Soviet Union, and Congress made a mistake in passing it."

The speech, however, was not a political harangue. Lew always spoke with great respect for the Commander-in-Chief. He knew millions of Americans listening to him loved Roosevelt. In fact, Lew's speech was visionary and simply asked that the magnitude and extent of our aid to the Soviet Union be re-evaluated by the President and Congress in light of constantly changing conditions and the possibility the Soviets might attempt to dominate their central European neighbors once the Nazi regime was destroyed. "A political vacuum will be created in eastern Europe that Soviet communism will attempt to fill," he said, in a sentence Dom didn't happen to remember.

Lew gave a thoughtful, tempered speech; one, he believed, that enhanced his reputation with voters in his district. In fact, he was convinced the speech assured his re-election. Some editorialists, however, seized that one sentence critical of *Lend Lease* to the Soviets. They used it to maintain that Thilman was not totally and truly committed to the defeat of Hitler from all sides at the earliest possible date with the smallest loss of American lives. He was, they wrote, what he always was: *a dyed in the wool isolationist masquerading in the garments of a reluctant interventionist posing as a foreign policy expert about a future no one, not even much smarter men than him, could possibly discern.*

That was not the image Lew Thilman wished to convey nor did it represent his true opinion, as he fully supported the American war effort. But in front of every group where he spoke or debated his opponents, he had to respond to the ever increasing attacks against the quality and depth of his commitment to defeating Nazi

Germany. No one cared about his vision of Europe after the war. No one wanted to think about the nature of the world after Hitler. "How could it be any worse," most people asked. No one cared when Lew mentioned Tocqueville's prophetic warning made a hundred years earlier when he envisioned the northern hemisphere divided between and dominated by America and Russia.

The national election for members of the House of Representatives on November 3, 1942, was a stunning success for Republicans. They gained forty-seven seats and would hold two hundred and nine seats to the Democrats two hundred and twenty-two in the Seventy-eighth Congress that convened in January, 1943. But not all races went the Republicans' way. In the Fifth Congressional District on Milwaukee's north side, the thirty-eight year old conservative incumbent, Lewis Thilman, was solidly beaten by an old, Irish Democrat. Lew was shocked; he couldn't believe he received thirty-six thousand fewer votes than in 1940. *My God,* he wondered, *where did all my support go?*

The next morning over breakfast, Anita asked, "What will you do now?"

Lew's eyes dropped. "I'm done January 3rd. I'll clean out my office and ship everything back here. Then, Anita, I have to do what every red-blooded American male must do: join the armed forces. Actually, I've decided to join the Navy. When we sailed to Europe in '39, I enjoyed the sea. I'll enter Officer's Training School. That won't be a problem for a former congressman with a law degree. I suppose I'll end up on a ship somewhere; serve my country that way."

"Harm's way is a far cry from the halls of Congress."

"Sure it is, but what can I do? Man, talk about getting kicked out . . . ."

"The newspaper editorials hurt you . . . ," Anita said.

Mary Louise poured Lew a second cup of coffee. ". . . with their lies. They defamed your character. Can't you do something about that?"

"It's a free press, Mother. Dom was right; I should not have given that speech. You know, sometimes Dom takes the opposite side of an issue just for the sake of being contrary, but this time he was right."

"You might have lost anyway," Anita said. "The district has changed."

"Maybe . . . ."

"And why do you have to join the Navy right away?" Mary Louise asked. "Couldn't you spend some time with us?"

"No, Mother." Lew knew what he must do. Nothing his mother or sister would say could dissuade him from serving his country. As a matter of highest honor, he had to enlist.

+ + +

Earlier that year John Helden had been ordered to report for induction into the Army. He took along his birth certificate – he turned forty in May – his sons' birth certificates, plus a letter from his industrialist uncle.

Peter Helden advised *To Whom It May Concern* that John had been assigned to work with the Defense Department's office in Chicago regarding the government's purchase of airplane refueling tankers from the Helden Company. These were just finding their way into mass production at the large south side plant where petroleum transport tanks were still being manufactured, as there was demand both domestically and militarily for that equipment as well. The Helden Company, because of excellent manufacturing methods and the commitment of their union workers, integrated both tank types into the same half-mile long production line. Shipped to air bases all over the world, the tankers delivered fuel to long rows of P-47 Thunderbolts, and B-17 and B-24 bombers parked on the matted, sacred grass of foreign fields.

John's work included trips to Chicago to discuss design and specification changes that the Army Air Corps constantly suggested to improve their equipment. He recognized an idea that could easily be implemented into the manufacturing process, or a costly one that John would point out to the purchasing officers. In 1942 and 1943, dozens of changes, some large – capacities were always being increased – but mostly small, were made in the design of the "refuelers", as they were called. John was one of thousands upon thousands of unsung engineers on the home front who produced and perfected the equipment necessary to wage and win the battles of modern warfare.

In early September, the Draft Board's second letter finally came. Anita didn't open it and didn't call John at his office because, she decided, they both had waited weeks anyway and could wait a few more hours. Mostly, she wanted to be at his side when he read it. When he got home, he smelled the pot roast cooking. His two boys ran to him, as they always did, while Anita greeted him with a grave expression. He asked, "What's wrong?"

"It came . . . ."

For a moment, he stared at the envelope before opening it. His visceral center drained, and his thinking slipped into the ill-defined subconscious. His eyes quickly scanned the letter.

John peered into Anita's eyes. "I've been rejected."

"Oh, John, thank God." She wrapped her arms around him. Overwhelming gratitude flooded their hearts.

To celebrate, Mary Louise served supper in the dining room. What she couldn't anticipate that summer evening in 1942 was how the voters would throw Lew out of office in November. The widespread influence of the good work Dr. Thilman had done for so many years in their congressional district failed to save Lew from a crushing defeat.

That night, after Michael and Johnny had been tucked in, Anita felt the full fear of John having to go to war dispelled by that most appreciated of government letters. Before he turned off the lamp, her breath whispered desire, and their eyes declared a shared passion. In the secret darkness, ecstatic arms encircled him.

+ + +

A week after the election, Lew returned to Washington. The morning he departed, he asked John, "Do you know that little flower shop on Lisbon Avenue, just a few doors east of Sherman – Carolyn's?"

"Oh, sure, I get Anita flowers there."

"Take this card; give it to Carolyn or the other girl – what's her name – Hildy? Have a dozen red roses sent to Mother. Here's five bucks . . . keep the change."

"Okay, thanks."

"My loss has been hard on Mother. I should have listened to Dom. It's like I was just obsessed to give that damn speech. Vanity,

John, and really bad judgment cost me the election. I gave the papers all the fodder they needed. Boy, I blame no one but myself. Stupid, really stupid . . . ."

"You knew the risk. You believed you were doing the right thing."

"Yeah, I know, but I let a lot of people down. Carolyn and her husband supported me, put my sign in their window, even donated a few bucks. There were so many like that; you'd be surprised. I feel I let every single one of them down."

After work, John stopped at Carolyn's. Hildy, in a blue dress and white apron, greeted him.

John asked, "How are you this chilly November evening?"

"I'm just fine . . . how may I help you?"

"I'd like a dozen red roses and this card delivered to my mother-in-law tomorrow morning if that's possible."

"Of course, would you like long stem or regular?"

"Long, I think. Actually, they're from my brother-in-law to his mother. Do you know Lew Thilman?"

"Yes, I do. He comes in every now and then. The Rabachs were supporters of his; they introduced me. He seemed very nice. In fact, we all voted for him, even my mother. We're sorry he lost."

"We all are."

"Tell me, Mr. Helden, how is your brother Julius?"

"Julius is in India, but I don't know exactly where."

"Is he . . . ?"

"He's an Army doctor; they made him a captain. He joined right after Pearl Harbor. Helen is raising their two little girls. It's kind of sad these days with loved ones in the war."

"Yes, these are difficult times."

When Hildy handed him his change, he spotted her diamond ring and wedding band. He hadn't noticed it before.

"Nice to see you again," John said. "Give my regards to Carolyn."

"Nice to see you too, Mr. Helden. I shall."

As John left the shop, he wondered how long it had been since he last bought flowers for Anita. *Long enough for Hildy to get married,* he realized.

+ + +

In Washington, Lew packed up his books, files, photographs, even the mounted sailfish he caught in the Gulf Stream off Key West in the fall of 1941, before the Lend-Lease vote for the Soviet Union. Looking at the fish now, he remembered its brilliant iridescence, as it was gaffed out of the emerald-blue water. He remembered exactly how the sunlight sparkled off the surface of a sea, only slightly broken by gentle trade breezes humming eastward along the string of tiny islands. It was a day, a moment, he'd never forget. Then he dreamed he'd be a member of the House for many years, knowing he desired that for the rest of his professional life.

His secretary, Rosalie, made arrangements to have his office belongings shipped back to Milwaukee. She even recruited carpenters from the Capitol staff to build a shipping crate for the five-foot sailfish. Rosalie hoped to become a secretary to one of the new, incoming Republican Congressmen. She put her name in the employment pool along with a letter of recommendation from her boss for the last four years. She liked Lew and regretted his defeat. She thought him outstanding though they never really became close friends. Lew kept distant in their relationship, only dating women whom he met through other congressmen's wives. *Now that he's out,* Rosalie thought, *maybe he'll find time to marry.*

Lew wouldn't meet his future wife for three more years and wouldn't marry for another two. When he finally did, at age forty-three, he fathered and raised five children. He often sat with them, admiring the sailfish that always found just enough space on one of the less prominent walls in their home. He relished telling about that bright, splendid day when, as a young congressman, he fished the Gulf Stream.

Many Democrats were clearing out their offices as well, but Lew was just one of a handful of Republicans leaving the House. Colleagues he had worked with stopped by to wish him well. Even a few of the losing Democrats stopped to express their condolences; Lew gladly reciprocated. Politically, he was glad to see so many Democrats leaving, but a sad camaraderie arose among the outgoing members that crossed party lines. Numbered among the ranks of the losers, Lew felt bitterly uncomfortable.

Most congressmen returned to their districts for Thanksgiving, but Lew decided to stay in Washington despite his mother's pleas to come home.

Monday morning after the long weekend, Lew Thilman went to the recruiting office in the Post Office Building on Pennsylvania Avenue. He met a young Navy lieutenant who was impressed when he learned Lew was a Member of Congress; it didn't seem to alter his attitude when Lew told him he'd be out of office on January 3, 1943. The Navy man appeared genuinely surprised that an ex-congressman Lew's age would decide to join the armed forces so quickly.

"We'll take you at thirty-eight for officer's school, you bet," the youthful lieutenant said. "Of course, we'll need your medical records. Fill out this application, and we'll start the process. Once you're in, you'll get another physical – our docs look you guys over pretty good."

At Christmas, Lew's family delighted in his homecoming. Mary Louise longed to comfort him or, perhaps, longed to have Lew comfort her. She found her son's defeat devastating because she shared his dream of remaining in the House for years to come. She coveted the prestige of being the mother of a United States Congressman. To have it snatched away by the ungrateful voters of the district, where her husband had labored so many years, was more than she could bear. Lew, however, hid his self-pity. Anita realized losing the election wasn't the end of Lew's career; he could always practice law. She felt he'd be successful whatever he chose.

Lew relaxed by roughhousing and wrestling with his nephews on the living room carpet, desperately trying to put out of his mind the worst defeat of his life. He even tried teaching the boys a carol at the piano, picking out the melody of *Silent Night* and repeating the words over and over. Michael, however, was too playful to take him seriously.

At the end of December, Lew flew to Washington. He delivered his medical records to the Navy recruiter then vacated his office on the last day of 1942. He thanked Rosalie for all her terrific help the past four years. They hugged goodbye, but she wasn't as sad as he had expected. She told him a newly elected Republican from Nebraska just hired her.

"Well, at least one of us gets to stay in the House," Lew quipped.

Since returning to Washington, Lew received not a single, social phone call. Of course, he didn't make an effort to call anyone either. If he had, he would have found all his House friends still out of town. On New Year's Eve he stopped at the Mayflower for an early dinner alone. Then he walked to his apartment and began packing. The furnished rooms meant no furniture to ship. His big Buick could haul clothes, bedding and books. He planned to drive home sometime after the new Congress was seated. Hopefully, the recruiting lieutenant would have Lew's first orders by then; if not, Lew would stay in Washington until he did. His landlord told him his apartment wasn't going to be occupied until February, so Lew could rent all of January if he wished.

On the morning of January 4, 1943, no longer a member of the House of Representatives, Lewis Thilman stopped at the recruiting office. The young lieutenant said his application hadn't been completely processed; he asked Lew to call him or come back in several days. It was then Lew realized how depressed he felt. He walked alone for hours along the Mall from the White House to the Lincoln Memorial and back towards the Capitol. As the early darkness came, he flagged a cab to the Mayflower for another lonely dinner over which he ruminated how badly he miscalculated everything about his re-election. He even misjudged the consequential bitterness he felt at no longer being a member of Congress.

The recruiter called the following Tuesday and asked Lew to come in; processing was complete. Now Lew wanted to get involved in the war effort. Officer's Training School sounded extremely appealing. He'd be in a warm climate, meet new people, and learn new skills. He could hardly wait. He even realized military service would look good on his record if he ever ran for public office again, presuming, of course, he'd survive the war.

"Mr. Thilman, sit down sir," the lieutenant ordered.

On his desk, a thin, manila file folder lay on top of Lew's medical records. The lieutenant opened it and leaned back in his chair, shuffling through the few sheets until he settled on one. "Primarily, we see you had a bleeding ulcer in your early twenties. Tell me about that . . . what's happened since?" He stared at Lew.

"It's under control with diet. It's not a problem."

"It's a problem for us, Mr. Thilman. The medical guys turned your application down."

Lew was stunned. "Why for God's sake?"

"The Navy can't make a special diet just to keep your ulcer in check. You have to eat Navy chow, Navy hash. Think your stomach can handle that?"

Lew slumped in his chair. "Probably not . . . ."

"That's what our doctors think. You're lucky; you get to sit this war out."

"What about the Army?"

The lieutenant shrugged. "Same standards . . . ." He handed Lew his medical records. "Thanks for volunteering; sorry it didn't work out." He extended his hand. "Good luck, sir."

"Yes, good luck to you too, Lieutenant." They shook hands.

Lew found it almost unbelievable. In an instant he comprehended his completely untenable situation: thrown out by the voters, only thirty-eight years old, and now rejected for military service, while the nation faced its greatest peril.

He stepped outside the Post Office Building onto the broad sidewalk of Pennsylvania Avenue. It was a mild winter day in Washington. Everyone hurrying by seemed to have such great purpose. He gazed to the southeast all the way up the wide avenue to the Hill and the sun-bright dome of the Capitol, white against a glorious azure sky. He wondered, *now what the hell do I do?*

Chapter 21 ~ 1948 [Part 1]

John Helden Sr., one of three founding brothers of the Helden Company, died in 1938 at the age of sixty-seven. While most of the company's employees thought him indispensable, his death prompted a period of great change. Since the company's early years, John served as *Works Manager*. Whatever his brother Peter conceived, John figured a way to build and, in many cases, improve. Transport tanks were first built with flat ends, no stiffer than the metal thickness itself. John Sr. thought to *dish* the tank end greatly increasing its rigidity, as well as providing a more pleasing appearance. He first proposed welding underground storage tanks in lieu of riveting. He conceived building milk transport tanks with welded stainless steel inner and outer jackets encasing thick, cork insulation. Everyone, especially his brothers, consulted John to determine if an idea was feasible knowing, very likely, he'd find an efficient way to fabricate it.

One person in the company, however, figured John Sr. could be replaced and rather easily at that. Peter Jr. realized an experienced mechanical engineer who had worked in the metal fabricating industry could succeed as Helden's Works Manager. Peter Jr. understood the power of education and experience. He thought it silly when his father, upon his brother's death, lamented, "I don't know what we're gonna do without John?"

After the company hired Jack Higgins, employees who thought John Sr. irreplaceable soon changed their minds. Higgins, a graduate engineer with twenty years' experience in metal fabrication, thoroughly understood every shop method the company utilized. Within a year he had actually improved manufacturing methods, creating new efficiencies that eventually led to greater profitability. For it, John Helden Sr. was nearly forgotten in the day-to-day operations of the shop. Peter Sr. had taken the advice of his son and for the first time recognized that Peter Jr. had made a significant contribution to the financial well-being of the company.

Joseph Helden celebrated his seventy-second birthday in 1939 and realized he should retire. In anticipation of that, Peter Jr. convinced his father to begin hunting for a graduate engineer who had solid design experience. They found the right man in Donald Anzia, but let Joe remain titular head of the engineering department.

When in late 1940 Peter Sr. asked Joe to review a complex specification from the Department of the Army, he realized it was time to get out. Tired of slaving over a drafting board, he regretted, like his brother, John, that he foolishly sold his company stock to Peter Sr. when times were tough. Peter never again offered Joe or John a chance for equity, even after the company became profitable. Joe resented the deterioration of sibling relationships. When Peter Sr. presented him a fine *Movado* watch on his retirement, Joe's bitterness prevented him from ever wearing it.

Peter Jr. hired a certified public accountant to replace old Mr. Schneider, the bookkeeper. Karl Albrecht quickly expanded his department with junior accountants and bookkeepers; the company now had hundreds of employees and generating the weekly payroll was a huge task. In a few years, after large, military contracts were secured, payroll would exceed a thousand.

By the autumn of 1943, strong allies of Peter Jr. headed the manufacturing, engineering and accounting departments. The Board of Directors thought highly of him for attracting such top-flight men. Peter Jr. still headed *Sales,* but didn't want it anymore. What he wanted was his aging father to retire. Peter Jr. coveted the presidency, though he still worried about his imagined rival, John Helden Jr. Throughout the years John had remained the top sales engineer, well-liked by customers and fellow employees. Peter Jr. knew, without John ever expressing it, that John wanted to head the department.

"Before my brother died, I promised I'd make John head of *Sales,*" Peter Sr. said. "I think he's earned it."

"I agree," Peter Jr. lied. "He's our best sales engineer by far."

"So why hire someone else?"

"It's not that I want to hire someone else. I just want to strengthen the company the same way we did in manufacturing, engineering, and accounting."

"You don't think John can strengthen the department? He's strengthened the company plenty. Look at his production."

"That's my point. We make him head of the department and he's not selling anymore. We lose our top producer. He'll have to run the department – manage it – that takes time."

"He's got a lot of energy."

"Sure he does, but why not keep that energy focused on sales? Why not bring in a *Marketing* guy to run the department? Let John do what he does best – make us money."

"Let me think about it," Peter Sr. said.

In December, Peter Jr. ordered John Helden Jr. to a sales convention in St. Louis. John had a bad cold and didn't want to go because it was clearly Peter Jr.'s responsibility. "If I were head of the department," John told Anita, "I'd gladly go. Peter just doesn't want to go before Christmas."

"Do you feel well enough?"

"I'm okay. What bothers me is that Peter always dumps the crap on me."

"Tell him *no*."

"I can't, not if I want to head the department someday."

John went to St. Louis in snowy, freezing weather. His cold didn't improve. His cough worsened. On the train back, several days before Christmas Eve, he felt exhausted and weak. When he finally got home, Anita palmed his forehead and found the fever.

"Just let me sleep," John said.

In the morning Anita sensed the seriousness of her husband's illness – his temperature shot above 103 – and begged the doctor to come.

"Pneumonia in both lungs," the doctor said. "He's got to be hospitalized."

John Helden Jr. descended into the valley of death the week of Christmas, 1943. While he fought for his life, a life Anita beseeched God to spare, his cousin, Peter Jr., recognized an opportunity. "Who knows when John might come back . . . six months, a year?"

Peter Sr.'s face revealed an uncommon sadness. "John could die . . . ."

"Yes, and then what? We've got to hire someone now."

"To replace John?"

"No, to head the department."

"But, Pete, I promised his father . . . ."

Now Peter Jr. had to make a compelling argument, for he knew, if and when John returned, his father might not be as receptive. Indeed, Peter Sr. could, out of mere sentimentality, appoint John head of *Sales* though Peter Jr. had vowed never to let that happen.

"Let's assume John dies," Peter Jr. began. "Do we hire someone to replace him? No, who could replace John? What we'd have to do is hire a sales and marketing guy who understands the principles of selling. Then he can train all our sales engineers to increase their production. Our men don't know these techniques, Father. These are modern, proven, scientific principles."

"Okay, okay . . . I'll take your word for it."

"Now let's assume John lives. Obviously, he's very weak. He won't have the strength to take on new duties. His strong suit will be what it's always been – sales – but only sales. We'd still have to hire a marketing guy to head the department. We'd still have to get someone who can increase the production of all our sales engineers, whether John lives or dies."

"Okay Pete, I understand. Let me think about it."

Tom Norris was a roommate of Peter Jr.'s at the University of Wisconsin, having majored in *Advertising and Marketing*. They kept in touch through the years and often talked of possibly working together. Peter Jr. called Tom and offered him the position to head the Sales Department, but he'd still have to pass muster with Peter Sr.

The interview went well. Tom was a sharp, tough guy who exuded tremendous confidence. Finally, after considerable persuasion from his son, Peter Helden Sr. relented, hiring Norris to manage the department that his nephew had, for years, dreamed of heading. Peter Sr. convinced himself it was the right decision. But that evening, alone in his study, his old promise to his brother nagged at him, and he wondered how his nephew would react to the decision. But then he concluded, *Pete's right . . . John's a sales engineer not a manager,* and thought of it no more.

A month into his illness, John Helden Jr., his body weak as a frail boy, struggled to regain his health with the herbs of faith and hope. He yearned to be well again, strong again; he craved to work again. Nothing fortified his resolve more than his longing to one day ascend to the head of Helden's Sales Department.

Without his father's knowledge, Peter Jr. called the local newspapers to announce Tom Norris's appointment. He wanted his sick cousin to learn of it that way. Dom Thilman brought it to Anita's attention. She clipped the article, hiding it in her recipe drawer where John never looked. She'd wait until he was stronger to break the news, knowing he'd be deeply disappointed. As the weeks passed, and John slowly regained his strength, Anita realized she had to tell him. One mid-morning on the living room sofa, Anita snuggled against him. It surprised him; she didn't do that often.

"What are you thinking?" he asked.

"Just glad you're better . . . ."

"Yes, I'm beginning to feel like my old self. I'll call Uncle Peter in a few days and tell him I'll be back April first. That gives me a couple more weeks."

"John, something happened while you were away."

"What?" He had no idea.

"They hired a man to head the Sales Department." Anita read the brief article aloud; when she finished, she handed it to John. In his eyes, she saw bewildered disappointment.

"I suppose I've been gone too long."

"Yes . . . I suppose they had to do something."

"My father told me, before he died, that Uncle Peter promised he'd appoint me . . . ."

"John, don't-"

"I don't think I could do it now. I'm not strong enough. I'll be happy just to have my old job back and not worry about the whole department."

"Oh, I'm glad." Anita stood, smoothing her dress. "You rest . . . I'll make lunch."

+ + +

To be an American on the home front in 1945 at the end of the Second World War – a cataclysm that claimed the lives of sixty million human beings of nearly all nationalities, races and creeds, most of whom were innocent victims of indiscriminate cruelty and violence – was an experience of such perfect elation and intense exhilaration that not to have been alive then places it forever beyond the realm of the most creative imaginations.

The joyous relief each man, woman, and child felt swelled into a national sense of exultation that transformed America's wartime resolve into the desire for a new, enduring, prayed-for peace that can only be understood by the sudden realization that an all-encompassing, massive, pervasive, violent war is, at long last, finally over.

However, for the suffering inhabitants of Britain, Poland, China, Russia, France, and, especially, for European Jews, it was tragically different. Within and across the destroyed cities, towns and countryside of defeated Germany, Italy, and Japan, the difference approached the indescribable. Only America, by the ordinance of geography and the limits of its enemies' air capabilities, had remained a safe sanctuary. Its shores and borders were never invaded; its cities never bombed. Nevertheless, its people, with so many of their uniformed loved ones in harm's way, longed for the war's swift end. Few Americans realized that America – from sea to shining sea – would never be so safe again.

In the days following Japan's surrender in August, 1945, after the horrifying atomic bombings that destroyed Hiroshima and Nagasaki, John Helden sat in the kitchen of his new home in Wauwatosa, while Anita put the finishing touches on the evening meal. They might not say much while listening to the chatter of Michael and Johnny, but suddenly one or the other would pronounce, "It's over." They'd look at each other, smile, and fall silent. Later in the evening, as the family visited in the living room before they all went to bed, one or the other would again exclaim, "It's over." This continued for days after the great news, but less frequently as time passed and then, after a month or so, it was said no more. But the joy they both felt at the war's conclusion – and apparently favorable resolution – lingered a long while, especially because their sons would not have to serve. Lew Thilman was wrong about the war's duration: for America it was over in less than four years. Michael Helden was ten then and his brother, Johnny, only eight.

The young American men and women who gained the victory of World War II, both on the home front and far away in Europe and the Pacific, rolled up their sleeves and went to work building the remarkable prosperity that America enjoyed for two decades. The war produced tough, seasoned veterans who longed to be lovers to the waiting, anxious, young women who yearned to be held by their heroes. That they were successful in this most wonderful transition from war to peace, soldier to civilian, warrior to lover, first became evident in the birth statistics of 1946. In the nineteen, halcyon years that followed, nearly eighty million bouncy, American babies were born in a boom. Once they began to come of age, America would never be the same. How appropriate that the children of those warrior-lovers born in the late 1940s would, only twenty years later, be chanting in the riot strewn streets, "Make Love, not War."

+ + +

During the winter and spring of 1945, across the eastern countries of Europe, the Soviet Army, made powerful by American *Lend Lease* and its thousands of tanks, trucks, and tons of critical supplies, swept all the way to Berlin, just as Lew Thilman had feared.

In early 1946, Winston Churchill gave his celebrated *Iron Curtain* speech in Fulton, Missouri, marking the formal acknowledgement of the *Cold War*. The former British Prime Minister warned America that it must meet the challenge of Soviet expansionism. The Soviet Union, the highly admired communist utopia of the American political left, and our chosen ally against Hitler, had devolved into a dangerous adversary. All of Eastern Europe and half of Germany fell behind Churchill's infamous and unforgettable oxymoron. Behind that cruel curtain, virtually all national sovereignty and human liberties were eliminated.

When Lew Thilman read Churchill's speech, he threw the newspaper on the floor in disgust. *Comes over here like he's some kind of prophet . . . that son-of-a-bitch couldn't crawl in bed with Stalin fast enough. Now he tells us we've got to get tough with the commies. You wasted our best chance, Winnie. It's too damn late now . . . .*

+ + +

In early 1946, two years after recovering from pneumonia, John Helden approached his Uncle Peter with a proposal: he asked to be appointed the company's sole distributor of petroleum and milk transport tanks in Wisconsin and northern Illinois. His cousin, Peter Jr., had been made Executive Vice President and was increasingly running the company, as Peter Sr. relinquished more of his every-day duties. Tom Norris ran the Sales Department, forcing John to realize he would never be anything other than a sales engineer unless he could convince his uncle that an independent distributor would increase the company's profits. John dreamed of having his own distributorship, for he realized he could no longer dream of having an executive position in the company. He couldn't compre-hend why his uncle always passed him over. It hurt John to the core of his being, but he never let his uncle or cousin know. And never did he suspect his cousin's sabotage.

A few months earlier, Dr. Julius Helden returned from the war to resume his medical practice on the south side. Peter Sr. also appointed him the company's physician. Julius would treat an injured worker, and the company paid the bill. Occasionally, he'd be called to the plant for an emergency, such as a sheared off finger or an eye pierced by a metal grinding. After dealing with it, he'd visit his uncle to check his blood pressure. Old Mr. Helden liked his youngest nephew and respected him for his military service. At one of those routine exams, Julius urged his uncle to consider John's request for the distributorship.

"I will, Juley, but it's up to your brother."

Peter Sr. was too smart to let his affection for his nephews influ-ence a decision concerning the continued profitability of his grow-ing company. On the one hand, during the war years, John's work habits, conscientiousness, ability to answer tough questions, and solve engineering problems had favorably impressed his wealthy uncle. On the other hand, he found John's personality less than pleasing. Without John really being aware of it, his salesman's per-sonality was always trying to sell *himself*. Peter Jr., especially, found it obnoxious. Nevertheless, his father understood that such a per-sonality was essential for a man in sales. So Peter Sr. was inclined, when he called John to his office, to make a decision at least par-tially in John's favor.

After they shook hands across the large, mahogany desk, Peter Sr. swiveled in his leather chair. "John, tell me why you think I should give you this distributorship?"

John had waited a long time to hear that question; in his mind he answered it a thousand times. "Uncle Peter, no one in Sales has better engineering knowledge of our products than me. No one in engineering can sell those products better than me because I know how to sell. I've proven that. Most of our customers know me and trust me. I totally believe in our products, and, for the rest of my career, more than anything else, I want to sell your equipment. I pledge to you, I will do everything in my power to sell a lot of it."

Peter Helden Sr., seventy years of age, but indefatigably young, appreciated his nephew's well-stated confidence. In it he recognized John's intelligence, ambition, and even passion. It echoed almost exactly the response he had hoped to hear.

"I'll tell you my thinking, John: I'll give you the distributorship for milk tanks, but not petroleum. Quite frankly, I don't think you can handle both – too many customers, too many product differences. You wouldn't do justice to either. We'll keep petroleum tank sales in-house, but you can have our territory for milk tanks." He looked at his nephew intently. He thought, *boy, you damn well better succeed.*

For forty-four year old John Helden Jr., that moment represented the realization of a desperate dream born in the disappointment of having been passed over to head the Sales Department. Now, his own company, *Helden Wisconsin Tank Sales,* would provide John, in the next ten years, success greater than he ever imagined. It would propel him, through hard work and brilliant salesmanship, to the forefront of all distributors in the Midwest and West. Only the largest Helden distributors in New York and Pennsylvania would garner greater sales. John's Uncle Peter never regretted granting John's request. It was the kind of decision made countless times over nearly fifty years that built Peter Helden's enormous wealth.

Peter Sr. never revealed that Peter Jr. had urged his father to give John the distributorship. While Peter Jr. no longer looked upon his cousin as a threat, he wanted him out of the company. He knew if John wasn't successful, milk tank sales could be brought back, but John wouldn't be brought back.

"You do understand," Peter Jr. said, "you're no longer an employee of this company . . . no more paychecks now or in the future."

"Yes, I understand."

+ + +

Lew Thilman spent the war years in Fort Lauderdale, Florida, working as a stockbroker. In 1946, he moved back to Milwaukee and lived awhile with his sister, Anita, and John Helden, and their two sons in the new home on Harding Boulevard. Several houses away, a slender, comely brunette with a soft, beguiling figure resided with her parents. Carol Lerner was twenty-four; Lew forty-three. That difference raised quite a few eyebrows in the family, especially among the country cousins. But Lew was youthful looking – as a couple they did look terrific together – and as long as Carol and Carol's folks didn't mind, it really didn't matter to Lew what anyone else thought, not even his mother, Mary Louise. Lew courted Carol, proposed to her, and, in the fall of 1947, married her.

Lew chose John Helden as his Best Man simply because Dom wasn't in town. He and Dorothy had moved to Tucson at the end of 1945 and would not return for the wedding.

Anita, insightful to a fault, remarked to John, "You know when Lew is seventy, Carol will only be fifty-one. It might not make much difference now, but as the years go by it will become a problem. When Lew's an old man, Carol will have to take care of him. Good heavens, he's old enough to be her father."

On their honeymoon, Lew and his young bride drove to Fort Lauderdale in Lew's new, yellow Buick convertible. As a stockbroker, skillful investing made him a well to do young man. He even made money lounging on the beach, for which Carol thought him rather brilliant. She didn't mind the morning phone call to his old broker friend nor the reading of the *Wall Street Journal,* nor the afternoon call, once she realized he profited simply by trading stocks. Lew did a lot of thinking on the beach, while Carol, in her bathing suit, closed her eyes against the November sun and dozed, only occasionally responding to one of Lew's comments. He was looking forward to 1948 because his political soul was stirring again, a stirring he hadn't felt for several years after his bitter defeat in 1942.

"Boy, if ever there was a vulnerable sitting president, it's Truman. It won't matter who the Republicans nominate. He'll beat old Harry in a landslide."

Certainly, in 1947 the conventional political wisdom ran along that line, especially after the congressional elections of 1946 when Republicans gained control of the Senate and House for the first time since 1930. Lew recognized the resurgent trend. It began in 1938 when he was first elected to Congress and would culminate, he believed, in the election of a Republican president in 1948. Lew intended to be part of that great victory.

A flat, low beach in Florida, however, wasn't a high enough perch to observe how greatly Lew's district had changed and continued to change, even as Carol and he lulled away their honeymoon in Florida's warm, winter sunlight. Negroes migrated to the northern cities in search of decent jobs and to escape the harsh, overt segregation in the South. Labor unions gained powerful entrenchment in Milwaukee's large industrial plants. Working people living in the older, inner city neighborhoods of Lew's district were much more likely to vote for a liberal Democrat with promises, be it a House member or presidential candidate, than a conservative Republican with ideals.

By 1948 Lew would have been surprised how few Negroes in the District even remembered his father who had delivered so many of them several decades ago. Now those men and women struggled to make a living for themselves and their families in postwar America where their civil rights as human beings, loyal citizens, and weary veterans were still not acknowledged, let alone enshrined.

Lew viewed his third election to the House of Representatives as difficult, but possible. The incumbent was the same old, liberal Democrat who beat him in 1942. Lew would have to win a crowded, Republican primary in September for the chance to challenge in November. He needed a campaign manager, workers to get enough printed flyers out to the middleclass neighborhoods, a few, well-placed ads in the newspapers, and frequent radio spots. For his manager he asked his brother, Dom, someone he never would have considered back in 1938. Dom, happily domiciled in Tucson, declined. He thought Lew crazy to run again. So Lew tapped one of his old, lawyer friends to raise money, write a few letters to the newspapers, and arrange as many speaking engagements as possible. "One every night if you can," Lew urged. "I'll speak to any group."

For workers, Lew enlisted his nephews, Michael, thirteen, and

Johnny, eleven, who for fifty cents and a chocolate malt distrib-
uted flyers to homes for hours at a time, each working one side of
a street, block after block. On most summer Sundays, Lew took the
boys to Old Heidelberg Park to place flyers under the windshield
wipers of the hundreds of cars parked there, while the music of
the polka bands floated through the elms. And Lew had another
angle or, perhaps, an angel to help him. Lew's decision to run for
Congress delighted Carol who believed, right from the start, that
Lew would win. He spoke so convincingly to her about everything.
She dreamed of going to Washington as the wife of a United States
Congressman, and, if Lew were elected, she'd also be going as a
mother-to-be.

"Carol, I want you to go door-to-door with me. You'll make a
terrific impression on the wives, and they'll tell their husbands. People want to see your fresh, wholesome, all-American look. Women
are important in these elections. If we can convince them, we'll win
this thing."

Lew seemed to be right. At the first several houses, women were
charmed that Carol campaigned with her husband and cheerfully
accepted Lew's literature. But at the fifth house they hit a snag. The
lonely lady wanted to know everything about Carol and Lew: how
they met, where they lived, what church they belonged to. The
woman and Carol even discussed recipes. Finally extricating his
wife from the talkative Republican, Lew said, "We can't get bogged
down like that. Time is precious here. We've got to keep moving . . .
you can't talk so much."

"But Lew, we have to show some interest. We can't just say *hello*
and run."

"You can't discuss recipes. This is a political campaign . . . when
I clear my throat, that's the signal to leave."

At the next three houses, conversations were brief, but at the
fourth the housewife enticed Carol into a discussion about neighborhood dress shops, probably because of the cute, summer print
Carol wore. She just didn't notice how often Lew cleared his throat.

Four hours of campaigning at only thirty-six houses exhausted
Lew who realized this wasn't one of his better ideas. Carol, however,
seemed amazingly fresh and eager to do it again. Lew explained
how he'd have to go alone, only because he could meet so many

more people by limiting each visit. "Now that you're pregnant," he argued, "it's probably better if you don't exert yourself." But Carol insisted she felt fine; the doctor assured her walking was beneficial. Plus, she promised Lew, she'd avoid lengthy discussions regardless of how talkative a voter might be. Lew relented. The second day's results weren't much better: fifty-three houses in five hours. Lew felt even more exhausted; Carol was noticeably tired, and both had sore feet. That night she acquiesced to her husband's wishes and never campaigned again.

More and more, Lew's strategy involved his nephews, Michael and Johnny Helden, who could distribute flyers to over two hundred homes in four hours. "That's twelve hundred homes a week, almost five thousand a month," Lew told Carol. "That's effective campaigning."

School didn't start for the boys until the Tuesday after Labor Day, which coincided with primary election day. Once back in school, they couldn't work during the week. To compensate, Lew, presuming he'd win the primary, decided to purchase more newspaper and radio ads.

The evening before the primary, John Helden asked, "Lew, do you think you'll win?"

"I think so. I'm sure there are enough Republicans who remember Dad and voted for me in '42. With five candidates, it won't take that many votes."

That same night, Lew's nephews read about their favorite uncle. The evening newspaper endorsed none of the five Republicans, but advised their readers, if they must participate in the Republican primary, not to vote for Thilman, a washed-up, political has-been. They claimed he had been on the wrong side of the intervention issue in 1941 and, after his defeat, failed to serve his country in the armed forces. They complained he was a staunch conservative, no friend of the workingman, and, even worse, favored the rich. He would become just another one of those *do-nothing* Republicans, as President Truman labeled the majority members of the Eightieth Congress. *In November,* the editorialists counseled, *the voters of the district would do well by returning the Democrat to the House.*

"Gee, they sure don't like Uncle Lew," Michael told Johnny.

In the morning paper, they learned their uncle finished third, receiving slightly less than six thousand votes. With surprising stoicism, Lew accepted that his political career was finally over, while Carol wept bitterly. When Lew told her being a congressman's wife and living in Washington weren't quite as wonderful as he had described, she didn't believe a word of it. What gave Lew real trouble, though, was that only eight years earlier in 1940, in the same district, he had polled 74,000 votes and now, *not even ten percent of that. Where did all my support go,* he wondered.

The family barely reacted to Lew's loss. John Helden expressed his and Anita's regrets in a brief telephone conversation. Dom learned about it from his mother and did little more than shrug, as he read the letter to Dorothy. Even Mary Louise with surprising resignation accepted the outcome and never talked about it again though she still, on occasion, bitterly reminisced about Lew's defeat back in 1942. In a few weeks it became ancient family history.

What became more important in all their lives was that next spring Carol would give birth to Mary Louise's third grandchild. Michael and Johnny especially looked forward to having a baby cousin, the first on their mother's side. They had six cousins on their father's side, but they weren't close though their father remained close to his brothers. Michael and Johnny wondered about that, but never asked why.

Chapter 22 ~ 1948 [Part 2]

The Heldens of Harding Boulevard spoke little about their fear of another war even though they felt hostilities might erupt after the Soviets blockaded Berlin in the summer of 1948. President Truman responded by ordering an around-the-clock airlift that delivered the vital supplies Berliners needed to survive. Thus, an armed conflict seemed to be avoided, but always somewhere in Anita's mind flitted the unbearable thought of her sons one day going off to war.

John Helden made plans to attend the Wisconsin Milk Haulers' Convention in late September. He had been invited by Lee Marnet, one of his best customers, who realized John should participate now that he was the distributor of the popular Helden milk transport tanks. Lee suggested John might even pick up some new business. Two more of John's best customers, Bill Donnelly and Buster Moore, also urged John to attend. Buster hauled in northern Illinois. He wasn't a member of the Wisconsin association, but was friendly with Lee who always brought him along for the good time: lots of food, a golf outing, socializing, and plenty of liquor, ingredients Lee and Buster loved. The last two years of the war forced the cancellation of the convention, but it resumed in 1946. As was the custom in those days, wives were not invited.

In July, John hired Russell Lynch, a salesman he had known for several years who had plenty experience selling rolling equipment. Russell served in the infantry during the First World War when only twenty. At the start of the Second, he was forty-four, too old to serve his country again. John invited Russell to the convention after Lee said it'd be all right. John planned to check in Thursday and play golf with Lee, Buster and Bill that afternoon. They had a two o'clock tee time. Russell wouldn't drive up until Friday.

Packed and ready to go, John was stopped by Anita. "You have to talk to Johnny."

"What's the problem?"

"He read something . . . I explained it because if I don't the boys just look it up."

"What?"

Anita sighed. "A doctor on the east side was accused of performing an abortion. Johnny read the article – don't ask me why."

"What did you tell him?"

"The truth – he got very upset, said he couldn't believe a doctor would do such a thing."

"Why didn't you tell me last night?"

"Because you came home too late. I'll get him."

On the living room sofa, John put his arm around his younger son. "You know Johnny, if you read newspapers, sooner or later you're gonna read some really bad stuff."

"Yeah, but why would a doctor do that?"

"I don't know. Maybe the woman wanted him to."

Johnny couldn't believe it. "Why would a lady want to kill her baby?"

"I don't know. Maybe she wasn't married. Maybe she just didn't want a baby. I honestly don't know."

"Mom said it's against the law, and the doctor will go to jail. But if the lady didn't want the baby, shouldn't she go to jail?"

"The doctor goes because he's the one who breaks the law. He shouldn't do that even if a woman wants it"

"Then why did he do it?"

"I don't know . . . maybe for money."

Johnny pushed away. "How can a doctor kill a little baby for money? How can that be?"

That the newspaper reported the unsubstantiated incident infuriated John. *Damn editors have no discretion at all,* he thought. "Johnny, I can't give you a good answer. Don't think about it. Your mother and I don't want you having bad thoughts. You gotta think good stuff. I don't want you upset while I'm gone. Okay?"

Johnny nodded.

"And no fighting with Michael . . . ."

"Would Aunt Carol do that?"

"No, no, no, Johnny . . . they're thrilled to have a baby. Don't think like that. Put it out of your mind now."

The boy's eyes rimmed with tears. "I'll try Dad."

"Johnny, you have to be strong – strong in your head." John stood, took his son by the hand, and led him to the kitchen.

"Anita, I've really got to go." He placed Johnny's hand in hers. "The convention's over Sunday morning. I'll be home for dinner."

"What about Mass," Anita asked.

"I'll find one." He kissed them both. "Say goodbye to Michael for me."

By the time John reached the highway to Madison, he realized he wouldn't arrive until two, at the earliest. He'd register at the resort then head to the course. He'd miss the tee time, but that wasn't a problem so long as Lee had the patience to let several other foursomes go ahead.

Lee Marnet, one of the largest milk haulers in southeastern Wisconsin, served the vast Chicago market and made a lot of money during and after the war. He paid his employees fairly and gave generous year-end bonuses. For it, no one in his company had any reason to challenge him. Men who represented a challenge – real or imaginary – stood outside his employ; John Helden fit that field. John and Lee got along reasonably well except when Lee drank. Then Lee turned mean.

John had one bad experience with Lee and vowed never to get entangled like that again. Arriving late now might anger Lee, an emotion John didn't want to incite. Only three weeks earlier, Lee asked for a quote on thirty, high-capacity milk transport tanks, one of the largest, non-military orders in the history of the Helden Company. John anticipated clearing five hundred dollars on each tank: fifteen thousand bucks – twice his salary his last full year as an employee – in just one deal. He felt great about the order. Finally, he had a chance to make some real money.

The bright September morning showed a tinge of yellow in the early changing foliage. Confident in his big, new, smoke-white, four-door Chrysler *New Yorker*, John hummed along at sixty miles an hour. He knew he had the brains to handle Lee regardless of how angry or drunk Lee got, or whatever else might happen. *Don't lose sight of the rabbit,* John told himself. For thirty tanks he'd put up with a lot of Lee's crap.

At noon he reached the outskirts of Madison then headed north. Occasionally, he thought of Johnny: *poor little kid . . . so sensitive.* He recalled when his brother, Julius, had shown Anita and him the tiny, aborted fetus, and how it disturbed Anita. *My God, that's eighteen years ago.*

In Portage at a small café he ordered a sandwich and chocolate malt. He asked the waitress about the nearest Catholic Church; Sunday he'd catch noon Mass on his way home. Leaving the restaurant, John knew he wouldn't get to the resort until two-thirty at the earliest. Lee's reaction concerned him, but not nearly as much as a pleasant weekend at a nice resort on a Wisconsin lake. *It's gonna be great,* he thought, *regardless of how Lee reacts.*

After another ninety minutes, John turned off the highway. He passed through a timber portal marked *Dolan's Lake Cavanaugh Lodge.* The gravel road snaked through pines and hardwoods. He lowered both side windows letting the sweet, forest air fill the car's interior. Red-roofed cottages first appeared to his left, then through trees, glimpses of a shining, silver surface. The road ended at a clearing with sweeping views of the radiant lake.

The main buildings of the resort clustered directly ahead of John's slowly rolling car. He parked, grabbed his suitcase, and hurried towards the lodge. The resort seemed deserted because all the men were at the golf course.

Summer months at Dolan's were strictly family vacations. In the fall, however, the resort hosted conventions that proved, with uninhibited alcohol consumption, far more profitable. This was the Milk Haulers' second year at Dolan's.

John approached the registration desk where a middle-aged woman greeted him. "Hello and welcome . . . I'm Lucille Dolan."

John introduced himself, as she offered her hand. He signed the guest register explaining that Mr. Lynch, the other member of his party, wouldn't arrive until tomorrow afternoon.

"Whenever he arrives is fine although I hope he won't miss our fish boil. We're famous for that."

She excused herself, retreating to the rear of the office. Through a passageway covered by an old, Indian blanket, she called, "Jerry." In a moment a boy about Michael's age appeared. He stared at John, but said nothing.

"Take Mr. Helden to *Fern Villa.*"

A voice in the midst of changing replied, "Yes, ma'am."

"I hope you'll enjoy your stay with us and the convention, of course."

"Oh, I'm sure I will. I'm really looking forward to it."

Faint shadows beneath Jerry's eyes made him appear older, more serious, and indeed almost sad. He carried John's suitcase along the narrow concrete walk leading to the cabins east of the lodge along the lakeshore that bent, John noticed, sharply to the south.

"Are you in school?"

"Yes sir."

"Do you work here?"

"Yes sir. My father's the hired man. I help out."

"Good for you . . . how old are you?"

"Thirteen."

"Where do you live?" John's curiosity always got the better of him.

"I live here . . . ." The boy stopped in front of the cabin where John would sleep the next three nights. "I mean *here,* at the resort. My mother's the cook."

He entered ahead of John who held open the screen door. A fieldstone fireplace separated the living room from the bedroom where Jerry placed John's suitcase. A second bedroom was on the opposite side. Both had their own small bathroom. At the rear of the cabin a screen porch overlooked the lake. Wooden stairs stepped down to a grassy area that sloped to the shoreline. White pines, scattered birches, and an occasional hardwood surrounded the cottages built years ago amid these old-growth trees.

Jerry motioned towards the fireplace. "Should I start a fire, sir?" Strips of newspaper were stuffed beneath a cast-iron grate that held a bundle of kindling. "The log box is on the porch."

"No, thanks . . . I'm heading out to the golf course."

Jerry stood waiting.

"Well, you're a very fine, young man. Thanks for helping me." John handed the boy a silver half-dollar.

"Thank you, sir." He slipped out ahead of any more questions.

On the porch, John reached for a cigarette, but changed his mind after inhaling the fresh, clean air. The wooded, distant shore blazed in the afternoon light. He spotted early deciduous reds and yellows among the bright, grey-green conifers. In an angled wedge of reflected sunlight, the breeze rippled small, unbroken waves that mirrored tiny, brilliant suns off thousands of their crests. *Anita and the boys would like this,* John knew. It reminded him of summers at Uncle Henry's on Basses Bay.

It was past four when John finally got to the course. *They should be coming up Nine fairly soon,* he figured. *Especially, if they teed off at two.*

Strolling to the Ninth green, he wondered what Lee's reaction would be to John's late arrival. Gazing down the fairway, he recognized Lee, Bill, and Buster striding towards the hole along with two other men. At the flag, John waved his arms in the direction of his three best customers.

They stood at what would be their third shots when Lee recognized John. "What the hell . . . that's that asshole Helden." Then he shouted, "Get the fuck off the green!"

From a hundred yards, John couldn't hear Lee's invective. Instead, completely indifferent to the etiquette of the game, he grabbed the flagstick, waving it above his head.

Lee turned to the tall, muscular man caddying for him. "I can't hit with that idiot on the green. Run up there and tell him to get the fuck off."

Frankie dropped Lee's bag and sprinted towards John. From fifty yards, he screamed, "Get the fuck off the green!"

John recognized Frankie. *Oh, man, why did Lee have to bring that goon?* He replaced the pin and walked off into the shadows of trees. A shadow, too, fell across his light-heartedness. Without even being aware of it, he lit a cigarette.

After Bill Donnelly finished putting, he approached John. "Nice to see you, Johnny." They shook hands. "Sometimes Lee likes to show just how low-class he really is. Don't let it bother you."

John forced a laugh. "It doesn't . . . ."

Bill Donnelly, by temperament and background, was far more compatible with John than either Lee or Buster. He and John got together with their wives for dinner whenever Bill came to Milwaukee. Both women came from fine families and took their roles as wives and mothers seriously. Even if John wasn't around, Anita enjoyed the Donnelly's company, whereas she abhorred being in the presence of Lee Marnet.

Lee and Buster approached John and Bill. Two tough looking guys, carrying their bags, followed.

"John, say hello to Frankie and Hubie. You remember them, I bet." Lee laughed.

"Ya, sure, hi fellas," John said, in a flat, lifeless voice. He didn't offer his hand, nor did they.

"What the hell took you so long?" Lee asked.

"I had a little problem. Sorry I couldn't make it, but you obviously didn't need me." He glanced at Frankie and Hubie.

"Oh for shit's sake, they ain't playing. They're our caddies."

Buster laughed at Lee's explanation then said, "Hi John."

John and Buster shook hands vigorously. Buster liked John, and his wife liked Anita. The four occasionally had dinner together. Buster's problem was Lee; Lee influenced him but never for the better. If Lee got drunk, Buster got drunk; if Lee swore, Buster swore; if Lee visited a strip joint, Buster gladly tagged along. However, when Buster was with his wife and John and Anita, he was as sweet and well behaved as an altar boy, which, as a youngster, he had been.

"We're playing nine more," Lee said. "Helden, we'll see you later. Come on boys." He headed to the Tenth tee. Hubie and Frankie followed.

Buster waved. "See you later Johnny."

Bill said, "I thought maybe Lee'd ask you to hike along."

"Nah, it's okay. I don't care to play. I'll see you guys back at the resort."

In fact, John didn't care – he wasn't a golfer – but he did care that Lee brought along Frankie and Hubie, his bodyguards, as John dubbed them. They drove trucks for Lee after serving in the Marines during the war. If, after work, Lee didn't have anyone to go out with for a few drinks and a steak, he'd invite them. Right from the start, he enjoyed their rough company. They drank bourbon, weren't shy about getting drunk in public, or making salacious comments about nearby women. Husbands couldn't do much about it because Frankie and Hubie were just as tough as they looked. Lee liked being with them; along with liquor they made him feel tough, and when Lee felt tough he really wanted to be in charge.

John regarded Frankie and Hubie as crude, uneducated men. Lee was crude too, but not stupid. Over the years, he bought a lot of equipment from the Helden Company. He became John's biggest customer, someone he sold to before the war, and someone John still had to cater to because he needed the business. Marnet Trucking was growing fast, hauling huge quantities of milk to the unquenchable dairies of Chicago. John always believed he could handle Lee one on one, but Frankie and Hubie tipped the balance against John. He knew Lee and those tough ex-Marines devised a dangerous trio.

+ + +

A year earlier, John called on Lee at his office near Delavan. The meeting lasted longer than anticipated, and Lee insisted John join him for dinner at Lee's favorite steak house. John agreed, never suspecting Lee would also invite Frankie and Hubie.

John attempted some intelligent conversation, but both truck drivers thought him little more than a pompous ass. Lee did nothing to dispel the notion. Frankie and Hubie weren't accustomed to the company of a cultured man who'd rather discuss the performance of a great pianist than the performance of a truck, even though he was an engineer.

John's presence didn't stop the three from drinking heavily nor did it raise the level of conversation, which, because of its incessant emphasis on vehicles, John found unbearably tedious. When dinner was over, he asked Lee to take him to his car. The four men got into Lee's Cadillac. With bourbon in his brain, Lee headed towards his office, but as he neared it, suddenly accelerated and shouted, "Helden, we're gonna take you to see some dancing girls."

As the car roared down the highway, Frankie and Hubie cheered.

"Damn it, Lee, turn around . . . take me back. I wanna go home."

"No you don't. You wanna see some tits and ass, right boys?" He turned to look at his henchmen in the back seat, as the car drifted into the empty, oncoming lane.

"Yes sir," they said, like smart Marines.

Lee drove and swerved for miles, terrifying John. After eleven, Lee crossed into Illinois. John, utterly powerless, turned his anger into a sulking silence. A drunken Lee didn't give a damn about John's emotions, wishes, or anything else. Finally, he pulled up to a clapboard sided, two-story house remodeled into a roadside tavern. A lighted sign proclaimed, *The Pink Pillow, Exotic Dancers.* Neon signs touting *Schlitz ~The Beer that Made Milwaukee Famous* shone in the windows.

"I'm not going in," John said.

Lee opened his door. "Oh yes you are." He got out, while Frankie and Hubie waited for their orders. "Bring him in." Lee slammed the door and weaved into the strip joint.

John turned and looked right at Frankie. "Keep your hands off me or I'll-"

"You'll what?" Hubie sneered.

"Get out, or we drag you out," Frankie said.

"I told you, I'm not going . . . ."

"Then we're dragging you," Hubie said.

Hubie grabbed John's right arm; Frankie pushed from the other side. John could not resist though he was a reasonably strong man. Furious but helpless, John resigned himself to being hauled into the strip joint.

They plopped him next to Lee at the end of a narrow table facing an elevated stage rimmed with pink-lens stage lamps. A dancer had removed most of her costume except for a g-string and tassels on her nipples. Her generous buttock and breasts bounced directly in front of John; he noticed beads of sweat and a look of boredom.

Lee leaned towards Frankie. "The heat's on . . . ."

"Oh, shit," he replied.

When the music stopped, the dancer left the stage under a thick, pink layer of cigarette smoke, while the sparse audience offered meager applause.

"John, whadaya want?"

"Nothing . . . I wanna get outta here."

Lee muttered, "Too bad, no naked tits for Helden . . . ."

A middle-aged waitress came. Lee ordered *Schlitz* all around.

"There's sheriffs all over this part of the county," she told Lee, whom she obviously knew. "The girls gotta keep their clothes on, or they'll haul 'em in and fine us to boot. Can you believe that? They haven't been here yet, but they will. Two other places called and tipped us off. We always know when the sheriff's snooping."

"Can we get laid?" Hubie asked.

"Not tonight. Sheriff's been trying a long time to prove we're a whorehouse. We gotta be careful." She took Lee's ten-dollar bill and walked away.

After they finished their beers – John, perspiring and thirsty, gulped half the bottle – Lee stood and snarled, "Let's get the hell outta here," just as a dancer was removing a fishnet bra that seemed barely able to contain her voluminous breasts.

John didn't get home until three in the morning. Exhausted, he vowed, *never will I let that son-of-a-bitch pull that kind of crap again.*

+ + +

Driving back to the resort from the golf course, John resolved not to let Lee and his henchmen spoil the weekend. The convention and resort, he realized, were big enough to avoid the three, most of the time, without slighting anyone.

He parked near the rear corner of the dining room – later when he reflected on it, he couldn't explain why – rather than taking the closest spot where everyone could admire his new Chrysler. That might have been a bit more convenient, but it didn't matter because the car would just sit there until the convention ended anyway.

John strolled onto the swimming pier. West of it, another pier docked motorboats plus an old, bobbing, wooden sloop. The lake was clean and clear. John's gaze traced the shallows dropping off. To his right, where the shoreline bent south, a sandbar stretched far out. He knelt to feel water way too cold for swimming. Jerry's father was working on the other pier; John headed over there. He said, "I'd like a boat for Saturday afternoon."

Saturday morning after breakfast an economist from the University of Wisconsin would give the plenary address. There were no meetings Saturday afternoon. John thought it'd be a pleasant time for Russell and him to fish. After Saturday's dinner, the new officers would be inaugurated, and then some *to be announced* entertainment would end the evening.

"Sure . . . fishing, sailing?"

"Fishing."

"Let me show you," the hired man said.

He led John to a sixteen-foot wooden boat with a ten horsepower Evinrude mounted on the broad stern.

"Lake's too big to row. If you wanna troll, there's oars."

John admired the varnished interior of the well-maintained boat. "It's fine."

"What's the name?"

"Helden, John Helden."

"It'll be ready after lunch. If you don't have gear, we got rods and reels. I can get minnows if you'd like."

"Yes, we'll need everything."

After thanking the man, John hiked the sandy-loam trail leading to the cottages along the west shoreline. The bank sloped steeply; in places the path rose five to ten feet above the water. White pines towered above. Behind the cabins a narrow road wound through the woods. Several spurs off the entrance road let guests drive to the cabins to unload luggage and gear.

The shore and shallows were strewn with rocks, rounded smooth by wave action since the last glacier trenched the lakes ten thousand years ago. When John reached the last cabin, he walked past, as the trail continued westward. Coming to a high vantage, he saw the lake bulge into a bay. The south shore curved in an arc of narrow sand until it met the far western shore that pointed north-ward almost on a line. The sun, setting now, red and magnified through the low, long atmosphere, hovered above the dark, distant trees. John felt a sense of simple, innocent wonder. He was glad to be alone amid the sacred silence, glad not to be with Lee, Buster, Frankie, and Hubie in some loud, smoky Nineteenth hole.

Once the sun dropped behind the tree line, the air felt cooler. John hiked back, as cars rumbled down the gravel road to park in the area between John's car and the porte cochere. He nodded a greeting to men he didn't know. At the cabin, he carried in several birch logs. He lit the strips of newspaper popping the kindling into flame. He placed logs on the kindling and reset the spark screen. He would have enjoyed just sitting there, but instead showered and shaved. The dinner bell rang at six-thirty, but before he left, he brought in more logs. The fire was burning well though he doubted it would survive until his return.

At the dining hall, John Helden entered alone and first for the opening meal of the convention. Lucille Dolan, all dressed up and smiling broadly, greeted him and asked whose party he was with.

She led him to Lee Marnet's table, one with four place settings. John sat so he could watch the entrance. Bill ushered in along with other men who quickly filled the room with the din of conversation. Finally, Lee and Buster showed up.

John asked Lee, "Where are your bodyguards?"

"I sent 'em back. They haul into Chicago tomorrow. I don't want 'em up here sitting on their fat asses when they can make me money."

Buster laughed. "They sure are strange bastards . . . ."

"Hell, whadaya expect? They were in the Pacific killing Japs. They served their fucking country damn well. What the fuck did you ever do?"

Buster shrank against his chair.

An older waitress took their drink orders. After she served them, Bill Donnelly proposed a toast. "Gentlemen, to a great weekend."

"I'll drink to that." In his mind, John Helden celebrated Frankie and Hubie's departure.

"Cut the crap, Bill," Lee said. "John, how're you coming with my quote? You've had it a couple weeks. What the hell's going on?"

"It's a big order. There'll be some significant savings in manu-facturing and materials. We're pricing it very carefully. It's to your advantage, Lee, to be patient. I guarantee it'll be a good quote."

"I'll give you another week, no more . . . besides, you gotta fig-ure it two ways."

"What do you mean *two ways?* There's only one way to figure a quote."

"Oh, nothing, John, nothing at all. Let's just have a great week-end. We'll talk business next week." Lee raised his glass, gulping half his martini.

The kick-off dinner consisted of fried chicken, mashed potatoes, gravy, green beans, homemade bread, and cherry pie à la mode. Afterwards, all two hundred conventioneers enjoyed coffee and cig-arettes. Lee and Buster claimed exhaustion and went to their cot-tage. Bill and John talked a while before calling it a night. Bill had a room in the lodge. John, in the chilly darkness, found the walkway back to his cabin.

Of the fire, only embers remained. John threw in kindling and piled on several logs. The cabin had no furnace. Shivering, he undressed into his pajamas. He crawled into the cold bed then realized he needed more covers. He grabbed several woolen blankets off the other bed and pulled on woolen socks. Eventually, he warmed up. Beyond the crackling fire, if he listened closely, he could hear waves lapping the shore. His thoughts drifted to Anita and the boys. He missed them, but they were safe and warm back in Wauwatosa. He'd see them Sunday evening. *Besides,* he thought, *with Lee's henchmen gone, this is gonna be a very pleasant weekend.* Then he wondered again what Lee meant when he said, "two ways." He began his prayers, but in minutes fell asleep.

At seven, the cold, unfamiliar room startled him. Rested and refreshed, he threw a blanket over his shoulders and fetched wood to rebuild the fire. The fragrant, moist air seemed warmer outside than in. Low sunlight shimmered through the dewy trees, as sparrows chirped all about.

He built a roaring fire and sat facing it, content and happy. At seven-thirty, the bell clanged the conventioneers to breakfast. When John got there, Lee, Buster, and Bill were already drinking coffee while waiting for their food. The waitress saw him, came right over, poured a cup of steaming coffee, and took his order.

The business of the convention commenced at ten o'clock when several speakers discussed issues of interest to the haulers. John and Bill attended a talk in the lodge given by a member of the Chicago Board of Health who discussed sanitation requirements for hauling bulk milk into Chicago. He warned that standards were going to get tougher, inspections more frequent, and violators fined. Repeat violations would draw heavy fines and could result in suspended licenses. "Eventually," he stated, "all major Midwestern cities will follow Chicago's lead. Where the public's health is concerned, there will be no compromise with safety."

He even mentioned, to John's satisfaction, that the welds joining the stainless steel sheets to create the milk tank interior had to be ground so perfectly smooth that not a single, tiny, bacteria-harboring pit could remain. That was exactly the manufacturing technique the Helden Company had perfected.

John whispered to Bill, "Lee and Buster should be hearing this . . . where are they?"

"Don't know."

Lee and Buster didn't show up for lunch either. In the afternoon, John and Bill heard an engineer from the Wisconsin Highway Department discuss truckloads on pavement and bridges and the trend towards increasingly heavier wheel loads and how this would affect future designs. John appreciated the insights. The speaker predicted new highways would bypass cities and towns, whereas now nearly all major roads went right through the congested heart of most communities. He pointed out that these modern highways would save haulers fuel and time. He closed his remarks by urging them to write their representatives in Madison to support all new transportation projects throughout the state.

When the talk ended, John stepped outside into the bright sunlight. He spotted Russell Lynch leaning against the tennis court backstop. He waved at John who was glad to see him. Russell, a pleasant guy to have around, provided a great counterbalance to Lee Marnet.

"So, you made it okay . . . ."

"Yeah, no problem at all. I'm settled in at Fern Villa. Pretty nice resort, I'd say."

"Yeah, and the food's good. Tomorrow I'm taking you fishing."

"I didn't bring any gear."

"They've got everything, including minnows."

Friday's fish boil served as an informal social event. On the beach, large, galvanized pails were heaped with chunks of lake ice and bottles of beer. Straddling a shallow fire pit, Mr. Dolan and Jerry's father set up two wooden A-frames supporting a steel rod from which hung a large, cast iron kettle. A stack of split, birch logs fired the water into a rolling boil and kept it there. Tom Dolan borrowed the old idea from resorts in Door County.

One hundred and fifty pounds of fresh walleye and perch, one hundred pounds of potatoes, and another hundred of white onions and carrots boiled in wooden-handled, wire baskets. It was an even bigger job to cart the food to the dining room. Mrs. Dolan called the groups alphabetically. Tail-enders endured the wait with beer and small talk, while the daylight slowly faded away.

"That food looks dangerous," Buster said. "Those onions are gonna produce a lotta gas."

"Then you keep your damn door shut," Lee responded. "I don't wanna hear you fartin' all night long."

"It isn't the hearing that would worry me," John said.

The four men laughed out loud, while a smiling Lucille Dolan, unaware of the crude humor, approached. "Mr. Marnet, your group is next if you'd like to stroll on up now."

Walking side by side, John said to Lee, "You know, Lee, I don't have the faintest idea what you meant by *two ways*."

Lee put his arm around John's shoulders. "Trade-ins, Johnny, trade-ins."

Melted butter soaked the fish and potatoes. Bowls of coleslaw, stacks of rye bread, and pitchers of beer anchored every tablecloth. Because the whole process took so long, dinnertime ran late. Afterwards, some younger men drove to town to check out the taverns. In the lodge, men played ping-pong or coaxed the pinball machines. Other men played serious poker, as silent clusters watched. In the center room where the program talks had been given, small groups conversed.

John said, "Lee, why would you even mention trade-ins? You know we don't take used equipment in trade."

Lee grinned. "Tell me, John, when you bought the *Chrysler*, did you trade in that old piece of shit you were driving?"

"Sure, but that's a car."

"Well, why can't I trade in some old tanks? I bought 'em from the Helden Co."

"That equipment's shot. That's why you're buying new. Those tanks have outlived their useful life."

"Maybe, maybe not . . . did your old *Nash* have any useful life left? I doubt it."

"There's a market for used cars, Lee. There's no market for used, beat up, milk tanks."

"That's not my problem. I'm going to bed." Lee left, not saying goodnight to anyone.

John turned to Russell. "He can't be serious . . . I can't take his junk."

"Oh he's serious. He'll do everything he can to make it your junk. We'll have to see what they're worth – scrap maybe – but he'll want a lot more."

John shook his head. "Well, I'm not taking them. He needs new tanks more than he needs dumping old ones off on me. He'll come around."

Saturday morning after breakfast everyone, including Lee and Buster, stayed to hear an economist from the University of Wisconsin speak on *The Fifties: Fabulous or Frightening. What can we expect?* The economy had been robust since the end of the war; businessmen wondered how long the good times would last. Most of these men struggled through the Great Depression. None wanted to experience anything like that again. The professor, after being introduced, began by telling a story.

"In the old days, an aging Mother Superior at a convent near Milwaukee became bossy and irritable, a striking change from her cheerful, younger self. Other Sisters, dismayed at her loss of good humor, decided they had to do something not only for Mother Superior's sake but for theirs as well. In fact, she was making their lives miserable. So, in desperation, they consulted their physician who suggested a shot of brandy in the evening before she slept. Well, Mother Superior, temperate by nature, adamantly refused. The doctor then suggested offering her a glass of warm milk with a tiny bit of brandy in it and increasing the quantity minutely each evening until the prescribed dosage of one, full shot was attained. Unfortunately, Mother Superior wasn't a milk drinker either, plus they had no cow."

A stirring of light laughter rustled the room.

"But the good Sisters, frugal by nature and vow, had saved enough over the years to purchase a lactating cow from a neighboring farmer. Again they suggested Mother Superior have a glass of warm milk every night before she slept even though she claimed she didn't want it. Finally, after much prodding, Mother Superior relented, and the brandy-tainted milk became a nightly elixir for the unsuspecting old nun."

Again light laughter fluttered through the room.

"To everyone's delight, as the amount of brandy gradually increased, Mother Superior's irritableness gradually decreased. It was regarded as something of a small miracle. Within several months Mother Superior not only regained her former good humor, but also began to display remarkable compassion, charity, and wisdom. Indeed, her words were so inspiring that the Sisters assigned a young nun to record her most insightful expressions.

"As the years passed, Mother Superior eventually failed. Sensing the end was near, the Sisters instructed the recording Sister to stay with Mother Superior day and night, as they wanted to capture her final words of wisdom. And then one night, after thoroughly enjoying her last, warm glass of spiked milk, she died.

"Ah yes, with heavy hearts they buried her. But they sought comfort in her words and, in particular, her very last words that were dutifully noted. After the funeral they all clamored, 'Please, Sister, share with us that we might forever remember her.' The young Sister opened her notebook, turned to the last page, cleared her throat, and said, 'our dear Mother Superior's final words were, and I quote, *whatsoever you do . . . don't sell that cow!*'"

That tough group of milk haulers laughed, whistled, clapped, hooted, and howled. John Helden said to Russell, "We should try that on Lee."

After the men settled down, the economist began his formal remarks. He foresaw a period of moderate, continuing growth in the late forties and early fifties. The national birth rate had increased in 1946 and 1947, which he attributed to the anxiousness of the returning veterans to start their families, but he didn't think it would continue for more than another year or two. Nevertheless, it would be good for the milk haulers because, as more babies were born, there would be more demand for dairy-fresh milk. In addition, new milk-based products would be developed so the demand for whole milk would increase even though, perhaps, the country might experience a mild or even significant recession in the early 1950s. He didn't foresee a depression, certainly nothing like the 1930s. He felt strongly that government fiscal policy had to be cautious and prudent to insure that a free-spending Congress didn't ignite the evils of inflation. At the same time, he advised that the Federal Reserve must be careful not to pursue too restrictive a monetary policy that could plunge the nation into recession. He was confident, however, that, after running up huge deficits to finance the war, Congress and future Congresses would act responsibly to avoid excessive spending and an increase in the national debt. In conclusion, he stated forcefully, "The most responsible thing any government can do is preserve the value of a nation's currency. In the 1920s, we all know what rampant inflation led to in Germany. Inflate the currency and you break the backs of the poor, you destroy the middle class, and you open the door to tyrants."

The conventioneers applauded vigorously. The professor, feigning modesty, raised and lowered his out-stretched palms to dampen their enthusiasm. A question and answer period followed, but few were asked, as the men were eager to get outside into the superb weather.

Everyone commented on the great speech, but talk quickly turned to the afternoon activities. Most of the men planned to golf again, but several, including John and Russell, intended to fish. All looked forward to the gala, steak dinner that was the high point of the convention with the installation of new officers and some unannounced entertainment to follow. The convention ended Sunday after breakfast, but check-out wasn't until noon. John Helden looked forward to twenty-four more hours of relaxation and fun.

After lunch, he and Russell met Jerry's father at the boat dock; he showed them how to prime the gas line, set the choke and gear shifter, then pull the engine to life. John swung the boat away from the pier, heading east towards a big bay. They were told it offered the best chance for pike. They hooked fathead minnows through the lips, used split shot to sink the bait, then cast their lines way out. Russell, manning the oars, pointed the bow towards the south shore. The northerly breeze let them drift deep into the bay.

"If a northern hits they hit hard; you set the hook right away," John said. "If it's a walleye, you barely feel it. Takes a delicate touch . . . ."

Russell lit a cigarette, cupping his hands against the breeze. "Should be a good dinner tonight."

"Right, and another good night's sleep."

The sky was bright with large, white cumulus, their edges backlit by brilliant sunlight. The men enjoyed the wonderful air, each other's company, and soaking minnows. John even remarked that the shoreline trees were showing more color than when he arrived just two days ago. He loved being on the water trolling for pike while searching the sky for eagles.

"Have you thought any more about Lee's trade-ins?" Russell asked.

"Nope, I don't intend to think about it till we're back."

As they drifted, John told Russell about the time Lee's henchmen dragged him into the strip joint. "When Lee drinks with Frankie and Hubie, he becomes wild. I'm really glad they left. When I saw them at the course I felt like going home."

Four times they drifted deep into the bay. They had several soft strikes. "Walleyes," John said, because the minnows were gone. They caught nothing, but it didn't matter; both men enjoyed the tranquility and glorious weather. It had been years since John fished on a peaceful, late summer day, forgetting his cares and concerns.

The afternoon sun was already low when they brought in their lines. Russell hauled in the minnow bucket, while John started the engine. They were back at the dock in minutes. They wanted to get cleaned up leisurely. Both men looked forward to a cocktail, good steak, and an enjoyable evening.

Because the nights turned cool, John decided to wear his wool suit rather than the summer model. Relaxed and in good spirits, Russell and he headed to the dining hall. The tables had been rearranged to accommodate the officers' table with a lectern in the center. To the right, a set of drums and a floor microphone suggested the evening's entertainment. As at every meal, tables displayed the host's name. They had to hunt for Lee's, which had been moved from the right side to the left. When Russell spotted *Mr. Lee Marnet,* John was puzzled. "Seven places?" He thought for a moment, then muttered, "Frankie and Hubie . . . they're back."

Chapter 23 ~ 1948 [Part 3]

The dining hall filled rapidly. Lee swaggered in with Frankie and Hubie, both wearing dark suits that looked a size too small for their broad, thick bodies. John Helden, hiding his displeasure, introduced Russell who shook hands with the three men.

Bill and Buster arrived. The seven sat chatting while waiting for a waitress to take their drink orders and how rare or well done they'd like their porterhouses. As liquor flowed, the convention-eers' voices created an unceasing din.

Lee barked, "John, I don't want you inflating your quote because of the trade-ins."

"I told you, Lee, I don't take trade-ins."

"Oh, yes you will – you don't take 'em, I'll buy from *Kold-Karry*."

John laughed. "No you won't. They make an inferior tank. You won't buy 'em, and you know it."

"Damn it, Helden, don't tell me what I will or won't do. You're gonna take those twenty tanks in trade, and that's it. You figure the fucking quotes, and you figure 'em good. Shit, I've given you a lot of business over the years. Why are you being such a prick about this? What's the big fucking deal?"

"Lee, I told you last night, there's no market for beat up, worn out equipment. You know it; I know it. Everyone in this room knows it."

Bill sensed the pointlessness of the argument. "Look, gentle-men, this is our last dinner here. Let's enjoy ourselves. I don't want to talk business."

"Me either," Buster said. "I wanna another drink."

When the waitress brought the soup and salad, Buster, Lee, Frankie, and Hubie ordered another cocktail.

"There's gonna be a show tonight," Buster said. "A girl singer and a magician, I heard."

Lee grinned. "Helden would prefer strippers with big tits, right John?" Frankie and Hubie laughed.

John didn't answer.

Lee attacked his steak. "You know, gentlemen, Andy Kane becomes President tonight. He hauls into the Twin Cities, Duluth, Superior. He's a *Kold-Karry* guy." He said it matter-of-factly, but John jumped on it.

"The outer jackets aren't stainless, just regular carbon steel. They gotta be painted; the whole damn tank has to be painted. Who at this table wants that kind of expense?"

Russell appreciated John's quick response. In Russell's opinion, no one in America was better able to defend or sell Helden milk transport tanks than John Helden.

"Andy Kane is a wild man," Bill interjected. "I can't believe he got elected."

"Yeah, he paints his tanks the ugliest two-tone brown you've ever seen," Lee said. "Who the hell would paint a fucking milk tank brown? They look like baby shit."

Frankie and Hubie laughed hard. They had loosened their ties, hung their suit jackets on the backs of their chairs, and rolled up their sleeves. They devoured their porterhouses like hungry, high school football players.

Lee continued ranting. "They call him *Sugar Kane*. He doesn't run his business. He's got some Harvard guy. I heard all he does is play golf and wine and dine customers. That's why he's such a fat slob. Look at that ugly son-of-a-bitch."

To the left of the lectern sat the incoming and, to the right, the outgoing officers. No one could miss Andy Kane. He sat there like an old bulldog chewing on a bone. But he was a smart, old bulldog who knew how to make money and gain influence.

Buster laughed. "Yeah, and he's your new president."

"I sure as hell didn't vote for him." Lee wanted to be an officer, but no one ever encouraged it. Sober, he didn't have the courage to toss his hat into the ring of his peers.

After dessert, Lee's attention returned to John. "You know, Helden, I'm the best damn customer you ever had, even before the war. You owe me a lot, and that's why you're taking those tanks in trade."

"I don't want to talk about it, Lee." John knew his assessment of *Kold-Karry* gained him the advantage. "We'll discuss it next week."

Lee pounded both fists on the table. "G--damn it, no we won't . . . we'll discuss it now!"

Lee's outburst aroused Frankie and Hubie. They glared at John in anticipation. If he made a move, they were ready.

Bill said, "Lee, this isn't the time or place to discuss business – forget it."

"No, g--damn it . . . ." Lee jabbed his index finger at John. "Your cousin said you could be a stubborn son-of-a-bitch. I didn't wanna have to tell you that, but your cousin told me if you balked, they'd force you. I told him you wouldn't, but damn it, John, you're proving me wrong."

John stared at Lee in disbelief. "You talked to Peter Jr. behind my back? You had no right to do that. I'm the distributor. I make the deal – not them. You gotta make it with me because you're my customer. Why the hell would you go behind my back?"

John stood, loosened his tie then pulled off his woolen suit coat. Frankie and Hubie thought he might charge Lee. They pushed back from the table, anxious for action, but after hanging his coat over the back of the chair John sat down.

Lee stammered the start of an answer, but a man at the lectern overwhelmed all the conversations with his amplified voice.

"Gentlemen, can I have your attention . . . we'd like to start the program."

In the first order of business, the outgoing president gave a brief farewell speech. Then the outgoing secretary administered the oaths for the new officers. Amused by excessive handshaking at the front table, the conventioneers clapped and whistled. After everyone settled down, Andy Kane gave his inaugural address with the usual remarks about working hard to build a better association and pledging to personally lobby in Madison on behalf of the milk haulers. In closing, he asked everyone to call him *Sugar* and reminded them that his door was always open to members in good standing, which meant those current with their dues.

"You know," he continued, "it's the new president's responsibility to provide entertainment at this event. And tonight, I promise you, nobody's gonna be disappointed. Now, order another drink and make it a double 'cause the waitresses ain't gonna be around after this last call."

That set off furious order taking. Sugar directed his new vice-president and secretary to close the Venetian blinds and curtains on every window except the transoms that stayed open for ventilation. Cigarette smoke flowed like a ghostly fluid out the high windows along the east wall.

Sugar motioned to the musicians waiting in the kitchen passageway. The drummer came first, followed by the trio's leader, an accordionist, and a double bassist who carried his instrument reverently. They began with a medley from the Broadway show *Oklahoma*.

John turned to Bill. "They sound terrific." He liked the tunes and kept his eyes on the musicians to avoid Lee.

When the trio finished, Sugar Kane shouted over the applause, "Now let's give a rousing, milk haulers' welcome to our songstress for the evening, the lovely Miss Jean Hathaway."

A beautiful blonde walked regally from the kitchen passageway to the microphone. Her tall, well-rounded figure intrigued every man in the room. They clapped out of sheer appreciation for her elegant, good looks. She glanced at the accordionist, smiled slightly, and nodded. He played the introduction to her first song, just as the waitresses began serving the last drinks. After an unrecognized verse, John Helden knew the refrain.

> *"It was just one of those things,*
> *Just one of those crazy flings,*
> *One of those bells that now and then rings,*
> *Just one of those things . . . ."*

When she finished, Lee said, "She's a much better looker than singer."

Buster laughed. "Hey, that's why she's singing for milk haulers."

"It's the northwoods . . . who'd you expect, Dinah Shore?" Bill asked.

John thought her second song better. He found her so lovely that it didn't matter her voice was less than perfect.

Sugar announced a short break before the magician's act. Bill, Buster, and Hubie went to the men's room in the lodge. While they were gone, Lee said, "Helden, we got a little surprise for you tonight."

"Yeah, I can only imagine." One surprise was enough for

John. He didn't know how he'd handle his cousin. John presumed Lee approached Peter Jr., but then he realized Peter might have approached Lee. For all John knew, Peter Jr. might have cooked the whole deal.

"Me and Buster and the boys are gonna visit a fine little establishment after the show. We thought we'd take you along."

"No, thanks." If, in fact, Peter Jr. initiated the deal with Lee, then John knew he was betrayed. *Good God, my own cousin . . . .*

Lee glanced at Frankie. "Sounds like John doesn't wanna join us."

"Oh, I think he will."

John snapped back to the moment. "Lee, what the hell are you talking about?"

"We're taking you to a fine, little whorehouse . . . my treat."

"I don't go to whorehouses."

"Well you are tonight. We're gonna get you laid," Lee said. "Right, Frankie?"

"Right, boss."

"My treat, John. These are high-class whores: voluptuous, good-looking, naughty women. You can have anything you want."

"I told you, I don't go to whorehouses." He turned to Russell. "Can you believe this idiot?" Russell glared at Lee.

Hubie returned and sat down. Lee began again, "John, how long you been married? All with the same woman . . . seems to me it's time you got yourself a fresh piece of tail."

"Absolutely not," John said. "That's completely against my religion."

"We'll get you over your scruples, right Frankie?"

Frankie grinned. "Oh, yeah, we'll get Saint John laid."

Bill returned. He heard nothing of what was said.

John wondered, *is Marnet serious? What does he think . . . I'd go? Oh, yeah, he'll have his goons abduct me. He did it before . . . .*

Sugar introduced the magician who pulled a couple rabbits out of a top hat, but it was the way he made the bunnies vanish that stumped the crowd. John Helden paid little attention. His emotions swelled into thoughts. *Lee planned this. They'll force me just like in Illinois. They'll kidnap me if they have to. By God, I will not let that happen.* He glared at Lee, realizing he hated the man.

After the magician finished, receiving a nice round of applause, Miss Hathaway returned for her final set. With her golden hair radiant in the spotlight, Lee quipped, "You know what Confucius says: blonde women have black hair, *by cracky*."

Buster howled, but Frankie and Hubie didn't catch the play on words. John found their befuddlement amusing, but now he feared them, for he knew what Lee would have them do.

Miss Hathaway sang,

"I'm wild again, beguiled again,
A simpering, whimpering child again,
Bewitched, bothered and bewildered am I . . . ."

She bowed to light applause, but before she could begin another song, Sugar grabbed the microphone. He sensed his members had had enough. "Hey guys, let's hear it one last time for the lovely Miss Jean Hathaway." He clapped enthusiastically, while the men were merely polite.

Again she bowed, cast a disapproving glance at Sugar, then exited the room. Passing through the kitchen, she noticed a sleazy looking man about thirty-five smoking a cigarette. He stared hard at Jean who found his face cruel. After collecting her coat, purse, and make-up case, she left without saying anything to anyone and walked to her car. She had been paid before she sang and now was anxious to get away from that roomful of liquored men. Seeing that tough-looking guy puzzled her. She couldn't imagine why he was just standing there.

At that moment, Sugar shouted into the microphone, "Hey guys, it's door prize time . . . door prize . . . ."

Most of the men stood, clapped, whistled, and shouted.

Bill leaned towards John and Russell. "Last year they gave away a new car, a *Plymouth* coupe."

Russell said, "That's pretty nice."

"Yeah," Lee interjected, "the year before, a boat and motor, but I heard Kane is gonna top that big time tonight."

"Maybe a *Piper Cub*," Buster suggested, drawing laughs.

"Gentlemen," Sugar began, "you gotta pay attention now 'cause I've arranged the greatest door prize in the history of this convention; hell, in the entire history of the world's conventions. Nobody will ever top old Sugar's door prize of 1948, nobody, guaranteed.

But you guys gotta listen to me . . . this is something special and something that is probably best forgotten after we all go home. Just remember: only one lucky son-of-a-bitch is gonna win this thing, and right now all you guys got the exact same chance so I don't want any fighting and no riots. I don't like sore losers . . . understand? There's only one door prize and only one lucky winner, and that's final. If any of you assholes give me any shit, I'll throw you outta here."

Lee asked, "What the hell's he talking about?" Then he shouted, "Get on with it, fat boy."

Sugar spoke into the microphone. "Everyone understand?"

There was a derisive, unruly rumbling that affirmed the question. The men were impatient and restless. Most had consumed way too much liquor.

"I have in this box" – he pointed at it – "two hundred some cards with three or four letters written on each. The first letter is the name of a cabin or the lodge, which is obviously 'L'. The last two or three letters are the initials of each man in this room except for last year's officers and the new officers. I regret my initials can't be in there, but those are the rules. Oh, yeah, the musicians ain't in there either."

He turned towards the trio. "Sorry boys."

Then Sugar continued. "So, I'm gonna give you morons an example. If I draw a card with the letters *L-A-B-C* that means whoever *A-B-C* is – and I hope he knows who the hell he is – and he's staying in the lodge because of the *L* . . . he's the winner. Got it? So if you're staying in the lodge and your name is Asshole B. Crapper, you're the lucky winner. Got it?"

Roars of laughter changed to a general hooting and hollering. "We got it, we got it. Get on with it. Come on, let's go."

Sugar shouted, "All you guys shut the fuck up!"

John leaned towards Bill. "Your new president is unbelievably crude. How'd he ever get elected?"

"Beats me . . . I didn't vote for him."

"This place is a mad house. I bet you, Russell, and I are the only sober guys in here."

"You're probably right," Bill shouted back.

The same men who had closed the window curtains moved a

small, three-stepped, wooden platform into position at the other end of the head table. Sugar, at the microphone, stood in front of the musicians who waited for their cue. Then the two men moved a tall, four-panel, folding screen in front of the platform so it and the passageway to the kitchen were no longer visible to the conventioneers. Sugar and the musicians, however, had a wide open, side view.

Sugar barked into the microphone, "Jack, lock the front door."

Before Jack could zigzag through the tables, another man got up, walked the few steps to the door and turned the dead bolt. At the same time, Sugar signaled to the man standing at the electrical panel in the kitchen passageway. He began throwing switches until only dim light from scattered ceiling bulbs diffused through the smoky air. The bright spotlight that shone on Miss Hathaway now aimed at Sugar.

The buzzing crowd quieted down after Sugar shouted, "Who bombed us at Pearl Harbor?" The question surprised everyone, but no one answered. "I'm asking you bastards, who the fuck bombed us at Pearl Harbor?"

Half the men in the room shouted, "The Japs . . . ."

"Right, and whose ass did we kick all the way back to Tokyo?"

Again the reply came, but this time louder. "Japs, the Japs . . . ."

"And who committed atrocities against our friends in the Pacific?"

Now the eager milk haulers shouted the same answer, but much louder. John leaned towards Bill. "What's he trying to do, restart the war?"

Sugar, his face flushed, sweated profusely. He loosened his tie and pulled off his coat. "Now I'm gonna tell you bastards something." He wiped his face with a handkerchief. "My boy was killed on Iwo Jima, my" – his voice faltered and broke – "my only son. Those g--damn Japs had no right, no fucking right or reason, to start a war with us. They had no fucking right or reason to bomb Pearl Harbor. They had no right to disturb the peace in half the fucking world. But you know what we did? We kicked their yellow asses all the way back to Tokyo because Harry Truman's the greatest president ever. He showed those yellow bastards, they might know how to start a war, but we sure as shit know how to finish one."

After that impassioned outburst, the dining hall exploded with applause. Frankie and Huble, along with nineteen other men, had served in the Pacific. Most of the men, including John Helden, had a brother, son, nephew, or cousin who served either in the Pacific or in Europe. Every man in the room agreed that the Japanese warlords and Nazis warmongers deserved the deadly fate American military power had dealt them.

Sugar had brought the crowd to an eager, edgy, emotional state. Again, he shouted into the microphone, "Quiet, quiet you bastards . . . shut-up, all of you!"

The men obeyed for Sugar's slain son had gained him control. He turned to the musicians and nodded. They began to play *Rose, Rose, I Love You* at a slow, lilting tempo. He lowered his voice because the room had fallen quiet. "What happens when a country starts a war and gets its ass kicked? What happens when those cocky Jap generals get the shit kicked out of 'em? What happens after Tojo swings from the gallows? Gentlemen, I'll tell you what happens."

Sugar signaled to the man at the electrical panel. The room went dark except for the spotlight that swung wildly away from Sugar and scanned the front of the room until it stopped at the large screen that hid the small, wooden platform. Still the trio played, hauntingly, *Rose, Rose, I Love You*, but no one could see Sugar. Their eyes were drawn to the circle of light on the shielding screen, but that was all they could see.

John Helden whispered, "What the hell's going on here?"

Then Sugar, hidden in darkness, continued. "Gentlemen, I'll tell you what happens. You've all heard this saying since you were schoolboys. Tonight I'm gonna prove it's still true in our day and age. Drummer . . . ."

The trio ended the slow, sad melody, while the drummer began a roll that grew louder, but couldn't overwhelm the booming crescendo of Sugar's amplified voice. "What saying, you ask? Well, gentlemen, this expression goes back to the Greeks and Romans . . . their armies lived by this rule. Gentlemen, gentlemen . . . remember this?" He screamed into the microphone, "To the victors belong the spoils."

Suddenly, the spotlight switched off. The room went completely black. No one could see anything. For a moment it was as quiet as a monk's funeral, but then came a low, restless stirring. No one knew, not a man there had the faintest suspicion of what old Sugar Kane was about to deliver for the grand door prize of 1948.

After some bumps and shoe shuffling in the vicinity of the screen, out of the blackness came Sugar's booming voice. "Gentlemen, to the victors belongs *this* . . . ."

Suddenly, the intense circle of light shone not on the shielding screen, for it was gone. Instead, illuminated on the pedestal, a stunningly beautiful Japanese girl stood naked with a single yellow rose in her long, black hair. Her milk-white skin was unblemished save for the deep, delicate pink of her nipples, the faint shadow of her shallow navel, and the blackness of her triangular pubic hair that pierced like an arrow the eyes of every man in the room. Her waist was tiny, her hips curvaceous, and her breasts perfectly formed in fullness with the proportions of her slender body. For an instant, the room maintained a stunned silence, but then it erupted. Shouts and screams became a roaring. John Helden saw the girl twitch with fear.

"Quiet, quiet, shut up," Sugar screamed, over and over, but the men would not. Not until they had exhausted their lungs, throats, and voices.

John's gaze, like all the men's, affixed onto the porcelain beauty of the girl, but her mind's gaze beheld the snowy, blue-white mountains of Nagano, the home of her girlhood. The vision explained the slight, enigmatic smile on her lips, for her soul was not in that room.

After the haulers slumped into silence, Sugar commanded, "Turn around Madam Butterfly."

The girl didn't move.

"Damn it, Madam Butterfly, turn around. We wanna see your cute, little yellow ass."

The conventioneers roared with laughter.

The girl remained motionless, gazing at her beloved mountains. Her indifference infuriated Sugar. He screamed into the microphone, "Turn around and show us your fucking backside, you stupid yellow bitch."

John realized the girl didn't understand Sugar's screaming. Out of the shadows a woman appeared, telling the girl, in her native tongue, to turn around. She obeyed, but unsteadily because she wasn't used to high heels. When the men saw her beauty from behind, they let out another deafening roar.

John Helden remained silent. An enormous sadness had overtaken him.

Finally, Sugar's harsh voice commanded, "Get her outta here – now – come on, Mother Butterfly, get her ass outta here."

The older woman extended her right hand so the girl wouldn't stumble in the treacherous heels. As soon as she stood safely, the woman wrapped a red, silken robe about the girl's narrow shoulders and whispered in her ear. The girl rid herself of the awkward shoes and left the room with the woman's arm around her.

Sugar, perspiring and breathing heavily, desperately needed water.

Lee grinned at John. "Bet you're really anxious to get to a whorehouse now, eh Helden? Once we know who wins the little Jap, we'll go. Frankie, you're driving."

"You got it boss." Frankie desperately wanted to win, but his and Hubie's initials weren't even in the box. Lee made sure of that.

After gulping water, Sugar recovered. "We're gonna take a ten minute break, and then we'll have the drawing. Like I said, there's only one winner, and he gets Madam Butterfly for the night. I don't want no problems, no riots. There's a honeymoon suite in the lodge. That's where one of you lucky bastards is gonna spend the greatest night of your life. And whoever you are, you owe Sugar big time."

Lee sneered, "Let's hope Helden wins this thing. You'd fuck her, right John?"

"Lee, you're talking like an idiot." Bill stood and walked away.

John looked at Lee. "No, I would not."

He and Russell followed Bill to the far side of the room leaving Lee, his boys, and Buster nursing their last drinks.

"He's really drunk, John," Bill said. "He won't remember any of this in the morning."

"I will," John replied.

"You do understand this is white slavery," Russell said. "Kane could go to jail."

"Yeah," John and Bill agreed, but neither uttered what they knew they ought to do.

Sugar returned to the microphone. "Okay, quiet down now.

Everybody take their seat. It's time one of you lucky assholes wins this thing."

As John sat down, Lee said, "Helden's not lucky; he won't win. But John, you're coming with me and the boys. We'll get you laid, and I'll pick up the tab. I guarantee she'll be fatter and uglier than the little Nip, but, what the hell, you can always shut your eyes."

Frankie and Hubie laughed hard.

"Shut up Lee," Bill said, just as Sugar asked for another drum roll.

Nonchalantly, John asked, "Hey, is that the Japanese girl?" He pointed past Lee's left ear. Instinctively, Lee turned, as did Frankie and Hubie.

Lee's glazed eyes searched for the girl. "Helden . . . where?"

When Lee turned back, John's chair was empty except for his draped coat. Lee scanned the room and found John unlocking the door's deadbolt. Lee cupped his hand at Frankie's ear and shouted, "Get that son-of-a-bitch!"

After John went out, a man reset the deadbolt, just as a sliding Frankie, with Hubie right behind, reached the door. Frankie grabbed the knob, pulled it violently though the deadbolt stopped the door after a sixteenth of an inch. "Shit," he muttered, fumbling with the lock.

As a boy, John ran like a rabbit; now at forty-six, his body lean and pumped with adrenalin, he still felt fast. He darted towards his car, but stopped cold after only five quick strides, just as Frankie and Hubie stumbled through the dining room door.

John sensed he was not alone, as though someone was watching him, as though someone was very near. Had he heard something, a noise above? He turned back just as a slight figure dropped feet first from a large, conifer branch about a foot above John's head. In the faint glow filtering through the dining room curtains, they looked at each other. John realized this shadowy person had seen and heard everything through the open transom windows. It was the boy, Jerry.

"There he is," Frankie shouted.

They charged towards John – no more than fifty feet away – while Jerry, like a phantom, disappeared. John barely had time to reach his car and certainly didn't have time to unlock it, get in, start the engine, and leave, as he planned. He knew they'd drag him out just like they did in Illinois. Instead, he sprinted towards the pole lamp that lit the area where the road to the highway began. His lead dwindled to twenty-five feet. Running harder than he had in years, he passed the lamp and raced towards the highway half-a-mile distant. After he entered the black darkness, he kept running, but finally stopped because he could see nothing, though his shoes still sensed the gravel road.

To Frankie and Hubie, John vanished. They stopped chasing much sooner than John realized, and, in the lamplight, they wondered how far he might have gone and what to do about it. Frankie ordered, "Go get Lee . . . I'll wait here."

Hubie trotted back to the dining room.

John bent over, hands on knees, to catch his breath. Safe in darkness and silence, he watched Frankie light a cigarette. John decided to wait for Lee to come. He wanted to hear what Lee would say.

"He ran up the road and disappeared." Frankie spoke with the conviction of having witnessed something preternatural.

"Aw shit, he's out there somewhere. He's gotta come back, either this way or the cabin path. Nobody could get through the woods. Hubie, you stay here. Frankie, go over there and wait . . . sooner or later he'll come. When you get him, take him to my cabin. Tie him up if you have to. Then, Hubie, you come and get me."

Frankie asked, "Are we still gonna visit the ladies?"

"Only if Helden's with us . . . make sure you get him."

"We'll get 'em, boss," Frankie said.

"Is the drawing over," Hubie asked. Lee ignored him and headed back to the dining room. "Did I win?" Hubie shouted.

Lee turned. "Shut up, you stupid son-of-a-bitch. Catch Helden, and I'll get you laid for a week."

John, his eyes well-adjusted to the darkness, heard every word. He went out the road until he reached the fork of the first spur leading to the cabins. He moved quickly, for he knew exactly what he would do.

Lamps left on in the cottages gave enough light to find Lee's Cadillac. At the right front wheel John knelt and uncapped the tire valve. He used his car key to depress the stem; air hissed out. John held it until the tire was nearly flat then did the same to the other front tire.

On the path he hiked Thursday afternoon, John headed back towards Frankie. As he neared the boat dock, he saw Frankie and Hubie commiserating under the cone of lamplight. Without hesitating, John slid down the bank to the water's edge. Several branches from the tangled foliage scratched his face. His palms scrapped hard against the rough gravel.

In an instant, he strode into the water, heading far out. Even with shoes, larger stones were difficult to maneuver; he slipped often. He trudged along until the chilling water reached his waist. He rubbed his hands to cleanse the abrasions. It was a moonless night, but the lodge lights guided him, as he struggled eastward.

Frankie and Hubie lounged near the pole lamp waiting for John to reappear. When he was in line with them, at least fifty yards beyond the end of the swimming pier, he saw the reddening tips of their cigarettes, as they inhaled. If John called their names, Frankie and Hubie would easily hear, but from where they stood, the lake was black and impenetrable.

The lake bottom sloped downward and water rose to John's chest. The faltering breeze blew from the north, as it had every day. He had to get back to his cabin fast. He had to strip, dry off, dress, pack, and leave because, sooner or later, Lee and his boys would show up there.

John trudged hard through the cold, heavy water. He recalled a sandbar jutted out ahead and, once reached, he'd be able to move faster. The water rose to his neck, forcing him to angle towards the lodge. Then the lake bottom sloped upwards; in minutes, John struggled onto the sandbar. He paralleled the shore, as it bent southward. The water dropped below his knees, but his soaked clothes felt like frozen wraps slapping against his raw skin. He tramped along, but was tiring fast. Finally, he spotted his cabin, lit by the single lamp he had left on before he and Russell went to dinner. With every step, in water now only up to his ankles, his body shivered violently. He tried to run, but the air through his sopping clothes beat against him like a blunt spray of icy pellets. He lurched onto the shore, staggering towards the cabin. Colder than he had ever been in his life, a freezing chill pierced to the core of his being.

Inside, he pulled off his ruined shoes, drenched socks, tie, shirt, wool pants, and underwear. He went into the bathroom, groping for a towel. He was drying and rubbing his shaking body when he heard the cabin door open. Russell, spotting water on the floor, followed the trail into John's bedroom.

When Russell encountered John shivering naked, he asked, "My God, John, what happened?"

Thin, red scratches streaked John's ashen face. His black hair, wet and matted, deepened the bluish cast of his lips. "The only way I could get back here was the lake. I gotta go, Russell. Lee and his goons want to take me to a whorehouse. He did that once before. If I stay and he tries it again, I swear I'll kill him."

Russell grabbed towels to wipe up the trail of water. "Lee could show up any minute. He was really mad you got away."

John pulled on dry underwear and pants just before they heard voices.

"That's them," Russell said.

John contorted into a flannel shirt, while slipping out the rear door. Barefoot and shivering, he nimbly descended the steps. He crouched beside the wood lattice that kept small critters from below the floor joists. He heard Lee pounding at the front.

Russell took his time. "What the hell do you want?"

"Where's Helden?"

"I don't know. Ask your boys . . . they did the chasing."

"Come on Russell," Lee implored. "We just wanna have a little fun with John. Where'd he go? His car's still here. He's gotta be around here someplace."

"I haven't seen him. For your sake, I hope he isn't hurt."

Lee looked into Russell's eyes. "Is he here?"

Russell opened the screen door. "Come on in . . . take a look."

It was a great bluff. If Lee hadn't fallen for it, he would have found John's soaked clothes twenty feet from where he stood. He stared, blankly, into the room, his mind beclouded by liquor. Hoping to distract, Russell asked, "What do you have against John, anyway? What's he ever done to you?"

"He's arrogant . . . thinks he's better . . . thinks I'm a horse's ass."

"You are a horse's ass," Russell said. Frankie coughed to cover his laugh.

"Yeah, but I don't like him knowing it."

"Everybody knows it. How the hell do you expect John not to know it?"

"It's his wife," Lee muttered. "She's an arrogant bitch . . . thinks she's better . . . won't have anything to do with me or my wife."

"It's not his wife," Russell said.

Lee turned away. "Let's go boys."

Unless they found Helden fast, Frankie and Hubie realized things did not look promising regarding their sampling of the local whores. Growling vulgarities, they followed a swaying Lee back to the lodge.

John came in, shivering uncontrollably. He put on a heavy sweater, opened his suitcase, and took out a small leather holster.

"Oh, John, no . . . ."

It was Uncle Henry's pistol. John showed Russell the loaded chamber. "I'll use it before I'd ever let that son-of-a-bitch kidnap me again." He put the gun back in the holster and set it aside. He pulled on dry socks and his fishing boots. He threw his clothes and toiletries into the suitcase and stuffed his soaked clothes and shoes into a pillowcase.

"I left my suit coat in the dining room. Will you bring it?"

"Sure." Russell stood in the bedroom doorway wondering why John just didn't tell Lee to go to hell. After seeing the handgun, though, he knew John had to leave. He never dreamed John would commit such a violent act, but then, he thought, *one never knows . . . .*

"So long Russell . . . thanks for your help. I heard your great bluff."

They shook hands. John picked up his suitcase, the soaked, stuffed pillowcase, and the holster. Russell held open the door. John hobbled across the narrow walk, then between two cabins. He passed behind the tennis court backstop, just steps from a deep hollow, dense with slender tamaracks. The dining room was dark. He heard the jukebox wailing in the lodge and saw groups of men in the lighted windows still socializing.

He gazed at the upper story and wondered about the beautiful Japanese girl forced by war, poverty, and cruelty to spend this night as a sex slave, raffled like some cheap trinket, a mere door prize for an American's amusement and lust. A world away, her country lay in ruins. Her own bleak city, the remnants of family and friends, her first love, her school, playmates, her girlhood, and innocence, everything lost forever to memory. John's eyes rose upwards until he beheld the black, cloudless sky ablaze with stars. He whispered, "Oh God, why, why . . . ?"

He scurried behind the kitchen and, at its far corner, reached his car. His eyes scanned the dimly lit parking area, but spotted no one. He opened the trunk, swung in the suitcase and pillowcase, then quietly shut the lid. He placed the holstered pistol on the passenger seat, put the transmission in neutral, and released the emergency brake, allowing the big *Chrysler* to roll backwards down the slight slope. At the flat bottom, he started the engine. When he reached the pole lamp – his car completely visible to anyone who might be looking – he turned on the headlights, accelerated, and was gone.

Lee, Frankie and Hubie never figured out how John escaped that night, nor did they ever suspect he flattened Lee's tires, enraging Lee Sunday afternoon when he was set to leave.

Passing through Dolan's portal for the last time, John turned onto the highway. He watched the engine temperature gauge creep upwards. In two hours he'd reach Madison. He'd be home in four. When the engine had warmed, he turned the heater to its highest setting. It took an hour for John to stop shivering, all the while fearing he'd catch pneumonia like he did in 1943.

John didn't know how he'd ever deal with Lee Marnet again. Nevertheless, the business of Lee buying thirty new tanks and the unpleasant issue of trade-ins remained. He had to confirm if Peter Jr. really made a commitment to Lee that only John had the right to make. John had to explain his actions to Bill and Buster because they tolerated Lee's stupidity more than John ever would. His mind raced over these matters again and again, always intermingled with thoughts of the Japanese girl. Her image – naked, beautiful, and terrified in front of two hundred wild men – would haunt him for the rest of his life.

Passing the small cafe in Portage where he ate lunch Thursday, he encountered not a person or moving car. He reached the Madison bypass and headed towards Milwaukee. Twenty miles east of Madison, he stopped at a wayside to urinate. No cars were parked there, and few passed on the highway. He turned off his headlights and stepped outside into the mild night. Exhausted, he longed for sleep.

John hated what had happened with Lee. When he first met Lee, years ago, he liked him. But twice now, John experienced Lee's drunken ugliness. Lee might be an unavoidable customer, but he wasn't a necessary friend. Besides, Anita never liked Lee. *She was right about him from the start*, John realized.

He smoked half a cigarette. The image of the Japanese girl returned again and again, and, alternately, it conjured a vision of sweet, illicit temptation or an insight that moved him to an ineffable pity. A car passed at high speed. John gazed at the brilliant, starry sky that he first beheld as a boy at Uncle Henry's, then got into his car and headed home.

He remembered how Juley, Uncle Henry, and he lingered on the pier at Basses Bay those long-ago summer nights, just loving the stars. Uncle Henry told of the old days: of his father in the Civil War, of his dear mother, of snowbound winters and golden summers, and how he loved and lost his darling Caroline, the only girl he ever wished to wed. At eighteen, she died of smallpox. She was Henry's one, true sweetheart. He told the boys, "One beautiful day I'll be with her in Heaven." Johnny Helden figured her death was why Uncle Henry took a little sipping whiskey now and again.

Then, out of John's deep memory, he heard Uncle Henry call, "Boys, say hello to these fine gentlemen."

John and Juley echoed, "Hello."

"These are my sister Augusta's boys. They're staying with me this summer. The little fella wants to be a doctor when he grows up . . . right Juley?"

"Yes, Uncle Henry."

"Don't know what the other wants to be. Johnny, do you know what you wanna be when you grow up?"

"Nope – I ain't got no special calling like Juley."

One of Henry's acquaintances asked, "What do you like?"

"Well, I sure do enjoy fishin'. . . ."

The men laughed.

"Show 'em what you got," Henry said.

They opened the burlap sacks. Each lifted out a large Northern pike held with a cord stringer through the gill and mouth.

One of the men remarked, "Those are beautiful fish   where'd you catch 'em?"

"Little Muskego," Henry lied, not wanting to disclose the abundant source in Basses Bay.

The interurban approached the station at Tess Corners. When it stopped, Uncle Henry said, "Boys, walk over and show the folks on the train. They'll get a kick outta that."

Two men dressed in fishing outfits stepped down from the center car. They eyed Johnny, and one asked, "Son, would you consider selling those fish?"

Johnny looked at Uncle Henry who nodded.

"Sure, mister," Johnny answered.

"How much do you want?"

Henry moved closer and asked, "How much you willing to pay?"

"A silver dollar for each . . . ."

Again Henry nodded.

"Sold, mister," Johnny said.

The man picked the coins from his leather purse and handed them to Juley who beamed. Johnny put both fish back in the burlap, but Henry removed the cord stringers. He'd use them again. Johnny handed one sack to the man who said nothing and the second to the man who had done the negotiating. "Thank you kindly, son," he said.

The conductor called, "'board . . . ," The men climbed on.

As the train rumbled away, Uncle Henry said, "Boys that's a fine day's work. How'd you like some supper?" He hankered for a cold beer.

In the quiet tavern, Henry and his nephews ate like starved boys. Over and over, they discussed the great successes of the day. As the afternoon waned, Uncle Henry ordered a little whisky. After a sip or two, he began telling again of his darling Caroline.

John wiped away his tears. *Grandpa Rosenberg died that day,* he remembered.

After three, he turned into his driveway and parked in front of the garage. He entered the house quietly, not wanting to startle Anita. In Michael's room, he stroked his son's forehead, bent down, and kissed him.

Michael whispered, "Night, Dad."

John peaked into Johnny's room, but he was too asleep to whisper anything.

In the bathroom mirror John Helden discovered the face of a worn, exhausted old man. In the bedroom, Anita slept peacefully, but John hoped she'd wake. As he undressed, she did.

"John?"

He sat on her bed, placing his hand on her hip. Anita turned on her back. He kissed her lips in the dim, borrowed light. He longed to embrace her.

"How come you're home?"

"It was cold in the cabin . . . a lot of drinking . . . I just didn't want to be there anymore."

"I'm glad, but do you mind if I sleep? I'm very tired."

"No, you sleep. I'm tired too. We'll talk in the morning."

She turned on her side, falling asleep in minutes. John washed, poured witch hazel into his hand, and patted his scratched, stinging face. Because his toothbrush was in the *Chrysler's* trunk, he rubbed tooth powder on his teeth. He rinsed his mouth, but the tobacco taste lingered. He put on clean pajamas and crawled into bed. It was almost four. On his back, exhausted and barely aware of Anita's slow, steady breathing, the stunning image of the Japanese girl overpowered his cluttered mind. Her lips bore the same mysterious smile when John first beheld her. *Gotta get her outta my head . . . .*

He tossed side to side, his mind wild with impressions. *I don't want to think this stuff . . . just let me sleep, please . . . .* He prayed the *Our Father;* then, *Hail Mary, full of grace, the Lord is with thee . . . .* Finally, he felt himself drifting, floating away, floating on the lake, slowly drifting off, remembering the freezing water, the air crushingly cold, drifting off, but warm in bed now, and slipping, just slipping away into a cavern of deep unconsciousness. There men were jostling him. Through the dispersing crowd, he spotted Buster, Russell and Bill.

John heard Lee shout, "The party's over."

Russell, his voice echoing and quiet, said, "You won, John. You won the drawing."

John struggled to understand. "Oh my God, no . . . ."

"You're one lucky son-of-a-bitch," Lee said. "Come on, we'll take you to Sugar Kane. You gotta prove you're the right guy."

"No, no, fellas, I couldn't have won. I was gone. I left."

Russell said, "Doesn't matter. Come on, Sugar's waiting."

Lee introduced him to Sugar Kane. "He's staying in Fern Villa and his initials are JH."

"Let me see your driver's license."

John fumbled with his wallet.

"Well, I guess you are Mister FVJH – congratulations." He grabbed John's tie, pulling him towards himself. "You owe Sugar big time . . . remember that Helden. Here's the key: top floor, honeymoon suite. She's waiting."

"No, no, I can't do this. I'm a married man. I can't do it . . . ."

"Shut up," Sugar said. "It ain't your decision. She's a spoil of war, nothing more. You won her fair and square. We won the war fair and square. She's a trifle for your pleasure . . . now get the hell over there."

"No, no, please, Russell, Bill, please. You know my wife," John sobbed, "our wives are friends. I can't betray her."

"Sure you can," Buster said. "Tonight the little Nip is your very own real live doll."

Buster, Bill, and Russell hustled John into the lodge. Men there began to chant, "Spoil of war, spoil of war, spoil of war . . . ."

The crowd let John's little entourage pass to the staircase. He sobbed all the way up. At the suite, John's friends waited until he unlocked the door and entered. Then they left.

In the room's soft light, the Japanese girl stood beside a curtained window. She wore a red robe; her long, black hair still adorned with a yellow rose. The honeymoon bed had been turned down. Somewhere, John heard the trio still playing *Rose, Rose, I Love You*, slowly and hauntingly. His mind struggled to discover. *Where are they?*

"Good evening, sir."

Her greeting startled him. "I shouldn't be here . . . ."

Taken aback, she asked, "And why not?"

"I'm married. I have a wife and sons . . . ."

"Oh, I understand. If you do not wish to make love to me, I will make love to you."

"No, I'm a Christian. I don't want to betray my wife. I don't want to commit adultery."

"I don't understand what you mean." She turned, gazing at the black lake.

The same lake I trudged through, but how, when? Confusion overwhelmed John's mind.

She faced him again. "But, sir, what of your deepest desires?"

"I want to go home to my wife. I don't want to betray her. I want you to go home. I don't want us to be here. I felt so sorry for you standing in front of all those wild men."

The girl laughed. "Oh you should not . . . they didn't harm me by looking. If they had lust in their hearts then they harmed only themselves."

"I won't hurt you. I wouldn't hurt you in any way. When I first saw you, I felt so sad."

"I know; you are a kind man. I can tell that. A cruel man would have already forced himself onto me, but you are a good man. To you I give myself freely."

"No, please, I don't want you to give yourself. You must understand. I'm a married man with sons. I love my family. I don't want to betray them."

"And I, too, do not want you to betray them. Stay with your wife forever. But you did say you wouldn't hurt me in any way. I must tell you, it will hurt me deeply if you do not allow me to give myself to you. Do you not understand that I need to be comforted, that I need to be caressed and kissed by a man who I know is a good man? My mother and I suffered terribly during the war. My father and brothers were killed. They were good men. Now we are alone. We are poor and have so little hope. May I not at least escape my sad life for a moment of sweet tenderness with you? May I not possess a few hours of joy to obtain at least one, happy memory for my uncertain future? This night let us give to one another the pleasure of our love. Too soon will the morning come, and the sweet songbirds sing. You may leave me then without so much as a single farewell. Your wife, your sons will never know. No one will ever know what happens between us this night, no one except you and me and the God of infinite mercy."

Against this gentle persuasion, John felt himself weakening.

Sensing it, the girl untied her robe, letting it slide from her delicate shoulders and fall to her ankles where it gathered in a crescent. She stood naked in front of him with the same inscrutable smile on her porcelain face.

He felt his entire being – body, heart, mind, and soul – overwhelmed by desire. He wanted her more than his honor, more than his own sacred vow, even more than the enduring love of his wife. The girl approached him and began unbuttoning his shirt. Aroused, he stood motionless. She placed her white arms around his neck, tugging gently, but he refused to bow to kiss her covetous lips. He was paralyzed by desire, incapable of protest. She placed her hand against his chest, moving it slowly and lightly in a downward arc.

"Who are you?" John asked.

"I am *Butterfly* . . . your *Butterfly*."

He heard music, hauntingly familiar, but from where? Melodies first and once encountered far away and years ago. Now a phantom violin serenaded sweetly above the rising sighs of an orchestra that he sensed could only exist in his exhausted mind. Then Butterfly sang with impassioned tenderness,

"Love me with a little love,

A child-like love,

The kind that suits me.

Love me, please . . . ."

Naked on the bed, they embraced until he raised himself above, letting his eyes gaze upon the beauty of her small, perfect body. Smiling, she spread her legs. Entering her, he experienced the intense pleasure of his powerful release.

He woke instantly, semen cooling rapidly on his leg. *My God, forty-six and still having wet dreams . . . .*

The pleasure of the dream amazed him, not merely the physical, but the emotional and mental pleasure, as well. It was as though he truly knew her and would see her again and possess her again and again. Now, in the darkest depths of his heart, he hungered for that.

On his back in the blackness, John lay motionless. He felt the deepest weariness. He had no idea how long he had slept. He glanced at the alarm clock: five thirty. *Maybe*, he thought, *I'll be able to get her outta my mind now.* But he could not.

He took off the soiled pajama bottom, wiped his leg, then

dropped the pants next to his bed on the side away from Anita. He wondered about the girl and wondered about himself, his courage, his character, his will.

Should I have done something? Should Russell, Bill, and I have done something? Could we? Could I? He tried to think of Anita, but Butter-fly and the sweet illicitness of the dream overwhelmed all. Finally, falling back to sleep, his last terrible thought was an unanswerable and unbearable question: *What has this night been for her?*

Chapter 24 ~ 1948 [Part 4]

The first thing John told his secretary, Lorraine, Monday morning was to hold his calls, and if Lee Marnet called to tell him she hadn't heard from John, didn't know where he was, and didn't know when he'd be in. He closed his office door, sat at his desk and pondered, just as he had while driving over, what Lee had said about Peter Jr. forcing John to take Lee's old equipment in trade. He was reaching for the phone when Russell walked in.

"You look a hellava lot better than Saturday night," Russell said.

"I feel better . . . had a couple good nights' sleep. How'd it go? What happened Sunday?"

"Lee didn't show up for breakfast, but Bill was there and Buster. He was pretty hung over. They were surprised you left."

"Did you see Lee?"

"We had lunch, but he was in bad shape. He wondered where you were. Claimed he didn't remember much about Saturday night . . . said he was gonna leave right after lunch. That's when I left."

John chuckled. "I guarantee Lee didn't leave when he wanted to. I gave him two flat tires."

Russell laughed hard. "Good for you."

"I gotta call my cousin now . . . find out if he told Lee he'd force me to take those tanks. That's really bothering me. "

"John, Sunday after breakfast, I met a hauler, a young vet from Little Chute. We got talking . . . said he owned only one tank, but there was plenty business around Green Bay. He just doesn't have the equipment to go after it. I asked if he'd consider buying used. He would if it could pass inspection and wasn't too beat up. If we end up having to take Lee's tanks, I think this chap might buy."

"That's really good, Russell. If I'm forced into it, I'll have my brother George check 'em. He's a hellava mechanic. Maybe we can fix 'em up for a couple hundred bucks and sell 'em for a little profit."

"That's what I was thinking," Russell said.

That conversation, however, didn't alter what John intended to tell his cousin. After Russell left, John called Peter Jr. who wasn't available. He returned the call after lunch.

"John, it's Peter. How are you? How was the convention?"

"Hello Peter, I'm okay . . . the convention? That depends . . . Lee Marnet was there."

"I should hope so. He invited you, didn't he?"

"Yes, he did, but he told me something I didn't like. He wants to trade in twenty old tanks on the thirty new ones."

"So what?" Peter asked.

"*So what?* I don't take worn out equipment in trade – that's what."

"Well, you're gonna have to. You don't take 'em, there's no deal. Of course you're gonna take 'em."

"Peter, you know damn well there's no market for used equipment. I can't have money tied up in Lee's old junk. I'd sit with those tanks forever."

"Look, John, cut the bullshit. You don't take 'em, we'll find someone who will, and we'll give him the distributorship."

"Peter, what the hell are you saying? I've sold a lot of tanks since your dad gave me the distributorship. Why threaten me? We're first cousins for heaven's sake."

John sat through a long pause.

Finally, Peter said, "Let me tell you something, John, and you remember this and remember it well."

John sensed Peter's anger.

"As far as our business is concerned, my father and I have no family. We have no relatives, blood or otherwise, understand? Don't ever bring that crap up again. My father and I abhor nepotism. You were given the distributorship because we thought you knew how to sell our equipment, not because you're his damn nephew, and certainly not because you're my cousin. We thought you'd cooperate, play ball, put the good of the Company ahead of your own selfish interests. Just remember, you'll never be shown any favors because you're a blood relative – never! This is business, understand? You either do what we tell you, or we take the distributorship away. It's that fucking simple. What the hell do you think . . . that you tell us what to do? If you're gonna act stupid and force us to take Lee's old tanks, then you lost the distributorship and don't ever come crawling back here looking for a job. Understand?"

The outburst stunned John. Never had Peter talked so brutally to him. John could not respond. Later, after reflecting on it, he realized he should have recalled that John's father was a co-founder and Works Manager until his death. It was he who devised most of the successful shop practices that made the company prosperous. John should have reminded Peter that John's two brothers, Clarence and George, labored for the company for years, since their tender boyhoods, and still labored there. He should have mentioned Uncle Joe who produced engineering drawings for over forty years, but died a broken man. More than anything, he should have reminded his cousin that through the years everyone in the family contributed to Uncle Peter's success precisely because they were blood relatives, because they were family. And finally, he should have reminded Peter Jr. that, as childhood playmates, they loved each other like brothers. But John didn't say any of it. He was too intimidated, too discouraged, too hurt.

"So what's it gonna be?" Peter asked.

"Did you tell Lee you'd make me take 'em if I balked?"

"I don't remember what was all said – maybe I did – so what? I mean, we gotta do this deal together, John. Thirty tanks is a damn big order, and we gotta do what it takes to make sure we don't lose it. You're smart; you understand that. Look, John, we want you as our distributor. You just gotta understand business is tough sometimes, conditions change. The government's gonna let haulers write off their equipment over a much shorter period of time. Haulers are gonna be replacing equipment a lot faster than they used to. In the future, you're gonna have to take used equipment in trade . . . plan on it. Run ads in trade magazines. Seek out smaller haulers. Sell to other distributors who might have a ready customer. We don't give a damn what you do, just don't rock the boat. Now, will you take them – yes or no?"

John muttered, "Yeah, I'll take 'em."

He stared out the window at the row of yellowing elms that bordered the warehouse across the street. His thoughts slid to the abstract, not ideas really, not concepts that could be articulated. John's feelings and thoughts commingled, plunging him into a problematic, more uncertain state where doubt danced freely among long-held principles, precepts, and notions that he had always believed to be true. He drifted towards a dreamlike subconscious from which the dream is never exactly remembered because something essential within it has been irretrievably lost.

He barely heard his cousin say, "Good, John, good work. Let's keep in touch . . . ."

John hung up the phone, and, as he did, became acutely aware of the movement of his hand and wrist. He observed his fine hands almost as though they were detached. He rotated them while studying the creased and scrapped palms and prominent blood vessels bulging on their backs. *I should play more,* he wished, thinking of his beloved music and Anita's Steinway.

The deal was this: Marnet Trucking would take delivery of five new stainless steel, milk transport tanks every two months for a year. With each new tank, Marnet would trade in one of their old tanks until all twenty had been transferred. For the last ten deliveries there'd be no trade-ins. John and Lee negotiated a trade-in allowance of four hundred dollars per tank, regardless of size or condition. The selling price John wrangled netted three hundred and fifty dollars profit per tank. That meant he had to pay fifty bucks out of his own pocket to the Helden Company every time Lee took delivery of a new tank. Surprisingly, not once in their lengthy telephone conversation did John or Lee mention what happened at the hauler's convention.

John Helden wouldn't see a dollar's worth of profit until the last four months, after he had shelled out a thousand bucks. The old tanks would be delivered to the big, gravel yard at the rear of John's office where the driver, most often Frankie, lowered the landing gear and disconnected the tank from the tractor. Frankie gave John the title for the old and a check for the new, less the trade-in amount. John's signed receipt enabled Frankie to drive to the Helden plant to hitch a new tank that he'd deliver to Lee in Delavan. Lee waited anxiously to inspect the long, gleaming, horizontal, five thousand gallon thermos on wheels. He saw it for what it really was: a moneymaker.

After Frankie arrived with the second old tank, parking it alongside the one he had delivered two weeks earlier, John and Russell went out to talk with him.

"Hello, Mr. Helden, Mr. Lynch," Frankie said, pleasantly. He, too, never mentioned what happened at the convention. Away from Lee, Frankie's politeness surprised John who still felt a lingering animosity towards Frankie. John knew Lee was a bad influence and regretted that Frankie didn't have the character and brains to escape it, or so he thought. "Mr. Helden, may I ask what you're planning to do with these old tanks?"

"We're gonna fix 'em up and sell 'em."

"Me and Hubie are thinking about going into business, but please don't tell Lee. He'd be madder than hell. I hear small haulers do okay. We meet a lot of 'em at truck stops. We were kinda thinkin' about buying one of these."

"Where would you get the money?" Russell asked.

John cut in. "We shouldn't pry into Frankie's financial affairs. If you get the money, Frankie, of course we'll sell you a tank. We're gonna recondition them almost like new . . . put 'em back in sanitary and safe running condition. We'll make 'em so pretty you won't believe it. Call Russell in about a month. You can take a look then. If you still want one, we'll sell it to you. But it's gotta be a cash deal or a cashier's check – okay?"

"Okay . . . I appreciate it, Mr. Helden. Mr. Lynch, I'll call you."

They shook hands with Frankie. Five weeks later with a cashier's check, he bought the first reconditioned, two thousand gallon milk tank. John and Russell could hardly believe it. John made over three hundred dollars after he paid Russell his commission. Then, six weeks later, Frankie and Hubie bought a three thousand gallon tank. Again, John could hardly believe it because he made over six hundred bucks.

Several Saturdays prior, John's brother, George, had assessed the work to recondition the first tank: inspect interior stainless for pits and cracks; new manhole dust cover and gasket; check manhole ladder; new outlet valve dust cover; a few new running lights and brake lights; some new hoses and fittings for the air brakes; pound out dents in running boards and rear bumper; check and grease landing gear; check brakes; wash entire stainless outer jacket with a muriatic acid solution; repaint running boards and rear bumper; wash wheels and tires.

George needed three Saturdays to complete the work, not including the acid wash and repainting. For that, John contracted with an industrial paint shop that had a tractor to haul the tank both ways. For ensuing tanks, if tires had to be replaced, the selling price increased accordingly. John found he could repair a tank for about five hundred bucks making his total investment about nine hundred. The good news was he sold the second tank for fifteen hundred because that's how much the banker said he'd lend Frankie and Hubie to buy it.

John envisioned none of this when Lee first told him he wanted to buy thirty new tanks. Never did John imagine he'd have to accept used equipment to make a sale. Regrettably, during October and November, John's only sales were to Frankie and Hubie. Lee had already taken delivery of four new tanks leaving two old ones standing idly in John's yard.

Lorraine, Russell's base salary, and the office rent had to be paid, plus John needed money for his family. Michael and Johnny wanted a television set. Some of their neighbors already had sets, and John wanted one too. Nevertheless, he was fortunate: Anita's inheritance from her father enabled them to avoid a mortgage. They had plenty equity in their home, but John didn't intend to borrow against it though he was reaching a point of desperation. He couldn't run his business without working capital, and he couldn't pay all the household bills. Finally, John asked his banker if he'd lend him money against the used tanks he took in trade.

"Absolutely not!" Of course, the banker had no problem putting a mortgage on the Helden home, urging, "Borrow ten thousand . . . you'll need money in reserve."

John had to sell Anita on the idea. When she understood John's financial plight, when she saw the worry in his eyes, when she reflected on how hard he had always worked for her and the boys, and how good he had always been to her mother, it proved an easy decision. John even told Anita about his horrible telephone conversation with Peter Jr., which shocked her. She said, "Peter Jr. has one interest in life – money. That's pathetic."

Several days after he signed the mortgage, his brother Clarence called. "Johnny, how'd you do on the Marnet deal?"

"Lousy. What have you heard?"

"What do you mean lousy?"

"Peter Jr. forced me to take twenty old tanks in trade. My profit is tied up in old equipment that's gonna have to be fixed up. Even then it'll be a tough sell, and it's gonna take time."

"You should've done a hellava lot better than that. Junior's been strutting around here like a peacock. I bought the stainless and carbon at damn good prices. We're making money on Marnet. Our accountant told me we'd make at least three thousand on each tank, ninety thousand pure profit. So, how come you couldn't get more?"

"Peter gave me a unit price. That was it. I asked him to take a hundred off, but he said it was impossible, said his costs were too high. And Marnet wouldn't pay any more, kept threatening to buy from *Kold Karry*. It was a classic squeeze."

"That's bullshit – he could've taken off two hundred. I'm telling you, Johnny, first cousin or not, Peter is one greedy son-of-a-bitch. Boy, do I see that now. Uncle Peter was never like that – his interest was building quality – making money came second. But now, more and more, Junior's running this place, and he's obsessed with money. It's unbelievable."

"What do you suggest?"

"You have to negotiate tougher. You're gonna have to threaten if he doesn't get his price down. Tell him you'll lose the deal, but also that you don't give a damn if you do. He'd just as soon see you make nothing. Johnny, you gotta be tough in business . . . clever. I know your true nature. You're my little brother; you're like Ma, too sensitive. You should've been a concert pianist like she wanted."

"Oh, Clarence, that dream is long gone. I'm in a tight spot, but I'll get out of it."

"Remember, Johnny, be tough with Peter Jr."

John left his office amid the waning, golden daylight of an October afternoon rich with falling leaves and mild, smoky air. He loved the remembrance of summer and the inevitableness of winter that autumn always conjured. *Strange*, he thought, *how the dying of the year can be so appealing.*

The six weeks after the Haulers' Convention were the most difficult in John's career. The problems, though, helped cure his infatuation with the Japanese girl, but forged an inattentive, disinterested husband. At home, Anita sometimes felt he was little more than an indifferent roomer.

Devastated by the realization he was thrown into a financial hole by a first cousin and the company he had devoted his life to, John appraised and questioned his thirty-two years of loyal, hard work. Peter Jr., the same age and worth more than half a million dollars, forced John to scrimp and scramble while knowing the company would make a tremendous profit. John told Russell, "I had to make dollar concessions to get the deal done, but I also had to endure Lee's crap and my cousin's betrayal." John wished Clarence hadn't even mentioned the Company's huge profit, which John found demoralizing. A strange melancholy came over him, a sadness he couldn't dispel.

The last Saturday of October, over the protestations of Michael and Johnny, John Helden drove to his office, as he was inclined to do every Saturday now because of the bleak feelings emanating from his financial situation. He refused to share those feelings with Anita. She couldn't dissuade him of weekend work though he could persuade her there was always something urgent. She resented it, but resigned herself to having him around only on Sundays. John's Saturday absence, however, disappointed his sons who were crazy about their dad and loved it when he touted an adventure.

At his office, John wrote several letters for Lorraine to type on Monday. He gazed out the window at his car on the empty street. There really was no pressing work, and John knew it. He never called customers on Saturday. He could write a few more solicitations, but they could wait until Monday. Finally, he decided to take his family to dinner and a movie. He hadn't done that for months. Driving towards Greenfield Avenue he had another idea. *I'll bring Anita flowers.* He'd stop at *Carolyn's* for roses, though he hadn't been there for years.

He parked a few blocks east because so many cars and trucks lined the curb. He crossed LaPointe Avenue barely noticing the elderly woman sweeping the front porch of the white, clapboard-sided house just beyond a small, triangular patch of grass. It was Mrs. Walker's house where Hildegard Neubauer once lived.

Suddenly, John stopped at the realization of something radically altered. The Rabachs' little shop, indeed the whole building, had vanished. As John approached, workers were painting yellow parking stripes on new, asphalt pavement where *Carolyn's* once stood.

He asked, "What happened to the flower shop that was here?" The question drew confused looks.

The foreman moved towards John. "What are you talkin' about?"

"There was a flower shop here, on this parking lot. What happened to it?"

"Mister, I don't have the faintest idea. I don't live around here."

"Oh, sorry . . . ."

John went into the pharmacy where he had often shopped. He spotted a white-coated clerk whom he didn't recognize. "Sir, excuse me; what happened to the flower shop that used to be next door?"

"I didn't know there was a flower shop next door."

"It was very nice. I used to buy flowers there for my wife."

"I've only worked here a year," the pharmacist said. "When I was hired, it was just an empty lot. Someone once mentioned a dilapidated building that the owner tore down. No one ever said anything about a flower shop. My boss put the parking lot in for our customers. Maybe he knows what happened."

"It's pointless, I suppose, for me to ask if you knew the two ladies who worked there."

"No, I didn't."

"Could I use your phone book?"

The pharmacist pointed at the telephone booth at the end of the soda fountain counter. John searched the white and yellow pages for *Carolyn's Flower Shop,* but didn't find it. Then he thought, *maybe Hildy took over the business when it moved.* He looked for *Hildy's* or *Hildegard's,* but that wasn't listed either. He thanked the pharmacist and left the store.

Where'd they go, John wondered. And again.

As he headed towards his car, a young man approached, handing John a *Vote for Truman* flyer.

"Oh, sorry, we're for Dewey." John returned the pamphlet.

"Too bad – Truman's the better man." The campaigner turned to hand flyers to the men painting the parking lot.

John chuckled. *Truman's gonna get trounced.* His brother-in-law, Lew Thilman, had been predicting it for months.

He drove west towards Wauwatosa. He'd stop at *Locker's* for Anita's roses, but Carolyn and Hildy stuck in his mind. *They were nice women, and Hildy said she knew Juley . . . I never mentioned that to him. When did I see them last? We moved in early '43 . . . must've been January or February of '43. No, that's not right. Wait . . . I got roses for Mary Louise when Lew lost in '42. Hildy was wearing a wedding ring . . . that was the last time . . . man, six years already.*

After he left the florist, he crossed North Avenue to Hayward's for a couple packs of cigarettes. Leaving the drugstore, someone behind him shouted, "Helden!"

John turned. He didn't recognize the man approaching. "You're John Helden, right . . . the engineer?"

"Yes, and you are?" John couldn't place the face.

"You don't remember me, do you?"

"Well, I can't seem to recall . . . ."

"I knew your brother, Julius."

"Did he introduce us?"

"Yeah, years ago . . . ."

"I'm sorry, I just don't-"

Annoyed, the man cut him off. "I'm Dr. Anthony Messert." He turned and walked away, slurring under his breath, "What a dimwit . . . ."

PART 3 ~ 1957 to 1976

Chapter 25 ~ 1957

In February, 1950, Peter Helden Sr. slipped and fell on icy steps at the front stoop of his home, struck his head on the brick edge, and lost consciousness. He suffered a skull fracture with severe concussion and lay in a coma for days. In the hospital, flat on his back, he contracted pneumonia. He never regained consciousness. Two weeks later he was dead at age seventy-four.

When John Helden Jr. learned of his uncle's death he wept, though Anita felt no such sadness. John and his brother, Dr. Julius Helden, were asked by the funeral director to serve as pallbearers. John's brother, George, was not asked. Clarence Helden had died in 1949.

On a bright winter morning, Peter Helden Sr.'s two youngest nephews, along with four other men, shoved his finely-crafted casket into a sepulcher in a sprawling mausoleum that resembled the brick and stone mansions along Lake Drive. His widow, Lisa, son Peter Jr., daughter-in-law, Harriet, and their only child, nicknamed Pete, observed in silence. All were stoic except twenty-two year old Pete who occasionally wiped his teary eyes.

Anita Helden, part of the crowd surrounding the entombment, studied Peter Jr. and Harriet's faces. Anita wondered why all those years they had never associated with John and her, although now she was well past caring. Peter Jr. noticed Anita and how good she still looked. She was forty-seven and strikingly beautiful in a mature way that intelligent men appreciate. Harriet had not fared as well. Her nose and high cheeks bore the badge of chronic rosacea, which

Anita blamed on alcohol. Indeed, Harriet enjoyed a *Manhattan* or two before dinner and a good *Burgundy* with her meal. Her husband knew she had a drinking problem, but he simply didn't care. His mother was a drinker, but he didn't give a damn about that either.

Harriet had grown plump, nearing a state of unattractive heaviness. It mattered very little to her husband, for their marriage had slipped into an arrangement of mutual indifference. Harriet lunched daily with friends and played lots of *Bridge*. Peter Jr.'s principal interest was making money, indeed, more than his wife could ever hope to spend. But Peter Jr. had another interest, well beyond the limits of house and yard: a slender, thirty-four year old, full-breasted, dark haired woman who lived in an apartment midway between his house and the Helden office. He lavished her with cash to pay the rent, utilities, groceries, and a clothing *allowance* because he refused to let that be an open-ended deal. It was bad enough it was open-ended for Harriet. He bought his special friend enough jewelry to restrict her sexual favors to him alone. In fact, Peter Jr. warned her, "I'll drop you in a heartbeat" if she ever two-timed him. Only once did she get pregnant, and then he paid for the little procedure. He brought her home from the doctor's office, made tea, scrambled eggs and toast, staying until she fell asleep after eating. Her gynecologist was well-known on the east side as a paragon of confidentiality. Though many women knew of this man, rarely was his name – *Messert* – mentioned above a whisper, but if a woman needed his services, never was his phone number withheld.

John Helden's mind, as he stood solemnly aside after fulfilling his pall bearing duties, dwelt on the deaths of family members, people dear to him: his brother Clarence, Uncle Frank in 1944, Uncle George in Chicago in '39, his father in '38, Uncle Henry in '32, his mother in '27, and then all the way back to 1910 when Grandpa Henry died. And now Peter Sr. was gone. Only Uncle Joe remained, and he refused to attend his brother's funeral because he had cast himself into a mold of unyielding bitterness for not sharing, though he was a founder, in the tremendous financial success of the company.

The funeral luncheon was at Peter Jr.'s private, downtown club, which was so crowded that John and Anita barely said "hello" to Peter and Harriet let alone having a few moments for small talk.

For the past year, Peter Jr. ran the company with minimal interference from his aging father. He literally hand-picked all key management and production people. Long tenured board members, associates of his father, were slowly being replaced by Peter Jr.'s younger, wealthy friends. The resultant company bore little resemblance to the familial business that John Sr., Uncle Joe, Clarence, George and John Jr. loved back in the first two decades of the century.

The estate of Peter Helden Sr. was reported in the newspapers at over eight million dollars, a sum that stunned John and Anita. Each of the seven living nieces and nephews received a mere thousand bucks, paltry indeed in comparison to the size of the estate. John was disappointed but Anita said, "I'm not the least bit surprised."

+ + +

In July, 1952, a sweltering Chicago hosted the Republican national convention amid a steamy sense that in November the GOP would finally end twenty years of Democratic rule. Senator Robert Taft of Ohio, son of the twenty-seventh president and a strong isolationist, was the odds-on-favorite, but a cadre of more outward-looking easterners was determined to gain the nomination for General Dwight D. Eisenhower. So highly regarded was Eisenhower that even the Democrats sought him as their candidate. After a raucous credentials fight, Eisenhower, the former World War II Supreme Commander, was nominated on the first ballot.

Initially, John Helden had no favorite, but when the convention ended he pronounced to his family, "We like Ike." John first voted Republican in 1940 because he didn't approve of President Roosevelt ignoring Washington's precedent not to seek a third term. The persuasiveness of his brother-in-law, Lew Thilman, convinced him to vote Republican again in '44 and '48. As the years went by, John grew increasingly conservative.

Eisenhower's campaign against the Democrat, Adlai Stevenson, was a crusade not so much against the studious, liberal, Illinois Governor as against President Truman's policies regarding Korea, communism, and the incumbent vice of corruption. Eisenhower promised he'd travel to Korea to end the war. He'd maintain a strong NATO abroad to oppose communism and a frugal, corruption-free administration at home. In November, Ike and his five-o-clock shadowed running mate, Richard Nixon of California, won in a landslide.

That same November, Wisconsin reelected Senator Joe McCarthy who had made a name for himself as a strident anti-communist and who, as one unimpressed editorialist wrote, *saw a communist under every rock and behind every tree.* John Helden had met McCarthy three years earlier, before McCarthy burst onto national prominence with a speech claiming the State Department was riddled with communists.

McCarthy's Irish heritage endeared him to the family of Joseph Kennedy of Massachusetts. Mr. Kennedy served as Ambassador to England during the Second World War. His son, John F. Kennedy, who served in the House and then the Senate, called McCarthy, "a great American patriot." John's younger brother, Robert, chose McCarthy as godfather for his first child, Kathleen, born July 4, 1951. That was remarkable given Robert's closeness to older brother, Jack. In 1953, Robert served as legal counsel on McCarthy's Senate Subcommittee on Investigations. Many people across the nation cheered McCarthy's return to the Senate.

Giving credibility to McCarthy's claim of communists in the government was the infamous espionage case of Julius and Ethel Rosenberg. They had been members of the Young Communist League and the American Communist Party from 1936 until 1943 when they left the Party to concentrate on Julius's espionage activities. On March 29, 1951, they were convicted of passing nuclear secrets of the United States to the Soviet vice consul in New York City. They were sentenced to death and executed on June 19, 1953. The sentencing judge held them responsible not only for espionage, but also for the deaths of American soldiers in the Korean War. He believed the information given the Soviets helped them develop the atomic bomb, which emboldened their North Korean surrogates to attack south across the Thirty-eighth parallel. When the Soviet Union tested their first hydrogen bomb in August, 1953, many Americans attributed that horrific development to the Rosenberg's treason. The government's star witness testifying against Julius and Ethel was David Greenglass, a machinist at Los Alamos who worked on the development of the first atomic bomb. David was Ethel's younger brother.

Twenty-five days after Eisenhower's election on November 4, 1952, Ike flew secretly to Korea where he revived the stalled peace talks. As a result of that clandestine mission an armistice was signed in July, 1953. Ike also had a personal interest in ending the war: his only living child, John, was serving as an army officer in Korea. After three years of intense fighting, American casualties exceeded 165,000 including more than 54,000 killed in action. Eisenhower, like all good military men, wanted the war over, if not by total victory then by imperfect truce.

+ + +

Shortly before the opening of the 1953 baseball season, the Boston Braves relocated to Milwaukee. The joy John Helden and his sons felt at getting a major league team was comparable to everyone else's in Milwaukee. Anita, however, had little interest in sports. When John decided to buy season tickets, he bought only three, but certainly not to exclude Anita. John wanted to attend every game, whereas Michael or Johnny frequently decided to do something else, especially if it involved girls. As a result, Anita went often. She enjoyed the fresh air, chatting with other women, and that attending ball games had become fashionable.

The Braves played good ball that season, finishing second to the great Brooklyn Dodgers. For John Helden, baseball provided a tremendous emotional and psychological lift. And while that remained the family's favorite topic into the early fall, John and Anita rejoiced when the Korean War ended. They feared for their sons, so close in age now to the military draft.

In late August during a week with no home games, John Helden took eighteen year old Michael to California where he had enrolled at a small, Jesuit college. It was their first trip to Los Angeles. For two days, John enjoyed seeing a slice of the sprawling city. By the time John got back to Milwaukee, his son, Johnny, had started his junior year in high school.

Things had gone well for John ever since he learned in 1948 that used equipment could make him money. The economy kept growing. For every tank he took in trade he found an enthusiastic buyer. His income peaked in 1951 at over fifty thousand dollars, but wartime taxes were still the law. In effect, John had worked six months for the federal government, another reason he voted for Eisenhower.

George Helden was one of two keys to John's success. He refurbished twenty tanks on weekends from the fall of 1948 until mid-1949, and though John paid him well, it took a toll on George's marriage. By the summer of '49, George's wife, Irene, decided she didn't want George working Saturdays and certainly not Sundays. Nevertheless, John couldn't afford to lose George because refurbished tanks could be sold profitably. Selling was the second key.

To placate Irene, John decided to hire George full time, away from the Helden Co. He promised that George would not have to work weekends. John found a vacant shop in West Allis big enough for a single tank, a brake, a shear, other equipment, and yet small enough to afford the rent. He was confident he could keep George busy forty hours a week. John also knew it would be pleasant, as they grew older, working together in the trust and friendship of brothers.

George, with unusual enthusiasm, presented the idea to Irene. She was skeptical; even though John agreed to match George's wage, Irene questioned if John could match the Helden Co.'s pension.

George Helden was a skilled mechanic, worth far more than the company ever paid him. As a union man he earned a union wage, though he possessed more experience and knowledge than most of his union brothers. Not all shop men were created equal though the union treated them that way. George and several others were exceptional. Most were average, while some were lazy and unambitious. George solved difficult fabrication problems, but his cousin, Peter Jr., never made him a foreman though he should have. Dedicated shop men like George were the ones who made money for the company. They knew how to build complex weldments efficiently; a process that involved cutting, bending, drilling, machining, welding, riveting, and bolting until the finished product was ready to ship.

When Peter Jr. learned John wanted to hire George, he decided not to let him go. Peter Jr. offered to sweeten George's pension. He also expressed doubt if John could remain in the repair business long enough for George to retire. As much as Irene liked her brother-in-law, she didn't want George forgoing the security and comfort a growing pension provided.

John asked George to inspect the building he intended to rent. He wanted his approval and suggestions on the layout. Ever enthusiastic, John gave George a grand tour of the small shop, while chattering about their future together. He sensed, however, his brother's distraction.

"George . . . what is it?"

"I... I... I can't do it, Johnny."

"Why not?"

"I can't give up my pension. I just can't. Irene's worried sick."

"I thought you said Peter would honor it."

"I thought he would, but he called me in, and said he won't. He doesn't want me leaving."

"I understand not wanting to lose you, but you paid that money in – it's yours."

"Company paid in, too."

"I know, but that was in the union contract. George, that money is yours whether you stay or leave."

"Peter said it's the company's decision"

"Oh, bull shit, George. He just doesn't want you working with me. That son-of-a-bitch doesn't give a damn about you or me."

"Johnny, if I stay he's gonna kick in an extra fifty bucks every month. Irene said I can't pass that up unless you could match it."

"I don't have fifty for my own pension let alone yours," John said.

John understood Irene's concerns. He bore no ill feelings towards either of them though he felt an incessant bitterness towards his cousin. He wondered why Peter Jr. always seemed more hindrance than help even though John sold so much equipment for the company since getting the distributorship. Uncle Peter showed more appreciation, but he wasn't as active anymore. Wisely, George never mentioned what Peter Jr. had said about John's probable inability to make the repair shop a success. That really would have angered John. George knew for years that Peter Jr. didn't like his brother, though he never understood why.

Now John had a big problem, and he knew it. He still had to

take used equipment in trade. The thought of hiring someone with half his brother's skill and experience was depressing, but likely. He had to rent a shop; that was necessary if he was going to get tanks repaired in a reasonable time and manner. And eventually he'd have to hire two men: a skilled mechanic and a helper. John had been George's helper many Saturdays in '48 and early '49.

Several weeks later, Peter Jr. told John that if he still wanted to get into the tank repair business, Helden had a proposition. The company repaired petroleum transport tanks, but wanted to get out of it, as they just weren't set up for sporadic repair work. Peter Jr. was willing to send that business to John, but he wanted the right man as John's partner.

Peter said, "We have to have assurance the repairs are done right." He suggested Ray Butler, a foreman who had been in charge of petroleum tank repairs for several years. "Ray knows how to repair both petroleum and milk a hellava lot better than your brother, plus he's a hellava lot smarter."

John ignored the insult. "Let me think about it."

That same evening John called George and asked about Butler.

"He's a foreman in charge of repairing petroleum . . . if and when one comes in. Those repairs, Johnny, aren't a big part of Helden's business."

"Does he know his stuff?"

"Ya, but like most foremen he thinks he's smarter than he is. He can be bossy as hell."

"Why is Peter Jr. willing to let him go?"

"Butler doesn't get along with Higgins, the works manager. I think Higgins wants him out."

"Why?"

"He expects foremen to do things his way, but Butler doesn't always do it. He's a real pain in Higgins's ass."

"Can he repair milk?"

"Oh, sure, Johnny, he builds milk."

"Do you think he'd be okay running a shop?"

George paused. "Make it clear, right from the start, you're the boss. Can he do the work? Ya, he can. But if you get real busy, he'll want more men."

What finally made the decision for John was not a gut feeling because his gut wasn't sure, never having met Ray. But then John got an order for seven new milk tanks from a big hauler in Eau Claire, with four used ones taken in trade. When John placed that order with the company, Peter Jr. told him he had two petroleum tanks to be repaired; if John and Ray could get *their* business up and running, he'd send those tanks John's way. Whatever concerns John had, he was hungry enough for all that business to make a decision in favor of Butler.

In their first meeting, John found Ray congenial and enthusiastic. A big, burly man, fairly nice looking with a thick neck and powerful arms and hands, he obviously had worked hard all his life. Any prejudice John might have held was dispelled. Both men came away with a sense they could work together. They agreed to a fifty-fifty partnership, splitting the monthly rental of a shop, the purchase of equipment, and any and all other capital expenditures. John had his brother-in-law, Lew Thilman, draw up a corporate agreement that Ray's attorney reviewed. They did not discuss Ray's salary, nor did Ray disclose that, as his first official act, he intended to hire his twenty-three year old son as his assistant. The important thing in John's mind was that, right from the start, he and Ray seemed to get along pretty well.

In West Allis they found a vacant, high-bay, industrial building with an overhead crane, perfect for their purposes. They formed a second partnership, separate from the repair business, went to John's bank, arranged a twenty year mortgage, and bought the property. Each man contributed five thousand dollars towards the down payment. After the closing, John Helden told Anita, "Things are looking pretty good." In a few weeks he knew that shop would be filled with four tanks plus two more waiting in the yard. Repaired and sold, John figured those tanks would make him a fine profit.

First, though, the shop had to be outfitted. Most of the heavy equipment was used; smaller equipment was bought new. After everything had been purchased, John was low on cash; he assumed Ray was too.

Ray set things up with the help of his son, Rob, a high school graduate who drove a truck for a living. Rob was a good-looking, athletic guy who Ray imagined good enough to play major league baseball. When Rob failed to impress in the tryouts, Ray told his son not to worry, he could always work with him.

John agreed to a thousand dollar monthly salary for Ray. George Helden's pay would have been less. When Ray told John he intended hiring his son because he needed a helper, John understood, but when Ray proposed a salary of five hundred a month, John balked. He pointed out that newly hired graduate engineers at the Helden Co. were paid only three, seventy-five. John would match that.

Ray replied, "hell no – my kid's getting five hundred."

Just as adamantly, John said, "No, he's not."

The next morning when John called the shop there was no answer, no answer in the late morning, none in the early afternoon. John headed out to the shop, but Ray wasn't there. Back at his office, he eventually reached Ray at home. "Why the hell aren't you at work?"

"I ain't coming in until you agree to pay Robbie what he's worth."

"He's a truck driver; he isn't worth five hundred."

"Don't insult my kid."

"That's not an insult. I'm just not paying him more than a graduate engineer."

"Well, you're unreasonable. How the hell do you expect him to support a wife and kid?"

"I didn't know he had a wife."

"Well, he's gonna have one. We gotta pay him a decent wage, for chrissake. We're gonna make you a lot of money, and you're nickel and dimeing me right off the g--damn bat."

"Four hundred," John said; "not a penny more."

Ray paused. He sensed John's resolve and agreed. Rob was thrilled to get it.

The first repaired milk transport tank that rolled out of Helden Tank Service, Inc.'s shop looked terrific, and John congratulated Ray and Rob for it. But when John analyzed the costs, he was horrified. Ray's labor was three times the average of the twenty tanks George had repaired. John suspected Ray padded the hours. He confronted him, but Ray just shrugged, saying, "actually, we really had to hustle to get done as fast as we did."

Ray had John right where he wanted. Ray could charge as many hours as he damn well pleased. It sickened John, knowing he couldn't control his costs and that his potential profit on every used tank would plummet. Essentially, his sales company earned all the money to pay Ray and Rob's salaries plus the mortgage; by the time other overhead was paid, John's share of the profits was depressingly small. Convinced he was overcharged on the first four tanks, John blamed his cousin, Peter Helden Jr., for putting him in an untenable situation by cajoling him to partner with Ray Butler. Gone forever were the sweet profits he had enjoyed when George did the repairs. After only three months, John knew he'd have to buy Ray out.

He called his brother, Julius, who asked, "Have you settled on a price, and did he offer to buy you out for the same?"

"We haven't talked price yet, but, yeah, he said he'd be willing to buy me out."

"Why don't you let him?"

"Because then he'd really have his way with me."

"Can't you negotiate the cost of a repair upfront?"

"He claims there's no way of knowing what they'll find once they start tearing a tank apart and, therefore, no way of estimating hours."

"Johnny, you're a distributor, pick up more manufacturers. Forget about taking used tanks in trade. Let Peter Jr. worry about that."

"Helden doesn't want me selling other people's equipment."

"They can't control what you do, Johnny. Think about it."

John did, but still decided to buy Ray out. He felt he had no choice because to sell new tanks, he had to take used ones in trade. That was the reality now. He didn't want to sell for other manufacturers; he had plenty of business with the Helden Co. Nevertheless, he'd have to manage his finances carefully and deny his family things they wanted.

After four arduous years, John called Anita and his sons together to explain his decision. He had painstakingly saved sixteen thousand dollars in government bonds, for that was the price he and Ray agreed to. Anita knew it was the right decision. With Ray running the shop, she observed how her husband's enthusiasm, his love for the piano, books, and baseball, his ability to laugh easily, and enjoy life had slowly drained away. And gone, too, was his sense of romance.

When the deal was finalized, the most important issue John faced was hiring an experienced shop man, a first-rate welder. He also had to hire a helper and, eventually, another welder. Robbie taught Michael how to drive the stick-shift pickup and tractor. He showed how to hitch to the fifth wheel and connect the airbrakes for moving tanks in and out of the shop. Then Michael taught Johnny.

In the summer of 1955, Michael worked in the office, while Johnny labored in the shop where he salvaged scrap metal, swept floors, cleaned the bathroom, and did some simple mechanical tasks. He also hand-delivered checks, some as large as twenty-five thousand, to young Pete at Helden for new tanks John had bought and resold. At twenty-seven, Pete had been appointed *Sales Manager*. When John heard about it, he told Anita, "Oh, great – good to see they still abhor nepotism."

Buying out Ray Butler proved a good decision. John hired two qualified men and tracked their time meticulously. He monitored all expenditures. He achieved enough cost reductions to increase his profit on every tank. He didn't do as well as when George did the repairs, but it was significantly better than when Ray and Robbie had their hands in his pocket. Now he was running both his sales company and the repair shop, challenging but heady days for John Helden. He worked more hours a week than he knew he should, and more than his family wanted, but he was setting things straight. Eventually, he hoped the outcome would lead to great prosperity.

+ + +

In late August, 1955, Michael headed back to Los Angeles on the Santa Fe *Super Chief,* while John and Anita drove Johnny to Notre Dame, the only university he applied to. John took the same honeymoon roads he and Anita traveled in 1932: south on US 41 through the tangle of Chicago, through Gary with its spewing, sprawling steel mills and refineries, and then straight east on US 20 into South Bend, Indiana.

Driving into Notre Dame's campus along a tree-lined avenue, John pointed out the stadium to the right. "It was brand new when we stopped here in '32." Straight ahead they saw the Golden Dome with the statue of Our Lady high on top. Johnny, in the back seat, felt anxious and nervous. After he and his father carried all his stuff up to his room in Cavanaugh Hall, he went down with his parents to say goodbye. John wanted to get back to Milwaukee.

"Johnny, write us, okay," Anita said. "Let us know how you're doing."

"I will."

"If you have any major problem, call us collect," John added.

"Okay, I will . . . thanks Dad."

John approached his younger son to kiss him goodbye, but for the first time in Johnny's life he backed away, embarrassed with so many guys walking past. Johnny hugged and kissed his mother. Then his father extended his hand, and Johnny shook it. He liked that.

John backed out the long, gravel road past the old Field House and Navy Drill Hall. He turned the big Chrysler around, spotting his son in the rear view mirror, still waving. Then he turned the corner, out of Johnny's sight.

"How do you feel about leaving him?" John asked.

"Mixed . . . ."

"Yeah, me too. You know, we haven't lived without a son in the house for twenty years. Think you can handle it?"

"What choice do I have?"

Nearing Chicago, Anita suggested stopping at the Drake Hotel where they spent their wedding night. "We need a good dinner and a good night's sleep. It'll bring back memories. It's been a long day. You must be tired."

"No, I wanna get home." John intended to be at the shop early next morning. His businesses consumed his thoughts. It was unfortunate. Anita, fifty-three years old and still a very beautiful woman, felt romantic.

Should I tell him, she wondered, but then decided, *no* . . . .

Chapter 26 ~ 1957 (Continued)

At Notre Dame, Johnny Helden felt homesick only the first night. His two roommates were great. He met other terrific guys and found the dining hall food better than expected, though that opinion changed soon enough. In splendid, late summer weather, he swam in St. Joseph's Lake, hiked the spacious, tree-filled campus, and attended all the orientation sessions on college life. In Washington Hall he enjoyed the 1940 film, *Knute Rockne All American,* which featured a young actor, Ronald Reagan, playing George Gipp – the *Gipper.*

West of Notre Dame across the Dixie Highway, St. Mary's College for women nestled beside a sharp bend in the St. Joseph River. The evening before classes commenced, the freshman girls from St. Mary's visited Notre Dame for a get-acquainted dance. There Johnny met Gilliane.

+ + +

In Los Angeles, Michael contracted infectious mononucleosis. His upper abdomen hurt when he touched or twisted it, and he felt so fatigued he could hardly attend classes let alone swing a golf club. He had made the team his freshman year, played well as a sophomore, and now looked forward to a great junior year. Unfortunately, the doctor ordered him home, as the contagious *mono* took several months to run its course. Deeply disappointed, Michael took the train back to Milwaukee. John and Anita Helden regretted their son's illness, but loved having him home again.

John Helden never heard of the disease so he took Michael to see his uncle. Dr. Julius checked Michael's vitals then probed his abdomen. Michael winced at the tenderness below his rib cages.

"Your liver and spleen," Julius said. "Classic symptoms . . . how'd it start?"

"I thought I had the flu. That went away, but I still felt tired. I went back to the infirmary. They did a blood test after the doctor did what you just did. Uncle Julius, how soon can I go back?

"It's a viral infection. Regrettably, Michael, I can't do much for you. It could be a couple months before you feel better, but you have to rest. I'm afraid you'll miss the whole semester."

"Then I'm off my course sequences; I'll miss the whole year."

John cut in. "That's all right. When you're better you can work for me."

As much as Michael loved his father, working for him during the cold winter months was no substitute for being in college in sunny Los Angeles. He wanted to play competitive golf, be with his buddies, and graduate there.

"You'll be a hundred percent by spring," Julius said. "Go back next September. In the meantime, once you start feeling better, work for your dad and play golf."

With undisguised enthusiasm, John Helden, agreed.

It wasn't what Michael wanted, but after several weeks he relented. It pleased his father. Things were going much better for John ever since his repair business regained profitability. He even began investing money in the stock market. At home he resumed playing the piano much to Anita's and his recuperating son's delight.

+ + +

After several months at Notre Dame, Johnny Helden was in terrific physical condition. He worked out with weights two or three times a week, hiked to St. Mary's on Friday or Saturday evening to date Gilliane, and on glorious, autumn Sundays they strolled the picturesque path between the two campuses.

Johnny had fallen hard for her, but in November, after the weather turned wet and gray, he felt troubled by a realization that overtook his infatuation. Gilliane gave every indication that she liked him just as much as he liked her. They even exchanged love letters. But Johnny, in spite of his intense feelings, began wondering, *how is this going to end?* She made it clear she wasn't interested in marriage. Johnny made it clear that he was, and he wanted children.

She shook her head. "No, no, Johnny Helden, motherhood's not for me."

Still they continued to see each other and made out as often as possible. But afterwards, walking back to campus and approaching the Grotto, he had to ask himself, *what's the point?*

Sundays when it rained they visited in the parlor at St. Mary's. Sometimes they joined a group; more often they sat alone. In December, Gilliane planned to go home to Quebec for Christmas vacation. She wasn't, however, looking forward to the long train ride.

"Come home with me," Johnny said. "It's only four hours."

"Oh, really . . . and have you talked to your parents about that?"

"I just got the idea."

"Well, I suspect your mother wouldn't be too pleased to see a little French girl in tow."

"My brother would."

Gilliane laughed; she liked Johnny's sense of humor. He recognized in her face a resemblance to the French actress, Leslie Caron. Gilliane possessed a cute, sexy figure. Johnny knew that Michael, for sure, would enjoy having her around for a while.

"No, it would send a bad signal."

"We're just good friends."

"Oh, darling, you know you want us to be lovers. You say it in so many words in all your letters. We kiss like lovers."

"You know I don't mean now – in four years – if things work out."

"I've told you, Johnny, I don't want babies."

"At twenty-two you might change your mind."

"Maybe you'll change yours."

"I don't think so. That's something I want in life."

"But I don't. Were I ever to get pregnant, I'd-" She stopped herself.

"What?"

"Nothing, nothing at all . . . I just don't want to get pregnant or be pregnant."

"You weren't going to say you'd kill yourself."

Gilliane laughed again. "Oh, good heavens no, what a terrible thing to suggest."

"I wasn't serious . . . ."

"You have to understand, Johnny, when I say something, I am serious. I mean what I say, and you should believe me. If you want to have babies, find some silly American girl and stop seeing me, stop calling, stop writing. I will not have your babies."

"Do you want to stop seeing me?"

"It doesn't matter what I want. You're the man; you'll decide what happens."

Johnny was quiet, thinking, wondering, but for his own sake he had to ask. "Were you going to say you'd have an abortion?"

Her eyes flashed with anger. "How do you know such things? Yes, I was. Now do you understand why I won't marry you? Even though, perhaps, I love you . . . even though I might want you as my lover. But no, Johnny, that will never happen – never!"

Three days before Christmas, Johnny Helden went home alone.

+ + +

By the middle of January, Michael felt well enough to start working for his father. It proved such a boost for John Helden that he almost felt giddy. He released the part-time secretary he had employed since moving his sales office to the shop. Michael picked up her work without missing a beat. In his spare time, he read the *Wall Street Journal,* not merely for financial news, but for book reviews, editorials, guest commentaries, and letters from readers. He clipped articles he thought significant, placing them on his dad's desk. John liked that because it gave them even more to talk about.

For Michael, though, working with his father proved more tranquil than satisfying. He rekindled friendships with high school buddies who now attended Marquette University. They all looked forward to playing golf in the spring. At the urging of his uncle, Lew Thilman, Michael began investing a little money in common stocks. He dated occasionally, but always, in the back of his mind, he longed to return to Los Angeles even though his friends kept pressing him to transfer to Marquette.

+ + +

In February, John and Anita drove to Notre Dame to visit Johnny and meet Gilliane. They had dinner at the Morris Inn, the campus hotel where the Heldens stayed. After the pleasant evening had ended, Anita told her son, "She isn't right for you at all. You should marry an American girl. She's too short, too dumpy. After two babies she'll weigh two hundred pounds. She's not right for you and certainly not right for your father and me."

John Helden scolded, "Anita, they're only eighteen; don't jump to conclusions."

"I'm nineteen," Johnny corrected. His birthday was in January.

Sunday morning after Mass at Sacred Heart Church, Johnny said goodbye to his parents. Anita made a few more comments about Gilliane's unsuitability, but John, sensing it really bothered his son, told her, "Forget it!"

Anita insisted on the last word. "No, you know I'm right."

As soon as they left, Johnny called Gilliane. She agreed to see him.

He hiked towards St. Mary's in the warm, bright February sunlight that shimmered across a crystal surface of snow. Rivulets of snowmelt trickled down the sloping, gravel road that ran between scattered islands of slick, brown grass. On the lakes, the silver ice had thinned, ready to disappear in the balmy winds of several more mild days.

In the clean, sweet air, Johnny recognized the problems. His mother was right, but not for the reasons she so tactlessly stated, but for something that would horrify her in the same way it had shattered the tender sensibilities of her son. She presumed, as any mother would, that this girl might want to marry her son, and she presumed Johnny foolish enough to ask. She presumed, as any mother would, that Gilliane wanted babies just like she knew her son did. And worst of all, she presumed Johnny might let himself be seduced.

But, wisely or foolishly, young love maintains a curious independence from parental influence. Johnny's incessant, deepest longings yearned for someone impossible to attain: a beautiful, young woman who would never be his wife or his lover though she had become his greatest love. He regarded himself too young though he didn't think Gilliane too young. He was ill-prepared for marriage though he realized she could marry at any time. Johnny couldn't imagine how to support a wife and children. She, however, was ready, indeed, eager to be a mistress or a wife. And he sensed, acutely, that one day Gilliane who claimed, sometimes passionately, that she loved him, would abruptly leave forever.

+ + +

When April finally came, Michael got out his golf clubs, cleaned his cleats, and hit the driving range; he practiced putting in the living room. John Helden never minded his son taking a couple afternoons off because Michael always got the work done. After two weeks of intense practice, Michael drove alone to *Whitnall Park* in Hales Corners and played eighteen holes. He paired with an older, retired man who marveled at how straight and far Michael hit the ball, marveled at his short game, and putting. Michael shot a true 71; his playing partner shot 94 with a few Mulligans along the way. The man complimented Michael, telling him what a pleasure to play with such a fine, young golfer. That first round of the season elated Michael. His second round would be with golfing buddies from Marquette, guys still urging him to transfer there.

+ + +

Easter Sunday, 1956, fell on April 1. Classes at Notre Dame ended the day before Holy Thursday. Johnny planned to take the train to Chicago, a cab to Union Station to catch the *Hiawatha* to Milwaukee, then home by ten. He saw Gilliane the Sunday before; she recalled an invitation he once made, but did not honor.

"Will you take me with you? You invited me at Christmas."

His mother, he knew, would never extend that invitation.

"What's wrong darling, cat got your tongue?"

"I'm sorry . . . I can't . . . ."

"Why not?" Gilliane knew the answer.

"I would have had to ask earlier so my mother could have prepared."

"Johnny, your mother doesn't like me. Of course, she wouldn't invite me."

"No, she liked you."

"Shame on you . . . don't lie. I don't care that she didn't. Your father did."

"Yes, he thought you were charming."

"And what did your mother say?"

Johnny would never reveal his mother's nasty comments or how wrong her thinking was. He knew Gilliane wouldn't be a suitable wife not because she'd get big and fat after having babies, but precisely the opposite: she wouldn't have babies at all. In spite of that, Johnny found it impossible to end their romance.

"Don't go home for Easter," Gilliane said. "Take me to Chicago." They leaned against an old oak, kissing passionately. She whispered, "Darling, I want you to be my lover."

Shocked at her boldness and the realization she would give herself without being married, he said nothing. And he was scared, for he was still a virgin.

Before she went into her dorm, she said, "Call me tomorrow." She climbed half the steps, but then turned and came down. She whispered, "Tell me, darling, would you rather spend ten days with your mother or ten nights with me?" She turned and ran up the stairs.

+ + +

Far from the isolation of Notre Dame and St. Mary's, and the scrutiny of the press, the United States government conducted the first airborne explosion of a hydrogen bomb in the spring of 1956 at the Bikini Atoll in the Pacific Ocean. This display of awesome power did not, however, prevent the Soviet Union from doing whatever it wanted behind the Iron Curtain.

In June, the Soviets crushed labor riots in Poznan, Poland, with a large loss of innocent life. In October, the Hungarians revolted against the pro-Soviet, puppet government. In response, the Red Army invaded. By the time the fighting ended, thousands of Hungarians had been killed, many more wounded, and a quarter million had fled their homeland. President Eisenhower chose not to intervene.

The American people, many of whom were of Polish and Hungarian heritage, understood the profound injustice of Eastern Europeans denied their God-given right to liberty. They also understood that intervention could lead to nuclear war. The grave moral question was this: could the loss of one hundred million lives in the United States and Soviet Union be justified to liberate the Hungarian people? Indeed, would there be any liberty of any value to any nation after a nuclear war? Obviously, Eisenhower didn't think so. He knew conventional warfare as well as any living man, but he also foresaw the unlimited horror of a nuclear war. He wanted no part of it.

Other ways to deal with the Soviets had to be found, even while many Americans worried that communism would eventually spread over the globe like heavy oil on a ball. Containing that pernicious spread would challenge every succeeding American administration. That Eisenhower and his State Department hadn't figured it out by 1959 was glaringly apparent in Fidel Castro's takeover of Cuba, which resulted in a communist state allied to the Soviet Union only ninety miles off the coast of South Florida.

Michael Helden, three weeks shy of his twenty-second birthday, cast his first vote in the 1956 national election for Dwight D. Eisenhower. His father and mother did the same. At Notre Dame nineteen year-old Johnny Helden briefly noted Eisenhower's reelection, as he never imagined Stevenson had a chance. Eisenhower won fifty-seven percent of the popular vote and forty-one of the forty-eight states. It was an incredible victory for the incumbent president, but the Democrats retained slender margins in both the House and Senate. The American people, enduring the *Cold War* peace and enjoying widespread prosperity, were comfortable with the status quo.

+ + +

After Johnny returned from Easter vacation, Gilliane refused to date him. Half-heartedly, he told himself to forget her. Instead, he kept pestering her. Slowly, his persuasiveness began to change her mind, simply because he remained what he had always been for her: just a wonderful guy to talk to and be with. By mid-May she agreed to see him.

She came down the steps of Holy Cross Hall and extended her hand. "Friends shake hands, you know . . . ."

"What about a friend you love?"

"Love? You said you loved me, but when I gave you the chance to prove it, you went home to your mother. I don't think I can ever forgive you for that."

Johnny thought about what his father taught him when his body began to change and what the Jesuits had taught in high school. He thought of his Faith and what he believed to be most sacred and true. It really seemed simple for him: fornication was a serious sin, an offense against God. Christ had taught that.

He replied, "Chicago would've been wrong."

"Wrong? When is love between a man and a woman wrong?"

"When they're not married."

She snapped, "I don't believe that."

"But I do."

They agreed to see each other once more after final exams, before they both went home for the summer. Gilliane was distant, while Johnny acted as though nothing happened. From his point of view nothing had, but from her perspective something profoundly significant both had and had not occurred.

Gilliane regarded Johnny if not a boy then certainly not yet a man, completely dismissing him as a lover though she was ready for one. She yearned for the deepest human intimacy without the risk of pregnancy. She had read. She knew what to do. Gilliane desired a man who would make passionate love to her without the slightest concern for any moral paradigm because she didn't possess such concern. But she didn't want just any man, and that was her dilemma. Johnny, sweet, smart, and so much fun, touched her heart. Gilliane wanted him.

She agreed to one last date only because she thought it would be amusing before going home to Quebec. In spite of her casual indifference, the scented air, lingering twilight, and a rising moon enchanted her just as it did Johnny. When he reached for Gilliane's hand, she let him take it. They strolled towards Notre Dame. Then in the long, secret shadows, he turned to kiss her. At first, she resisted, but Johnny pressed against her, and she responded. They kissed passionately, while his hand found her breast. He whispered, "I love you."

She pushed him away. "How dare you say that? Don't ever tell me that again. If you loved me you would have taken me to Chicago. You don't love me; you don't know what it means to love a woman. You have silly, childish feelings that mean nothing to me – nothing." She turned and ran towards St. Mary's.

Johnny easily caught her.

"Let me go," she pleaded.

But he held her against his hard body, gazing at her beautiful face in the bright darkness of the moonlight. "I'm sorry I can't be what you want."

Her forehead fell against his chest. Tears glistened her eyes. "I am, too."

He kissed her lips tenderly. "Goodbye, Gilliane."

He let her go, turned, and walked away. It wasn't at all what she expected. She called after him, but he never looked back. She watched him disappear, while her heart swelled with sadness. That he behaved as he did made a disturbing, ill-defined impression upon her.

In the middle of August, after waiting weeks for a reply to his June letter, Johnny received a letter from Gilliane. She wrote that she had a very interesting summer and hoped he had too. She enclosed a small black and white photograph of herself against a backdrop of ornate, nineteenth century buildings that Johnny assumed was a street in old Quebec. In the photo she held a small overnight case. On the back she had written, *This was a very pleasant weekend*. He got the message.

Saddened as much as hurt, he realized how desperately Gilliane needed to end their romance, even to the point of cruelty. He wished she had simply written, *Johnny, it's over. I never want to see you again.*

He consoled himself with the realization they would never marry. He wanted a family, she did not. Thinking logically, Johnny could accept her decision, but emotionally the thought of him ending the romance proved difficult.

After returning to Notre Dame, he had no idea if Gilliane even came back to St. Mary's. He never called to find out. Then a friend told him he had seen her in South Bend with a group of girls. Johnny shrugged. "So she's here," he said. "So what?"

For several days he tried not to think of her, but the memories of a nearby, beautiful girl can wear a young guy down. In early October, he abandoned his stolid resolve. He called St. Mary's and got her floor telephone number.

"Why didn't you call me sooner," she demanded.

Johnny couldn't believe it. "You made it extremely clear it was over."

"A woman has many moods; I wrote that letter, Johnny, in a

very bad mood. You have to learn to understand a woman. We don't always mean what we say."

"You once told me you always mean what you say. What am I supposed to believe?"

Gilliane laughed. "Ask me out . . . ."

The next Saturday evening he hiked to St. Mary's and waited in the parlor till she came, just as he had almost every weekend his freshman year. He was thrilled to see her, for she looked even more beautiful than he remembered. She greeted him warmly, tenderly squeezing his arm as she took it.

"Darling," she said, "I'm so happy to see you. I've missed you terribly."

Their romance began again almost as though the four month interlude never occurred. Johnny had no idea how to reconcile his intense feelings for Gilliane with what he knew of their hopeless future. Nevertheless, he loved being with her, loved kissing, and caressing her. He put the marriage dilemma out of his mind. Weeks went by. At Thanksgiving, Gilliane went to a classmate's home in Cleveland, never teasing Johnny for an invitation she knew would never come.

In January, after returning from Christmas break, Johnny detected a change in Gilliane, but said nothing because, if anything, she became even more amorous. As the semester finals approached, they agreed not to see each other until exams were over. When they met again, they felt the exhilaration of having their tests behind them. In Gilliane's mind it was the perfect moment for something else, something she had thought about for a long while.

"I want to say this very carefully," she began, "because it has nothing to do with how I feel about you. I've tried to show you how I feel."

He peered into her eyes.

"Johnny, I'm not a good future for you, and you are not the future I want for myself. I've decided to leave St. Mary's."

He was stunned. Gilliane obviously decided this during a period Johnny thought was the apex of their romance. But, in spite of her feelings, she remained resolute and clear-minded. She would never have him for her husband. She would never bear his children, and she certainly did not want his mother as her mother-in-law.

She knew it was the correct decision, and, as much as she cared for Johnny, he had no choice but to accept. If he reacted badly, all the more reason for her to leave.

"Where are you going?"

"A college in Massachusetts, closer to Quebec; I'll write when I'm settled." Johnny started to say something, but she touched his lips. "Please, no questions, just accept . . . ."

After that night, he never saw Gilliane again. He received a letter postmarked New York City. She told him she loved him very much, that she regretted it had to end the way it did, and that she'd never forget him though it would be better if he forgot her. She did not give a return address, but ended the letter, *Farewell dear Johnny Helden. You were the boy I loved the most.* The word *boy* seared his memory.

+ + +

In May, 1957, Senator Joseph McCarthy died in Bethesda Naval Hospital. He drank heavily after the Senate censured him for his ruthless conduct in accusing persons of being communists or their sympathizers. His friend, Senator John Kennedy of Massachusetts who was recovering from back surgery, missed the roll call in the Senate chamber. Kennedy indicated, however, he would have voted to condemn his Irish-American compatriot. Sixty-seven senators exiled Wisconsin's junior senator to isolation, irrelevance, and historical infamy. At age forty-nine, McCarthy died of acute hepatitis having ignored his doctor's advice to quit drinking. Obviously, McCarthy didn't care to live.

"He was a happy-go-lucky guy when I met him in '49," John Helden told Michael after the news of McCarthy's death. "That was before he started accusing everyone of being a communist."

"Well, if there really are commies in our government, they'll sleep better tonight."

"Good point," his father said.

+ + +

On Friday, October 4, 1957, the Soviets launched the first earth orbiting satellite: a one hundred, eighty pound, basketball-sized *Sputnik I*. Before long, television commentators warned, "The United States is losing the space race."

That evening, Johnny Helden took the train back to Milwaukee for the third game of the World Series against the Yankees on Saturday. On that beautiful October afternoon, the Yankees clobbered the Braves 12 to 3. Mickey Mantel hit a towering home run whose majestic arc thrilled Johnny. Tony Kubek, the Yankee left fielder and a twenty-year old Milwaukee native, hit two more.

Sunday noon, Johnny headed back to South Bend, while his parents and Michael, now attending Marquette, headed for Game Four.

The following Thursday, the Braves beat the Yankees in New York to win the seventh game, setting off the biggest celebration in Milwaukee since the end of World War II. John Helden was overjoyed. Only four years after leaving Boston, the Braves had won the World Series.

Eyeing John's good mood, Anita enlisted him to work around the house on Saturday when the happy triumph would still linger in his heart and mind. She wanted to start in the basement, but he refused because the bright, fall day was too beautiful to work indoors. So he raked leaves first, piled them in the barren petunia bed, then started cleaning the garage.

"What's this old bureau," Anita asked.

"That was Uncle Henry's . . . ."

Anita wobbled it. "It's been here ever since we moved in." With effort, she pulled out the top drawer stuffed with papers, as was the second.

"I saved that when we cleaned out Uncle Henry's place on Basses Bay in '32. His Bible and a few other books were in there."

"That's twenty-five years, John. Get rid of it. And that wood . . . you've kept that ever since we moved in. You'll never build anything."

"That's good birch trim."

"Burn it," Anita ordered. "The boys haven't used their bikes in years; I'll give them to the *St. Vincent de Paul*. Can you get rid of those old tires?"

"Sure, at the shop."

So John dragged everything out of the garage, spread sweeping compound, grabbed the big push broom, and went to work. Satisfied, Anita went inside to make sandwiches.

After lunch, John began to put things back.

"Not the wood or that bureau," Anita insisted.

He crisscrossed the wood on top of the leaf pile, sensing the breeze would die later in the day. He'd burn it then. In the house he watched the fourth quarter of the Notre Dame-Army game. Notre Dame's last minute, game-winning field goal thrilled him, as he knew it did Johnny.

Outside again, the late afternoon sun streaked the high cirrus clouds in reddish amber. Burning leaves scented the air, as the temperature dropped. *Good for sleeping,* John thought.

When Uncle Henry died, John and George went through his papers and found the deed for the property on Basses Bay. Nothing else seemed important, as John never had reason to open the bureau again. Now he removed all the papers and letters, placing them on the grass in the windless air. He put the drawers on top of the burn pile. In a minute the leaves flamed, and the wood popped. The drawers burned easily for being old, dry pine.

Kneeling on the grass, John went through Henry's papers. Many were faded and illegible. He had no idea what they were, so he crumbled them into the fire. A more substantial, brown envelope contained his grandfather's honorable discharge dated June 8, 1865, and signed at Lincoln General Hospital, Washington, D.C., by a Surgeon of the Army whose faint signature John could not discern. He went into the house, gave it to Anita, telling her she'd find it interesting and to save it. John carried the remaining papers into the garage. Under the light of two ceiling bulbs he spread everything on his car hood. Sheets that seemed of no importance John tore and tossed onto the fire. Using a steel rake, he pulled the burning pile into a tight circle. Then he placed the chest on top; within minutes the fire raged.

Back in the garage he went through the old letters. A packet tied with ribbon was addressed to his uncle in a woman's decorative hand. *Love letters,* John suspected, *from Uncle Henry's beloved Caroline.* He opened one, but it was badly faded. He held it towards the ceiling bulb; light passed through the ink almost as easily as the thin paper. *I should respect their privacy,* he decided. He retied the packet and set it aside. Then he spotted an envelope addressed by a masculine hand. It was to John's mother, *Augusta Rosenberg, Tess Corners. Before she married Pa,* he presumed. He examined the front of the envelope and noticed – what he could see of it – a partial post-mark date of *364*. It puzzled him until he realized, *1864. My God, that must be Grandpa Henry's handwriting as a young man.* He withdrew the letter to his grandmother and unfolded it. Even in the bright garage the fancy handwriting was faint and faded, illegible save for a scattering of words and half words. He could make little sense of it, so he refolded and slipped it back inside the fragile envelope. He examined other letters, but it was all the same: the faded ink barely readable.

He gathered everything, went back to the burn pile and knelt beside it. In his left hand he held envelopes, while his right dealt them like playing cards into the flames. They burned brightly orange. Finally, through his hands passed the once longed-for letter from a soldier-husband in the Civil War that Veronica Watry had lovingly placed in Augusta Rosenberg's anxious hand that Christmas evening, ninety-three years ago.

John watched as the fire consumed the clump of letters. All the tender words of lovers and loved ones, all their hopes and dreams, all the expressions of fidelity, separation, and longing, all the poetic and prosaic words transformed into mere smoke, vapor, and ash, lost forever from the eyes, minds, and hearts of those whose blood flowed after. The fire burned down to a smoldering.

"John," Anita called, "supper's ready."

Chapter 27 ~ 1962

After forsaking his desire to graduate from the small Jesuit college in Los Angeles, Michael Helden went straight *A* his last semester at Marquette, earning his degree in Finance in June of '58. He intended to leave for California within weeks, but his father persuaded him to stay a few more months to build a bigger stake just in case he couldn't find a decent job out there. That made sense to Michael, but, as so often happens, a few months stretched to six, then nine, and, finally, a year. He still worked for his father when Johnny graduated from Notre Dame.

Johnny's academic finish wasn't nearly as auspicious. He had majored in the *Great Books Program* that Dr. Mortimer Adler introduced at the University of Chicago after World War II and then installed at Notre Dame. Driving home with his parents, Johnny felt ill-prepared for a career in business or anything else. Most of his classmates sought advanced degrees in Philosophy, English, or Law. Johnny's latent interest pointed elsewhere.

John Helden invited Johnny to work for him until he decided on a career. In less than a month, though, he grew bored. The brothers realized there wasn't enough work for two. When Johnny expressed interest in actually learning how to repair milk transport tanks, his father adamantly refused. So Johnny quit, leaving Michael right where he didn't want to be.

By August, Johnny decided to enroll at Marquette to study engineering, which is what he originally intended at Notre Dame. His father dissuaded him then, arguing, "You don't want to spend your life slaving over a drafting board." That convinced Johnny at eighteen, but not at twenty-two. Now he wanted to know how men designed bridges and skyscrapers. When constructers erected the great steel framework for Milwaukee's baseball stadium, he asked, "Who figures all that stuff out?" His father answered, "That's what engineers do."

John Helden didn't object when Johnny quit, in fact, he

welcomed it, hoping Michael might stay for another year or two. Michael, though, longed to return to California. Not a day passed that he didn't dream of heading west on Route 66.

Johnny entered Marquette's Engineering College in September of '59, while Michael continued working for their father. On weekends, the three watched the Green Bay Packers on television. Anita thought it one of the family's happiest times. Only Michael felt discontent; he hid it from his father, rarely hinted to his mother, but often confided in his brother.

"Somehow I've got to convince Dad to let me go. I can't go on like this."

"He wants you to stay right where you are."

"He knows I wanna get back to L.A."

"Maybe, but the longer you stick around, the harder it's gonna be to break away."

Michael slumped in his chair. "I know."

"Maybe you should just pack up and leave. I'll help until he hires someone."

"It might come to that."

Months passed, but the status quo held. Michael longed for a life in Los Angeles. He had friends there, loved the climate, and recognized the opportunities. Nevertheless, living at home was pleasant and cheap; he paid no room and board at his father's insistence. His job was easy, giving him time to read, study the stock market, and discuss investments with his uncle Lew who had become a broker after the demise of his political life.

Michael played golf from May into October and dated occasionally though he told his brother he intended someday to marry a Southern California beauty. Plus he saved money. His stake had grown by smart investing and frugality so that on his twenty-sixth birthday, Michael had six thousand dollars, while Johnny, twenty-four, had barely a tenth of that. Michael's life was, in fact, comfortable and easy, only lacking the one thing he craved most: a life in Los Angeles.

Johnny studied year round, delivered mail at Christmas, attended summer school, and worked part-time for his father as a *gofer*, relieving Michael of some of the chasing around. He met great guys at Marquette: Dick Straub had transferred from Michigan

State; Jim Kasdorf enrolled in engineering after he earned a degree in Business Administration.

Johnny hoped to graduate in two years, but only "if the course sequences work out," his advisor cautioned. He studied during the week, but went out Friday and Saturday evenings. He realized, once he had his engineering degree, he'd land a decent-paying job.

His father advised, "Get financially established, then think about your future."

On a Friday evening in March, 1960, Jim Kasdorf and Johnny Helden drove to *Beek's* on the east side, a great place to see old friends and meet new people, especially young women. Tony, a personable Negro, played terrific piano, the drinks were reasonable, and everyone smoked cigarettes, including Johnny. Occasionally he got a phone number.

That night, through the crowd, he noticed the extraordinary beauty of a girl's profile. After someone lit her cigarette, she gracefully tilted her head to exhale. Johnny, content to stare, checked himself, as she glanced his way. He realized he had to give this a try, so he elbowed towards her. Unable to think of a clever line, he said, "Hi, I'm Johnny Helden."

"Hi Johnny Helden, I'm Karen Anderson."

Fortunately, they had something in common: both went to Marquette. She majored in English and lived in a dorm. Johnny studied engineering and lived at home. They chatted for an hour before Johnny suggested they get some fresh air.

"A capital idea," she said.

The mild, March night refreshed them. The sidewalk filled with the exit surge from the last show at the Downer Theater, so Johnny headed the other way. At the corner he took Karen's hand, crossed the street, but then, wisely, let her hand go. They walked several blocks past the gracious homes on Belleview Place to Wahl Avenue where they crossed to Lake Park. The swollen moon had risen above Lake Michigan; its reflected light pointed with inevitable fidelity right at them. They gazed across the black, wide bay of Milwaukee towards the lights strung along the far southern shore.

"This is one of my favorite spots," Johnny said.

"It's very beautiful. I didn't realize the lake was so close here."

"Close, but no cigar . . . or cigarettes."

Karen laughed. "I don't go to smoky bars very often. In fact, I've never been to *Beek's* before. My girlfriends asked me."

"I'm glad."

They looked at each other; the moonlight revealed an interest in his eyes. Karen didn't hesitate. "Johnny, I'm going with a guy. He got his M.D. at Madison, interns at County General, puts in long hours . . . I rarely see him on weekends."

In silence, they headed back towards *Beek's*. Approaching Downer Avenue, Johnny asked, "Are you engaged?"

She laughed. "No, curious though; wondering where it might lead, that kind of thing."

"He must be a little older."

"Six years . . . my, you're perceptive."

"Sometimes."

Outside *Beek's,* Jim paced the sidewalk. He spotted Johnny. "Hey, Helden, let's go."

"I've really got to get back to my friends," Karen said. "Goodbye."

The next seven Fridays, Johnny went back to *Beek's* in hopes of seeing Karen again. He never did. But he met a lot of people, including a guy pursuing, in Madison, the same engineering degree as Johnny at Marquette. They both expected to graduate in 1962. His name was Bob Schmitt.

Bob grew up in Whitefish Bay; summers he worked for his father who owned a metal fabricating company on the north side. SMF, Inc. served as subcontractor to some of the largest manufacturers in Milwaukee, building specialty weldments along with fabricating some structural steel for the construction industry. Bob told Johnny that structural steel was his great interest; he intended in the years ahead to increase that side of his father's business. Johnny liked Bob's aggressiveness, confidence, and intelligence. Eventually, they became friends.

+ + +

In 1953, Chevrolet introduced the Corvette, a powerful, rakish, sports car beautifully designed with a body of molded fiberglass. Young Pete Helden ordered one as soon as they came out. The car gave him the idea to build milk tanks out of molded fiberglass, abandoning the welded, seamless, stainless steel design the company perfected twenty-five years earlier. He persuaded his father, Peter Jr., that fiberglass was the material of the future: lighter, cheaper than, and nearly as strong as the proven, polished steel. Everyone in the engineering department caught Pete's enthusiasm until his father finally said, "Okay, let's give it a try." Then they had to go to work.

The chief engineer, Donald Anzia, put together a team of his best engineers, swearing them to secrecy. Research had to be done in the strength and behavior of the fiberglass and the radically different fabrication methods. Material and machinery suppliers had to be found; destructive and non-destructive testing had to be performed. Finally, the design engineers hit the drawing boards. And always there lurked the cheerful, enthusiastic, impatient presence of young Pete Helden who never studied engineering a day in his life. In that regard, he and his father were equals.

They built the prototype in secrecy. The foreman didn't ask George Helden to join the team. George snooped plenty, but nobody told him anything. Never could George have imagined that the company would abandon their proven techniques for building milk tanks. In the early and mid '50s, the Helden tanks were, unquestionably, the finest milk transports in the world.

John Helden and other distributors from around the country received invitations to a cocktail reception where a new product in the Helden line would be introduced. Guests were led to a curtained-off, cleaned-up bay in the large manufacturing plant. They ate, drank, and mingled with Peter Jr., Pete, and other executives and sales engineers. After an hour, office personnel and shop men joined the party. All had been invited to attend the preview showing of a new product that had been described in the invitation as *revolutionary*. A large curtain bearing the Helden nameplate hid the thing, and then, when all were in good spirits, Peter Jr. stepped to the microphone. After welcoming everyone, he said, "Today, ladies and gentlemen, we unveil the latest in quality Helden products, a new milk transport tank that will revolutionize the industry."

John Helden could hardly believe it. He had absolutely no inkling it would be a milk tank.

"This is a breakthrough in design and fabrication . . . I think you're gonna like what you see," Peter Jr. said. "Okay boys, open the curtain."

John went speechless at the unveiling of the sleek, white, stream-lined, five thousand gallon, fiberglass beauty. Everyone cheered and applauded wildly. Visually, the tank was a stunning success; so much more aesthetically-pleasing than the traditional design that a comparison of Pete's Corvette to a 1937 Buick roadster would be apt. And somehow, as everyone's comments filled the large space, the new tank came to be called a *plastic* tank.

"This will revolutionize the milk hauling industry," Peter Jr. told the crowd. "The tank is lighter. Haulers will need less fuel, and that's gonna save your customers a lot of money. And look at it . . . it's beautiful, the wave of the future. Gentlemen, this tank will destroy our competitors and their carbon steel monstrosities. This will be the death kneel for *Kold Karry*. Gentlemen, we are proud to present this money-making winner."

The crowd cheered again, as young Pete shuffled next to his father.

When things quieted down, Peter Jr. said, "Now I'm gonna give you another winner . . . this is my son Pete. He's the genius who thought of using fiberglass. Pete, say something."

The men clapped and cheered. Pete was only thirty. "Gentle-men, thank you. I just wanna say this g--damn tank is gonna make us all a hellava lot of money."

"When can we start selling 'em?" John Helden shouted.

"Right away." Peter Jr. nodded at his cousin. "We've printed beautiful brochures. The production line is up and running; as fast as you sell 'em, we'll ship 'em. And you're gonna like the price; these beauties cost less than stainless. We're phasing out stainless. After the New Year, fiberglass is the only thing you're gonna be selling."

Pete leaned into the microphone. "And it'll be a damn easy sell. Nobody's ever gonna wanna buy those steel dinosaurs again."

John Helden caught his cousins' enthusiasm. He mailed the new brochures to his customers with a cover letter explaining that stain-less steel milk transport tanks had gone the way of the *Dodo* bird. He liked what he wrote and sent copies to his cousin and young Pete, but they didn't respond.

He heard first from Lee Marnel who barked into the phone, "What the fuck . . . you expect me to buy plastic?"

John emphasized fiberglass's lighter weight, cost savings, and the futuristic design, which Lee really liked. "I'll buy one just to show it off. I'll drive that plastic fucker into Chicago myself."

Bill Donnelly called, conceding the tank's good looks, but asked, "Was it road tested?"

"Oh, I'm sure it was," John said. "I can't imagine not . . . Anzia's too good of an engineer."

"Okay," Bill said. "I'll buy one."

It proved a good week for John: two new fiberglass tanks sold without trade-ins. But then he got a call from Lee's old driver, Frankie, who hauled in the central part of the State. Frankie and Hubie had bought a dozen used tanks from John.

"Thanks for sending me that brochure . . . kind of funny, though, 'cause I just heard that *Kold Karry's* gonna build all their tanks now with stainless outer jackets, just like Helden."

"They're way behind . . . Helden isn't building stainless anymore. Molded fiberglass is the wave of the future."

"I don't know about that . . . I think I'll stick with stainless."

"Someday, Frankie, I predict I'll sell you used fiberglass."

Frankie laughed, suspecting it might well happen.

A 5000 gallon milk transport tank carries a load of 43,000 pounds. The top, center manhole allows for cleaning and filling as well as access for sanitary inspections. Tanks are built without baffles; they have to be filled completely to prevent a sloshing of the heavy liquid, as it navigates the smooth and bumpy roads leading to the big city dairies. The tare weight of the tank is known so a truck scale can verify the weight of the load. The tank is emptied by gravity flow through an outlet valve at the bottom rear. If the operator begins emptying without opening the top manhole, a vacuum is created inside the tank that will allow the giant, invisible hand of air pressure to crush it. John Helden repaired several crushed steel tanks in his shop. He supposed molded fiberglass would collapse the same way, that is, if an operator were careless.

+ + +

Two weeks and a day after she met Johnny Helden, Karen

Anderson accompanied Jack Cutler to the *Doctor's Ball* at the Schroeder Hotel. Jack would complete his residency by the end of May and begin his professional life as a gynecologist at a clinic in Racine. His chosen specialty impressed Karen; she believed he respected women because of it. Jack never gave her reason to think otherwise.

Attending the prestigious Ball thrilled Karen, especially because Jack worked such long hours and many evenings. Their date also offered an opportunity for Jack to meet her parents. Karen wore a lovely deep-pink formal gown that displayed her slender, well-rounded figure. When Jack picked her up he found her really beautiful, and almost told her so.

In a black tuxedo with red cummerbund, Jack Cutler made a fine impression: six feet tall, broad, square shoulders, light brown hair, and with what Karen's two sisters called "dreamy, blue eyes." He shook hands with her father and again when they left, but did not offer his hand to her mother, nor did she extend to him. She wasn't ready to give such an easy sign of acceptance where her eldest daughter was concerned. Karen's sisters, Katherine, seventeen, and Jane, eleven, came down to meet Jack, too. They thought Jack very good looking and told their parents, as soon as Jack and Karen left, that their sister "should marry that guy."

At the Ball, Jack's colleagues eagerly met Karen. Jack liked having her by his side and even hinted, after introducing her to his closest classmates, that she was his soon-to-be fiancée. It shocked Karen. At an aside, she reprimanded him not because she thought she would or wouldn't marry Jack, but simply because it was way too early in their dating. Nevertheless, she forgave the presumption, smiling at him often enough to indicate Jack needn't worry. They danced and socialized until the end of the Ball, then, with a large group, went to a popular Italian restaurant in the Third Ward. Some of the older doctors drank heavily. Karen appreciated that Jack did not.

She got home at three. She thanked Jack for a wonderful evening and kissed him goodnight. He held her a little too long. She whispered, "I really must go in."

They both felt, as he walked to his car and she ascended the stairs to her bedroom, that something wonderful had happened between them.

The following Thursday, the evening they most often saw each other, Karen took the bus to 68th Street, walking the block and a half north to *Rosetti's*. Weary of winter, she longed for spring yet loved the beauty of the silent, windless snow. There was little traffic and no one else on the sidewalk. Spheres of light at each street lamp filled with thousands of snowflakes, sparkling and suspended, as though too pure and delicate to be affected by something as insistent as gravity. She wore a burgundy knit cap with a matching scarf slung over her left shoulder. Her face glowed with anticipation. In the distance, Karen spotted a shadowy figure, a blur in the snow, but then felt a surge of excitement recognizing Jack.

After last Saturday night she realized her feelings for him had intensified. *Do I really want an infatuation at this point,* she wondered. *Could it be a prelude to love? Could I really love Jack Cutler?* He had promise, no question: intelligent, physically attractive, strong and healthy, and in a few months he'd finish his residency. She realized she could be a doctor's wife if she pursued him now. Yet, for all the times they had been together, Jack never disclosed anything deeply personal. She knew little about his deceased parents and didn't know much about Jack's younger sister either, his only sibling.

Jack, hatless, gloveless, and bootless, ran towards her. His coat, open at the collar, exposed a white, starched pinpoint open at the neck. He was oblivious to the weather or wanted to give that impression. When he reached her, they embraced and kissed like lovers.

She said, "Oh, Jack, Jack . . . ," in a way he had never heard before.

He gazed upon her loveliness caught in the lamplight; her eyelashes and hair flecked with crystal flakes, eyes shining with happiness. Still Jack couldn't muster the words to express his feelings. When he wrapped his arm around her, she snuggled into him.

Rosetti's, rich and warm with fine aromas of Italian cooking, jukebox music, and soft lighting, held enough of a crowd to make it appealing. Oddly, the Christmas decorations were still up – old Mr. Rosetti was funny that way – though now they seemed perfectly appropriate with the fresh, falling snow. The hostess knew Jack and Karen from prior Thursdays. She led them to a table along the south wall, far from the front door and just the right distance from the jukebox where Sinatra crooned.

"What would you like?" Jack asked.

"Hot chocolate would be nice."

"*Schlitz,*" he said, glancing at the waitress.

In moments she returned with a steaming cup and a cold beer.

"Would you like to see the menu?" The waitress knew Jack and Karen always ordered pizza, but asked anyway.

Jack lit a cigarette and offered one to Karen. They discussed the dance; Karen teased him about all the young interns addressing one another as "Doctor" in lieu of their first names. Jack asked if she had a good time in spite of his little faux pas. She answered, "I had a wonderful time." She also remarked, without giving it any thought, that she was surprised how many of the couples she met were engaged.

"Hey, interning is tough . . . new docs need some comforting." Jack grinned. Karen got the message and looked away.

The pizza, Jack's supper, was hot and delicious. Karen left most of the pie for him. He ordered another beer and another hot chocolate for Karen. Neither of them wanted the evening to end. Karen had finished her assignments; when she got home she'd go to bed. Jack was scheduled for floor duty at eleven-thirty.

"How late will you stay up?"

"Don't know . . . depends what happens."

"Doesn't beer make you sleepy?"

"I suck coffee."

"How busy does your weekend look?"

"Very . . . what'd you have in mind?"

"Well," Karen elongated the word, "my mother invited us to dinner Sunday."

"That's really nice, but I'm scheduled Sunday."

"Oh, Jack, can't you get a substitute?"

He laughed. "I am the substitute; you know that."

"Don't you want to get to know my parents and sisters? They all think you're very nice."

"Of course, but I gotta work."

"It will only be a couple hours . . . ."

"I really wish I could, Karen, but now to the end it's gonna be tight. After I finish, I'll have plenty time. We'll be together a lot."

"You'll be in Racine."

"That's not far."

"Jack, if I had the chance to spend time with your family, nothing would interfere."

"Well, that just can't be, can it?" Jack swigged his beer then lit another cigarette.

Karen let her eyes reveal her disappointment. She wanted her parents and sisters to get to know Jack so Karen's thoughts and feelings could be confirmed or confronted. And she wanted Jack to know her family. Her senior year in high school she resolved to make a good choice for a husband because she couldn't imagine anything worse than an unhappy marriage. A wise nun had advised the girls, "bring your fella home to your parents. Put him under *their* microscope."

"I'm sorry I said that, Jack. You're too young to have lost both."

"I'm over it."

Then Karen asked, "How did your father die?"

Jack decided to answer, for he knew, sooner or later, he'd have to tell. "Some drunken idiot ran a red light; hit my dad's car broadside . . . spun it like a top. He was thrown out the passenger door. Witnesses said it happened unbelievably fast. A truck was coming the other way . . . driver tried to stop, but my dad was pitched right in his path. The truck ran him over. Ten minutes later, in the middle of the road, he died from what's called massive internal injuries."

Karen's face blanched. "Oh, Jack, that's horrible."

They fell silent. She held his hands across the table until he lit another cigarette. She noticed his changed expression, as though telling of his father's death recalled tremendous pain that etched itself into his fine face. Karen regretted asking, but it was something she needed to know, and now she wanted more.

"Would you tell me about your mother?"

"How she died?"

"Well, yes . . . what she was like."

"She was an RN, very intelligent, but she took my dad's death extremely hard. She wasn't the same after that."

"That's understandable. Did she ever think of remarrying?"

"Not that I ever knew." He fell silent again, his face expressionless.

Finally, Karen asked, "How did she die?"

Jack realized, *no sense in putting it off.* "I just finished premed. My mother and sister came for graduation."

"Where did they live?"

"Dubuque . . . afterwards, my mother suggested Wendy stay with me awhile to get to know Madison because she was thinking of going to UW. She graduated from high school that same June."

Karen interrupted. "Wendy's your sister?"

"That's what I said, right?" His voice revealed irritation.

"Yes, sorry, I won't interrupt."

"Originally, we lived in St. Paul, but after my dad died, my mother moved us to Dubuque. She wanted to get away from there."

"Of course."

"My mother drove back to Dubuque, and Wendy stayed at my place. Maybe she'd stay a week or even longer. Whatever we decided because my mother didn't really care, knowing Wendy was with me. I was gonna show her around campus that morning, but then a friend of mine, George Brower, called and asked if we wanted to spend the day at his folk's place on Lake Mendota. He had met my mother and Wendy at graduation. Wendy was pretty cute, and George probably liked the idea of her coming over. So we drove out there.

"It was one of those perfect June days. George invited a few other friends, guys and girls, and everyone was really nice to Wendy so she had a great time. We went waterskiing, swimming, just had a lot of fun. George's mother made lunch. We had a couple beers, but I wouldn't let Wendy drink even though those idiots wanted me to so she'd get a little more relaxed and, you know, maybe a little friendlier. Those guys were a bunch of horny bastards."

"Jack . . . ."

"Well, they were – no big deal – that's the way guys are. Anyway, after lunch we took it easy, talked, listened to music . . . just hanging out. It was fun, and Wendy really enjoyed herself. Towards evening George built a bonfire. We sat around singing, drinking beer, laughing . . . having a great time. George did cozy up to Wendy, and she was okay with it because he didn't come on too strong. He wasn't drunk or anything – none of us were – well, maybe a little high. George got some blankets. We looked at the stars and just had one of those great nights, you know?

"Yes," Karen answered.

"We left around midnight. When we got back to my place, I noticed a guy leaning against a car right in front. As we walked past, he said, 'Excuse me, sir, are you Jack Cutler?' It surprised us. I told him I was and asked who the hell he was. He said he needed to talk to me, but wondered who the young lady was so I told him she was my sister. At first, he didn't believe me. He asked if he could come in. I asked what the hell for. Then he pulled out his ID. He was a cop, a Madison detective. That's when I got concerned.

"We went in. I had a lower flat with a small living room that wasn't real tidy. He asked us to sit down, but he wanted to see our driver's licenses. Wendy was really tired, and so was I, so I asked the guy what the hell this was all about.

"He looked at Wendy and again asked what relationship she was. That pissed me off because I had already told him, but he was thinking maybe she was my girlfriend. Once we got that straightened out, he started with the usual bullshit, 'I regret to . . . .'

"Then he stops and looks at Wendy 'cause she was kinda dozing off. He motioned for me to nudge her. I bitterly regret that I did. I should've let her sleep, dream of the great day we just had. I should've kicked that asshole out of there. But she woke up, and we sat there waiting for him to do his g--damn job. Of course, he wasn't enjoying himself either.

"Finally, he started again. 'I regret to inform you . . . your mother, Annette Cutler, was killed in an auto accident.'"

Karen gasped. "Oh my God!"

"I couldn't believe it. My sister shrieked. I asked, 'How . . . where?' He told us, 'Near Mineral Point about ten in the morning.' Then he said, 'I've been waiting for you a very long time.'

"Obviously, we couldn't sleep. The feelings I had that night were something I will never forget and never want again. Wendy cried and cried. Finally, the cop left. I know he tried to help, but he was worthless. He gave me his card, said I should call in the morning because we had to identify the body. I held Wendy all night.

Finally, towards dawn she fell asleep, but I didn't sleep a wink. In the morning I felt like shit, but I had to arrange to see the body."

"He should have waited 'til morning so you two could've gotten a good night's sleep."

Jack gazed out the front window at the falling snow. A profound sadness had altered his expression. Karen realized, perhaps, she shouldn't have asked about his mother.

"We drove to the morgue, met that cop, and identified our mother. I couldn't believe my eyes. Her face, shoulders, chest were battered, smashed . . . everything purple and black. It was horrible. Wendy burst into tears. I was numb. It was like my emotions died. Then we had to ship the body to a funeral parlor in Dubuque. We had to call my mother's sister in Des Moines, get the death certificate, and bury her. It was the worst week of my life."

Karen looked away from him and down, shaking her head in sad disbelief.

"Wendy, though, proved pretty tough. She surprised me. She contacted a lawyer, the insurance company, and even arranged to sell the house. She decided she didn't want to live in Dubuque, Madison, or anywhere else in the Midwest. She decided she wanted to go to college in California. She said, 'I'll find my way,' and she has. She's smart. She's done well out there."

"How could your sister afford to do that?"

Jack felt a little high from the beer, and that's probably why he decided to answer. "When my dad was killed there was a hundred thousand dollar life insurance policy."

Karen gasped again. "What did your father do?"

"He was a chemist, but his best friend sold life insurance."

"My God, that's a fortune."

"There was a similar policy on my mother."

Karen stared at Jack, realizing for the first time that he was a wealthy young man.

"My sister and I each inherited over a hundred thousand." Jack grinned, thinking Karen now regarded him as even more desirable, but she wasn't thinking that at all. Finally, she was learning about Jack's life, and that's what she deemed valuable.

She wondered aloud, "What kind of auto accident?"

"Aaah," Jack drew out the sound. "That's where things get interesting."

He ordered his fourth beer and lit another cigarette. "After my mother's funeral I stayed in Dubuque. About a week later I told my sister I had to go to Madison, but I called that cop and asked if he'd show me where my mother died. At first he balked, but I told him he had to so he said to meet him in Mineral Point. From there I followed him to the site. It was on a curve. In the accident report, he claimed she fell asleep, missed the curve, and hit a tree.

"I told him my mother never napped during the day, much less the morning.

"So he said, 'Well, maybe she blacked out.' That was possible I suppose; she was fifty.

"Anyway, we walked a little ways and came to a spot where the brush was all matted down, which he said was from the tow truck that pulled her car out. We headed towards a big tree that was mangled. You could tell a car hit it hard. He said the ambulance drove in there to get her. Must've been off the road maybe seventy-five yards . . . .

"Then we walked back towards the highway. When we reached it, I looked back at the tree and noticed something I hadn't noticed when we walked in. The ground sloped down away from the road. The curve was on top of a hill that sloped down and away."

Jack raised and extended his arm; with his hand he drew an imaginary downward sloping arc that stretched from Karen's eyes across to the adjacent table.

"What's so unusual about that?"

"Had my mother fallen asleep or blacked out, the car would have followed the slope of the ground, away from that tree. The car would have ended up down the hill. Do you understand what I'm suggesting?"

"I'm not sure I do. What's your point?"

"The point is my mother drove straight into that tree. She deliberately hit it. My mother committed suicide. That's my g--damn point."

Karen put both hands to her mouth. "Oh, Jack, no, no . . . ."

"Don't be so shocked . . . . The cop wasn't. He told me, 'Don't think those thoughts, son. I wrote the report, and I ain't changing it.'

"I said, 'Fine, leave it, but just between the two of us, we both know she hit that tree deliberately.'

"So again he says, 'Son, don't think those thoughts.' Dumb shit . . . what the hell was I supposed to think? Something I knew wasn't true?"

"But, Jack, you can't prove that. Your mother had no reason to commit suicide. She just saw you graduate."

"You don't get it, do you? The only way her car could hit that tree was if my mother steered into it; otherwise it would have gone down the hill."

"No, she must have fallen asleep or blacked out. Or the steering locked . . . ."

"She would have braked."

"Not if she blacked out."

"Damn it, Karen, don't argue. I tell you clear, simple facts, but you believe something stupid. For God's sake, think!"

"Don't insult me. I can express my opinion. Your mother had no reason to commit suicide, especially the day after you graduated."

"Not true . . . she did because of my dad's death. They were close. She was lonely. She didn't want to live without him. Her kids were grown up. She knew we could take care of ourselves. She presumed some dumb cop would think she fell asleep at the wheel or blacked out, and he did. She knew we'd get the insurance money. It was all planned."

Karen refused to believe it. She couldn't look at Jack for his rudeness, but she asked, "How did you ever get over losing your parents?" As soon as she said it, she thought it a foolish question because she suspected he hadn't.

"You can get over anything. You can get used to anything."

"Oh my God, I'd hate to lose my parents."

"I'm telling you, you can adjust to anything."

"I'm not so sure. If you do, it must come at a bitter price."

Jack shifted uncomfortably. "You gotta develop emotional toughness; that's what I did."

"Did you? Some things people never get over, and, quite frankly, I don't think you're over your parent's deaths, especially your mother's. I'm not sure you ever will."

Jack stared hard at her. "Bullshit, I'm over it. I know how she died. I didn't let my emotions obscure the truth. You have to deal with truth. So many people create false realities. They let their emotions dominate, which is really stupid."

"Do you think I'm emotional?" Karen asked.

"Women are by their nature."

"Then I suppose you consider women basically stupid."

"That's not what I mean. My mother was intelligent, far more rational than emotional. I respected that."

Something dark within Karen prodded her to say, "If she committed suicide, then to my way of thinking, she was stupid, really stupid."

It enraged him. He decided to put her in her place. "Listen, if you became a prostitute you could adjust to it if you had the right mental attitude and controlled your silly emotions. You could adjust regardless of how distasteful you think prostitution is."

"Jack, what a terrible thing to suggest."

"No, no, I don't mean you." Jack realized his blunder. "I'm speaking in general. I'm just saying if a person uses reason to control their emotions then you, anybody really, could make the adjustment to that kind of life or any kind of life."

"I certainly could not. Do you think I'd so easily abandon my moral principles?"

"See, that's my point. Now you're reacting emotionally. If you dealt with it strictly on an intellectual basis, you could handle it."

"Don't say that. I'm not reacting emotionally. One doesn't choose to debase oneself and then rationalize it by discarding the moral principles one has always lived by. *That* would be unbelievably stupid."

"What I'm saying is we're adaptable. We can adjust to anything if we have to and if we choose to. Survival is the strongest instinct not abstract moral principles."

"Oh, really . . . then how can you believe your mother committed suicide? Or wasn't survival her strongest instinct? Why couldn't she adapt to losing her husband?"

"My mother did adapt. She adapted to choose suicide rationally – not emotionally."

"You don't know that." Karen's voice reeked sarcasm.

"I knew my mother . . . ."

"People who commit suicide suffer from unbearable despair. Did your mother?"

"Of course not, I would've known. My sister would've known. I'm telling you, she made a calm, rational decision: no despair, no emotion, just the desire not to live anymore."

"That's nonsense; everyone loves life. Obviously, your mother was mentally ill."

"Damn it, Karen," Jack's voice was thick with anger, "this is pointless. I gotta go." He threw enough money on the table for the bill and tip. His arrogance prevented him from conceding that Karen got the better of the argument. In his mind he screamed, "Girl, you're an idiot."

"You're the one who brought up suicide," she said, coldly.

Outside it was still snowing. The night was as beautiful as the evening, but now it didn't matter to either of them.

"Will you drive me back," Karen asked.

"Oh, shit, not tonight."

"Jack, it's late. I don't want to take the bus."

"I gotta get back . . . I'm on at eleven thirty."

She stopped pleading. Jack bent to kiss her, but she turned away. He pressed his lips hard against the side of her mouth then let her go. Walking towards the bus stop she felt agitated and unsettled. Three hours earlier, seeing Jack thrilled her, but now she felt as though she had been with a different guy, a stranger, someone she didn't even like. *What a jerk,* she thought. Her feelings of infatuation were completely gone. *I need to know more,* she told herself and then, letting her innate compassion come to the fore, *he's suffered deeply in ways I haven't. Next time I'll handle it differently.*

Chapter 28 — 1962 (Continued)

In July 1960, the Democrats nominated Senator John F. Kennedy of Massachusetts for President of the United States, while the Republicans chose the incumbent vice president, Richard M. Nixon, setting the stage for an intense, spirited campaign and the closest presidential election in the nation's history. Kennedy's Catholic faith made the race even more interesting. After his nomination, the old anti-Catholic bias that smeared Al Smith in 1928 began rearing its ugly head.

Candidate Kennedy, nicknamed Jack, addressed the Houston Ministerial Association in early September. He successfully defused Protestant suspicions of divided loyalty by emphasizing his allegiance to the Constitution were it ever in conflict with the teachings of his Church.

American Catholics always had a separate identity apart from the Protestant mainstream. They had their own schools, hospitals, and holidays called "Holy Days." Catholics looked to the Church – whether their parish priest or the Pope – for instruction and guidance on issues of faith and morals.

By 1960, the Catholic Church in America was confident and self-assured. Kennedy's self-assurance shone in his televised debates with Richard Nixon. He spoke eloquently, while Nixon stumbled and faltered. Once Nixon slipped, referring to his serene opponent as "President Kennedy." The youthful senator embodied charisma, good looks, and style. He possessed the intellect of a scholar. His rhetorical skills and quick wit were Shakespearean. He loved touch football, poetry, sailing, good cigars, and beautiful women. The one he married, Jacqueline Bouvier, captured the hearts of her countrymen.

Upon his election as president, Kennedy represented the nearly complete acceptance of American Catholics into public life. The initial furor regarding his religion seemed trifling. Indeed, Jacqueline remarked to a journalist that the religious controversy surrounding her husband mystified her because, she said, "Jack is such a poor Catholic."

Michael and Johnny Helden liked Kennedy, but their parents were too Republican to be changed by his charm. At the dinner table several weeks before the election, Johnny extolled Kennedy's intelligence and eloquence. John Helden responded, "Don't vote for a Democrat . . . they always get us into war." John remembered Wilson for the First World War, Roosevelt for the Second, and Truman in Korea. Nevertheless, Michael and Johnny were too enamored with Kennedy to be swayed by a non sequitur.

"As Catholics," Michael said, "I think we have a moral obligation to vote for Kennedy."

"Nonsense," John Helden replied. "You vote for a man's political philosophy not his religion."

So the household split: two for Kennedy, two for Nixon, mirroring the percentages in the national popular vote: 49.7 for Kennedy, 49.5 for Nixon. A question, though, quickly arose in certain quarters of the press: "Did Chicago's Democratic mayor, Richard J. Daley, stuff the Cook County ballot boxes with enough fraudulent votes to put Illinois in Kennedy's column?" When Nixon was presented with hard evidence supporting the claim, he declined to pursue it, citing the potential for a Constitutional crisis. It probably marked Nixon's greatest, single act of statesmanship.

On January 20, 1961, Anita, Michael, and Johnny watched Kennedy's *Inaugural Address* on television. John Helden went to work even though he was beginning to warm to the new President. Early in his speech, Kennedy affirmed that "the rights of man come not from the generosity of the state, but from the hand of God." Michael thought, *good – he's not afraid to oppose communism.* Kennedy concluded by saying, "Let us go forth to lead the land we love, asking His blessing and His help, but knowing that here on earth God's work must truly be our own."

"Wow, what a speech," Johnny said.

"It was very good," Anita, the life-long Republican, admitted.

"Come on, it was brilliant." Michael jumped up from his chair. "Man, the secular humanists must be going crazy with all those references to God."

Kennedy's idealism and vision inspired Michael. Finally, he

told his father that, as much as he liked working for him, he decided to return to Los Angeles to "find my life out there."

At first, John seemed to accept it, but as days passed, he ruminated and grew angry. "Why the hell would he wanna live out there," he asked Anita. "Why can't he find his life here? I've got a good business . . . he could take it over."

But Anita understood. Michael had every right to pursue his own happiness wherever he wanted. At twenty-six, who were his parents to interfere?

John ignored his wife. Indeed, it angered him even more that Anita sided with Michael. Johnny told his father he'd help him until he found a new secretary, but John ignored that, too. He didn't want Michael leaving under any circumstance. He browbeat him to such an extent that one Saturday morning after John went to his office, Michael hurriedly packed, loaded his car, and said goodbye to his mother and brother. "Tell Dad I'm sorry . . . not to worry." As Michael's car disappeared down the 96th Street hill, Anita wept.

When John Helden returned and Anita told him Michael had left, John's anger erupted. She knew she had to stand defenseless before him, taking the vicious verbal attack not only for Michael's sake, but also, in a strange, twisted way, for John's as well. The cruel, vulgar, irrational tirade blamed Anita for Michael's leaving, for not understanding John's business problems, and even for John's own loss of happiness. It lasted nearly half an hour until, slamming the door behind him, he left.

Anita might as well have been physically beaten, so battered were her mind and heart. In the past, Johnny witnessed similar attacks. He observed how his mother withdrew more and more from her husband, for her pain was cumulative and permanent.

In silence, Anita and Johnny ate supper alone. By now, they suspected Michael neared St. Louis, but neither had any idea where John Helden might be. Johnny called the office, but there was no answer. When they went to bed they had trouble falling asleep: hoping, waiting and listening for John's car to roar up the driveway. It never came.

Sunday morning they went to Mass. They had heard nothing from John Helden. After church, Anita became nauseous, vomited, and went to bed. She closed her door, but Johnny, walking past, heard her sobs. He tried to comfort his mother, but she could not stop weeping.

By Sunday night, John still hadn't called. Anita remained in bed, declining to eat. Monday, Johnny attended his classes. When he returned, he sat with his mother attempting to calm and soothe, but still she wept on and on.

Finally, that evening John Helden called. Johnny got angry. "Why didn't you call sooner? Mother is extremely ill . . . worrying about you, worrying about Michael. What right do you have to hurt her? You have to apologize . . . she's my mother. What right do you have to hurt any of us? I don't blame Michael one damn bit for leaving. He had every right . . . you don't own him. Why treat us like dirt? My God, we're your family. You're supposed to love us." Johnny slammed down the receiver. Now he didn't care what his father did. *Leave us forever,* he thought, rejoicing that his brother had finally broken away from the stunted life beneath his father's dominating will.

John Helden returned despondent, apologetic, and sorrowful. Weeping, he knelt at his wife's bedside and begged forgiveness. Like so many times before, she gave it. Anita and Johnny realized John's anger wasn't caused solely by Michael's leaving, but by other disappointments and frustrations that John had suffered and endured for many years. He unwillingly bore that enormous pain because he felt utterly helpless how to get rid of it.

John could never accept his own father's decision to leave the company he had founded. He could never accept his own family locked out forever from the great wealth the company had amassed. He never understood why he wasn't made an executive at the company where he sold more new equipment than the next three men combined. He never understood why his cousin, Peter Jr., his boyhood playmate, rejected his friendship as a man. He never understood why Peter Jr. denied John the pleasure of working with his brother, George, while foisting Ray Butler on him, causing John several years of costly trouble. And now his older son deserted him and withdrew his wonderful companionship, leaving John alone with enduring frustrations and seemingly never-ending problems. Anita and Johnny were deeply scarred by John's ugly reaction to Michael's departure, but they also felt great pity for John without even knowing that a terrible secret hid in his afflicted heart. Life once granted John Helden the opportunity to rescue a young Japanese girl from sexual slavery, but he chose not to because of a man's worst failing – cowardice.

Another big disappointment loomed in John's immediate future. The Helden Company's new molded fiberglass milk transport tanks were creating problems. Apparently minor at first, but once thoroughly understood, they led to the complete demise of the Helden Company's milk transport tank manufacturing business. Subjected to the vicissitudes of aging roads and highways, the fiberglass tanks developed small, random cracks that bled milk into the insulation between the inner and outer jackets. Initially, no one paid much attention when slightly less than five thousand gallons were received at the dairy. But after several more runs, the driver noticed an odor. Then an inspector noticed a four hundred pound increase in the tare weight of the tank. Several loads had high bacteria counts and were dumped. The tanks began to cost their owners money. Once Lee Marnet had all the facts, he figured it out real quick: the tanks could not withstand the stresses and strains of long-distance hauling. Lee took his anger out on John Helden.

"What the fuck kind of leaking lemon did you sell me?"

"Helden's got their best engineers studying it. They'll figure it out and repair at no cost to you. Peter Jr. pledged that to all the distributors."

"Bull shit," Lee replied. "I don't want band aids. I want my money back. I never shoulda bought a g--damn plastic tank. This is gonna kill you and Helden. Your cousin and his kid are fucking idiots."

Lee proved correct on all accounts. Helden's engineers never found an acceptable fix because the original thickness of the fiberglass was simply inadequate. The only possible design change meant thicker material that would increase the tare weight unacceptably. But, fix or no fix, it didn't matter. Word spread among the milk haulers throughout the Midwest and East that the plastic tanks had failed. Less than three years after their introduction, the Helden Co. recalled every single one and returned the entire purchase price to angry buyers.

Initially, Peter Jr. demanded John Helden return his commissions to his customers, a crushing blow. But John refused. It wasn't his fault the company gave him an inferior product to sell. He told Peter Jr. he wouldn't do it. When Peter Jr. got furiously angry, John said, "I'll take my chances in a court of law." Peter Jr. consulted his attorneys and never made an issue of it again. The Helden Company paid back to John's customers all the commissions he had earned. Ethically, it was the right thing to do, but for it, Peter Jr. never forgave his cousin.

By 1962, The Helden Company, the world's undisputed leader in milk transport tanks for over thirty years, ceased building them. Peter Jr. and Pete never showed any regret, at least not publicly, because the demand for petroleum transport tanks continued to increase, and the long, milk assembly line easily converted to petroleum. Overall sales dipped for a few years, but eventually the petroleum business carried Helden to record sales. Kold Karry, now building their milk tanks with stainless steel outer jackets, captured Helden's entire former market share. John Helden, star salesman of the Helden stainless steel milk transport tank for a quarter of a century, found himself without a product to sell.

+ + +

Mild temperatures in Milwaukee in early December can deceive. The weather changes violently when the trailing cold front of an *Alberta Clipper* races across the State. Sleety wind, snow, and stinging rain dispel the beguiling gentleness of the last Indian summer day. Most people aren't prepared for it.

She didn't know what to do. Coming out of Johnston Hall after her last class, she realized she wasn't dressed for the seven block hike back to her dorm, plus there wasn't a bus in sight. She huddled at one of the doorways to Gesu's basement church, ducking in when she couldn't bear the cold. When the late afternoon Mass ended, people streamed up the stairs. A young man looked at her with surprised recognition. "Hi Karen Anderson," he said.

"Oh, my God . . . Johnny Helden . . . hi."

"You look like you need a ride."

"Yes, desperately. Oh, my goodness, how lucky you're here. For me, I mean."

"I'll get my car; it's got a good heater. I'll honk right in front of this door . . . wait for me."

He rushed, thinking, *she's prettier than I remember*. He started the car, scraped the ice from the windows, and in minutes pulled in front of Gesu. Karen came running out. She thanked him again and mentioned how they hadn't seen each other since the night they met last March.

"Yeah, eight months, pretty long," Johnny said. "I don't get to the lower campus very much except occasionally for Mass."

"And I certainly don't get to the engineering building."

He laughed. "Not many girls do."

Johnny drove slowly on the treacherous streets. He had often thought of Karen and wondered if she got engaged to the doctor she was dating. So he asked.

"We broke up in June . . . irreconcilable differences."

It surprised Johnny. "I wish I had known."

"Maybe it's better you didn't. I needed time to think about things."

"Are you . . . ?"

"I'm not dating anyone . . . kind of concentrating on school."

"Yeah, me too." He parked in front of her dorm. She thanked him again. "It's like you were heaven sent. I really didn't know how I'd get back."

"I'm glad I went to Mass."

She waited for him to say more, then opened the door. The wind pushed it back.

"Karen, look . . . I was wondering . . . could I call you?"

"Yes, I think I'd like that." She tore paper from a notebook, wrote a phone number, and gave it to him. "I'll be at my parents this weekend."

The first telephone conversation lasted an hour. Had it been up to Johnny, it would have lasted two. Their first date he met her parents and sisters, none of whom were nearly as impressed as they had been with Dr. Jack Cutler. Karen's mother pointed out that Johnny wasn't wearing a tuxedo. "That makes a big difference." Mr. Anderson commented, "Nor is he a doctor." Little Jane noticed, "His eyes aren't even blue."

At the end of the evening, Johnny asked Karen for another date before Christmas, but she declined. "I've just too much to do." Nor did she know Johnny well enough to invite him to a family celebration. A second date would have to wait.

+ + +

It was the first Christmas Eve of Johnny Helden's life without his brother who spent December job hunting in Los Angeles. When Anita learned Michael wouldn't be coming home, she decided not to put up a tree. Instead, she placed the Nativity set on the piano, surrounding it with balsam boughs plus a string of colored lights. John bought two poinsettias to flank the fireless fireplace; on the mantel, Anita placed tall tapered red candles.

John Helden had patched things up with Michael; now they talked on the phone at least once a week. John suspected Michael's job search was not going well. Michael had enough money to last a year, but John speculated, *if he doesn't find a job by June, he'll come home.*

Anita made a simple supper. Afterwards, in the living room, Johnny gave her a large, leather bound album for family photos, which she truly appreciated. He gave his father a two-record, boxed set of *Madama Butterfly,* featuring the great Swedish tenor, Jussi Bjorling, and the angelic soprano, Victoria de Los Angeles. The gift delighted John Helden who hadn't heard the opera in its entirety since his honeymoon. He asked Johnny to play it. So, instead of carols sung by a choir, Act I filled the house. The music affected John just as it did on a long ago, distant, April night.

He recalled the happiness of that honeymoon day in New York City twenty-eight years ago. He looked longingly at Anita who sat with her gift on her lap, her face devoid of expression, eyes unwilling to meet her husband's, and a memory unwilling to recollect. *So many years,* John realized. George Pohlman was dead ten years already; they hadn't heard from Linda for at least five. They never did return to New York, as Anita promised.

Then John thought of his own *Butterfly* and the bittersweet sadness of the remembrance of a dream. It all rushed back: the horror of an incident and a night he could never forget, but never tell. And guilt he could never erase.

At the end of the first act, Anita excused herself and went

upstairs to bed. John and Johnny wished her, "Merry Christmas."
Anita could barely reply. Her vapid heart had filled with sadness
and regrets that she simply was unable to share with her husband,
her mother, her brothers, her sisters-in-law, or her sons.

+ + +

Johnny Helden's second date with Karen Anderson fell on the
Wednesday between Christmas and New Year's Eve. They went to
an early movie and then to *Zaffiro's* for ravioli and Chianti. After
finishing their meal, they smoked cigarettes, sipped a little more
wine, and talked for an hour. Then Karen wanted to go home. At
her door, Johnny asked what she was doing New Year's Eve. Karen
told him her aunt and uncle always have a family get-together. She
never imagined Johnny might want to spend that special night with
her. "I'm sorry," she said.

"It's alright . . . my uncle Lew and Aunt Carol invited me."

They said goodnight; Johnny sensed her reserve. He suspected
her breakup with Jack Cutler wasn't pleasant and her guardedness
perfectly normal. Nevertheless, he called her the next day and asked
her out in the New Year, 1961. They talked for an hour. He liked the
way she expressed herself. She was smart and her family seemed
nice. He was physically attracted to her in a way he hadn't felt since
Gilliane. Unlike Gilliane, Karen casually remarked that someday
she'd like children of her own.

+ + +

In Los Angeles, Michael found a job with an insurance company. He made it clear to the entire family, including Uncles Lew
and Julius that he would not return to work for his father. John Helden resigned himself to it, for he had no choice save anger, which,
he realized, was fruitless. His repair business was still doing reasonably well. He missed Michael, but compensated for it by hiring an efficient, pleasant secretary just as he adjusted to not selling
new equipment – only refurbished used. What he could not easily
accept, though, was his declining income. He turned fifty-nine in
May, realizing in only six years he'd be collecting Social Security.

+ + +

By the end of January, Johnny and Karen were dating every Saturday night. Some days after late classes they'd see each other for a bite to eat. In February, they also began to date Fridays. It became quite obvious to families and friends that they had become a couple.

The first Saturday evening in March, Johnny Helden paused at the doorway of his father's small den. "Goodnight, Dad."

"Goodnight Johnny . . . Karen I suppose?"

"Yes. What are you reading?"

"Mr. Irving's *Sketchbook*."

"And Beethoven's *Sixth* on the stereo . . . at least I know you'll have a pleasant evening."

His father laughed. "I hope so. Depends on . . . ." John's left index finger jabbed at the living room below where his wife watched television.

Anita sat on her French provincial sofa, her head turned towards Hollywood.

"Goodnight, Mother."

Without turning, Anita asked, "Where are you going?"

"I've a date with Miss Anderson."

"That's what I thought. You see her a lot."

"Yes."

"How come so much?"

"I like her."

"You should stay home and watch Lawrence Welk with me." The television show's bubbly music just began.

"No thanks," Johnny said.

"It's a good show . . . the best." She slapped the armrest to make her point.

"I'm glad you enjoy it."

"Watch with me . . . it's such a wonderful show."

"Mother, I've got a date."

"Call, tell her you'll be late."

"No." He moved towards the hall.

"You should keep me company."

"Father's home."

"He's no fun."

"Well, I can't help that."

"Yes you can . . . stay with me. Oh look, pretty Bobby Burgess is going to dance."

Johnny glanced at the television. "Mother, I've got to go."

"Your father just sits in his den . . . ."

"He's reading and listening to Beethoven."

"Why would anyone on a Saturday night listen to the music of an old, dead German?"

"Well, Mother, if you don't know by now . . . ."

"I don't care to know. Just sit for a few minutes and watch . . . oh my, look at that boy dance. Your father couldn't dance like that. He was a pump-handler."

"Mother, I've really got to go." Again Johnny glanced at the screen.

"You're seeing so much of her I suppose you should bring her home sometime."

"Yes, that'd be very nice," Johnny said.

"Come on a Saturday . . . we'll watch Lawrence Welk together. That'll force your father to come down."

"No, Mother, that I will not do."

"You're terrible . . . ."

"I've got a date; that's perfectly normal."

"No, you're terrible not to like Mr. Welk."

"I don't know the man."

She glared at Johnny. "You know very well what I mean."

Johnny stepped back into the living room. "Let me put it to you in verse. You like poetry . . . this is in the form of a couplet." He had made it up in the shower.

"Tell me," she said.

"Promise not to get upset."

"I won't."

Johnny said, gravely, "I would rather be gored by a wild bull elk than bored by the music of Lawrence Welk."

"Oh," Anita screamed. "You're terrible . . . go to your Miss Anderson . . . leave me alone."

From the top of the stairs John Helden shouted, "What's the matter?"

"Your son is depraved." Only Johnny heard it.

"Goodnight Mother." He bent to kiss her.

"No, don't kiss me," she said. "I don't like you anymore."

Johnny called, "Goodnight Dad." John Helden stood bemused at the top of the stairs, the open *Sketchbook* in his hand. His younger son left quickly and quietly.

+ + +

By the spring of 1961, Johnny Helden and Karen Anderson were infatuated with each other. The mild, breezy weather, suppers at *Zaffiro's* with a bottle of Chianti, and, afterwards, gazing from the Brady Street footbridge across the harbor to the shore lights in Bay View, all conspired to make them content and happy. Inevitably, they began to embrace and kiss and experience the sweetest, visceral feelings.

That summer Johnny worked for his father at the shop in West Allis, while Karen worked downtown. They spent three or four evenings a week together and, other nights, talked on the phone. In September they began their last year at Marquette; both looked forward to graduation and good jobs. In the back of their minds, the slumbering subject of marriage waited.

The following spring, Johnny asked Karen to marry him. Her acceptance delighted their families though a date wasn't set. Anita proposed a celebratory dinner party for the Andersons on a Saturday evening. She suggested that during the meal, Mr. Welk's bubbly music should float into the dining room. John Helden said, "That's fine, but we'll serve champagne to make it bearable."

At Marquette, the recruiters arrived. Johnny interviewed with several companies. He accepted a job for five hundred and twenty-five dollars a month with a national firm that held the contract for designing the proposed expressway interchange downtown. When he received the commitment letter he realized he could, at the grand age of twenty-five, finally get married and start a family.

Karen found employment in the Milwaukee public high schools as an English teacher. Johnny's salary exceeded hers, but she understood engineers earned more. Karen's uncle was an engineer who earned a fine salary, according to Aunt Beth.

After much soul-searching, Johnny and Karen decided to elope. With two, beautiful, younger sisters, Karen knew a large, fancy wedding would be a financial drain on their father who wasn't a wealthy man. She gladly gave it up. Johnny knew his mother would be disappointed, but he had to respect his fiancée's wishes more than his mother's wants. Ultimately, the major question for Johnny and Karen simply was: *Who will marry us?*

The Anderson sisters loved their Aunt Beth, the wife of their mother's brother, Paul Peterson. Elizabeth was a businesswoman; her husband was a senior vice president at one of Milwaukee's largest manufacturers. They had no children, lived in the Highlands subdivision, traveled regularly, and led a comfortable life. Karen confided to Aunt Beth that she and Johnny had made the decision to elope and would not be dissuaded. Elizabeth, wisely, supported the decision. It was Aunt Beth who referred Karen to Father Jim.

After Father James Fahey retired from Marquette University, he became chaplain for the Sisters and young women at Mount Mary College. Father Jim offered Mass, heard confessions, and counseled students, faculty, college employees, and anyone else who rang his doorbell. He knew Karen's aunt for many years.

From the little orchard beside Father Fahey's red-roofed house, the high bell tower of Mount Mary College stood square and black against a long, narrow band of fading light. In silence, Johnny and Karen watched the dusk change the sky from red to deepest blue, and in the black east, the appearance of the first, dim stars.

The housekeeper showed them to the parlor. Father Fahey appeared in a minute. They all shook hands.

Karen began, "Father, may I ask how you know my aunt Elizabeth?"

"How do I know anyone in this town? I met her at Marquette . . . must be over twenty years already. She told me you both just graduated . . . congratulations."

"Thank you, Father."

"And what would you like to talk about? Your aunt refused to say."

"We'd like you to marry us," Karen said.

"Wonderful!" He then tried to convince them a small church ceremony with a reception just for the family would be, "more loving and more considerate." He advised costs be shared three ways or even four if Johnny's parents would chip in. "You don't want to disappoint your folks." But they were adamant. They wanted to get married quickly and quietly.

"Father," Johnny said, "we believe the size of the wedding has absolutely nothing to do with marital happiness. My parents had a big, lavish wedding . . . ."

"I know my father will be grateful," Karen said. "He's not a wealthy man, and both my sisters will probably want fancy weddings."

"So you're willing to make that sacrifice?"

"I don't see it as a sacrifice at all, Father."

They had to furnish birth certificates, copies of Baptismal and Confirmation Certificates, apply for the marriage license, and take blood tests. State law required all marrying persons to be checked for the sexually transmitted diseases of syphilis and gonorrhea. In addition, they needed two witnesses. In a letter, Johnny asked Michael who agreed to come home, while Karen asked Aunt Beth. The date was set for the last Saturday in August.

The day before the wedding, Johnny and Michael snuck their best suits and ties to Jim Kasdorf's house. They'd dress there so John and Anita wouldn't question where they were going all spiffed up on an early Saturday afternoon. Leaving in casual clothes, Michael fibbed, "We're golfing . . . ."

They met Karen and her aunt at Father Fahey's at two. Johnny and Michael found Elizabeth charming, guessing her age in the mid-forties. At fifty-two, she did look younger. Stylishly dressed with a lovely figure, she possessed an interesting face that became more appealing as both brothers, discreetly, studied it. And she did something so thoughtful in bringing them boutonnières, and for Karen a lovely bouquet of white and yellow thorn-less roses. She snipped the thorns herself. In the dining room, away from the priest and brothers, she whispered to Karen, "White is for your purity, yellow for your passion." It brought tears to Karen's eyes.

Father Fahey read several nuptial readings from the Old and New Testaments before asking Johnny and Karen to stand before him to express their vows for Aunt Beth, Michael, and God to hear. They exchanged plain, gold wedding bands after which the priest said, "I now pronounce you man and wife." All knelt as the priest offered the sacrifice of the Eucharist, which all received. Finally, he imparted God's blessings one last time, while Johnny gazed into Karen's eyes. They kissed, and though it was brief, enormous passion hid within their hearts, a passion emanating from the chaste and exquisite anticipation of their consummated love.

+ + +

For Johnny and Karen Helden, indeed, for most Americans, October 15, 1962, began as an ordinary, back-to-work, autumn Monday, but it proved far from ordinary for those who analyzed the reconnaissance photographs that revealed Soviet missile launch sites under construction in Cuba. Next morning at breakfast President Kennedy, still in his pajamas, was informed.

In 1962, the Soviet Union lagged far behind in the arms race. Soviet missiles could only reach Europe, but American missiles could strike anywhere in the Soviet Union. In 1961, the United States installed fifteen intermediate range *Jupiter* missiles in Turkey, a mere sixteen minute chip shot across the Black Sea to Moscow. The Soviet Premier, Nikita Khrushchev, conceived the brilliant counter-move of placing equivalent-range missiles in Cuba, a deployment that would provide a deterrent to a preemptive American nuclear attack against the Soviet Union.

Since the failed Bay of Pigs invasion in 1961, which President Kennedy had authorized, Fidel Castro, Cuba's dictator, searched for a strategy to defend his island from another American assault that he felt was inevitable. As a result, he welcomed Khrushchev's plan to install missiles in Cuba. Throughout the summer and early fall of 1962, the Soviets worked feverishly to build their bases.

On Wednesday, October 17, another high-altitude reconnaissance flight over Cuba discovered intermediate range nuclear missiles that, with the exception of the states of Washington and Oregon, could reach every major city in the continental United States.

On Thursday, October 18, a majority of Kennedy's advisers recommended a naval blockade of Cuba, an idea that the President liked because it proffered the Soviets a way out of the crisis. Kennedy, though, instructed his writers to draft two different speeches for the American people: one would announce not a blockade, which is an act of war, but a quarantine, which is merely keeping something unwanted out of a particular area. The second speech would announce a far riskier air strike against the missile sites that some of Kennedy's top advisers still advocated. At that point, the President could not glean the proper course.

Monday evening, October 22, Kennedy, in a televised address, announced to the American people the discovery of the missile installations in Cuba and his decision to impose a naval quarantine around the island. He stated, unequivocally, that any nuclear missile launched from Cuba against the United States would be construed as an attack by the Soviet Union itself. Kennedy demanded the Soviets remove all their offensive weapons, both missiles and bombers, if they truly wished to avoid the possibility of all-out nuclear war.

Johnny told Karen, "If there's nuclear war, Milwaukee will be wiped out."

"My God, what can we do?"

"Nothing . . . pray . . . ."

Tuesday, Kennedy ordered low-level reconnaissance flights over Cuba every two hours. On Thursday, the 25th, he raised military readiness to its highest level ever. At the United Nations his Ambassador, Adlai Stevenson, confronted the Soviets directly. When Stevenson asked about the missiles, the Soviet Ambassador refused to comment; Stevenson said he'd "wait till Hell freezes over" for a reply. Then in the most dramatic moment in the history of the United Nations, Stevenson showed the low-level reconnaissance photos of the missile sites. The effect was stunning: unmistakable evidence of the Soviet military presence in Cuba.

Johnny and Karen watched in disbelief. *Now,* Johnny believed, *war is inevitable.*

On Friday, the 26th, President Kennedy received an impassioned letter from Premier Khrushchev to resolve the crisis. Khrushchev proposed removing Soviet missiles and personnel if the United States would publicly guarantee not to invade Cuba. That same day, Kennedy received a second letter from Khrushchev demanding the removal of American missiles in Turkey in exchange for the removal of the Soviet missiles in Cuba. The President's brother, Attorney General Robert F. Kennedy, suggested ignoring the second letter, but informing Khrushchev of Kennedy's agreement with the first.

The American people were not informed of this sudden, bright, burst of hope. As Johnny drove home that evening into the fading October daylight, the copper sky polished as a pot, he wondered if he and Karen would survive the weekend. A feeling of abject and massive regret engulfed him. Their married life might end before it had really begun.

Entering their apartment, he asked, "Aren't you watching?" The television was off. "My God, Karen, we're on the brink of war. Don't you realize our lives might be over?"

She had been crying, but smiled at him. "Johnny, no, no . . . ."

"How can you smile?"

"Because we must live . . . ."

"We have no control over that . . . we control nothing."

"We can pray. You said that. We can thank God . . . ."

"For what – the end of the world?" His voice rang with bitterness.

She moved towards him, placing three fingers gently upon his lips. Her eyes were radiant and joyous. She whispered, "No, Johnny, for our baby . . . ."

+ + +

Later that night, Robert F. Kennedy, a month shy of his thirty-seventh birthday, went alone to the Soviet Embassy. Ambassador Dobrynin argued that Soviet missiles in Cuba were justified because of American missiles in Turkey. Kennedy suggested, wisely, that the Turkish missiles could possibly be included in a potential settlement, but he had to confer with his brother, the President. When he returned, he told Dobrynin that the President was ready "to examine favorably the question of Turkey." After Kennedy left, Dobrynin cabled the Kremlin.

Saturday, October 27, dawned into the darkest day of the crisis. The Soviets shot down a high altitude reconnaissance plane over Cuba. The American people presumed it would force Kennedy to respond militarily, leading to all-out war.

Sunday morning, Americans went to church in droves, praying that war would be averted. And then, what seemed miraculous to many, tensions began to ease. That afternoon Khrushchev publicly announced he would dismantle the Cuban installations and return the missiles to the Soviet Union. He expressed his trust that the United States would honor its commitment to never again invade Castro's totalitarian island. He made no mention of Kennedy's secret pledge to dismantle and remove the *Jupiters* from Turkey. Kennedy knew they weren't strategically necessary, but he also recognized they were the key to ending the crisis.

The world had never come closer to bilateral nuclear war. Save for the intelligence, patience, and wisdom of two extremely disparate men, President John F. Kennedy and Premier Nikita Khrushchev, *Hell* was averted.

On May 3, 1963, Karen Helden gave birth to twin boys.

Chapter 29 -· 1968

A fter the birth of Nicholas and John in 1963, Karen Helden took the summer off, but started teaching again in September. Karen named Nicholas for her father, a name she loved. Johnny Helden didn't mind, for it was his and his father's middle name, as well. The second son they decided to call John Junior or *JJ* for short.

Karen's mother agreed to baby sit the twins, but two years later, after the birth of a daughter, Ann, Karen quit teaching for good. She preferred staying home, caring for her three little ones.

A year after Ann's birth, Johnny joined a firm that did architectural and industrial work. He had tired of designing concrete box-girder bridges, one after another, month after month. Buildings and special structures, he believed, would prove more interesting.

In 1967, Karen gave birth to another daughter, Kristin. With that, Johnny considered their family complete.

They bought a three-bedroom, 1930's bungalow in Wauwatosa, a suburb just west of Milwaukee. The living room, dining room, and kitchen lined up front to back with each room getting successively smaller. When Karen's father-in-law, John Helden, first saw the kitchen he commented, "Remember, Karen, the size of the kitchen doesn't determine the quality of the meal." She smiled, for she knew he enjoyed her good cooking. Often Karen invited John and Anita to visit their grandchildren and stay for dinner.

The birth of twin boys and then a little girl thrilled both families. By the time Kristin came along, though, babies weren't such a big deal. Karen's younger sister, Katherine, had married and was pregnant. The youngest sister, Jane, a senior in high school, had enrolled at the University of Wisconsin for the fall semester of 1968 and, with irrepressible enthusiasm, looked forward to the fun she intended to have in Madison.

Without older sisters, Jane found home life boring. Only phone calls to friends made it bearable. She had no interest in current events particularly the war in Vietnam. When at the end of January the Vietcong and North Vietnamese launched seventy thousand troops against the American and South Vietnamese forces in the so-called *Tet Offensive,* she maintained an adamant disinterest. If her parents talked about it, she left the room. The last thing she wanted to hear was that nearly a thousand young Americans were killed during the two week battle. She hated such awful news. She was young, energetic, carefree, and fun-loving. Jane told her mother, "I refuse to think about what's happening in some stupid corner of the world."

+ + +

Once, after inviting her in-laws for dinner, Karen, with Anita's help, cleaned the kitchen before putting the children to bed. Joining her husband in the living room, she heard John Helden exclaim, "This is the war I feared the Democrats would get us into."

"Come on Dad, you never heard of Vietnam," Johnny replied.

"That's true, but they always seem to get us into a war somewhere."

Johnny turned off the television. "Yeah, but Kennedy kept us out of nuclear war. I'm not sure Nixon could've."

"Nonsense," John replied. "Nobody's that stupid."

"I despise war," Anita said. "It's tragic for a family to lose a son. We were always so worried that Michael and Johnny would be drafted."

"Yes," John said. "I was too young for the First World War and too old for the Second. Our sons were too young for Korea and now too old for Vietnam. We've been blessed. We have to be grateful."

"But how blessed are the sons that do serve?" Anita asked. "How do their parents feel? Believe me, we're far more lucky than blessed. If we were blessed there wouldn't be any wars. That there are tells me something is terribly wrong with the way men think."

"I agree," Karen said. "War never settles anything."

"That's not true," Johnny said. "We saved South Korea, defeated Japan . . . got rid of Hitler."

"And got Stalin in his place," John Helden said. "The Soviets are just as bad."

"That's exactly right," Johnny said. "So should we not oppose communism . . . just let them conquer and oppress every country in the world because we're not willing to fight? Let them deny people their liberty, ban religion, free speech, owning property, everything we supposedly cherish, but don't care enough to defend for others?"

"That won't happen," John answered. "They don't have the resources, plus I doubt they have the will." He glanced at Anita who seemed content.

"They have surrogates: North Korea and now North Vietnam. Castro's only ninety miles from Florida. Are you suggesting we do nothing, just sit back and enjoy our fun and games, while the rest of the world goes up in flames? And don't forget, Dad, they always do it brutally. Good people die . . . teachers, newspaper publishers, priests . . . ."

"You know," John Helden said, "I've often wondered what America would be like if we hadn't fought the Civil War."

Johnny laughed. "Dad, what's that got to do with anything?" He glanced out the front window. "It's raining."

John Helden looked to see how hard. "Well, back in the 1860s or '70s, without the Civil War, I believe slavery would have died a natural death. The abolition movement was growing. As old slaveholders died off, younger generations would have recognized the evils of slavery and, eventually, set their slaves free without government edict or war. Had Lincoln not used force after Fort Sumter, had he just let things quiet down without resorting to military action, who knows how things might've turned out?"

"Dad, that's debatable, but pointless," Johnny said. "You can't rewrite history."

"I'm not trying to; I'm just speculating. Another example: what would the world be like if we hadn't gone into the First World War?"

"You mean not help the British and French?"

"Exactly – we helped defeat Germany, but what did we get for it? The British and French imposed extremely harsh conditions at Versailles, which led to tremendous resentment in Germany and, eventually, gave rise to Hitler. What did Hitler say to gain power? He simply told the people that war reparations were unjust, that Germany had every right to stop paying them so the country could begin to work to restore its national prestige and wealth. That made sense to Germans. But Hitler seethed with anger and hatred to avenge Germany's defeat in 1918. Had we not allied ourselves with Britain and France, the war would have ended in stalemate because it had been stalemated since 1916. That would have resulted in a more just truce. Very likely, Hitler never would've gained power."

"Dad, you have to accept history as it is. It's pouring outside . . . ."

"We hear," Karen said. "Let your father finish."

"If there was no Second World War and even though the communists took over Russia, they wouldn't have been able to move into Central Europe, as they did in 1945 when they drove Hitler back to Germany. It's very possible Poland, Hungary, Czechoslovakia, Yugoslavia, and East Germany might have remained free."

"You sound like Uncle Lew," Johnny said.

"Well, not exactly, though he made a good point. Had we not gone into the First World War and had there not been, because of it, a second war in Europe, then Japan would have been far more cautious in her ambitions. They attacked Pearl Harbor because they knew we'd fight to save Europe. They would have been very reluctant to attack us if we only had to fight them."

Karen turned towards Johnny. "Your father knows he can't rewrite history. He's making a case to avoid future wars because the consequences of going to war are so unpredictable."

"That's right," John said. "Next time a president beats the drums of war for some perceived threat, that is exactly when we shouldn't go to war unless, of course, we're directly attacked. What we need is better diplomacy. Look at Vietnam . . . what a mess. Where will it lead? How will it end? How many will die? MacArthur warned never get involved in a land war in Asia."

"Yeah, but he fought one in Korea," Johnny said. "That's Asia."

"Truman ordered it. That was small, manageable peninsula, but we still couldn't win once the Chinese communists poured in. We lost tens of thousands of young men. Had we not gone into the First World War, the Korean War might never have happened."

"Boy, Dad, I'd sure love to peer into your backward-gazing crystal ball," Johnny said.

"Johnny," Karen said, "its future wars your father hopes to avoid. He's just saying our leaders have to think more seriously before rushing into some stupid war."

"I understand. I'm just not convinced we'll ever have such

wisdom in our leaders or such accommodating adversaries. Usually, it's because someone threatens or attacks. Look at South Korea. Because of what we did it's still a free country and our ally."

"True, but we still should evaluate future threats more intelligently," John said. "More deliberately, more cautiously; and we have to stay strong. We disarmed after the war, and that emboldened North Korea. Our rationale for overwhelming military power should be to never have to use it because an adversary would so fear that power. This is why diplomacy is so important. Incompetent diplomats usually end up turning matters over to the generals. War signifies death – the death of diplomacy and the death of innocents."

"John, it's raining very hard; we should go," Anita said. "I'm tired and I'm sure Karen is, too."

+ + +

In Los Angeles, Michael quit the insurance company to work for a financial public relations firm. His knowledge of finance and his ability to write about it impressed the partners. Michael quickly grasped an understanding of the business and, for the first time in his early career, found real satisfaction in his job.

+ + +

When President Kennedy sent military advisers to Vietnam, he stated that the United States had to help our friends resist the spread of communism whenever and wherever it occurred. If we didn't stand in South Vietnam, he argued, other countries in Southeast Asia – Laos, Cambodia and Thailand – would fall like dominos. Kennedy's assassination on November 22, 1963, elevated Vice President Lyndon Johnson to Commander-in-Chief. Thereafter began a long, slow slide into a protracted jungle war.

In August, 1964, Johnson claimed North Vietnamese torpedo boats in the Gulf of Tonkin had attacked American destroyers without provocation. In retaliation, Johnson and his advisers decided to launch air attacks against North Vietnam. They also asked Congress to pass a resolution granting the President authority to repel attacks against American forces and to take all steps necessary for the defense of our allies in Southeast Asia. The problem with all of this was that the alleged torpedo attacks never occurred. As later revealed, it was a fabrication, a massive deceit that led eventually to the deaths of over fifty-seven thousand young Americans.

Johnson and his ministers expanded the war in South Vietnam from a limited, focused, localized reaction against communist guerrillas, the Vietcong, to an all-out war against North Vietnam. Little did Johnson's imperious cadre care about the right of the American people to know the truth, and little did they anticipate the tenacious toughness of their anointed foe.

On March 31, 1968, Johnson, realizing his once broad support had sharply contracted, announced he wouldn't run for reelection. He still possessed, though, nine months to escalate the increasingly vicious war making extrication that much more difficult for his successor. *And who might that be,* people wondered: Vice President Humphrey, Senator Eugene McCarthy of Minnesota, Senator Robert F. Kennedy of New York, or, perhaps, Nixon that washed-up Republican who couldn't even win the California governorship in 1962?

"Good riddance," John Helden, his wife, sons, and daughter-in-law all agreed after Johnson's unexpected withdrawal.

+ + +

John Helden hadn't sold a new milk tank since the debacle with the plastic tanks, and while there were many Helden tanks still on the road, his repair business floundered. Haulers near Milwaukee still brought tanks in for minor repairs, but if John wanted to make money by selling something, he had to scavenge for an old, beat-up tank, repair it, and then hunt for a buyer. "It's a tough way to make a buck," he told Anita.

With a bewildered melancholy, he often recalled those lucrative years after the war and in the early fifties when he took for granted that the good times would continue right up to his retirement. His old customers, Lee Marnet and Buster Moore, died of heart attacks; Bill Donnelly sold out before he retired. Others began trading in their old Helden tanks to purchase the stainless steel beauties that rolled out of Kold Karry's plant. Kold Karry gladly took used Helden tanks in trade. They emerged dominant and profitable precisely because Helden no longer was a competitor.

Observing Kold Karry's great success and his own lack of it, John Helden, in the declining years of his career, blamed his cousin. The Helden Company grew more profitable than ever selling petroleum transport tanks. Neither Peter Jr. nor Pete gave a damn about losing the milk tank business. "We didn't need it," they agreed whenever they discussed its demise, never recalling their own egregious mistake that caused the downfall. The last thing they cared or thought about was John Helden's financial plight, as he neared retirement. Peter Jr. hadn't talked to John in years, vacationing every winter in Florida while letting Pete run the business.

When John mentioned his retirement to Anita, she reacted with mixed feelings, for she couldn't foresee how life might unfold having her husband home all day. At least, when he went to work she didn't have to worry about his moods. He decided to officially retire the last day of May, 1968, several weeks after his sixty-sixth birthday.

John still had to find a buyer for the shop building to pay off the remaining mortgage. He intended to sell his equipment, for he needed every dollar he could get if he was going to have a halfway decent retirement. He advertised in the newspapers and had one serious inquiry about purchasing the building, but the man wanted to buy it on a land contract. John's brother-in-law, Lew Thilman, suggested John should offer to rent the building though John claimed the buyer wouldn't agree to that. Actually, the deal appealed to John because the land contract would cover the last two years of mortgage payments. Then for the following thirteen years the income would augment his Social Security.

"I'll be eighty-one at the end of the contract," John told Anita. "I might be dead."

John sold the building and all its equipment on the buyer's terms. Because Helden milk transport tanks still roamed the roads, John continued selling replacement parts not made by Helden – valves, dust covers, electrical parts, etc. – out of his home. Some months he earned several hundred dollars. And he had his two other primary interests: the piano and reading. When the day of the land contract closing came, he left the shop for the last time, feeling pretty good about it.

+ + +

Shortly after the start of the New Year, 1969, Johnny Helden was let go by the consulting firm he had joined in 1966. The boss called him in, claiming they just didn't have enough work going forward. He told Johnny to pack his books and gear and leave immediately.

"I've got work on my board," Johnny protested. "Don't you want me to finish?"

"We know what you're doing," Collings answered. "I need this to be your last day. We'll mail your check."

"This is kind of a shock . . . ."

"John, use me as a reference. I'm pleased with what you did for us, but we can't keep you. We just don't have the work."

Johnny assured a distraught Karen that he'd find a new job real quick because he had every reason to believe his previous employers would speak well of him. By the first of March, B & X Engineering, another national firm, hired Johnny at a salary fifty dollars a month less than his previous job. He was glad to have it. He met Phil Heller there; with the passing months they became good friends. Heller, intelligent and a seasoned structural engineer, was seven years older than Johnny. From him Johnny would learn much.

Johnny's new boss, Robert Jaffray, mentored the younger engineers. Johnny gained from that, as well. B & X served the city's best architects doing the largest and most notable buildings including hospitals, schools, and other large commercial and industrial projects, exactly the kind of engineering Johnny wanted to practice. He passed the sixteen hours of written exams to become a licensed Professional Engineer, indispensable for his future career. As the end of March approached, Karen and he looked forward to the coming of spring.

+ + +

On the evening of April 4, 1968, in Memphis, Tennessee, an assassin murdered Dr. Martin Luther King, Jr. Dr. King had agreed to lead a march in sympathy with striking garbage workers. Not five years had passed since the assassination of President Kennedy, and now two of America's finest and most idealistic men had been slain by despicable descendants of John Wilkes Booth.

In 126 cities across America, sorrow and anger in black neighborhoods erupted into riots that killed forty-six people and injured over three thousand. A year earlier, racial confrontations in Newark and Detroit sparked a race riot in Milwaukee; though it was deemed relatively minor by the press, three people died, a hundred were injured and 1,740 arrested. In 1968, however, it was almost as though Milwaukee's black community was too profoundly saddened, too deeply hurt, almost as though they knew – to their great credit – that Dr. King wouldn't want them reverting to violence.

"That Monday I went to work, remember?" Johnny asked Karen, recalling the summer of 1967. "A curfew was in effect, but Mr. Jaffray called and asked me to come in and, if I got stopped, just tell the police we were working on a government project under deadline."

"Yes, I remember very well because I didn't want you to go."

"I passed cops in squad cars with their rifles sticking out the windows. That looked unbelievable strange, so foreign . . . ."

"Pointed at you?"

"No, no, towards the sky."

"Well, let's hope there won't be another," Karen said.

"Blacks are suffering; sooner or later there'll be a reaction. My dad always points out that it's a hundred years since the Civil War. Man, you'd think we'd be further along."

"They don't get the education."

"Why not? You were a good teacher. You had black kids."

"Many come from homes that don't value education. The parents aren't educated."

"So it's generational. How can that be changed?"

"When I was still teaching, we were told to move kids through, whether they passed or not. People think that's terrible, but what's a school supposed to do with some seventeen year old kid, strong as a horse, who won't work to pass freshmen English his third time around? Those guys are tough. They can create bedlam in a classroom. Administrators have only one choice: give them a *D minus* and get them out. And that's exactly what we did because we realized some situations are kind of hopeless. Some kids just don't care to learn."

"But of the black kids that wasn't a majority, was it?"

"No, many were good, especially girls. But if every public high school every year has ten or twenty really bad students – white or black – you're talking about a lot of kids coming out with very poor educations. What can they do? What kind of jobs can they get? What kind of futures do they have?"

"They're drafting those guys and shipping them to Vietnam."

"I know," Karen said. "So what do they do when they get back? If they get back . . . ."

"I don't know."

Three days after Dr. King's assassination, Mary Louise Thilman celebrated her ninetieth birthday. John and Anita hosted a dinner party, inviting Johnny, Karen, the four grandchildren, plus Lew, Carol, and their five children, ages nine to twenty. Michael, Dom, and Dorothy remained out west though Anita pleaded for their return.

At dinner, Mary Louise, still mentally sharp, expressed horror at the assassination of Dr. King, telling again the old stories of how her husband had gone out in the middle of the night to deliver Negro babies over a period of so many long years until he was physically exhausted. She even boasted, "Dr. King would have been very proud of my husband."

+ + +

On the first of June at breakfast, John Helden announced to his unsurprised wife that he was now officially retired though he hadn't done much of anything since the sale of the shop several weeks earlier. After his coffee, he went up to his den and called brothers George and Julius, son Michael in Los Angeles, Johnny at B & X, his brother-in-law, Lew Thilman, and several friends and business acquaintances to inform them of his retirement after forty-five years of selling, and twenty years of servicing, milk transport tanks.

John regarded selling spare parts more hobby than business. He enjoyed calling former customers who still needed replacement parts. He wanted to keep his name "out there." In addition, he had his reading, piano playing, helping with household chores, as well as chauffeuring Anita and her mother on domestic and medical errands.

John's remaining but ever diminishing ambition focused on the piano. He attained his greatest technical proficiency at age twenty. Now, occasionally, he'd peruse pieces he learned then: Chopin's *Third Ballade,* Beethoven's *Moonlight Sonata,* Mendelssohn's *Rondo Capriccioso,* and marveled that he once played them, for now they seemed far beyond his aging technique.

Anita knew the importance of music in her husband's life and encouraged John. Initially, he practiced with great fervor. After three months, though, his rigorous schedule had been abandoned. In fact, he found practicing two hours a day just too much. He preferred reading, walking, and talking on the phone. Regaining his youthful artistry lingered, however, like a recurring dream.

John and Anita's relationship had eroded to the point where they never discussed their deepest thoughts and feelings. They enjoyed talking about the grandchildren and agreed almost rapturously that Nick, JJ, Ann and Kristin were beautiful and smart. But, as years passed, they let the romance of their early love slowly slip away. They withdrew from each other because they didn't possess the simple wisdom to use the marriage bed to stay bound to one another. Indeed, it was forsaken for separate bedrooms. Anita moved into Johnny's old room. John kept the master. By that time, the link of conjugal love had been broken irrevocably.

Anita found the arrangement acceptable, more so than she dare say. Occasionally, John felt desire for his wife yet suppressed it, believing intimacy the last thing she'd be interested in, while she suspected he had lost his sexual interest entirely and so never mentioned it. In any event, it would have been extremely difficult for Anita because John had too often been abusive: not physically, but emotionally and mentally.

Anita never could repel John's verbal onslaughts, never could counter or deflect them. She absorbed their full brutality into her heart, holding it there secretly. She deceived John and her sons into believing that when she forgave him, as she always did, she also forgot. But the pain remained ever present, haunting and frightening, because, even though John was growing older, he still exhibited dark moods that often foretold the coming of the verbal violence. Usually, it was just a matter of time before the same old things began to corrupt his mind and memory: failures, disappointments, mistakes, perceived and real injustices, his forsaken dreams, and, sadly, what John assumed to be Anita's unloving heart when, in fact, it was a heart too often battered and broken by him. Intuitively, she could sense the coming attack, but she never devised a preemptive, protective strategy or an adequate defense save one: she ceased loving her attacker.

With both sons gone, the house on Harding Boulevard became a strange sanctuary with an inverted emphasis. For John, it was his place to leave; for Anita her place to stay. Almost daily, John went to lunch with old cronies or headed downtown just to look around. In the fall, he'd drive to the country for apples and cider. He liked visiting his old boyhood neighborhood around 31st and Lincoln, saying prayers at his parents' graves at Mount Olivet, or hiking along the Menomonee River. He even did the grocery shopping alone because it got him out of the house. He joked with clerks, something Anita had no patience for because she knew it was John's salesman's personality oddly craving the facile attention of strangers.

Often he drove alone to Basses Bay. He parked his car so he could sight the little lake between Uncle Henry's old cottage – it had been enlarged and remodeled – and the neighbor's. Then John recalled his boyhood memories, while melancholy filled his heart. *Was it really so long ago,* he pondered. *Is so much of my life already over?* Only God knew where such questions might lead. When he returned to his clean, comfortable house, he could always count on a good, home-cooked meal because, in that regard, Anita was absolutely dependable.

Unlike her husband, Anita enjoyed staying home. When he left, the house became her haven. She read the newspaper and wrote letters to Michael, Dom and Dorothy in Tucson, and her cousins, especially Susie. She cleaned, did laundry, and worked on her photo albums without worrying and wondering what might be churning in John's shadowy mind.

Anita's memories of girlhood summers with her maternal grandmother in the little farming town of Belgium, north of Milwaukee, lingered in her heart. She loved those sweet days when her grandmother washed Anita's hair in the soft rainwater saved in the cistern, and when she so often played with her little friend, Louie, across the road. *He tried to kiss me once, but I was only seven so I pushed him away, but now, I think, it would have been alright.*

Every day at four, Anita called her mother. They talked for an hour. At five, she began preparing dinner. She needed time to steel herself against John's return, for she never knew how he might be. A good dinner, she reasoned, was to her advantage. Sadly, with John home, pleasant as it often seemed, she knew she was never entirely safe.

+ + +

On June 5, 1968, an assassin shot Robert F. Kennedy at point blank range moments after Kennedy acknowledged his victory in the California Democratic presidential primary. In a rented room only seven blocks from the Ambassador Hotel where the crime occurred, Michael Helden had fallen asleep before the midnight murder. He didn't learn of it, like Johnny and Karen, until the morning when Kennedy died.

"My God, what is happening to this country," Karen asked. She liked Kennedy.

"I don't know," Johnny answered. "I think law enforcement's gotta devise better ways to protect public figures. Obviously, there's a lot of hatred when you kill someone just because you dislike their ideas or the color of their skin."

"Kennedy was a very good man, very idealistic."

"He certainly was a good Catholic . . . ten kids, another on the way."

"Oh, how terribly sad . . . ."

"Yeah, lucky for his wife they're rich."

"Good heaven, Johnny, money can't make up for the loss of a husband and father."

"I know, but it'll make things easier."

"That won't lessen her sorrow."

"Karen, I understand. I'm not talking about that. I'm just saying it'll be easier for her to raise their kids alone because he was a wealthy man. Why do you think they had ten kids? It's because they could afford them."

"I suppose, but they obviously wanted a large family. He came from a large family."

"They could afford it. No way could we have ten, not with what I earn. We can barely afford four."

"Well, I think that's perfectly valid. Poorer people should limit the size of their family."

"That's not what the old song says." Johnny sang, "Oh, the rich get rich and the poor get children . . . ."

Karen rolled her eyes.

What troubled him was the issue of birth control. The Catholic Church adamantly opposed it so Karen and he abstained from love making when Karen thought she might be ovulating, which to Johnny seemed like all the time. Karen made it clear right from the start that she believed in the Church's teaching.

The introduction of the so-called "birth control pill" in 1960 changed people's attitudes, inside and outside the Church. For the first time, the pill put women in complete and secret control of their bodies. Only they would decide when to allow the possibility of pregnancy. It was first believed the pill granted this freedom without any apparent negative side effects, but by the mid-sixties, contrary evidence was beginning to accumulate. Most complaints were minor: nausea, bloating, weight gain, and depression, but there were more serious side effects as well, especially, blood clots and strokes. Even so, Karen's doctor recommended the pill knowing she wasn't planning another child. Johnny asked Uncle Julius about it because Karen wasn't convinced.

"I wouldn't make my wife take it. I don't think you should make Karen, too many unknowns. What do you do now?"

"Abstain."

Julius chuckled. "The old rhythm method, eh?"

"Yeah," Johnny answered.

"Stick with it. Abstinence increases desire just like hunger builds an appetite. I've found that true my entire married life."

Relieved by Julius's advice, Karen rejected the idea of a daily pill all the way to menopause.

"So what it really boils down to," Johnny said, "if you're rich and can afford ten kids, then you get to make love more than a poor guy."

Karen laughed out loud. "Only you, Johnny Helden, would think such a thing."

"Well it's true. We abstain because we're afraid you'll get pregnant because we both know we can't afford it."

"Life isn't necessarily fair . . . ."

"That's why I think the Church is wrong," Johnny said. "Do we or do we not have the right to limit the size of our family?"

"Oh I believe we have that right, absolutely."

"Then I think we should be able to use some type of birth control – other than the pill, I mean."

"No, Johnny. If we, for whatever reason – money, health, emotions – decide not to have any more kids, then we have to abstain on days I could get pregnant. If we freely choose to have only four, which I believe is our God-given right, then we have the responsibility to avoid intercourse when I might get pregnant. That's the right way. The Church is absolutely correct. There has to be that quid pro quo."

"Why do people make love?"

"What do you mean?"

"Do they make love just to procreate? The Church teaches sex is primarily for procreation, but let's analyze that. We're married six years. How many times have we made love? Let's say once a week, fifty times a year, three hundred times since we're married. We have four kids. So you tell me: what's the primary purpose of sex? The Church says procreation, but look at the disparity, look at the ratio. We've had intercourse seventy-five times for each kid. I believe the primary purpose is the love of husband and wife, the desire to bond emotionally and spiritually, something we've always agreed on, plus the joy intimacy brings. It isn't children. You got pregnant three times; two hundred and ninety-seven other times you didn't. So tell me: what do you think the *primary* purpose of sex really is?

"Johnny," Karen drew out his name. "Sex is an appetite. It's like hunger."

"Right, and when I'm hungry I eat. Just because I ate a thousand times last year doesn't mean I don't want to eat tonight."

"Yes, but if I make porterhouse every night you'll get sick of it. I make it once a month, and you love it. If we make love without that relatively short time of abstinence – and what's seven or ten days – you'd tire of me. You know how you get, and I love that. But it's precisely because we have that time off that builds our desire. If we use birth control I think you'd tire of me."

"I doubt it."

"Well, you never know, and I don't care to find out. Our love making has always been wonderful . . . you've always told me that. Are you saying you're profoundly unhappy just because we have to abstain a few days every month?"

"No, it's just that sometimes I'm in the mood, but I can't express it. That seems unnaturally repressive. I work hard. I try to be a good husband and father, and making love rewards that. But if I have that desire – sorry – the Church decrees I either have to run the risk of another child we can't afford, or I have to abstain. I cannot, however, under any circumstances use birth control."

"Johnny, I broke up with Jack Cutler because he wanted to use birth control. He didn't even want kids until I insisted. Then he told me – oh, he was such a chauvinist – after two kids I had to use birth control."

"Are you suggesting we'd split over this? Hey, I forgot about that Cutler guy."

"No, what I'm saying is the more one overindulges an appetite, the less that appetite is satisfied."

"I'm not talking about overindulgence. I'd just like it when the desire is there."

"True love is sacrificial, you know that. If you truly love me then make that little sacrifice. I promise you, when we do make love, I will do anything to satisfy your deepest desires. Please, Johnny, try to see it my way."

"I just don't believe, for people like us, it's wrong."

"It'd be wrong for me, Johnny. I'll make love anytime you wish, but then we have to accept the consequences."

"We can't afford another child unless I make more money.

"Then you have to see it my way."

He said nothing. He knew the strength of her convictions. He decided not to mention it again and prayed only once, "Dear God, if Karen does get pregnant, let it be just one."

+ + +

Intense conversation about Kennedy's assassination consumed Johnny's office. Mr. Jaffray strolled through, reminding everyone it was an engineering office not a newsroom. After work, as they walked to their cars, Phil Heller told Johnny, "It's too easy to get handguns. Any deranged idiot can get one."

"The real danger lurks in the human heart."

"Yeah," Phil agreed, "but there still should be some kind of registration. You have to register a car and earn the license to drive."

"That wouldn't compel criminals. Deer hunters would register their rifles, but I doubt criminals will register stolen or black market handguns."

"John, something has to be done. This country can't go on like this. King and Kennedy were killed by guns."

"No, Phil, they were murdered by evil men. Maybe we should teach all of our children, *Thou shalt not kill.* Oh, sorry, we can't teach that in the public schools anymore."

"Come on, the guy was a deranged Palestinian."

"So, you think he would've registered his handgun?" Johnny laughed out loud. It irritated Phil who didn't appreciate John's cavalier attitude. Phil felt the same bitter frustration so many Americans felt. They wanted the Government to do something – anything.

+ + +

Bob Schmitt called Johnny earlier that spring wondering if B & X could prepare plans for remodeling an old warehouse at SMF's plant, widely regarded as a neighborhood eyesore. Without knowing if his boss would take such a small project, Johnny said, "Sure."

When Johnny told Mr. Jaffray, he responded enthusiastically. "Of course, meet with your friend. See what he needs."

Bob wanted the old, beat-up metal siding on the warehouse replaced with concrete block and architectural wall panels. It seemed feasible to Johnny, and Mr. Jaffray agreed. "See if they have any old plans. If not, you'll have to field measure . . . record your time."

It took Johnny three weeks to do the job during which he and Schmitt had several meetings. At the last one, Bob's father, the sole owner, approved the proposed appearance of the remodeled warehouse. He liked what he saw then left, barely acknowledging Johnny. Wisely, he ignored the slight. What impressed him was how closely Bob resembled his father. "No one would ever doubt whose son you are," Johnny told Bob.

After the building permit was issued, Bob treated Johnny to lunch. They had associated more in 1961 and '62, but now, after working together, Bob suggested they start golfing again. They set a date that turned out to be the Saturday after Kennedy's death. Karen mentioned that Aunt Beth was coming over that morning to discuss flowers for the gardens.

Bob had reserved a ten o'clock tee time. He pulled up at the Heldens just minutes after Aunt Beth arrived. Johnny invited Bob in to say hello to Karen who was in the backyard with her aunt.

At the rear door Bob shouted, "Hi Karen." He turned to leave.

"Oh, Bob, wait; I'd like you to meet my Aunt Elizabeth." Looking back she was surprised that Beth stood several steps behind. She had stopped the instant she saw young Bob Schmitt.

"Hello," he said, in a disinterested, monotonic voice.

Elizabeth was speechless. An insistent fear quickened her heart. *My God, he looks just like his father . . . .*

"Aunt Beth," Karen said.

"Oh, yes . . . how do you do?"

"I do wonderful, but we gotta go. Goodbye."

Johnny, clubs slung over his shoulder, glanced at Karen. Elizabeth's awkward and hesitant reaction in meeting Bob Schmitt bewildered them both. They couldn't possibly suspect that Schmitt possessed the same despicable, mustached face that many years ago Elizabeth prayed she'd never encounter again.

+ + +

In early August, 1968, a self-resurrected Richard Nixon won the Republican nomination for president. Two weeks later, Soviet tanks rumbled into Prague, crushing the tender blossoming of liberty known as the *Prague Spring,* the Czechoslovakian experiment with liberalized communism. The Johnson Administration did nothing, citing as precedent Eisenhower's failure to confront the Soviet Union in Hungary in 1956.

It became obvious to the American people that their Government had abandoned Central and Eastern Europe to the ruthless tyranny of the Soviets, but gave every indication it would defend

Western Europe even if it meant nuclear war. The Government, however, didn't seem to have any reservation sending armed forces half way around the world to fight communism in the small countries of Southeast Asia, countries dangerously close to Communist China. But now more and more Americans were beginning to see the war in Vietnam as a senseless quagmire.

At the Democratic National Convention in late August, violent clashes occurred between anti-war protestors and Illinois National Guardsmen along with the Chicago police. After a tumultuous convention, a weakened Vice President Hubert Humphrey was nominated for president. Many Americans linked him to the failed war policies of Johnson's Administration.

Nixon had the great political advantage of being able to promise that his new leadership would end the war in Vietnam. An eager reporter once asked Nixon if he had a secret plan to end the war. Nixon replied that "to tip my hand" would interfere with the Paris peace negotiations with the North Vietnamese. So, while he never used the phrase, he let the gullible public believe that there did exist – in his mind – a secret plan.

John Helden was all for Nixon. He abhorred Lyndon Johnson and didn't think much of Humphrey either. He told his brother, Julius, that Nixon's secret plan would end the horrible war, which John despised even more than the Korean War. Julius, far more skeptical, responded, "Yeah, Nixon's secret plan is so secret even he doesn't know it."

John stammered, "Well, you shouldn't say that. He's a man of integrity."

"We'll see . . . ."

Nixon was elected on November 5th in a count almost as close as his loss to Kennedy in 1960. Democrat Governor George Wallace of Alabama, champion of States Rights for the unholy cause of continuing segregation in the Deep South, garnered almost ten million votes. Had he not been in the race, who knows what the outcome might have been?

John Helden called Julius the next morning after Nixon's win was finally confirmed. "Now we'll see what Nixon can do."

"I wish him well," Julius replied. "Getting out of that damn war won't be easy. I don't care how good his secret plan is."

"Yeah, the war is just draining the life out of this country. He's got to end it."

"You know, Johnny, I often wonder if this would've happened had Kennedy lived. I always thought he had a better understanding of the world. He handled that Cuban missile crisis extremely well. I just don't believe he would've gotten us in so deep in Vietnam."

+ + +

At sixty-six, Anita Helden decided she'd host Thanksgiving yet another year. She could hardly expect her daughter-in-law to prepare a big dinner with four little ones under foot, though Karen gladly would have done it. Nick and little Johnny were five, Ann, three, and Kristin just a year. Anita's brother Lew, his wife Carol, and their five children celebrated their own feast with Carol's elderly parents. Michael decided to stay in Los Angeles so Anita's guests included only her mother Mary Louise Thilman, Johnny, Karen, and the children.

Several days before Thanksgiving, Mary Louise became ill. The doctor suspected indigestion – her heart sounded okay – but antacids helped not at all. Thanksgiving morning Mary Louise called Anita, stating she was too sick to come. She asked, though, if Johnny and Karen would stop and visit, as she always enjoyed seeing her great-grandchildren. Mary Louise developed some dull, achy pains in her arms and shoulders, but chose not to mention them to Anita, taking a couple aspirins instead.

The children delighted her. She remarked, "My, Karen, you certainly know how to make pretty babies." Johnny noted her good spirits though she moved slowly.

Friday morning Mary Louise called and asked Anita to come. After a bad night, she felt exhausted and sick. John dropped his wife off then went home to play the piano. Anita helped her mother to the bathroom and then back to bed.

Anita heated the plate of food she had brought along. Mary Louise ate only a little before pushing the tray away. Moments later she vomited, soiling her bedding.

Anita wiped her mother's mouth, stripped the sheets, and changed the foul blankets. When she asked her mother if she'd like to get back into bed, Mary Louise could not rise from the chair.

Anita struggled to help, shocked at her mother's sudden loss of strength. She called her brother, Lew Thilman, who told her to call the doctor right away. Then she called her husband, but didn't think to call a priest.

They all arrived within the hour. Now Mary Louise was slipping in and out of consciousness. The doctor listened to her heart and lungs. "Her heart rate is very slow, very weak . . . ."

Lew asked, "Should she be hospitalized?"

The doctor shook his head.

Mary Louise whimpered, ". . .'nita, help me." Within minutes she died.

Born ninety years earlier in 1878, she was the youngest of eleven children, a farm girl who never finished high school, but read widely and loved learning. She was beautiful in face and form and smart enough to marry a doctor for whom she bore three children, including a son who was twice elected to the House of Representatives. After the birth of her last child, she underwent a complete hysterectomy because of multiple, intrauterine tumors. She blamed the tumors on a mishap she suffered when, at sixteen, helping with the haying, she fell hard against the rounded end of a wooden handled pitchfork.

When doctors discovered a large tumor in Anita Helden's uterus after the birth of Johnny in 1937, Anita's father advised her to have just the tumor removed rather than the complete hysterectomy that Anita's gynecologist recommended. Her father told her, "A hysterectomy ruined my marriage. I don't want it ruining yours."

The Tuesday morning after Thanksgiving, Johnny and Karen Helden attended Mary Louise Thilman's funeral Mass and the wintry burial next to her doctor husband who died in 1938. The entire family was there: Anita and John, Michael who flew in from Los Angeles, Lew, Carol, their children, and Dom and Dorothy who flew in from Tucson. Most of Anita's country cousins came to show respect for their beloved aunt.

After the luncheon, Lew Thilman rose to say a few words. He thanked everyone for coming before saying, "The death of my mother represents the end of that generation of the Pierron family born in the two decades after the Civil War. She was the youngest of eleven and lived the longest, and the fact is that the bonds among all her descendants and relatives will not remain nearly as strong, now that she's gone. She was a cohesive figure for the Pierron family. I well know from observing other families how the loss of such a matriarchal presence has a splintering effect on the survivors. I wish it weren't that way, but it will . . . ."

John whispered to Anita, "He should tell some funny stories from the old days."

"These gatherings," Lew continued, "are unique in the sense that we shall never be so gathered together again." The room grew exceedingly quiet. "We'll leave here today and joke with one another: 'hope to see you soon, but not at another funeral.' Then we'll laugh and hug each other and go our separate ways. Before we know it, two or three years will have flown by. Some of us will have gone to the Lord. That's just the way life is. And in five years? Well, all bets are off."

When it was over, everyone made light of Lew's somber remarks, even teasing whose funeral might be next. Many of the country cousins were in their seventies and eighties and possessed robust senses of humor, if not robust health.

Anita Helden glanced at her husband, resolving in her heart, *I shall outlive you.*

Chapter 30 ~ 1971

Karen Helden's baby sister, Jane Anderson, registered at the University of Wisconsin in the isthmus, capital city of Madison at the end of August, 1968, with giddy enthusiasm and a haughty confidence that she'd have the best college career of anyone, meaning of course, her two, older sisters.

Clothes shopping, phone conversations, packing, repacking, and parties consumed Jane's last several hectic weeks at home. She relished every minute. Never had she felt so excited about life. Never did she feel such a rush of anticipation, nor was she ever so ready to have fun. Her parents had to remind her that she was going to a great university, not a never-ending party, and she had to study and do well in her courses. Jane barely heard it. She knew what she had to do and didn't need her parents telling her anything.

Karen remarked to Johnny, "She's so immature."

"She'll be fine."

"She's not ready to go away. She doesn't take things seriously."

"When I went to Notre Dame, I wasn't ready. What kid's really ready to go away to college? It's like marriage; nobody's ever ready for it. People learn, adapt. Jane will too."

At Jane's going away party, Johnny asked her, "You gonna go to football games?"

"Wouldn't miss a one. They'll be great."

"Yeah, right . . . the Badgers didn't win a game last year."

"Doesn't matter," Jane giggled. "They'll be great this year."

When she got to the university, its intensity surprised her: meeting people, learning the vast campus, registering, buying books, eating in a rush, and never getting quite enough sleep. She hoped, once those pressures passed and classes started, her life would settle down. Though the first school week seemed easy enough, after a few weeks the work piled up, and she found herself lagging behind, not other kids, necessarily, but where the syllabus told her she should be.

On weekends, coursework forced her to study, but she wanted some fun, too. She befriended girls who felt the same; they started going places that welcomed the college crowd. They even tried sneaking into some of the popular beer bars where upper classmen went with such apparent joy. She resented having to be twenty-one to drink alcohol although now she could smoke without her parents' hounding. Within a few weeks she reached a pack a day.

The Wisconsin Badgers lost their season opener to Arizona State in Tempe by the outrageous score of 55 to 7, which caused derision among many in the student body. Serious students simply didn't care. Jane screamed her support at the home opener, which Wisconsin lost to Washington, 21 to 17. She consoled herself with the closeness of the score and looked forward to the next game against Michigan State. She told her new acquaintances, "We'll beat 'em; you'll see." They laughed at her naive optimism.

At the end of the game, the scoreboard in Camp Randall Stadium read *Michigan State 39, Wisconsin 0*. Jane heard the comments. "Shit, if they don't beat Utah, we oughta drop football." The following Saturday the Badgers lost to Utah State.

Jane called her mother. "Football games are so bad. People boo all the time. They can't even score touchdowns . . . stadium's half empty . . . it's no fun at all."

"How's your schoolwork?"

Jane snapped a perfunctory, "Fine."

"What are your favorite classes?"

"I don't want to talk about it. I deal with that all week."

"Jane, take school seriously. Your father won't send you if you don't."

"I know."

Jane decided to study harder because she knew her father would pull her out if she didn't. Football bored her. The Badgers kept losing, and Jane never went to another game. The beer bars proved hard to get into because her fake ID wasn't credible. Plus, she didn't like any of the guys who showed some interest in her. *I might as well study,* she concluded, because the thought of living at home and *getting some stupid job* was sufficiently depressing to compel her to achieve first semester grades that were, at least in her mind, pretty good: four *C's* and one *B*.

+ + +

On February 1, 1968, during the *Tet Offensive,* South Vietnamese General Nguyen Ngoc Loan killed a young, defenseless Vietcong prisoner with a single shot to the temple. Eddie Adams of the Associated Press photographed the incident earning him a Pulitzer Prize. It became an iconic photograph that helped galvanize opposition to the Vietnam War and strongly suggested all that was supposedly wrong with America's involvement in it.

After the photo garnered worldwide attention, Adams was assigned to accompany General Loan on his military rounds. His troops regarded Loan a hero, as did the Vietnamese people for whom he had successfully built hospitals throughout South Vietnam. Moments before the infamous picture was taken, several of General Loan's soldiers had been gunned down. The Vietcong launched their attack during the holiday of *Tet,* breaking the truce they themselves had agreed to. Many of the Vietcong's victims were defenseless. In a mass grave outside of Hue, three thousand South Vietnamese were discovered by American forces. *Tet* proved to be a military failure for the North Vietnamese and Vietcong, but it was a huge public relations victory because of its potent negative effect on the resolve of the American people.

For General Loan, the execution of the Vietcong insurgent was an act of just reprisal. The *Tet Offensive* occurred when the South Vietnamese civilians least expected it. The Vietnam War degenerated into civil war. Adams' photograph captured but one of thousands of heinous incidents committed by both sides in the long conflict.

Jane Anderson first saw Adams's photograph months after it was taken. It horrified her. At home, she had ignored the war, but that was impossible at the university. Everywhere she went, students talked and argued about it, while liberal professors condemned it.

When Jane came home at Thanksgiving, she found it unbelievable that her family seemed almost oblivious to the war. She mentioned it to Karen.

"We've been talking about it for a long time," Karen said. "Before you went to Madison you had no interest, and now you think we don't have enough. I voted for Nixon because I believe he's sincere about getting us out of Vietnam."

"He's an asshole."

"Is that how they teach you to converse?"

"Well, he is . . . ."

"Jane, he's not even in office yet."

Mary Louise Thilman's death the day after Thanksgiving kept Karen occupied with Johnny's family; she only saw Jane again for a few moments before Jane went back to Madison. Karen thought her little sister far too angry about the war. It was the only thing she wanted to talk about, and when she did, she was insulting, rude, and demeaning even when others agreed with her. Johnny understood the root of Jane's contemptuous opinions.

"UW is extremely liberal; she's been influenced. There's a lot of anger on that campus."

"It's not just that," Karen said. "Her language is atrocious. My mother said Jane uses vulgarities all the time. Jane claims everyone at school talks like that."

"She'll outgrow it."

+ + +

Nixon was inaugurated on January 20, 1969. Johnny stayed home to watch Nixon's speech with Karen. At its conclusion he said, "So, Nixon the peacemaker . . . let's hope so."

John and Anita thought the speech excellent. Michael found it not nearly as inspiring as Kennedy's in '61, and doubted it would ever be remembered and revered to the same extent. *Unless Nixon gets us out of Vietnam fast,* he wrote Johnny.

Ten months before Nixon took office, the United States Army perpetrated a tragic massacre of five hundred unarmed, civilian South Vietnamese at *My Lai.* The American people did not learn of the horror until near the end of 1969. More than any other single event it turned Americans against the war.

+ + +

Jane completed her freshman year with a straight *C* average, one grade below her parents' expectations. Her father was reluctant to send her back. Jane promised to work hard that summer. If he'd relent, she'd save and contribute to the cost of her education.

Aunt Elizabeth offered her a job, but Jane suspected working at a floral shop would be boring and socially isolating. She certainly didn't like the idea of living with her parents and having "to deal with their constant nagging," as she told Karen.

She answered an ad for college-age waitresses at a resort 150 miles north in Door County and was hired sight unseen. All she had to do was show up by the tenth of June. Her parents thought she needed more time at home to balance the long months away at school, but her sisters convinced them to let her go.

Worse in her parents' minds was that Jane no longer had any interest in going with them to Sunday Mass. She adamantly refused regardless of how they insisted until, to end the harassment, she lied about attending Mass at a different time. She drove aimlessly for an hour and a half to sell the deception.

Jane's behavior bewildered her parents. She had been a wonderfully spirited little girl, a somewhat restless teenager, and now a rebellious college sophomore who gave every indication she could barely tolerate being in her parents' presence. To some degree, she was confrontational with everyone in the family. Even when Aunt Elizabeth mentioned that being a waitress was a worthy but demanding profession, Jane lashed out. "What would you know about it?" When Elizabeth told how she had worked as a waitress as a young woman, Jane turned away.

Johnny Helden explained, "She's just a kid who wants to discover life on her own terms, without other people's prejudices."

"Then she's stupid," Karen said. "The school of hard knocks is the dumbest."

"She's young; she wants new experiences."

"Johnny, why do you always defend her? You of all people. You're the most thoughtful, cautious guy in the world, while she's the exact opposite."

"Karen, let me tell you something. I know Jane is headstrong, but your parents' lectures accomplish nothing. They should be more curious about what's really going on in her mind and heart. Instead, they criticize how she dresses, how she talks, her smoking, her hair; they're just driving her away."

"She was rude to Aunt Elizabeth for absolutely no reason."

"Of all people, your aunt will excuse it most easily. She understands Jane."

That was true. So true, in fact, that Elizabeth drove Jane downtown to catch the train to Green Bay. In high spirits and eager for adventure, Jane said a hasty "goodbye," glad she wouldn't be home until three days before she was to return to Madison. Her dismayed parents let Elizabeth convince them Jane would be fine. The resort was a family place with a good reputation, and even Aunt Beth had left home at nineteen. "Jane will be a better person for the experience," Elizabeth predicted.

For the most part, Elizabeth's opinion proved correct. Jane became a competent waitress, worked hard in the kitchen, and made friends with other college girls and young men who worked at the resort, especially, a guy named Don. She even learned to water ski. When Don saw her in a two-piece bathing suit his interest piqued. Within weeks she fell for him, and they began making out whenever they could. He suggested going "all the way," but her Catholic upbringing still convinced her to resist.

Working with girls her own age, enjoying the pleasant camaraderie of staff and guests, having fun in her free time, and Don always being so sweet conspired to create in Jane happy and contented feelings. She forgot her family in Milwaukee, school in Madison, and the distant war in Vietnam.

Besides, as far as Jane could tell, everyone at the resort seemed oblivious to the war. Jane never once watched television or read a newspaper. She settled into a genteel state of mental isolation, allowing none of the war's ugliness to intrude upon her idyllic summer.

By the time she returned to Milwaukee for the last weekend before the start of school, the war had receded from her whimsical consciousness. But when she got back to Madison, the intensity of war opposition amazed her. Soon enough, it seized her again.

She exchanged a few letters with Don, but after a month they both lost interest. She met a new guy, York, who passionately opposed the war. He took her to parties where people drank beer, smoked marijuana, and bitterly criticized America's involvement in Vietnam.

Then, like a bomb burst, the news of *My Lai* hit: gruesome evidence that American officers and soldiers had killed helpless women, children, and babies.

York told Jane, "Everything we ever learned about this country is bullshit. The government's evil, Nixon's evil, the fucking military's evil."

"What's evil," Jane said, "is the killing of innocents."

My Lai sharpened Jane's thinking. She didn't seek to escape with alcohol or drugs though now she drank beer and occasionally smoked pot. Every day she thought of My Lai and used it to sustain her anger and justify the rejection of her parents' middle-class values. She used it to intensify her self-awareness of maturing in knowledge, opinion, and even, she believed, wisdom.

At Thanksgiving, her mother persuaded her to come home. Unrelenting in anger and confrontation, willingly intent upon disturbing the family's tranquility, Jane so exasperated her father that he told her to go back to Madison. At the apex of his anger, he shouted, "Get the hell out of here . . . I don't ever want to see you in this house again."

Her mother begged Jane, "Just forget the war for a few days, be kind to your father."

Such pleadings meant nothing to Jane. "You're all blind to what's happening in the world, and you think I'm the problem."

"Jane, please, your father just wants a little peace."

"Bull shit, he just doesn't want to pull his head out of his ass."

"Jane, shame on you, how dare you speak that way about your father?"

When she walked out the front door, she said nothing. Her father said nothing, while her mother fought back tears. Aunt Elizabeth drove her to the train station. They spoke very little. As Jane got out of the car, Elizabeth said, "Be careful, Jane . . . careful with your body. Your emotions are so raw, you might not act rationally. The last thing you need is to get pregnant."

Startled, Jane wondered, *can she possibly sense I've already had intercourse?* She looked at her aunt and for the first time recognized the incredible depth of understanding in Elizabeth's eyes. Something impelled her to hug her aunt. "Goodbye, Aunt Beth," she said, "and thank you. I don't know when I'll see you again."

At the Christmas break, Jane went with friends to San Francisco to check out Haight-Ashbury. They had only two days to look around before heading back to Madison. At the end of the semester, Jane's dismal grades - all *D's* - were mailed to her parents. Her father demanded she return home, for he'd no longer pay her tuition. She never bothered to respond, but went ahead and enrolled in only one course, *Political Science 201*. She got a job in the Student Union cafeteria, but her interest in staying at the university had waned. She stumbled through her class until early May, 1970. Then another event stunned the nation. Four students at Kent State University were killed by Ohio National Guardsmen with another nine injured. For Jane and several of her friends it was the last mask ripped from the viciously cruel face of government. She attended one more class then dropped out for good.

In the aftermath of Kent State, her professor began, "Now we see the raw evil of this government. The U.S. military kills innocents in Vietnam, while the so-called National Guard kills innocent students at home. This is so outrageous that I'm really struggling to maintain my belief in the philosophy of non-violence, a philosophy I've held for many years."

A young man shouted, "Violent revolution is the only way now."

"No," the professor said, "it isn't the way at all. Government structures and reactionary forces are too powerful; so in control of the military and police that I really believe they'd welcome violent demonstrations just to get rid of us anti-war folks. And make no mistake: Kent State was nothing. They'll slaughter thousands on the campuses if necessary, including all of you. Nixon would welcome it. He desperately wants to eliminate the opposition. No, what we need is a leftist president, someone truly progressive and antiwar." Then, grinning, "We need one of you as president."

The class laughed.

"No, seriously, in '72 we need to elect a progressive Democrat. You young people can, whoever it is, get him elected. We want to gain power constitutionally. Believe me, that's the key. In '68 the leftists were outside the convention. In '72 they have to be inside, controlling it. The American people, as ignorant as so many of them are, will be so damn sick of Vietnam that a leftist will have an excellent chance. Nixon is history . . . trust me on that. One term, no more. The war isn't going to get any better, and things are going to get much worse at home, especially, if you guys stay active in the anti-war movement."

Jane, wild to do something to rid the country of Nixon and end the war, asked, "Should we . . . like maybe . . . join the Democratic Party?"

"Absolutely – young progressives and leftists have to take it over if we're ever going to have any hope for real peace. Republicans are the reactionaries, but Vietnam will bring them down just like Johnson and Humphrey. Look, '72 is the year when the political left, the true progressives, must triumph. Otherwise, we'll have violent revolution."

Another student asked, "But why would reactionaries in the Democrat Party give up control?"

"That's what '68 was all about, wasn't it? The reactionaries ran that convention with an iron fist. No, the key is for you guys to get involved at the local level . . . ease the old reactionaries out the door. That's the way it works, but you have to get involved. In this country, revolution starts at the ballot box. Where does it end? Well, we'll have to wait and see."

After class, Jane packed her jeans, shirts, sweatshirts, underwear and toiletries, and waited for her second ride to California. She thought her professor incredibly naïve. Jane and her friends had big ideas for protest and action. She was going with the same two guys and young woman she had gone with at Christmas. All were angrily anti-war. Three were from Wisconsin; Jane's boyfriend, York, came from New Jersey. All four vowed never to return to Madison.

"Fuck school," York told his comrades. "We're going to California to do something about the fucking war. I don't know exactly what, but it's gonna be fucking spectacular."

+ + +

On August 24, 1970, shortly before four in the morning, the most destructive domestic terrorist bomb in the history of the nation to date exploded outside Sterling Hall on the University of Wisconsin campus in Madison. Twenty-six buildings were damaged and, sadly, a lone physics researcher, Robert Fassnacht, working in the small hours of the night, was killed. The bombers' target was the *United States Army Mathematics Research Center*, a Department of Defense project on the second floor that sustained very little damage. The blast, however, destroyed the physics department in the basement and first floor. People thirty miles away heard the explosion. Four student anti-war radicals built and detonated the bomb. Three were brought to justice, served prison time then paroled; the fourth suspect was never apprehended.

The president of the university expressed his opinion that the violent act was in response to increasing repression by civil authorities against campus protesters. Later he wrote: *There's a sharp difference between protesting, even vigorous protesting, and violence. In like fashion you can also have repression; you can crack down too hard.*

John Helden called his brother, Julius. "I hate the war, but I find it hard to believe people would resort to blowing up buildings. They killed a young father . . . ."

"It's a criminal act, Johnny. It might not be murder one, but it is murder two. Did you read that the university president suggested the civil authorities cracked down too hard?"

"That makes no sense. That's like blaming the cops for the crime," John said.

"Some of those anti-war punks are just as violent as the war they oppose."

"And how can you ever make restitution to a young widow and her kids?"

+ + +

When York, Jane, and the other couple arrived in San Francisco, York went straight to a bank. What he did there he never disclosed, and no one asked. He rented a shabbily furnished one-bedroom apartment for all of them and bought most of the food so nobody felt inclined to ask him anything. Clearly, he was their provider and leader.

After several months they still hadn't figured out what action they'd take to hasten the end of the war. They joined several anti-war demonstrations, but that was it. Marijuana, actually, had become a bigger part of their daily lives. York bought that, too. But then they heard the stunning news of the bombing in Madison, jarring them back to an awareness of their mission.

York screamed at his little cadre, "You were crazy to leave Madison," even though it was his idea. "Madison," he now claimed, "is obviously the true center of the violent revolution to come. It was right under our fucking noses, and we missed it. We have to go back."

The other couple agreed, but Jane kept a cooler head. She remembered what her professor had said about the enormous power reactionary forces possessed. When she told York she wasn't returning, he tried to change her mind, but when he realized she was adamant, muttered, "fuck you" and left. Not a single word of tenderness, not so much as a goodbye hug, nothing at all for the comely, young woman who gave him her virginity.

+ + +

At B & X, Phil Heller was named project engineer for the new library science building at the University of Wisconsin in Madison. Phil enlisted Johnny Helden to design the foundation for the massive, eight-story structure, including the perimeter wall and interior column footings. The news of the Madison bombing and the tragic death of Robert Fassnacht, a husband and father of three young children, shocked both men.

"Anarchy in our midst," Phil said.

"How ironic that some idiot blows up a university building, while we're designing a new one. Maybe someday some nutcase will blow this one up," Johnny responded.

At home, Johnny told Karen, "I'm working my butt off, while these stupid anarchists are blowing up buildings. They could blow up a thousand buildings, but it wouldn't change a thing in Vietnam. If anything, it'll turn people against the anti-war movement. *My Lai* had a much bigger impact in changing minds than blowing up a building. Watch the coverage on television; that'll change your mind."

"Johnny, Aunt Elizabeth called; she got a call from Jane. Guess where she is?"

"I haven't the faintest idea."

"Los Angeles . . . she wants Michael's phone number . . . can I give it?"

"Sure, what's her problem?"

"Same as always – money. She asked Elizabeth for another loan, said she's going to get a job as a waitress in LA, and hoped Michael would be willing to give a reference. Elizabeth said Jane needs a dressy outfit for interviews. What do you think?"

"Michael always liked Jane. He'll give her a reference."

"Maybe Michael could kinda keep an eye on her."

"If she lets him. Your sister knows how to disappear. You only hear something when she needs help. If she starts hitting Michael for money, he won't be a second Aunt Elizabeth."

"Elizabeth is the only one she's ever asked. She won't pester your brother."

"Okay, give Elizabeth his phone number. Tell her Jane should call Michael whenever she wants. I'll let him know."

A month later, near the end of September, Karen gave birth to Joseph Thomas Helden. He resulted, one cold winter night, from Johnny's passion in spite of Karen's suspicion she was ovulating. The third son pleased them, but the baby was a hardship. Johnny still worked for what could best be described as a subsistence level salary for a family of seven. Engineering was not a high-paying profession. All the engineers at B & X knew it, grumbled about it, complained to the boss, but, in the end, accepted it because they loved the wonderful work engineering challenged them to do.

John and Anita were thrilled with their fifth grandchild. Joey was a beautiful baby, and everyone in the family was crazy about "such a cute, little fella," as John Helden liked to say.

"And such a good baby," Karen told her mother.

Jane's bitter estrangement, however, gravely compromised her parents' happiness. Jane's dropping out of school, not writing or calling, and leaving an unpaid tuition bill for her last political science course took a heavy toll on Mr. Anderson. Jane only wrote Aunt Elizabeth, but refused to divulge her address. All anyone knew was that Jane lived somewhere in Los Angeles and received mail at a post office box. Her mother wrote, but her petitions never earned a reply.

In Los Angeles, hearing from Jane delighted Michael Helden who gladly agreed to be a reference. He suggested she check out the fine-dining restaurants on the west side. "That's where the big tippers go," he said.

He offered to take her out to dinner, but Jane declined, telling him she wanted to get a little more settled before she'd see him. Searching the want ads for waitress jobs she found a restaurant on La Cienega Boulevard that was hiring. She got dressed up – she was a very attractive young woman – took a cab and entered the restaurant with such confidence that she almost willed the interviewing manager to hire her on the spot. Next day she got the job.

Two months later Jane was amazed how much money she had saved. She vowed she'd never be broke again. Her experience at a busy, family resort in Door County proved a tremendous advantage. She actually found the fine-dining job easier because she didn't have to bus or wash dishes. And she really turned on her flirtatious charm when she sensed it might augment her tip. Men approached her, but the manager made it clear nothing could be arranged on the premises. Jane wasn't interested. She wanted to save money, wanted a nice place to live, a car, and stylish clothes. She resolutely put the war in Vietnam out of her mind. None of the staff and customers seemed to have much interest in it anyway.

She fell in love with the mild Southern California climate, grateful to be away from the dingy streets of Haight-Ashbury and the clock-like fog and damp chills of San Francisco. She made a new friend at the restaurant, a bright, young woman named Polly Laffner. Like Jane, Polly wanted money. Waitress work was tough, but many nights the tips were phenomenal. Occasionally, Polly hinted to Jane about a much easier way to earn extra income. First, though, Polly invited Jane to live with her and share expenses in a nice, two-bedroom she found near Hancock Park. When Jane saw it, she immediately agreed. Polly had a late-model car and helped Jane move her things from the downtown YWCA.

By the first of November, Jane's checking account brimmed with dollars. She repaid all her loans to Aunt Elizabeth. She came to realize what a jerk York was, telling Polly how stupid she had been to associate with "that lazy, son-of-a-bitch . . . a total waste with him and his worthless friends." She hadn't smoked pot since leaving San Francisco, and she quit drinking beer. After two more weeks, she felt ready to have dinner with her brother-in-law's brother, Michael Helden.

When Michael picked Jane up on her night off, she invited him to see their third floor place. Unfortunately, Polly was working, but Jane promised Michael he'd meet her soon. The nicely furnished apartment surprised Michael, and he said so. He took Jane to a good Italian restaurant. The evening started pleasantly because Michael told her she looked absolutely beautiful. Jane liked hearing it. Michael realized if there wasn't such a big age difference he might be interested, but he was fifteen years older and felt, *it's just too much*. What really surprised him, though, were Jane's opinions.

"I was involved in the anti-war movement in Madison and San Francisco. But I left Madison before the bombing."

"Yeah, that was terrible . . . killing that young researcher. He had three little kids."

"What's that compared to the thousands of kids we've killed in Vietnam?"

"I'm not sure of that number, Jane, but however many it's tragic. I despise the war. I want it over as much as anyone, but you can't condone killing an innocent man."

"So what are you doing about it? You don't look like an anti-war person to me."

Michael laughed. "Neither do you." Actually, he thought Jane looked more like a Hollywood starlet.

"I'm biding my time. I wanna save money . . . then see what I can do in the *Movement*."

"Movement?

"Peace movement – my main interest now is peace. War sickens me. I hate our government for what it's doing in Vietnam. I think if I had the chance, I'd kill Nixon."

"Jane, come on, don't talk stupidly. If you really hate the killing in war, why would you want to kill another human being?"

"Because Nixon's evil!"

"Blame Johnson . . . he got us in so deep it'd be difficult for any president to get us out. Plus, the Vietcong is every bit as vicious. It's always the same, though, with the anti-war crowd; the USA is the perennial bad guy. We live in a free society so, day after day, we see the terrible things our military does. The press and media focus on that. Eventually, it turns people against the war. Rarely, though, do they focus on the enemy's atrocities. You can be sure that's not happening in North Vietnam. They just show our viciousness.

"You ask what I'm doing about it. Absolutely nothing . . . so long as those images appear on television every night, the American people will end the war in the next election. At some point, Congress will stop funding it. Then there'll be a mad scramble to get out of Vietnam. All the resources we've poured in there and the lives lost will have been in vain. South Vietnam will fall to the communists."

"That's fine with me. At least the Vietnamese people will have some peace."

"That's incredibly naïve, Jane. There'll be purges. People will lose their lives. A lot of innocent people will die, people perceived as enemies of the new regime."

"If they helped America, maybe they should die."

Michael shook his head. "Oh, Jane, come on . . . ."

He realized nothing would change her mind, while Jane felt her opinions were absolutely *right-on*. She thought Michael reactionary and unenlightened. *Were he to spend time with me, I'd change him.* She rather liked Michael and regretted he was a little older, but that was okay. He was a nice guy, and she needed a nice guy now. When he dropped her off, she made it very clear she wanted a goodnight kiss, but he balked.

"Jane, I'm thirty-six. I'm just . . . I mean . . . I don't think we should get involved . . . not with Johnny and Karen being our siblings."

That's stupid, she thought; *so typical of a repressed male.* "Goodnight," she said, coldly.

+ + +

When Polly told Jane about her work in motion pictures and the extra money she earned, Jane was thrilled.

"They're independent producers," Polly explained, "but they make fun, entertaining films and pay very well. I'm sure they'd hire you."

"I've never acted."

"The key to acting is being natural. If I ask you to walk across the room you'll walk natural, but if there's a camera here and you're aware it's filming you, then how natural would you walk? The good actresses walk exactly the same with or without a camera filming."

"Oh, Polly, that's so good . . . will I have to take lessons?"

Polly laughed. "You don't need lessons. Just remember what I told you about being natural. Walk natural, stand natural, do everything natural. That's all that's expected."

"What about my lines?"

Polly laughed again. "No, Jane, when you start, there's no speaking parts."

"So I'm like an extra?"

"Not really, more important than that. You're so pretty and shapely you'll probably get close-ups right away . . . I mean if you're hired."

"When can I interview . . . how soon can I start? What must I do?"

Polly smiled and peered hard into Jane's eyes. "You have to," she paused, wondering how Jane would react, "take all your clothes off."

"What," Jane screamed, more surprised than shocked.

"The films are what people in the business call *nudies*."

+ + +

As Christmas approached, Johnny and Karen analyzed their finances. 1970 wasn't a good year for local and statewide engineered construction and, hence, not good for architects, their consultants, including B & X, and all the employees. Johnny had practically no overtime, which in prior years provided significant extra income. Christmas bonus was a measly fifty bucks. They agreed Joey had to be their last child though Karen still strongly opposed artificial birth control. Johnny accepted it because he was happy in his marriage: happy with Karen's personality and character, as well as her efforts to keep herself slender and attractive. In addition, he was finding it easier to control his passion.

Christmas Eve provided a sweet reprieve. Karen invited her parents and in-laws. After dinner, the children opened gifts from their grandparents. John Helden mentioned that Michael had seen Jane about a month earlier; he said she looked terrific and had a good job at a high-class restaurant. "Don't worry," John assured the Andersons. "Michael will keep an eye on her."

Jane's parents longed to hear from her, to know she was safe and well, that she was living intelligently, and associating with decent people. Not a day passed that their hearts didn't ache for the love of their youngest daughter, and Jane's father, Nicholas Anderson, didn't bitterly regret the unloving intolerance he had shown her.

Nick and JJ were seven, Ann was five, and Kristin three. Without overspending, Karen and Santa made them happy Christmas morning. Playing with the ripped-off wrapping paper kept baby Joey content. John and Anita Helden gave a hundred dollars, which was an enormous help, but Karen's mother insisted on buying presents for her daughter and son-in-law even though they preferred cash. Instead of exchanging gifts, Johnny and Karen decided to have dinner alone some evening after Christmas.

Most of their friends were in similar financial straits except Bob Schmitt who had no wife, no kids, and plenty of money. Everyone understood the correlation. After the first warehouse project in 1968, Bob hired B & X to remodel the SMF offices and then two smaller projects. When those jobs arose, Bob and Johnny drew closer; summers they played golf.

None of their friends, though, paid anything but cursory attention to the anguish of the Vietnam War. People were too busy raising kids, paying bills, and scraping to put money aside for either a larger house or their kids' college educations.

Johnny and Karen were more aware only because of John Helden. The war took a tremendous toll on him, emotionally and mentally. The relentlessly depressing television news drew him in. "This damn war never should've been fought," John repeated dozens of times. He well understood that the suffering caused by widespread death and destruction was utter madness. Obviously, Nixon's secret plan proved a pathetic sham.

Early in the new year of 1971, Johnny and Karen went out to dinner as their Christmas treat. They left the children with their favorite babysitter and dined at *Karl Ratzsch's*, a wonderful, old, German restaurant downtown. On the drive home they fell silent, but then Johnny remembered an incident he hadn't thought of in years.

"I think I was twelve . . . Michael fourteen."

"What year?"

"If I was twelve . . . 1949."

"The year Jane was born, almost twenty-two years ago."

"It was early July, but an overcast day. We were fishing with my dad on a lake in Northern Wisconsin. I always sat in the bow seat, my dad at the stern with Michael between us, manning the oars. You have no idea what a great boy Michael was. He was only fourteen, but really strong and so willing to work. Had my dad asked, he would've rowed us around that lake ten times and never complained.

"My dad was casting for muskies along the west shore of this big peninsula that split the lake. He caught a few smallmouth bass, but threw 'em back. He wanted to catch a musky. He wanted us to see that because they're such great, fighting fish. I was looking at my dad and the back of Michael's head so only my father was looking past the bow towards the south. He'd glance at Michael or me then cast this big, black bucktail towards shore."

"What's a bucktail?"

"It's a popular lure for musky fishing."

"Oh . . . ."

"Once I thought my dad was staring at me, but he was looking at the far south shore. He pointed and said, 'look at those dogs.' Michael and I turned around, but they weren't dogs. It was a doe and her fawn, wonderful to see, but then something incredible happened."

"What?" Karen asked.

"A bald eagle swooped down and hovered with open talons above the fawn, as though it was going to try to pick it up."

"Oh my goodness . . . what happened?"

"Well, the doe stood on her hind legs just like a horse and thrashed with her front legs at that eagle, no more than a couple feet above. She thrashed wildly, while the fawn cowered beside her. The eagle just hovered there waiting for the deer to tire, falter, so it could attack the fawn."

"What an incredible thing to witness."

"Yes, it truly was."

"What happened then?"

"The doe never stopped thrashing her legs. She stood on her back legs all that time, kind of hopping in place and thrashing wildly at that big eagle until, finally, it rose and flew off."

Karen twisted against her seat belt to look at Johnny. "That's remarkable . . . ."

He glanced at her. "Karen, I can still see it in my mind's eye, as though it were yesterday."

"I imagine very few people, Johnny, have ever seen such a life and death encounter in the wild."

"I know. It was terrifying, but wonderful – a true triumph – I mean because she saved her fawn. Just think how powerful that doe's maternal instinct was."

"Yes," Karen said. They fell silent. She thought of her own precious children and how she would do anything to protect them even to the point of death. She closed her eyes, praying ineffably. Then she thought of her own mother and, somewhere far away in the City of Angels, her dear little sister, Jane.

Chapter 31 ~ 1973

A s often happens in a man's life, a missed opportunity with a beautiful woman comes back to haunt. Jane's enchanting femininity lingered in Michael's mind and heart, eventually proving irresistible. At first, he thought it wise not to have succumbed to Jane's very obvious invitation for a goodnight kiss. As time passed, however, he recognized his foolishness in refusing something so delightfully innocent. *Most likely*, he reflected, *it would have led to nothing*. After all, how could a romantic spark for a much older man be lit in Jane's tender heart? It probably would have led merely to a pleasant friendship that might have benefited them both, particularly, as it would have enabled Michael to keep an eye on Jane, as he had promised his sister-in-law.

Of course, he reasoned, had it led to romance there wouldn't be anything so terrible about that either. His uncle Lew was nineteen years older than Carol, and that marriage proved fruitful indeed. As for Jane's radical opinions, she just needed the guidance of an older and wiser man. He ruminated for several weeks before deciding to call Jane again.

Those same weeks for Jane were filled with change. She accompanied Polly to the location of her next filming and met the director and producer, men who seemed nearly Jane's father's age. She wasn't completely comfortable or ready for the interview, but did observe a dozen other girls, including Polly, frolic nude in front of the rolling cameras. It certainly didn't appear the girls had to work very hard.

Both the director and producer suggested Jane wait a little while to adjust to the idea of performing naked. Then they'd want to see how she acted in front of the camera doing the simple things all the girls had to do: undress, take showers, play volleyball, sunbathe, splash and lounge around the pool, and any other innocuous activities they dreamt up. All the girls Jane met agreed that after several days it became the easiest thing in the world. The money didn't hurt either. The criteria for a girl in nudie films were simple: a beautiful face, full breasts, flat tummies, cute rear ends, and a willingness to spend four to five hours nude in front of the male production crew. On location, only the make-up and hair specialists were women.

Jane overcame her modesty and was hired before she redressed. With Polly's encouragement, she endured her first few days of filming, received her first pay and giggled as she deposited almost two hundred easy dollars into her savings account. She continued working at the restaurant, performed in nudies as often as they called her, and loved the double income. Within a month she bought her first car.

Polly and Jane associated with men who took them to fine places and fancy parties. They had no trouble attracting and meeting good-looking, wealthy men whether at the restaurant or in their film work. They led busy social lives and were out so much that Michael Helden's calls at all hours of the day and evening went unanswered. When he finally reached Jane, he made a big deal out of it. But Jane felt Michael muffed his chance when she needed a nice guy. Since their date a few months ago, she had met lots of nice guys and didn't have much interest in Michael anymore. She agreed to go out again only because he practically begged to let him take her to the same, good, Italian restaurant.

"I'm still waitressing, but I'm also doing some film work. Polly got me into films, and I'm doing great . . . bought a used convertible, and you saw our place . . . not too shabby huh?"

"What kind of film work?" Michael asked.

"Oh, I'm little more than an extra, but the pay is good."

"What studio?"

"They're independent."

"When's it coming out?"

"What?"

"The film you're in."

Jane laughed. "Oh, I don't know . . . they don't tell us that. But, Michael, sometimes I can save over five hundred a month; once I saved over eight hundred."

"That's really good, Jane. Have you thought about investing in the stock market?"

"I know nothing about that."

Michael sensed an opportunity. "Would you like to learn?"

"Not now . . . I prefer cash in the bank. When I get five thousand, maybe . . . I'll see."

"Have you talked to Karen recently?"

"No, but I talked to Aunt Elizabeth. I paid her all the money I borrowed. I told her to tell everybody I'm fine."

"That's good, but you should call Karen. She'd love to hear from you."

"Oh, I will . . . eventually."

+ + +

Nick Ut began taking photographs in Vietnam for the Associated Press when he was only sixteen. He succeeded his brother who had been killed while photographing combat action in the Mekong Delta in 1965. In early June, 1972, the South Vietnamese air force launched a napalm attack against the village of Trang Bang, a suspected Vietcong stronghold. As five terrified village children ran to escape the inferno, Nick Ut stood waiting on the road. He raised a camera to his eye as a naked, nine year old girl, Kim Phuc, running for her life, appeared in his viewfinder. She had been badly burned, except her feet, and had torn off her flaming clothes to save herself. Terrified, she screamed in agony, as she ran straight towards Nick's lens. Her older brother ran in front; the deep, black hollow of his open mouth conveying the pure horror of an eternal scream. Her younger brother lagged behind, staring back at the dark smoke of destruction, while two of her little cousins, terrified and fleeing, were to her left. Behind the children, seven South Vietnamese infantrymen, seemingly nonchalant, strolled away from the burning village. Only two gazed back towards the carnage.

Like her brothers, Kim's mouth was open; the same deep, black hollow conveyed terror and unbearable pain. In the evocative silence of a photograph, her scream would be forever heard by every human being whose eyes fell upon it. Kim Phuc ran towards the cameraman for she saw him as her savior. He was. He carried her in his arms and drove her ten miles to a hospital. Nick Ut, at age twenty-one, in a single day of his life, had saved a precious, nine year old girl, earned a Pulitzer Prize and, unwittingly, turned countless more Americans against the war.

John Helden wept when he saw the photograph. Anita, in a rare moment of comforting affection, placed her hand on the back of his heaving shoulders. She said nothing for there wasn't anything to say.

"All my life I saw war as senseless; so much death and destruction and for what? It never changes, and it never ends. We try helping our friends, but it always breaks down into the ugly reality of innocent people suffering and dying. I can't deal with it anymore, Anita, I just can't."

Their twin grandsons, Nicholas and JJ, were nine, the same age as Kim Phuc. When John and Anita pondered Ut's tormenting photograph, it was impossible not to think of their grandchildren. *My God, will we ever see such horror here,* John Helden wondered.

Johnny and Karen were just as shocked. "Madness," Johnny said.

In Los Angeles, Jane Anderson, too, wept over the photograph. It angered her because of its unimaginable violence. It deeply pained and saddened her because of its profound cruelty. In Kim Phuc's straight, slender, pre-pubescent body, Jane recognized her own skinny, undeveloped figure before it transformed into voluptuousness. She remembered how she hated her child body only because she was forced to compare it to the mature bodies of her sisters. Their breasts were beautiful before Jane even budded. They possessed curvaceous hips and narrow waists, while she retained a boyish straightness.

Now, at twenty-three, and possessing a stunning figure, she decided to use it to her financial advantage. Just like My Lai, Jane would never let herself forget Kim Phuc, or that she, too, had once been the same kind of straight, skinny girl frightened by so many things until she crushed her fears by doing everything her parents warned her not to do.

If Kim was forced by a napalm bomb to run naked towards a camera, *a bomb made by an American company employing the same kind of stupid Americans as my parents,* Jane thought, then, *I will freely run naked in front of a camera.* She would reject everything she believed as a child and everything her parents and sisters still believed: their small-town, middle-class values, their conservative politics, and their Catholic faith. She envisioned herself a future film star.

She knew what the filmmakers wanted, and she would do it. They had promised her payment beyond her wildest dreams; with that money she would somehow and someway avenge Kim Phuc and the innocents of My Lai.

+ + +

Johnny Helden got a call from an architect, an acquaintance of Bob Schmitt, who worked for a large retailer in southeastern Wisconsin. The architect needed an engineer to design loading docks in an existing warehouse that required large new door openings in a masonry wall. Johnny mentioned it to Mr. Jaffray who told him to meet with the client, find out all he could about the project, and then Jaffray would write the proposal. It was the fifth job Johnny brought to the firm; in appreciation he received a raise. In those days, fifty cents an hour, a thousand dollars a year, was meaningful. It boosted Johnny's annual salary to twelve thousand. Karen was very pleased, and Johnny, for the first time, felt like he was really getting somewhere. They even talked about buying a larger house.

The retailer's architect, Cliff Lorenz, and Johnny got along well right from the start. Cliff expressed his desire to eventually open his own architectural practice in Chicago. He told Johnny that he should think about going into private practice someday as well. "I'll need a structural engineer, but I don't want to hire a big firm . . . too much overhead I'd end up paying for."

+ + +

In the summer of 1972 in Miami Beach, the Democrats nominated for president one of the most liberal men in the United States Senate. George McGovern, a true progressive, had been a bomber pilot during the Second World War, earning the *Distinguished Flying Cross*. He rarely mentioned it during the campaign because having seen the horror of war he became a man of peace.

McGovern advocated the immediate and complete withdrawal of all American forces from South Vietnam. He also proposed handing out a thousand dollars to every American citizen, but when that was widely criticized as fiscal foolishness, he dropped the idea. Yet he was a man of courage and conviction. On the Senate floor in September, 1970, he harshly criticized his colleagues. "Every Senator in this chamber is partly responsible for sending fifty thousand young Americans to an early grave . . . . This chamber reeks of blood . . . . It does not take any courage at all for a Congressman or a President to wrap himself in the flag and say we are staying in Vietnam, because it is not our blood that is being shed."

John and Anita Helden would have agreed with McGovern's searing condemnation, but they never heard or read it. Their sons would have agreed, as well, but that did not mean any of them would vote for McGovern. He was perceived as too radically liberal. Fairly or unfairly, the electorate saw him as favoring amnesty for draft dodgers, abortion rights for women, and the legalization of marijuana.

On the Republican side, the incumbent Richard Nixon had, in 1972, ordered the development of the Space Shuttle, oversaw the *Paris Peace Talks* to vainly try to end the war in Vietnam, visited China, and met with Mao Zedong to normalize relations. Nixon also oversaw the signing of the *Biological Weapons Convention* to ban biological warfare, signed the first *Strategic Arms Limitation Treaty* with the Soviet Union, and on August 23 announced that the last American ground troops had been withdrawn from Vietnam. It was far too much for McGovern to overcome. Nixon won forty-nine states. The Electoral College tally was a lopsided 520 to 17 with only Massachusetts and the District of Columbia dropping into McGovern's column. Forty years after Franklyn Delano Roosevelt's landslide victory, the once proud Democratic Party, now clearly betrayed by its far left-wing, was in shambles.

In Los Angeles, Michael Helden voted for Nixon. Jane Anderson and Polly Laffner failed to register, though both intended to vote for McGovern. "It didn't really matter," they agreed when they learned McGovern lost by eighteen million votes.

+ + +

Business at B & X seemed to be picking up. Jaffray dropped hints that several nice projects had filled the pipeline. He mentioned two general classroom buildings: one for the university in Madison, the other at a satellite campus upstate. He told Johnny about a large shopping center with a two-story department store and mentioned to Phil Heller a large suburban office building. When one of the classroom building projects went ahead, it appeared that, along with assorted small jobs in the office, overtime would be required. Suddenly B & X was busy and its employees, including Johnny Helden, enlisted to work extra hours. Everyone wanted to make more money before Christmas.

+ + +

The United States Supreme Court made two profoundly far-reaching decisions in 1973: the first, *Roe v. Wade* in January, and the second, *Miller v. California* in June.

The first decision ruled that state laws against abortion violated a woman's constitutional right to privacy under the *Due Process Clause* of the *Fourteenth Amendment.* This ruling extended to women the right to abort an unborn child for any reason whatsoever up to the point of viability, that is, the point at which the child is able to live outside the womb even if artificial aid is required. Viability usually occurs at about twenty-four to twenty-eight weeks although babies have survived as early as twenty-two weeks after conception. In a companion case, *Doe v. Bolton,* the Court ruled that women had the right to abort after viability when necessary to protect their health.

Two associate justices dissented in *Roe v. Wade:* Byron R. White and William H. Rehnquist. Justice White had been appointed to the Court by President Kennedy in 1962 after serving as the number two man at the Justice Department under Attorney General Robert F. Kennedy. In dissent he wrote: *I find nothing in the language or history of the Constitution to support the Court's judgment. The Court simply fashions and announces a new constitutional right for pregnant mothers and, with scarcely any reason or authority for its action, invests that right with sufficient substance to override most existing state abortion statutes. The upshot is that the people and the legislatures of the fifty States are constitutionally disentitled.* White went on to criticize the Court for *creating a constitutional barrier to state efforts to protect human life while . . . investing mothers and doctors with the right to exterminate it.*

Justice Rhenquist was born and raised in Milwaukee and appointed to the Supreme Court by President Nixon in January 1972. His dissent faulted the historical analysis of the majority. He wrote: *By the time of the adoption of the Fourteenth Amendment in 1868, there were at least thirty-six laws enacted by state or territorial legislatures limiting abortion. While many States have amended or updated their laws, twenty-one of the laws on the books in 1868 remain in effect today.* He went on to conclude that *the drafters did not intend to have the Fourteenth Amendment withdraw from the States the power to legislate with respect to this matter,* i.e. abortion.

The second decision in June reiterated the traditional jurisprudence that obscenity was not protected by the First Amendment. Thus, recognizing that it had to define obscenity, the Court established what came to be known as the *Miller Test* for determining what constitutes obscene material: three conditions were required for a book, magazine, or film to be considered obscene. In addition, the Court ruled that all three conditions had to be satisfied.

When certain California lawyers realized what the Court had done, they knew they could successfully defend clients who wanted to produce sexually explicit material. It would be nearly impossible for all three conditions to be met because the so-called average person of the first condition represented an exceedingly broad spectrum of opinion and taste. In effect, *Miller v. California* opened the front door of America's theaters and bookstores to the vilest pornography imaginable. Not the intended consequence, perhaps, of the nine, noble justices, but the real consequence nevertheless.

+ + +

Jane Anderson and Polly Laffner were completely unaware of the rulings of the Supreme Court. In Jane's high school government and history courses she showed little interest in the division of powers among the three branches of the Federal government. In college, she hated the war in Vietnam, and Johnson and Nixon for it, but beyond that, the laws, rulings, and workings of the national government meant almost nothing to her.

Now, however, Jane's decision to take leading roles in the production of the new, X-rated adult films really did mean something. The producer and director were amazed at her willingness to perform the most intimate sexual acts in front of cameras and film crews that often were within several feet of the bed, couch, table, chair, stairs, or floor on which she and her male partner were performing.

But Jane, a tough negotiator, demanded much in return. By the end of 1973, she had earned over fifty thousand dollars having sex in films with twenty different men. She quit waitressing, as did Polly, though Polly never displayed the same raw enthusiasm for performing sex acts that Jane did. Polly didn't mind performing nude, but nobody was making nudies any more precisely because sex acts in films could now be shown with absolute impunity in thousands of theaters across the country. Polly performed, but her innate reluctance was apparent to the director. He relegated her to secondary roles, and, as a result, Polly earned considerably less than Jane. Their friendship, however, deepened even as Jane became more successful.

Both of them felt a waning interest in dating men. If they went to dinner or a movie, they went with each other. They stopped frequenting the popular bars where single men and women congregated, and they never accepted an invitation from a guy they had performed with.

Jane said, "I get fucked so much I have absolutely no interest in going out with men."

Polly sighed. "I feel the same." And then, "Jane, I was thinking about something . . . ."

"And what might that be, dear Polly?"

"I don't know how much you've saved, but I've saved quite a bit, and I was wondering if we should buy a house together. Something on the west side: Beverly Hills or even Santa Monica . . . close to the ocean. Let's get away from the city . . . go somewhere to enjoy those ocean breezes. Maybe even have our own pool . . . ."

"Oh, Polly, that's a capital idea," Jane blurted. Instantly she thought of her sister, Karen, who often used that expression.

+ + +

By early 1973, the engineers and draftsmen at B & X had plenty work and were grateful for it. Phil Heller was named project engineer on the general classroom building. Ron Dietmann did preliminary design work for the shopping center, while Johnny helped on both projects. When the six-story suburban office building broke, Mr. Jaffray called Johnny into his office and appointed him project engineer in appreciation for not only bringing jobs to the firm, but also for the good work he had done since being hired in 1968. He showed Johnny the architect's elevations; it thrilled him to be in charge of the structural design of such a handsome building.

"I think a steel frame with either precast concrete floors or steel joists, but do a cost analysis first," Jaffray said. "A simple, one-bay prelim, but don't forget if you go precast, the columns and foundations will have to be larger."

"Have soil borings been taken?"

"Not yet . . . just presume three thousand. We should have 'em in a couple weeks."

"I'll have Bob Schmitt give me prices for the steel."

"Good . . . hopefully, he'll bid the job."

Johnny glanced at the architect's title block. "The Messert Building," he read aloud.

"He's a wealthy doctor, developing this for his own clinic and rentals. I guess a law firm's going in plus some other tenants. He'll need those to get financing."

"Who's my contact?"

"Oh, the architect invited us over. I guess the client wants to meet the design team.

"Who's the client?"

"Messert, Dr. Anthony Messert, you'll meet him."

+ + +

Michael Helden had his last Italian dinner date with Jane in September. Her indifference to her family surprised him. "What's the point of not calling your mother or Karen? They'd love to hear from you."

"I have my own life now. Someday, when it feels right, I'll get in touch. Occasionally I call Aunt Beth."

"How often?"

"That's none of your business."

"Jane, I promised Karen I'd look out for you. Just give her a call; tell her you're okay and that we see each other now and then."

"I don't want you looking out for me and, please, don't tell me who to call."

The evening ended with Jane fleeing his car. Dismayed, Michael let a month go by before calling Jane again, but her number was out of service with no new number provided. He called *Information*, but no public listing for Jane Anderson or Polly Laffner was available. At their apartment, their names had been removed from the directory. He inquired of the building manager who wouldn't release any information regarding any tenant, past or present. "Besides," he said, "they didn't tell me where they were going."

Michael recalled that first evening when Jane so sweetly offered to kiss goodnight. Had they kissed, he believed, things would be completely different. He blamed himself for her hostility, for losing her friendship, and now her whereabouts.

+ + +

After the rooms were painted, the bathrooms and kitchen re-wallpapered, new carpeting installed, new furnishings purchased, and after they felt settled again, Polly and Jane decided to dine at the restaurant where they formerly worked and first met. They dressed plainly and wore no makeup. Men paid them scant attention. No one suspected they performed in films, let alone pornographic films. They owned a beautiful home on the west side, drove new cars, had plenty of money, and expected to make a lot more. Triple X-rated adult films featured Jane in starring roles for which her agent wrangled lucrative fees for her uninhibited services. Polly had the same agent, but received considerably less for her more reserved, secondary billings. Consistent with their industry, their pseudonyms were salacious and silly.

+ + +

Mr. Jaffray and Johnny Helden walked the few blocks to the architectural offices of *Davis, Gordon & Mayer* to meet the client and the entire design team for the proposed Messert Building. Kyle Davis, the most pompous of the three partners, ran the meeting and introduced all the participants: his chief designer, the architect in charge of working drawings, the two mechanical engineers, the electrical engineer, and, lastly, Mr. Jaffray and Johnny, the structural consultants. Business cards were exchanged. Davis excused himself, returning in several moments with his client.

"Gentlemen, it is my distinct pleasure to introduce Dr. Anthony Messert. Dr. Messert, a highly respected member of the medical community in southeastern Wisconsin, has specialized in gynecology for over forty years. He's developing this marvelous building, not only as a commercial venture, but as a tribute to his long career serving the reproductive health needs of many women. Now if you would, please, I'd like each of you to stand and introduce yourself and describe to Dr. Messert your role in this exciting project."

Jaffray rose last. He stated his name and then, "B & X will be doing the structural design of the building frame, which includes roof and floor beams and girders, columns, footings, and walls for all required loads, as stipulated by Code. In addition, a wind load analysis will be performed, and all critical structural connections will be detailed. My project engineer is with me." He turned towards Johnny. "He'll be doing the bulk of the analysis and design. His name is John Helden. He's been with our firm for over five years and is a highly competent structural engineer."

Mr. Jaffray sat down. Johnny saw no reason to stand and reintroduce himself, and everyone in the room seemed to agree until Dr. Messert said, "Well, young Mr. Helden, aren't you going to say something?"

Without waiting for a nod from his boss, John Helden rose and said, "Call me Johnny!"

Everyone laughed at the unexpected salutation. Dr. Messert stared hard at Johnny for he recognized in his face the man who was his father. He said, "Tell me, *Johnny*, is Dr. Julius Helden a relative of yours?"

Johnny smiled. "Yes, he's my uncle. Do you know him?"

Wanting to offend, Messert said, "Not really . . . I just pulled his name out of my ass."

+ + +

Until Michael Helden could discover the whereabouts of Jane Anderson, he evaded Johnny and Karen's inquiries. After much soul-searching, Michael realized he had no choice but to hire a private investigator. He interviewed a former cop who, in addition to giving references, claimed he had plenty experience finding missing persons. The detective guaranteed he'd get back to Michael soon enough with solid information if Jane was still in Los Angeles. If she wasn't, it might take longer. Michael paid the retainer and put the matter out of his mind. His intuition told him Jane was relatively near.

+ + +

After the meeting with Dr. Messert, Johnny called Uncle Julius.

"I knew him in med school; we were friendly then. We did our residency at County General until he left to complete his at Columbia Hospital. That was back in the early thirties. I haven't had any contact with him since."

Johnny mentioned Messert's crude remark.

"He was just as crude back then. What's the project about?"

"It's a large office building: six stories, ninety thousand square feet."

"Is he the owner?"

"Yes, this is his new clinic plus tenant space."

"Did you catch any names?"

"No, but the architect said something about modern healthcare for women. He made a big deal how Messert, over the years, has helped so many women."

"Under the banner of reproductive health care, I suppose. I suspect he's an abortionist, but I should verify that. I'll let you know."

His uncle's verification of Messert's specialty deeply troubled Johnny. Karen and he, indeed, everyone in both their families, were horrified that the Supreme Court ruled abortion a woman's legal right.

Julius said, "It gave Messert and other gynecologists a green light. However, a mutual acquaintance told me abortion has always been a part of Messert's practice, long before Roe versus Wade. At a new clinic, I'm absolutely certain he'll perform abortions."

"Then I can't be part of it," Johnny said.

Julius replied, "That's a decision only you can make."

Karen discussed serious matters with her aunt Elizabeth the same way Johnny did with his uncle Julius, and now she wanted to know what Elizabeth thought about *Roe v. Wade*. She knew her husband's opinion and her parents', but her aunt sometimes thought differently about things. "Can you come for coffee?" Karen asked.

After they settled comfortably in the living room, Karen

wondered aloud about the court's decision. Elizabeth said, "I'm just as shocked as anyone."

Karen sighed. "I can't imagine being in such a situation. Before I was married there was no way I'd let myself get pregnant. I was a virgin . . . ."

"What if you got pregnant now?" Elizabeth asked.

"We'd have the baby even though it'd be a financial strain."

"Well, many people nowadays think differently about these kinds of things . . . ."

"I suppose if a girl is poorly educated without a strong, supportive family or from a broken home and some guy takes advantage of her, forces her-"

"I'm not so sure," Elizabeth interrupted, "that it has to do with those things as much as with human nature. Young people become infatuated. Passions are easily aroused, and sex is such a powerful drive. It happens to the best girls in the best families."

"So do you think Roe versus Wade was a good decision?"

"No, I don't . . . I see it as a profound mistake."

Karen poured her aunt a second cup of coffee. "Why?"

"Because it gives people a way to avoid the consequences of irresponsible behavior. I suspect, Karen, from now on we'll be shocked at how many abortions will occur."

"Johnny knows a doctor who does abortions. He's planning a new clinic, and B & X has the job. Johnny was named the project engineer, but he won't work for a known abortionist."

"Oh for heaven's sake . . . ."

"It was his uncle Julius who told him about the man. He knew him years ago."

"Johnny's Uncle Julius?"

"Yes, remember our family get-together after we were married? We wanted you to meet him because he's such an interesting man, but he and his wife were out of town."

"Oh, yes, of course, I remember Dr. Julius Helden." Suddenly Elizabeth recalled a day: distant, grey, sad, the air cool and moist against her pallid face.

Karen noticed her aunt's dreamy, faraway look, like a haunting of memory though indiscernible, for Elizabeth's expression was an amalgam: plaintive, winsome, and enigmatic.

"A penny for your thoughts . . . ."

Elizabeth laughed. "Oh, it's nothing."

"Can you stay awhile?"

"Of course . . . ."

"I can't imagine how horrible I'd feel being pregnant in a hostile family with an angry boyfriend who'd want me to abort. The thought of killing an unborn child terrifies me."

"Yes, it's a terrible dilemma for a young girl."

"I can't imagine what I'd do," Karen said. "I suppose I'd run away. I would not kill my baby."

"It's terribly difficult for a young girl, but a mature woman who carelessly – let's say in an affair – gets pregnant with all the birth control available and then has an abortion, well, that's despicable because she's destroying a new life so capriciously. Some men act very irresponsibly and women can be lax, too. Abortion looks like an easy way out, but a price will be paid, and it will be women who pay it." Elizabeth set her cup aside.

"But abortion is birth control, the ultimate form of birth control. It's not contraception, but the result is the same: no child, no new life. We heard a priest once say that contraception and abortion are the bitter fruits of the same barren tree."

"That's true."

"So what can be done?" Karen glanced outside and waved at the mailman.

"I've joined a group of very determined women opposed to abortion. Their idea is to educate young people, especially girls, to avoid premarital sex, or if they do get pregnant to give their babies up for adoption."

"Educate where . . . in schools?"

"Schools, television, newspaper ads, even billboards . . . ."

"Sounds expensive."

"Yes, but we also need volunteers. If a single girl gets pregnant, we want to encourage her to carry the baby to term and offer it for adoption if, for one reason or another, the girl or her family can't raise the child."

"That sounds very worthwhile."

"Would you consider . . . ?"

"Yes, I think I need something now."

Elizabeth rose to leave. "Next meeting, come with me."

+ + +

Johnny Helden asked Mr. Jaffray for a private meeting. Without hesitation, qualification, or equivocation he denounced Anthony Messert as an abortionist and stated he couldn't, in good conscience, design Messert's new building. Jaffray listened, impassively. Then Johnny said, "B & X should turn the job down, let some other firm do it; it's blood money."

"No, I won't do that, but I can switch you," Jaffray said.

"What . . . why?"

"Ron can do Messert's building. You do the shopping center."

"I think the firm should take a principled stand here."

"A lot of people accept the Court's ruling. Abortion is legal now."

"It might be legal, but killing an unborn child is inherently immoral regardless of what the Court rules."

"Well, you're not a woman, Johnny. A lot of women feel if they want an abortion they have that right. It's their body, and the government shouldn't be telling women what they can or can't do with it. That's not unreasonable."

"But it isn't their body; it's someone else's . . . the child's."

"Johnny, look, I'm not a philosopher. I'm an old engineer. I've got employees here. I've got to make a little money for the firm, or there'll be no firm. I'm not interested in anything other than having good work for my staff that puts bread on all our tables."

"Messert's building isn't good work . . . abortion is evil."

"I don't want to discuss it anymore. You tell Ron I said you're to do the shopping center. He can do Messert's building."

"But Mr. Jaffray . . . ."

"End of discussion, Johnny. Go tell Ron!"

+ + +

At the heart of Johnny's understanding of human reproduction was his belief that life begins at the moment of conception. "Ultimately, science and religion have to agree on that," he told Uncle Julius. "If human life doesn't begin at conception, what is it that does begin then?"

"Speaking as a scientist, I agree," Julius replied. "Human life is this marvelous continuum from conception to death. Within that, there are degrees of development, stages of growth and degeneration, but at every moment along the way, it's all human life."

"Yes."

"In Roe, the Supreme Court ignored the *Declaration of Independence.*

"How?" Johnny asked.

"Well, doesn't it say that every American is endowed by his or her Creator with the right to life, liberty and the pursuit of happiness? Unless I'm missing something here, isn't it true that Jefferson meant – because of the specific order of his words – that life supersedes liberty just as liberty supersedes the pursuit of happiness?"

"I never thought of that," Johnny answered.

"In Roe versus Wade, seven men decided that a certain class of Americans doesn't have that fundamental, God-given right to life. A mere seven men ruled that those unborn human beings – unfortunate enough to be conceived in the wombs of females who simply don't want to be pregnant – don't have that fundamental right to life."

"Yeah but a woman could be pressured by the guy . . . ."

"Oh, I'm sure that happens, but here's the point, Johnny: the Court ruled that the liberty of the mother to kill her unborn child was of greater value than the child's life. That's an inversion of Jefferson's word order and, I'm sure, an inversion of his philosophical intent.

"In a completely arbitrary way, the Court ruled that it's more important for a woman not to be burdened with an unwanted pregnancy than it is to protect, preserve, and then safely deliver her unborn child. The tragedy is that the aborted child could be given for adoption if the woman doesn't want it. There's absolutely no reason to waste a human life."

"My freshmen year at Notre Dame we had a course in moral theology. That was 1956. We discussed abortion, and when, if ever, it was moral to have one."

Julius responded, "Ectopic pregnancy, principle of self-defense, that kind of thing . . . an ectopic pregnancy cannot lead to a live birth. It would kill a woman."

"Yes, that's exactly what we talked about."

"Johnny, I've had several patients with ectopic pregnancies, but they're rare. I sent those women to a gynecologist who performed the abortion. Normal pregnancies aren't inherently dangerous. Pregnancy isn't a disease. Roe isn't about pregnancy threatening the life of the woman. It's about women not wanting to be pregnant. They and their partners failed to abstain or use birth control so abortion becomes the birth control of last resort.

"Mark my words, Johnny – there'll be a lot more abortions in this country now. Not because women's lives are in danger, but simply because some women don't want to be pregnant. All this talk about birth control all these years; yet look how carelessly people behave. Now a guy can think, *I don't need to use birth control . . . if she gets pregnant let her get an abortion.*"

"Wow . . . ."

"Roe's going to have bad consequences."

"How many lives will it take," Johnny asked.

"For what?"

"How many abortions before Roe versus Wade is overturned?"

"I hope not many, but we shall see . . . ."

+ + +

Michael Helden got the call and next day, after work, went to the private investigator's office.

"How'd you find her," Michael asked.

"Combing through real estate transactions; she bought a house."

Michael laughed. "How could she afford to buy a house? She came to LA broke."

"I'll tell you, but you're not gonna like it."

"I have to know . . . I have to let her family know."

"She has a housemate; her name is Polly Laffner."

"Yeah, I met her once."

"The two of them bought a house in Beverly Hills. I've got the address and phone number. It's quite a nice house, actually – pool, landscaping – certainly more house than you'd expect a couple of waitresses to own."

". . . big mortgage, I suppose."

"Actually, big down payment . . . a relatively small mortgage."

The investigator detected bafflement in Michael's eyes.

"It's their profession that enabled them to buy this place." He slid a photograph of the house in front of Michael.

"Very impressive." Then the word *profession* jarred his mind. "What profession? They're waitresses."

"Mr. Helden," the investigator fumbled with his typed notes, "the subject of my search – one Jane Anderson, age twenty-four, born and raised in Milwaukee, Wisconsin, parents still living there – is, at the present time," he paused, "an adult film star."

Horrified, Michael stared at the man in disbelief.

"She performs explicit sex acts in pornographic films that show in theaters throughout the country. She's one of the top performers. Her screen name is" – he scribbled on a piece of paper then pushed it in front of Michael who groaned – "and her income, while I wasn't able to learn the exact amount, my sources tell me is probably in the low six figures.

"It appears – though I can't really verify this – that she and her housemate are lesbian lovers. I tracked them for a long time; neither of them dates men. They go out together and come home together. I've never seen either of them with a man except in their films. And speaking of which, if you know her well and like her and don't want to see how she's degraded, I suggest you stay away from her films. They're very, very raw . . . nothing's left to the imagination."

Michael's head and body slumped. His heart nearly broke. He couldn't believe that Jane Anderson, his sister-in-law's beautiful kid sister, had chosen such an immoral life. *My God, doesn't she care about her immortal soul?*

Driving back to his place, Michael wondered, *how could I ever divulge such information? How could I tell Karen or Johnny? How can I reason with Jane? How can I persuade her to abandon that evil life?* And, finally, *how can I save her?*

+ + +

Joey Helden turned three in September, 1973. The bungalow in Wauwatosa had shrunk into crowdedness, and Johnny and Karen knew they'd have to buy a bigger house. Johnny expected '74 to be a good year; possibly with overtime, he could earn fifteen thousand.

Then news came that the second general classroom building

went unfunded by the State legislature, Mr. Jaffray was actually relieved. All four design engineers – Jaffray, Ron, Phil and Johnny – and the two draftsmen had plenty of work. Then, unexpectedly, the developers of the shopping center canceled the project for failing to secure financing. Johnny was left with nothing to design and no project to manage.

Messert's building engrossed Dietmann, while Phil wrapped up the design of the general classroom structure. He made it clear that without more drafting help, the contract drawings wouldn't be done by the deadline. Jaffray had no choice, but to call Johnny into his office.

"I'd like you to help Phil . . . he needs another draftsman."

"Mr. Jaffray, I'm a Professional Engineer. I need a project of my own."

"I'm not a magician, Johnny. I can't pull a job out of my hat."

"Have you called-?"

"I've called everyone. Did you call Lorenz and Schmitt?"

"Yes, nothing."

"What I really need are a couple good draftsmen."

Johnny shook his head. The last thing he wanted was the back-bending, eye-straining tedium of drawing plans and complex structural details nine hours a day.

"You know with your salary I could hire two . . . ."

Distracted by the recollection of his father telling him years ago not to go into engineering because he'd spend his life slaving over a drafting board, Johnny missed Jaffray's point. "I'm sorry; what did you say?"

"I could hire two draftsmen with your salary."

"What exactly do you mean?"

"Johnny, I'm sorry. I'm gonna have to let you go."

Chapter 32 ~ 1975

Karen Helden, nee Anderson, broke up with Jack Cutler in June, 1960. She had many reasons, but, certainly, his reluctance to get to know her family topped the list. Many times Karen's mother invited Jack to dinner, and nearly just as many he declined. When he did accept, he was noticeably uncomfortable, saying little during the course of the meal, so little in fact that Karen's father once asked, to screams of sisterly laughter, "Is your fella mute?"

Thinking about it, Karen suspected the early, tragic deaths of Jack's parents contributed to his sullenness while dining with her noisy family. Then, too, Jack thought his scientific education far superior to Karen's literary one and just about everyone else's as well. Karen admitted the point; after all, he was a Doctor of Medicine. But when he said her education was, "quite frankly, inferior," she realized the depth of his intellectual conceit. No one in her family was capable of talking science, which, in Jack's eyes, diminished them all. Nevertheless, his quiet personality, good looks, and powerful physicality remained attractive to Karen.

Her girlfriends, as well as her sisters, believed she'd eventually marry Jack. Had people known of his inherited wealth they would have been even more convinced. And occasionally, Karen did fantasize about being his wife. However, after that fateful March evening when he revealed how his parents had died, Karen realized Jack was so deeply affected by his mother's death that she doubted he'd ever get over it.

Karen questioned whether she'd want to live with Jack's dark memories haunting their marriage, wondering if his love for her was sufficient to supplant them. She believed having children would help, but his initial response was negative. He didn't want any children. In time, she convinced him that children were the essence of marriage, and she wouldn't consider marrying him unless he was willing to father at least two. Jack agreed, but stated with emphatic authority that after the second child he expected Karen to use birth control.

At that, Karen – suddenly and cleanly – broke it off, stunning Jack just as much as her parents, sisters, and friends. No wily argument in his favor had any effect on her decision at all. When he called begging to see her again, she told him that his indifference to her family, his inability to get over his mother's death, and his insistence that she use birth control would prevent them from ever attaining a happy marriage. She wished him well, said goodbye, and hung up the phone. At the other end Jack muttered, "Bitch!" He never dated a Marquette girl again.

+ + +

An old, well-respected obstetrics and gynecology clinic in Racine hired young Dr. Cutler. Within days after completing his residency, he rented a spacious apartment and commenced his professional life. At the clinic, his serious manner, excellent work ethic, and likeability drew the admiration of his colleagues. Of course, several of the physician's wives considered him a highly eligible bachelor who should meet this friend's daughter or that friend's cousin. They invited Jack to dinner parties where he comfortably scrutinized the proffered candidate. Most of the young women were sufficiently attractive to gain at least one date with the young doctor, sometimes two, but rarely three. This pleasant social life lasted several years until Jack finally met what he was looking for: an absolute knockout.

Cheryl Williams worked as a receptionist for a law firm whose senior partner was good friends with a doctor at Jack's clinic. This partner's wife suggested inviting Cheryl to a dinner party at the doctor's home, knowing any man would find her beauty and stunning figure highly attractive. Cheryl's status, twenty-five and unmarried, suggested a discriminating young woman. Actually, her innate desire to marry a wealthy man had kept her from the altar. She presumed young doctors, if not wealthy at the start of their careers, would certainly end up that way so she had an immediate interest in Jack. His physical attractiveness, natural reserve, calm manner, and occasional witticism made him a pleasant dinner guest. Jack asked Cheryl out before the evening ended. People commented that it obviously was love at first sight. The more accurate word, however, was *lust*.

Cheryl's father abandoned his wife and daughter when Cheryl was only four. She never saw or heard from him again. Her mother claimed he "went to war," but Cheryl didn't know where that place was. When she learned the meaning of the word, she asked her mother, "What did Daddy do in the war?"

"I don't know what he did, where he went, nothing . . . I don't care to know, and you shouldn't either. He's a worthless, shiftless bum. Don't waste your time thinking about him." With that she hoped Cheryl would stop annoying her about a man for whom she had nothing but contempt.

Once, Cheryl found a photograph in her mother's dresser of a nice-looking, mustached man, his arm around her mother who smiled as though she had been ordered to. Cheryl believed with all her heart that this handsome, commanding man must be her father. She feared confirming it, however, because she knew her mother would lash out screaming, "forget that good-for-nothing son-of-a-bitch."

Sometimes when her mother invited a gentleman to their dimly lit apartment, Cheryl sensed, in the aromas that floated about him, another man whom she barely remembered, but didn't want to forget. A man who, when she was close to sleep, bent to kiss her cheek with something like a brush that tickled, and with a hand, large and rough, that tenderly stroked her hair. She discovered aromatic memories in a stranger's cigar, his overcoat, or his shaving scent, and even in the sweet-sour, juniper-berry breath of her mother: odors, so long as they weren't excessive, Cheryl found evocative and strangely comforting.

As Cheryl grew up, her mother grew slovenly. She only tidied the apartment and herself when a man came for the evening and often for the night. Eventually, Cheryl discovered the nature of those nocturnal visits and attained the disgusted realization that if her mother wasn't a whore, she certainly was a slut. Cheryl just didn't understand how her mother could know so many men. After Cheryl finished high school, her best friend asked if she'd like to share an apartment. Cheryl's mother encouraged it.

Cheryl vowed to marry only one kind of man: a wealthy one.

That, she knew, would prove her classiness compared to her pathetically low-class mother. Cheryl believed money the root of all happiness, but, if not happiness then certainly comfort, and if not comfort, then absolutely the root of all fun. She swore she'd have at least two of those for the rest of her life. When she met Jack Cutler she sensed she had found the man who offered both the money and the class she so ardently craved.

With two strangers as witnesses, a judge in the Racine Courthouse married Jack and Cheryl. They cared not a bit that they disappointed Cheryl's mother, friends, and acquaintances and, in Jack's case, distinguished colleagues and their match-making wives. Religion had no place in their lives so the last thing they wanted was a pretentious church wedding followed by a tedious reception that Jack neither wished to pay for nor endure. Cheryl would have enjoyed a fancy party to show off her ring, dress, hair, nails, shoes, and even her new husband, but she deferred to his wishes because she was giddy at having learned Jack inherited enough money to render him a rich man by her rather humble standard. She ignored the unsocial nature of their wedding and concentrated on something she had never before experienced: two weeks away from Racine. When Jack asked Cheryl what she'd like to see on their honeymoon, she answered, "Ceilings." It aroused him on the spot.

They spent their wedding night at the Drake in Chicago, the same hotel John and Anita Helden stayed at in 1932. Jack intended a leisurely drive to St. Louis then north along the Mississippi to Dubuque where he lived with his mother and sister several years before going to college. From there he'd drive to Madison along the same highway where his mother ended her life. He'd even hunt for the curve where her car left the road, seeking the tree that so cooperatively killed her. He didn't think it particularly morbid, but decided not to tell Cheryl until they were actually there if, indeed, he could find the exact spot. If he couldn't, "no big deal."

Cheryl's morning sluggishness, leisurely breakfast, perpetual interest in shopping on Michigan Avenue, along with Jack's desire to return to bed, his impatient waiting, as Cheryl modeled new lingerie, room-service drinks in the late afternoon, and then dinner with a bottle of wine at a first-class restaurant: all of it rendered the trip to St. Louis superfluous. Days passed, all spent the same hedonistic way. After the first honeymoon week they decided to stay the second, for both agreed they were "having the time of our lives." Their indulgently lazy routine consisted of breakfast, sex, nap, drinks, lunch, shopping, sex, cocktails, dinner, sex, and sleep repeated in various combinations for ten days after which Jack grew weary and bored, but said nothing. He had promised Cheryl a two week honeymoon, and that's what she'd get. Her only legitimate complaint, had she thought of it, was that she saw the same ceiling over and over, day after day, night after night.

Idle silence marked the short drive back to Racine. They had nothing more to say for they had raved *ad nauseam* about the restaurants, hotel, shopping, and even their love making, but now they had only the empty, streaming moments in the car and, come Monday morning, their jobs to look forward to.

"I don't want to go back," Cheryl said.

"Quit."

"I can't."

"Why not . . . I make enough."

"Everybody loves me."

"Then go and don't complain."

"I don't want to. I want you to make love to me, bring me breakfast in bed, and rub my feet."

Jack laughed. "Great, we'll make love, but you're making breakfast."

If Karen Anderson's education was inferior, Cheryl's was non-existent. Jack found she had nothing interesting to say: not a thought, idea, opinion, nothing. She was incapable of meaningful conversation so he endured her small talk until he got so bored that he ordered her to "be quiet now." She obeyed because she believed Jack when he told her he suffered a strange kind of earache, especially in the car.

Jack wasn't merely anxious to get back to work; he desperately needed to get away from his wife of less than three weeks. Not until his desire returned would he seek her out again. Cheryl was oblivious to his ruminations, noticing nothing. Jack was young, strong, and sought her often.

He worked weekdays and Saturday morning, fifty weeks a year. Except for Saturdays, Cheryl worked the same as the receptionist for a group of middle-aged lawyers who never tired of slyly admiring her curvaceous figure. Jack and Cheryl took two-week vacations; for several years they went back to Chicago to grasp the same sensual indulgences they relished on their honeymoon. After five years, Cheryl wanted to see New York City so they went, but only for a week. She liked Chicago better. The next year they found a resort in Missouri's Ozarks to be terribly boring. One summer they went to Washington D.C., which Cheryl found unbearably hot, humid, tedious, and tiring. One winter they went to Florida and got bad sunburns. For it, Cheryl was miserable and untouchable. Jack got so disgusted he booked an early flight back to Chicago.

They hardly spoke on the drive to Racine and the same apartment Jack rented when he first was hired. He wanted to buy a house, as his colleagues urged, but Cheryl was content in their cozy place, cluttered now with years of accumulated stuff, mostly hers. Since neither of them wanted children, Cheryl asked, "What's the point of having a house and yard?"

Their tenth anniversary snuck up like a stealthy mini-tide on a flat, Caribbean beach. They celebrated with a weekend in Chicago, but it was contentious and unpleasant. After ten years, Jack didn't have the faintest idea why he married Cheryl other than sexual gratification. But even that seemed ever more elusive. Finally, he realized, something had to change.

For entirely different reasons, Cheryl also wanted some kind of change. Years earlier, she tired of her job and yearned to quit. She told Jack she wanted to move to Chicago. Jack suggested Milwaukee, which he liked from his residency days. She asked about restaurants and shopping. He said the restaurants were great, but he didn't know anything about stores. The prospect of moving to a larger city pleased Cheryl. She decided, once resettled she'd never work again. And if Jack didn't like it, *he can go to hell.*

+ + +

In June, 1973, the United States Congress passed, with a veto-proof majority, the *Case-Church Amendment* that prohibited any further American military involvement in Southeast Asia. This presented communist North Vietnam an opportunity, whenever they so decided, to again invade democratic South Vietnam without fear of retaliatory bombing. In September, 1974, Congress appropriated seven hundred million dollars in aid for South Vietnam. It wasn't nearly enough to fund an army whose morale and preparedness had already declined precipitously.

President Nixon resigned in disgrace at noon on Friday, August 9, 1974. John and Anita Helden watched and listened to his farewell speech with mixed and bitter feelings. John thought him a brilliant man who failed tragically. He voted for Nixon three times. He believed the President had no knowledge of the Watergate fiasco or its cover-up, but John was wrong. In fact, Nixon traded the honor of the presidency to protect a cadre of criminal cronies. When John learned that, he realized how deeply flawed Nixon's character truly was and how profoundly he betrayed the American people.

By the end of April, 1975, the North Vietnamese army had encircled Saigon, the capital of South Vietnam, the Paris of the Orient. Thirty thousand South Vietnamese troops in the city were stranded without leadership. When rocket fire began to fall on civilian areas, panic and chaos erupted. President Gerald Ford ordered helicopter evacuation of seven thousand Americans and South Vietnamese from the besieged city. Frantic civilians, terrified of the inevitable communist takeover, swarmed the air base hoping to board the helicopters. The evacuation effort shifted to the walled American embassy secured by Marines who struggled to resist the thousands of civilians desperate to escape.

Off the coast of Vietnam, three American aircraft carriers stood by. South Vietnamese air force pilots flying American-made helicopters landed on the carriers, but the quarter million dollar choppers were dumped into the sea to make room for more incoming escapees. Finally, the last morning of April, ten remaining United States Marines were air-lifted from the embassy grounds. The North Vietnamese army poured into Saigon. Before noon, the Vietcong flag flew above the presidential palace. The long war in Vietnam was over. America had been defeated, expelled, and its world and self-image gravely diminished.

+ + +

After losing his job at B & X, Johnny Helden decided to go into the private practice of consulting engineering. It worried his father because of his own tough experiences as a small businessman. It worried Karen, and it worried Johnny even though he tired of working for firms that were forced on occasion to fire people.

Johnny had two potential clients: SMF, a manufacturer of steel products and fabricator of structural steel, and Cliff Lorenz, a young Chicago architect who once suggested Johnny strike out on his own. Johnny called his friend, Bob Schmitt at SMF, who had no upcoming projects, but supported Johnny's decision. Then he called Lorenz who had a contract to design a large supermarket in Chicago. He invited Johnny to his office to preview the project. If they could agree on a fee, it would become Johnny's first job as an independent consultant.

1974 proved a tough year. Johnny completed only a handful of projects. In his abundant free time he solicited people he knew and wrote firms he didn't know. By the end of December his income squeaked past fifteen thousand, marking the year a modest success.

He called Bob Schmitt on a regular basis. Bob mentioned an idea he had. "I'll get back to you," he said.

In early February, Johnny took his friend to lunch. Bob explained, "In high-bay industrial buildings, oftentimes floor space is used for offices or parts storage, but they don't need eighteen foot ceilings. That's all wasted space above."

Johnny nodded.

"I want to manufacture steel mezzanines that can be built nine or ten feet above the floor and used for either additional offices or storage or both."

"Are you thinking all pre-engineered?"

"Exactly."

"There're a lot of variables."

"Yeah, I know: bay sizes, column heights, stair locations . . . ."

"And loads: office is fifty pounds per square foot. Storage can vary from a hundred to two fifty, or more."

"Yeah, and bays can be thirty by thirty, forty by forty or even larger."

"That's right," Johnny said. "But you can't add new loads to the existing columns. You'll have to put your columns at smaller centers to keep your beam sizes down."

"Why can't we use the existing columns?"

"You'd overload the footings."

"So what do we do?"

"There's an old adage in structures: columns are cheap, beams expensive, which simply means columns on smaller centers result in smaller, lighter beams. Columns on large centers require expensive, heavy beams."

"Okay," Schmitt said. "Can you do this?"

"I can do it, Bob, but it looks like a lot of time."

"What's your hourly?"

"Twenty."

"Agreed," Bob said. "Come in next week. We'll define the parameters."

During the year, Cliff Lorenz gave Johnny several nice projects. Cliff had two draftsmen who prepared the structural contract drawings under Johnny's supervision relieving him of that odious task. He drove to Chicago once a week to keep the jobs moving.

As Christmas of 1975 approached, Johnny's income approached twenty-five thousand. Karen was enormously proud of her husband and both realized they could afford a larger house. Aunt Elizabeth suggested the *Highlands* where she and Paul lived. Karen loved the thought of being within walking distance of her dearest aunt. Johnny didn't object because it was a beautiful old neighborhood. It was just a matter of finding the right house.

+ + +

Early summer of that year, Jack Cutler interviewed with Dr. Anthony Messert. In the clinic's waiting room, two young women, sitting widely apart, idly paged through glossy magazines. The receptionist, a well-dressed, middle-aged woman, led Jack to a sparsely furnished corner office. A light tan, textured paper covered walls devoid of pictures or photographs save for the framed degrees and medical licenses above the credenza. A fine leather chair stood at the uncluttered desk. The lack of personal photographs on both the credenza and desk caused Jack to recall that he once kept a framed photo of Cheryl on his desk, but no longer. Gazing out the window he spotted his car in the parking lot then sat down. Moments later a slender man, his gray hair combed straight back, entered the room.

Jack started to rise, but the man said, "No, no, sit . . . ." They shook hands. "I'm Dr. Anthony Messert – you are Dr. Cutler, I presume?"

"Yes, how do you do," Jack said.

"Any trouble finding me?"

"None at all."

"Good. I built this clinic this far west to be closer to Madison. We get patients from Madison, Milwaukee, and all points in between."

"I see."

"I didn't realize you were so young."

Jack laughed. "I'm forty."

"Tell me about yourself."

"How far back?"

"Just your professional life."

"I graduated from Madison's Med School in '60, did two years residency at County General in Milwaukee, then joined an OB-GYN clinic in Racine where I've been for the past ten years. I'm in good health, quit smoking a couple years ago, drink a little on occasion. That's about it."

Messert studied Jack's fine face. "Well, Doctor, these are good times to be a gynecologist, are they not? I've been practicing gynecology for many years, but the opportunities today and in the future are exceptional."

"When isn't it a good time to be a physician?"

"You miss my point: these are particularly good years, especially for someone as young as you – I mean looking ahead – to be a gynecologist."

Jack laughed again, not understanding Messert's emphasis. "Surgeons and anesthesiologists do pretty well."

"Yes, they do. So what do you think of obstetrics?"

Jack winced. "I'm way down the list in Racine. Most of the other doctors deliver big time, but I guess I've always been more of a GYN man."

"Actually, that's good; I'm glad to hear it. We're completely out of OB here. Our focus and what I see in current trends lead me to believe that women's reproductive health care is going to be an ever expanding and even more lucrative field in the near future, but not necessarily obstetrics."

"How can a women's clinic be out of OB?" Jack asked.

"We have a different emphasis here. There are plenty of baby doctors."

"Am I not interviewing for an OB-GYN position? I'm not entirely sure what you're getting at."

"Well, Doctor Cutler," Messert smiled, "the times are such that the nature of OB-GYN is fundamentally changing, whether you're mindful of it or not. My clinic is devoted to helping women, especially young women, who find themselves in a difficult situation and need an understanding and skilled physician to help them. More and more, our practice is devoted to ending unwanted pregnancies. In other words, now that it's legal, my clinic – and I'm proud to say this – is one of the leading abortion providers in southeast Wisconsin. And Doctor, this is going to be a growing practice. This is going to be a bigger part of everyone's practice, and, as conscientious doctors, we have a social and ethical responsibility to help women who find themselves unintentionally pregnant."

"Interesting," Jack said. "The clinic I'm at now won't do abortions. We've done therapeutic D & Cs, but never just to get rid of a healthy fetus."

"I bet your colleagues are Catholic guys."

"Some, not all . . . ."

"Those guys wear horse blinders; abortion's legal now. They'll have to do 'em."

"I don't think so. They're strongly opposed."

"I've argued the point with Catholic doctors for years. I've been doing abortions since the early '30s. The reality is that most sexually active teenagers and young women don't want to be pregnant, and, as conscientious gynecologists, we have an obligation to help them."

At mention of the 1930s, Jack wondered about Dr. Messert's age. Instead, he said, "They should use birth control."

"Doesn't always work; passion overwhelms reason. Putting on a condom interferes with the spontaneity of the act."

"That's the beauty of the pill."

"Perhaps . . . ." Dr. Messert gazed out the window, then turned towards Jack again. "So, you've done therapeutic D & Cs?"

"Quite a few, actually . . . menopausal women with those unending monthly flows."

"Well, actually, there's a tad more to a D & C where a fetus is involved," Messert said. "It's not quite the same simple procedure as a therapeutic, so we're able to charge a higher fee for a first trimester."

"How is it different?" Jack asked.

"The curettes are different. For an abortion the curette is a hooked-shaped knife that we use to cut the fetus into pieces and then scrape it all out. If I were careless – which I am not – and some fetal remains are missed, there's the possibility of infection, which would require a therapeutic D & C to clean things up . . . plus antibiotics, of course."

"Does that happen often?"

"Not to me. I've had a lot of experience, Doctor. I know what I'm doing. I've done thousands of first trimesters. If you join us, I'll train you well."

"You said you charge more?"

"Look, if it's an unwanted pregnancy we're justified in charging more because girls get pretty desperate, and they're willing, or their boyfriend, or even their parents, to pay a significant fee. That's just the way it is. They see us as providers of a very valuable medical and social service, and they're willing to pay for it. On our end, it's a lot simpler. We don't deal with insurance . . . strictly credit card or cash."

Jack came to the interview thinking traditional OB-GYN. Messert caught him off guard with his prediction that abortions would become a significant part of a gynecologist's practice. Jack doubted that, but was intrigued, nevertheless, because an abortion *Dilation and Curettage* was a procedure he thought he ought to learn. Messert's lack of an obstetrical practice wasn't disconcerting to Jack at all.

"I guess, Doctor Cutler, you have to be comfortable doing abortions. I don't want you if you have some kind of scruples about that. Are you religious?"

"Let me think about it . . . no, I'm not."

"Good." Messert chuckled. "I'll thoroughly train you, of course. You'll be surprised at some of our techniques and equipment. You could make a lot of money here, more than with a bunch of stingy, old baby doctors." He laughed. "My doctors do very well. Abortion's gonna be big business . . . now that it's legal, I mean. Roe versus Wade has become the law of the land. I, for one, intend to profit from it."

"Well, let me think about it. Are you offering me a position?"

"Yes, I am, Doctor," Messert replied. "You seem like a nice chap . . . good credentials, plus you've had good experience. Talk to your wife. I'll guarantee a hundred thousand your first year, and I'll put it in writing. This is the wave of the future. You'd be wise to ride it."

+ + +

Jane Anderson kept in touch only with Aunt Elizabeth whom she called once every couple months, nothing regular, but sufficiently often to keep Elizabeth unworried. Now, thirteen weeks had passed, and Elizabeth grew concerned. She mentioned it to Karen who told Johnny. He called Michael to see if he knew what was going on with Jane, and if he'd seen or talked to her.

After Michael learned Jane was performing in pornographic films, he spoke briefly with her, but she was just as cold and indifferent as before. She revealed nothing of her life, and Michael didn't pry. He called several times after that, but finally Jane told him not to call anymore, as she just didn't see any point in having any kind of relationship. She turned down one last invitation to dinner, hung up, and never spoke to Michael again.

When Johnny asked Michael to call Jane, he was reluctant, but did offer to track her down and make sure she was all right. He drove past her home several times, but never observed any activity other than a car or two parked at the front curb, while the typically dense foliage that shields a Beverly Hills swimming pool hid the back. Michael decided to hire the same private investigator who found her before, in hopes he could find her again. The detective assured him he would.

+ + +

Pete Helden surprised John Helden by inviting him to his office "to wrap up some old business." John hadn't heard from Pete or his father in years and couldn't imagine what Pete was referring to. John asked his son to tag along. Johnny had met Pete several times in the '50s when Johnny, as a teenager, delivered payment checks for equipment his father had sold. Back then, Pete never showed any interest in getting to know Johnny.

They parked across from the plant in front of the old Helden office building where John had worked as a sales engineer from his early twenties until he left in 1946, at age forty-four. He had been there the day in 1925 when Uncle Peter broke ground and eighteen months later when all the scattered office departments finally gathered under one, new roof.

Johnny commented about the few cars on the street and the apparent lack of activity.

"I think the plant's been shut down for about a year."

"What about office people?"

"John pointed west. "They park in that far lot."

"Oh yeah, I see." Johnny looked at his father's troubled face. "Dad, this can't be anything serious. Don't worry."

Pete greeted them vigorously. He had the enthusiasm of a typical salesman though he hadn't been in Sales for years. "Good to see you guys. John, you've been a stranger around here for a hell of a long time – how come?"

It so disarmed John, he couldn't respond. Ever since the failure of the plastic milk transport tank, he had no business dealings with Helden. Pete and his father never once called him or invited him to the Helden Co. office. And now, John couldn't bring himself to say any of that, just as he couldn't years ago.

"Sit down. Make yourselves comfortable. Want a soda . . . *Coke, Pepsi?*"

"No thanks," they said.

Pete began, "You don't know, and I wouldn't want you reading it in the papers, but we're moving our corporate offices out of Milwaukee."

Surprised, John said, "I thought it was just-"

"Manufacturing's gone, and it ain't coming back. It's more efficient if our offices are closer to the main plant in Arkansas."

"Are you and your wife moving down there?"

"Hell, yes . . . Arkansas's an up-and-coming state with low taxes.

Here we've got real estate taxes, income taxes, and those damn personal property taxes have killed us. Hell, we pay taxes on our toilet paper."

For years, the Helden Company moved unsold equipment into John's yard so when the city assessor came around, there'd be a dozen or more transport tanks he couldn't count for taxing purposes. By the time an assessor got to John's place, the tanks had been hauled back to the Helden plant. It was a widespread practice because the personal property tax on unsold equipment was regarded as counter-productive, short-sighted, and confiscatory. It helped push many manufacturers out of Wisconsin. Foolishly, John let the Helden Co. park their equipment in his yard for free.

"Will there be any local presence," John asked.

"Only our attorneys . . . we'll keep those leeches on board for a little while." Pete laughed.

"Hard to believe," John said, "when I think of what it used to be . . . ."

"Oh, hell, the union and taxes killed us. Companies can't operate profitably here. We won't be the last to leave."

"What about your father?"

"They moved to Florida, permanently. I doubt he'll ever step foot in Wisconsin again."

"I didn't know . . . ."

"Well, you know how that goes. He had lots of loose ends." Pete knew how indifferently his father felt about his relatives from the poor side of the family. Peter Helden, Jr. called none of his cousins to inform them of his move, not even Dr. Julius, the most highly regarded.

Noticeably impatient, Johnny asked, "Why did you ask my father here?"

Pete glanced at him with annoyance, suggesting Johnny should keep his mouth shut. Addressing John, Pete said, "One of the things the lawyers want us to do is close any open accounts or agreements, any loose ends, that kind of thing. We've got inactive accounts with your two old businesses. Accounting and legal want to terminate, in more of a formal way, our past relationships, that you were a distributor for us and a customer for parts, that kind of thing."

"How?"

From a file folder, Pete pulled out a typed page and carbon copy. "This is a standard mutual release agreement. We use the exact same legalese with everybody, but you'll see your two companies named and you personally." He pushed the copy towards John. "Read and sign it," he said.

John read then handed it to Johnny who said, "I want to talk to my father about this in private."

"Yeah, sure, go ahead . . . ." Pete hid his displeasure.

In the hall, Johnny asked, "You understand this, right?"

"Yes," his father answered. "They won't sue me, and I won't sue them. They don't owe me money, and I don't owe them. I see no reason not to sign it."

"I know, but I think you should balk . . . just to see how he reacts."

"No, Johnny. I'll sign, then let's get out of here."

"Dad, please, trust me."

John Helden didn't know what his thirty-eight year old son was thinking. "Okay, but don't make it a big deal."

They went back into Pete's office. From behind his desk, he grinned broadly. "Yeah, nice to see you again, John . . . been a long time." He handed John a pen, but Johnny snatched it.

"We don't really see the necessity to sign this. We have absolutely every confidence that Helden has no reason to sue my father."

It caught Pete off guard. "So what are you saying, kid – your dad won't sign?"

"No, I'm saying we want to talk about it."

"Okay, let's talk."

"Maybe we ought to discuss," Johnny paused, "if my father has reason to sue Helden."

"What the hell are you talking about?"

"The plastic tank . . . your great invention." Johnny's voice reeked sarcasm.

Pete's face reddened. "We got outta that business, you know that. What the hell does that have to do with anything?"

"Getting out of that business destroyed my father's livelihood."

John Helden put his hand on his son's arm. "Johnny, no, don't go there."

"Listen to your father, kid. John, sign the g--damn agreement!"

"No," Johnny said, placing his hand on his father's. His eyes pleaded for trust. "Not until we know why."

"Why what?" Pete asked.

"Why you decided to build milk transport tanks out of plastic when you were the country's leading producer of stainless steel?"

Pete could hardly believe his ears. Years ago, he remembered Johnny as a skinny, pimple-faced punk, an errand boy who used to bring him checks. He'd take the thousands of dollars and dismiss Johnny with a wave and a perfunctory, "thanks kid." Now Johnny had the audacity to question him, as though he possessed authority.

Pete said, "What the fuck are you talking about?"

"My father was a successful distributor of Helden milk tanks until the failure of your plastic tanks. You built an inferior product that cost my father his livelihood, at least to the extent that he never made any money selling your equipment again. You breached the trust my father placed in you: the reasonable expectation that you'd continue manufacturing the best milk tanks in the world. Once you switched to plastic, my father's business was ruined, destroyed by your deliberate and foolish decision to switch from stainless to plastic. It seems to me that's the basis for a lawsuit – breach of contract."

Pete struggled to control himself. "It wasn't plastic, dammit, it was fiberglass. We did plenty research . . . it was time for a change. Hell, that tank was the best looking milk tank ever built . . . revolutionized the industry-"

John Helden cut in. "It leaked. What good is a leaking milk tank?"

"We were way ahead of our time . . . ."

"Then why isn't anyone building plastic tanks today?"

"Man, you guys just don't get it." Pete faked a laugh. "First of all, let me explain it very clearly: they weren't plastic; it was fiberglass. Call it that." He glared at them. "It was a research project. After we discovered the problems we lost all interest in building milk tanks. They weren't profitable – understand? We make a hellava lot more money building petroleum. The fiberglass experiment provided the opportunity to stop building milk . . . something we had wanted to quit for years. Building milk tanks was for shit. Petroleum's where the money's at."

"I know better," John said. "You forget my brother, Clarence, was Helden's purchasing agent. He knew how profitable milk tanks were."

"Clarence didn't know shit. You think we'd share our financials with that fat slob? Besides, he's been dead forever."

"When he was alive, he told me the tremendous profits you made," John said.

"You didn't answer my question," Johnny said, calmly. "The fact is, you didn't have the faintest idea when you started selling the plastic tanks if they'd hold up because you never did any road testing."

"Fiberglass, dammit . . . ." Pete's palm slammed the desk. "Show a little g--damn respect. Where the fuck do you come up with this shit? How the hell do you know what we did or didn't do? We road tested that tank plenty."

"What roads? What kind of loads? How many miles? Where are the logs?"

At that Pete lost it. "Listen you punk kid, who the fuck do you think you are? I could buy and sell your skinny ass a thousand times over. Who the fuck do you think you're talking to?"

As calmly as before, Johnny said, "We knew an engineer on the design team. He told us your road testing program was minimal at best and non-existent at worst."

Pete glared at Johnny. He stood and ordered, "Get the fuck outta here." Then to John Helden, "You'll be hearing from our attorneys . . . ."

In the car, Johnny said, "Dad, I bet ten bucks you'll never hear from his attorney or Pete." John Helden shook his head. At seventy-three, he feared Pete's threat, but his son won the wager.

+ + +

In Los Angeles, Michael Helden, for the second time, hired Bill Kangas, private investigator, to find Jane Anderson, his sister-in-law's sister.

Bill learned his trade working as a cop and detective in several police departments in Southern California. After twenty years he went out on his own. His style, like his successful peers, was methodical, thorough, and relentless. Most of his cases were domestic or small business matters: a husband cheating on his wife or vice versa, business fraud relating to fire or theft, a business owner stealing from a partner, families dissatisfied with a police investigation or even the outcome of a murder trial in the case of a loved one, and, of course, missing persons. He considered himself a true professional, never letting his emotions becloud his judgment or intuition. He was presumptuous only when there was nothing else left for him to be. He knew every human being always and invariably left some kind of trail.

In the case of Jane Anderson, the first thing he checked was the missing person reports. Nothing. Second thing, he asked his contact in the adult film industry to track Jane down. He couldn't. The third, not waste his time staking out her west side home, but check real estate records to see if she and Polly still owned it. Bill wasn't a bit surprised to learn they sold it several months prior. He searched utility records, and, in every case, accounts were in the name of P. Laffner. Only the property title had been recorded in both women's names. Polly left a forwarding address at the Post Office, but Jane did not. That raised Bill's curiosity. When a trail turned cold so quickly, his relentless nature kicked into a higher state of unyielding determination. He knew he'd find Jane eventually, but first he'd have to find Polly Laffner.

Polly witnessed the changes in the adult film industry in its degeneration from rather tame nudies to explicit sex acts, and she hated it. She hated the drug and alcohol use so many girls succumbed to. She hated the toughness of so many men on both sides of the camera, and she certainly hated the risk of catching a venereal disease. After she realized Jane wanted to end their relationship and sell the house, she knew it was time to quit the porn industry. She didn't have to work as a waitress anymore. She wanted a break from Los Angeles and had saved enough money to do nothing for a few years. She decided to return to her parents in the small Texas town where she grew up. She wanted to get far away from the life she had led for the past several years and to get over her attachment to Jane. Jane had made it perfectly clear she no longer wanted what she and Polly had so carefully nurtured: a loving relationship.

Bill Kangas wrote Polly stating his credentials and that he had been hired to determine Jane's whereabouts. He received no reply, so he wrote a second letter three weeks later, literally begging for

Polly's help. This time she answered, but claimed she didn't have the faintest idea where Jane was and hadn't seen or talked to her since the closing on the sale of their home. He wrote a third time, pleading that she'd talk with him, at least on the phone. A week later they talked, but Polly offered no new information. It became obvious to Bill that Polly and Jane's parting was not amicable. Polly said something to the effect that "some asshole turned Jane's head" leading to "our break-up," indicating that theirs was indeed a romantic relationship. Bill asked about the guy, but Polly didn't know his name, what he did, where he lived, indeed, nothing for they never met, and Jane revealed very little. Polly did say, however, that Jane always expressed an interest in visiting Hawaii; she and Polly had talked about going there, but it never happened. It was a good lead, and Bill thanked her. He had an associate in Honolulu who could track Jane down anywhere on the islands.

Lastly, Bill requested if Polly ever heard from Jane to "please let me know." She promised she would, but doubted it, knowing the finality of their break-up. He was ready to hang up, but then thought to ask if Polly knew where Jane banked. "Where I banked," she answered.

He checked passenger lists for flights to Hawaii for the months after Jane and Polly sold the house; he found two J. Andersons: one flew roundtrip, the other one-way. He wrote his associate in Honolulu, asking him to search for Jane. Along with Jane's personal information, Bill included a copy of the photograph Michael Helden had given him.

Bill checked her auto and driver's license registrations; both bore Jane's old address. He combed marriage licenses in Los Angeles, Orange, and Ventura counties, and in Las Vegas and Reno. He checked passport applications. He went to her bank, but was told that without a subpoena they couldn't give him any information. Bill's wife, however, knew someone who worked there, and from her Bill learned that Jane's account had been closed. When he checked the date, he realized it happened before the closing of the sale of the house. That puzzled him. *What did she do with her proceeds and the money she withdrew,* he wondered. He searched other airline records picking Milwaukee – Jane's hometown – New York, Miami, and New Orleans as possible destinations. His file of empty leads grew thicker. After two months of intensive work he had learned little.

Bill called Michael, explained how he had come up empty and asked if he wanted him to continue. When Michael learned Bill's charges to date, he told him he couldn't afford to go on. Michael realized Jane simply didn't want to be found. Bill, however, suspected something would eventually turn up, serendipitously.

As part of his routine, Bill Kangas regularly checked police bulletins downtown. Six months after Michael told him to stop searching for Jane, Bill came across a homicide bulletin from Oregon involving a Caucasian woman. He was intrigued by the remoteness of the discovery and the description of the body – that of a shapely, young woman – and, in spite of his doubts, felt compelled to check it out. He never forgot about Jane Anderson even though he couldn't invoice Michael for the many hours spent chasing fruitless leads. It was a long drive to Eugene so he asked his wife to accompany him. She was even more skeptical, but he promised her they'd make a little vacation out of it, spending a night in Sacramento on the way up and, on the drive back, a night or two in San Francisco.

Three weeks earlier, hikers found a woman's body in rugged terrain near the east edge of the *Siskiyou National Forest*. They had been camping, but were so disturbed at what they found that they packed up and sought out the nearest law enforcers.

The site of discovery was analyzed as a crime scene before the body was transported north to the morgue in Eugene. Fingerprints were sent to the FBI; the results were received several days before Kangas arrived to view the body. If the dead woman was not a felon, very likely she had never been fingerprinted. If that were the case, identification would be almost impossible. The young woman had been decapitated.

In spite of an extensive search by the canine unit, her head was never found. Gunpowder residue, however, discovered on the upper torso indicated that she had been shot in the head, execution style, before the decapitation. Nearly everything about the woman's death indicated that whoever killed her did not want anyone to discover who the victim was.

Kangas, deeply troubled by what he learned, thanked the officer who helped him and left Eugene with a copy of the woman's fingerprints. He wondered why the killer or killers hadn't thought to cut off the young woman's thumbs. *Stupid guys*, he realized.

In San Francisco, Bill and his wife stayed at a motel on Lombard Street near the base of Russian Hill. Bill dropped his wife off at Union Square for shopping then drove to the police station. He knew Jane had resided awhile in San Francisco before moving to Los Angeles. He presumed she wasn't a felon, but maybe she'd been picked up on a misdemeanor. He found several files marked *Jane Anderson*, pulled them, and sat at the visitor's table in the Records Room.

The first slight folder concerned a middle-aged woman picked up for prostitution; the second, a black woman for shoplifting, and the third, a young, Caucasian woman for disorderly conduct and possession of marijuana. He stared hard at the mug shot, for it was indeed the visage of the person he yearned to find: *Jane Anderson: born in Milwaukee, Wisconsin, 1949*.

He stared at her youthful, defiant, pretty face. He had seen her in a pornographic film and knew how beautiful she was. *What a waste*, he thought. Then he pulled out her fingerprint card and placed it on top of the small stack of closed manila folders.

His heart racing, Bill reached inside his sport coat for the envelope containing the fingerprints of the headless, female torso he had pondered in horror in Eugene. He struggled to remain calm.

He easily recognized the perfect match that induced visceral and triumphant feelings for having solved the mystery of a dear person lost. At last, he had found Jane. Finally, he had kept his promise to Michael Helden. He had done his job without any expectation of remuneration. Though he didn't know the killer yet, he knew the killer's greedy motive.

Bill Kangas – tough cop, tenacious detective – couldn't suppress tears from glistening his eyes, as he whispered to himself, *jackpot!*

Chapter 33 ~ 1976

A month after his interview, Dr. Jack Cutler joined the Messert Clinic. His wife, Cheryl, was thrilled with his salary and didn't give a second thought that her husband decided on a career in women's reproductive health. She told him, "I'm very pro-choice."

Anxious to quit her job and move to Milwaukee, Cheryl took charge of cleaning their place and packing. In the interim, Jack rented, close to the clinic, a furnished studio apartment where he slept weeknights. On weekends they'd get together to house-hunt. Jack needed a tax write-off; he gained nothing by renting. Cheryl, however, didn't like the idea of owning a house simply because it meant more work for her.

Driving around the lake country west of Milwaukee with the newspaper real estate section and a county map, they discovered the little town of Delafield where they found a house under construction. Impetuously, Jack stopped and said, "Let's have a look." Cheryl had no interest in a half-built house, but he ordered, "Come anyway!"

Large window openings faced a narrow channel two hundred feet from the rear of the structure. Jack inspected the rough carpentry framing as though he knew what he was looking at, while Cheryl simply looked bored. Jack helped her step off the deck, dropped her hand, then headed under a vault of old hardwoods towards the channel. From its grassy bank they gazed northeast at the sun-bright, open water of Lake Nagawicka. The beautiful vista reminded Jack of the summer days he spent at George Brower's home on Lake Mendota in Madison. It reminded Cheryl of nothing. Jack said, "Let's buy this place."

Cheryl reacted with an angry, "Absolutely not!"

As Jack drove off, he turned onto a street with a large, old, oak tree in the middle of the roadway. Spotting it, he accelerated. As the car raced towards a collision, Cheryl screamed. Laughing, Jack swerved away, as the pavement forked, straddling the tree's massive trunk.

"You scared me," Cheryl cried. "What's wrong with you? Are you crazy?"

"Sorry." Sudden remembrance of his mother's death at the trunk of another tree stunned Jack into silence.

+ + +

Karen Anderson and her aunt, Elizabeth, worked together for several years with a group of women who passionately disagreed with the Supreme Court's ruling in the *Roe v Wade* case. The committee defined their mission as twofold: educational and political. They knew television was the most effective way to reach large audiences, but it was expensive. After their first ad urging adoption instead of abortion, which the members themselves paid for, they realized they needed a fund-raising strategy.

Politically, they worked to elect men and women to the State legislature who were pro-life and would support legislation to somehow limit Roe's far-reaching effects. What alarmed the women was that, according to recently published State records, over ten thousand abortions had been performed in Wisconsin in 1974. Karen asked her aunt, "How can we go from zero to over ten thousand in a single year?"

"Before Roe, doctors performed abortions in secret," Elizabeth answered. "Now abortion's legal, and the State wants to know the numbers . . . doctors comply."

Shortly after the first of the year, Elizabeth volunteered to publicly debate the question of whether the Court's ruling in *Roe v Wade* was good for America. She spent hours at the library reading, taking notes, and organizing her thoughts relating to the legal, scientific, social, and moral aspects of the ruling. Her opponent, who would argue the affirmative, headed a local women's reproductive rights group. The debate was scheduled for Thursday, January 22, three years to the day after the Court's decision.

Karen invited her parents and sister, Katherine, and her husband. Johnny asked his parents, Uncle Julius, and Aunt Helen. About two hundred people gathered in the high school auditorium. The organizers agreed that those opposed to the Court's decision should sit on the right, as they entered the hall, and those in favor on the left. Johnny noticed the stark setting: two podiums on either side of the moderator's desk that faced the audience; behind the desk an American flag on a floor staff. The backdrop was black.

John and Anita sat next to Julius – Helen didn't come – with Johnny and Karen right behind, about a third of the way back in the auditorium. Karen spotted her parents and waved. Within minutes, the moderator and debaters came on stage. The moderator introduced both women: Ms. Susie Tybern, president of *Families by Design,* received enthusiastic applause from people on the left. Elizabeth received about the same from those on the right.

The moderator began. "First, I want to thank all of you for joining us this rather chilly, snowy evening and welcome you on the third anniversary of the historic Roe versus Wade ruling. Tonight's debate concerns the question: *Was the Court's decision good for America?* Ms. Susie Tybern will argue the affirmative. Mrs. Elizabeth Peterson will argue against.

"We all know that Roe has been one of the most controversial rulings in recent years, but the organizers and I believe that public debate can shed better understanding on highly contentious issues. I ask all of you, regardless of how you feel about Roe versus Wade, to treat both debaters with respect. I request that your applause be restrained and, please, refrain from any verbal outbursts. You will note two of Milwaukee's finest" – she pointed at the police officers stationed at the two rear exits – "are in attendance to assure law and order." At that the crowd stirred.

Johnny studied Elizabeth's appearance, realizing how good she looked for a woman of sixty-five. Other men in the audience, including his father and Uncle Julius, also studied her face with curiosity. Johnny thought Ms. Tybern younger, *perhaps forty-five to fifty.* He had every confidence Elizabeth would hold her own, for they had discussed the issue several times.

Again, the moderator: "We'll begin by posing this question: *Was Roe versus Wade a good legal and political decision for the United States?* Ms. Tybern, arguing in the affirmative, you may begin."

A full head of reddish-brown hair framed Ms. Tybern's pretty, round face. "I, too, thank everyone for attending and for this opportunity to defend what should no longer be in need of defending.

Of course Roe versus Wade was a good decision, and one that was long overdue. When you think of back-alley abortions, suppression of a woman's right to control her own body, the lack of privacy in the most intimate decisions of a woman's life . . . the Supreme Court acknowledged all of it and ruled properly and responsibly."

There was an outbreak of applause.

Elizabeth, nervous, a bit shaky, and not thanking anyone, replied, "It certainly was not a good legal decision. Many constitutional scholars maintain that abortion is one of those matters that clearly should have been left to the individual States. The Court claimed that state laws against abortion violated a woman's right to privacy and due process. That is not true because another human life is involved. Let me define abortion very clearly: it is the willful killing of the unborn child. I think everyone here can accept that definition. Would one argue, for the sake of a woman's privacy and due process, that she has the right to kill her newborn infant in the secret space beneath the basement stairs?" Elizabeth had written the rhetorical question in advance.

Some in the audience hissed. The moderator tapped her gavel.

Ms. Tybern replied, "Let me state even more forcefully that abortion is not the killing of an unborn child. The Court clearly ruled that abortions can be performed up to the point when the fetus becomes viable. You're not talking about another human person until after viability. The Court clearly recognized and affirmed that."

Elizabeth responded, "Actually, the Court also ruled that women have the right to abort after viability to protect the health of the mother. An unborn child can be aborted at any time to protect the so-called health of the mother."

"And what, may I ask, is wrong with that? Don't you value the life of a woman?"

"I value the life of a woman as much as anyone in this room, but I think everyone needs to be reminded that pregnancy is not a disease, let alone a fatal one. Only rarely does pregnancy threaten the health or life of the mother."

"It can affect a woman psychologically and emotionally very deeply, especially if she doesn't want to be pregnant. That is part of a woman's health, too, and the Court, in its wisdom, recognized that."

Elizabeth faced her opponent. "Ms. Tybern, you said that abortion is not the killing of an unborn child. You also said the fetus isn't a human being until it's viable. Then it is your responsibility to tell us two things: first, what is killed in the act of abortion, and second, if it isn't a new human being, what exactly is it?

Vigorous applause came from the right side, earning the gavel's pounding.

"Okay, I'll be happy to explain that," Ms. Tybern responded. "What is eliminated – not killed – is a tiny, ill-defined clump of cells and tissue roughly resembling one of those funny, little, curved peppers, but much, much smaller. Certainly, it is not a human being. In fact, it resembles any number of other mammals during early gestation. Regarding what it is, I will concede that it's a byproduct that sometimes results from the act of sexual intercourse."

Johnny Helden whispered to Karen, "That's weak – your aunt is doing very well." Karen nodded.

Elizabeth countered, "This 'ill-defined clump,' as Ms. Tybern calls it, is what each and every one of us was from the very beginning of our existence, that is, from the moment of our conception. First, we are an embryo, then a fetus, and then, when we finally begin to twitch a little inside our mother's womb, then and only then does she concede that we've become a legal person even though, technically, we're still a fetus.

"But think for a moment about some other words we use to describe the various stages of our human growth and development: infant, child, juvenile, adolescent, young person, adult, elder, and geriatric. All those words indicate a specific stage of human growth, development, and, ultimately, decline. In the meaning of every single word, everyone in this auditorium must admit that it is the growth, development, and decline of human beings that we're talking about. Embryo and fetus are no less proper words for describing the growth and development of very young human beings than the words elder and geriatric are for describing the decline and diminishment of older human beings.

"Those words, collectively, define the many possible gradations of physical and mental immaturity or maturity. They portray the continuum of human life from conception to death. All are equally valid for describing developing or developed human beings. To pick an arbitrary point before which we describe an embryo or fetus as an 'ill-defined clump' is completely illogical and unscientific. We are human beings from the moment of conception to our death."

Again applause. Before Ms. Tybern could respond, the moderator tapped her gavel. "Ladies, I also want you to address whether it was a good political decision. Ms. Tybern, please . . . ."

"Yes, of course, it was. But first let me respond to what Mrs. Peterson just said. It's obvious she has nothing but disdain for the reasoning of the Court. She recites her little word litany as though she can infer from late and later development a scientifically unknown state of very early development. It's like pointing at a tree and saying 'see the acorn.' Sorry, the acorn is not a tree, and the embryo is not a human being.

"Now, politically, had we waited for the States to change their anti-abortion laws, millions of American women would have suffered the burden of sexual and reproductive oppression. They would have been forced to seek what so many of our predecessors suffered: mutilation or even death at the hands of back-alley abortionists. This ruling came none too soon for all American women."

Vigorous applause came from the room's left side. The moderator said, "Mrs. Peterson, you may make the last statement here, and then we'll move on."

Elizabeth sipped some water, aware of the irregular beating of her heart, something she had never noticed before. She glanced at her notes. "My understanding of how laws are created in this nation is through a Legislative body with the consent of the Executive, all duly elected by a majority of citizens. For the Court to rule, as it did in Roe, strikes me as political tyranny of a mere seven men. Let me remind everyone that in 1858, the Court's Dred Scott decision denied full humanity and citizenship to American Negroes. That judicial tyranny was regarded as so outrageous, so profoundly evil that the Civil War was fought to correct the terrible error in the Court's thinking. My point is this: the Supreme Court doesn't always get it right. They didn't get it right regarding slavery, and they didn't get it right in Roe versus Wade. Therefore, it will remain, I believe, a politically divisive issue for years to come."

The right side of the hall broke into applause. The moderator rapped her gavel to quiet things down.

One of the men in the audience, who thought Elizabeth looked familiar, had cared for her in a brief encounter forty-five years ago. Dr. Julius Helden suddenly recognized in her mature face the unique beauty of her youth. He recalled exactly when and where he had treated Elizabeth.

The moderator began again, "Now, ladies, we'll next discuss the question: *Was Roe versus Wade a good or bad scientific decision?* Again, Ms. Tybern, because you speak in the affirmative, you may begin."

"The main scientific question, really the only scientific question is: when does human life begin? But before I answer that, just let me correct an error of Mrs. Peterson's. She said the Civil War was fought to correct the Dred Scott decision. It is my understanding, and I'm quite sure a majority of American historians would agree with me, that the Civil War was fought to preserve the Union because the South seceded. Lincoln fought to preserve the Union.

"Now, regarding when human life begins, the Court is quite clear and specific. Human life begins with viability. They received plenty of input confirming that from the scientific community. The Court and the scientific community have spoken definitively. Responsible citizens must obey the law of the land. We are a nation of the rule of law, are we not?"

Elizabeth responded, "Yes, we are supposed to be a nation of the rule of law, but, as I said, Congress never passed a law authorizing unlimited abortions for any reason for the full nine months. Only seven, old, black-robed men created such a ruling. That doesn't constitute the rule of law. It constitutes a judicial tyranny.

"But I do want to address the scientific question because Ms. Tybern obviously did not. I maintain that human life begins at the moment of conception, for if it isn't human and if it isn't alive until viability, then what are we dealing with? In fact, after only fifteen days, the baby's heart begins to form. At twenty days the brain begins to form. At four weeks the limbs start growing. All this development occurs before a woman even knows for sure that she's pregnant.

"Let me give an example: we all know who Shakespeare and Beethoven are – the greatest English writer and the world's greatest composer. But, they weren't that when they were a year old, or a month, or a week; then they were merely infants. Had both of them died at a tender age what would the effects of their deaths have been? Would we have Shakespeare's plays or Beethoven's symphonies? No, the world would have neither. But they lived, they learned, grew and experienced life – its joys and sufferings – and so we have their wonderful art. But now let's suppose they both had been aborted very early, long before viability, that is, long before they became, according to the Court's definition, persons. If they weren't persons, but were, in Ms. Tybern's words, ill-defined clumps, then surely had they been aborted the world should have lost nothing. But, again, any honest, thoughtful, logical person must admit that had Shakespeare and Beethoven been aborted, the world would never have known the beauty and greatness of their art. Therefore, human life, as we know and understand it, must necessarily begin at the moment of conception. Every person in this room began his or her unique life at conception."

Lively applause rose from the right side.

"Ms. Tybern, you may respond."

"Well . . . where to begin? No pun intended." Some in the audience laughed. "No one denies the potential of an embryo to grow into a living person. But we must not forget that the Court based its decision on the best scientific information available. Scientifically speaking, what the embryo really is . . . is a parasite. Here's some simple, but very powerful logic: a parasite is not a person; an embryo is a parasite; therefore, an embryo is not a person." She paused and added, dramatically and with great emphasis, "and, thus, can be aborted."

Some, but not all, on the left side of the auditorium clapped.

"Mrs. Peterson, one more response and then we'll move on."

"Ms. Tybern's definition of an embryo is laughable. If I remember my high school biology correctly, a parasite is a plant or animal that lives off another species, causing harm to that species. An embryo is human, same as the mother – indeed, half of it is the mother. Its inherent nature is certainly not to harm the mother. So, Ms. Tybern is wrong. The embryo is not a parasite and, therefore, must not be aborted."

Now vigorous clapping came from the right side of the room. The moderator tapped her gavel.

Another doctor in the audience, an older man, sitting on the left at the center aisle also thought Elizabeth looked familiar. He nudged his younger companion, whispering, "I think I know that woman." He, too, recalled treating her years ago.

"She's pretty good," the younger man whispered back, evoking a scowl.

The moderator said, "Well, ladies, so far this has been very interesting, but now we're going to ask you to address another question: *Has Roe versus Wade had a positive or negative affect on our society?* Ms. Tybern?"

"Yes, but just let me quickly clarify my last point: an embryo is no more a person than an acorn is a tree. An acorn needs soil, water and sunlight to grow and develop into a tree. So, too, does an embryo need enormous amounts of nutrients from the woman to grow and develop into a person."

Elizabeth, frustrated that Ms. Tybern snatched the last word no matter what the moderator directed, cut in, sharply. "This is ridiculous. She's the affirmative. I'm to have the last word. She's done that three times already." At that, some in the audience booed.

Before the moderator could respond, Elizabeth said, "An embryo is certainly a human being, though extremely small and immature. Anything that has the potential to become a mature human being is itself necessarily *human*. It was procreated by humans and never could become something other than human. And it's a *being* because it possesses life; that is, it is capable of growth and development. It is a *human being* and, therefore, a person. Is it dependent upon the mother for nutrients and a safe womb? Absolutely, and in precisely the same way that a newborn is dependent upon the nutrients in the milk of her mother's breasts and the safety of her arms."

"That's hardly a last word," Ms. Tybern shouted. "That was a speech – same old tired argument ad nauseam."

"Please, Ms. Tybern," the moderator said. "You agreed to have an equal number of statements. You go first; therefore, Mrs. Peterson gets the last word. So, please continue."

Throughout the debate John Helden struggled to recall when and where he had encountered Elizabeth. It wasn't recently, for when he looked at her he was reminded of a much younger woman. Finally, he remembered. *Oh, yes, that little flower shop . . . .*

"What's the question again," a shaken Ms. Tybern asked.

"Has Roe versus Wade had a positive or negative affect on our society?"

"Good grief, of course it's had a positive social effect." Ms. Tybern's exasperation was apparent to everyone. She agreed to the debate because she felt it would be an easy win. Instead, she found Elizabeth's persistence frustrating and her arguments formidable. She went on, "At long last, women are the social and sexual equals of men. Finally we have the legal right to control both our sexual lives and our reproductive lives. Without abortion, unwanted pregnancies would lead to unwanted children. Do we really need thousands more unwanted, illegitimate, delinquents running around? Do we really want to build more orphanages? Do we really need more wards of the State?"

"My goodness," Elizabeth replied, "with all the different kinds of contraception, abortion shouldn't be necessary at all."

"Obviously, Mrs. Peterson doesn't understand the impulsive nature of sexual passion."

The slur drew boos, laughs, hoots, and hisses from both sides of the aisle.

"I certainly do," Elizabeth protested. "I'm just suggesting a couple should use contraception to prevent an unwanted pregnancy, or they should abstain."

At the sound of that word, snickering scattered throughout the audience. Ms. Tybern picked up on it. "Oh, now I understand where you're coming from. Sex is only for having babies. It's that crazy Catholic thing. Well, I've got news for you," she turned towards the audience, "sexual passion even trumps the Catholic Church."

Vigorous applause erupted from the left side of the auditorium. The moderator pounded her gavel.

"No," Elizabeth cried. "One does not have to be Catholic to understand that people have to be responsible. Our human sexuality must be used properly because the consequences can be so profound. Whether it's an unwanted child or an abortion, both are bad social consequences, especially for women."

"Ah, ha," Ms. Tybern began. "Now she's beginning to see the importance of women having complete control of their bodies. The Supreme Court finally acknowledged the only authority over a woman's body is the woman herself. To deny – as Mrs. Peterson consistently has – that a woman has the right to decide when she will or will not reproduce would be the greatest tyranny imaginable."

Again, vigorous clapping from the left side of the hall prompted the moderator's restless gavel.

"I have not consistently denied that a woman has the right to decide when she'd have a baby," Elizabeth began. "She not only has that right, she also has the prior right and responsibility to decide if and when she wishes to become pregnant. She also has the prior right and responsibility to decide if and when she wishes to have intercourse and with whom. If she decides to have intercourse, she'd better first decide if she wants to get pregnant. If she doesn't want to get pregnant, she can either not have intercourse or use contraception. My point is, if she's careless and has intercourse without contraception and becomes pregnant, then she does *not* have the right to kill her unborn child. My whole point is that people have to use their sexuality responsibly."

Ms. Tybern couldn't wait to answer. "Here's the way life really is: women and men enjoy sexual intercourse far more if it's spontaneous without giving it much prior thought at all. Good heaven, Mrs. Peterson, there is such a thing as passion, you know. In our modern, enlightened society, sex has nothing to do with marriage or having babies. Indeed, sometimes it has very little to do with love. Sexual intercourse is a highly desirable animal act of great pleasure. Sometimes, couples use contraceptives. Fine, I'm all for it. But, sometimes they don't. And sometimes a woman gets pregnant when she really doesn't want to. The man might not want it either, but he can walk away. Now, thanks to the Supreme Court, a woman can do something about an unwanted pregnancy, and she can do it safely, without guilt or condemnation so she can get on with her life."

The left side burst into applause.

Elizabeth recognized how difficult it would be to counter Ms. Tybern's last statement let alone change any of the audience's opinions. She scanned her notes, found something and then, after the room quieted down, began. "Two things are obvious from Ms. Tybern's last statement: first, she has no respect for the traditional view that the proper place for sexual intimacy and procreation is in the married state. Second, she sees abortion as a quick, easy, consequence-free way to get rid of an unwanted pregnancy.

"Throughout the ages and in all cultures, marriage has been regarded as the sanctuary for sexual intimacy, procreation, and the rearing of children. Yes, I'm aware there's been a sexual revolution recently that holds a radically different view: the view of free love. It advocates that men and women can have sex whenever and with whomever they wish, and because of Roe versus Wade, an unwanted pregnancy can be terminated. But that vision is a false vision. For a single woman to get pregnant and then get an abortion is a profoundly negative experience. Not all women are so hard of heart that they're not emotionally and psychologically scarred by having an abortion. If an unmarried woman gets pregnant and chooses to keep her baby, her life can be very difficult as a single parent. Then there's the possibility of contracting a venereal disease. It seems to me, and I think it should seem so to every thoughtful person, that casual sex is a dangerous activity. It used to be called promiscuous behavior. Now Ms. Tybern calls it enlightened."

The moderator interrupted. "Mrs. Peterson, I'd like to give Ms. Tybern a chance to respond."

"Thank you," Ms. Tybern said, sweetly. "Here again, Mrs. Peterson is talking about a society and social mores that no longer exist. The most important social principle of modern enlightenment is that women and only women are in control of their sexuality and their bodies – end of discussion."

At that, another outburst broke from the left side of the room.

Elizabeth sipped a little water. She knew what she had to say. "Sexual intercourse outside marriage is socially irresponsible. It is very unwise for women to engage in it. Men, even so-called modern men, lose respect for women who are sexually easy. That's just the way men are. If a woman gets pregnant and the man deserts her, she's left with two very difficult choices. Hopefully, she would choose to keep her baby. Sadly, many choose to destroy their baby. Though it happens often now, abortion was and always will be a socially reprehensible act. Even though a woman freely chooses it, it still is an act of terrible violence against her dignity as a mother and her defenseless child's right to life. It represents profound irresponsibility of both the man and the woman, for it is the most extreme and radical form of birth control. Contraception really isn't birth control, though it's referred to that way. Only after conception occurs can there be such a thing as 'birth control.' Abortion truly is birth control for it denies birth to the unborn child who waits – silently, helplessly, and patiently – to be born."

The audience responded with silence. "Ms. Tybern, you may reply."

"What if a woman is raped or raped incestuously? What if she and her husband have several kids, but don't want another, and she gets pregnant? What if she's close to menopause and gets pregnant? In those cases," – she turned towards Elizabeth – "are you really suggesting that a woman has no control over the contents of her womb?"

"You and I know that abortions due to rape and incest represent only a tiny fraction of the total. There were ten thousand abortions in Wisconsin last year; I suspect only a tiny number were from rape and incest. Regarding a husband and wife who want to limit their family: there is abstinence or contraception if they can use it with a clear conscience. In this day and age, to suggest that parents need or should use abortion to limit the size of their family is utterly ridiculous. My God, people have to exert some degree of personal responsibility."

Applause came from the right, but on the left, Elizabeth's arguments angered one of the two doctors who recognized her. He muttered something after virtually every comment, but his companion couldn't make sense of it.

The moderator said, "Let's move on now to our last question which is: *Has Roe versus Wade had a positive or negative moral effect on our nation?* Ms. Tybern?"

"Just let me say, there's a higher moral law than what some ancient astrologers conjured up in some medieval monastery. It is the moral law based on reason and a woman's ability to think for herself. We are all independent persons, and, in so many matters that affect our lives, we must think for ourselves. Occasionally, as with Roe versus Wade, the Supreme Court intervenes on behalf of reason, freedom, privacy, and independent thinking. I've said it before in this debate, and I'll say it again: where a woman's body, sexuality, and reproductive life are concerned, there is only one absolute authority, and that is the woman herself. The

Supreme Court recognized that, and I would like to suggest that these so-called 'pro-life' people begin to respect the law. Not to do so is not only illegal but immoral. Did Roe have a positive moral effect on our nation? It did for thinking people. It did for women. It did for all those who truly value individual freedom and privacy. But now my opponent will drag out all those silly religious arguments so be warned."

The moderator cut in. "Ms. Tybern, there are to be no personal attacks. You are not to presume anything about Mrs. Peterson's arguments. You are to hear them before you challenge them. Mrs. Peterson, you may respond."

"Thank you. In spite of Ms. Tybern's ridicule, the fact remains that our nation was founded on the principles of Judeo-Christian morality. It was not founded on a specific religion, but the founders were religious men and women, mostly Christians, and they utilized those moral principles to guide them in forming the nation. I came across a quote by John Adams, our second president, years before the American Revolution. In 1756 he wrote: *Suppose a nation in some distant region should take the Bible for their only Law Book, and every member should regulate his conduct by the precepts there exhibited. What a paradise would this region be!*

"In the Old Testament, in the Jewish Torah, and the Mosaic Law, the commandment states: 'Thou shalt not kill.' In the Declaration of Independence, Thomas Jefferson wrote that: *all men are created equal, that they are endowed by their Creator with certain unalienable Rights that among these are Life, Liberty and the pursuit of Happiness.*

"Our laws against murder are based on that ancient commandment. We are not to kill other human beings. In the Declaration, the first right that Jefferson names is the *Right to Life*. Liberty is subservient to it. Let me give an example: the liberty of a slave woman in 1860 was more important than the happiness of the slaveholder who derived wealth and material comfort from owning slaves. Because Jefferson recognized that liberty takes precedence over the pursuit of happiness, the call for the eventual abolition of slavery was inherent in the Declaration of Independence. Did the slaveholder have the liberty to beat and kill a slave? Absolutely not because the slave's right to life took precedence over the liberty of the slaveholder to abuse and kill."

Ms. Tybern broke in, shouting, "The slavery we should be talking about is the slavery that unwanted pregnancies force upon women."

Her outburst caused loud grumbling on both sides of the aisle. The moderator pounded her gavel. "Order please . . . Mrs. Peterson, are you finished?"

"No, I am not."

"Then you may continue. Ms. Tybern, please, do not interrupt. You will have your chance to rebut."

Elizabeth began, "The analogy is easily drawn. The life of the unborn child takes precedence over a woman's liberty to abort that child. And the liberty of the unborn child to grow and develop to birth takes precedence over a woman's pursuit of happiness."

At that, the left side of the auditorium exploded with boos, hisses, shouts, and rants all garbled together so no one could understand anything. People on the right clapped and shouted, "quiet, sit down, quiet," while the moderator pounded her gavel. After a few minutes order was restored.

Several rows from the stage on the aisle, a slender, older man rose, his gray hair slicked back. At first he said nothing, but then in a loud, shrill voice and pointing straight at Elizabeth, he screamed, "You lying bitch – you had two abortions."

Most of those sitting in front and to the sides of the old man heard it. People in the rear caught only some of the accusing words; they asked each other, "What'd he say?" Again, the hall erupted in a tumult of gasps, shouts, boos, and hisses. On the stage the moderator pounded her gavel fast and hard, but to no avail.

Elizabeth stood frozen, speechless; her face blanched.

The moderator pointed at the offender still standing there and shouted into her microphone, "Police, get that man out of here." They raced down the aisle, gripping the old man's thin arms, and dragging him towards a rear exit.

John Helden faintly recognized the man, but Johnny and his uncle clearly did. Julius realized, *My God . . . Anthony Messert.*

A younger man trailed behind the cluster of Messert, two cops, and several others. With shocked disbelief, Karen Helden looked right at him, while he stared hard at her. It was Jack Cutler.

Paul Peterson bounded up the side stairs, put his arm around his wife, and escorted her to the wing of the stage, out of sight.

Ms. Tybern, grasping the situation, shouted into her microphone. "Ladies and gentlemen, don't leave! This debate is far from over. I want to question my opponent about her two abortions. That should be fun . . . ."

The moderator said, loudly, "Ladies and gentlemen, this debate is over. Ms. Tybern, please, turn off your microphone."

Ms. Tybern, however, wasn't through. People were filing out, but few turned to look back when she shouted, "abortion is moral because anything that enhances a woman's freedom is moral." At that, several young women cheered.

Finally, the moderator signaled, and the sound system was turned off.

Karen desperately wanted to reach Elizabeth. Seeing Jack Cutler stunned Karen, but what that old man screamed horrified her. If nothing else, she longed, not to ask a single question, but to comfort her dear aunt.

Johnny and Karen rushed down the side corridor to the stage door. John, Anita, and Dr. Julius followed, for both Helden brothers wanted to meet again the woman they once knew, years ago, as *Hildy*.

+ + +

Six months had elapsed since Michael Helden discharged Bill Kangas from continuing his search for Jane Anderson. When the call came, it surprised Michael. Kangas said, "You gotta come to my office."

"Nice to see you again," Bill said, without meaning it. The dirty necessity of informing young Mr. Helden that his sister-in-law's sister had been brutally murdered easily erased Bill's self-satisfaction at having linked a headless woman's body in Oregon to a pretty girl's set of fingerprints in San Francisco.

"Did you find her," Michael asked.

"Yes, I did . . . sit down, please."

Kangas told Michael everything: how he drove to Oregon, how he matched the prints in San Francisco, how he presented the case to the Los Angeles police, and how they obtained the body, did the forensics to verify Jane's execution-style murder, and delved into Jane's banking history to establish a motive. Lastly, and particularly difficult, Kangas told of Jane's decapitation.

Michael slumped in his chair. A hand at his forehead hid his eyes. He uttered, over and over, "No, no, no . . . ." He began to sob, to weep. The unfathomable reality of Jane's murder crushed his spirit, his joy of life, his deepest longings, and shattered his highest ideals. He who boastfully assured Karen Helden that he'd keep his eye on her baby sister, now felt responsible for Jane's death. *Had I only kissed her . . . had I only started a relationship to stay close . . . had I only acted more decisively . . . had I only been her friend . . . .*

"She got in with a bad crowd. That porno business is rough. She's not the first girl to die, and she won't be the last."

"Who killed her?"

"We don't know yet, but we will."

+ + +

Wahl Avenue curls off Lake Drive just north of St. Mary's Hospital. Impressive homes and mansions on the west side of the street overlook the resplendent lake from the high bluff that extends northward for miles, though the avenue itself is modestly short. Sturdy wooden benches face the great lake, inviting strollers to sit awhile and enjoy the luminous, ever-changing silver, grey, and blue palette of sky, clouds and sea.

On a mild February day, Elizabeth Peterson and Karen Helden decided this would be a good place to walk and talk. Karen parked near Lake Drive, close enough that when they glanced southward they could see the lovely, old, stone water tower that stands in the roundabout, marking the hospital's main entrance. Strolling northward, Elizabeth took Karen's arm, comforting them both. Karen waited for her aunt to speak, but they walked a full block before she did.

"Paul and I wanted children, but I just couldn't conceive. I was almost thirty when we married, and Paul's five years older. We went to doctors, tried different diets, positions, exercises, all kinds of things, plus we prayed very hard. Time went by . . . I worried that what I had done injured me, thinking maybe that was the reason I didn't conceive. I felt Paul had a right to know, so I told him. It was difficult and strained our marriage, but he eventually forgave me."

"As well he should," Karen said.

"Paul suggested we tell my doctor – about the abortions, I mean – and see what he had to say. Well, there was no evidence of injury. I was built normally, no tipped uterus or anything like that: nothing that would prevent me from getting pregnant. Then we learned Paul had a low sperm count, and, given our ages, that probably was the reason I didn't conceive. At least that's what the doctor thought. Of course, we were very disappointed."

"Did you consider adopting?"

"We did, but Paul was working so much overtime during the war, and then I had the opportunity to buy the flower shop where I worked. I decided if I couldn't have children I wanted to be a businesswoman, to see if I could run a business successfully. After the war things got pretty good. Eventually, I owned three shops, but it was just too much work. I sold two, and now even one is too much. I'm sixty-five, Karen, time to retire."

"You don't look that old. You're still beautiful."

"Oh, dear, dear Karen, thank you. After the debate, I felt very old and very beaten." She paused, and then, "Paul and I have decided to sell the business, but if we can't, we'll just close the doors."

They approached the *Lion Bridge* that crossed a deep, wooded ravine. Elizabeth fell silent until Karen asked, "You're not cold?"

"No, I'm fine."

Then Karen asked what she was most curious about. "How did you know Johnny's father and Dr. Helden?"

A sadness brushed Elizabeth's face. "When I was very young and foolish, Dr. Helden cared for me at County General. Actually, he did the first abortion."

Karen gasped.

"It was therapeutic; without it, I would have died." She paused then whispered something that Karen did not hear.

They paused on the bridge and leaned against the stone balustrade, gazing through naked trees at the silver-grey, ice-stricken lake. Karen didn't know what to say.

"Dr. Helden was extremely kind to me. I could never forget that."

"And Johnny's father?"

Elizabeth smiled at the memory. "He was a customer at Carolyn's, the flower shop where I worked. Oh, John Helden was very nice: tall, dark, and handsome. He often bought roses for his wife."

"Oh my goodness . . . my in-laws. So you knew him just from his coming into the shop?"

"Yes, we got to know all our customers. Once I worked up nerve and asked if he knew Dr. Julius Helden. He told me that was his brother."

"And they both knew you as Hildy?"

"Yes. In those days," she laughed, winsomely, "I was Miss Hildegard E. Neubauer, but everyone called me Hildy."

"Oh, that's so lovely. Why did you ever change?"

"Well, marriage changed my last name, and I decided to use my middle name first, because Hildy sounded too girlish. I thought *Elizabeth* far more elegant."

Karen laughed, while Elizabeth tugged her arm playfully. When they neared the pavilion in Lake Park, they turned and headed back.

Neither spoke until they reached the bridge again. Elizabeth said, "Karen, what I did was wrong. At the time, I was terribly frightened and embarrassed and didn't want to be pregnant, let alone have a baby. I was young and stupid. Mostly, I feared my parents, but I shouldn't have. That baby was their grandchild. They never had another. For years, I was haunted by the realization that I had done the worst thing any woman could do by destroying the innocent child in my womb. I alone decided to deny that precious child the joy of life. My maternal instinct and my guilt rebelled against my desperate longing for spiritual peace. No one said what I had done was wrong. No one condemned me. But my conscience, that tiny, secret, inner voice told me it was not natural, not normal, and not right to have killed my own little child."

"How did you ever overcome that?"

"For many years I didn't, and because I aborted one child, I aborted another."

Karen was horrified. "My God, what are you saying?"

"Several years later, I met a man who never would have shown any interest in me if I hadn't had the first abortion. When I met him, I would have been the mother of an illegitimate three-year-old. He was far too selfish to love another's man child. I learned too late that he only wanted the pleasure my body gave him. He deceived me. He led me to believe he wanted to marry me. He seduced me, but I allowed it, Karen, and I became pregnant. When I told him, thinking he'd be happy, he told me I was a liar, of easy virtue, unworthy to kiss his mother's shoes. I never heard from him again."

"Oh, my God, how incredibly cruel . . . ."

"I was hurt, angry, my heart so filled with revenge that I had his baby aborted."

"Not by Dr. Helden?" The possibility horrified Karen.

"Oh, heavens no. By Dr. Messert, the old man who screamed at me."

In silence they walked back to Karen's car. Saying little, they drove to Elizabeth's home for a cup of hot tea. Once settled, Elizabeth said, "You asked how I ever got over it . . . ."

"Yes, how did you? You seem, you've always seemed so, oh, I don't know, content. At peace with everything."

"I had friends: the people who owned the little flower shop where I first worked as a bookkeeper. They were Catholic, and because of them, and others, I converted. They taught me about the Sacrament of Confession and how it liberates from the guilt of sin. By then, I was absolutely desperate to rid myself of the terrible guilt I had lived with for so many years. After my Baptism, I went to Confession, even though the priest told me that all my sins were washed away by the waters of Baptism. I told him everything. In telling it, in repenting of it, I finally felt the guilt drain from my heart and mind. When he said the words of absolution, I finally believed with every fiber of my being that God forgave me because my sorrow for those sins was so immense and true."

"That's wonderful."

Elizabeth sighed. "Yes it was, and the priest who heard my confession – oh, he was such a dear man – died several years ago. Do you know who that was?"

Karen shook her head. "I have no idea."

"It was Fr. Fahey, the priest who married you."

+ + +

Good police work got the guy. Someone always knows something, and it's usually just a matter of asking enough people enough questions until, eventually, a cop catches a break: just a small, slight lead, but something that puts him on the true trail. What really helps police in their work is that human nature doesn't like keeping secrets, especially, if they involve something illicit or horrific.

The investigation focused on guys and girls who performed regularly in the pornographic film business and had worked with or knew Jane. Finally a break came: after questioning dozens, a smart, tough detective sat down with a hanger-on type, a porn star wannabe, a real talker who knew a guy who owned a twenty-eight foot power boat that had been used for filming sex scenes. That didn't sound like much, but when questioned, the owner mentioned that he had once helped a guy get rid of something. And while the owner didn't know what the guy did for a living, he knew he wasn't involved with the adult film industry. The two had met casually at the marina. Though the yacht owner claimed he didn't know what it was to be gotten rid of, he did brag to the detective that the two of them figured out how to dispose of it so "no one in the world will ever know."

Under intense questioning, the boat owner finally revealed how this guy had snatched a couple bricks from a building site, placing them into a large tote bag along with what he "had to get rid of." He stuffed the bag into one of those red and white, beer and soft drink, carry-on coolers so common to recreational boating. On a fair-weather weekday, the two men cruised out about five miles, far from other boats, opened the cooler and heaved the weighted tote overboard. They watched it sink into a thousand feet of black, Pacific water, never to be seen again. They exchanged a couple high fives, then cruised back to the marina.

The yacht owner admitted that he was paid two thousand bucks for something "so fucking easy." And finally, under the threat of prosecution for aiding and abetting a crime, he gave the detective the name of Jane's killer.

The police released Jane Anderson's body only after they had confirmed, by the killer's admission, that Jane's head could never be recovered. The coffin was sealed and, at the coroner's directive, marked *Do Not Open. Advanced Decomposition.*

At the news of Jane's grisly death, her father collapsed.

Michael Helden agreed to accompany the coffin on the long

flight back to Milwaukee. It was the least he could do, for the opportunity to do more had been forever lost. A small obituary appeared in the newspapers without any notice of public visitation or mention of the private funeral mass for the immediate family. Jane's mother asked her sister-in-law, Elizabeth Peterson, to give the eulogy.

After the priest read the long account of *The Raising of Lazarus* from St. John's Gospel, Elizabeth went to the lectern. She had jotted some notes for the eulogy, but wondered, *what can I possibly say that will comfort anyone?* She resolved not to break emotionally.

"I have often thought the supreme act of a woman's love is carrying and giving birth to a child." She looked at Jane's mother. "You did that three times, and three times you bore a beautiful baby girl. I've also thought that the most painful experience for a mother, indeed, for both parents, is to experience the death of a child. How do parents cope with that? Is there less sorrow if their child, as in Jane's case, had attained adulthood?"

Karen reached for Johnny's hand, squeezing it hard.

"No, I'm afraid not. The suffering that comes with the death of a child of any age is far beyond anyone's feeble words to explain or comfort. And the death of a child by murder is way beyond the limit of bearable human pain. At twenty-six, Jane was a mature woman: independent and willful, yes. But she did not deserve – no one deserves – to be murdered.

"I believe with all my heart that God is particularly merciful to one who is murdered, especially, a young person. Our dear Jane was denied the happiness that would have unfolded throughout the remainder of her life. She was denied all those earthly joys – and sorrows – that we all come to experience and so often take for granted. Jane was denied her future years to discover, not only the fullness of her own life, but the beauty of God's love, His mercy, and forgiveness. The murderer, however, distorts that by bringing death prematurely and, thus, unnaturally thwarting the will of God by stealing years of life that Jane was entitled to live. The act of murder is so profoundly evil because the murderer violently puts his will ahead of the will of God."

Elizabeth gazed into the eyes of Jane's parents. "Jane was your youngest daughter. The youngest child is usually the most free-spirited, and that certainly was true of Jane. She grew up in the shadow of two outstanding sisters, and she felt – I know because she told me – always a little bit inferior. I explained she was just younger. Eventually she'd catch up. Sadly, she never did. But Jane loved people, loved having fun, and living life to the hilt. She was hard working, independent, and hated the horrors of war. Like so many young people today she was rebellious. But if I look at the world critically, I guess maybe she had some pretty good reasons to rebel."

Elizabeth paused. She felt she hadn't said nearly enough, sensing the tiny gathering desired more, yet only a few written sentences remained. She hoped they would suffice.

"I believe it's important for us to recall our Lord's words to the Good Thief on Calvary, as they both hung waiting to die. Christ said, 'this day you will be with me in Paradise.' Today all of us must believe with all our hearts that Jane is with her Blessed Savior in Paradise, and that she is at peace. And so, we say farewell dear Jane with the firm and steadfast hope that one day – one happy day – we shall all embrace you again."

Elizabeth stepped down. Without looking at anyone, she walked to the pew where her husband, Paul, waited. He took her hand and glanced at her, his heart filled with admiration.

Michael Helden thought it *a perfect elegy*. But nothing Elizabeth said or might have said could ever diminish the haunting realization that he had, in some very real way, contributed to Jane's tragic Los Angeles life and death.

In the front pew, Jane's mother and sisters wept softly, while her father wept uncontrollably. He had not forgotten, indeed could never forget, the last words he spoke to his beautiful, youngest daughter back in 1969, after a ruined Thanksgiving weekend when he told her in his strongest, sternest, most authoritarian, and disgusted voice, "Get the hell out of here . . . I don't ever want to see you in this house again!"

PART 4 ~ 1980 to 1991

Chapter 34 ~ 1980

In 1976, Lewis Thilman favored the governor of California, Ronald Reagan, as the Republican nominee over the incumbent president, Gerald Ford. Lew agreed with Reagan's more conservative philosophy. However, Reagan's quest for the nomination failed. In November's general election, Democrat Jimmy Carter defeated President Ford. Most observers attributed Ford's loss to the pardon of his predecessor, Richard Nixon, for the crimes of Watergate.

Shortly after Carter's inauguration in 1977, Lew began writing his memoirs. He focused on the years from his first election to Congress in 1938 to his defeat in the Republican congressional primary in 1948.

After finishing the first draft, Lew mailed a copy to his brother-in-law, John Helden. John made copies and gave them to his sons, Michael and Johnny. He circled one paragraph that he thought insightful. It read:

The two fundamental flaws of political liberalism are that it rewards those who are irresponsible and incompetent and punishes those who are competent and responsible. On the basis of the first flaw, liberalism is called compassionate. The flaw of political conservatism is not that it rewards those who are responsible and competent, which it does, but that it ignores those who are irresponsible and incompetent. On that basis, conservatism is called cruel.

Reagan's mid-twentieth century American conservatism, however, was far less personal. It stood for four fundamental principles: first, constitutional limits and the division of power among the three federal branches of government are to be strictly maintained; second, matters not expressly dealt with in the Constitution are to be left to the States; third, fiscal responsibility is required at all levels of government: federal, state and local; and, fourth, a strong military is necessary to defend the nation from aggression, particularly, Soviet aggression. Reagan believed in massive, retaliatory military power not because he thought the United States could win an un-winnable nuclear war, but precisely the opposite: he wanted to preserve the sacred and beneficent peace against a powerful foe far too willing to exploit any weakness.

Elected to the presidency in 1980, Reagan vowed to remake the federal government into a lean, restrained, prudent, and humble servant of the American people. Unfortunately, he simply had no idea how resistant and reluctant to change the thriftless Congress and the leviathan of bureaucratic government would prove to be. In the face of it, Reagan turned his attention to foreign affairs and decided it was time to win the *Cold War*.

+ + +

Jack Cutler rarely scanned the obituaries in the evening newspaper; he didn't know enough people in Milwaukee to warrant it. His eyes spotted the top name in the listing only because it was familiar: *Anderson, Jane*, the kid sister of an old girlfriend he knew years ago. The brief obit listed only parents and two sisters with their husband's first names in parentheses. *So, Karen is now Mrs. John Helden*, Jack discovered. A sense of sadness at Jane's death overcame him, for he remembered her as a bright, bubbly, eleven year-old. Things didn't easily shock Jack, but this death disturbed him. He found it hard to believe. It bothered him for days.

Jack had seen Karen at the *Roe v Wade* debate earlier in the year and was just as surprised as she obviously was to see him. He couldn't recall what her husband looked like or if she even was with a man, for when he spotted her, he saw only her. His own marriage had grown loveless and dull. When he thought of Karen, he easily convinced himself that she would have made a far better wife save for one inconvenient reality: Karen wouldn't marry him. Still he wondered about her because he thought her very high-class compared to his crude, uneducated wife. After ten years with Cheryl,

Jack had grown so bored and uninterested that he almost found it laughable were it not, in fact, such a miserable situation.

After several days of lingering wonderment about Jane's death, Jack decided to call Karen and express his condolences. He couldn't imagine, other than an auto accident, what fate claimed the delightful, little – for he still thought of her that way – Jane Anderson. Jack found Karen's phone number and decided to call midweek, presuming her husband would be at work. Of course, Jack couldn't possibly have known that Johnny's office was in the basement of their home.

She answered, "Hello . . . ."

Even though he recognized her voice he said, "I'd like to speak to Karen Helden, please."

"This is she."

He paused, debating if he should hang up or speak.

She repeated, "Hello?"

"Karen, this is Jack Cutler."

"What?" She paused. "I don't believe it."

"It's me, Karen . . . I just-"

"Why in heaven's name would you call?" She calculated then said, "It's sixteen years . . . ."

"I saw in the paper that Jane died. I couldn't believe my eyes. I just wanted to express my sympathy."

"Well, I suppose that's considerate of you, but, good heaven, totally unnecessary."

"Karen, I was so shocked I-"

"And inappropriate, I might add."

"I didn't mean to offend . . . ."

"I'm a married woman. We have five children. I'm grieving. My parents are grieving. Just what did you expect?"

"Nothing."

"Goodbye, Jack."

"Karen, wait, just answer one question, please . . . ."

"What?"

"Are you happy, I mean in your marriage and everything?"

"Yes, I am."

"Good, I'm glad. When I saw you at that debate you didn't look very happy."

"What," she cried again. "My dear aunt was viciously attacked. What did you expect me to do: smile, wave, blow you a kiss? I was concerned about her. Now may I go?"

"I didn't know she was your aunt."

"How could you? How could you know anything about me? You had no interest when you had the chance, certainly no interest in knowing my family, let alone my aunt."

"That's not true. I was interning . . . under tremendous pressure. I had no time for myself let alone anyone else. I didn't want our relationship to end. Once I had some time, you never gave me a chance."

"Oh please, Jack, spare me. I knew we wouldn't be happy together, and I made that very clear, at least, I thought I did. You weren't what I needed, and I certainly wasn't what you wanted."

"I didn't know what I wanted."

Karen's curiosity got the better of her. "Why were you there?"

"Where?"

"At that debate . . . ."

"I'm a gynecologist. You know that."

"Well, I hope you don't do abortions."

"Yeah, well, no, I-"

She cut him off. "Goodbye Jack. Please don't call again."

At the tumultuous end of Elizabeth and Ms. Tybern's debate, when two cops forcibly escorted Dr. Messert from the auditorium, several persons had slipped in front of Jack so it didn't appear he was with the old abortionist. Completely surprised at seeing Jack, Karen had no reason to believe he performed abortions or didn't perform them, for that matter. In fact, she didn't wonder about it until after she hung up.

+ + +

Johnny Helden's consulting practice proved a constant struggle right from the start. He couldn't compete with large engineering firms for the big, prestigious projects, but instead had to compete with well-established one or two-man shops for smaller jobs. Occasionally, if Johnny got a larger project, he'd hire his free-lancing friend, Jerry Summers, a young draftsman he had met at B & X to prepare the drawings.

In 1977, Erv Shaffer, a senior architect Johnny had befriended while at B & X, handed him a large industrial account. American Leather Corporation, the sprawling tannery north of downtown, produced so much high quality finished leather that its weekly output was measured in acres.

Johnny still worked for Chuck Lorenz in Chicago. His architectural firm provided good fees when Lorenz had decent contracts. Unlike Bob Schmitt's ongoing project at SMF to design structural steel mezzanines, however, Lorenz's work never generated a steady income stream.

Johnny referred to those clients as his top three. He knew other architects including a talented, young designer, Joe Albert, who now and then sent Johnny an interesting project though never anything big. Once, Joe asked him to design a complex, three-story office building. The negotiated fee was sufficient to support Johnny's family for two months. Unfortunately, Albert's client couldn't secure financing, so the young architect and Johnny were never paid. It was a devastating setback for both, as Albert also had a family. For the Heldens, instead of two months' expenses accounted for, it meant two more months of scraping by, deferring bills, and going a little deeper into debt. Two more months without the financial reprieve Johnny so desperately needed; two more months when Karen could not avert the worried look in his eyes. Fortunately, Bob Schmitt and his ongoing mezzanine project provided monthly income and with it, an ever closer friendship.

From what John and Anita Helden could surmise, their son, at age forty-three, had become a reasonably well-established consulting engineer. While he hadn't accumulated any wealth except for the slow, steady buildup of equity in his house and life insurance, he at least was able to shelter, clothe, and feed his wife and five children. What loomed ominously, though, was that Nick and JJ would finish high school in '81; both had every intention of going to college. Nick wanted to study engineering like his father and was content to do it at Marquette, but JJ wanted to attend Notre Dame. He didn't know exactly what he'd study, but knew it wouldn't be engineering. JJ's interests were more like his mom's. Being a great reader, both Johnny and Karen thought he'd choose something in the liberal arts.

+ + +

Karen's father, Nicholas Anderson, began drinking heavily after Jane's death. As the years passed, he made no effort to quit, ignoring his wife's pleadings with an indifference that emanated from a broken heart. By 1980, he couldn't even allow the beauty of seven grandchildren to overcome his unrelenting guilt and crushing sorrow for the lost life of his murdered daughter. He never was a flat-out, fall-down drunk, but whenever he came home or visited his daughters' families, the stale stench of alcohol and cigarettes permeated his presence. After a while nobody enjoyed being with him save his steadfast wife who constantly overlooked all. As so often happens, the curious workings of her mind shuttled a terrible sense of guilt back and forth between her brain and heart that eventually smeared her with a shared blame for Jane's tragic death. Then Mrs. Anderson began to drink. Witnessing this sad parental degeneration, Karen felt helpless, unable to initiate any healthy change. Inevitably, her parents slowly drifted away.

+ + +

Orders for structural steel mezzanines manufactured by SMF nearly always required some modifications. Johnny and Bob Schmitt worked out the modular column spacing, stair framing, and standard loads for the first brochure. Once the sales reps got that material, orders began to flow in regularly. Neither Bob nor Johnny minded the additional engineering work; SMF passed those costs on to the customer. Every modification was incorporated into the large design file, and every attempt was made to standardize so that customization, as months and years went by, would become less time-consuming.

Johnny performed stress analyses and deflection calculations and drew many fabrication details at his home office. After several months, though, he spent one or two days a week at SMF in the small office set aside for him. Bob would review all the work Johnny completed since their last meeting, an arduous task. Every shop detail had to be meticulously checked, for Bob was a perfectionist and rightly so. Any mistake on a drawing would waste time and steel; Bob wouldn't tolerate that. After several months, Johnny got to know the office employees, the works manager, and some men in the shop. But a new, young receptionist, Dana Buckley, really charmed him.

Johnny guessed Dana in her early twenties; *young enough to be my daughter,* he realized. A sweet, pretty, pleasant girl, Johnny always enjoyed her cheerful greeting. At first, she was a temp, but after several months, because of her intelligence and work ethic, she was hired full-time.

Karen invited Bob Schmitt to dinner several times, or they all, occasionally, went out for a fish fry. Usually, Bob had a date, but sometimes not. This time, Bob invited Johnny and Karen to his apartment for drinks, and dinner – his treat – at a classy restaurant overlooking the Milwaukee River. When they rang Bob's doorbell, a lovely young woman greeted them happily, her face bright with pleasure. It was Dana Buckley.

+ + +

Dr. Anthony Messert didn't note Jack's fifth anniversary at the clinic until day's end when he suggested they go out to dinner. In those five years, several doctors had left, and several new men had been hired. Jack, without effort, gained seniority. Messert liked Jack; liked his calm, conscientious, no-nonsense style as a physician, and his quiet, controlled personality as a friend and even as a prodigy. Messert, in his own words, was "a damn good mentor" to the younger doctors. He thoroughly instructed them in the best practices and procedures for successful first trimester abortions. Second trimesters he did himself, but always asked one of the other doctors to observe and learn. He was getting older, finding it more difficult to cut, carve, and dismember the fetus. He knew that a younger man would eventually have to take over that part of the practice. His preference was Jack, though he displayed only a perfunctory interest.

That Messert, however, showed no interest in helping his clients avoid the possibility of a second or even a third abortion became a contentious issue between the two men. Jack wanted to help prevent a young woman from becoming a repeater, but Messert argued, "We're not offering a fix for the failures of public school sex education." They did have a few repeaters, and Jack thought it senseless and sad for the girl. Messert said, "If they're so g--damn careless, let them suffer the consequences. Besides, it's good for my bottom line."

Messert enjoyed Jack's company, insisting he join him at least once a week for dinner at a good restaurant. Jack went because it usually kept him out past Cheryl's bedtime. Messert thought Jack a good conversationalist for one, simple reason: he let the old doctor expound. They'd have a couple drinks before dinner, eat slowly, then go to Messert's home for a Scotch nightcap in his comfortable den.

Miguel, Messert's man servant, followed them into the room. Dr. Messert motioned to Miguel who came back in minutes with a nearly full bottle of *Chivas Regal* and two tumblers.

"It was a tough day, Jack, a tough week, but Miss Regal knows how to soothe."

"Not so tough . . . ." Jack settled down in the leather chair across from the old doctor who relished the fine whiskey.

"I did five D, D & E's this week; five of 'em, Jack. Until you do one yourself, you don't understand how difficult they are."

"Why the hell do they wait so long?"

"Stupidity," Messert answered.

"Actually, they change their minds. One of the girls you did told me she broke up with her boyfriend, so she decided to get rid of his kid. She said she wanted the baby until they split."

"The bimbos have a million stories, Jack. Don't believe any of 'em. They all come with some self-serving tale. I've heard 'em all. Fact is, they wait too damn long because they're lazy, stupid, or both."

"They should come in as soon as they know."

Messert didn't reply. He took a full swallow of Scotch. "You wanna listen to a little Montavani?"

"Whatever." Music didn't matter much to Jack.

The old doctor rang a little bell. Miguel came and put on one of Messert's favorite albums.

Messert began again. "The problem with late terms is they're just inherently difficult plus risky. There's just not a lotta room up there . . . risk of perforation, cutting, tearing, that kind of thing. I have to be damn careful. Let me tell ya, Jack, fetal tissue is tough. It's like cutting raw chicken with a butter knife, and I'm just not as strong as I used to be, especially my hands. That's why you should take over. You're a strong guy and could do 'em a lot easier. You have to account for every tiny piece of flesh though: fingers, toes, whatever, and lay 'em all out and fit it together to make sure you got the whole body." He idly turned the glass in his hand. "Of course, that's why we can charge more. That's the upside, I suppose."

"I don't know," Jack said. "I'm not sure I wanna do late terms."

"You're not as emotionally tough as you should be, Jack. Of course, you might want to do them if we could ever figure out a better way than this damn dismemberment. It's the cutting apart that's so difficult."

"Like what . . . a caesarean?" Jack laughed at the absurd suggestion.

"Oh, hell no. We could never sell that. I don't know exactly. I've heard what some guys are experimenting with; some of it sounds promising."

"Like what?"

"There're a few doctors on the coasts who deliver the fetus feet first after inducing labor or, more usually, a forced dilation. They turn the fetus so they can grab the feet with forceps. Then they pull the body out feet first, but only part way."

"Kinda like a breech?" Jack asked.

"Yeah, but the butt never comes out first. Ultrasound guides 'em so they can turn the body if they have to, grab the legs with forceps, and just pull the body down feet first into the birth canal. In effect, they deliver the whole body except the head, which they purposely keep lodged just inside the cervix."

Messert searched Jack's face for any sign of a reaction. Jack looked straight ahead as though lost in abstract thought. His hand hung limply over the end of the armrest, holding his half empty glass of Scotch at a downward angle.

"This is a great arrangement," Messert said of *Moon River*.

"Yeah," Cutler said, indifferently.

"You know, Jack," Messert continued, "a D & C is relatively simple. You're right; it's wonderful if the bimbos come in early. You prefer it; I prefer it. But what if they come late second or even third trimester? This is when it gets really tough – for me. First of all, we have to charge a hell of a lot more for late terms, which is perfectly just. You can't compare a D & C to a dilation, dismemberment and extraction. And if at that point we could avoid dismembering the damn thing, just bring it down and get rid of it before its head is delivered, my life would be a hell of a lot easier. You follow me on this, Jack?"

"Are you thinking what . . . lethal injection?"

"Well, we could do that I suppose, but this method is different."

"How do you get the head out? You might have to do an episiotomy." Jack's questions pleased Messert, for they revealed no feeling of repugnance.

"If the head were to pop out, so long as it's dead, so much the better, I suppose. But I'd want to avoid an episiotomy, as do the bimbos. This is the brilliant thing these doctors are doing, really clever to avoid both a lethal injection and an episiotomy. If there's no lethal injection and if the head pops out and it's alive, then, yes, legally, we've got a little bit of a problem. But if the head is still in there, above the cervix, then technically if we kill it in that position at that location it's still a legal abortion. Follow me?"

"That'd never fly," Jack said. "Girls don't want to be cut and sewn."

"Yes, that's exactly the problem. They don't want anything to interfere with a rapid resumption of their sex life." Messert laughed. "They want to heal as fast as possible, and that's understandable. As doctors, we have to facilitate that. So what do you think we should do?"

"Forget about it," Jack replied. "Educate to get 'em in early: first trimester, simple D & Cs. It seems to me this practice should be widely promulgated by now."

"No, no, Jack, that's not the way science advances. A scientist must never be afraid to search for something new."

"That doesn't sound like science," Jack said. "It sounds like infanticide. That would be drawing the thinnest imaginable line between abortion and infanticide."

"Maybe, maybe not," Messert said. "In fact, there's a far better way than lethal injection and episiotomy."

"Such as?"

"That's the brilliance of this new method. It's actually been used thousands of times already." Dr. Messert had a wry smile on his thin lips. "Have any idea?"

"None at all."

Anton poured Cutler and himself another Scotch. He wore an expression of pleasurable anticipation at what he was about to reveal. "You know, Jack, you're not as smart as you sometimes think you are." He chuckled. "Here's the genius in this: they deliver the entire body except the head, which is still up there in legal territory. Very simple up to this point, right? Yes, there's inducement, or forced dilation, prep, and all that crap, but that only affects the bimbo. It's all very easy for the staff and doctor. So, once the body's out, everything but the head, then you take long, surgical scissors and very skillfully – remember you're in the birth canal now – insert them into the back of the head at the base of the skull to create an opening. Then you open and twist the scissors a few times to increase the size of the hole."

"What the hell are you talking about?"

"Just listen now . . . this is what's so brilliant. You remove the scissors and insert a suction catheter. You suck the brains out, and, presto, the skull collapses. The head is rendered small enough to deliver without an episiotomy."

"Oh, God," Jack said.

"Neat, huh?" Dr. Messert laughed. "Simple, dimple . . . clean as a whistle."

"That crosses the line. That's not abortion; that's infanticide. You're killing a fully formed baby that's partially born, one that you just delivered."

"I'm not convinced of that, Jack. That baby ain't really been born yet. So long as it's not completely out, we are allowed to kill it. Roe versus Wade . . . it's between a woman and her doctor, a woman's right to privacy. We're all concerned here with the health of the mother, right? Besides, these guys have been doing a lot of late-terms using this exact method. No one's thrown them in jail, and no one's going to."

"They do 'em clandestinely," Jack replied. "I've never read anything about it. That gets out in the public domain, those guys are gonna end up in jail."

Messert resented Jack's harsh judgment. "I doubt it."

"If that gets out in the papers, the right-wingers and pro-life people will pound the hell out of us. You know damn well that baby at that point is viable. It could survive."

"You're wrong, Jack. Don't ever underestimate our allies – the feminists, the ACLU, our many friends in the Senate, most of the press – everyone who believes it's a private matter will support it. They'll defend it, or, at the very least, they won't oppose it."

"Bullshit . . . it's infanticide anyway you look at it. I couldn't do it."

Dr. Messert sighed. "You know, Jack, you're just not the hard-nosed professional you ought to be. I've told you a hundred times, we're blameless. It's the woman who makes the decision to kill – not us. It's a woman's legal right, upheld by the g--damn Supreme Court, and she can kill it whenever she wishes – throughout the whole nine months – if it in any way affects her mental or physical health, which it always does. We bear no responsibility other than providing skillful surgical methods. We are mere facilitators, nothing more, nothing less. But you know what, Jack? You don't believe that. You have your g--damn delicate conscience telling you this is all a very dirty little business. Yet you don't have the fucking courage to quit because you love the money. You're a hypocrite, Jack. You are a true hypocrite, and you certainly should know how Christ hates hypocrites." Dr. Messert laughed out loud.

"Bullshit. I'm comfortable doing early D & Cs. You're talking about killing a fully formed, viable infant that can live outside the womb. That's infanticide. You don't give a shit because you'll do anything for money."

"Come on, Jack, extend your thinking. Listen, at the next provider's convention a guy's gonna make a presentation. He's gonna bring videos showing the procedure. I'm gonna learn it, and I'd like you to learn it too." He raised his hand to keep Jack silent. "Before you say 'no,' do me a favor: at least think about it . . . keep an open mind. Come with me: Las Vegas, all expenses paid. We'll have a look see. This'll make late-terms a piece of cake."

"I'm not interested."

"You know, Jack, with this procedure guys are gonna make big money. Last year I turned away at least fifty who were too far along. That represented a small mountain of cash. It's important we learn this and provide it."

Messert fell silent. He looked at Jack, but turned away as Jack drained the last of his Scotch. Both men were tired. Miguel appeared in the doorway, but Messert waved him away. Jack poured himself more Scotch and then, unexpectedly, sat upright. Turning towards his colleague, he asked, "Do you believe in life after death?"

Messert let out a surprised yell, laughing hard. Finally, he said, "Hell no, but I do believe in death before life."

The comment bemused Jack. "What the hell's that supposed to mean?"

"Well, think about it, Jack. It's the most perfect definition anybody ever gave for what abortion really is: death before life." Messert laughed even harder.

"Oh shit, I ask a serious question, and I get bullshit."

"Hey . . . just a little food for thought."

"Well, what was it," Jack asked.

"What was what?"

"Your answer . . . ."

"I told you, hell no. Don't you listen? I absolutely do not believe in life after death – never did, never will. What do you think I am, Jack? Some kind of religious nut who fancies he's gonna end up with wings, sitting on a g--damn cloud strumming a fucking harp?"

"That's not what I was thinking." Jack's seriousness disturbed Messert who was too tired and drunk to be serious about anything. In spite of that, Jack continued. "I'm thinking more about the idea of being judged for what we do with our lives."

"Aw, shit, Jack, don't get religious on me. You know you're not a religious guy. Religion is the silly dreaming of the perpetually asleep. We're men of science, damn it, science."

"Well maybe this isn't all there is," Jack said. "This life, I mean. Could be more . . . who's to say? I read an article about near-death and out-of-body experiences where the soul floats above the body like on an operating table when a surgeon says 'hey, we're losing this guy' and the guy is up near the ceiling looking down on the whole scene, and he doesn't give a damn about anything because there's this wonderful, warm light calling him to come over to the other side."

"What the fuck are you talking about?" Messert's voice reeked ridicule. "What kind of bullshit is that? You can't possibly believe that crap?"

"Near-death experiences, out-of-body experiences, the soul being drawn to a loving light . . . that stuff actually happened. It was recounted in a book by a respected scientist."

"Ya, Jack, and I'm an alien from another planet come down here to wipe out the human race, and abortion is the only way I can figure out how to do it. Don't believe everything you read. That's pure, unadulterated bullshit."

"Maybe, maybe not . . . eventually we'll know, right? When we croak?"

"No we won't . . . only if there'd be consciousness after death. If there isn't, and I'm damn sure there isn't, we'll never know anything. How the hell can you know something if you're not conscious to know it?"

"I meant if there is life after death, if there is consciousness after death. Then we'll know."

"We'll know nothing. I don't wanna talk about this shit. It's stupid speculation. When you're dead, you're dead. You think the g--damn fetuses we rip apart and throw in the dumpster are up in heaven playing on a fucking swing set?"

"I don't know . . . I hope so. They're innocent."

"Bullshit – they're medical waste, garbage, trash, worthy only of incineration or a landfill."

"Oh, man, and you tell me to extend *my* thinking." Jack shook his head.

"I'll tell you what I believe, Cutler. Life is nothing more and nothing less than a brief moment of consciousness between two infinite, black voids. It's that way for an elephant in Africa, that way for the mouse in your kitchen, and it's that way for you and me. There are only two variables: the length of the period of consciousness and the degree of intelligence within the context of that consciousness. People are not created equal. I know all about those so-called promises of eternal life, but it's all bullshit, Jack. We are dust, and to dust we shall return. There is no heaven, no hell, and no immortal soul.

"I can reflect perfectly on that first, black void. They claim the universe is thirteen billion years old; well, I, for one, had no fucking problem waiting all that time to be born. I'm here right now. Those thirteen billion years seem like a drop in the proverbial toilet. And why is that? Because I didn't possess consciousness, and you know what? The next thirteen billion ain't gonna seem like anything at all either, because I won't have consciousness and neither will you. Now get the hell out of here."

Jack rose wearily from his chair.

"Sleep off your stupid opinions," Messert ordered. He walked Jack to the front door. "I'll see you tomorrow, bright and early."

He'd never reveal it, but Jack's comments disturbed him. *I hate that kind of crap,* he thought. Now he'd have to read something inane to get it out of his head so he could sleep.

+ + +

Actor and ex-governor of California, Ronald Reagan was elected the nation's fortieth and oldest president on November 4, 1980. He won in a landslide gaining 489 electoral votes to only forty-nine for the incumbent, Jimmy Carter. At age seventy-eight, John Helden admired Reagan. When he read that Reagan in his youth had saved seventy-seven persons from drowning in the Rock River in Illinois, John judged Reagan a man of outstanding character and would have voted for him on that commendation alone.

During Carter's presidency the nation, burdened and marred by low economic growth, high inflation, higher interest rates, and intermittent gasoline shortages, struggled to shed its malaise. Reagan suspected the American people were tired of high taxes and sick of sending so much of their paychecks to profligate congressmen and the nodding bureaucrats in Washington.

In addition to Carter's domestic failures, fifty-two American diplomats, held hostage in Iran for 444 days, proved to be an international humiliation. More than anything else, Carter's inability to figure out how to free them sealed his fate and assured Reagan's destiny.

On election night, delighted that Reagan won, John Helden called Johnny to revel for a few moments in the Republican landslide.

"Dad, it's no surprise. Carter was a disaster. He made it easy for Reagan."

"Yeah, let's hope for Carter's sake, he runs his peanut farm better than he ran the country," John quipped.

Chapter 35 ~ 1982

By the time they graduated from high school in 1981, Nick Helden and his fraternal twin, John Jr., or JJ as he was called, were as different in face, mind, body, personality, and interests as brothers born years apart. Right after their births, the parents and grandparents assumed they were identical, but by the third week everyone knew they weren't. As boys, Nick always stood a little taller, a little stronger, and a little more rugged. As a young man, however, JJ grew two inches taller than his brother, while developing tremendous interest in golf and tennis. Nick, the better natural athlete, loved football and baseball, but also played tennis and golf nearly as well as JJ who practiced for hours. No jealous rivalry, though, ever diminished the joy of brotherly competition. JJ won far more than he lost, but Nick came close enough to keep himself in the game. Besides, Nick knew he couldn't play football and baseball all his life, but golf and tennis the brothers could always enjoy, and, eventually, he thought, *I'll kick JJ's butt.*

In grade school their academic differences showed early: JJ, more naturally studious, loved reading, writing, and history, while Nick had far more interest in math, science, and geography. "If only we could merge their report cards," John told Karen; "we'd have a brilliant student, top to bottom." JJ loved story books. Nick loved magazines, especially, *Popular Mechanics* and *Flying*. The one magazine they fought over was *Sports Illustrated*.

Their social skills also differed: JJ was outgoing and friendly, while Nick took some time warming up to people. JJ had lots of acquaintances and a new best friend every couple months. Nick developed deeper friendships that lasted year after year. In high school, JJ was the life of the party; Nick hung around in his quiet way, but before the party ended he'd make the funniest comment or tell the funniest story. By Nick's senior year, he had a sweet, pretty girlfriend who had every intention of marrying him. Maggie proved a big factor in Nick's decision not to go away to college.

Nick enrolled in Marquette's College of Engineering with every intention of majoring in *Structures* just like his dad had. Johnny Helden was thrilled about it because he never pressured Nick, just as Karen never pressured JJ to major in *English* at Notre Dame. In fact, JJ majored in *Economics* with a minor in *English*. His uncle, Michael Helden, advised him that economists were needed in virtually every field. The minor in *English* satisfied JJ's love of literature.

Johnny Helden presumed that after Nick graduated he'd be more than willing to work with his father. That thought kept Johnny motivated because even with student aid, college costs for both sons proved a major burden. Nevertheless, JJ's decision to apply to Notre Dame and his acceptance delighted Johnny.

JJ didn't want a big sendoff. Karen cooked one of his favorite dinners. Afterwards his younger siblings presented him a color photo of themselves in a clear plastic box frame that he could place on his desk. Nick gave him a pack of ballpoint pens and a piercing look, as they shook hands. "I'll miss you," he said.

"Yeah, I'll miss you, too, Nick. Good luck at Marquette."

Next morning, Ann and Kristin actually had tears in their eyes when they embraced JJ after the car was loaded and ready to go. He saw his sisters differently then and realized for all their bickering, quarreling, and fights over the years, he did love them. "I'll be home at Thanksgiving," he said. "That's not so long."

Eleven year old Joey followed JJ around all morning. In spite of their seven year age difference, JJ and Joey grew close. They played catch, ping pong, tennis, and anything else Joey wanted to play. They even invented the game of tackle basketball in the family room that almost drove their mother and sisters crazy. The raucous game induced howls of laughter and wild screaming until it peaked at Karen's decibel limit, prompting her to shut it down. Now, all set to leave, JJ saw the sadness in Joey's eyes. He knelt and hugged and kissed his little brother. "I'll miss you, too, Joey. Write me some letters okay?"

Karen decided not to accompany them, though Johnny wanted her to, especially for the drive home. Once on the expressway, they wouldn't encounter a stop light until exiting the toll road in South Bend. John and JJ enjoyed conversing, as John reminisced about his first weeks at Notre Dame twenty-six years ago. His enthusiasm for the greatness of the place prejudiced his son in just the right way.

After they hauled JJ's belongings up to his dorm room, his roommate stumbled in. The young men met with great enthusiasm. John chatted with the boy's parents who drove over from Toledo, but then, glancing at his watch, cut it short. He told JJ he wanted to get going. JJ walked his father to the car. They hugged, shook hands, and said goodbye. John realized JJ wasn't going to have any difficulty adjusting, just as he hadn't. His sociable son was anxious to get back to his room, his roommate, and his new life.

Before John left, he hiked to Our Lady's Grotto and prayed three *Hail Mary's* for JJ's well-being. He then lit a votive candle in holy remembrance of his sister-in-law, Jane Anderson. He wondered if anyone else at Notre Dame had ever lit a Grotto candle for a murdered porn star.

Gazing westward at the rising road to St. Mary's, he thought of his innocent romance with Gilliane a quarter-century ago. The memories came with longings, but not for her. They were deep within: visceral, true, yet forever gone. At forty-four, his happy, carefree years at Notre Dame receded from his present life like a rocket, ever accelerating. *I'm out twenty-two years already . . . married nineteen . . . five kids . . . dear God, where did it all go?* Beneath the high vault of ancient, apostolic trees, he headed back to his car.

+ + +

The next time John and Karen Helden socialized with Bob and Dana they detected a playful coyness in the couple that just begged for a question. Dana hinted "nothing, nothing at all," while Schmitt grinned. Karen blurted, "Bob, you popped the question, didn't you?" Dana's joyous eyes confirmed it.

"What?" Schmitt's question slid downhill. He enjoyed their attention.

"So when is the happy day," Karen asked.

Dana look lovingly at Bob who answered, "We're not gonna rush this thing."

"Right . . . ." Dana's voice limped with facetiousness. "At our age, we certainly mustn't rush into anything."

"That's right. We've got plenty time. Courtships are important."

"Not that important, Bob. You're pushing forty-two," Johnny said.

Schmitt glared at him. He hated references to his age in Dana's presence.

"Well, it's not uncommon at all for older men to marry younger women," Karen said.

"My uncle Lew was forty-three when he married," Johnny said. "They had five kids . . . boom, boom, boom! My aunt was twenty years younger . . . fertile as a rabbit."

Karen popped in, "Bob, you're only forty-one. Dana could have six."

Three laughed, while Schmitt barked, "Cut the shit – what the hell's wrong with you people? I live in the moment. We take one day at a time, right Dana?"

"Right . . . ." Dana's sarcasm stretched the word.

Karen sensed they had teased Bob enough. "So, when are we gonna see a nice big rock on Dana's finger?"

Schmitt liked the question. "We're working on it." He smiled at Dana, though the upturn was barely visible beneath his droopy mustache.

"Let's go fry some fish," Johnny said. "I'm hungry."

+ + +

John and Anita Helden both marked their eightieth birthdays in 1982. In early spring they observed their fiftieth wedding anniversary. John made a dinner reservation at Ratzsch's for the immediate family, including Michael who flew in from Los Angeles. *It's a curious event,* he thought of his parents' golden milestone. *More an acknowledgment of endurance than a celebration of marital bliss.*

Johnny and Michael knew their parents' marriage wasn't the happiest, but Anita and John felt a curious satisfaction at surviving five decades in spite of the loss of their young love. Years of John's cruel, verbal attacks, and Anita's bitter, painful retreats caused unspoken and unresolved sorrow in their isolated hearts. Yet, in the ephemeral presence of their grandchildren, they suppressed whatever sadness they bore, allowing those bright, youthful lives to momentarily lift their spirits with the hope for five wonderful futures.

+ + +

In the late seventies, Dr. Julius Helden and his wife retired to a quiet community near San Diego. A year later, Lewis Thilman moved his wife and two school-age children to Orange County, south of Los Angeles, where Michael Helden welcomed the news of both uncles' relocations. Before Reagan's election in November, however, Julius and Lew died of massive heart attacks. *How ironic,* Michael thought. *They came west to escape Milwaukee's harsh winters, but instead found the warm, sunny places where they were destined to die.*

Also in 1980, several years after selling their floral business, Elizabeth and Paul Peterson bought a three-bedroom home in Sarasota, Florida, where they decided to reside from early November to late April. They enjoyed its spacious lanai and small swimming pool. As they became familiar with Sarasota, they discovered the charm of the long, thin barrier island of Siesta Key. They parked in the public lot near Crescent Beach then strolled for miles on the broad, fine, white quartz sand. The blue-green water of the Gulf swept over their bare feet high onto the flat, hardpan and then receded, dissolving their shallow footprints behind. They loved watching the mighty pelicans dive for dinner or glide down like Navy fighters coming in for a carrier landing. Many times they drove to the restaurant at the south end of Midnight Pass Road, across from the park at Turtle Beach. They dined alfresco on the deck that overlooked the island rookery in Little Sarasota Bay where the great blue herons gathered serenely, and white egrets sat like birds of snow in the fading winter light.

Florida summers, however, proved too hot and humid for Paul and Elizabeth, so they bought a condominium in Milwaukee, spending May through October there. Those fair weather months enabled closer contact with Paul's sister and her broken husband, Nicholas Anderson, who suffered serious health problems caused by excessive drinking and smoking.

While in Milwaukee, Elizabeth invited her nieces, Karen and Katherine, to lunch at least once a month. They appreciated nice restaurants; the *Tuscan Bicycle Club* in Elm Grove was a favorite. Seated at a window table, the three ordered a glass of Chardonnay and perused menus, as the dining room began filling up. They finished placing their orders when a group of four men entered. Karen glanced indifferently, but then looked again. Dr. Jack Cutler caught her eye.

"Who is it," Elizabeth asked, noticing Karen's double-take. Katherine didn't recognize any of the men.

Karen explained she had dated the heavy-set one, a doctor, twenty years ago and how shocked she was, after all that time, to have seen him at Elizabeth's debate. She mentioned, too, that Jack called after Jane's funeral to express sympathy.

"He's never gotten over you," Elizabeth said. "That's understandable. You're very special."

"Well, I hope he doesn't notice us."

Katherine said, "I never would have guessed that was Jack. When you were dating, he looked really good: well-built, slender . . . ."

"He's middle-aged now, and it shows," Karen said.

Minutes later, Jack spotted Karen across the room. After a quick sandwich and cup of coffee, Jack and his companions rose, heading towards the exit, away from Karen's table.

"He's leaving," Katherine whispered.

But Jack wasn't. In the lobby he told his associates, "Wait a minute." He went back into the room and zigzagged towards Karen. Elizabeth noticed him first. Sipping hot tea, the women ceased chatting, as he approached. He faced and greeted Karen.

She uttered a perfunctory, "Hello Jack," but made no effort to introduce him to her aunt and sister. Jack had buttoned his suit coat, as he walked over, but his protruding stomach pulled the jacket apart at the pinch of the button. The three noticed the unattractive bulge.

Dr. Cutler began, "I wanted to tell you that I've given thought to what we talked about on the phone. I realize you're absolutely right. I apologize for being so uncooperative, I mean, when I had the chance . . . with your family and everything."

"Good heaven, Jack, that's almost twenty years . . . it's a bit late, don't you think?"

A sticky sense of discomfort settled like syrup onto the four. Elizabeth and Katherine refused to speak, though a silly comment might have rinsed the feeling away. Karen felt she had said enough, while Jack, unable to express his own muddled feelings, stood there suffering a terrible, unanticipated anxiety. *Man, what the hell did you expect?* Suddenly, he blurted, "I should have married you . . . ."

It embarrassed Karen, but then, at the preposterousness of the statement, she broke into a high-pitched, wailing kind of laughter. It shocked her aunt and sister. They detected in Jack's eyes the humiliation of ridicule.

After composing herself, Karen stared at Jack and said in a calm, controlled voice, "I never wanted to marry you. I never regretted for an instant not marrying you, but I suspect you'll regret having made a fool of yourself today. Now, please, once and for all, go away."

Karen's incivility shocked Elizabeth and Katherine.

Instantly, Jack turned and strode out of the room. Katherine whispered, "Karen, that's not like you."

Elizabeth said, "I would not have handled it that way . . . no doubt those are your true feelings, but discretion and tact always serve us better."

Karen didn't need much time to realize her mistake. "You're right. Now I'll have to apologize to *him*. Good God, what was I thinking?"

+ + +

For Johnny Helden, the end of 1981 marked eight years in private practice. Work came from his three best clients and an intermittent stream of referrals. His income rose modestly, year after year, but with his children growing older and Nick and JJ in college, he never had enough to invest in stocks, as some friends of his did or claimed they did. Many of his jobs were getting more difficult, especially the tannery work and several complex buildings for Chuck Lorenz. One night, after working fifteen straight hours in Chicago, Johnny got home at three in the morning. Four and a half hours later, Bob Schmitt called. When Karen told him Johnny was still sleeping, Bob accused John of being "the laziest son-of-a-bitch I've ever known." Karen tried to explain, but Bob slammed down the phone.

Johnny worked fifty to sixty hours every week for years. His only break was a two week vacation with his family at the same resort in northern Wisconsin he went to as a boy. By the end of that pleasant reprieve, urgent messages filled his office answering machine with fresh problems: a contractor's mistake in the field and "how the hell" to fix it; a change in the design of a mezzanine that he finished two months ago; conflicts on shop drawings; a disturbing call from an attorney, or a promising one from a new client with a rush job. And then he'd have to scrape money together to pay the resort's bill, and in a few more weeks all five kids would be starting school again. Every month he'd project his unpredictable income against his certain expenses; half the time he came up short. He had no choice but to drop a little deeper into the dark hole of debt.

On Johnny Helden's forty-fifth birthday, he fretted more about his fiftieth. Driving to and from a client's office, he often reminisced rather than searching for solutions to the tough engineering problems of the moment. Without realizing it, he was becoming more like his father. He daydreamed of his boyhood with a melancholy that made him long for something that could never be defined let alone grasped. Memories of his youth seemed more like an illusion: dreamlike, elusive, filled with shadows, or flashes of light: a long, absurd gestation, a quarter century of anguished and incomplete learning replete with folly and waste, too little knowledge acquired, and too few skills mastered, more dreamer than man, an impossible soldier, cowardly, but thrilled by heroes, passionate with the undying belief that somehow and someway his fog-shrouded future would unfold into the flower of a splendid life.

Now, within the full maturity of his manhood, he contemplated and analyzed, but always an irrepressible doubt hinted that *this* life was not the perfection he dreamed he was destined to attain. Nevertheless, within his simple heart, a strange, deep wisdom taught him to use the ordinary, the prosaic, and the plain, the difficulties and the failures, the general mediocrity, the mundane and the routine to mold and shape himself into a man of true character. His integrity, founded on a ruthless, brutal honesty and self-awareness, revealed a profoundly deficient man. In spite of that, he would become a good man, a man of duty, of virtue, and a man of love. He never shunned the difficulties presented him. He strove to be open and loving towards others whereas, in his past, he often turned away with chilling indifference. He bore heavy burdens, but would not disclose their weight to anyone so others never knew. Even those closest to him never really understood how long and hard he worked; they never sensed and he never explained how extremely difficult so much of his work was, and how he struggled to endure and persevere when every fiber and cell in his body cried out for rest and ease. Those struggles went on for years. Through it all, he remained reluctant to share it with anyone, even Karen, though her insight was deepest. Eventually, his character and strength of will, sustained by his Christian faith, enabled him to not merely endure, but to prevail.

+ + +

Sunday morning Dana Buckley woke early, but could not, though exhausted, fall back to sleep. Wildly unfocused, she struggled to brew a pot of coffee. The same horrid thought dominated ever since she left the clinic. She could not stop thinking of what she had done and could not stop crying. The same, tiny essence of an infant that had given her so much joy when she first realized she was pregnant – a child, she believed, conceived in love – she allowed to be destroyed a mere eight weeks later.

Dana could not bear thinking of it, yet the unyielding pain of that repugnant reality was inescapable. Nor could she bear thinking of Schmitt. Her feelings for him were so drastically altered, she didn't know what they were. Dana wondered if it was him she loathed or herself, though she didn't feel self-hatred, as much as a profound, ponderous, debilitating regret. The mere thought of seeing Schmitt again was abhorrent to her.

Weeping, Dana showered, letting the warm water comfort her weakened body. She toweled off, dressed, and, without realizing it, began to cry again. After her third cup, the coffee tasted rancid. She brushed her teeth, then rinsed with an antiseptic wash. In the vanity mirror she found a tired, puffy, old-looking, young woman. Dana could not remain in her apartment, so she drove aimlessly, crying as often as not, while thinking the same terrible thoughts over and over.

She couldn't tell her parents, not her sister or brothers, no relative, and she didn't care to talk to her girlfriends because she suspected they'd minimize what she had done. She imagined they'd say, "It's no big deal. It's legal, why worry about it. You'll get over it." Then she thought of Karen Helden who always seemed so understanding. It was the friendship of their men that brought them together. They weren't close, but did like each other, though Karen was eighteen years older, old enough to be Dana's mother. Dana decided that's who she'd tell.

Trembling, she rang the Helden's doorbell. Karen frowned when she saw Dana's face.

"Dana, what is it?" Whether Karen wanted it or not, Dana fell into her arms weeping. On the sofa, Dana rocked in Karen's hug like a teen-age daughter, her body pulsating with grief. Johnny peeked in from the hall, but backed away when Karen's glance warned against entering. Finally, Karen whispered, "My God, Dana, what is wrong?"

With an outpouring of words and tears, and in a few, brief moments, Dana told Karen she had been pregnant with Bob Schmitt's child until last Friday afternoon, forty-eight hours ago, when she had the baby aborted. Then silence, save for her soft weeping. As Karen rocked her, she felt Dana's body slowly calm down. Dana had made her confession, shared her sorrow and guilt, and deeply sensed Karen's innate compassion and understanding.

"Did Bob want you to have the abortion?"

"He demanded it."

"Did you want that?"

Dana looked into Karen's eyes. "Oh, my God, no, never . . . ."

"Then why?"

"Because he told me if I didn't, everything was over between us."

"You're his fiancée. You're to be his wife." Karen noticed Dana wasn't wearing the diamond Bob had given her.

"I don't think so."

"Have you talked to him?"

"Talk? My God, I can't bear the thought of looking at him."

"Are you working tomorrow?"

"I'm supposed to, but I'm not sure I'm strong enough."

"Don't go . . . get your strength back. Take a few days . . . make him wonder."

"He hasn't even bothered to call."

"Does he know?"

"Yes. A couple weeks ago he put a note on my desk."

"What did it say?"

Dana paused. It pained her to repeat it. "He told me to 'get rid of it.'"

"Oh, my God," Karen groaned.

"He wouldn't talk to me, wouldn't look at me, didn't call at night . . . nothing."

"What did you do?"

"In the note, he wrote the phone number of a clinic. I called and asked if they did abortions. The woman said 'yes,' so I made an appointment for a pre-op visit. I was so distraught I didn't know what to think. I felt I still loved Bob. I didn't want to displease him; I wanted to marry him. That's why an abortion seemed so stupid. It was our child. He told me he loved me, said he wanted to marry me. So why couldn't we move the date up a few months? That's not so terrible. It happens."

"Did you tell him that?"

"I tried, but he walked away. You know what he's like. He said, 'no talking until after you do what you're supposed to do.' He said I should call him when it's done."

"But you haven't . . . ."

"No, and I'm not going to. If I don't work tomorrow I'll go in Tuesday, but I know I won't even be able to look at him."

Karen sighed, but was at a loss what to say. She wished Aunt Elizabeth was there.

Dana wiped her tears. "I feel better for telling you."

"Oh, Dana, I'm so sorry. Men can be such unbelievable jerks."

"I'm as much to blame."

"I doubt it."

"I tried to resist, but believe me, he was aggressive. I told him I wouldn't make love until we were married. Then one night, a few weeks later, he got on his knees, proposed, and pulled out that big, beautiful ring. I was just overwhelmed and said 'yes.'"

"You can't blame yourself for that. I did the same when Johnny asked me."

"Afterwards, though, he began pressuring me again. Not too much at first, but, as weeks went by, he talked about getting married and our honeymoon and the house we'd buy and I ate it all up . . . believed every word."

"He wore you down . . . ."

"Yes, completely, and then, Karen, I gave him my virginity. Before I knew it, we were making love every time we got together. It was inevitable that I'd get pregnant."

"How did he react when you told him?"

"Well, he seemed okay at first, but after a day or two, things changed. He told me I had to get rid of it, as though it was an ugly dress or a bad hairdo or something. And that's when he turned cold. I mean he treated me like I wasn't even there."

"Did you talk?"

"Very little . . . he stopped calling me evenings. At work it was all business."

"What did you do? What were you thinking?"

"That he'd change. He knew I wanted that baby. It was our love child, or so I thought. I really believed he'd come 'round."

"Obviously, he didn't."

"No, and then he put that note on my desk, and I had to make a choice. And, Karen, I made the wrong one. I should have kept my baby. If he didn't want the two of us, so be it."

"Yes, I agree. That's what I would have advised."

"At least I'd have my baby because now I have nothing. I certainly don't want him."

"How can you continue working there?"

"I can't . . . I have to quit. I couldn't possibly work for him anymore. I know what he'd try. He'd sweet talk me. Knowing myself, I'd probably go back."

"Do you love him, Dana?"

"Friday morning, before the abortion, I thought I did. Driving home after I left the clinic, I realized he doesn't love me. No man who loves a girl would force her to have an abortion. Do I love Bob? Did I love him? Maybe I was just infatuated, but it sure felt like the real thing, so I don't know. When I see him again, I'll have a better sense, I suppose. But even if I think I still love him, I realize I can't be with a man who made me kill my child – *our* child."

The women fell silent. Karen didn't know what else to say or ask.

After a moment, Dana said, "The doctor at the clinic said some really strange things. He told me not to think of what was to be done as ending my pregnancy. He called it a PRP, a *Period Restoration Procedure*. Can you believe that? When I used the word *baby* and *abortion,* he scolded me. He told me not to think of it in those terms. Oh, my God, he was an awful man."

Karen's curiosity got the better of her. "What was the name of the clinic?"

"The Messert Clinic . . . it was Dr. Messert who said those things."

"Did he perform the abortion?"

"Oh, God no, he's an old man. He just did the interview."

"Who did?"

"A younger man . . . quite nice, actually."

"What was his name?"

Suddenly, Dana realized, *what difference does it make? Why would Karen want to know? It's not important at all.* She detected in Karen's eyes a longing.

"Dana?"

"Yes."

"Who did the abortion?"

"What does it matter? Why would you even ask that? I did the most terrible thing a woman can do, the most unnatural thing anyone could ever do . . . I killed my own child. The doctor just did the dirty work." Dana began to weep.

"Oh, Dana, I'm so sorry. I just . . . ." Karen faltered. "I didn't mean to be-"

"His name was Dr. Cutler."

+ + +

It had been slipped under his locked office door. It puzzled him, but when he picked it up and pinched it, he knew exactly what it was. "Shit," he muttered. He ripped open the envelope. The ring slid onto his desk. Staring at it he thought, *stupid bitch.* There was a note. It read: *You told me to get rid of it. I did. Now I'm rid of you.* In silence, he screamed, "fuck . . . ."

A sense of emptiness permeated the outer office because Dana Buckley never came. Bob called right away, but her phone just rang and rang, infuriating him. He stayed angry all day. Everyone kept their distance. No one mentioned Dana; when Schmitt asked if anyone had heard from her, no one had. She had done something he despised. It wasn't that she didn't show up for work, or gave the impression she quit, or even that she gave the ring back. It was her rejection of him. He detested anyone who would ever dare that. He rejected others, but no one rejected him. He would not allow it. His pride revolted against rejection. Now he felt an uncontrollable hatred and rage because Dana – "that stupid little bitch" – had done precisely that.

He called John Helden and ordered, "Get here right away!" Johnny suspected it might be about Dana, but knew it could also be mezzanine business because Bob, in four words, wasn't easy to read. Johnny arrived mid-afternoon and encountered the barren outer office, making him wonder about Dana. Bob heard the door open and hollered in a flat, unfriendly voice, "Helden, if it's you, get in here."

"What's up," Johnny asked.

"Fuck . . . I'll tell you what's up. Shut the g--damn door."

Johnny did, saying, "Bob, calm down."

"Don't tell me to calm down. That fucking bitch left this on my desk." He held up the ring.

"Just the ring . . . no note?"

"Just the fucking ring." His teeth clenched in anger. "She didn't come to work – didn't even call. I haven't talked to her since last week. She didn't work Monday. I don't have the faintest g--damn idea what the fuck is going on."

"Did she work yesterday?"

"Yeah, but we didn't talk. She left early, never even said good-night. I was on the phone and just had a gut feeling she'd sneak out."

"When did she put the ring on your desk?"

"Fuck," he muttered, realizing he'd be caught in his lie.

He called Louise, his assistant, into his office. She greeted Johnny then faced her boss.

"What do you know about this?" Bob held up the ring.

"I believe that's the ring you gave Dana."

"You know damn well it is. How the hell did it get back to me?"

Louise fidgeted, but feared Bob so she told the truth. "Yesterday Dana gave me an envelope and asked me to put it on your desk, but I never had the chance so this morning, before you got here, I slid it under your door."

Johnny piped in, "Bob, you said Dana left the ring on your desk?"

"Shut up, Helden. Did she say anything else?"

"No," Louise said.

"Did she say she was quitting?"

"No."

"Can you tell me anything?"

"Just that she said she wrote you a note-"

"Get out," he ordered.

Johnny jumped on it. "You said there was no note. Why'd you lie? What'd she say?"

Fury showed on Bob's scowling, pock-marked face. "None of your fucking business."

"Dana made it our business. She came over Sunday and told Karen what happened."

"Oh, shit, what'd she say . . . what fucking lies?"

"That you demanded she get an abortion."

"Oh, bullshit, she wanted it as much as me."

"That's not what she told Karen. You wouldn't even talk to her unless she got the abortion."

"That bitch tells Karen exactly what you guys want to hear, so I look like a real prick. Let me tell you something, Helden . . . ." Bob's right elbow perched on the desk; his index finger jabbed at Johnny. "That g--damn little slut wanted it. She gets pregnant and thinks she can pull it off with a quickie, hurry-up wedding. Let me tell you something: my mother has a nose for that kind of shit. I'll be damned if some pregnant twit is gonna drag me to the altar. You know damn well I said courtships are important. So why the fuck didn't she use the pill? Is she so fucking stupid or was it entrapment? Well, at least I learned what I needed to know. Good fucking riddance."

Johnny felt a loathing for his old friend. He saw in Schmitt's eyes a hatred, but for what, he wondered. *A wonderful girl whom he impregnated; his fiancée whom he treated with brutal cruelty; a young woman he rejected unless she killed her own child?*

"You're the problem, not Dana. I believe every single word she said. You're the liar. You never loved her. You just used her. She gave the ring back because it means nothing to you."

"Fuck you," Schmitt said.

"What'd she say in the note?"

"None of your fucking business."

"What's so pathetic about all this is the happiness you've destroyed. You've broken Dana's heart. You killed your own child – your parents' grandchild – and you denied yourself the happiness that comes from a loving wife and children. You think she's stupid? You're the dumbest asshole I've ever known."

Schmitt looked at Johnny with a piercing hatred. "Get the fuck out of here."

"What did Dana say in her note?"

Schmitt jumped from his chair, screaming, "Get the fuck outta here!" In the adjacent offices everyone, especially Louise, shuddered.

Johnny stood and headed towards the door. When he reached it, he stopped and turned towards Schmitt. "You know, you really are to be pitied. I don't give a damn how much money you have or how much you accumulate. You'll die wealthy, I suppose, but you're gonna end up with exactly what you deserve – nothing."

Schmitt glared at him and howled, "You're through here, Helden . . . you'll never work for me again. The easy money is over, so go fuck yourself!"

Chapter 36 ~ 1985

Nick and JJ earned their undergraduate degrees in four years; neither failed a course and, at age twenty-two, both were eager to start their careers. Nick had joined the Army Reserve Officers' Training Corps at the start of his sophomore year. For it, he was awarded a partial scholarship that bound him to three years of military service after his graduation.

When Nick told his parents what he intended, Johnny Helden said, "We're not a military family; you know that." But John relented in the face of Nick's unyielding determination and Karen's unwavering support for her son's decision. It didn't hurt, either, that joining the ROTC program reduced the cost of Nick's education.

Johnny Helden lost SMF as a client in 1982 after his falling out with Bob Schmitt. Several months later, Chuck Lorenz abandoned his architectural practice in Chicago during a drought in commercial construction. With two sons in college, those losses caused significant financial strain in the Helden household. Fortunately, American Leather constantly strove to increase production with new, more automated equipment that required frequent modifications to their old, heavy timber buildings and even several modern additions to the downtown tannery. Johnny and Jerry Summers produced all the architectural and structural drawings. New tannery projects came in so frequently that John's two lost clients mattered not nearly as much. Initially, his income declined, but then slowly recovered.

JJ interviewed with several major stock brokerages; in August, Curran, Oswald & Trotta, a well-regarded regional firm, hired him. His training included studying for his Series Seven exam, which he passed with high marks. He started with a small base salary and commenced cold calling to build his *book*. At the outset, he found the telephone work mindlessly easy, but with dozens upon dozens and then hundreds upon hundreds of rejections, he realized making a living as a stock broker was not as easy as he first believed. He often became dispirited, but overcame it with a resilient determination to keep calling regardless of how frequently he was told "no." His carefully scripted pitch was rejected at least fifty times for every new client acquired, but some of those actually had a lot of money and invested with JJ. After several years of arduous work, he established a foothold. After several more years, he was established.

Nick married his high school sweetheart, Maggie McNeil, seven months into his military service. Noreen Schuler, another girl both he and JJ knew in high school, bumped into JJ a week after he started working as a broker. They kept bumping into each other so often that they started dating. Eventually, it led to marriage two years after Nick and Maggie's wedding.

After Nick was commissioned a Second Lieutenant, and JJ got his own apartment, the home in the *Highlands* became remarkably calm in a way that unsettled Johnny Helden. He missed the easy banter with his twin sons and the frequent, lengthy conversations with one or both. He complained to Karen about it.

She responded, "I think it's time you learn to converse with your daughters."

The Heldens celebrated daughter Ann's twentieth birthday in 1985. Her high school achievements were exceptional: in addition to high grades, she displayed a remarkable talent for acting and singing. Senior year she played *Nellie Forbush* in the great Broadway show, *South Pacific*. For all the received acclaim, especially from her grandparents, her quiet, undemanding personality hid the depth and sensitivity of her feelings and insights. She sensed her father's preference for his sons, sensed his less-than-subtle favoritism, but cared not to compete in a situation she felt should never be competitive. So she demanded nothing of her father and little from her mother, though she was Karen's secret favorite by far. When she began her freshman year at Marquette and chose to live in a dorm, the Helden home became even more tranquil.

Also that year, daughter Kristin began her last semester in high school. Her first three years of solid *C minus* achievement proved the futility of her carefree approach, while reinforcing her decision to avoid college. Her willful nature made John and Karen realize it was pointless to force her into higher education. Her senior year, she took not a single college prep course; when she told her father she was the only girl in the weightlifting class, John shook his head in disbelief and disappointment. Kristin wanted to do *something* . . . get out, get a job, earn money. What Johnny and Karen did not detect was Kristin's natural ability to sell. She inherited her grandfather's salesmanship, which made her remarkably successful, eventually taking her to Manhattan where, as a young woman, she earned more than her father.

Long before Joe Helden turned fifteen, Ann and Kristin recognized between him and their father the same closeness that Nick and JJ enjoyed. It appeared so natural and normal, there was no point in complaining about it. At home, Ann just passed through with a quiet grace making few demands on either parent. What she didn't know was her father's difficulty in expressing his feelings for her. He observed her quietly, passively, but in his heart felt tremendous love and pride because she had been a wonderful girl and was now becoming an exceptionally fine young woman. Once he told Karen, "Ann will make a mark in this world."

Karen smiled and said, "I think so."

+ + +

After breaking-up with Bob Schmitt, Dana Buckley decided to move to Denver. She had a cousin there who worked for an oil company that was hiring. The prospect of a new job, the lure of the Rockies, and love for her cousin enticed Dana to relocate. John and Karen hated to see her leave.

"Schmitt should go away, not you," Karen said.

"He'd never leave his company," Dana replied. "I'm not comfortable here, so I'll be the one. I'm tired of looking over my shoulder all the time."

"I haven't heard from Schmitt," Johnny said. "I sent an invoice at the end of the month. He paid it, but he's never called, and I'm not going to call him. I think he's nuts."

"He's selfish," Karen said, "and foolish. It's like he's incapable of understanding how much he's lost."

"Maybe being selfish is nuts," John said.

"Perhaps," Dana said. "All I know is that it's better for me to leave."

"You won't tell him where you're going," Johnny said.

"Oh, my God, no," Dana answered. "And, please, don't you tell . . . ."

"We won't," Karen said. "I've a feeling we'll never see him again."

Johnny could only wonder.

+ + +

Dr. Jack Cutler and Cheryl, his wife of almost twenty years, had attained a marital state of comfortable and complacent indifference. They inhabited a spacious house in a western suburb, but really didn't live together. Only infrequently did they act like a couple. They made love rarely. When they did, it was not satisfying. Jack no longer found her desirable, while she showed little interest in sex. Cheryl's friends determined their social life; wives set the agenda. Jack tagged along Saturday nights to parties, restaurants or the theatre, just like the other dutiful husbands.

Evenings at home, Jack and Cheryl ate at the same table, but conversed little. Afterwards, they watched different television shows in different rooms, or Jack read. Eventually, he moved into another bedroom under the pretense of different hours: he was early to bed, Cheryl the opposite, and the morning mirrored that. While Cheryl knew what Jack did and earned, he didn't really know what she did with her weekday time, and, frankly, he didn't care. Jack had no idea how much money Cheryl spent. She paid the bills and kept the household checkbook. That she had lots of clothes, shopped regularly, and went often to lunch with her girlfriends was apparent to Jack, as that was what she talked about. But he never bothered to quantify it monetarily, for he really didn't think that way. Not yet, at least.

For years, Jack complained that unemployed Cheryl had plenty of time to take better care of the house. His nagging irritated his wife who had little interest in housework. Finally, she hired a sturdy cleaning lady who came every Tuesday morning, after Jack went to the clinic, and left an hour before Jack came home. Cheryl paid the woman in cash so Jack wouldn't find her in the checkbook. For a few weeks, Jack believed Cheryl had a change of attitude, complimenting her on the tidy house. But she was a liar at heart, telling him she decided to do a major cleaning every Tuesday. She also suggested that Jack should make an effort to be a little neater in his personal habits. Jack agreed, but when he eventually learned that Cheryl, in fact, wasn't doing the housework, he never made an issue of it. He had his reasons.

Tuesday evenings, Cheryl insisted Jack take her out to dinner. She claimed she worked too hard and didn't want the kitchen messy again. A fine dining meal was her little reward. Wednesday evenings, Jack had dinner with Dr. Cutler, as he had for years. Thursdays, Cheryl heated a frozen pizza, while on Fridays, Jack picked up *Chinese*. That way, the kitchen stayed tidy four days straight. At most, Cheryl cooked two dinners a week, but they certainly weren't culinary masterpieces. The Cutlers were not eating well or wisely, and, in time, it affected them.

As the years passed, they both put on useless weight. Jack often suggested they shed a few pounds, but his wife chose a different approach: she bought a new wardrobe to fit. Every fall, after a few summer pounds were gained, Cheryl went shopping. In the spring, after adding more winter pounds, she went shopping again. Ever-larger sizes of clothes moved into her closet just as smaller sizes were regularly shipped to the resale shop. In her new clothes, Cheryl – "the empress of pleasant indulgences," as Jack secretly ridiculed her – never felt she looked bad at all. Her body's changes were so gradual, so subtle, and seeming such a normal progression as she aged that after fifteen years of marriage she hardly noticed her spectacular, wedding night figure was gone for good. Her narrow waist had vanished. Her breasts sagged onto the stomach's fatty rolls. The splendid, hourglass figure that thrilled Jack in the early years had been destroyed by knife, fork, spoon, a lack of exercise, and copious quantities of moderately priced wine. When Cheryl occasionally detected a hint of self-destruction, her girlfriends assured her she looked "great," just as she assured all of them they did too. Jack called it, "mutual self-delusional reinforcement." With each passing year, as Cheryl's girth expanded, their sexual intimacy diminished. Jack appeared indifferent to the situation, as did Cheryl. *After all,* she thought, *we're getting older.* They decided years ago they didn't want children, so now they resigned themselves to a passionless marriage. Cheryl never suspected that Jack found her repugnant.

Wednesdays, Cheryl also dined out, often with a girlfriend, but many times alone. She ate as well as her doctor husband and drank nearly as much: a cocktail before, wine with her meal and, oftentimes, a cognac after.

Usually, after their midweek dinner ritual, Dr. Messert invited Jack to his home for *Scotch on the rocks*. After suffering through Jack's marital complaints, and finally settled in his comfortable den, Messert asked, "Why the hell did you marry her?"

Jack held his cupped hands in front of his chest, about eight inches out. "Big ones," he answered.

"Oh shit, there's got to be more than that."

"Hey, she seemed very nice. She was beautiful in those days."

"Let me tell you something," Messert said. "There are three kinds of women: the first you wouldn't spend a minute with; they're most plentiful. Second kind you'd spend a few hours with just for the fun of it – they're called sluts. The third kind is most rare: they're the women you'd spend your life with, the kind you'd marry. Unfortunately, I think you married the second kind."

"Yeah, you're right . . . just my luck."

"What's luck got to do with it? Get a divorce, Jack. The sooner you end it the better."

Jack swigged more Scotch. "I knew the third kind once." He thought of Karen Anderson.

"So why didn't you marry her?"

"She turned me down."

Messert laughed. "I find that hard to believe. You must've really screwed up."

"It wasn't me. It was my last year interning. I worked long hours . . . had to . . . pissed her off. She was demanding. Couldn't deal with it, so she broke it off. Claimed it was all my fault."

"Console yourself Jack. If she really wanted you, she would've hung in there."

"Yeah, I told her she had to have a little patience."

"Nonsense, she dumped you because she didn't desire you. That old black magic wasn't there."

Jack swallowed more Scotch. He felt unsettled, tense, yet calm in a strange, resolute, and fated way. He knew he was drinking too much, but had no intention of stopping. It marred his memory. An old, sad feeling settled into him, accompanied by a stirring of resentment. But what did he resent? Who did he resent? *Not Karen Anderson,* he realized. Sober, he always thought well of her regardless of what she had decided. He didn't blame her for the breakup. He knew it was his fault. He realized, for the most part, he ignored her simplest wishes, failed to accommodate her little requests, failed to make the effort to be a bit more social, as she had asked, especially with her family. He looked back at those times often, knowing that he, himself, was the reason Karen broke it off. He was just a guy she had pizza with on Thursday nights, but that wasn't enough. She had every right to expect more, but he was too dumb to give it; too stupid to realize that his wit and charm over pizza and a couple beers, even his becoming a doctor, simply didn't cut it with such a fine young woman. And yet, there were moments, he recalled, when there was so much promise, so much hope for their future together. *I took it all for granted,* he realized. After that last, medical school ball twenty-five years ago when they met again and were so thrilled to see each other and kissed so passionately that long ago snowy night, Jack grew complacent. He thought their future together was inevitable. She would be with him throughout his residency, his first job in Racine, and then into their married life. *And a better life than this,* he knew. So what did he resent? Who did he resent? Turning towards his colleague, he answered the same, as he always had so many bitter times before.

"What the hell are you thinking now," Messert asked.

"I don't like my wife or my life, for that matter."

"Yeah, but you do nothing about it."

"I had envisioned myself a well-respected physician. So what am I? An abortionist barely in the shadows of respectability with a fat, stupid wife . . . ."

Messert laughed derisively. "You are exactly what you have chosen to be."

"Bullshit." Jack took another swallow of Scotch. "I married wrong. That makes a huge difference."

"So did I," Messert said; "but I got rid of her." He sipped more Scotch. "Besides, you should be proud of what you do. You should march into a crowded room, shouting, 'I'm an abortionist. I help women, and I'm damn proud of it.' That's what I'd do. Of course, I don't have to because everyone in town knows what I do."

"I'm a gynecologist who happens to do early abortions. Don't call me an abortionist."

"You just called yourself one. I hate to tell you this, Jack, but you're a coward. You're afraid to say what you are, plus you're afraid to divorce your wife. What you do not fear, of course, is the easy money. Sorry, Jack, but you are one, big fucking coward."

Jack gulped his Scotch. He stared straight ahead. If Messert had been at all observant, he would have seen anger coloring Jack's face.

"You'll go home tonight and beg for sex. That, too, is cowardly, knowing you can't stand the woman."

The ludicrous suggestion mitigated Jack's anger. He laughed out loud.

"That's nothing for you to laugh at. It's pathetic."

"We don't do that anymore, you idiot."

"Don't call me names, Cutler."

"Don't make stupid suggestions."

"Don't tell me about your pathetic sex life."

Again Jack laughed. "I have no sex life. I amuse myself other ways."

Messert eyed him suspiciously. "How?"

"I gave Cheryl a secret, special name," Jack slurred. "Around the house I say it under my breath, but she can't decipher my mutterings so she always asks, and I just say *nothing* . . . drives her nuts."

"Tell me."

"No, you'll tell her."

"I never see your wife."

"You'll tell her anyway. You'll call her and tell because the name is so brilliant."

"Jack, for chrissake, tell me. We need a good laugh."

"First, promise you won't tell."

"I promise," Messert said.

"If you tell" – he paused, smiling oddly – "you have to let me kill you, okay?"

The remark stunned Messert. "Why the hell would you say something like that?"

"Hey, just joking old man, just horsing around . . . now promise."

"Okay, I promise, but don't ever say anything like that again. Now tell me."

"I saw her fat, cellulite ass once and was so disgusted that I came up with a perfect name. Now, when I think of it or say it, it always amuses me. Laughter's the best medicine, right?"

"Okay, Jack, enough of this crap. Tell me the fucking name and then get the hell out of here. I need sleep dammit."

"Her name is . . . ," Jack chuckled, *"Rumpledbuttskin."*

+ + +

Other than her close family, the tenth anniversary of Jane Anderson's death was marked by only one person: Michael Helden in Los Angeles. He kept a written record of significant events in his life and happened to notice that horrible date approaching. On the day, he went to noon Mass, offering his Eucharistic intention for the repose of Jane's immortal soul. That night he called his eighty-three year old father, John Helden.

"No, I didn't remember it."

"Not the kind of thing one cares to remember. Did Johnny or Karen mention it?"

"No."

"Dad, I feel bad about something . . . ."

"What?"

"I've never told anyone . . ."

"What?"

". . . that I had a chance to stay close to Jane, but failed to take it. I feel responsible for her murder. Had I done only one thing differently, I believe she'd still be alive."

"Oh, Michael, no, what was it?"

"I had the chance to start a little romance with Jane, but I turned it down. It's haunted me all these years."

John paused and thought of an incident that for thirty-seven years haunted him. Now he wondered if he should tell.

"Dad, you there?"

"Yes, Michael . . . I was thinking of something that's haunted me for a very long time."

"Something you'd like to share?"

"I've never told anyone."

"Tell me. Maybe it'll help us both."

The images were as vivid in John's mind as the night a beautiful

Japanese girl was offered as *The Grand Door Prize of 1948.* "It happened at a Milk Hauler's Convention after the Second World War. I was there with Russell Lynch and Bill Donnelly – you remember them – and Lee Marnet and Buster Moore. Lee and Buster were heavy drinkers and rough guys. At the gala dinner, the new president, trying to outdo his predecessor, always raffled a spectacular door prize: one year a boat, the next a car. That year everyone wondered what it would be. Well, Michael, it was a beautiful Japanese girl . . . for the night."

"You mean for sexual purposes?"

"Yes."

"That was a crime."

"I know, and I did nothing about it."

"Could you have?"

"I think so; if I had gotten Russell and Bill to help, and we fetched the sheriff."

"Were there a lot of men there?"

"Couple hundred . . . ."

"Was there a sense of outrage?"

"No, none . . . the place went completely wild."

"Dad, what exactly do you mean?"

"When they showed her, Michael, she was stark naked. The place went crazy. Everybody screamed and hollered . . . everyone except Russell, Bill and me. We couldn't believe it."

"So what did you do?"

"Nothing. I left. I got outta there as fast as I could. But, Michael, had I been courageous, I would have rescued her."

"Maybe she didn't want to be rescued. Maybe she needed the money. Maybe she was forced. Had you gotten involved, who knows what might have happened to you and to her."

"I was a coward, Michael. It's haunted me ever since."

"You're not a coward, Dad. I know what you all endured in your life."

"What I endured had little to do with courage."

"Dad, you're not thinking logically. Obviously, you were emotionally affected, and now in hindsight you believe you could have saved her. But I doubt it. Had you tried, there were enough guys there to make sure you didn't. They might've beaten you up. You just don't know what would've happened. I think you were wrong to let it bother you all those years."

"No, Michael, of course I knew I couldn't physically intervene. But when I left I could've gone to the sheriff. All I had to do was report it, but I did nothing."

"Well, yeah . . . maybe . . . ."

"It bothered me so much I went to a priest. He said, 'we are always' – *always, Michael* – 'to be our brothers' and sisters' keepers.' I made a terrible mistake. I could have saved her. That was one of the things in my life that God expected of me, but I failed to act. I failed because I was a coward, and that realization spoiled the rest of my life."

+ + +

In Sarasota, Elizabeth Peterson met women on Siesta Key who collected seashells: univalves, bivalves, and the multi-colored Coquinas, all of which delighted her. She bought a softcover on Florida's famous seashells and decided to take up the hobby. Early in the morning she'd cross the Stickney Point Road Bridge, park in the public lot, then head south across Crescent Beach towards the Point of Rocks where even earlier risers already searched for the precious, little treasures the sea so haphazardly pitched ashore. She loved the early, pale, grey-white light, and the first, fresh breezes, as she hunted the edge of the sea in the shadows of the waking shore. Finally, the yellow sun rose above the buildings and trees on the west side of the Key. She'd check her watch: Paul by now was waiting for her to come and have breakfast. One time, heading back to her car, she decided, *Paul should try fishing*.

Pouring his coffee, she said, "Some morning I'd like you to come with me."

"One sheller in this family is enough."

"No, I mean to watch the men fish. They catch beautiful fish there."

"I gave away all my rods and tackle."

"You could just watch to see if you might have an interest.

"Well, maybe . . . .

"Then, Paul, we'd experience the loveliness of the morning together."

One day when Elizabeth went shelling, Paul tagged along to observe the fishermen casting far out near the Point of Rocks. He talked to several of them, learned their equipment and bait, and decided to give it a try. His first day proved a great success: he caught a three pound Red Snapper plus a tremendous number of congratulations from all the others who knew he was a novice. Elizabeth, delighted by Paul's good luck, knew how to prepare the milk-white fillets just perfectly. They had two delicious dinners from that first, fresh fish.

Paul and Elizabeth had married in 1938, when she was still called Hildy. They bought *Carolyn's Flower Shop* right after the war in 1945, renaming the business *Flowers by Elizabeth*. From then on, she preferred using her elegant, middle name.

At home though, and in private, Paul never stopped calling her Hildy; he fell in love with Hildy, and that would forever remain his lover's name. Paul had a good sense of humor that offset his innate seriousness. He easily made her laugh, but there were long stretches when he just didn't care to converse. She knew he was, as people used to say, the strong, silent type. Sometimes after dinner they spoke only a few words until they whispered "goodnight."

Radio shows and reading assured his evening silence, letting him reflect on things, especially his work. As a mechanical engineer, he derived incredible pleasure and considerable income from his job. In problem solving, in design, manufacturing methods, even shipping, he always searched for improvements. It didn't take long for his company to make him a vice president.

They wanted a family, a boy and girl would be wonderful they agreed, but Elizabeth didn't conceive. After a year, they began to wonder about it. After two, they became concerned, especially Elizabeth, because she thought maybe something she had done in her youth injured her in some terrible way that prevented conception. Her esteem for Paul made her ponder if she should tell him, if she should disclose things about herself that she never thought she'd disclose. Yet, perhaps, she reasoned, *he has a right to know.* Indeed, if she learned that she had been harmed in such a way that prevented having children, she would even consent to a divorce if Paul's desire for offspring was imperative in his life.

She decided to tell Paul rather than first going to her doctor to determine her capability to conceive. It proved a terrible mistake.

She told Paul she miscarried when she was only twenty, though she could never reveal what she had done to herself to lose that baby. Then she told of her affair with Arthur, getting pregnant, and finally aborting their child out of sheer hatred for the father and his brutal rejection of her. She told all those things as calmly and delicately as she could, but they had a devastating effect. Paul knew she wasn't a virgin when they married, but neither was he. Never, however, did he suspect his wife of being so careless as to let herself get pregnant by two men she didn't love, didn't care to marry, or who didn't care to marry her.

Stunned, he withdrew in a massive, emotional, and physical retreat that lasted for weeks. Only after a month did her weeping and pleadings begin to soften his heart. He never stopped loving her. When they married, he realized how blessed he was to love a woman with all his body, mind, heart, and soul. Now, struggling to repress his emotions, he agreed she should be examined by a top gynecologist. The results were favorable: she was a healthy thirty year old woman; there was no injury or abnormality in her reproductive organs, plus her regular menstrual cycle was a positive indicator. The specialist found no reason why Elizabeth could not get pregnant. "It could be your husband," he said. "He should be checked, as well."

Paul scoffed at the idea that he might be the cause of his wife's failure to conceive, but he realized all possibilities had to be examined. The conclusion of the urologist's laboratory analysis revealed a sad biological truth: *The patient has an unusually low sperm count that precludes procreation.*

It battered Paul's psyche nearly as much as Elizabeth's two premarital affairs crushed his heart. It devastated his self-image as a strong, robust father-to-be. Suddenly, *he* was the problem, and all his musings turned inward toward his own profound deficiency as a man. Elizabeth and he hadn't been intimate for months, not since she disclosed the two tragedies of her early life. After learning of his pitifully low sperm count, Paul retreated again.

In bed, night after night, Hildy whispered, "Paul, it doesn't matter." Then one, sleepless night, she decided she wanted her husband back. The following evening, she set the table with her fine china and crystal, prepared one of his favorite dinners, lit candles, and had him open a bottle of wine. Slowly he began to relax and relinquish his emotional guard. The conversation became pleasant and easy again. When they finished, she cleared the table, poured him the last of the wine, and excused herself. Minutes later she returned wearing new, black lingerie that just barely hid the incredible beauty of her figure. They bonded that night, passionately pledging to stay bound for the rest of their lives. They came to accept that they couldn't have their own children. Though they talked about adopting, they finally decided against it. Elizabeth still wanted to work at *Carolyn's*, while Paul knew, with the likelihood of America getting involved in the war in Europe in 1941 or 1942, that he'd be working long hours for a company well-positioned to gain huge military contracts. And that was, for both of them, exactly what happened.

In 1979, the year before they moved to Sarasota, Hildy realized Paul was becoming impotent. He had some successes, always more widely spaced, but by his mid-seventies, his sexual prowess was gone. It was difficult for him to accept, as he still desired his wife who at almost seventy years of age maintained her attractive, curvaceous figure. *It's a curious thing,* he realized, because he truly did desire her, but simply could not perform. *Well, she's not making a big deal out of it . . . maybe I shouldn't either,* he rationalized. *I've given up work, all my technical reading, the house, driving . . . maybe it's a normal regression. What is death, but having to give up everything one knows and loves?*

Thoughts of death, his death, came more frequently now. *Then what,* he wondered. *Is there consciousness, or do we give that up too? Maybe consciousness is heaven? Hell might be nothingness, no consciousness at all, but then how much of a punishment would that be? How bad is it if one doesn't know one is being punished? How could there even be suffering without consciousness?*

Though Paul's mind stayed sharp, his body was aging rapidly. When he and Hildy returned to Milwaukee for the summer, his nieces and their husbands noticed his frailty immediately. Karen and Johnny Helden suspected that Paul, at eighty, didn't have much longer to live.

Nevertheless, in November of 1985, Paul and Elizabeth headed back to their winter home in Sarasota. Elizabeth drove every mile. Right before Christmas, life presented one of those unanticipated, unpleasant, and unwanted surprises. Hildegard Elizabeth Peterson, nee *Neubauer,* died unexpectedly. She was seventy-five.

Chapter 37 ~ 1988

The sudden death of Elizabeth Peterson in late 1985 deeply saddened her nieces, especially, Karen Helden. From Karen's earliest Christmas memories, those seemingly idyllic family gatherings
always included Aunt Beth and Uncle Paul. As Karen grew into
adolescence and young womanhood, Aunt Beth became a friend
and confidant. She and Karen conversed regularly and, more often
than not, celebrated the meeting of their hearts and minds. Karen
knew she would miss her aunt terribly.

Several months later, Karen's blood uncle, Paul, died. She
mourned his passing hardly at all. The loss of his beloved Hildy,
left Paul literally helpless and unwilling to live on. At eighty-one
he had enjoyed a long, productive life.

Karen's parents, however, worried her constantly, for their
health seemed precarious at best. Her mother slipped away after
years of ignoring tell-tale signs of failing health; her father succumbed three months later. Karen well knew her parents died of
broken hearts, never able to overcome the sorrow of their youngest
daughters' brutal murder in 1975. The horrible manner of Jane's
death and the realization of her chosen profession proved unbearable for their suffering souls.

By Karen's forty-eighth birthday, she had lost five persons
who were most dear to her. Without question, Jane's death was the
most difficult to comprehend and endure. As a young girl, Jane's
high-spirited nature delighted the entire family. Her youthful
demise shattered the family's early expectations of Jane leading a
happy and worthwhile life within the context of family, friends, and
faith. Karen, conjuring all the strength of her will, refused to submit
to unending regret over the death of her sister, but chose life in the
raising of her children and the love of her husband.

Yet, many times when alone at home making beds or folding
laundry, she thought of Jane and how, in only a few, short years,

her precious life disintegrated. As painful as that memory always proved, Karen refused to place all the blame on her father, nor would she entirely blame Jane. Something in Jane's temperament, Karen suspected, must have impelled and enabled her to live so dangerously. That Jane's sensitive soul, however, could become so hardened as to work in the pornographic film industry, Karen found almost beyond belief. Karen never knew, and no one in the family could ever have imagined that it was the suffering of innocent children in Vietnam that drove Jane to act so recklessly. Jane wanted to help those children, wanted to hug, hold, and care for them, taking them far from the ugliness of war. To do that, Jane believed she needed money. Thus, while money was the apparent reason she became a porn star, her coveted savings, tragically, provided the motive for her barbaric murder.

+ + +

In Los Angeles, Michael Helden never really got over Jane Anderson's death or his imagined role in the tragedy of her life. *How could Jane,* he wondered, *having been raised in the same Christian home as Karen, choose such an immoral life?* Michael hated the pornographic film industry in his midst; he regarded it as a moral cancer poisoning the soul of the nation. He understood America in all her flawed complexities, but his idealism longed for something far better. As he grew older, he became more introspective and began writing a journal in which he recorded his deepest thoughts and strongest opinions.

He often sent his brother, Johnny, his written thoughts. He rarely revealed what prompted him to write, but he had been thinking of Jane and her murder when he composed the following:

> *The elegant concept of individual liberty, contrary to the repulsive fashion of unbridled personal freedom, is essential to preserve the democratic Republic the Founders so brilliantly conceived. Liberty, they hoped, would exhort each individual citizen to high self-governance by means of an educated intellect and a well-formed conscience. The Founders counseled that failure to educate the young, both academically and morally, would result in the eventual loss of liberty for all.*
>
> *Ideally, citizens of a democratic Republic are not to be governed*

by their appetites and emotions, for this inevitably leads to personal and social anarchy. Those suffering the hell of their own addictions and passions eventually affect others who, far too often, are senselessly and brutally harmed. Drugs and drunkenness, laziness, lying, greed, gambling, gluttony, pornography, fornication, adultery, and worst of all, murder, not only deeply harm the perpetrators themselves, but also innocent victims and family members, friends, neighbors, the larger community, and even the nation itself.

Sufficiently widespread, these reprehensible acts lead to an enormous expansion of state and federal behavioral statutes, police activities, courts and judiciaries, jails and prisons, all in a vain and hopeless attempt to control the wretched and violent conduct of so many tragically uneducated citizens. Such lawlessness deserves punishment: fines and loss of privilege and, in many cases, incarceration. Incarceration then becomes a profound indicator: if a large percentage of a nation's citizens are imprisoned, it can be reasonably concluded that efforts to educate many of its youngsters, in the principles of true individual liberty, have tragically failed.

Johnny replied in a post card: *An excellent piece! Unfortunately, moral behavior can't be taught without the inspiration and guidance of religion. Don't expect much help in the matter from the public schools.*

+ + +

John Nicholas Helden, born in 1902, third son of John and Augusta, began to fail noticeably in the summer of 1987. He gave up driving, had difficulty managing his medications, suffered short-term memory problems, lost his interest in conversing, reading, and playing the piano. He wanted only the company of Anita, his oft maligned wife of fifty-five years. The fight was finally out of John, his strength gone. He could hardly help Anita flip and turn their twin mattresses, something he always did with ease. He lost weight at an alarming rate and once showed himself to Anita who gasped when she saw he had been reduced to little more than skeleton and skin. Somewhere in his body cancer flourished; it had come quickly and devastatingly. By September, they both knew he was facing death. Day after day they waited for *something*. Finally it came. He could not urinate.

Rushed to the hospital, biopsies discovered cancer in the prostate and bladder. Surgery was recommended. Both Michael and Johnny felt they had to approve it, though they held little hope. Nevertheless, the operation to remove the prostate and part of the bladder went well. The surgeon, when asked about a prognosis, answered, "Six months to a year." The sons were grateful to hear it.

Michael and Johnny should have questioned the anesthesiologist. Their father never woke from the deep coma he sank into during the lengthy surgery. His body could not overcome the pernicious effect of the anesthetic. John Helden never regained consciousness and died the first week in October.

Several days after John's burial on a glorious autumn day, the kind of day he loved, Michael suggested that Anita sell the house on Harding Boulevard and move to Los Angeles to live with him. During a good real estate market, the house sold quickly. Most of the possessions were assigned to an auction house, but a few precious things were shipped to California. By mid-December, 1987, Michael and his mother were on the Interstate heading west.

+ + +

Nick Helden completed his three year commitment to the Army Corps of Engineers at the end of June, 1988. With wife Maggie and baby Jennifer, Nick returned to Milwaukee for what everyone in the family believed would be a permanent stay. John Helden looked forward to welcoming Nick into his consulting practice, while Karen couldn't wait to fall in love with her first grandchild. JJ planned on playing a lot of golf and tennis with his twin. His sisters, thrilled to be aunts, were delighted to have Nick and his family domiciled in town for good. John and Karen had a *Welcome Home* party, but John never had a chance to talk with Nick about working together, so he invited Nick, Maggie, and the baby to stop over the following evening.

"It's nice to see you in civilian clothes again," John said. "You know, Nick, we haven't talked about you working with me for a long time. I thought maybe tonight we could discuss that."

"Okay," Nick said.

Maggie looked at her husband apprehensively. She knew this moment had to come, and *better now than later*, she realized.

John asked, "Did you do any structural engineering in the Corps?"

"Very little."

"I'm surprised . . . ."

"Actually, I preferred field work. I was a survey crew chief and then got into transport logistics and support."

"No design of buildings, structures?"

"None."

"Well, I can bring you up to speed real quick."

Karen noticed Nick's discomfort. Maggie shifted the baby arm to arm, all the while studying Nick's face. Uncomfortable as he was, Nick knew this was the right moment. Finally he said, "Dad, I think before we go any further, you should know that I've decided to re-enlist."

Johnny and Karen were shocked. Neither suspected that.

"You've got to be kidding," John said. "You know I've looked forward to you joining me ever since you graduated. Now you tell me you wanna re-enlist with the Corps . . . I can't believe that."

"Well, to a certain extent, you shouldn't. Actually, I'm not re-enlisting with the Corps. I've decided to join the Special Forces."

"Nick, come on, that's insane. You got your degree in Structures; I run a structural consulting firm. We talked for years about you coming in and building up the practice together. In ten years I'll retire, and you can take it over. Now you tell me you're joining the Special Forces? I'm sorry, but I find that damn hard to accept."

"They're better known as the Green Berets."

"I know."

"They were active in Vietnam."

"I know that. And now you think you want to join them?"

"Yes, I do."

"What the hell for?" John glanced at Karen, her head shaking in disapproval.

"I've decided to make the Army my career."

When John digested that, like some foul tasting fish, his disgust showed in his face, the squirming of his body, and his voice. "Nick, you can't possibly be serious . . . ."

"Dad, I've given this a lot of thought. Maggie supports my decision. It's a tremendous opportunity to work with outstanding people, doing some really great things."

"But not engineering . . . ."

"No, but they did say my engineering background would help."

"Why the hell did you study engineering in the first place?" John's voice reeked ridicule.

"Because I wanted to learn and understand what you know and do."

"Then why the hell won't you join me?"

"Because Dad, I don't want to do what you do. I saw how hard you worked and never really earned as much as you deserved. I just don't want that for my family."

John scoffed. "Do you really think you'll do better in the Army?"

"Dad, I'm glad I'm a graduate engineer, but I want my career in the military. It's that simple."

"I told you before, Nick, we're not a military family. We have no history of service."

"That's not true," Nick said. "Your great grandfather was in the Civil War. Uncle Julius was in World War Two. Grandpa Anderson was in the Navy before he got married. That's a history of service."

"No, no, I meant my Helden lineage – me, my father, my grandfather who was a life-long pacifist, and his father who left Germany to save four sons from serving in the Prussian army. Had he not done that, none of us would even be here. It's an anti-war heritage, Nick. Militarism is not in your background, not in your blood."

"Well, maybe it's time someone in our family finally serves to justify all the blessings we've had as Americans."

"Nick, please, think it over before you decide. Think about what I've said. Try to see this from your mother's and my point of view."

Karen cut in. "Johnny, leave me out of it. Nick is a man with a wife and child. He can do whatever he wishes, and besides, we've had no war since Vietnam."

"In this world we could be in another war in a week," John replied. "And you Nick . . . with a family? I'm sorry, but I think you're crazy."

Maggie rose. "Nick, the baby's fussing. We have to go." That John Helden stooped to insult her husband stung her heart.

Standing, Nick said, "Dad, I have thought it over – many times I'm re-enlisting. I'm sorry if you can't accept that."

After they left, John's anger turned towards Karen. "You shouldn't have sided with Nick. If you feel that way, you should have, out of respect for me, said nothing. For God's sake, don't you understand how much this means to me? I've looked forward to Nick joining me for years, and now you encourage him to re-enlist."

"I didn't encourage him. I just acknowledged that he can do whatever he wants with his own life. Apparently, that's beyond your ability to grasp."

"It's not his own life; he's got a wife and child. He's putting himself in harm's way. If we get in another war, Nick will be in it. I know about the Special Forces. I know what they do. Maggie and the baby will be left stateside, while he's off in some God-forsaken country behind enemy lines. What the hell kind of life is that for a man with a family? I want what's best for Nick. You've got this stupid idea he can do whatever he wants, but I know the dangers. I don't want that for my son, and you shouldn't either."

"Johnny, we're not at war. There's no world crisis on the horizon. Besides, you always said you believed in a strong military, so there wouldn't be another war. I guess you just want other people's sons to serve. That is so hypocritical. You should be proud that Nick wants to be part of the strong military that you've always advocated."

"Nick has a valuable professional education. He has a family. He serves his country best if he works as an engineer and provides for his wife and little girl."

"That is not for you to decide. Nick is a responsible man. He has all the rights that come with being free."

"Yes, and if something happens to Nick, then what . . . then how will you feel?"

"He'll be fine, Johnny. We're not at war. Just let him leave with your love and support. Don't make it hard for him. You told me how hard your father made it for Michael when he decided to move to Los Angeles. You totally sided with Michael then because you knew he had the right to pursue his own happiness – however he wished. Why can't you see that now for your own son? You told me you detested your father's behavior, and now you're acting just like him. You'll make Nick react just like Michael. Don't you see you're driving him away, and that's so terribly wrong?"

"Michael wasn't joining the military. He wasn't that stupid."

"That's a terrible thing to say . . . to insult your own son and every American who's ever served. Sometimes I just don't understand you, Johnny. Why are you so selfish where Nick is concerned? He's so outstanding in everything. Don't answer – I'm too tired to argue. Besides, it's pointless. Nick is going to do what he wants, and I'll support him a hundred percent, and you should, too. Now I'm going to bed."

Repudiated and alone, John brooded.

+ + +

Jack and Cheryl Cutler divorced in 1987 after twenty-two years of a lustful, barren, loveless marriage. In the early years, amidst plenty of passion, Jack mumbled several times in close succession a gigantic lie: "I love you." Yet in all those years, they never became friends. Initially, their emotional bond had all the overwhelming fluff of teenage infatuation. Spiritually, though, they never approached that deep, visceral oneness indicative of true friendship irrespective of gender. A psychologist acquaintance of Jack's once commented, "There's no guarantee lovers will become friends, but there's a damn good chance friends will become lovers." When Jack heard that, he laughed out loud knowing *Rumpledbuttskin* was the last human being he'd ever want to be friends with. Nevertheless, she was – in fact and sad fancy – his legal wife.

Jack could only shake his head in wonderment that he had made, at age thirty-one, such an unbelievably bad choice. But then he'd justify it because he remembered how powerless he felt in the face of his enormous and relentless sexual desire for Cheryl. Finally, the prodding insults of Dr. Anthony Messert convinced Jack to see a lawyer and initiate the action.

Cheryl, speechless for just a moment, spewed a stream of obscenities that sent Jack barging out the door. He hated her filthy mouth that always came into play when he said or did something that, in the slightest way, angered or irritated her. He decided he'd never "listen to that shit again." He didn't mind men using offensive language, but hated it in women because he never once heard his mother or sister voice crude vulgarities.

Jack's lawyer informed Cheryl's well-known divorce attorney that Jack would be "utterly fair" in the financial settlement. Cheryl calmed down after Jack offered the house free and clear, everything in it, and half his financial assets. There'd be no fighting over material things because Jack didn't want any of them. He would not, however, grant alimony. Cheryl grudgingly accepted that because her attorney advised that the house, free and clear, was "a very big bird in the hand," whereas alimony wasn't a sure thing. Jack's attorney knew where to draw the line.

In the courtroom, amidst a palpable sense of mutual contempt, Jack felt almost nauseous listening to Cheryl's inane answers to her lawyer's questions. Overdressed, wearing too much makeup and a silly little smirk on her plump face, Jack could barely stand looking at her.

The judge expressed gratitude that children weren't involved. "You obviously can't stand each other, so you should be divorced," he said. "I advise you never to see each other again."

Leaving the courthouse and driving back to Messert's clinic, Jack, repeatedly and out loud, vowed on the words "stupid bitch" that he'd never remarry. His revulsion and hatred for Cheryl overwhelmed him in disgust and anger. Other motorists, noticing Jack's mumblings and wild gesticulations, must have thought him crazy.

Finally, drained of emotional energy, his mind regained control. The outburst, though, *felt damn good* and, in fact, was necessary before he could turn his thoughts to work. He tried to remember if he had one or two abortions scheduled that afternoon. *Doesn't much matter,* he thought. Then he realized he had nothing else to look forward to.

During several months of heavy drinking and physical dissipation, Jack's mind fought to eradicate every memory of Cheryl, an impossible task. Nevertheless, a strange and curious idea supplanted all the ugly thoughts of his ex-wife. A new hatred and its ultimate resolution gave him tremendous pleasure. Since his divorce, he possessed a sense of enormous freedom and control, not only over his own life, but the lives of others. Cheryl destroyed his chance for marital happiness, but now that meant nothing to Jack.

He was rid of her. What was important was a profound need to reorder his life, to finally make everything right. He concluded, "My life's a fucking disaster," but he imagined he knew how to salvage it in one grand gesture. He knew he had made two fatal choices in his life: one involved a woman, the other a man. He believed both had deceived and nearly destroyed him. Now, with only the man remaining, Jack decided, "It's time I'm free of that worthless son-of-a-bitch once and for all."

+ + +

Johnny Helden's harsh comments, regarding Nick's decision to make the Army his career, hurt his daughter-in-law, Maggie, far more than his son. Nick even defended his father because when Nick was younger he did allow and, in some respects, even encouraged his dad to believe that one day Nick would join and eventually take over his father's consulting practice. He wasn't surprised by his father's negative reaction. He really couldn't blame him, but Maggie resented her father-in-law calling Nick "insane" and "crazy." Nick argued that his father referred to Nick's decision, not him, personally. But Maggie saw something in John Helden she had never seen before: a selfishness and possessiveness towards a young man who everyone in the family knew was an exceptional son, brother, and husband – a shining star – and John's favorite, as well.

John refused to admit his bias. If Karen pointed it out, as she occasionally did, he adamantly insisted he loved all his children equally, but his actions belied his words. In fact, it was easier for him to understand and relate to his sons, just as he imagined it was easier for Karen to understand and relate to her daughters. He believed it normal parental behavior, nothing to be concerned about, and certainly nothing for Karen to make an issue of.

When Nick and Maggie were alone she told Nick, "I used to think your dad respected his kids, but it really hurts that he talked to you in such an insulting way."

"He's respectful, but he's always been against war, and he fears for my safety. He doesn't understand how sophisticated everything has become and how covertly the Special Forces operate."

"No, Nick, it was his tone . . . like no one in your family is allowed to think differently."

"Oh, I don't know. I always thought my dad was pretty open-minded."

"I don't think so. He's happiest when everyone in the family agrees with him. He obviously was upset when your mother took your side."

Nick laughed. "Well, maybe a little . . . ."

"Nick, he was demeaning."

"My dad apologized, and I forgave him. I hope you will, too."

"I don't know. I'm not sure I can trust your father anymore."

"Maggie, don't say that. That's extreme."

"I have to be honest, Nick. He doesn't own you. You're my husband and a father."

"He knows that better than anyone. He just worries about our happiness, that's all."

"Well, we'll see . . . ."

Johnny Helden had no choice but to accept his son's decision. After apologizing to Nick, they resumed their friendly conversations. At the end of July, Nick, Maggie, and the baby said goodbye to their families and headed for Fort Bragg, North Carolina. John sensed a change in his daughter-in-law's attitude. Her "goodbye" lacked its usual warmth. He felt her stiffness when they briefly hugged. John kissed her cheek, but she did not reciprocate, as she always had. She backed away, her eyes averting his yearning gaze.

Shaking hands and hugging Nick, John wished him, "God's blessings and a great career. I'll miss you, Nick. Keep in touch . . . ."

"I will," Nick said; "and, Dad, don't worry; there's nothing to worry about."

Karen said, "Take good care of yourself and your family. I'll miss you and little Jenny, terribly. Oh, how I wish you all were staying in Milwaukee."

"First leave we'll be home," Nick promised.

John Helden said nothing more. He was too bewildered by Karen's last wish.

+ + +

1988 marked the thirteenth year that Jack Cutler had worked at the Messert Clinic. He attained the position of Chief Surgeon, specializing in second and early third trimester abortions. Dr. Messert, at eighty-two, still actively mentored his doctors, did some pre-op consultations and examinations, and watched over the clinic's business affairs. With patience and persistence, Messert, over a period of several years, convinced Jack to learn and master the more difficult procedure – *dilation, extraction, and dismemberment* – for second and third trimesters.

Initially, Jack showed little enthusiasm, but Messert wisely started by having Jack abort a four month pregnancy where the fetus was only about five inches long; then a five month at about eight inches and, finally, a six month African-American female with a weight of about a pound and a half and a length of twelve inches. As he grew older, Messert lost most of his strength. Of all the clinic's doctors, Jack proved most qualified to take over late term abortions. He possessed a calm, controlled personality, tremendous hand strength, dedication to his work, and an intellect that Messert could always appeal to if he sensed Jack's emotions starting to sway his thinking. He often told Jack he wanted his clinic to provide, in absolutely every case, "professional excellence coupled with personal indifference." He emphasized the need for both safe surgical procedures and complete emotional detachment, and prided himself that no girl or woman ever died at his or his clinic's hands.

As the years passed, the two doctors' Wednesday night dinners went from weekly to biweekly to monthly. During his marriage, Jack used the frequent dinners with Messert to get away from Cheryl, but after his divorce, he and Messert agreed to dine together only on the first Wednesday of the month. Jack still possessed a robust appetite, but Messert, as he grew older, cut back. One cocktail at the restaurant sufficed; for dinner he ordered a small filet mignon and a salad. Afterwards, they'd go to Messert's home for a tumbler or two of Scotch on the rocks. In spite of the relaxing mood, many times the night ended in contentious disagreements, which by the following morning seemed trivial. Even after so many years, neither man considered the other a close friend. They were professional colleagues who enjoyed each other's company one night a month; that was enough considering how much time they spent together at the clinic.

Messert's supercilious personality never softened; his harsh political and societal opinions, and narrow tastes in food, drink, and music, remained static for decades. His lifestyle included travel twice a year, a fine home and manicured yard, tailored clothing, remarkably good health that he attributed to his abstemious eating habits, a loyal man-servant, and a hoard of cash along with significant investments in stocks. In addition, his office building appreciated greatly since he built it back in the 1970s. By itself, it provided sufficient income for Messert to live comfortably.

In contrast, Jack Cutler lived in a messy apartment, gained weight, never exercised, rarely socialized, and traveled little. Even after giving Cheryl half his assets, plenty money remained along with tremendous income potential all the way to retirement. Every two years he treated himself to a new Buick *Riviera*. His work became his life. He regarded himself a gynecologist who specialized in abortions, just as Messert had urged. After Jack's divorce, he drank heavily, but abandoned that at Messert's insistence because it badly impacted Jack's work. He knew drinking to excess was stupid, but he enjoyed a couple drinks before dinner. One night a month at Messert's for several Scotches certainly didn't seem excessive.

Jack had two lady friends whom he occasionally took, separately, to dinner. They in appreciation took him to bed. To his credit, he made it clear he had no interest in remarrying. As divorcées and still physically attractive, the women possessed rapacious appetites for men. One vigorous gal proudly told Jack that he was her twenty-fifth lover. Then she asked what would happen to her sex drive in menopause. Jack glibly answered, "You don't have a thing to worry about."

Sports and movies on television along with non-fiction reading occupied the bulk of Jack's leisure time. He never read novels or 'story books,' as he called them years ago when he dated Karen Anderson. He had no particular or partisan interest in politics. When Messert told him the importance of *Roe v Wade,* Jack commented, "That's the Supreme Court . . . it's got nothing to do with politics." Messert knew better, but convinced himself and Jack that the controversial decision would never be repealed.

Back in 1976, when Karen's aunt debated the issue, Jack thought she got the better of it even though Jack believed a woman does have a legal right to an abortion. Whatever his feelings on abortion, they rarely challenged his thinking. In his early years with Dr. Messert, when Jack first beheld a larger, aborted fetus, he realized something was very strange, brutal, and unnatural about such a tiny, mutilated corpse. But then, Messert always offered some powerful argument that eased Jack's inherently open mind.

"We're not the killers, Jack. It's the woman who wants the abortion; she's the killer, not us. Does the employed executioner kill the condemned criminal, or is it the State? Was the poor chap who guillotined the Queen guilty of murder, or was it the French masses? Is the soldier guilty when he kills the enemy, or does the blood belong on the hands of the Commander-in-Chief? Is the hit man guilty, or is it the godfather?

"Jack, you and I are innocent as lambs. It's the person who wills that another dies that is guilty of murder, not the person who executes that will. If I believed in God – which I do not, and you shouldn't either – I would stand fearlessly before him and say, 'I've done nothing wrong in my life, not a thing. I only helped women . . . helped those ignorant sluts out of a sense of true, Christian compassion.' That, Jack, is what I'd say to God. I am blameless of all sin, and he would welcome me into Heaven with open arms." Messert laughed heartily.

"That's a pretty good argument," Jack conceded.

"It's a brilliant argument because it's true. For what we do, I feel absolutely no guilt. None!"

"Well, actually, sometimes I'm not sure what I feel . . . ."

"That's alright Jack. But you know what? The bimbos do, and rightly so, because they are the killers." Messert laughed. "Hell, I respect a street hooker more than the sluts who come to us. At least, a whore demands payment. Nowadays these young girls spread their legs for nothing at all. It's unbelievable to me. They get knocked up then shell out damn good money to get rid of their nasty, little problem. I can't respect such profound stupidity. I've seen it thousands of times. Girls party, get drunk, then drop their panties for any jerk who tells 'em they're cute."

"Man, you are one, cynical son-of-a-bitch," Jack said. "You claim you help women . . . shit, Doctor, you hate women. Most of these girls are in relationships or school or just starting out. It's just not the right time to have a baby."

Messert laughed out loud. "You're a gullible bastard, Jack. That's what they all say. Don't believe that shit. They get knocked up at frat parties. They're that stupid."

"You're a woman hater, old man."

Again Messert laughed. "I admit it, but no female in my care would ever suspect it. Besides, guys are just smarter. When they decide to get married, they certainly aren't gonna pick some campus dick socket that's had a couple abortions. Those bitches are gonna end up fat, alone, broke, and miserable, just because they couldn't say 'no,' and you know what, Jack?"

"What?"

"They deserve it."

Jack shook his head. "Your compassion is overwhelming."

"I understand things . . . cause and effect. Scientific analysis has no column or row for compassion. Look at sex education in the public schools. They teach sex in the classroom, but the lab's in the back seat of a car. The girl gets knocked up and – presto – she's at our door."

"They're supposed to teach condoms, birth control, safe sex . . . ."

"Yes, Jack, I'm sure they do a splendid job." He laughed hard again. "That must be why there are only a million abortions every year."

Both swigged more Scotch. Jack noticed the tremble in Messert's hand. *No way could he ever do what I do anymore,* he realized.

"Jack, you need remember only three things: first, what we do is legal; second, we provide a valuable service; and third, we provide excellent surgical skills. Think of nothing else; don't let any stupid argument against abortion get in your head. For us, abortion must never be a moral issue . . . only the woman who chooses it. We're the facilitators – nothing more, nothing less. For us it's completely legal, financially beneficial, plus we do the best we can to make it medically safe. That's it."

Jack poured himself another full tumbler of whiskey. "When you put it in those terms it makes sense, but the reality is something far darker."

"Thanks," Messert said, cheerfully, ignoring the trailing phrase. "But, Jack, I shouldn't always have to put your g--damn mind at ease. I've had to do that for years. You're a good surgeon. You've become a damn good abortionist. Be proud of that."

"Oh, shit," Jack said, "kiss my fucking ass! I'm proud of nothing. You think I enjoy ripping limbs off, looking at mutilated fetuses, seeing their tiny, clenched fists, seeing that death mask horror locked on their little faces?"

"Don't speak so vulgarly in my presence, Cutler. Is that what your mother taught you? All surgeries are bloody messy . . . you know that."

"My mother was a refined woman, a surgical nurse who helped save lives. She'd puke if she saw what I do."

"Then have the fucking courage to quit."

Messert said it many times before, but Jack, especially in the early years, always rationalized that most of his procedures were first trimesters, which his mind and emotions dealt with comfortably. Besides, Messert paid Jack more than any other clinic, so Jack stayed. He swallowed more Scotch. Messert went to the bathroom. When he returned, to ease the tension, he said, "Actually, Jack, I'm very much in favor of some vulgarities . . . ."

"Tell me . . . I'll use 'em."

"Quite frankly, I very much appreciate the visual vulgarities one finds in pornography."

"You look at porn? Shit, old man, what the hell's wrong with you?"

"Not for me, asshole. For kids, young studs . . . sexy movies, dirty magazines, sexy sitcoms, anything that titillates the young. And do you know why, Jack? Because it's good for our business . . . cause and effect. I'd like every bimbo in this country to have two or three abortions before they turn twenty. Then we'd really be rolling in dough."

"You think crazy thoughts, old man."

"Yes, indeed . . . did I ever tell you my definition of hard-core pornography?"

Uninterested, Jack slumped lower in his chair.

"Hard-core porn is public exhibition of sex acts everybody loves to do in private." Again Messert laughed hard.

"Pornography is for guys who can't get a woman. They're to be pitied."

"Oh, shit, Cutler, you talk like some bleeding heart."

"No, no, I was thinking of you." Now Jack laughed hard.

"Shut up, asshole . . . I've got a damn good sex life, probably better than yours."

"At eighty-two?"

"Yes, at eighty-two."

"You hire hookers, right?"

"They are not hookers . . . very refined ladies of the night."

"Yeah, I'm sure."

"Very clean, very high class . . . ."

Jack fell silent. The thought of going to a prostitute was repugnant. After a night with one of his lady friends, he had no interest in sex for weeks. As a gynecologist, there was nothing sexually alluring about a woman's genitalia without several strong drinks, dim lighting, soft music, and lovely perfume. In the depths of his mind dwelt horrible images, grotesque images he fought to suppress: images of mutilated and nearly decapitated fetuses wrenched from wombs, extracted bloody and bruised, but perfectly formed and ready for life had the women simply made the other *choice.*

"You wanna call it a night, Cutler?"

"No, I'm not drunk enough . . . ."

"Good." He filled Jack's tumbler.

Jack drank, put his glass down, but said nothing.

After a moment, Messert said, "Do you realize we had five nigger girls this past week? That's the most we've ever done."

"That's a very offensive word."

"I'm from an older and wiser generation, Jack. That word is perfectly acceptable to me."

"Times have changed. You should say 'African-American' or 'black.'"

"Oh, excuse me, Doctor, I didn't mean to offend your g--damn sensibilities. We had five African-American black niggers." Messert laughed, but then turned serious. "It's unusual. They mostly go to that inner city clinic."

"You gotta problem with that?"

"Not at all. I welcome it. I suppose the nigger clinic was too busy."

Jack didn't respond. He glared at Messert before swallowing more Scotch.

"Actually, I enjoy aborting blacks. I feel like I'm doing a public service."

"What the hell are you talking about?"

"I'm talking about the stinking carrion of murderers, whores, and AIDS infected faggots."

"You're a g--damn racist."

"Yes I am."

"And a misogynist."

"Definitely!"

"Anyone else you hate?"

"Just the usual – Jews, Catholics, homos . . . ."

"Why do I listen to this shit?"

"Then get the fuck out," Messert growled.

But Jack, his body warm from whiskey and his mind beclouded by it, suddenly felt aggressive. "Fuck you, old man. We're drinking all night."

"Bullshit – you get the hell out of here right now." Messert tried to sound tough.

Jack laughed. "Shut up, you fucking faggot."

The slur stunned Messert. "What did you call me?"

"A *fucking faggot*, faggot!"

Messert rose uneasily from his chair, his voice quivering. "You get the hell out of here. Nobody talks to me like that. What the hell's wrong with you?"

Jack emptied his glass, reached for the bottle, but accidentally knocked it over, spilling about an inch of whiskey onto the carpet.

"You clumsy idiot," Messert screamed. "What the hell's wrong with you?"

Jack hollered, "Miguel!"

Within seconds Miguel appeared in the doorway. "Yes, sir?"

Without looking at him, Jack waved the empty bottle above his head. "Bring me another."

"You do nothing of the kind," Messert countermanded. "Get a towel and clean this up." He pointed at the carpet. "Cutler, you get the hell out of here. You're drunk."

"Shut your fucking mouth," Jack slurred. "Sit down . . . ."

Messert moved to leave the room. Jack sprang from his chair, grabbing the old man by his thin upper arms. "I told you to sit down, faggot." The strength in Jack's hands surprised Messert, as he was spun down into his chair.

"We're not done drinking," Jack said. "Miguel!"

Messert glared at Jack, but suddenly feared him in a way he had never feared anyone. He felt himself trapped in a narrow slot of danger. He realized Jack had too much to drink, wasn't rational, and might turn violent. "Jack, please, go home," he pleaded. "Get a good night's sleep. I'm tired; you're tired. We'll talk in the morning."

While Jack sulked, Messert feared to move. Miguel returned with a fresh bottle of Scotch and a roll of paper towels, hoping to appease both men. He set the open bottle on the table next to Jack then bent down dabbing the carpet to absorb the wasted Scotch. A stain remained, but Messert, wisely, said nothing.

With Miguel out of the room, Jack, for no apparent reason, did something violently irrational: he grabbed the fresh bottle of Scotch and threw it full force against the fieldstone fireplace where it exploded, spewing whiskey and shards of glass onto both men. Messert, stunned into speechlessness, stood and forced a scream: "Miguel – call the police!"

Jack darted into the kitchen, grabbed the handset from Miguel and ripped the phone off the wall, popping wires. "Go in the other room," he ordered.

Messert, searching for any kind of weapon, grabbed the log poker from the fireplace and waited. "I'll kill that son-of-a-bitch," he muttered.

Jack reentered the den and saw Messert standing there trembling. Jack laughed. "What's wrong old man . . . afraid of me?" He hadn't spotted the poker.

Messert waited, his thoughts wild, heart pounding, body shaking.

"What's that?" Jack asked. Then he recognized the pointed cast-iron tool. "What the fuck?"

Raising the poker above his head, the old man lunged at Jack, but there was such a disparity in strength and reflexes that Jack easily grabbed the poker in its downward stroke, ripping it out of Messert's hands. "What the fuck do you think you're doing?"

Messert, fearful and speechless, backed away.

"I see hatred in your eyes, old man. You wanted to kill me, didn't you?"

"You son-of-a-bitch – I taught you everything you know, and this is how you act? You go crazy on me. I made you a rich man. You should kiss my feet."

Jack laughed. "Just think, the old faggot would like to kill me."

Slowly, Messert's mouth turned into a thin smile. He looked past Jack. "Yes, I would, I certainly would . . . and now I will."

Jack turned. Standing ten feet behind, Miguel held a small caliber pistol in his trembling hand.

"Shoot him Miguel," Messert screamed.

Jack said, "You kill me Miguel, and he'll let you hang for it."

"Miguel, kill him . . . shoot him!"

Miguel started shaking and weeping. His hand dropped to his side. Jack reached for the gun and took it without a struggle. Turning back towards Messert, Jack laughed. "Now, old man, I'm afraid I have to kill you."

"No, no," Miguel screamed.

Messert fell onto his knees, hands over his head, groveling for his life. Jack found it contemptible and ludicrous. He had no intention of killing the old man, but intuitively felt Messert didn't deserve to live. Jack just didn't want to be *the idiot who kills such a worthless piece of shit.*

Jack grabbed Messert by the back of his shirt, pulled him up, saying, "In the basement . . . Miguel, you too."

Miguel went down first. Jack pushed Messert towards the stairs thinking the old man would grab the handrail. But Messert was not quick or strong enough. He screamed, as he crashed and twice tumbled over, banging and bruising every part of his fragile head and body on the pine treads. When he landed on the concrete floor, Miguel screamed in horror. Messert groaned. His bony body twitched several times then slumped silent and motionless. Miguel thought him dead.

Jack went down with the pistol in one hand and the log poker in the other, convincing Miguel that Jack would kill him, too. Jack spotted an old, heavy, wooden armoire. He opened one door just a crack, stuck his hand in and, hoping the sound would be muffled, discharged the pistol into the wood back. He then dropped both the gun and poker onto the wardrobe floor.

Jack felt incredible rage when he realized Messert wanted Miguel to shoot him, but, wisely, controlled himself. He knew Messert didn't have the strength to kill him, but Miguel, sneaking up behind with a pistol, surprised him. He realized he should have suspected Messert had a gun in the house, but he was right about Miguel. No way did he possess the anger and hatred to pull the trigger. He was a kid, early twenties at most, without a stomach for killing a mouse let alone another human being. *I wonder if Miguel knows what we do*, Jack thought. *I wonder if he knows his boss once drowned a little girl aborted alive.*

Though nearly drunk, Jack now knew exactly how this night would end. He had thought about it for months, but never imagined that an unplanned confrontation with Messert would provide the final impetus.

Miguel's pitiful terror amused Jack because he had absolutely no intention of harming him. "Miguel, go upstairs and make a pot of very strong coffee. And don't be afraid. I'm not going to hurt you."

Miguel had to step over Messert's motionless body to ascend the stairs. Jack knelt beside Messert, gripping his throat for a pulse. He found a weak one.

At the top of the stairs, Jack said, "He's not dead." Jack's throat was as dry and grainy as sun baked sand. "Get me a glass of water."

Miguel brought it then stood mutely at the coffee maker. When the coffee was brewed, he poured a cup and pushed it across the counter towards Jack.

"Now, Miguel, here's what you have to do. Messert will live. But you have to give me time to get away before you call the police. Understand?"

Miguel nodded.

"It's almost one-thirty . . . give me until two before you call. Is there a phone upstairs?"

Again Miguel nodded.

"You have to give me at least thirty minutes to get away – understand?"

"Yes," Miguel answered.

"If you call even a minute before two, I'll come back – someday, somehow – and I'll kill you. Do you understand?"

Miguel nodded, his eyes filled with tears and terror.

Jack finished his coffee, but then did something Miguel thought extremely odd. Jack extended his hand, saying, "Good-bye Miguel and good luck. I have nothing against you, and I had no intention of killing Messert. Had I wanted to, I could have killed him with his own gun. You know that; you saw that. Make sure the police understand . . . I am not a murderer."

Miguel stood trembling, as he watched Jack move to the front door and leave.

Later, when the police interviewed Miguel, he told how calmly Jack said and did all of these things, convincing them that Jack's attack on Messert was premeditated.

Jack figured he had plenty of time. By two, he'd arrive safely at his destination. Then it was just a matter of following his plan, and that wouldn't take long. If Miguel obeyed, things would probably be over before the police would even know enough to start searching for Jack. Now it was important to drive normally, sensibly, not too fast, not too slow. Jack knew if a cop spotted him, he'd check him out, having nothing better to do. Even if he was pulled over, though, it'd be okay provided Miguel hadn't called the police. Jack worked his way towards Blue Mound Road then past the miles of strip shopping malls, fast food restaurants, and office parks leading to Goerke's Corners. There he'd pick up I-94 west to Madison, just as he did every workday going to the clinic. But, unlike those mornings, tonight he knew he need not drive that far.

Like I'd ever work for that asshole again . . . worthless son-of-a-bitch. Man, he was scared when I got the gun. Maybe I should've killed him. No, no, not your style, Jack. I should've toyed with him a little more though . . . put the fucking gun in his mouth. He would've shit in his pants. Man, if he only knew . . . oh, shit, no way. He'll be hospitalized for a month. Maybe he's brain dead . . . actually, that'd be very good. I wonder if the motherfucker has a will . . . I bet that's where Miguel comes in . . . maybe Miguel doesn't even know.

Jack headed west at sixty miles an hour. He felt better for the water and coffee. He figured he'd be at his exit in fifteen minutes.

No hurry . . . nice and easy. Wendy's the only one, but she'll be okay

*. . . surprised, but what the hell . . . she'll understand better than anyone.
Should've stayed closer to her . . . California's too damn far . . . after Mom
we drifted apart . . . too bad . . . she was a good kid sister . . . one of the few
I could trust . . . next of kin . . . my only kin . . . yeah, she'll be okay. All the
others assholes . . . and none bigger than Messert . . . worthless son-of-a-
bitch . . . oh, and good old Rumpledbuttskin . . . she'll be surprised as hell,
but she never gave a shit anyway . . . and Karen Helden . . . what an arrogant bitch she turned out to be. There'll be a lotta stupid chatter by all of 'em
. . . a lot of moronic questions . . . unless Messert lives . . . then the lies will
flow like cow shit in the rain, but fuck it . . . who gives a shit. Like I really
give a rat's ass what anyone thinks . . . all assholes . . . a world of assholes.
Rumpledbuttskin will be surprised . . . maybe the most . . . damn, she was
beautiful . . . beautiful, but too stupid to keep it. And Messert . . . what an
asshole he turned out to be . . . what an asshole I was to work for that prick
. . . amazing how money corrupts. And why the fuck I ever bothered to get
married I'll never know . . . that sucked. Face it, Jack, you fucked up. So,
what are we gonna do about it? How are we gonna make amends? Well, I
think we gotta go out in glory . . . self-respect . . . that's what's important
. . . even if you don't have it, but you get it in the end. Gotta have that damn
self-respect . . . super important now . . . it just is . . . everybody craves it.
Courage is good, really good . . . the root of all self-respect. It proves it . . . the
one thing that always gets the respect of all the cowards out there. Besides
Jack, you've done it a thousand times . . . no big deal. Mental preparation
down to the tiniest detail . . . you know exactly what must be done. Courage
gains respect . . . everybody admires courage. Mom was courageous . . . but
she didn't give a shit either . . . didn't give a g--damn about either one of us.
Dad did, though . . . then run over like a g--damn dog in the middle of the
road. If he had lived, I wonder where I'd be . . . not here, no fucking way . . .
he would have been the difference for all of us . . . .*

Jack groaned; within him surged waves of incredible pain.

*Dad . . . Dad . . . why'd you have to die like that? I needed you . . .
Wendy needed you . . . Mom needed you. Why were you there then . . . why
weren't you home? Why'd it have to end like that? Nothing's been right
ever since. I didn't give a shit about anything . . . now I can't remember the
stuff you said I was supposed to. You said you'd always be there for me . . .
always there to explain things. Now, I can't even remember what you look
like. Dad . . . I've missed you so much for so long . . . don't you realize nothing went right without you? Why'd you have to die? Dad, why . . . why?*

Tears streamed down Jack's face. After a moment, in the lonely darkness of the car, he muttered, "I'm so fucking lost . . . I've been lost for so fucking long." He just exited the freeway.

His car crawled through the intersection onto the road that curved along the southwest shore of Lake Nagawicka. A few lamps shone above the doorways of the buildings facing the street. Across the watery blackness several lights dotted the far northern and eastern shores.

Concentrate now . . . no more thinking . . . find that street.

Since exiting the Interstate, he encountered not a single car. He glanced at the dashboard clock. *Three minutes until Miguel calls the police.* The silent darkness and absence of headlights, in front and behind, convinced him that Miguel had obeyed.

You're home free and safe Jack . . . the worst is over. Now, everything according to plan . . . simple, dimple . . . you know you've got that special stuff . . . .

For a moment his thoughts turned abstract, inexpressible, but then, *yes, you've got it, Jack . . . you were born with it . . . in your genes, in your blood . . . a mother's gift. If you didn't, there'd be no self-respect . . . , but now I'm feeling it Jack . . . for the first time in a long time, I'm really feeling it.*

The street sign caught just enough light for Jack to read *Oak*. He turned and let the *Riviera* creep north until the road angled left in front of the house Jack and Cheryl had looked at under construction back in 1975. The home's carriage lamps revealed the front facade, the mature landscaping, and the fine roof lines.

Focus, Jack . . . focus . . . . Do what you know you must . . . .

A wide bend in the road let Jack make a U-turn. He swung the Buick south, aiming directly at the same large, old, oak tree less than a quarter mile distant that he once swerved to avoid, while his young wife screamed in terror. He unfastened his seatbelt.

Now . . . no more thinking . . . focus, Jack, focus . . . no more thoughts . . . do it now.

The car accelerated slowly, but then he muttered, "What the hell . . . ."

He floored it. Twenty . . . twenty-five . . . thirty . . . thirty-five . . . forty . . . fifty . . . sixty . . . sev- **Impact!**

Chapter 38 ~ 1991

Early morning programs broke the stunning news: a middle-aged doctor beat an elderly colleague nearly to death and then committed suicide by crashing his car into a tree at high speed. Local television stations and the press couldn't get enough of the sensational story, especially, after learning both men were abortionists. Two days later it made national headlines. Messert's lawyer released a statement claiming that Dr. Jack Cutler had been harassed at the Messert Clinic for months by extreme, right-wing, anti-choice protesters. They called him ugly, vile names, while screaming at patients not to have "your baby killed." Messert's statement implied that Dr. Cutler suffered severe depression due to the continual and vicious protesting. In fact, only a handful of peaceful, pro-life demonstrators picketed the clinic once a month, but that was never reported anywhere.

Dr. Messert went on to describe his cordial friendship with Dr. Cutler and how they had worked together for thirteen years with tremendous mutual respect. He also emphasized that he forgave Dr. Cutler for his irrational behavior, regretted his death, and hoped that all reasonable persons would finally come to appreciate the wonderful work that doctors like Jack and he did, in helping women from all walks of life and all races, colors, and creeds.

The death of Jack Cutler horrified Karen Helden. She had known Jack when they were young, liked him, and even felt infatuated for a while. Then she decided, because of differences relating to children, birth control, and religion, Jack was not the man she wanted to marry, but still considered him an appealing guy who, she presumed, would have a successful career as an OB-GYN specialist. It wasn't until she learned that he aborted Dana Buckley's pregnancy that she had misgivings about the kind of man Jack had become. It didn't surprise her at all that he was divorced and childless. What surprised her was Messert's additional claim that Jack's "nervous system had suffered terribly." She knew Jack was a lot tougher than that.

Her sister, Katherine, called. "Can you believe it?"

"No. I was shocked . . . stunned . . . I still am."

"To think your first serious boyfriend committed suicide."

"Well, I guess I don't find it entirely unbelievable."

"Karen, how come . . . how can you say that?"

"I never told you this, but his mother committed suicide."

"Oh, my, did he tell you that?"

"Yes, he did."

"I didn't realize you knew him so intimately."

"It wasn't that. His parents were dead. I wanted to know how they died. Is that so intimate?"

"No, I suppose not. It's just so sad. He was so young then."

"Yes, very sad then and very sad now, especially, because he committed suicide the exact same way as his mother."

"You mean by hitting a tree?"

"Yes, she deliberately drove into a tree. At first when Jack told me, I didn't believe it, but that's exactly what happened."

"Oh my God . . . ."

"Her suicide became the model for his."

"Oh, Karen, that poor man."

"Yes, a terrible end to what was once a promising life, although, I suspect, a sad life."

"Because he was an abortionist?"

"Well, yes, that and divorced . . . no children. I knew him as an idealistic, young doctor. Never in my wildest dreams did I imagine he'd end up an abortionist."

Then Katherine recalled something. "Remember years ago when we had lunch with Aunt Elizabeth, and Jack was in the restaurant and came to our table?"

"Yes."

"Remember what he said about wanting to marry you?"

"Yes."

"And remember how you kind of put him in his place and told him you never would have married him, and he should go away, and Aunt Elizabeth kind of scolded you for being so harsh?"

"Yes, I remember."

"Did you ever call him to apologize?"

Karen experienced a sudden, deep blush of regret, but said nothing.

"Karen?"

"I'm here."

"Did you ever apologize to Jack?"

After a long pause, Karen finally answered, "No, I never did."

+ + +

Of all the American presidents who served after the Second World War, only Ronald Reagan believed communism and the Soviet Union could be defeated, not by military means alone, but by condemnation, shame, and the power of the idea of liberty. Like the founding fathers, Reagan believed every human being possesses a divine liberty, a liberty that is the bestowed gift of the Creator himself.

In Eastern Europe in 1988 and '89, Soviet-style communism began crumbling. The people of Poland, Hungary, Czechoslovakia, Yugoslavia, and East Germany yearned for freedom or at least, after forty years, to be rid of Russian domination. The Soviet Union's Mikhail Gorbachev let it happen without the harsh military intervention that had crushed popular uprisings in the past.

Reagan knew that in hundreds of millions of persons behind the Iron Curtain there dwelt on their imprinted souls the longing for liberty, the yearning to be free. He called the Soviet regime evil. He told Gorbachev to "tear down that wall!" Suddenly, millions who had been intimidated by ugly cadres of the East German secret police realized the mighty power of the people.

The communist East German government on November 9, 1989, unexpectedly allowed its imprisoned citizens to move freely through the border checkpoints leading to West Berlin and West Germany. The action stunned people on both sides of the Berlin Wall: that hated concrete and steel barrier that manifested Churchill's mythical *Iron Curtain*. Ecstatic crowds gathered to celebrate, while young men and boys climbed the high, brutal wall and began beating it with chisels and hammers.

On October 3, 1990, East and West Germany reunited into a single German state. Soon, the waves of freedom and patriotism that swept across Eastern Europe pounded against the totalitarian walls of Russia itself. There arose in Moscow a big, burly, vodka-drinking, bear of a man named Yeltsin. It appeared, at long last, that the cruel, heinous communism of the Soviet Union was shoveled into the ash can of history.

As much a victory for Reagan's doctrine of 'peace through strength' and for the haunting doctrine of 'mutually assured destruction,' better known by its simple acronym *MAD*, it was far more the eastern European and Russian people's yearning for freedom that finally ended the long, Cold War.

+ + +

Nick, Maggie, and the baby had been gone over a month, and Johnny and Karen still hadn't heard from them. It didn't bother Karen, but it bothered her husband. Finally, Johnny said, "You know, Nick promised he'd keep in touch. It's over a month now and not a word, not even a phone call. I told him he could call us collect."

"They're fine Johnny. He's in school, plus he's a husband and father. That comes first. Just relax . . . we'll get a letter soon enough."

"I bet Maggie's folks have heard from her."

"That's different. She's younger, and I'm sure she likes to talk about the baby with her own mother."

"Well, Nick has a mother, too."

"Oh, Johnny, please, don't make it a competition."

It bothered him every day for eight weeks until a letter came. Nick, instead of writing about Maggie, baby Jenny, and how they were adjusting to living in North Carolina, wrote what he had learned, was learning, and would learn. In Infantry School he was taught everything about small arms plus larger armament like howitzers and heavy mortars. After that his class went to the Army Airborne School for three weeks of intensive training to prepare for jumping from an airplane. *I couldn't wait to do it*, he wrote. *It was an incredible thrill especially having a thousand percent confidence in my chute. I passed everything fine including my five jumps. I earned my Silver Wing and can't wait to jump again. All the guys feel that way. That's why we're all here, I guess. Next week we begin the Special Operations Prep Course, thirty days where they're going to teach us how to navigate on unmarked terrain among other things. Should be interesting. Okay, that's it for now. Maggie and Jenny are fine. Love, Nick. P.S. We probably won't be home again until next summer.*

John put the hand-written sheet down. "That's as impersonal a letter, as we've ever received."

"He's a professional soldier, John. Our son is a very serious man now."

"You'd think he'd at least write that Maggie and Jenny send their love."

"Well, yes, you'd think so . . . ." Karen slid the letter back into its envelope.

"I know what it is."

"What?"

"Maggie." The name jumped off John's lips.

"What about Maggie?"

"When they left she was very cold. She was never like that before."

"Do you know why?"

"I haven't the faintest idea."

"Well, I'll tell you," Karen said. "When Nick told us he was joining the Special Forces and wanted to make the Army his career, you insulted him. You said his decision was insane and he was crazy. I know you apologized to Nick, but that deeply offended Maggie. Regardless of how easily Nick lets those remarks roll off his back, it isn't pleasant for her to listen to you insult her husband. She loves Nick, and she's not going to let you say things like that without some kind of reaction. You'll have to apologize."

"Oh, man, Karen, did she tell you that?"

"No, Nick did. You don't realize sometimes, Johnny, how what you say can hurt someone. And once spoken, you can't take those words back. You'll have to apologize, but, who knows, maybe even then Maggie won't ever think of you, as she used to."

John sighed. "You know I didn't mean to insult Nick and certainly not Maggie. It just seemed so out of character for a Helden to choose the military."

"Let it be, John . . . just let it be."

+ + +

Succeeding Reagan after his second term, George H. W. Bush was elected in 1988 to the presidency. His family had long been in public service. As a young Navy pilot, he served heroically in the Pacific during the war against Japan. After the peaceful revolutions in Eastern Europe and with Bush at the helm, Johnny and Karen Helden felt confident there'd be no wars during Nick's tour of duty.

That summer, Nick and his little family returned to Milwaukee for a visit. Everyone was delighted to see them. The only problem John Helden needed to resolve involved his daughter-in-law, Maggie. He apologized to her and a second time to Nick; while Nick forgave easily, Maggie retained a remnant of feminine skepticism. She found John Helden a little too overbearing towards his wife and children, all over twenty-one except Joe who'd turn nineteen in September. Maggie simply wouldn't tolerate an intrusive father-in-law, though she revived her pleasantness towards him. When Nick, Maggie, and Jenny left again for North Carolina, the entire Helden family, in great spirits, united in a happy sendoff.

+ + +

In the spring of 1990, in the Western Asian city of Baghdad, a council of war was convened by the truculent Iraqi ruler, Saddam Hussein. His target was Kuwait, the small Arab emirate south of Iraq that possessed the world's fifth largest oil reserves. The Rumaila oil field spread over both southern Iraq and Kuwait; the Iraqis suspected that Kuwait was slant drilling beneath the sand-swept border to tap into Iraq's oil reserves. Iraq owed Kuwait money for its help in Iraq's eight year war against Iran; they asked for forgiveness of the debt, but Kuwait refused. It was enough to convince Saddam's council to wage war. On August 2, 1990, Iraq invaded Kuwait. Three days later, President Bush declared, "the invasion will not stand."

+ + +

In early December, Nick called his parents. He chatted with his mother about little Jenny and how she was growing and then mentioned, "Oh, by the way, Maggie is pregnant."

Karen's eyes shone with happiness. She whispered the news to John before handing him the phone.

"Congratulations Nick, and Maggie too   ."

"Thanks, Dad. I didn't tell Mom, but in a few days my unit is being shipped overseas for six to eight weeks of additional training. Maggie and Jenny will stay here.

"Where are you going?"

"They haven't told us yet. It's just part of our on-going training."

"I hope it's not Iraq. Although now that the *UN* authorized force to get Saddam out of Kuwait, I think there's actually less chance of war."

"Why do you think that?"

"Because I can't believe the Iraqis would willingly invite all that death and destruction. I looked in the *Atlas*. They're an easy, wide-open target. We can hit 'em from Turkey and Saudi Arabia."

"I hope you're right. You know there's a deadline . . . ."

". . . for Iraq to get out, yeah."

"The *UN* has given them until January fifteenth."

"Right . . . two days before my birthday."

"Then I better wish you a happy birthday now, Dad, because I don't know where I'll be on the seventeenth."

"Thanks, Nick . . . okay. Call us when you get back."

"I will."

"Oh, and Nick . . . ."

"Yeah . . . ."

"God bless you, Maggie, Jenny, and your new baby, too.

"Thanks, Dad. God bless you and Mom. So long . . . ."

+ + +

John turned fifty-four in January, 1991. For many years, Karen invited John's parents to his birthday party, but that ended with his father's death and his mother's move to Los Angeles with Michael at the end of '87. So now, only JJ, his wife Noreen, Ann, Kristin, and Joe were invited. "Strictly a family affair – just the way I like it," John told Karen. But when they all sat down at the dining room table, one was conspicuously missing.

"Where's Ann," John asked.

"Oh, I forgot to tell you," Karen said. "She called . . . said she couldn't make it."

"Why?" John asked.

"She had a commitment and forgot it was your birthday. She said she couldn't break it . . . something about a new job."

"I find that a bit strange. She's only known my birthday for a couple decades."

At that, Kristin snapped, "Mom, why can't you just tell?"

Karen glanced at Kristin. "Quiet."

"Tell me what?" John asked.

Sensing something unpleasant, Joe suggested, "I'm hungry . . . let's eat."

"Eating is sometimes wiser than talking," JJ advised.

Karen rose to get the lasagna, while Kristin poured herself a second glass of Chianti. John said, "Take it easy . . . ."

"Dad, don't tell me that. I'm twenty-three."

"True, but it affects you like you were twelve."

JJ smirked at Kristin. She rolled her eyes, disgusted with both parents.

Karen placed the large, steaming glass dish on the table and began to cut and serve. The tossed salad got passed around.

"So, Karen," John said, "what did Kristin want you to tell me?"

"I'm sure she's forgotten."

"No, I haven't," Kristin said. "You're afraid. That's pathetic."

"Karen, what's going on," John asked. "Since when are you afraid to tell me anything?"

Kristin said, "She's afraid to tell you the real reason Ann isn't here. Maybe if you weren't always so critical of us and didn't react so badly to everything . . . ."

"Kristin, don't be disrespectful of your father," Karen said.

"You think I'm disrespectful? Good God in heaven, Mother. What's disrespectful is that Ann isn't here and the reason she isn't here."

"Kristin, that's enough. Stop it right now," Karen said.

JJ asked, "Since when is Dad always so critical of us?"

Kristin scoffed. "You're not a girl. You and Nick always were his favorites . . . now Joey."

"Leave me out of it," Joe said. "I'm the baby. I'm supposed to be spoiled."

Noreen said, "I don't think your dad is so critical. He's always been great to me."

"You're not his daughter," Kristin said.

Again John asked, "Karen what's going on? Kristin, don't interrupt."

Karen stammered. "Well, it's just that Ann doesn't live here anymore . . . ."

"That I know," John replied. "Tell me something I don't know."

Karen raised her wine glass to her lips, held it there for a moment, but couldn't think of a way out of the jam Kristin stuck her in. More than anything, Karen realized, especially on Johnny's birthday, this was not how she wanted him to learn that their older daughter was living with a man twelve years her senior. Karen suspected this *something* would wreak family havoc, but saw it now as inevitable.

Then Kristin aimed at her father. "Dad, if you didn't live in a perpetual fog, maybe you'd figure out what's going on around here. Maybe you'd see your children for what we really are. Ann is living with a guy. Your favorite little angel is shacking up. They're not married, Dad, and he's pushing forty. They didn't elope with the help of some obliging priest like you and Mom. Do you get it, Dad? They're living in what you and Mom like to call *sin*."

John said nothing. He stared at Karen who spotted the sudden, sad bewilderment in his eyes that revealed just a fraction of the hurt in his heart, but she saw no anger. Then he looked at Kristin who asked, "Aren't you going to say something?"

"You've said enough . . . ."

"Dad, I'm really sorry, but I can't help feel, if it were me, all hell would break loose."

"Maybe it would, but what good is that? Do you want me to call Ann and scream at her? Should I scream at you, or your mother, or the four walls?"

"You could give Ann a good lecture on the evils of fornication."

"Christ did that several times. She's heard it; you've heard it; we've all heard it. If she doesn't care to recall it now, do you really think my reminding her will make any difference? She's twenty-five years old, you know."

Kristin, devastated for breaking her sister's confidence and spoiling her father's party, stared at her plate. Secret tears came to her eyes.

"So, Dad," JJ said, "other than that, how are you enjoying your birthday?"

John smiled, Noreen chuckled, Joe laughed, Kristin groaned, and Karen, grateful for JJ's wit, stood to clear the table before bringing the cake. Then the phone rang. Karen went to answer. It was Ann. "Mom, turn on *CNN*. The war has started . . . they're bombing Baghdad."

Shocked and confused, Karen had let Johnny convince her there'd be no war. She thought of Nick, but then of her husband. "Ann, you have to wish your father a happy birthday."

"No, I can't now. I have to get back. I just wanted to let you know. Tell Dad 'Happy Birthday' for me. I'll try to call tomorrow."

"Ann," Karen said, "your father knows . . . ."

Ann paused to absorb the blow. "Oh, no, Mom . . . I asked you not to tell him, to let me tell in my own way, in my own time. Why'd you do that?"

"It was Kristin."

"Oh, my God, what is wrong with her? I suppose Dad's furious."

"No, not angry, just hurt. You should have been here. It wouldn't have come out."

John called, "Is that Ann?" At that, a wave of regret rolled through Kristin's heart. She stood and left the room.

"Ann, we'll talk tomorrow. Maybe you should come over . . . ."

"I'll call, but make sure you answer. I'm just not ready to deal with Dad."

Karen hung up and went back to the dining room. She stood at the table and announced, "War has started . . . they're bombing Baghdad. It's on television." She was relieved she had a far worse transgression to report than Ann's.

Everyone rushed into the family room. Joe turned on *CNN*. The white flashes of exploding American bombs in the blackness of the Iraqi night stunned them into silence. Kristin looked into the room. She had her coat on. "War is stupid," she said.

"Where are you going?" Karen asked.

"Out for air . . . I'm too buzzed to sit."

"I'll go with you," Noreen said, sensing Kristin's need for company.

John, Karen, JJ, and Joe watched the bombing of Baghdad in silence until the reporter's inane comments became tedious.

"So, now we're at war again," John said. "Well, God bless dear Nick wherever he is."

"Wherever he's training," Karen said. "I'll serve the cake."

"Probably on alert now or something," JJ said. "Mom, I'd like ice cream with mine."

"Could be," John said. "Karen, give me a little scoop, too."

"Me too," Joe said, "but much bigger."

"War casts a shadow over people's lives," John Helden began. "How long is it gonna take to get Saddam out of Kuwait? At what price in terms of our boys' lives? And right now, innocent people are dying even though *CNN* claims we only strike military targets. If we take out their electricity and water supply, innocents will suffer plenty, especially children. It won't be another Vietnam though. This war is all about oil. We buy Kuwait's oil. Bush won't let Saddam interfere with that."

Joe asked, "How long do you think it'll last?"

"I haven't the faintest idea."

Karen said, "Come on, let's sing *Happy Birthday.*"

John replied, "Let's wait until Kris and Noreen get back."

"No, Dad, I wanna eat some cake," JJ said. "They might not be back for a while." He began to sing, Joe joined in, and then Karen.

"Thanks," John said, "but I don't really feel like celebrating something as trivial as my birthday given this damn war."

Fifteen minutes later, Kristin and Noreen walked in. JJ stood and told Noreen to keep her coat on. "I'm tired. I wanna go," he said.

Karen wrapped a big chunk of cake for them to take home and gave a piece to Kristin. After JJ and Noreen left, Karen said, "John, I'm going to bed . . . I'm sorry about Ann, but I'm just too tired to talk."

"We'll talk in the morning."

"Goodnight, Mom," Joe said.

Kristin sat on the sofa next to her father. She put her hand on his. "I'm sorry for telling about Ann . . . for ruining your birthday."

"You didn't ruin my birthday. This war did. Sooner or later, it had to come out about Ann. I won't hold that against you. You and I both know your mother should have told me."

"She was sworn to secrecy. We both were."

"Then Ann should have told me."

"No way, Dad; she's afraid how you'd react."

"She shouldn't fear me. If her guy's pushing forty, she should fear his history. What does she think . . . she's his first? That's laughable. Affairs are risky business for young women. Ann should have a heart-to-heart with his prior mistresses. She'd find out what a jerk he really is."

"Dad, that's insulting. You don't even know the guy. It's terrible to suggest your own daughter is someone's mistress. Why even say things like that? You can be so judgmental, and for what? For your information they are planning to get married . . . okay?"

"We shall see. I just hope you don't make the same mistake."

"I don't want to talk about it," Kristin said. "I'm going to bed. Happy birthday Dad . . . I love you . . . most of the time."

"I love you, too. Thanks for making my old age so interesting."

Kristin smiled. "You're not old Dad." She waved at her younger brother. "Goodnight Baby Spoiled."

Joe laughed; then, at his father's motioning, turned off the television. Now the two of them sat alone in the soft light of the family room. John said, "You know, Joey, bombing a city is a terrible thing. We see those horrific blasts from the comfort of our home, almost like watching fireworks. Maybe we don't fully comprehend that men, women, and children are suffering and dying. My God, can you imagine how terrifying it must be for those poor people?"

"No, I don't think I can."

"I can't either, but once, a long time ago, I had an experience that helps me grasp it a little better."

"What was that?"

"It must have been September of 1945. I was only eight. The Second World War had just ended a few weeks earlier. Everyone was so relieved, and my parents kept saying, "it's over; it's over," almost like a mantra. They were very happy . . . everybody was. Even I, as a little boy, felt differently after learning the war had ended because it overshadowed everything. Young as I was, I sensed that.

"Well, one day – it must have been a Saturday because my dad was home – he was shaving, and I was keeping him company when we heard the faint rumbling of thunder far in the west. But then we realized it was sunny outside. My dad thought maybe a storm was gathering. A few seconds later we heard it again. It was definitely louder, and then pretty soon it was constant and growing, by which time we knew it couldn't possibly be thunder. Joey, this was a roaring like a hundred freight trains barreling down on us."

"They say that's what a tornado sounds like," Joe said.

"Right . . . well, we went out on the airing porch on the second floor, hearing this incredible sound coming closer and closer, and then my dad spotted them. Just above the tall elms on the next street we saw the first row of planes – B-29s, what they called *Superfortresses* – headed right over our house on Harding Boulevard. They were flying very low, and wave after wave of those giant bombers swept over us. In my memory their undersides looked black as night. The sound was so deafening that we had to press our palms tight against our ears, but even then I could still hear that thunderous roaring."

"How many were there? Did you count 'em?"

"No, but I'll bet a hundred . . . maybe more. Of course, I was a boy so it's hard now for me to say. At the time it seemed endless."

"Was there anything in the papers about it: where they were going, how many?"

"My father never said he read about it, but I saw it, and I can still see it in my mind's eye. Maybe President Truman wanted to show the American people what our factories built to win the war. Maybe he wanted to show off the power of the Air Force. Maybe they just had to fly over Milwaukee to get wherever they were going. I really don't know, but, in thinking about it, I came to understand how terrible it must have been for the Japanese people to see those planes with their bombs raining down towards their children and homes. Where could they hide? Where were they safe? For everyone who was ever bombed, regardless of nationality or the reason for the war, it had to be a terrifying, hellish experience. Tonight it's terrifying for the people in Baghdad. My God, Joey, my father, your Grandpa Helden, would be horrified that it's us doing the bombing."

"Yeah, but Saddam refused to negotiate."

"Grandpa maintained that war is always a failure of diplomacy.

I believe that's true, and that's exactly why there are so many wars. Ordinary people seem to know better how to talk to one another, how to live in peace with their neighbors. It'd be wonderful if diplomats of all nations could learn that."

"I don't know, Dad; tyrants and war mongers seem like a fairly regular occurrence in this world."

"Yes, sadly that's true, but we've got to figure out a better way to deal with them." Then John thought of something else. "When I was at Marquette, before I started dating your mother, I knew a girl from Germany. Her name was Karla. She came here with her parents several years after the Second World War."

"Did you date her?"

"A couple times, but the chemistry wasn't there. She worked for an assistant dean. I'd see her in the halls, so I just started talking to her. Actually, she was a very lovely person, but she didn't seem to have much interest in me. She was interesting, though, and told me an incredible experience she had during the war."

"Lucky for me she wasn't interested in you. I doubt I'd be here."

John laughed. "That's right." For a moment he recalled the Karla of thirty years ago.

Joe said, "Dad, tell me."

"Well, let me think: Karla was a year younger than me. During the war, as a little girl, she lived in Germany. When she was six or seven, maybe early '45 when Germany was collapsing, she and her mother were walking on a road back to their house. She told me they saw an American plane not far from them, but heading in the opposite direction. They didn't pay much attention to it until they heard a roaring behind them. They turned around and here comes this fighter with its guns blazing.

"Her mother pushed her into the drainage ditch alongside the road. She said it contained filthy water, but her mother pushed her right down into it – not her face – and covered her with her own body. She said they could hear the bullets smacking the road and ground, but miraculously they weren't hit. Karla cried, but her mother told her not to move, and sure enough that son-of-a-bitch came back a second time. She said he passed by low and probably saw them, but they played dead, and he never returned.

"But just think, Joey, how easy it was for him to decide to kill two innocent people. He's got this fast plane with machine guns; from the air he spots a mother and her daughter walking along a road, a threat to no one. *Germans*, he presumes and then, *kill 'em*. His thought process might have taken less than a second. He turns the plane, gets a bead on, and pulls the trigger. Karla said it was a miracle they weren't hit. Then she told me something I've never forgotten. She said, 'Johnny, you think you understand war, but you can never really know what war is unless you experience being shot at, or being bombed, or have loved ones who are killed.'

"You know, Joe, she's right. Americans, except our front line soldiers, don't really know what war is. We've been profoundly blessed. Modern warfare has never come to our country. Enemy bombers and missiles have never invaded our skies. Let's pray we can keep it that way."

+ + +

Two weeks after the bombing of Baghdad, John and Karen received a letter from Nick.

> *Dear Mom and Dad,*
>
> *I've finished most of my training, all of which was excellent, and not a single guy in our final group washed out. Our instructors said that was something we can really be proud of. We're closely knit and have tremendous morale. All the guys are really great, and I'm glad I'm part of it. Now we're waiting for our first deployment and everyone's hoping for Iraq, but that's not likely because we've had no briefing on that situation. All of us would love to get into the war even if we're just a support mission. Tomorrow we're having a briefing. I'll know more then.*
>
> *By the way, Maggie is friends with some of the wives of my S.F. buddies back in N.C. That's good because some of them are mothers or expecting so she's got company. She said she's feeling much better, and not as sick with that morning sickness stuff. She said her doc told her that's usually the way it is with the second. Hey, we're hoping for a little boy, a little Nick Jr. (We'll leave Johnny Five for JJ and Noreen – if they ever figure out how to have one.) Of course, it could be another girl – ours I mean. Man, I don't know what we'd name her.*

I feel really good. I'm in great shape and love the Special Forces. Plus they've been feeding us really good so don't worry about that. Sorry I can't tell you where I am, but that's the way it is, especially now with the war in Iraq. Thanks for your last letter. It takes a while, but I always enjoy getting them so keep writing and tell Ann, JJ, Kristin and Joey to write, too. Hi to everybody.

Love, Nick

"Well, that's a very nice letter," Karen said.
"Yeah," John agreed. "I just wonder where he goes next."

+ + +

By January 30, 1991, United States military forces in the Persian Gulf exceeded half a million men and women. The American news media warned of Iraq's vaunted military ground forces, while many Americans, including John and Karen Helden, braced for a long, bloody conflict. But then, on February 28, a mere one hundred hours after the start of the ground campaign to expel Iraq from Kuwait, President George H. W. Bush ordered a cease fire. The Iraqi army had been routed.

A peace conference was arranged with an agreement signed on March 3. By March 8, the first troops began to return home. They were welcomed by Americans grateful the *Desert Storm* war ended swiftly and with so few casualties. But two nefarious matters remained: the first, America would deal with; the second, she would not.

When the retreating Iraqi troops fled Kuwait they ignited, by order of Saddam Hussein, more than seven hundred oil wells resulting in an environmental disaster of monstrous proportions. Private American companies were brought in to extinguish the fires, but it took eight arduous months, each day of which consumed six million barrels of oil.

The second matter involved broadcasts from *The Voice of Free Iraq* that urged, as early as February 2, a Shiite Muslim uprising in southern Iraq. Supported by the Arabic service of the *Voice of America*, the messages contained clear inferences that America would provide military assistance. President Bush, however, instead of ordering an assault on Baghdad and overthrowing the Baathist Sunni regime, allowed Saddam to remain in power. Shortly after American forces evacuated the Persian Gulf, Saddam turned his vicious attention to the Shiite uprising and crushed it ruthlessly.

In northern Iraq, the Kurds mistakenly presumed American military support would be forthcoming and began fighting against Saddam's loyalist generals. Just like in the south, that uprising was brutally crushed.

Johnny Helden liked President Bush, but when he learned what happened to the Shiites and Kurds he told Karen, Kristin, and Joe, "When you have the opportunity to kill a rat, you have to take it. Truman and Eisenhower never would have left Hitler in power. It's a mistake for Bush to leave Saddam."

Karen said, "Johnny, be grateful the war is over. You thought it might be another Vietnam. Now it's over in less than two months."

"You're absolutely right. I am grateful, tremendously grateful, especially for Nick's sake."

"And now Noreen is pregnant . . . and Maggie again."

"So I'll be an uncle four times already," Joe said. "I'm hoping Reeny can do her birthing stuff on my birthday. It'd be cool for my nephew and me to share the same day. I'd really like that."

"Three times," Kristin corrected. "And how do you know it's a boy?"

"Just a hunch."

"Any other hunches?"

"Yep, Maggie is going to have twins."

John, Karen, and Kristin laughed out loud, laughter that felt amazingly deep and good.

"Boys or girls," Karen asked.

"One of each," Joe answered with tremendous conviction. "You shouldn't laugh . . . ."

John and Karen struggled to control themselves.

"My baby brother's clairvoyant," Kristin said.

Karen wiped tears from her eyes. "You should learn about stocks and bonds. Maybe you could help JJ."

"Maybe I will," Joe replied. "I'd like that."

"Before you start picking stocks, let's wait and see how right you are about your sisters-in-law," John Helden said. "If you get them right, count me in."

Karen stood in front of her husband, daughter, and son, and in a gesture of profound gratitude raised her face and arms heavenwards. "Stocks don't matter, gender doesn't matter. What matters is life – new life! Our children's children, the future of our family, our old age, even our country. Oh, Johnny, don't you understand how blessed we are?"

He knew. They all felt her joy. But Johnny Helden felt, as well, a gnawing sadness that he and his beautiful older daughter, Ann, were still estranged, a separation that had worsened since John's birthday. Ann and her reputed fiancé' didn't visit, at least not when John was home. There were no friendly 'I miss you' greeting cards exchanged, no phone calls, nothing at all. Karen blamed her husband for failing to reach out to Ann or, as John judged her, but only to himself, "my prodigal daughter."

He sensed, hoped, imagined, and prayed that Ann would remember from her Catholic upbringing that she was not living a moral life. He hoped she'd acknowledge her sin, leave the guy, and return to the felicity of family and Church. But she was twenty-five: old enough to make mature decisions, even bad ones, without input from anyone, especially her father.

What John didn't know was that Ann had abandoned her Catholic faith and, in that abandonment, found it much easier not to deal with her father. She suspected he'd react to her loss of faith and her living arrangement as he reacted to certain other decisions she had made: badly. She had no use or time for that anymore. She put the moral question of fornication out of her mind, just as she put the unpleasantness of their estrangement out of her mind. More young women she knew and knew of, were living with guys. *Things have changed,* she convinced herself, though she knew her father would rant that the traditional moral principles remain eternally immutable. With such a profound difference of opinion, it simply became easier for Ann not to concern herself, and besides, she thought, *in a year or two I'll be married and everything will be fine. Dad will come around.*

Several evenings later, John and Karen declared "opera night" in the Helden home, an event of somewhat irregular occurrence,

but always pleasant when it came. They decided to listen to the long-playing recording of Verdi's *Aida* with the renowned soprano, Leontyne Price.

"It's appropriate," John said, "given the great victory in Iraq."

"Yes," Karen said. She called to Joe and Kristin, conversing upstairs. "Curtain going up."

Halfway through the first act, John said, "Someday I'd like us to see this at the Met."

"Oh, Johnny, that's a capital idea. I'd love to go to New York again."

In the second act, as the glorious music for the triumphal procession filled the house, John said, "I've read they have horses, sometimes even an elephant."

From upstairs Kristin shouted, "It's too loud – turn it down."

Karen moved to lower the volume.

"Come sit next to me," Johnny said.

She snuggled under his arm. "I'm sure it's spectacular . . . truly grand."

"Oh, yeah, the grandest of operas."

"And we'd go out to dinner?"

"Of course . . . I'll even order champagne."

The suggestion delighted Karen. "Sometimes, Johnny Helden, you really do have capital ideas."

Then something ordinary but unusual happened that had never before occurred on a late opera night. The doorbell rang.

John wondered aloud, "Who the heck could that be?" He glanced at his watch. "It's after nine."

Karen prayed it was Ann, but only Ann.

John went to the front door, opened it, and was stunned at the sight. There stood Maggie and three-year-old Jenny.

"Maggie, Jenny, my God, what a surprise . . . come in, come in."

They shuffled past him. Maggie's gaze bore deeply into John's confused and questioning eyes. In a soft, heartbreaking voice, she uttered, "Nick is dead . . . he was killed in Iraq."

She slumped, weeping, into John's arms.

The End.

www.ingramcontent.com/pod-product-compliance
Lightning Source LLC
Chambersburg PA
CBHW061504020726
47502CB00006B/1926